A Time to Laugh

Romance Collection

Laughter Unites Hearts in Five
Contemporary Stories

WANDA E. BRUNSTETTER,
GAIL SATTLER, JANICE THOMPSON

BARBOUR
PUBLISHING

Talking for Two © 2001 by Wanda E. Brunstetter
Clowning Around © 2003 by Wanda E. Brunstetter
Secret Admirer © 2004 by Gail Sattler
What's Cooking? © 2005 by Gail Sattler
Sweet Harmony © 2009 by Janice Thompson

Print ISBN 978-1-62416-740-9

eBook Editions:
Adobe Digital Edition (.epub) 978-1-62836-355-5
Kindle and MobiPocket Edition (.prc) 978-1-62836-356-2

Published by Barbour Publishing, Inc., P.O. Box 719, Uhrichsville, Ohio 44683, www.barbourbooks.com

Our mission is to publish and distribute inspirational products offering exceptional value and biblical encouragement to the masses.

Member of the
Evangelical Christian
Publishers Association

Printed in Canada.

Contents

Talking for Two

by Wanda E. Brunstetter

Dedication

To my son, Richard Jr., who first suggested I learn ventriloquism.
To my daughter, Lorina, the best ventriloquist student I ever had.
To Clinton Detweiler, a talented ventriloquist:
Much thanks for all your helpful insights

Chapter 1

"Miss Johnson, will you make Roscoe talk to us again?" Four-year-old Ricky Evans squinted his pale blue eyes and offered up a toothy grin so appealing that Tabitha knew it would be impossible for her to say no.

She pulled the floppy-eared dog puppet from its home in the bottom drawer of her desk and quickly inserted her hand. Thankful she was wearing blue jeans and not a dress today, she dropped to her knees and hid behind the desk, bringing only the puppet into view. Roscoe let out a couple of loud barks, which brought several more children running to see the program. Then Tabitha launched into her routine.

"Did you know I used to belong to a flea circus?" the scruffy-looking puppet asked. The children now sat on the floor, completely mesmerized, waiting for what was to come next.

"Really and truly?" a young girl called out.

Roscoe's dark head bobbed up and down. "That's right, and before long, I ran away and stole that whole itchy show!"

The children giggled, and Roscoe howled in response.

Tabitha smiled to herself. She was always glad for the chance to entertain the day care kids, even if she was doing it behind a desk, with a puppet that looked like he'd seen better days.

Five minutes and several jokes later, she ended her routine and sent all the children to their tables for a snack of chocolate-chip cookies and milk.

"You're really good with that goofy puppet," came a woman's soft voice behind her.

Tabitha turned to face her coworker and best friend, Donna Hartley. "I enjoy making the kids laugh," she said, pushing an irritating strand of hair away from her face. "It makes me feel like I'm doing something meaningful."

Always confident, always consoling, Donna offered her a bright smile. "Just helping me run Caring Christian Day Care is meaningful."

Tabitha blinked. "You really think so?"

Donna pulled out a chair and motioned Tabitha to do the same. "You know what you need, Tabby?"

Tabitha took a seat and offered up a faint smile, relishing the warm, familiar way her friend said her nickname. Donna began calling her that when she and her parents moved next door to the Johnsons, nearly twenty-three years ago. That was when Tabitha had been a happy, outgoing child. That was when she'd been an only child.

Shortly after she turned six, her whole life suddenly changed. The birth of blond-haired, blue-eyed sister Lois, had turned talkative, confident Tabby into a timid, stuttering, introverted child. Her father, who'd once doted on her, now had eyes only for the little girl who looked so much like him. Tabby's mother was a meek, subservient woman; rather than stand up to her controlling husband and his blatant acts of favoritism, she had merely chosen to keep silent while Tabby turned into a near recluse.

"Are you listening to me?" Donna asked, jerking Tabby's thoughts back to the present.

"Huh? What were you saying?"

"Do you know what you need?"

Tabby drew in a deep breath and blew it out quickly. "No, but I'm sure you can't wait to tell me."

Donna snickered. "Okay, so I'm not able to keep my big mouth shut where you're concerned. Old habits die hard, you know."

Tabby tapped her foot impatiently. "So, what do I need?"

"You need to attend that Christian workers' conference we heard about a few weeks ago."

"You know I don't do well in crowds," Tabby grumbled. "Especially with a bunch of strangers. I stutter whenever I talk to anyone but you or the day care kids, and—"

"But you won't be in a crowd," Donna reminded. "You'll be in a workshop, learning puppetry. You can hide behind a puppet box."

Tabby shrugged, letting her gaze travel to the group of happy children sitting at the table across the room. "No promises, but I'll think about it."

🌺

Seth Beyers had never figured out why anyone would want to buy an ugly dummy, but the customer he was waiting on right now wanted exactly that.

"The uglier the better," the young man said with a deep chuckle. "The audiences at the clubs where I often perform seem to like ugly and crude."

Seth had been a Christian for more than half of his twenty-six years, and he'd been interested in ventriloquism nearly that long as well. It just didn't set right with him when someone used a God-given talent to fill people's heads with all kinds of garbage. While most of Seth's customers were Christians, a few secular people, like Alan Capshaw, came to his shop to either purchase a ventriloquist dummy or have one repaired.

"Okay, I'll do my best for ugly," Seth said with a slight nod. "How does Dumbo ears, a long nose, and lots of freckles sound?"

"The big ears and extended nose is fine, but skip the freckles and stick a big ugly wart on the end of the dummy's snout." Alan grinned, revealing a set of pearly white teeth.

The dummy may turn out ugly, but this guy must really attract women, Seth mentally noted. Alan Capshaw not only had perfect teeth, but his slightly curly blond hair, brilliant blue eyes, and muscular body made Seth feel like he was the ugly dummy. He never could figure out why he'd been cursed with red hair and a slender build.

Seth waited until the self-assured customer placed a sizable down payment on his dummy order and sauntered out the door—and then he allowed himself the privilege of self-analysis. Sure, he'd had a few girlfriends over the past several years, and if he were really honest with himself, he guessed maybe he wasn't too bad looking, either. *At least not compared to the ugly dummy I'll soon be constructing.*

Whenever Seth went anywhere with his little buddy, Rudy Right, folks of all ages seemed to flock around him. Of course, he was pretty sure it was the winking dummy to whom they were actually drawn and not the hopeful ventriloquist.

Seth scratched the back of his head and moved over to the workbench. This was the place where he felt most comfortable. This was where he could become so engrossed in work that his troubles were left behind. He'd started fooling around with a homemade sock puppet and a library book on ventriloquism soon after he was old enough to read. When he turned twelve, his parents enrolled him in a home-study course on ventriloquism. In no time at all, Seth Beyers, normal, active teenager, had turned into a humorous, much sought-after ventriloquist. It wasn't long after that when he began performing at local fairs, school functions, and numerous church programs. About that time, he also decided he would like to learn how to make and repair dummies for a living. He'd always been good with his hands, and with a little help from a couple of books, it didn't take long before he completed his first ventriloquist figure.

Seth now owned and operated his own place of business, and people from all over the United States either brought or sent their ventriloquist figures to him for repairs. When he wasn't performing or teaching a class on ventriloquism, Seth filled special orders for various kinds of dummies. All but one of Seth's goals had been reached.

He wanted a wife and family. He'd been raised as an only child and had always longed for brothers and sisters. Instead of playing with a sibling, Seth's best friend was his sock puppet. Then Mom and Dad had been killed in a plane crash when he was fourteen, and he'd been forced to move from Seattle to Tacoma to live with Grandpa and Grandma Beyers. He loved them both a lot, but it wasn't the same as having his own family. Besides, his grandparents were getting on in years and wouldn't be around forever.

Seth groaned and reached for a piece of sandpaper to begin working on a wooden leg. "What I really need is to find someone who shares my love for Christ and wants to serve Him the way I do." He shook his head. "I wonder if such a woman even exists."

The telephone rang, pulling him out of his reflections. He reached for it quickly, before the answering machine had a chance to click on. "Beyers' Ventriloquist Studio." Seth frowned as he listened. "Glen Harrington's had a family emergency and you want me to fill in?" There was a long pause. "Yeah, I suppose I could work it into my schedule."

Seth wrote down a few particulars then hung up the phone. The last thing he needed was another seminar to teach, but he didn't have the heart to say no. He'd check his notes from the workshop he'd done in Portland a few months ago, and if everything seemed up to date, maybe there wouldn't be too much preliminary work. Since the seminar was only for one day, he was sure he could make the time.

He closed his eyes briefly as his lips curled into a smile. *Who knows, maybe I'll be able to help some young, talented kid hone his skills and use ventriloquism as a tool to serve the Lord.*

❋

Tabby stared dismally out the living room window in the converted garage apartment she shared with Donna. It was raining again, but then this was late spring, and she did live in the suburbs of Tacoma, Washington. Liquid sunshine was a common occurrence here in the beautiful Evergreen State.

Normally the rain didn't bother her much, but on this particular Saturday, it seemed as though every drop of water falling outside was landing on her instead of on the emerald grass and budding trees. She felt as if it were filling up her soul with agonizing depression and loneliness.

Tabby wrapped her arms tightly around her chest, as a deep moan escaped her lips. "Maybe I should have gone to Seattle with Donna and her parents after all." She shivered involuntarily. Tabby disliked crowds, and there was always a huge flock of people at the Seattle Center. No, she was better off here at home, even if she was lonely and miserable.

A sharp rap on the front door brought Tabby's musings to a halt. She moved away from the window and shuffled toward the sound. Standing on tiptoes, she peered through the small peephole, positioned much too high for her short stature.

Tabby's heart took a dive, and her stomach churned like whipping cream about to become butter. She didn't receive many surprise visits from her sister. Maybe this one would go better than the last. At least she hoped it would. Tabby drew in a deep breath, grasped the door handle, then yanked it open.

A blond-haired, blue-eyed beauty, holding a black, rain-soaked umbrella and ensconced in a silver-gray raincoat, greeted her with a wide smile. "Hi, Timid Tabitha. How's everything going?"

Tabby stepped aside as Lois rushed in, giving her umbrella a good shake and scattering droplets of cold water all over Tabby's faded blue jeans. Lois snapped the umbrella closed and dropped it into the wrought-iron stand by the front door. With no invitation, she slipped off her raincoat, hung it on the nearby clothes tree, then headed for the living room. Sitting carefully on the well-worn couch, she hand-pressed a wrinkle out of her pale blue slacks.

Tabby studied her sister. It must be nice to have her good looks, great taste in clothes, and a bubbling personality besides. Compared to Lois's long, carefully curled, silky tresses, Tabby knew her own drab brown, shoulder-length hair must look a mess.

"So, where's your roommate?" Lois asked. "On a rainy day like this, I figured the two of you would probably be curled up on the couch watching one of your favorite boring videos."

"Donna w–went to S–Seattle with her f–folks, and *L–Little W–Women* is not b–boring." Tabby glanced at the video, lying on top of the TV, then she flopped into the rocking chair directly across from her sister. "The b–book is a c–c–classic, and s–s–so is the m–movie."

"Yeah, yeah, I know—little perfect women find their perfect happiness, even though they're poor as scrawny little church mice." Lois sniffed, as though some foul odor had suddenly permeated the room. "The only part of that corny movie I can even relate to is where Jo finally finds her perfect man."

"You've f–found the p–p–perfect man?" Tabby echoed.

Lois nodded. "Definitely. Only mine's not poor. Mike is loaded to the gills, and I'm about to hit pay dirt." She leaned forward, stuck out her left hand, and wiggled her ring finger in front of Tabby's face.

"Wow, w–what a r–r–rock! Does th–this m–m–mean what I th–th–think?"

"It sure as tootin' does, big sister! Mike popped the all-important question last night, right in the middle of a romantic candlelight dinner at Roberto's Restaurant." Lois leaned her head against the back of the couch and sighed deeply. "Six months from now, I'll be Mrs. Michael G. Yehley, lady of leisure. No more humdrum life as a small potato's secretary. I plan to spend the rest of my days shopping till I drop."

"You're g–getting m–married that s–soon?"

"Don't look so surprised, Shabby Tabby." Lois squinted her eyes. "And for crying out loud, stop that stupid stuttering!"

"I—I—c–can't h–h–help it." Tabby hung her head. "I d–don't d–do it on p–purpose, you—you know."

"Give me a break! You could control it and get over your backward bashfulness if you really wanted to. I think you just do it for attention." Lois pursed her lips. "Your little ploy has never worked on me, though. I would think you'd know that by now."

"I d–do not d–do it for a–attention." Tabby stood up and moved slowly toward the window, a wisp of her sister's expensive perfume filling her nostrils. She grimaced and clasped her trembling hands tightly together. *Now I know I should have gone to Seattle. Even a thousand people closing in around me would have been easier to take than five minutes alone with Lois the Lioness.*

"Are you going to congratulate me or not?"

Tabby forced herself to turn and face her sister again. Lois was tapping her perfectly manicured, long red fingernails along the arm of the couch. "Well?"

"C–c–congratulations," Tabby mumbled.

"C–c–congratulations? Is that all you've got to say?"

"Wh–wh—what else is th–there to s–say?"

"How about, 'I'm very happy for you, Lois'? Or, 'Wow, Sis, I sure wish it were me getting married. Especially since I'm six years older and quickly turning into a dried-up, mousy old maid.'"

Lois's cutting words sliced through Tabby's heart, and a well of emotion rose in her chest, like Mount Saint Helens about to explode. How could anyone be so cruel? So unfeeling? She wished now she had never opened the front door. This visit from her sister wasn't going any better than the last one had. Blinking back unwanted tears, Tabby tried to think of an appropriate comeback.

"Say something. Has the cat grabbed your tongue again?" Lois prompted.

Tabby shrugged. "I—I th–think you'd better just g–g–go."

Her sister stood up quickly, knocking one of the sofa pillows to the floor. "Fine then! Be that way, you little wimp! I'm sorry I even bothered to stop by and share my good news." She swooped her raincoat off the clothes tree, grabbed the umbrella with a snap of her wrist, and stormed out the front door without so much as a backward glance.

Tabby stood staring at the door. "My little sister doesn't think I'll ever amount to anything," she muttered. "Why does she treat me that way?"

Lois is not a Christian, a small voice reminded.

Tabby shuddered. Why was it that whenever she felt sorry for herself, the Lord always came along and gave her a nudge? Tabby's parents weren't churchgoers, either. In fact, they had never understood why, even as a child, Tabby had gotten herself up every Sunday morning and walked to the church two blocks from home. Without Jesus' hand to hold, and the encouragement she got from Donna, she doubted if she would even be working at the day care center.

With a determination she didn't really feel, Tabby squared her shoulders and lifted her chin. "I'll show Lois. I'll show everyone." But even as the words poured out of her mouth, she wondered if it was an impossible dream. What could she, Timid Tabitha, do that would prove to her family that she really was a woman of worth?

Chapter 2

"I still can't believe I let you talk me into this," Tabby groaned as she settled herself into the passenger seat of Donna's little red car.

Donna put the key in the ignition then reached over to give Tabby's arm a reassuring squeeze. "It's gonna be fine. Just allow yourself to relax and have a good time. That's what today is all about, you know."

A frown twisted Tabby's lips. "That's easy enough for you to say. You're always so laid back about everything."

"Not always. Remember that blind date my cousin Tom fixed me up with last month? I was a nervous wreck from the beginning to the end of that horrendous evening."

Tabby laughed. "Come on now. It couldn't have been all that bad."

"Oh, yeah?" Donna countered as she pulled out into traffic. "How would you have felt if the most gorgeous guy you'd ever met took you on a bowling date, only because your matchmaking cousin set it all up? I didn't mention it before, but the conceited creep never said more than three words to me all night."

Tabby shrugged. "That would never happen to me, because I'm not about to go on any blind dates. Besides, have you thought maybe the poor guy was just shy? It could be that he wasn't able to conjure up more than three words."

Donna gave the steering wheel a slap with the palm of her hand. "Humph! Rod Thompson was anything but shy. In fact, he spent most of the evening flirting with Carol, my cousin's date."

Tabby squinted her eyes. "You're kidding."

"I'm not. It was probably the worst night of my life." Donna wiggled her eyebrows. "It was nearly enough to throw me straight into the arms of our preacher's son."

"Alex? Has Alex asked you out?"

"Many times, and my answer is always no."

"Why? Alex Hanson is cute."

Donna released a low moan. "I know, but he's a PK, for crying out loud! Nobody in their right mind wants to date a preacher's kid."

Tabby's forehead wrinkled, and she pushed a lock of hair away from her face. "Why not? What's wrong with a preacher's kid?"

Donna laughed. "Haven't you heard? The pastor and his entire family live in a fish bowl. Everyone expects them to be perfect."

"If Alex is perfect, then what's the big problem?"

"I said, he's supposed to be perfect. Most of the PKs I've ever known are far from perfect."

Tabby chuckled. "I have a feeling you really like Alex."

"I do not!"

"Do so!"

"Do not!"

Their childish banter went on until Tabby finally called a truce by changing the subject. "Which workshop are you going to register for at the seminar?" she asked.

Donna smiled. "Chalk art drawing. I've always been interested in art, and if I can manage to use my meager talent in that form of Christian ministry, then I'm ready, able, and more than willing."

Tabby glanced down at the scruffy little puppet lying in her lap. "I sure hope I won't have to talk to anyone. Unless I'm behind a puppet box, that is." She slipped Roscoe onto her hand. "If I'm well hidden and can talk through this little guy, I might actually learn something today."

"You're just too self-conscious for your own good. You've got such potential, and I hate to see you waste it."

"Potential? You must have me mixed up with someone else."

Donna clicked her tongue. "Would you please stop? You'll never build your confidence or get over being shy if you keep putting yourself down all the time."

"What am I supposed to do? Brag about how cute, smart, and talented I am?" Tabby grimaced. "Take a good look at me, Donna. I'm the plainest Jane around town, and as I've reminded you before, I can barely say two words to anyone but you or the day care kids without stuttering and making a complete fool of myself."

"You want people to accept you, but you don't think you can ever measure up. Am I right?"

Tabby nodded.

"That will all change," Donna insisted. "Just as soon as you realize your full potential. Repeat after me—I can do it. I can do it. I can do it!"

Tabby held Roscoe up and squeaked, "I can do it, but that's just because I'm a dumb little dog."

❧

The foyer of Alliance Community Church was crammed with people. Tabby gulped down a wave of nausea and steadied herself against the sign-up table for the puppet workshop. She was sure that coming here had been a terrible mistake. If not for the fact that Donna was already in line at the chalk art registration table, she might have turned around and bolted for the door.

"Sorry, but this class is filled up," said a soft-spoken older woman behind the puppet registration table.

"It—it—is?" Tabby stammered.

"I'm afraid so. You might try the ventriloquist workshop." The woman motioned toward a table across the room. "If you like puppetry, I'm sure you'd love to try talking for two."

Tabby slipped quietly away from the table, holding Roscoe so tightly her hand ached. There was no more room in the puppet workshop. Now she had a viable excuse to get out of this crowded place. She turned toward the front door and started to run. Pushing her way past several people, she came to a halt when she ran straight into a man.

"Whoa!" his deep voice exclaimed. "What's your hurry?"

Tabby stared up at him in stunned silence. She was rewarded with a wide smile.

Her plan had been to make a hasty exit, but this young man with soft auburn hair and seeking green eyes had blocked her path.

He nodded toward the puppet she was clutching. "Are you signed up for my class?"

Her gaze was drawn to the stark white piece of paper he held in his hand. "I—uh—th–that is—"

"I hope you're not self-conscious about using a hand puppet instead of a dummy. Many ventriloquists use puppets quite effectively."

Tabby gulped and felt the strength drain from her shaky legs. The guy thought she wanted to learn ventriloquism, and apparently he was the teacher for that workshop. The idea

13

of talking for two and learning to throw her voice did have a certain measure of appeal, but could she? Would she have the nerve to sit in a class with people she didn't even know? Could she talk for her puppet without a puppet box to hide behind? *Maybe I could just sit quietly and observe. Maybe I'd never have to say a word.*

✿

As she studied the handout sheet she'd just been given, Tabby wondered what on earth had possessed her to take a ventriloquist class, of all things! She felt about as dumb as a box of rocks, but as she pondered the matter, an idea burst into her head. Maybe she could do some short ventriloquist skits for the day care kids. If they liked Roscoe popping up from behind a desk, how much more might they enjoy seeing him out in plain view? If she could speak without moving her lips, the kids would think Roscoe really could talk.

From her seat at the back of the classroom, Tabby let her gaze travel toward the front. The young man with short-cropped auburn hair had just introduced himself as Seth Beyers, owner and operator of Beyers' Ventriloquist Studio. He was holding a full-sized, professional ventriloquist figure with one hand.

"I'd like to give you a little rundown on the background of ventriloquism before we begin," Seth said. "Some history books try to date ventriloquism back to biblical times, citing the story of Saul's visit to the witch of Endor as a basis for their claim." He frowned. "I disagree with this theory, though. As a believer in Christ, I take the scriptural account literally for what it says. In fact, I don't think the Bible makes any reference to ventriloquism at all.

"Ventriloquism is nothing more than an illusion. A ventriloquist talks and creates the impression that a voice is coming from somewhere other than its true source. People are often fooled into believing the ventriloquist is throwing his voice. Ventriloquism has been around a long time. Even the ancient Greeks did it. Romans thought ventriloquists spoke from their stomachs. In fact, the word ventriloquism comes from two Latin roots—*venter*—meaning belly, and *loqui*—the past participle of the verb *locuts*, which means to speak."

Seth smiled. "So, the word ventriloquism is actually a misnomer, for there is really no such thing as stomach talking. A ventriloquist's voice comes from only one place—his own throat. Everything the ventriloquist does and says makes the onlooker believe his voice comes from someplace else."

Positioning his foot on the seat of an empty folding chair, Seth placed the dummy on top of his knee. "Most of you will probably start by using an inexpensive plastic figure, or even a hand puppet." Gesturing toward the dummy, Seth added, "Later on, as you become more comfortable doing ventriloquism, you might want to purchase a professional figure like my woodenheaded friend, Rudy."

Suddenly it was as though the dummy had jumped to life. "Hi, folks! My name's Rudy Right, and I'm always right!"

A few snickers filtered through the room, and Seth reprimanded his little friend. "No way, Rudy. No one but God is always right."

"Is that so? Well, in the dummy world, I'm always right!" Rudy shot back.

Tabby leaned forward, watching intently. Seth's lips didn't move at all, and the sound supposedly coming from Rudy Right was nothing like the instructor's deep voice. If common sense hadn't taken over, she might have actually believed the dummy could talk. *A child would surely believe it. Kids probably relate well to what the dummy says, too.*

Yanking her wayward thoughts back to the happenings at the front of the room, Tabby giggled behind her hand when Rudy Right accused his owner of being a bigger dummy than he was.

"Yep," spouted Rudy, "you'd have to be really dumb to wanna be around dummies all the time." With the wink of one doeskin eye, the woodenhead added, "Maybe I should start pullin' your strings and see how you like it!"

When the laughter died down, Seth made Rudy say good-bye then promptly put him back in the suitcase from which he'd first appeared. With a muffled voice from inside the case, Rudy hollered, "Hey, who turned out the lights?"

In the moment of enjoyment, Tabby laughed out loud, temporarily forgetting her uncomfortable shyness. Everyone clapped, and the expert ventriloquist took a bow.

"I see a few of you have brought along a puppet or dummy this morning," Seth said. "So, who would like to be the first to come up and try saying the easy alphabet with the use of your ventriloquist partner?"

When no one volunteered, Seth pointed right at Tabby. "How about you, there in the back row?"

Her heart fluttered like a bird's wings. She bit her bottom lip then ducked her head, wanting to speak but afraid to do so.

Seth took a few steps toward her. "I'm referring to the young woman with the cute little dog puppet."

If there had only been a hole in the floor, Tabby would have crawled straight into it. She felt trapped, like a caged animal at the Point Defiance Zoo. She wanted to tell Seth Beyers that she wasn't ready to try the easy alphabet yet. However, she knew what would happen if she even tried to speak. Everything would come out in a jumble of incoherent, stuttering words, and she'd be completely mortified. Slinking down in her chair, face red as a vine-ripened tomato, she merely shook her head.

"I guess the little lady's not quite up to the task yet," Seth responded with a chuckle. "Is there someone else brave enough to let us critique you?"

One hand from the front row shot up. Seth nodded. "Okay, you're on!"

An attractive young woman with long red hair took her place next to Seth. She was holding a small boy dummy and wearing a smile that stretched from ear to ear. "Hi, my name's Cheryl Stone, and this is my friend, Oscar."

"Have you done any ventriloquism before?" Seth questioned.

Cheryl snickered. "Just in front of my bedroom mirror. I've read a book about throwing your voice, but I haven't mastered all the techniques yet."

"Then you have a bit of an advantage." Seth flashed her a reassuring smile.

Tabby felt a surge of envy course through her veins. Here were two good-looking redheads, standing in front of an audience with their dummies, and neither one looked the least bit nervous. Why in the world did she have to be so paralyzed with fear? What kept her locked in the confines of "Timid Tabitha"?

"Okay, let's begin with that easy alphabet," Seth said, breaking into Tabby's troubling thoughts. "All the letters printed on the blackboard can be said without moving your lips. I'll point to each one, and Cheryl will have her dummy repeat after me."

Cheryl nodded. "We're ready when you are."

Seth moved toward the portable blackboard positioned at Cheryl's left. "Don't forget to keep your mouth relaxed and slightly open, biting your top teeth lightly down on the bottom teeth." Using a pointer-stick, Seth began to call out the letters of the easy alphabet.

Cheryl made Oscar repeat each one. "A C D E G H I J K L N O Q R S T U X Y Z."

She'd done it almost perfectly, and Seth smiled in response. "Sometimes the letter Y can be a problem, but it's easy enough if you just say ooh-eye."

"What about the other letters in the alphabet?" an older man in the audience asked. "What are we supposed to do when we say a word that has B, F, M, P, V, or W in it?"

"That's a good question," Seth replied. "Those all get sound substitutions, and we'll be dealing with that problem shortly."

Oh, no, Tabby groaned inwardly. *This class is going to be anything but easy.*

"Let's have Cheryl and her little friend read some sentences for us," Seth continued. Below the easy alphabet letters he wrote a few lines. "Okay, have a go at it."

"Yes, I can do it." Cheryl opened and closed her dummy's mouth in perfect lip sync. "She had a red silk hat, and that is no joke!"

Everyone laughed, and Cheryl took a bow.

Seth erased the words then wrote a few more sentences. "Now try these."

"I ran across the yard, heading to the zoo. I need to get a key and unlock the car."

Tabby wrestled with her feelings of jealousy as Cheryl stood there looking so confident and saying everything with no lip movement at all. Tabby sucked in her bottom lip and tried to concentrate on learning the easy alphabet. After all, it wasn't Cheryl's fault she was talented and Tabby wasn't.

"That was great, Cheryl!" Seth gave her a pat on the back.

She smiled in response. "Thanks. It was fun."

The next few hours flew by, with only one fifteen-minute break for snacks and use of the restrooms. Tabby's plan had been to sneak out during this time and wait for Donna in the car. The whole concept of ventriloquism had her fascinated, though, and even if she wasn't going to actively participate, she knew she simply couldn't leave now.

By the time the class finally wound down, everyone had been given a video tape, an audiocassette, and several handouts. Everything from the easy alphabet to proper breathing and sound substitutions had been covered. Now all Tabby had to do was go home and practice. Only then would she know if she could ever learn to talk for two.

Chapter 3

"You're awfully quiet," Donna said, as they began their drive home from the seminar. "Didn't you enjoy the puppet workshop?"

"I never went," Tabby replied.

"Never went?"

"Nope. The class was filled up."

"If you didn't go to the workshop, then where have you been all morning, and why are you holding a bunch of handouts and tapes?"

"I was learning ventriloquism."

Donna's dark eyebrows shot up. "Ventriloquism? You mean you took the workshop on how to throw your voice?"

"Yeah, and I think I threw mine away for good."

"It went that badly, huh?"

Tabby's only reply was a slow sweep of her hand.

"What on earth possessed you to take something as difficult as ventriloquism?" Donna questioned. "I'm the adventuresome type, and I'd never try anything like that."

Tabby crossed her arms. "Beats me."

"Did you learn anything?"

"I learned that in order to talk for two, I'd need talent and nerves of steel." Tabby groaned. "Neither of which I happen to have."

Donna gave the steering wheel a light rap with her knuckles. "Tabitha Johnson, will you please quit putting yourself down? You've got plenty of talent. You just need to begin utilizing it."

"You didn't say anything about nerves of steel, though," Tabby reminded. "Being shy is definitely my worst shortcoming, and without self-confidence, I could never be a ventriloquist."

"I wouldn't be so sure about that."

"Right! Can't you just see it? Timid Tabitha shuffles onstage, takes one look at the audience, and closes up like a razor clam." She wrinkled her nose. "Or worse yet, I'd start to speak, then get so tongue-tied every word would come out in a jumble of uncontrollable stuttering."

Donna seemed to be mulling things over. "Hmm. . ."

"Hmm. . .what?"

"Why don't you practice your ventriloquism skills on me, then put on a little program for the day care kids?"

"I've already thought about that. It's probably the only way I could ever talk for two." Tabby shrugged. "Who knows—it might even be kind of fun."

"Now that's the spirit! I think we should stop by the Burger Barn and celebrate."

"You call that a place of celebration?"

Donna laughed. "Sure, if you love the triple-decker cheeseburger—and I do!"

Tabby slipped Roscoe onto her hand. "Okay, girls, Burger Barn, here we come!"

❀

In spite of the fact that he'd lost a whole morning of work, Seth had actually enjoyed teaching the ventriloquism workshop. With the exception of that one extremely shy young woman, it

17

had been exciting to see how many in the class caught on so quickly. The little gal holding a scruffy dog puppet had remained in the back row, scrunched down in her seat, looking like she was afraid of her own shadow. She never participated in any way.

Seth had encountered a few bashful people over the years, but no one seemed as self-restricted as that poor woman. Whenever he tried to make eye contact or ask her a question, she seemed to freeze. After a few tries he'd finally given up, afraid she might bolt for the door and miss the whole workshop.

A muscle twitched in his jaw. *I really wish I could have gotten through somehow. What was the point in her taking the class, if she wasn't going to join in? But then, who knows, the shy one might actually take the tapes and handouts home, practice like crazy, and become the next Shari Lewis.*

He chuckled out loud. "Naw, that might be stretching things a bit."

Gathering up his notes, Seth grabbed Rudy's suitcase. He needed to get back to the shop and resume work on Alan Capshaw's ugly dummy. There would be another full day tomorrow, since he was going to be part of a Christian workers' demonstration at a church in the north end of Tacoma.

Seth didn't get to worship at his home church much anymore. He was frequently asked to do programs for other churches' Sunday schools, junior church, or special services that might help generate more interest in Christian ministry. Between that and his full-time business, there wasn't much time left for socializing. Seth hoped that would all change some day. Not that he planned to quit serving the Lord with the talents he'd been generously given. No, as long as the opportunity arose, he would try to follow God's leading and remain faithfully in His service.

What Seth really wanted to modify was his social life. Keeping company with a bunch of dummies was not all that stimulating, and even performing for large crowds wasn't the same as a meaningful one-on-one conversation with someone who shared his interests and love for God.

"Well, Rudy Right," Seth said, glancing at the suitcase in his hand, "I guess it's just you and me for the rest of the day."

※

The Burger Barn was crowded. Hoping to avoid the mass of people, Tabby suggested they use the drive-through.

"Part of the fun of going in is being able to check out all the good-looking guys," Donna argued.

Tabby wrinkled her nose. "You do the checking out, and I'll just eat."

A short time later, they were munching their food and discussing the workshop.

"Tell me about the chalk art class," Tabby said. "Did you learn anything helpful?"

Donna's face lit up. "It was wonderful! In fact, I think I'm gonna try my hand at black light."

"Black light?"

"You hook a thin, black light over the top of your easel. The pictures you draw with fluorescent chalk almost come to life." Donna motioned with her hand, as though she were drawing an imaginary illustration. "I wish you could have seen some of the beautiful compositions our instructor put together. She draws well anyway, but under the black light, her pictures were absolutely gorgeous!"

Tabby smiled. "I can see she really inspired you to use your artistic talent."

"I'll say. I thought maybe you and I could combine our talents and put on a little program during Sunday school opening sometime."

"You're kidding, right?"

"I'm not kidding at all. I could do a chalk art drawing, and you could put on a puppet show. You might be able to use that old puppet box down in the church storage room." Donna gulped down her lemonade and rushed on. "It's not like you'd have to try your new ventriloquist skills or anything. You could hide behind the puppet box, and—"

Tabby held up one hand. "Whoa! In the first place, I have no ventriloquist skills. Furthermore, I've never done puppets anywhere but at the day care. I'm not sure I could ever do anything for church."

"Sure you could," Donna insisted. "Tomorrow, during our morning worship service, we're going to be entertained and inspired by some of the best Christian education workers in the Puget Sound area."

Tabby's interest was piqued. "We are? I hadn't heard. Guess I've been spending too much time helping out in the church nursery lately."

Donna smiled. "There will be a puppet team from Edmonds, Washington, a chalk artist from Seattle, a ventriloquist, who I hear is a local guy, and several others."

Tabby stared out the window. *Hmm. . .seeing some professionals perform might be kind of interesting. No way does it mean I'll agree to Donna's harebrained idea of us performing at Sunday school, though. I'll just find a seat in the back row and simply enjoy the show.*

❀

The church service would be starting soon, and Seth hurried through the hall toward the sanctuary. Someone had just come out of the ladies' restroom, head down and feet shuffling in his direction. Thump! She bumped straight into his arm, nearly knocking little Rudy to the floor.

From the startled expression on her face, Seth could tell she was just as surprised to see him as he was to see her. "Oh, excuse me!" he apologized.

"It's—it's o–o–okay," the young woman stammered. "It w–w–was probably m–m–my fault."

Seth smiled, trying to put her at ease. "I was the instructor at the ventriloquism workshop you took yesterday; do you remember?"

She hung her head and mumbled, "Y–y–yes, I kn–kn–know who y–y–you are. S–s–sorry for g–g–getting in the w–way."

"Naw, it was all my owner's fault," Seth made his dummy say in a high-pitched voice. "He's got two left feet, and I guess he wasn't watchin' where he was goin'." The vent figure gave her a quick wink then added, "My name's Rudy Right, and I'm always right. What's your name, sister?"

"My name's Tabitha Johnson, but you can call me Tabby." She reached out to grasp one of the dummy's small wooden hands.

Seth grinned. By talking to her through his partner, Tabby seemed much more relaxed. She was even able to make eye contact—at least with the dummy. *I should have tried that in the workshop yesterday. She might have been a bit more receptive.*

Seth had used his ventriloquist figure to reach frightened, sick, and even a few autistic children on more than one occasion. They had always been able to relate better to the dummy than they had to him, so maybe the concept would work as well on adults who had a problem with shyness. He also remembered recently reading an article on stuttering, which seemed to be Tabby's problem. One of the most important things a person could do when talking to someone who stuttered was to be patient and listen well. He thought he could do both, so Seth decided to try a little experiment. "It was nice having you in my workshop," he said,

19

speaking for himself this time.

Tabby's gaze dropped immediately to the floor. "It w–w–was good."

"Did ya learn anything?" This question came from Rudy.

Tabby nodded, looking right at the dummy, whose eyes were now flitting from side to side.

"What'd ya learn?" Rudy prompted.

"I learned that ventriloquism is not as easy as it looks."

No stuttering at all this time, Seth noted. *Hmm. . .I think I may be onto something here.*

"Are you gonna be a ven-trick-o-list?" Rudy asked, giving Tabby a wink.

Tabby giggled. "I'd like to be, but I'm not sure I'd have the nerve to stand up in front of people and talk."

"Aw, it's a piece of cake," Rudy drawled. "All ya have to do is smile, grit your teeth, and let your dummy do most of the talkin'." The figure's head cranked to the left. "Of course, ya need to find a better lookin' dummy than the one I got stuck with!"

At this, Rudy began to howl, and Tabby laughed right along with him.

Seth's experiment had worked, and he felt as if he'd just climbed to the summit of Mount Rainier.

"I'm surprised to see you here today," Tabby said, directing her comment at Rudy.

The dummy's head swiveled, and his blue eyes rolled back and forth again. "My dummy was asked to give a little demon-stration during your worship time. I just came along to keep him in line."

"And to be sure I don't flirt with all the cute women," Seth added in his own voice.

Tabby's face flushed. "I—uh—it's been n–nice t–t–talking to you. I th–think I sh–should g–go find a s–seat in the s–s–sanctuary now."

"Maybe I'll see you later," Seth called to her retreating form.

✿

Tabby slid into a back-row pew, next to Donna.

"What took you so long? I thought I might have to send out the Coast Guard, just in case you'd fallen overboard or something."

Tabby groaned at Donna's tasteless comment. "I ran into the ventriloquist who taught the workshop I took yesterday."

"You did? What's he doing here?"

"He's part of the demonstration. He brought along his cute little dummy."

"I guess he would, if he's going to do ventriloquism." Donna sent a quick jab to Tabby's ribs with her elbow. "Did he talk to you?"

"Who?"

Another jab to the ribs. "The ventriloquist, of course."

"Actually, it was the dummy who did most of the talking. He was so funny, too."

Donna nodded. "I guess in order to be a ventriloquist, you'd need a good sense of humor."

Tabby twisted her hands together in her lap. How in the world did she think she could ever talk for two? Humor and wisecracking didn't come easy for someone like her. She was about to relay that to Donna, but the church service had begun. She turned her full attention to the front of the room instead.

Mr. Hartung, the middle-aged song leader, led the congregation in several praise choruses, followed by a few hymns. Announcements were given next, then the offering was taken. After that, Pastor Smith encouraged the congregation to use their talents to serve the Lord, and he introduced the group who had come to inspire others to use their talents in the area of Christian ministry.

The first to perform was Mark Taylor, a Christian magician from Portland, Oregon. He did a few sleight-of-hand tricks, showing how sin can seriously affect one's life. Using another illusion, he showed the way to be shed of sin, through Jesus Christ.

Next up was Gail Stevens, a chalk artist from Seattle. She amazed the congregation with her beautiful chalk drawing of Christ's ascension into heaven, adding a special touch by using the black light Donna had been so enthusiastic about. This illuminated the entire picture and seemed to bring the illustration to life, as Jesus rose in a vibrant, fluorescent, pink cloud.

There were oohs and ahs all around the room, and Donna nudged Tabby again. "That's what I want to be able to do someday."

Tabby nodded. "I'm sure you will, too."

A group of puppeteers put on a short musical routine, using several Muppet-style puppets, who sang to a taped version of "Bullfrogs and Butterflies." Tabby enjoyed their skit but was most anxious for the upcoming ventriloquist routine.

Joe Richey, a gospel clown from Olympia, did a short pantomime, which he followed with a demonstration on balloon sculpting. He made a simple dog with a long body, a colorful bouquet of flowers, and ended the routine by making a seal balancing a ball on the end of its nose. Everyone clapped as Slow-Joe the Clown handed out his balloon creations to several excited children in the audience.

Seth Beyers finally took his place in the center of the platform.

"There he is," Tabby whispered breathlessly. "And that's his cute little dummy, Rudy."

Seth had already begun to speak, and Tabby chose to ignore her friend when she asked, "Who do you really think is cute? The funny-looking dummy or the good-looking guy who's pulling his strings?"

"I would like you all to meet my little buddy, Rudy," Seth boomed into the microphone.

"That's right—I'm Rudy Right, and I'm always right!"

"Now, Rudy, I've told you many times that no one but God is always right."

Rudy's glass eyes moved from side to side. "Is that so? I guess we must be related, then!"

"The Bible says that God made people in His own image, and you're certainly not a person."

There was a long pause, as if Rudy might be mulling over what the ventriloquist had said. Finally, the dummy's mouth dropped open. "I may be just a dummy, but I'm smart enough to pull your strings!"

Seth laughed, and so did the audience.

Donna leaned close to Tabby, "This guy's really good. His lips don't move at all."

Tabby smiled. "I know." Oh, how she wished she could perform like that, without stuttering or passing out from stage fright. What a wonderful way ventriloquism was to teach Bible stories and the important lessons of life.

A troubling thought popped into Tabby's head, pushing aside her excitement over the ventriloquism routine. *What would it feel like to have someone as good looking, talented, and friendly as Seth Beyers be interested in someone as dull and uninteresting as me?*

Chapter 4

Wasn't that program great?" Donna asked, as she steered her car out of the church parking lot. "Could you believe how gorgeous the chalk art picture was under the black light?"

"Uh-huh," Tabby mumbled.

"And did you see how quickly Gail Stevens drew that picture? If I drew even half that fast, I'd probably end up with more chalk on me than the paper."

"Hmm..."

Donna glanced Tabby's way. "Is that all you've got to say? What's wrong with you, anyway? Ever since we walked out the door, you've been acting like you're a million miles away."

Tabby merely shrugged her shoulders in reply.

"Since my folks are out of town this weekend, and Mom won't be cooking us her usual Sunday dinner, should we eat out or fend for ourselves at home?"

Tabby shrugged again. "Whatever you think. I'm not all that hungry anyway."

"What? Tabitha Johnson not hungry?" Donna raised her eyebrows. "Surely you jest!"

Tucking a thumbnail between her teeth, Tabby mumbled, "I've never been much into—'jesting.'"

Donna reached across the short span of her car to give Tabby's arm a quick jab. "I've seen the little puppet skits you put on for the kids at our day care. I think they're quite humorous, and so do the children."

Tabby felt her jaw tense. "You're just saying that to make me feel better."

"Uh-uh, I really do think your puppet routines are funny."

"That's because I'm well out of sight, and only the silly-looking dog is in the limelight." Tabby grimaced. "If I had to stand up in front of an audience the way Seth Beyers did today, I think I'd curl up and die right on the spot."

"You know, Tabby, ventriloquism might be the very thing to help you overcome your shyness."

"How can you say that, Donna? I'd have to talk in front of people."

"Yes, but you'd be talking through your dummy."

"Dummy? What dummy? I don't even have a dummy?"

"I know, but you could get one."

"In case you haven't heard—those lifelike things are really expensive. Besides, I'm only going to be doing ventriloquism for the kids at day care. Roscoe's good enough for that." She inhaled deeply. "Of course I have to start practicing first, and only time will tell whether I can actually learn to talk for two."

🌱

As Seth Beyers drove home from church, a keen sense of disappointment flooded his soul. The realization that he hadn't seen Tabby Johnson after the morning service didn't hit him until now.

During his little performance with Rudy, he'd spotted her sitting in the very back row. After the service he had been swarmed by people full of questions about ventriloquism and asking for all kinds of information about the dummies he created and repaired.

Tabby had obviously slipped out the door while he'd been occupied. He would probably never see her again. For reasons beyond his comprehension, that thought made him sad.

He reflected on something Grandpa had recently told him: "Everyone needs to feel as if they count for something, Seth. If you recognize that need in dealing with people, you might be able to help someone learn to like themselves a bit more."

Seth knew his grandfather's advice was good, and as much as he'd like to help Tabby, he also knew all he could really do was pray for the introverted young woman. He promised himself he would remember to do so.

※

Tabby had been practicing ventriloquism for several weeks. She'd often sit in front of the full-length mirror in her bedroom, completely alone except for Roscoe Puppet. Not even Donna had been allowed to see her struggle through those first few difficult attempts at talking for two. If Tabby were ever going to perform for the day care kids, it wouldn't be until she had complete control of her lip movement and had perfected those horrible sound substitutions. There was *th* for v and f, *d* for b, and *n* for m. It was anything but easy, and it was enough to make her crazy!

Tabby took a seat in front of the mirror, slipped Roscoe onto her hand, and held him next to her face. "What do you think, little buddy? Can we ever learn to do ventriloquism well enough to put on a short skit for the kids?"

Manipulating the puppet's mouth, she made him say, "I think we can. . . . I think we can. . . . I think I have a bang-up plan. You throw your voice, and let me say all the funny stuff."

Tabby smiled triumphantly. "I did it! I said the sound substitutions without any lip movement!" She jumped to her feet, jerked open the door, and bolted into the living room. Donna was there, working on a chalk drawing taped to her easel. Tabby held Roscoe in front of her face. "I think I'm finally getting the hang of it!"

Donna kept on drawing. "The hang of what?"

Tabby dropped to the couch with a groan. "I'm trying to tell you that I can talk without moving my lips."

Donna finally set her work aside and turned to face Tabby. "That's great. How about a little demonstration?"

Tabby swallowed hard, and a few tears rolled unexpectedly down her cheeks.

Donna was at her side immediately. "What's wrong? I thought you'd be thrilled about your new talent."

"I am, but I wonder if I'll ever have the nerve to actually use it." She swiped at the tears and sniffed. "I really do want to serve God using ventriloquism, but it seems so hard."

"God never promised that serving Him in any way would be easy," Donna said. "And may I remind you of the acts you already do to serve the Lord?"

Tabby sucked in her bottom lip. "Like what?"

"You teach the day care kids about Jesus. You bake cookies for the residents of Rose Park Convalescent Center. You also read your Bible, pray, and—"

Tabby held up one hand. "Okay, okay. . .I get the picture. What I want to know is, are you saying I should be content to serve God in those ways and forget all about ventriloquism?"

Donna shook her head. "No, of course not. You just need to keep on trying and never give up. I believe God wants all Christians to use their talents and serve Him through whatever means they can."

Running a hand through her hair, Tabby nodded. "All right. I'll try."

With fear and trembling, Tabby forced herself to do a short ventriloquist routine the following day for the day care kids. Fifteen little ones sat cross-legged on the carpeted floor, looking up at her expectantly.

Tabby put Roscoe on one hand, and in the other hand she held a small bag of dog food. Drawing in a deep breath, she began. "R–R–Roscoe wants to tell you a little st–st–story today."

Tabby couldn't believe she was stuttering. She never stuttered in front of the kids. *It's only my nerves. They'll settle down in a few minutes.*

Several children clapped, and one little freckle-faced, redheaded boy called out, "Go, Roscoe! Go!"

Tabby gulped. It was now or never.

"Hey, kids—what's up?" the puppet said in a gravelly voice.

So far so good. No lip movement, and Roscoe's lip sync was right on.

"We just had lunch," a young girl shouted.

Tabby chuckled, feeling herself beginning to relax. "That's right," she said to the puppet. "The kids had macaroni and cheese today."

Pointing Roscoe's nose in the air, Tabby made him say, "I think I smell somethin' else."

"They had hot dogs, too. That's probably what you smell."

"Hot dogs? They had hot dogs?"

Tabby nodded. "That's right, now it's time for your lunch."

"Oh, boy! I get a nice, big, juicy hot dog!"

"No, I have your favorite kind of dog food." Tabby held the bag high in the air.

Roscoe's furry head shook from side to side. "No way! I hate dog food! It's for dogs!"

The children laughed, and Donna, standing at the back of the room, gave Tabby an approving nod.

Tabby's enthusiasm began to soar as she plunged ahead. "But, Roscoe, you are a dog. Dogs are supposed to eat dog food, not people food."

"That's easy for you to say," Roscoe croaked. "Have you ever chomped down on a stale piece of dry old dog food?"

"I can't say as I have."

"Dog food makes me sick," Roscoe whined.

"I never knew that."

Roscoe's head bobbed up and down. "It's the truth. In fact, I was so sick the other day, I had to go to the vet."

"Really?"

"Yep! The vet took my temperature and everything."

"What'd he say?" Tabby prompted.

"He said, 'Hot dog!' " The puppet's head tipped back, and he let out a high-pitched howl.

By the time Tabby was done with her routine, Donna was laughing so hard she had tears rolling down her cheeks. As soon as the children went down for their afternoon naps, she took Tabby aside. "That was great. You're really good at talking for two."

"You think so?"

"Yes, I do. Not only have you mastered lip control and sound substitutions, but your routine was hilarious. Where did you come up with all those cute lines?"

Tabby shrugged. "Beats me. I just kind of ad-libbed as I went along."

Donna gave Tabby a quick hug. "Now all you need is a good ventriloquist dummy."

With an exasperated groan, Tabby dropped into one of the kiddie chairs. "Let's not get into that again. I can't afford one of those professional figures, and since I'll only be performing here at the day care, Roscoe will work just fine!"

🌸

Seth was nearly finished with the ugly dummy he was making for Alan Capshaw. While it had turned out well enough, it wasn't to his personal liking. A good ventriloquist didn't need an ugly dummy in order to captivate an audience. A professional ventriloquist needed talent, humor, and a purpose. For Seth, that purpose was sharing the gospel and helping others find a meaningful relationship with Christ.

In deep concentration at his workbench, Seth didn't even hear the overhead bell ring when a customer entered his shop. Not until he smelled the faint lilac scent of a woman's perfume and heard a polite, "Ahem," did he finally look up from his work.

A young, attractive woman with short, dark curls stood on the other side of the long wooden counter.

Seth placed the ugly dummy aside and skirted quickly around his workbench. "May I help you?"

"Yes. I was wondering if you have gift certificates for the dummies you sell."

Seth smiled. "Sure. For what value did you want it?"

"Would three hundred dollars buy a fairly nice dummy?"

He nodded. "Prices for ventriloquist figures range anywhere from one hundred dollars for a small, inexpensive model to seven hundred dollars for one with all the extras."

"I'd like a gift certificate for three hundred dollars, then."

Seth went to his desk, retrieved the gift certificate book, accepted the young woman's check, and in short order, the business was concluded.

"Are you a ventriloquist?" he asked when she put the certificate in her purse and started to turn away.

She hesitated then pivoted to face him. "No, but a friend of mine is, and she's got a birthday coming up soon."

"You're giving her a professional figure?"

"Sort of. She'll actually be the one forced to come in here and pick it up."

"Forced?" Seth's eyebrows arched upward. "Why would anyone have to be forced to cash in a gift certificate for a ventriloquist dummy?"

"My friend is extremely shy," the woman explained. "It's hard for her to talk to people."

"Your friend's name wouldn't happen to be Tabby Johnson, would it?"

"How did you know that?"

"I thought I recognized you when you first came in. Now I know from where." Seth extended his right hand. "I'm Seth Beyers. I saw Tabby sitting with you during the Christian workers' program at your church a few weeks ago."

"I'm Donna Hartley, and Tabby and I have been friends since we were kids. She said she spoke with you. Well, actually, I guess it was more to your dummy."

Seth nodded. "I could hardly get her to make eye contact."

"That's not surprising."

"Whenever she talked to me, she stuttered." His forehead wrinkled. "She could talk a blue streak to my little pal, Rudy, and never miss a syllable."

Donna shrugged. "To be perfectly honest, besides me, the day care kids are the only ones she can talk to without stuttering."

"Day care kids?"

"Our church has a day care center, and Tabby and I manage it. It's about the only kind of work Tabby can do. Her self-esteem is really low, and I seriously doubt she'd ever make it around adults all day."

Seth couldn't begin to imagine how Tabby must feel. He usually didn't suffer from low self-esteem—unless you could count the fact that he hadn't found the right woman yet. Occasionally he found himself wondering if he had some kind of personality defect.

"Do you think ventriloquism might help Tabby?" Donna asked, breaking into his thoughts.

He shrugged. "Maybe."

"Tabby did a short routine at the day care the other day. It went really well, and I think it gave her a bit more confidence."

Seth scratched the back of his head. He felt like taking on a new challenge. "Hmm. . . Maybe we could work on this problem together."

Donna's eyebrows furrowed. "What do you mean?"

"You keep encouraging her to perform more, and when she comes in to pick out her new dummy, I'll try to work on her from this end."

Donna's expression revealed her obvious surprise. "You'd do that for a complete stranger?"

" 'Whatever you did for one of the least of these brothers of mine, you did for me,' " Seth quoted from the book of Matthew.

"I like your Christian attitude," Donna said as she turned to leave. "Thanks for everything." After the door closed behind her, Seth let out a piercing whoop. He would soon be seeing Tabby again. Maybe he could actually help her. Maybe this was the answer to his prayers.

Chapter 5

"I wish you weren't making such a big deal over my birthday," Tabby grumbled as she and Donna drove home from the grocery store one evening after work. This time they were in Tabby's blue hatchback, and she was in the driver's seat.

"It's just gonna be a barbecue in my parents' backyard," Donna argued. "How can that be labeled a big deal?"

Tabby grimaced. "You ordered a fancy cake, bought three flavors of ice cream, and invited half the city of Tacoma!"

"Oh, please! Your folks, Lois, her boyfriend, your grandma, me, and my folks—that's half of Tacoma?" Donna poked Tabby on the arm. "Besides, your folks live in Olympia now."

"I know, but being with my family more than twenty minutes makes me feel like it's half of Tacoma," Tabby argued.

"It isn't every day that my best friend turns twenty-five," Donna persisted. "If I want to throw her a big party, then it's my right to do so."

"I don't mean to sound ungrateful, but you know how things are between me and my family," Tabby reminded.

Donna nodded. "Yes, I do, and I know your parents often hurt you by the unkind things they say and do, but you can't pull away from them and stay in your cocoon of shyness. You don't have to like what they say and do, but you've got to love your family anyway." She sighed. "What I'm trying to say is, you've gotta love 'em, but you can't let them run your life or destroy your confidence, the way you've been doing for so long. It's high time for you to stand up and be counted."

"Yeah, right. Like that could ever happen."

"It could if you gained some self-confidence and quit letting Lois overshadow you."

"Fat chance! Just wait till you see the size of her engagement ring. It looks like Mount Rainier!"

Donna laughed. "How you do exaggerate."

"She's only marrying this guy for his money. Did I tell you that?"

"Only about a hundred times."

"I think it's disgusting." Tabby frowned. "I'd never marry anyone unless I loved him. Of course, he'd have to be a Christian," she quickly added.

"I'm beginning to think neither of us will ever find a husband," Donna said. "You're too shy, and I'm too picky."

"I can't argue with that. Unless I find a man who's either just a big kid or a real dummy, I'd never be able to talk to him."

"Maybe you can find a ventriloquist to marry, then let your dummies do all the talking."

Tabby groaned. "Now there's a brilliant idea. I can see it now—me, walking down the aisle, carrying a dummy instead of a bouquet. My groom would be waiting at the altar, holding his own dummy, of course."

Donna chuckled. "You are so funny today. Too bad the rest of the world can't see the real Tabitha Johnson."

❀

The birthday party was set to begin at six o'clock on Saturday night, in the backyard of

Donna's parents, Carl and Irene.

"I still say this is a bad idea," Tabby grumbled, as she stepped into the living room, where Donna waited on the couch.

"Should we do something special with your hair?" Donna asked. "We could pull it away from your face with some pretty pearl combs."

Tabby wrinkled her nose. "I like it plain. Besides, I'm not trying to make an impression on anyone." She flopped down next to Donna. "Even if I were, it would never work. Dad and Mom won't even know I'm alive once Lois shows up with her fiancé."

"I've got a great idea," Donna exclaimed. "Why don't you bring Roscoe to the barbecue? After we eat, you can entertain us with a cute little routine."

Tabby frowned. "You're kidding, right?"

"No. I think it would be a lot of fun. Besides, what better way to show your family that you really do have some talent?"

"Talent? What talent?"

"There you go again." Donna shook a finger in Tabby's face. "Self-doubting will never get you over being shy."

Tabby stood up. She knew Donna was probably right, but it was time to change the subject. "Do you think this outfit looks okay?" She brushed a hand across her beige-colored slacks.

"Well, now that you asked. . .I was thinking you might look better in that soft peach sundress of mine."

"No thanks. I'm going like I am, and that's final."

❦

The warm spring evening was a bit unusual for May in rainy Tacoma, but Tabby wasn't about to complain. The glorious weather was probably the only part of her birthday that would be pleasant.

The smoky aroma of hot dogs and juicy burgers sizzling on the grill greeted Tabby as she and Donna entered the Hartleys' backyard. Donna's father, wearing a long white apron with a matching chef's hat, was busy flipping burgers then covering them with tangy barbecue sauce. He stopped long enough to give both girls a quick peck on the cheek but quickly returned to the job at hand.

His petite wife, who looked like an older version of Donna, was setting the picnic table with floral paper plates and matching cups.

"Is th–there anything I can d–do to help?" Tabby questioned.

Irene waved her hand toward the porch swing. "Nope. I've got it all covered. Go relax, birthday girl."

"That's a good idea," Donna greed. "You swing, and I'll help Mom."

Tabby didn't have to be asked twice. The Hartleys' old porch swing had been her favorite ever since she was a child. Soon she was rocking back and forth, eyes closed, and thoughts drifting to the past.

She and Donna had spent many hours in the quaint but peaceful swing, playing with their dolls, making up silly songs, and whispering shared secrets. *If only life could have stayed this simple. If only I could always feel as contented as when I'm in this old swing.*

"Hey, big sister. . . Wake up and come to the party!"

Lois's shrill voice jolted Tabby out of her reverie, and she jerked her eyes open with a start. "Oh, I—I d–didn't kn–know you w–w–were here."

"Just got here." Lois gave Tabby an appraising look. "I thought you'd be a little more dressed for tonight's occasion."

28

Tabby glanced down at her drab slacks and pale yellow blouse then she lifted her face to study Lois's long, pastel blue skirt, accented by a soft white silk blouse. By comparison, Tabby knew she looked like Little Orphan Annie.

Lois grabbed her hand and catapulted her off the swing. "Mom and Dad aren't here yet, but I want you to meet my fiancé, the successful lawyer, whose parents have big bucks."

Tabby was practically dragged across the lawn and over to the picnic table, where a dark-haired, distinguished-looking young man sat. A pair of stylish metal-framed glasses were perched on his aristocratic nose, and he was wearing a suit, of all things!

"Mike, honey, this is the birthday girl—my big sister, Tabitha." Lois leaned over and dropped a kiss on the end of his nose.

He smiled up at her then turned to face Tabby. "Hi. Happy birthday."

"Th–th–thanks," she murmured.

Michael gave her an odd look, but Lois grabbed his hand and pulled him off toward the porch swing before he could say anything more.

Donna, who had been pouring lemonade into the paper cups, moved toward Tabby. "Looks like your sister brought you over here just so she could grab the old swing."

Tabby watched her beautiful, self-assured sister swagger across the lawn, laughing and clinging to Michael like she didn't have a care in the world. She shrugged. "Lois can have the silly swing. She can have that rich boyfriend of hers, too."

"Oh, oh. Do I detect a hint of jealousy?"

Tabby knew Donna was right, and she was about to say so, but her parents and grandmother had just come through the gate, and she figured it would be rude to ignore them.

"So glad you two could make it." Donna's father shook hands with Tabby's parents then turned to her grandmother and planted a noisy kiss on her slightly wrinkled cheek. "You're sure lookin' chipper, Dottie."

"Carl Hartley, you still know how to pour on the charm, don't you?" Grandma Haskins raked a wrinkled hand through her short, silver-gray hair and grinned at him.

Up to this point, no one had even spoken to Tabby. She stood off to one side, head down, eyes focused on her beige sneakers.

Grandma Haskins was the first to notice her. "And here's our guest of honor. Happy twenty-fifth, Tabitha."

Tabby feigned a smile. "Th–thanks, Grandma."

"Yes, happy birthday," Mom added, placing a gift on one end of the table.

Tabby glanced up at her mother. She knew she looked a lot like Mom. They had the same mousy brown hair, dark brown eyes, and were both short of stature. That was where the similarities ended, though. Mom was much more socially secure than Tabby. She was soft spoken, but unlike Tabby, her words didn't come out in a mumble-jumble of stammering and stuttering.

Tabby's gaze went to her father then. He was still visiting with Donna's dad and never even looked her way. Lois got her good looks from him, that was for sure. His blond hair, though beginning to recede, and those vivid blue eyes were enough to turn any woman's head. *No wonder Mom fell for Dad.*

Donna's mother, Irene, the ever-gracious hostess, instructed the guests to be seated at the picnic table, while she scurried about to serve them all beverages.

Even though Tabby was the only one in her family who professed Christianity, they all sat quietly through Carl's prayer. When he asked God to bless Tabby and give her many good years to serve Him, she heard Lois snicker.

Tabby had a compelling urge to dash back home to her apartment—where she'd be free of Lois's scrutiny and her dad's indifference. She knew it would be rude, and besides, the aroma of barbecued meat and the sight of several eye-catching salads made her feel as if she were starving. The promise of cake, ice cream, and gifts made her appreciate the special party Donna had planned, too. It was more than her own family would have done. With the exception of Grandma, she doubted whether any of them even cared that today was her birthday.

"Please don't sing 'Happy Birthday' and make me blow out the dumb candles," Tabby whispered when Donna set a huge cake in front of her a short time later. It was a beautiful cake—a work of art, really—German chocolate, Tabby's favorite, and it was covered with thick cream-cheese frosting. Delicate pink roses bordered the edges, and right in the middle sat a giant-sized heart with the words Happy Birthday, Tabby.

"Don't spoil everyone's fun," Donna said softly.

Tabby bit back a caustic comeback, forcing herself to sit patiently through the strains of "Happy Birthday."

"Okay, it's time to open the presents." Donna moved the cake aside then placed the gifts directly in front of Tabby. The first one was from Lois. Inside a gold-foil-wrapped gift box was a pale green silk blouse and a makeup kit. It was filled with lipstick, blush, eyeliner, mascara, and a bottle of expensive perfume.

At Tabby's questioning look, Lois said, "I thought it might spark you up a bit. You always wear such drab colors and no makeup at all."

Tabby could have argued, since she did wear a touch of lipstick now and then. "Th–thanks, L–Lois," she mumbled instead.

Grandma Haskins reached over with her small gift bag. "Open mine next, dear."

Tabby read the card first then drew a small journal from the sack.

"I thought you might enjoy writing down some of your personal thoughts," Grandma explained. "I've kept a diary for many years, and I find it to be quite therapeutic."

Tabby and her maternal grandmother exchanged a look of understanding. Despite the fact that Grandma, who'd been widowed for the last ten years, wasn't a Christian, she was a good woman. Tabby felt that Grandma loved her, in spite of all her insecurities.

"Thank you, Grandma. I th–think it'll be f–fun."

"This one's from your folks," Donna said, pushing the other two gifts aside.

There was no card, just a small tag tied to the handle of the bag. It read: "To Tabitha, From Mom and Dad."

Tabby swallowed past the lump lodged in her throat. *They couldn't even write "love." That's because they don't feel any love for me. They only wanted me until Lois came along; then I became nothing but a nuisance.*

"Well, don't just sit there like a dunce. Open it!" her father bellowed.

Tabby ground her teeth together and jerked open the bag. Why did Dad always have to make her feel like such an idiot? As she withdrew a set of white bath towels, edged with black ribbon trim, her heart sank. Towels were always practical, but white? What in the world had Mom been thinking? She was sure it had been her mother's choice because Dad rarely shopped for anything.

"Th–thanks. Th–these will go g–good in our b–b–bathroom," she stuttered.

"I was hoping you'd put them in your hope chest," Mom remarked.

Tabby shook her head. "I d–don't have a h–hope chest."

"It's high time you started one, then," Dad roared. "Lois is only nineteen, and she's planning to be married soon."

As if on cue, Lois smiled sweetly and held up her left hand.

"Your engagement ring is beautiful," Donna's mother exclaimed. "Congratulations to both of you."

Michael beamed and leaned over to kiss his bride-to-be.

Tabby blushed, as though she'd been kissed herself. Not that she knew what it felt like to be kissed. The only men's lips to have ever touched her face had been her dad's, when she was young, and Carl Hartley's, whenever he greeted her and Donna.

Donna cleared her throat. "Ahem! This is from Mom, Dad, and me." She handed Tabby a large white envelope.

Tabby's forehead wrinkled. Donna always went all out for her birthday. A card? Was that all she was giving her this year?

"Go ahead, open it," Donna coached. She was smiling like a cat who had just cornered a robin. Carl and Irene were looking at her expectantly, too.

Tabby shrugged and tore open the envelope. She removed the lovely religious card that was signed, "With love, Donna, Irene, and Carl." A small slip of paper fell out of the card and landed on the table, just missing the piece of cake Grandma Haskins had placed in front of Tabby. Tabby picked it up, and her mouth dropped open. "A gift certificate for a ventriloquist dummy?"

"Ventriloquist dummy?" Lois repeated. "What in the world would you need a dummy for?"

Before Tabby could respond, Donna blurted out, "Tabby's recently learned how to talk for two. She's quite good at it, I might add."

If ever there had been a time when Tabby wanted to find a hole to crawl into, it was now. She swallowed hard and said in a high-pitched squeak which sounded much like her puppet, "I–I'm just l–l–learning."

❧

By the time Tabby and Donna returned to their apartment, Tabby's shock over the surprise gift certificate had worn off. It had been replaced with irritation. She knew Donna's heart was in the right place, and Tabby didn't want to make an issue out of it, but what in the world was she going to do?

Tabby placed her birthday gifts on the kitchen table and went out to the living room. Donna was busy closing the miniblinds, and she smiled when she turned and saw Tabby. "I hope you enjoyed your party."

Tabby forced a smile in response. "It was nice, and I really do appreciate the expensive gift you and your folks gave me."

Donna nodded. "I sense there's a 'but' in there someplace."

Tabby flopped into the rocking chair and began to pump back and forth, hoping the momentum might help her conjure up the courage to say what was on her mind. "It was an expensive birthday present," she said again.

Donna took a seat on the couch, just opposite her. "You're worth every penny of it."

Tabby shrugged. "I don't know about that, but—"

"There's that 'but.'" Donna laughed. "Okay, let me have it. What don't you like about the idea of getting a professional ventriloquist dummy?"

Tabby stopped rocking and leaned forward. "I—uh—"

"Come on, Tabby, just spit it out. Are you mad because my folks and I gave you that certificate?"

"Not mad, exactly. I guess it really would be kind of fun to own a dummy, even if I'm only going to use it at the day care."

"That's exactly what I thought," Donna said with a satisfied smile.

"The gift certificate says it's redeemable at Beyers' Ventriloquist Studio."

"That's the only place in Tacoma where ventriloquist dummies are bought, sold, and repaired."

"I know, but Seth Beyers owns the business, and he—"

"Oh, I get it! You have a thing for this guy, and the thought of being alone with him makes you nervous."

Tabby bolted out of the rocking chair, nearly knocking it over. "I do not have a thing for him! I just can't go in there and talk to him alone, that's all. You know how hard it is for me to speak to anyone but you or the kids. Wasn't that obvious tonight at the party?" She began to pace the length of the living room. "I couldn't even get through a complete sentence without stuttering and making a complete fool of myself. No wonder my family thinks I'm an idiot."

Donna moved quickly to Tabby's side and offered her a hug. "You're a big girl now, Tabby. I can't go everywhere with you or always be there to hold your shaking hand."

Donna's words stung like fire, but Tabby knew they were spoken in love. "What do you suggest I do—call Seth Beyers and see if I can place an order over the phone?"

Donna shook her head. "Of course not. You need to take a look at what he's got in stock. If there isn't anything suitable, he has a catalog you can look through."

"But I'll stutter and stammer all over the place."

Donna stepped directly in front of Tabby. "I suppose you could always take little Roscoe along for added courage," she said with a teasing grin.

Tabby's face brightened. "Say, that's a great idea! I don't know why I didn't think of it myself."

Chapter 6

Tabby knew there was no point in procrastinating. If she didn't go to Beyers' Ventriloquist Studio right away, she'd have to endure the agony of Donna's persistent nagging. Since today was Friday, and she had an hour off for lunch, it might as well be now.

Tabby slipped Roscoe into the pocket of her raincoat, said good-bye to Donna, and rushed out the door. She stepped carefully to avoid several large puddles then made a mad dash for her car, because, as usual, it was raining.

"Why couldn't it have done this last night?" she moaned. "Maybe then my birthday party would have been canceled." She slid into the driver's seat, closed the door with a bang, and pulled Roscoe out of her pocket. "Okay, little buddy, it's just you and me. I'm counting on you to get me through this, so please don't let me down."

※

Seth had been up late the night before, putting the finishing touches on a grandpa dummy someone in Colorado had ordered from his catalog. He'd had trouble getting the moving glass eyes to shift to the right without sticking. Determined to see it through to completion, Seth had gone to bed shortly after midnight. Now he was feeling the effects of lost sleep and wondered if he shouldn't just close up shop for the rest of the day. He didn't have any scheduled customers that afternoon, and since it was raining so hard, it wasn't likely there would be any walk-ins, either.

Seth was heading over to put the CLOSED sign in the window, when the door flew open, nearly knocking him off his feet. Looking like a drenched puppy, Tabby Johnson stood there, holding her purse in one hand and a small, scruffy dog puppet in the other.

"Come in," he said, stepping quickly aside. "Here, let me take your coat."

"My—my c–coat is f–fine. It's w–w–waterproof."

Seth smiled, hoping to make her feel more at ease, but it didn't seem to have any effect on the trembling young woman. "I've been expecting you," he said softly.

"You—h–have?"

"Well, maybe not today, but I knew you'd be coming in sometime soon."

Tabby slipped the dog puppet onto her hand and held him in front of her face. "How did you know Tabby would be coming here?" she made the puppet say.

Seth had no idea what she was up to, but he decided to play along. "Tabby's friend was in the other day," he answered, looking right at the puppet. "She bought a gift certificate for a dummy and said it was for Tabby's birthday."

Tabby's hand slipped slightly, and Roscoe's head dropped below her chin.

Now Seth could see her face clearly, and he had to force himself to keep talking to the puppet and not her. "Say, what's your name, little fellow?"

"Woof! Woof! I'm Roscoe Dog!"

She's actually doing ventriloquism, Seth noted. *Doing a pretty good job at it too. Should I compliment her? Maybe give her a few encouraging words about her newfound talent? No, I'd better play along for a while and see if I can gain her confidence.*

Seth moved over to the counter where he usually did business with customers. He stepped behind it and retrieved one of his catalogs from the shelf underneath. "Are you planning to help Tabby pick out a dummy?" he asked, again directing his question to the puppet.

Roscoe's head bounced up and down. "Sure am. Have ya got anything on hand?"

"You don't want to look at the catalog?" This time Seth looked right at Tabby.

She squirmed under his scrutiny, but in a well-spoken ventriloquist voice she made the puppet say, "I'd rather see what you've got first."

Seth frowned. Tabby seemed unable to carry on a conversation without either stuttering or using the puppet, and she still hadn't looked him in the eye when he spoke directly to her. What was this little woman's problem, anyhow?

❀

Tabby tapped the toe of her sneaker against the concrete floor as she waited for Seth's response to her request.

"Okay, I'll go in the back room and see what I can find," he finally mumbled. When Seth disappeared, she took a seat in one of the folding chairs near the front door. She didn't know what had possessed her to use Roscoe Puppet to speak to Seth Beyers. He probably thought she was out of her mind or acting like a little kid. If she'd tried to talk to him on her own, though, she'd have ended up stuttering like a woodpecker tapping on a tree. Tabby knew it was stupid, but using the puppet helped her relax, and she was able to speak clearly with no stammering at all. *Guess this little experience will be something to write about in my new journal,* she thought with a wry smile.

The telephone rang sharply, causing Tabby to jump. She glanced around anxiously, wondering whether Seth would hear it ringing and return to answer it. For a fleeting moment she thought of answering it herself but quickly dismissed the idea, knowing she'd only stutter and wouldn't have the foggiest idea of what to say.

She was rescued from her dilemma when Seth reappeared, carrying a large trunk, which he set on one end of the counter. "Be right with you," he said, reaching for the phone.

Tabby waited impatiently as he finished his business. She was dying to know what was inside that huge chest.

Five minutes later, Seth finally hung up. "Sorry about the interruption. That was a special order, and I had to be sure of all the details."

Tabby moved back to the counter, waiting expectantly as Seth opened the trunk lid. "I didn't know if you wanted a girl, boy, or animal figure, so I brought a few of each," he explained. Tabby's eyes widened as Seth pulled out several dummies and puppets, placing them on the counter for her inspection.

"They all have open-close mouths and eyes that move from side to side. Would you like to try one?"

Roscoe was dropped to the counter as Tabby picked up a small girl dummy dressed in blue overalls and a pink shirt. The figure's moving glass eyes were blue, and her brown hair was braided. Tabby held the figure awkwardly with one hand, unsure of what to say or do with it. The telltale sign of embarrassment crept up the back of her neck, flooding her entire face with familiar heat. "H—how do you w—work it?"

"Here, let me show you." Seth moved quickly around the counter until he was standing right beside Tabby. She could feel his warm breath against her neck, and she shivered when his hand brushed lightly against her arm. She wondered if she might be coming down with a cold.

Seth pulled the slit on the dummy's overalls apart, so Tabby could see inside the hollow, hard plastic body. "See here. . .that's where the wooden control stick is hidden. You turn the rod to the right or left for the figure's head to move." He demonstrated, while Tabby held the dummy.

"When you want to make her talk, you need to pull sharply down on this." He gave the small metal handle a few tugs. "The right lever makes the eyes move from side to side."

When Tabby nodded, Seth stepped away, allowing her access to the inside of the figure's body. "Okay, now you try it."

The control stick felt stiff and foreign beneath Tabby's trembling fingers, and it took a few tries before she got the hang of it. "Hi, my name's Rosie," she made the dummy say in a high-pitched, little-girl voice. "Will you take me home with you?"

Tabby pretended to whisper something into the figure's ear.

"She wants to know how much I cost," Rosie said to Seth.

His sudden frown made Tabby wonder if the girl dummy cost a lot more than the value of her gift certificate.

"This little game has been fun," Seth said kindly, "but if we're gonna do business, I think Tabby should speak for herself."

Seth's words hadn't been spoken harshly, but they still had an impact, causing Tabby to flinch, as though she'd been slapped.

"I'm sorry, but I get in enough dummy talk of my own," he apologized. "I'd really like to speak to you one-on-one."

Tabby lifted her gaze to finally meet his, and their eyes met and held. "I—I h–have a ph–phobia about sp–speaking in p–public or to p–people I–I'm uncomfortable w–w–with."

Seth grinned, but his eyes remained serious. "I know all about phobias."

"Y–you do?"

"Yep. I studied them in one of my college psychology classes." He pointed at Tabby. "Your phobia is called phonophobia—fear of speaking aloud. I think everyone has at least one phobia, so it's really not such a big deal."

"W–we do? I m–mean, other p–people have ph–phobias, too?"

"Oh, sure. In fact, I believe I'm plagued with one of the worst phobias of all."

Tabby shot him a quizzical look. "R–really? W–what's your ph–ph–phobia?"

"It's arachibutyrophobia—peanut butter, sticking to the roof of my mouth."

She giggled, in spite of her self-consciousness. "Y–you're m–making that up."

He shook his head. "No, that's the correct terminology for my phobia."

Tabby eyed him suspiciously.

He raised his hand. "I'm completely serious. I really do freak out every time I try to eat peanut butter. If it gets stuck to the roof of my mouth, which it usually does, I panic."

If Seth was trying to put her at ease, it was working, because Tabby felt more relaxed than she had all day. She tipped her head toward Rosie. "So, h–how much does she cost?" she asked, stuttering over only one word this time.

"Three hundred dollars. Your gift certificate should pretty well cover it."

"W–what about tax?"

He rewarded her with a quick wink. "My treat."

"Oh, no, I c–couldn't let you do th–that."

Seth shrugged. "Okay. You treat me to a cup of coffee and a piece of pie, and we'll call it even."

"I—I have to get b–back to w–w–work," she hedged, beginning to feel less relaxed and fully aware that she was stuttering heavily again.

"You can give me your address and phone number, which I'll need for my customer records anyway," Seth said with a grin. "I'll come by your house tonight and pick you up."

Tabby's heartbeat picked up considerably. "P–p–pick me u–up?" Her knees felt like they could buckle at any moment, and she leaned heavily against the counter for support.

Seth's grin widened. "How's seven o'clock sound?"

She was keenly aware of his probing gaze, and it made her feel even more uneasy. All she could do was nod mutely.

"Great! It's a date!"

🌸

"How'd it go? Did you get a dummy? Where is it, and how come you don't look overjoyed?"

"You'd better go take your lunch break," Tabby said as she hung her wet raincoat over the back of a chair. "We can talk later."

Donna shook her head. "I ate with the kids, and now they're resting. We have plenty of time to talk."

With a sigh of resignation, Tabby dropped into one of the little chairs.

Donna pulled out the chair next to her and took a seat, too. "Don't keep me in suspense a moment longer. Where's the dummy?"

"Right here," Tabby said, pointing to herself. "I'm the biggest dummy of all."

Donna's forehead wrinkled. "I don't get it."

"I'm supposed to take Seth Beyers out for pie and coffee tonight." Tabby's lower lip began to tremble, and her eyes filled with unwanted tears.

"You've got a date with Seth Beyers, and you're crying about it? I sure hope those are tears of joy."

Tabby dropped her head into her hands and began to sob.

"Please don't cry," Donna said softly. "I would think you'd be thrilled to have a date with someone as good looking and talented as Seth."

Tabby sniffed deeply. "It's not really a date."

"It's not? What is it, then?"

"He covered the tax for Rosie, so I owe him pie and coffee."

Donna shook her head. "I have absolutely no idea what you're talking about. Who's Rosie?"

Tabby sat up straight, dashing away the tears with the back of her hand. "Rosie's my new dummy. She's out in the car."

"Okay, I get that much. What I don't get is why you would owe Seth pie and coffee."

"I just told you. He covered the tax. My gift certificate was the right amount for the dummy, but not enough for the tax. Seth said if I treated him to pie and coffee, he'd call it even."

Donna smiled smugly. "Sounds like a date to me."

🌸

Seth had spent the better part of his day thinking about the pie and coffee date he'd made with Tabby. He wasn't sure why the thought of seeing the shy young woman again made his heart pound like a jackhammer. His mouth felt as though he'd just come from the dentist's office after a root canal. Maybe his interest in Tabby went deeper than a simple desire to help her climb out of the internal cell that obviously held her prisoner. If Seth were being completely honest, he'd have to admit that he was strangely attracted to Tabby. She might not be a beauty queen, but she was a long way from being ugly. In fact, he thought she was kind of cute. Even so, it wasn't her looks that held him captive. *What is it then?* he wondered.

Seth shrugged into a lightweight jacket and started out the door. "Guess I'll try to figure it all out tonight, over a piece of apple pie and a cup of coffee."

❧

Tabby passed in front of her full-length bedroom mirror and stopped short. For a fleeting moment she thought she saw a smiling, beautiful woman staring back at her. No, that wasn't possible, because she was ugly. *Well, maybe not actually ugly,* she supposed. *Just ordinary. Shy and ordinary.* How could timid, stuttering Tabitha Johnson with mousy-colored brown hair and doe eyes ever look beautiful? Tabby's navy blue cotton dress slacks with matching blue flats weren't anything spectacular. Neither was the red-and-white pin-striped blouse she wore. She'd curled her hair for a change, and it fell in loose waves across her shoulders. It was nothing compared to her sister's soft, golden locks, though. What then, had caused her to think she looked beautiful?

Tabby studied her reflection more closely. A hint of pink lipstick was all the makeup she wore. However, her cheeks glowed, and her eyes sparkled with. . .what? Excitement? Anticipation? What was she feeling as she prepared for this outing with Seth Beyers?

"Nervous, that's what I'm feeling!" Tabby exclaimed, pushing that elusive lock of hair away from her face. She reached for the doorknob. "Guess there's no turning back now. A promise is a promise," she muttered as she stepped into the living room. She began to pace, wondering if the butterflies, so insistent on attacking her insides, would ever settle down.

"Would you please stop pacing and sit down? You're making me nervous!" Donna patted the sofa cushion beside her. "Have a seat."

Tabby flopped onto the couch with a groan. "I hate waiting."

When the doorbell rang, Tabby jumped up like someone who'd been stung by a wasp. "Do you think I look okay?"

"You're fine. Now go answer that door."

As soon as Tabby opened the front door, her mouth went dry. Seth stood there, wearing a beige jacket, an off-white shirt, and a pair of brown slacks. His auburn hair looked freshly washed, and his green eyes sparkled with the kind of happiness she so often wished for. "Hope I'm not late," he said in a jovial tone.

"I—I th–think you're r–right on time."

"Are you ready to go?"

Tabby hesitated. "I—uh—let me g–get my d–dummy first."

Seth's eyebrows shot up. "I thought this was a pie and coffee thing." Without waiting for an invitation, he pushed past Tabby and sauntered into the living room. His gaze went to Donna, sitting on the couch. "You're Tabby's friend, right?"

She nodded. "Last time I checked."

"Can't you talk some sense into her?"

Donna shrugged and gave him a half smile. "She's your date."

"Quit talking about me like I'm not even in the room!" Tabby shouted. "I need the dummy so I don't stutter."

Seth and Donna were both grinning at her. "What? What's so funny?" she hollered.

"You're not stuttering now," Seth said, taking a seat in the overstuffed chair nearest the door.

"I—I was angry," Tabby shot back. "I usually d–don't stutter when I'm mad."

Seth chuckled and gave Donna a quick wink. "Guess maybe we should keep her mad at us."

Donna wiggled her eyebrows. "You think that might be the answer?"

Tabby dropped to the couch. "Would you please stop? This is no l–laughing m–matter."

Donna looked at Seth and smiled, and then she glanced back at Tabby. "Can't you see yourself sitting at the pastry shop, holding your dummy and talking for two?" She grabbed a throw pillow and held it against her chest, making a feeble attempt at holding back the waves of laughter that were shaking her entire body.

"You never know," Seth said with a chuckle. "We might draw quite a crowd, and Tabby could become famous overnight. I'd probably drum up some ventriloquist business in the process, too."

Tabby didn't know whether to laugh or cry. She sat there several seconds, watching her best friend and so-called date, howling at her expense. When she'd had all she could take, Tabby jumped up and stormed out of the living room. Jerking open her bedroom door, she stalked across the carpet and flung herself on the bed. "I may never speak to Donna again," she wailed. "Forget about the dumb old tax. Seth Beyers can buy his own pie and coffee!"

Chapter 7

Astream of tears ran down Tabby's face, trickling toward her ears. She jumped off the bed, fully intending to go back into the living room and give Seth and Donna a piece of her mind, but she stopped short just after she opened the door.

"Tabby has real potential," she heard Donna say. "She's just afraid to use her talents."

"She needs lots of encouragement," Seth responded. "I can see how shy she is, but I didn't think taking the dummy along on our date would help her any. In fact, if someone were to laugh at Tabby, it might make things even worse. I really do want to help her be all she can be, but I'm not sure how to go about it."

"I think you're right," Donna said. "Taking the dummy along would be a bad idea."

Tabby peered around the corner. She could only see the back of Seth's head, but Donna was in plain view. She ducked inside her room. Now probably wasn't a good time to reappear. Not with the two of them talking about her.

Tabby crawled onto her bed again and stared at the ceiling. When she heard a knock at the door, she chose to ignore it. The door opened anyway, but she turned her face to the wall.

"Tabby, I'm sorry." The bed moved under Donna's weight, and Tabby felt a gentle hand touch her trembling shoulder. "Seth and I were wrong to laugh at you. It was all in fun, and we didn't expect you to get so upset."

Tabby released a sob and hiccupped. "Seth must think I'm a real dummy."

"I'm sure he doesn't. He only wants to help you."

Tabby rolled over, jerking into an upright position. "Help me? You mean he thinks I'm some kind of neurotic nut who needs counseling?" She swiped the back of her hand across her face. "Is he still here, or has he split by now?"

"He's still here."

Tabby bit her lip and closed her eyes with the strain of trying to get her emotions under control. "Just tell him the pie and coffee date is off."

Donna hopped off the bed and started for the door. "He's your date, not mine, so you can tell him yourself."

Tabby grabbed one of her pillows and let it sail across the room, just as the door clicked shut.

❀

Seth paced back and forth across the living room—waiting, hoping, praying Tabby would come out of her room. He needed to apologize for his rude behavior. The last thing he wanted was to hurt Tabby's feelings.

"Maybe I should have kept my big mouth shut and let her drag the dumb dummy along on our date. The worse thing that could have happened is we'd be the laughingstock of the pastry shop," he mumbled. "It sure wouldn't be the first time I've been laughed at. Probably not the last, either."

When Tabby's bedroom door opened, Seth snapped to attention. His expectancy turned to disappointment when Donna stepped from the room without Tabby. Seth began to knead the back of his neck. "She's really hoppin' mad, huh?"

Donna nodded. "Afraid so. She wouldn't even listen to me."

"Will she talk to me?"

Donna shrugged and took a seat on the couch. "I doubt it, Seth. She wanted me to tell you that the date is off, but I told her she'd have to tell you herself."

Seth chewed on his lower lip. "And?"

"She threw a pillow at me, but it hit the door instead."

Seth groaned. "She may be shy, but she's obviously got quite a temper."

Donna shook her head. "Not really. In fact, I've never seen her this angry before. She usually holds in her feelings. She must have it pretty bad."

Seth lowered himself into a chair. "Have what pretty bad?"

Donna opened her mouth to reply but was stopped short when Tabby stepped into the room.

Seth could see she'd been crying. Her eyes were red, and her face looked kind of swollen. It made him feel like such a heel. He jumped up from his chair and moved swiftly toward her. "Tabby, I—"

She raised her hand, and he noticed she was holding a checkbook. He fell silent. It was obvious that a simple apology was not going to be enough.

❦

Tabby shifted from one leg to the other, wondering what to say. She was keenly aware of Seth's probing gaze, and it made her feel uneasy. She was sure he already thought she was an idiot, so it shouldn't really matter what she said at this point. After tonight, Seth would probably never want to see her again anyway.

Tabby continued to stand there, shoulders hunched, arms crossed over her chest. She felt totally defeated. "Y—you h—hurt me," she squeaked. "You h—hurt me b—bad."

Seth nodded. "I know, and I'm sorry for laughing at you. It's just that—"

"You d—don't have to—to explain," Tabby said with a wave of her hand. "I know it w—would embarrass you if I t—took my d—dummy, but I can't t—talk right w—without her."

Seth took a few steps toward Tabby, which brought his face mere inches from hers. "Your stuttering doesn't bother me, but if you'd be more comfortable bringing Rosie, then I'm okay with it."

Tabby gulped and drew in a deep breath. She was sure Seth was only trying to humor her. Taking the dummy into the pastry shop would be even dumber than taking her puppet to Seth's place of business earlier that day. She held out her checkbook. "Let's forget about pie and coffee, okay? I'll write you a check to cover the tax due on Rosie."

Running a hand through his hair, Seth frowned. "You don't want to go out with me?"

She glanced at him anxiously then dipped her head, afraid of the rejection she might see on his face. "I d—don't w—want to embarrass y—you."

"Look, if it would make you feel more at ease, we can get our pie and coffee to go. We could take it to the park and eat it in the car."

Tabby shifted uneasily. She really did want to go, but—

Donna, who'd been sitting silently on the couch, spoke up. "Would you just go already? You two are driving me nuts!"

"I th—think she w—wants to get rid of me," Tabby said, giving Seth a sidelong glance.

He wiggled his eyebrows playfully. "Her loss is my gain."

Tabby's heartbeat quickened at his sincere tone. He did seem to be genuinely sorry. "Okay, l—let's go. Without R—Rosie, though. One d—dummy is enough for y—you to h—handle."

"I hope you're not referring to yourself," he said with a puckered brow.

"She is," Donna said, before Tabby had a chance to answer. "She's always putting herself down."

Tabby shot her friend a look of irritation before retrieving her raincoat from the hall closet. "We'll talk about this later."

Donna shrugged. "You two have fun!"

"We will," Seth called over his shoulder.

❧

"I was impressed with your ventriloquism abilities when you were in my shop today," Seth said. He and Tabby were sitting in his black Jeep, at a viewpoint along the five-mile drive in Point Defiance Park.

Tabby took a sip of her mocha latte. "I'm just a beginner, and I know I still have lots to learn."

"But you're a quick learner. I saw no lip movement at all."

She shrugged. "That's what Donna's been telling me. She thinks I should do a ventriloquist routine for our Sunday school opening sometime."

Seth's face broke into a smile. "That's a terrific idea!"

"Oh, I couldn't."

"Why not?"

"I stutter."

Seth chuckled. "Not when you're really mad. . .or doing ventriloquism." He snapped his fingers. "Do you realize that you haven't stuttered once since we pulled into this parking spot? I don't know if it's the awesome sight of the lights on Narrows Bridge that has put you at ease, or if you're just beginning to feel more comfortable around me."

Tabby contemplated that for a few seconds. Seth was right; she hadn't been stuttering. For the first time all evening Tabby didn't feel nervous. In fact, she felt more relaxed than she had all day. Donna and the day care kids were the only people she'd ever felt this comfortable around. Maybe Seth could be her friend. Maybe. . .

Tabby grimaced. Who was she kidding? Seth was confident, good looking, and talented. He'd never want someone like her as a friend. In his line of work, he met all sorts of people. Probably had lots of close friends. She was sure none of them stuttered or turned cherry red every time someone looked at them. Why did she allow herself to hope or have foolish dreams? Would she spend the rest of her life wishing for the impossible?

"Tabby, did you hear what I said?" Seth's deep voice broke into her thoughts, and she forced herself to look at him.

"Huh?"

He rested his palm on her trembling hand. "You don't have to be nervous around me. I'm just plain old Seth Beyers, fearful of eating sticky peanut butter."

Tabby swallowed hard. Seth's gentle touch made her insides quiver, and she looked away quickly, hoping to hide the blush she knew had come to her cheeks. At this moment, she felt as though *her* mouth was full of gooey peanut butter. How could she not be nervous when he was touching her hand and looking at her with those gorgeous green eyes? She closed her own eyes and found herself wondering how Seth's lips would feel against her own.

"My fear may not affect my relationship with people," Seth continued, "but it's real, nonetheless." He trailed his thumb across her knuckles, marching a brigade of butterflies through her stomach. "I'd like to be your friend, Tabby. I want to help you overcome your shyness. You have potential, and if you'll let Him, I know the Lord can use you in a mighty way."

Tabby blinked away stinging tears. How she wished it were true. She'd give anything to face the world with confidence. It would make her life complete if she could serve God without fear or bashfulness—even if it wasn't in a mighty way, like Seth was doing with his ventriloquist skills.

"Will you allow me to help?" Seth asked.

Tabby felt drawn to his compassionate eyes, and she sensed he could see right through her. *I could drown in that sea of green.*

"Tabby?"

She nodded. "I–I'm not expecting any big m–miracles, but yes, I w–would like your help."

For the next several days Seth's offer of help played itself over and over in Tabby's mind. When he dropped her off at the apartment that night, after pie and coffee, he'd said he would give her a call, but he never explained how he planned to help her. Would he offer to get her speech therapy? If so, that would never work. Her parents had sent her for all kinds of therapy when she was growing up. Nothing helped. There wasn't a thing wrong with Tabby's speech. If there had been, she would have stuttered all the time, not just in the presence of those who made her feel uncomfortable. It was her low self-esteem and shyness that caused her to stutter, and she was sure there wasn't anything that could be done about it.

"You're awfully quiet today," Donna remarked, pulling Tabby out of her musings.

Tabby glanced over at her friend in the passenger seat. They took turns driving to work, and today they'd taken Tabby's car.

Tabby gave the steering wheel a few taps. "I was just thinking."

Donna laughed. "Thinking's okay, as long as you pay attention to where you're going."

"I am."

"Oh, yeah? Then how come you drove right past the church?"

Tabby groaned as she glanced to the left and saw the corner of Elm Street. She cranked the wheel and made a U-turn.

"Oh, great, now you're trying to get yourself a big fat ticket," Donna complained. "What's with you this morning?"

"Nothing. I'm just preoccupied." Tabby pulled into the church parking lot and turned off the ignition.

"Thinking about Seth Beyers, I'll bet."

Tabby opened her mouth, but before she could get any words out, Donna cut her off. "I think that guy really likes you."

"Seth's just friendly. He likes everyone." Tabby didn't like where this conversation was going, and she'd have to steer it in another direction soon, or they might end up in an argument.

"I know Seth is friendly," Donna persisted, "but I think he's taken a special interest in you. You should have seen how upset he was when you ran into your room the other night."

"How about this weather? Can you believe it hasn't rained in the last half hour? We'd better get inside before it changes its mind and sends us another downpour."

Donna clicked her tongue. "You're trying to avoid the subject, and it won't work. I have something to say, and you're gonna hear me out."

"We'll be late for work."

Donna glanced at her watch. "We're ten minutes early. So, if you'll quit interrupting, we still have plenty of time to talk."

Tabby drew in a deep breath and let it out in a rush. "Okay, get whatever it is off your chest. I really want to get on with my day."

Donna gave her a reproachful look. "What I have to say isn't all that bad."

"All right then, let me have it."

Donna blinked. "My, my, you're sure testy. It's Seth, isn't it?"

Tabby remained silent.

"I really do think the guy likes you."

Tabby wrinkled her nose. "You already said that. I think Seth's the type of person who's kind to everyone. It's obvious that he takes his relationship with Christ seriously."

Donna raised her dark eyebrows. "And you don't?"

Tabby shrugged. "I try to, but I'm not outgoing and self-confident the way he is. I don't think I'm a very good Christian witness."

"You could be, Tabby. You have a wonderful new talent, which you should be using to serve the Lord."

"I—I still don't feel ready to do ventriloquism in front of a crowd."

"Maybe you need to take a few more lessons. I'm sure if you asked, Seth would be more than willing to help you."

Tabby drew in another long breath, and this one came out as a shuddering rasp. "He said he'd help, and I even agreed."

"That's great. I'm glad to hear it."

"I've thought it over thoroughly," Tabby said. "I like Seth too much to expect him to waste his time on someone like me."

Donna shook her head. "Now that's the most ridiculous thing I've ever heard. If you like the guy, then why not jump at any opportunity you have to be with him?"

"Aren't you getting this picture? I don't stand a chance with someone like Seth Beyers. He's totally out of my league."

Donna held up both hands. "I give up! You don't want to see your potential or do anything constructive to better yourself, so there's nothing more I can say." She jerked open the car door and sprinted off toward the church.

Tabby moaned and leaned against the headrest. "Maybe she's right. Maybe I need to pray about this."

Chapter 8

S eth had been thinking of Tabby for the past few days. In fact, he couldn't get her out of his mind. The other night she'd told him where she worked, and he had decided to stop by the day care for a little visit. One of the fringe benefits of being self-employed was the fact he could pretty much set his own hours and come and go whenever he felt like it. Today, he'd decided to take an early lunch and had put a note in his shop window saying he wouldn't be back until one.

Seth pulled his Jeep into the church parking lot, turned off the engine, and got out. He scanned the fenced-in area on one side of the building. There were several children playing on the swings, so he figured that must be part of the Caring Christian Day Care.

He ambled up the sidewalk, and was about to open the gate on the chain-link fence, when he caught sight of Tabby. She was kneeling on the grass, and a group of children sat in a semicircle around her, listening to a Bible story. The soft drone of her voice mesmerized him, as well as the kids, who were watching Tabby with rapt attention. She wasn't stuttering at all, he noticed. It was uncanny, the way she could speak so fluently with these children, yet stutter and hang her head in embarrassment whenever she was with him.

"And so, little ones," Tabby said as she closed the Bible. "Jonah truly learned his lesson that day."

"He never went on a boat again, right, teacher?" a little red-haired, freckle-faced boy hollered out.

Tabby smiled sweetly, and Seth chuckled behind his hand. She still didn't know he was watching her, and he decided to keep it that way for a few more minutes.

"Jonah's lesson," Tabby explained, "was to obey God in all things. He could have drowned in that stormy sea, but God saved him by bringing the big fish along in time."

"I wonder if the fishy had bad breath," a little blond-haired girl piped up.

Tabby nodded. "The inside of that fish probably smelled pretty bad, but Jonah was kept safe and warm for three whole days. When the fish finally spit him out on dry land, Jonah was happy to be alive."

"And I'll bet he never went fishing after that," said the freckle-faced boy.

Tabby laughed softly. Her voice sounded like music to Seth's ears. How could anyone so introverted around adults be so at ease with children? *She'll make a good mother some day,* Seth found himself thinking. *She has a sweet, loving spirit, and the kids seem to relate really well to her.*

Seth opened the gate and stepped inside the enclosure just as Tabby stood up. She brushed a few blades of grass from her denim skirt, and the children all stood, too.

"It's time to go inside," she instructed. "Miss Donna is probably ready for us to bake those cookies now."

A chorus of cheering voices went up, and the kids, including those who had been swinging, raced off toward the basement door.

Tabby started to follow, but Seth cleared his throat loudly, and she whirled around to face him. "Oh, you—you sc–scared me. I d–didn't know you w–were h–here. How l–long have you–you been st–standing there?"

Seth grinned at her. "Just long enough to hear the end of a great story. The biblical account of Jonah and the big fish is one of my favorites."

"It's m–my favorite too," she murmured.

"You're really good with the kids," he said, nodding in the direction of the disappearing pack of children.

"Th–thanks. I love w–working w–with them."

"It shows."

There was a moment of silence, as Seth stood there staring at Tabby, and she shifted from one foot to the other.

"Wh–what br–brings you here?" she finally asked.

"I came to see you," he said with a wide smile.

Her only response was a soft, "Oh."

"But now that I'm here, I think maybe I should follow the kids into the day care and see what kind of cookies they'll be making." Seth offered her a wink, and she blushed, dropping her gaze to her white sneakers.

"We're m–making chocolate ch–chip," Tabby said. "We'll be t–taking them to R–Rose Park Convalescent C–Center tomorrow m–morning."

He nodded. "Ah, so you're not only a great storyteller, but you're full of good deeds."

Her blush deepened, and she dipped her head even further. "It's n–nothing, really."

"I think you're too modest," Seth replied, taking a few steps toward her. When he was only inches away, he reached out and gently touched her chin. Slowly, he raised it, until her dark eyes were staring right into his. "There, that's better. It's kind of hard to carry on a conversation with someone who's staring at her feet."

Tabby giggled, obviously self-conscious, and it reminded him of one of her day care kids. "Wh–what did you w–want to see m–me about, Se–Se–Seth?"

"I thought maybe we could have lunch and talk about something," he answered, stepping away. "I saw a little deli just down the street, and I'm on my lunch hour, so—"

"Th–that would be nice, but I've got c–cookies to b–bake," she interrupted. "D–Donna and I w–will pr–probably be baking l–long after the k–kids go down for their n–naps."

Seth blew out his breath. "Okay, I guess I can call you later on. Will that be all right?"

She nodded. "Sure, th–that will be f–fine. Do y–you have m–my ph–phone number?"

"It's on the invoice I made out for your dummy purchase the other day."

"Oh." She turned toward the church. "I–I'd better g–get inside now. T–talk to you l–later, Seth."

He waved to her retreating form. "Yeah, later."

❀

"You're wanted on the phone, Tabby!"

Tabby dried her hands on a towel and left the kitchen. When she entered the living room, Donna was holding the receiver, a Cheshire-cat grin on her pixie face.

"Who is it?"

"Seth."

Taking in a deep breath, Tabby accepted the phone then motioned Donna out of the room.

Donna winked and sauntered into the kitchen.

"H–hello, Seth," Tabby said hesitantly. Her palms were so moist, she hoped she could hold on to the receiver.

"Hi, Tabby. How are you?"

"I'm o–okay."

"I'm sorry we couldn't have lunch today, but I said I'd call later. Is this a good time for you to talk?"

She nodded, then realizing he couldn't see her, she squeaked, "Sure, it's—it's f–fine."

"Good. You see, the reason I wanted to talk to you is, Saturday afternoon I'll be doing an advanced ventriloquism class," Seth said. "I was hoping you'd agree to come."

Tabby twirled the end of the phone cord between her fingers. "I—uh—really c–can't, Seth."

"Can't or won't?"

She flinched, wondering if Seth could read her mind.

"Tabby?"

"I—I wouldn't feel comfortable trying to do v–v–ventriloquism in front of a b–bunch of strangers," she answered truthfully. "You know h–how bad I stutter. They'd probably l–laugh at me."

There was a long pause, then, "How 'bout I give you some private lessons?"

"P–private lessons?"

"Sure. We could meet once a week, either at your apartment or in my shop."

"Well. . ."

"I'd really like to see your talent perfected. Besides, it would be a good excuse to be with you again."

He wants to be with me. Tabby squirmed restlessly. Did Seth really see her in some other light than a mere charity case? Could he possibly see her as a woman? An image of little Ryan O'Conner, the freckle-faced boy from day care, flashed through her mind. He had a crop of red hair, just like Seth. *I wonder if our son would look like that?*

"Tabby, are you still there?" Seth's deep voice drew Tabby back to their conversation.

"Yes, I'm—I'm h–here," she mumbled, wondering what on earth had been going on in her head. She hardly knew Seth Beyers, and fantasizing about a child who looked like him was absolutely absurd!

"Are you thinking about my proposal?" Seth asked, breaking into her thoughts a second time.

"Pro–proposal?" she rasped. Even though she knew Seth wasn't talking about a marriage proposal, her heat skipped a beat. They'd only met a short time ago. Besides, they were exact opposites. Seth would never want someone as dull as her.

"So, what's it gonna be?" he prompted.

She sent up a silent prayer. *What should I do, Lord?* A few seconds later, as if she had no power over her tongue, Tabby murmured, "O–okay."

"Your place or mine?"

Tabby caught a glimpse of Donna lurking in the hallway. "You could come here, but we'll probably have an audience."

"An audience?"

"Donna—my r–roommate."

Seth laughed. "Oh, yeah. Well, I don't mind, if it doesn't bother you."

Actually, the thought of Donna hanging around while Seth gave her lessons did make Tabby feel uncomfortable. It was probably preferable to being alone with Seth at his shop, though. "When do you w–want to b–begin?" she asked.

"Is tomorrow night too soon?"

She scanned the small calendar next to the phone. Tomorrow was Friday, and like most other Friday nights, she had no plans. "Tomorrow n–night will be f–fine. I d–don't get home till six thirty or seven, and I'll need t–time to change and eat d–dinner."

"Let's make it seven thirty, then. See you soon, Tabby."

❦

Seth hung up the phone and shook his head. He could just imagine how Tabby must have looked during their phone conversation. Eyes downcast, shoulders drooping, hair hanging in her face.

His heart went out to her whenever she stuttered. He felt a hunger, a need really, to help the self-conscious little woman. He wanted to help her be all she could be. Maybe the advanced ventriloquism lessons would enable her to gain more confidence.

Seth turned away from the phone. *If I work hard enough, Tabby might actually become the woman of my dreams.* He slapped his palm against the side of his head. "Now where did that thought come from? I can't possibly be falling for this shy, introverted woman."

Back when he was a teen, Seth had made a commitment to serve God with his ventriloquist talents. He'd also asked the Lord for a helpmate—someone with whom he could share his life and his talent. Since he'd never found that perfect someone, maybe he could make it happen.

He sighed deeply. The way Tabby was now, he knew she'd only be a hindrance to his plans. He could just imagine what it would be like being married to someone who couldn't even talk to a stranger without stuttering or hiding behind a dummy. Unless he could draw her out of that cocoon, there was no possibility of them ever having a future together.

"What am I saying?" Seth lamented. "I hardly even know the woman, and I'm thinking about a future with her!" He shook his head. "Get a grip, Seth Beyers. She's just a friend—someone to help, that's all. You'd better watch yourself, because you're beginning to act like one of your dummies."

❦

"I don't know what you're so nervous about. You've already mastered the basic techniques of ventriloquism, so the rest should be a piece of cake," Donna said with a reassuring smile.

Tabby nodded mutely as she flopped onto the couch beside Donna. The truth was, she was a lot more nervous about seeing Seth than she was about perfecting her ventriloquism skills. She liked him—a lot. That's what frightened her the most. She'd never felt this way about a guy before. She knew her childish fantasies about her and Seth, and children who looked like him, were totally absurd, but she just couldn't seem to help herself.

"Tabby, the door!"

Donna's voice broke through Tabby's thoughts, and she jumped. She hadn't even heard the doorbell. "Oh, he's here? Let him in, okay?"

Donna grinned. "Since he's come to tutor you, don't you think *you* should answer the door?"

Tabby felt a sense of rising panic. "You're not staying, I hope."

"If you're gonna do ventriloquism, then you'll need an audience," Donna said.

The doorbell rang again, and Tabby stood up. When she opened the front door, she found Seth standing on the porch, little Rudy cradled in the crook of one arm, and a three-ring binder in his hand. "Ready for a lesson?"

She nodded then motioned toward the living room. "We h–have our audience, j–just as I expected."

"That's okay. It's good for you to have an audience," Seth answered. "It'll give you a feel for when you're onstage."

Tabby's mouth dropped open. "Onst–st–stage?"

Seth laughed. "Don't look so worried. I'm not suggesting you perform for a large crowd in the next day or two. Someday you might, though, and—"

"No, I won't!" Tabby shouted. "I'm only d–doing this so I can per–perform better for the kids at the d–day care."

Seth shrugged. "Whatever." He followed her into the living room. "Where's your dummy?"

"In my room. I'll go get her." Tabby made a hasty exit, leaving Seth and Donna alone.

❦

"She's a nervous wreck," Donna remarked as Seth placed the notebook on the coffee table then took a seat on the couch.

"Because you're here?"

She shook her head. "I think you make her nervous."

"Me? Why would I make Tabby nervous?"

"Well, I'm pretty sure. . ."

"I–I'm ready," Tabby announced as she entered the room carrying Rosie.

Seth stood up. "Great! Let's get started."

"Sh–should I sit or st–stand?"

"However you're the most comfortable." Seth nodded toward the couch. "Why not sit awhile, until you're ready to put on a little performance for us?"

"I—I may never be r–ready for that."

"Sure you will," Seth said with assurance. He wanted her to have enough confidence to be able to stand up in front of an audience, but from the way she was acting tonight, he wondered if that would ever happen.

"Tabby, show Seth how you can make Rosie's head turn backwards," Donna suggested.

Tabby dropped to the couch and held her dummy on one knee. She inserted her hand in the opening at the back of the hard plastic body and grabbed the control stick. With a quick turn of the stick, Rosie was looking backward. "Hey, where'd everybody go!" the childlike voice squealed.

Not one stuttering word, Seth noted, as he propped one foot on the footstool by Donna's chair. *Talking for two seems to be the best way Tabby can converse without stammering.* "We're right here, Rosie. Come join the party." This came from Rudy Right, who was balanced on Seth's knee.

"Party?" Rosie shot back. "We're havin' a party?"

"Sure, and only dummies are invited." Rudy gave Tabby a quick wink.

She giggled then made Rosie say, "Guess that means we'll have to leave, 'cause the only dummies I see are pullin' someone else's strings."

Seth chuckled. "I think we've been had, Tabby." He scooted closer to her. "Would you like to learn a little something about the near and far voice?"

"Near and far? What's that?" The question came from Donna.

"The near voice is what you use when your dummy is talking directly to you or some-one else. Like Tabby and I just did with our two figures," Seth explained. "The far voice would be when you want your audience to believe they're hearing the dummy talking from someplace other than directly in front of them." He pointed to the telephone on the table by the couch. "Let's say you just received a phone call from your dummy, and you want the audience to hear the conversation." Seth reached over and grabbed the receiver off the hook.

"Hi, Seth, can I come over?" A far-sounding, high-pitched voice seemed to be coming from the phone.

"Sure, why don't you?" Seth said into the receiver. "We're having a party over at Tabby and Donna's tonight, so you're more than welcome to join us."

"That's great! I love parties!" the far voice said. "Be right there!"

Seth hung up the phone and turned to face Tabby. "Do you have any idea how I did that?"

"You used the power of suggestion," Donna said, before Tabby had a chance to open her mouth. "We saw a phone and heard a voice, so it makes sense that we thought the sound was coming from the receiver."

Seth looked at Tabby. "What do you think?"

"I–I'm not sure, but I think m–maybe you did something different in your th–throat."

Seth grinned. "You catch on fast. I tightened my vocal chords so my voice sounded a bit pinched or strained. There's an exercise you can do to help make this sound."

"Oh, great! I love to exercise," Donna said, slapping her hands together.

Seth could tell from Tabby's expression that she was more than a bit irritated with Donna's constant interrupting. He wished there was some way to politely ask her well-meaning friend to leave.

"Actually, Donna, it's not the kind of exercise you're thinking of. It's only for ventrilo-quists, so. . ."

Donna held up both hands. "Okay, I get the picture. You want me to keep my big mouth shut, right?"

"You are kind of a nuisance," Tabby replied.

Wow, she can get assertive when she wants to. Seth wondered what other talents lay hidden behind Tabby's mask of shyness.

"I'll keep quiet," Donna promised.

Tabby raised her eyebrows at Seth, and he grinned in response. "Now, let's see. . . . Where were we?"

"An exercise." Donna ducked her head. "Sorry."

"The first thing you do is lean over as far as you can," Seth said as he demonstrated. "Try to take in as much air as possible, while making the *uh* sound."

Tabby did what he asked, and he noticed her face was turning red. How much was from embarrassment and how much from the exercise, he couldn't be sure, but he hoped it wouldn't deter her from trying.

"Now sit up again and try the same amount of pressure in your stomach as you make the *uh* sound." He placed one hand against his own stomach. "You'll need to push hard with these muscles as you speak for your far-sounding voice. Oh, and one more thing. It's best to keep your tongue far back in your mouth, like when you gargle. Doing all that, try talking in a high, whisper-like voice."

"Wow, that's a lot to think about all at once!" The comment came from Donna again, and Seth wondered if Tabby might be about to bolt from the room.

"There is a lot to think about," he agreed, "but with practice, it gets easier." He leaned close to Tabby and whispered, "Ready to try it now?"

She sucked in her bottom lip and nodded. "Hi, I'm glad you're home. I was afraid nobody would answer the phone."

Seth grabbed her free hand and gave it a squeeze. "That was awesome, Tabby! You catch on quick. A natural born ventriloquist, that's what you are."

A stain of red crept to her cheeks, but she looked pleased. "Th–thanks."

Seth pulled his hand away and reached for the notebook he'd placed on the coffee table.

"I have some handout sheets to give you. Things for you to practice during this next week and a few short distant-voice routines to work on."

Tabby only nodded, but Donna jumped up and bounded across the room. "Can I see? This has all been so interesting! I'm wondering if maybe I should put away my art supplies and come back to your shop to look at dummies." She grinned at Tabby. "What do you say? Should I take up ventriloquism so we can do some joint routines?"

Chapter 9

By the time Tabby closed the door behind Seth, she felt emotionally drained and physically exhausted. Tonight's fiasco would definitely be recorded in that journal Grandma had given her. Donna had done nothing but interrupt, offer dumb opinions, and flirt with Seth. At least that's how Tabby saw it. Her best friend was obviously interested in the good-looking ventriloquist. What other reason could she have for making such a nuisance of herself?

Well, she's not going to get away with it, Tabby fumed. She headed for the living room, resolved to make things right. *Friend or no friend, I'm telling Donna exactly what I think.*

Donna was sitting on the couch, fiddling with the collar on Rosie's shirt. "You know what, Tabby? I think your dummy might look cuter in a frilly dress. You could curl her hair and—"

"Rosie looks just fine the way she is!" Tabby jerked the ventriloquist figure out of Donna's hands and plunked it in the rocking chair. "I'd appreciate it if you'd mind your own business, too."

Donna blinked. "What's your problem? I wasn't hurting Rosie. I was only trying to help."

Tabby moved toward the window, though she didn't know why. It was dark outside, and there was nothing to look at but the inky black sky. "I've had about enough of your opinions to last all year," she fumed.

Donna joined Tabby at the window. "I thought your lesson went really well. What's got you so uptight?"

Tabby turned to face her. "I'm not uptight. I'm irritated."

"With me?"

Tabby nodded. "You like him, don't you?"

"Who?"

"Seth. I'm talking about Seth Beyers!"

Donna tipped her head. "Huh?"

"Don't play dumb. You know perfectly well who I mean, and why I think you like him."

"I think Seth's a nice guy, but—"

"Are you interested in him romantically?"

"Romantically?" Donna frowned. "You've gotta be kidding."

Tabby sniffed deeply. "No, I'm not. You hung around him all night and kept asking all sorts of dumb questions."

Donna's forehead wrinkled. "You're really serious, aren't you?"

"I sure am."

"I think we'd better have a little talk about this. Let's sit down." Donna motioned toward the couch.

Tabby didn't budge. "There's nothing to talk about."

"I think there is."

"Whatever," Tabby mumbled with a shrug.

Donna sat on the couch, but Tabby opted for the rocking chair, lifting Rosie up then placing the dummy in her lap after she was seated.

"I'm not trying to steal your guy," Donna insisted. "He's not my type, and even if he were, you should know that I'd never sabotage my best friend."

The rocking chair creaked as Tabby shifted; then she began to pump her legs back and forth. "Seth is not my guy."

A smile played at the corner of Donna's lips. "Maybe not now, but I think he'd like to be."

Tabby folded her arms across her chest and scowled. "Fat chance."

"There might be, if you'd meet him halfway."

"Like you did tonight—with twenty questions and goofy remarks?"

"I was only trying to help."

"How?"

"Before Seth arrived, you said you were nervous."

"And?"

"I was trying to put you at ease."

"By butting in every few minutes?" Tabby gulped and tried to regain her composure. "How was that supposed to put me at ease?"

Before Donna could say anything, Tabby stood up. "All you succeeded in doing tonight was making me more nervous."

"Sorry."

Donna's soft-spoken apology was Tabby's undoing. She raced to the couch, leaned over, and wrapped her friend in a bear hug. "I'm sorry, too. I—I'm just not myself these days. I think maybe I. . ." Her voice trailed off, and she blinked away tears, threatening to spill over. "Let's forget about tonight, okay?"

Donna nodded. "Just don't let it ruin anything between you and Seth."

Tabby groaned. "There's nothing to ruin. As I said before, there isn't anything going on. Seth and I are just friends—at least I think we are. Maybe our relationship is strictly business."

Donna shrugged. "Whatever you say."

"I think I'll take my next ventriloquist lesson at Seth's shop," Tabby said as she started toward her room. "Tonight made me fully aware that I'm not even ready for an audience of one yet."

❋

Seth wasn't the least bit surprised when Tabby called the following week and asked to have her next lesson at his place of business. Her friend, Donna, had turned out to be more than a helpful audience, and he was sure that was the reason for the change of plans. The way he saw it, Donna had actually been a deterrent, and it had been obvious that her constant interruptions made Tabby uptight and less able to grasp what he was trying to teach her. Even though they might be interrupted by a phone call or two, Beyers' Ventriloquist Studio was probably the best place to have Tabby's private lessons.

A glance at the clock told Seth it was almost seven. That was when Tabby had agreed to come over. His shop was closed for the day, so they should have all the privacy they needed.

"She'll be here any minute," he mumbled. "I'd better get this place cleaned up a bit."

Not that it was all that dirty, but at least it would give him something to do while he waited. If things went really well, he planned to ask her on a date, and truthfully, he was more than a little anxious about it. What if she turned him down? Could his male ego take the rejection, especially when he'd planned everything out so carefully?

Seth grabbed a broom out of the storage closet and started sweeping up a pile of sawdust left over from a repair job he'd recently done on an all-wooden dummy brought in a few weeks ago.

As he worked, he glanced over at Rudy Right, sitting in a folding chair nearby. "Well, little buddy, your girlfriend, Rosie, ought to be here any minute. I sure hope you're not as nervous as I am."

The wooden-headed dummy sat motionless, glass eyes staring straight ahead.

"So you're not talking today, huh?" Seth said with a shake of his head. "I'll bet you won't be able to keep your slot jaw shut once Tabby and her vent pal arrive."

Talking to Rudy like this was nothing new for Seth. He found that he rather enjoyed the one-way conversation. It was good therapy to talk things out with yourself, even if you were looking at a dummy when you spoke. He was glad there was no one around to witness the scene, though. If there had been, he might be accused of being a bit eccentric.

Seth chuckled. "Maybe I am kind of an oddball, but at least I'm having fun at my profession."

The bell above his shop door jingled, disrupting his one-way conversation. He grinned when Tabby stepped into the room, carrying Rosie in her arms. "Hi, Tabby."

"I—I hope I'm not l–late," she said. "Traffic was r–really bad."

Seth glanced at the clock again. "Nope, you're right on time."

"Are—are you r–ready for my l–lesson? You l–look kind of b–busy."

"Oh, you mean this?" Seth lifted the broom. "I was just killing time till you got here. My shop gets pretty dirty after I've been working on a dummy."

She nodded. "I g–guess it w–would."

Seth put the broom back in the closet and turned to face Tabby. "Are you ready for lesson number two?"

"I—I th–think so."

"Let's get started, then." He motioned toward one of the folding chairs. "Have a seat and I'll get my notes."

❧

Tabby watched as Seth went to his desk and shuffled through a stack of papers. *Why is he taking time out of his busy schedule to work with me?* she asked herself. *I'm sure he has much better things to do than give some introverted, stuttering woman private ventriloquist lessons.*

"Okay, all set." Seth dropped into a chair and graced her with a pleasant smile. "Did you get a chance to practice your near and far voices?"

"I p–practiced a little."

"How about a demonstration, then?"

"N–n–now?"

"Sure, now's as good a time as any." Seth pointed at Rosie. "If it would be any easier, you can talk through her instead of a pretend object or the telephone."

"How c–can I do th–that?" Tabby asked. "If I t–talk for R–Rosie, won't that be m–my near v–voice?"

Seth scratched his head. "Good point. I'll tell you what—why don't you set Rosie on a chair across the room, then talk for her. Make it sound as though her voice is coming from over there, and not where you're sitting."

Tabby bit down on her bottom lip and squeezed her eyes tightly shut. She wasn't sure she could do what Seth was asking, and she certainly didn't want to make a fool of herself. She'd already done that a few times in Seth's presence.

"You can do this," Seth urged. "Just give it a try."

Tabby opened her eyes and blew out the breath she'd been holding. "All r–right." She stood up and carried Rosie and a chair across the room then placed the dummy down and returned to her own seat. "Hey, how come you put me way over here?" she made Rosie say in a childlike voice.

"You're in time-out."

"That's not fair, I'm just a dummy. Dummies should never be in time-out."

"Oh, and why's that?"

"Dummies are too dumb to know how to behave."

Tabby opened her mouth, but Seth's round of applause stopped her. She turned to look at him and was surprised when he gave her "thumbs-up."

"D–did I do o–okay?"

He grinned from ear to ear. "It was more than 'okay.' It was fantastic, and you never stuttered once. I'm proud of you, Tabby."

Tabby could feel the warmth of a blush as it started at her neckline and crept upward. She wasn't used to such compliments and was unsure how to respond.

"In all the years I've been teaching ventriloquism, I don't think I have ever met anyone who caught on as quickly as you," Seth said sincerely. "You mastered the basics like they were nothing, and now this—it's totally awesome!"

"You really th–think so?"

"I know so. Why, you—"

Seth's words were cut off when the shop door opened, jingling the bell. In walked Cheryl Stone, the attractive redhead who had demonstrated her talents at Seth's beginning ventriloquism workshop, where Tabby first met him.

Cheryl gave Seth a smile so bright Tabby was sure the sun must still be shining. "Hi, Seth, I was in the neighborhood and saw your lights on. I was wondering if you've finished that new granny figure for me yet?"

Seth gave Tabby an apologetic look. "Sorry about the interruption," he whispered. "I wasn't expecting anyone else tonight, and I forgot to put the closed sign in my window."

"It's o–okay," Tabby murmured. "I'll j–just w–wait overth–there with R–Rosie w–while you take c–care of b–business." She was stuttering heavily again, and it made her uncomfortable.

Seth nodded. "This will only take a minute."

Tabby moved quickly toward Rosie, hoping Cheryl wouldn't stay long. She watched painfully as the vibrant young woman chatted nonstop and batted her eyelashes at Seth. *She likes him, I can tell. I wonder if they've been seeing other socially.*

Tabby shook her head. It was none of her business who Seth chose to see. Besides, if she were being totally honest, she'd have to admit that Seth and Cheryl did make a striking pair. They were both redheads, had bubbling personalities, and could do ventriloquism. What more could Seth ask for in a woman?

Chapter 10

It was nearly half an hour later when Cheryl finally walked out the door. Seth gave Tabby an apologetic look. "Sorry about that. Guess she's a little anxious to get her new dummy." He offered Tabby one of the most beautiful smiles she'd ever seen. "Before we continue with your lesson, I'd like to ask you a question."

Her heart quickened. Why was he staring at her that way? She swallowed against the tightening in her throat. "What question?" she squeaked.

Seth dropped into the seat beside her. "I have to go to Seattle tomorrow—to pick up an old dummy at the Dummy Depot. I was wondering if you'd like to go along."

Tabby's mouth went dry. He was asking her to go to Seattle. Was this a date? No, it couldn't be. Seth wouldn't want to go out with someone as plain as her. Why didn't he ask someone like cute Cheryl Stone? From the way the redhead kept flirting with him, Tabby was sure she would have jumped at the chance.

"Tabby?" Seth's deep voice cut into her thoughts.

"H–huh?"

"Are you busy tomorrow? Would you like to go to Seattle?"

She blinked. "Really? You w–want m–me to go along?"

He nodded. "I thought after I finish my business at the Dummy Depot we could go down by the waterfront. Maybe eat lunch at Ivar's Fish Bar and check out some of the gift shops along the wharf. I think it would be fun, don't you?"

Tabby gazed at the floor as she mulled this idea over. Tomorrow was Saturday. She wouldn't be working, and she had no other plans. She hadn't been to the Seattle waterfront in ages. Despite the amount of people usually there, it wasn't closed in the way so many of the buildings in Seattle Center were. The waterfront was open and smelled salty like the sea. Besides, it was an opportunity to spend an entire day with Seth.

"Tabby?"

She looked up. "Y–yes. I'd l–like to go."

❧

Tabby didn't sleep well that night. Excitement over spending a whole day with Seth occupied her thoughts and kept her tossing and turning. She was sure Seth wouldn't appreciate her taking Rosie to talk through, but she was concerned about her stuttering. Seth had told her several times that her speech impediment didn't bother him. It bothered her, though—a lot. She'd have given nearly anything to be confident and capable like normal people.

If only God hadn't made me so different, she wrote in her journal before turning off the light by her bed.

Tabby let her head fall back as she leaned into the pillow. *Maybe it wasn't God who made me different. It's all Lois's fault. If she just wasn't so beautiful and confident—everything Mom and Dad want in a daughter—everything I'm not.* She squeezed her eyes tightly shut. *Guess I can't really blame Lois, either. She can't help being beautiful and confident. It would take a miracle to make Mom and Dad love me the way they do her. They think I'm a failure.*

The thrill of her upcoming date with Seth was overshadowed by pain. She needed to work on her attitude. It wasn't a good Christian example, not even to herself. She released a shuddering sigh, whispered a short prayer asking God to help her accept things as they were, then drifted off to sleep.

🌸

When Tabby entered the kitchen the following morning, she found Donna sitting at the table, sketching a black-and-white picture of a bowl of fruit.

"All ready for your big date?"

Tabby shrugged. "It's not a real date."

"What would you call it?"

"I'd call it a day in Seattle to—" She giggled. "Maybe it is kind of a date."

Donna laughed, too. "You came home last night all excited about going, and it sure sounded like a date to me. I'm kind of surprised, though."

"About what?"

"I didn't think you liked Seattle."

Tabby dropped into a chair. "I don't like the Seattle Center, or shopping downtown, but we're going to the waterfront. I love it there, even with all the people."

Donna grinned. "I think you'd go to the moon and back if Seth Beyers was going."

"Don't even go there," Tabby warned. "I've told you before, Seth and I are just friends."

Donna shrugged. "Whatever you say."

Tabby glanced at the clock above the refrigerator. "Seth will be here in an hour, and I still need to eat breakfast, shower, and find something to wear." She reached for a banana from the fruit bowl in the center of the table.

"Hey! You're destroying my picture! Why don't you fix a fried egg or something?"

Tabby pulled the peel off the banana and took a bite. "Eggs have too much artery-clogging cholesterol. Fruit's better for you." She glanced at Donna's drawing. "Besides, you've already got some bananas sketched, so you shouldn't miss this one."

Donna puckered her lips. "You never worry about cholesterol when you're chomping down a burger or some greasy fries."

Tabby gave her a silly grin. "Guess you've got me there."

"How'd the lesson go yesterday? You never really said," Donna asked.

Tabby was tempted to tell her about Cheryl's interruption and how much it had bothered her to see the two redheads talking and laughing together. She knew it would only lead to further accusations about her being interested in Seth.

She flicked an imaginary piece of lint from the sleeve of her robe and replied, "It went fine."

"Great. I'm glad."

Tabby felt a stab of guilt pierce her heart. She was lying to her best friend. Well, not lying exactly, just not telling the whole story. "Seth got an unexpected customer, and we were interrupted before we really got much done."

"But you continued on with the lesson after they left, didn't you?"

Tabby grabbed an orange from the fruit bowl and began to strip away the peel. "The customer was a redheaded woman named Cheryl. I think Seth likes her."

"But it's you he invited to Seattle," Donna reminded.

"He probably feels sorry for me."

Donna dropped her pencil to the table. "Is there any hope for you at all?"

Tabby sighed. "I wish I knew. Sometimes I think there might be, and other times I'm so full of self-doubts."

"What makes you think Seth likes this redhead, anyway?" Donna asked.

"She's cute, talented, and outgoing. What guy wouldn't like that?" Tabby wrinkled her nose. "They looked like a pair of matching bookends."

Donna snickered. "Well, there you have it! If Seth can look at this redheaded gal and see himself, then he's bound to fall head over heels in love with her."

Tabby pushed away from the table. "Seth and Cheryl make a perfect couple, and I'm just a millstone around Seth's neck."

"If he saw you as a millstone, he sure wouldn't be asking you out. Normal people don't go around asking millstones to accompany them to Seattle for the day."

Tabby stared off into space. "Maybe you're right."

❁

Seth arrived on time. Not wishing to give Donna the chance to say anything to him, Tabby raced out the front door and climbed into his Jeep before he even had a chance to get out.

"I was planning to come in and get you," Seth said as she slid into the passenger seat.

She smiled shyly. "That's okay. I was r—ready, so I f—figured I may as w—well s—save you the b—bother."

Seth smiled. "You look nice and comfortable."

Tabby glanced down at her faded blue jeans and peach-colored sweatshirt, wondering if she was dressed too casually. Maybe she should have chosen something else. She considered Seth for a moment. He was wearing a pair of perfectly pressed khaki-colored pants and a black polo shirt. His hair was combed neatly in place, parted on the left side. He looked way too good to be seen with someone as dowdy as her.

"So, w—where exactly is th—this Dummy Depot, and w—what kind of d—dummy are you b—buying there?" she asked, hoping to drag her thoughts away from how great Seth looked today.

Seth pulled away from the curb. "The Dummy Depot sells mostly used dummies. Harry Marks, the guy who runs the place, recently got one in that needs some repairs. He asked if I'd come get it, since his car isn't running and he didn't want to catch a bus to Tacoma. I thought it might be kind of nice to mix a little pleasure with business," Seth said, giving Tabby another one of his heart-melting smiles.

Tabby nodded. "Makes sense to me." She leaned her head against the headrest and released a contented sigh. Maybe he really did want to be with her. Maybe there was a chance that. . .

"Have you known Donna long?" Seth asked, breaking into her thoughts.

"Huh?"

"How long have you and Donna been friends?"

"Ever since we w—were kids. Her folks m—moved next door to us when we were b—both two."

"Tell me a little about your family," he pried.

"There's nothing m—much to tell."

"There has to be something." Seth tapped the steering wheel with his long fingers. "Do your folks live nearby? Do you have any brothers and sisters?"

Tabby swallowed hard. The last thing she wanted to do was talk about her family. This was supposed to be a fun day, wasn't it? "My—uh—p—parents live in Olympia, and I h—have one s—sister. She l—lives in a high-rise apartment in d—downtown Tacoma, and sh—she's a secretary. There's n—nothing m—more to tell."

"You're lucky to have a sister," Seth commented. "I grew up as an only child. My folks were killed in a car wreck when I was fourteen, and my grandparents took me in."

"I'm so s—sorry," she murmured.

57

"Grandma and Grandpa Beyers were good to me, though. They taught me about Christ and helped me learn to use my talents for Him." Seth smiled. "I'll never forget the day Grandpa informed me that when he and Grandma were gone, the house would be mine."

Tabby knew the house he was referring to was the one he lived in now. The basement had been converted into his ventriloquist shop. Seth had told her that much when she'd had her lesson the evening before. What he hadn't told her was that the house had been his grandparents', or that they'd passed away.

"I'm s–sorry your g–grandparents aren't l–living anymore. It must be h–hard not to h–have any family," she said with feeling. As much as she disliked many of the things her own family said or did, she couldn't imagine what it must have been like growing up as an only child or not having her parents around at all, even if they did make her feel like dirt most of the time.

Seth chuckled. "Grandma and Grandpa aren't dead yet."

"They're n–not?"

"No, they moved into a retirement home a few years ago. Said the old house was too much for them to handle." Seth cast her a sidelong glance. "Grandpa thought the place would be well suited to my business, not to mention a great place to raise a bunch of kids someday."

Tabby wasn't sure how to respond to that statement. She'd always dreamed of having a big family herself, but the possibility didn't seem very likely.

"There sure is a l–lot of traffic on the f–freeway today, isn't there?" she said, changing the subject again.

Seth nodded. "Always is a steady flow of cars on I–5, but the weekends are even worse. Things will level off a bit once we get away from the city."

Tabby turned to look out the passenger window. They had just entered the freeway and were traveling over a new overpass. As busy as the freeway was here, she knew it would be even worse once they got closer to Seattle. It made her thankful Seth was driving. She'd be a ball of nerves if she were in the driver's seat.

"Mind if I put a cassette in the tape player?" Seth asked.

"Go a–ahead."

When the soft strains of a familiar Christian song came on, Tabby smiled. Seth liked the same kind of music she did. She closed her eyes and felt her body begin to relax. She wasn't sure if it was because of Seth's rich baritone accompanying the tape, or simply the fact that she was with him today. Tabby was glad she'd accepted Seth's invitation to go to Seattle.

❧

Seth glanced over at Tabby. Her eyes were shut, and she was sitting silent and still. He wished he could read her mind. Find out what thoughts were circling around in her head. *She reminds me of a broken toy. She didn't have much to say about her family. I wonder if something from her past is the reason for her terrible shyness. If she's hurting, then maybe her heart can be mended. There's even a chance she could actually be better than new.*

The only trouble was, Seth wasn't sure how to find out what kind of pain from the past held Tabby in its grip. She was a mystery he wanted to solve. Since Tabby seemed so reserved and unable to communicate her feelings to him, maybe he should talk to Donna about it. Tabby said they'd been friends most of their lives. Surely Donna would know what made Tabitha Johnson tick. A little bit of insight might help him know what direction to take in making her over into his perfect woman.

Seth hugged the knowledge to himself and smiled. *As soon as I get the chance, I'll get together with Donna and find out what gives.*

Chapter 11

The Dummy Depot was located in downtown Seattle, in a small shop near the busy shopping area. While Seth talked business with the owner, Tabby walked around the room studying all the figures for sale. It didn't take long to realize she could have bought a used dummy for half the price she'd paid for Rosie. She consoled herself with the fact that most of the figures looked well used and had lost their sparkle. Rosie, on the other hand, was brand new, without a scratch, dent, or paint chip on her entire little body. Besides, she'd purchased the dummy with the birthday gift certificate from Donna and her parents. They'd wanted her to have a new one or else they wouldn't have given it to her.

"Ready to go?" Seth asked suddenly.

"Sure, if y–you are."

Holding the damaged dummy under one arm, Seth opened the shop door with his free hand. "I don't know about you, but I'm getting hungry. I think I can actually smell those fish-and-chips wafting up from the waterfront."

Tabby's mouth watered at the mention of eating succulent cod, deep fried to perfection, and golden brown fries, dipped in tangy fry sauce. "Guess I'm kinda h–hungry too," she admitted.

Ten minutes later, they were parking in one of the huge lots near the waterfront. Seth reached for Tabby's hand as they crossed the street with the light.

Her hand tingled with his touch. *This does feel like a date,* she thought, though she didn't have a whole lot to gauge it on, considering she'd only been on a couple of dates since she graduated from high school. Those had been set up by Donna, and none of the guys had held her hand or acted the least bit interested in her. Of course, she hadn't said more than a few words, and those had come out in a mishmash of stammering and stuttering.

Groups of people were milling about the waterfront. Tabby clung tightly to Seth's hand, not wishing to get separated. As they headed down the sidewalk toward one of the fish bars, she spotted a young man walking a few feet ahead of them. He had two sizable holes in the back of his faded blue jeans, and long, scraggly brown hair hung halfway down the back of his discolored orange T-shirt. That was not what drew her attention to him, however. What made this man so unique was the colorful parrot sitting on his shoulder. With each step the man took, the parrot would either let out an ear-piercing squawk or imitate something someone had just said.

"I'm hungry! I'm hungry!" the feathered creature screeched. "The ferry's coming! The ferry's coming! Awk!"

Tabby glanced to her left. Sure enough, the Vashon Island ferry was heading toward one of the piers. Enthusiastic children jumped up and down, hollering that the ferry was coming, and the noisy parrot kept right on mimicking.

"I don't know who's more interesting—that guy with the long hair or his obnoxious bird," Seth whispered to Tabby.

She giggled. "The b–bird has my vote."

"I heard this story about a guy who owned a belligerent parrot," Seth remarked.

She looked up at him expectantly. "And?"

"The parrot had a bad attitude, not to mention a very foul mouth."

"So, what h–happened?"

"The guy tried everything from playing soft music to saying only polite words in front of the bird, but nothing worked at all."

"Did he s–sell the parrot then?"

Seth shook his head. "Nope. He put him in the freezer."

Tabby's mouth dropped open. "The freezer?"

"Yep, for about five minutes. When he opened the door again, the parrot calmly stepped out onto the guy's shoulder, a changed bird."

"He didn't use b–bad words anymore?"

"Nope. In fact, the parrot said, 'I'm truly sorry for being so rude.' Then the colorful creature added, 'Say, I saw a naked chicken in that icebox. What'd that poor bird do?'"

Tabby laughed, feeling happy and carefree, and wishing the fun of today could last forever.

Seth sobered, nodding toward the edge of the sidewalk. "You see all kinds down here."

Tabby watched with interest as a group of peddlers offered their wares to anyone who would listen. Everything from costume jewelry to painted T-shirts was being sold. Several men lay on the grass, holding signs announcing that they were out of work and needed money. An empty coffee can sat nearby—a place for donations. Tabby thought it sad to see people who were homeless or out of a job, reduced to begging. These few along the waterfront were just the tip of the iceberg, too.

"It's hard to distinguish between who really needs help and who's merely panhandling," Seth whispered in her ear.

She nodded, wondering if he could read her mind.

"Ivar's has a long line of people waiting to get in," Seth said. "Is it okay with you if we try Steamer's Fish Bar instead?"

Tabby glanced at the restaurant he'd mentioned. The aroma of deep-fried fish drifted out the open door and filled up her senses. "One fish-and-chips place is probably as good as another," she replied.

They entered the restaurant and placed their orders at the counter then found a seat near a window overlooking the water. Tabby watched in fascination as several boats pulled away from the dock, taking tourists on a journey through Puget Sound Bay. It was a beautiful, sunny day—perfect weather for boating.

"Would you like to go?"

Seth's sudden question drew Tabby's attention away from the window. "G–go? But we j–just got here," she said frowning.

Seth grinned. "I didn't mean go home. I meant, would you like to go for a ride on one of those tour boats you're watching so intently? We could do that after we eat, instead of browsing through the gift shops."

"Do w–we have t–time for th–that?"

Seth glanced at his watch. "I don't see why not. My shop's closed for the day, and I don't have to be back at any set time. How about you?"

Tabby shook her head. "I have all d–day."

"Then would you like me to see about getting a couple of tour-boat tickets?"

Tabby felt the tension begin to seep from her body as she reached for her glass of lemonade. "Actually, if I h–had a choice, I think I'd r–rather take the ferry over to V–Vashon, then ferry from there b–back to Tacoma."

Seth's face brightened. "Now that's a great idea! I haven't ridden the ferry in quite a while."

❈

Tabby hung tightly to the rail as she leaned over to stare into the choppy waters of Puget Sound Bay. The wind whipped against her face, slapping the ends of her hair in every direction. It was exhilarating, and she felt very much alive. Seagulls soared in the cloudless sky, squawking and screeching, as though vying for the attention of everyone on board the ferry. It was a peaceful scene, and Tabby felt a deep sense of contentment fill her soul.

Seth was standing directly behind Tabby, and he leaned into her, wrapping his arms around her waist. "Warm enough?" he asked, his mouth pressed against her ear.

Tabby shivered, and she knew it was not from the cool breeze. "I'm fine."

Seth rested his chin on top of her head. "This was a great idea. I've had a lot of fun today."

"Me, too," she murmured.

"It doesn't have to end when we dock at Point Defiance."

"It doesn't?"

"Nope. We could have dinner at the Harbor Lights."

Tabby glanced down at her outfit and grimaced. "I'm not exactly dressed for a fancy restaurant, Seth."

He chuckled. "Me neither, but I don't think it matters much. A lot of boaters pull into the docks at the restaurants along Tacoma's waterfront. I'm sure many people will be dressed as casually as we are."

Tabby shrugged. She was having such a good time and didn't want the day to end yet. "Okay. . .if you're sure."

"I'm positive," Seth said, nuzzling her neck.

She sucked in her breath. If this was a dream, she hoped it would last forever.

❈

Seth sat directly across from Tabby, studying her instead of the menu he held in his hands. She was gazing intently at her own menu, which gave him the perfect opportunity to look at her without being noticed. When had she taken on such a glow? When had her eyes begun to sparkle? He shook his head. Maybe it was just the reflection from the candle in the center of the table. Maybe he was imagining things.

Tabby looked up and caught him staring. "What's wrong?" she asked with furrowed brows. "Don't you see anything you like?"

Seth's lips curved into a slow smile.

"What's so funny?"

He reached across the table and grasped her hand. "Two things are making me smile."

She gave him a quizzical look.

"You haven't stuttered once since we left Seattle."

Tabby's face turned crimson, making Seth wonder if he should have said anything. "I didn't mean to embarrass you. It makes me happy to know you're finally beginning to relax in my presence."

She returned his smile. "I do feel pretty calm tonight."

He ran his thumb across the top of her hand and felt relief when she didn't pull it away. "You said there were two things making you smile. What's the second one?"

He leaned further across the table. "Just looking at you makes me smile."

A tiny frown marred her forehead. "Am I that goofy looking?"

Seth shook his head. "No, of course not! In fact, I was sitting here thinking how beautiful you look in the candlelight."

"No one has ever c–called me b–beautiful before," she said, a blush staining her cheeks.

Great! Now she's stuttering again. So much for making her feel relaxed. Seth dropped her hand and picked up his menu. "Guess I'd better decide what to order before our waiter comes back. Have you found anything you like yet?"

Tabby nodded. "I think I'll have a crab salad."

"You can order whatever you want," Seth said quickly. "Lobster, steak, or prime rib—just say the word."

"Crab salad is all I want," she insisted.

Seth was about to comment when the waiter returned to their table.

"Have you two decided?" the young man asked.

"I'll have prime rib, and the lady wants a crab salad." Seth handed both menus back to the waiter. "I think we'll have two glasses of iced tea as well."

As soon as the waiter left, Seth reached for Tabby's hand again. "I didn't mean to make you blush a few minutes ago. How come you always do that, anyway?"

"Do what?"

"Turn red like a cherry and hang your head whenever you're paid a compliment."

Her forehead wrinkled. "I—I don't know. I'm not used to getting compliments. You don't have to try and make me feel good, you know."

"Is that what you think—that I'm just trying to make you feel good?"

"Well, isn't it?"

His throat tightened. "I don't pass out false compliments so someone will feel good, Tabby."

Her gaze dropped to the tablecloth. "Let's forget it, okay?"

Seth offered up a silent prayer. *Should I let this drop, Lord, or should I try to convince her that I'm really interested in her as a woman, and that. . .* He swallowed hard. What did he really want from this relationship? When he'd first met Tabby, he'd felt sorry for her. He could sense her need for encouragement and maybe even a friend, but when had he started thinking of her as a woman and not just someone to help? There was a great yearning, deep within him, and he wondered if it could be filled by a woman's love. Tabby might be that woman. He had thought about her nearly every day since they first met. That had to mean something, didn't it?

Seth felt a sense of peace settle over him as he heard the words in his head say, *"Go slow, Seth. Go slow."*

Chapter 12

I can't believe you were gone all day!" Donna exclaimed when Tabby entered their apartment. Tabby dropped to the couch beside her and released a sigh of contentment. "Today was probably the best day of my life."

Donna's eyebrows shot up. "Did Seth kiss you?"

"Of course not!"

"You're turning red like a radish. He must have kissed you." Donna poked Tabby in the ribs. "Tell me all about it, and don't leave out one single detail."

Tabby slid out of Donna's reach. "Don't get so excited. There's not that much to tell."

"Then start with when Seth picked you up this morning and end with a detailed description of his kiss."

Tabby grimaced. "I told you, there was no kiss!" Her inexperience with men was an embarrassment. If she'd been more coy, like that cute little redhead, Cheryl, maybe Seth would have kissed her.

"Then what has you glowing like a Christmas tree?" Donna asked, pulling Tabby out of her musings.

"Seth is a lot of fun, and I had a good time today," she mumbled.

Donna released a sigh. "That sure doesn't tell me much."

Tabby leaned her head against the back of the couch. "Let's see. . . . We drove to Seattle, and freeway traffic was terrible." A long pause followed.

"And?"

"When we got to Seattle, we went to the Dummy Depot to pick up a ventriloquist figure Seth needs to repair." Another long pause.

"Then what?"

"We went down to the waterfront, where we had a great lunch of fish-and-chips."

"You must have done more than that. You've been gone all day."

Tabby glanced at her watch and wrinkled her nose. "It's only a little after eight. Besides, you're not my mother, and I'm not on any kind of a curfew."

Donna squinted her eyes. "You look like you're on cloud nine, so I figure you must have done something really exciting today."

Tabby grinned. "We did. We rode the ferry from Seattle to Vashon Island, then we caught another one to Point Defiance." She closed her eyes and thought about Seth's arms around her waist and his mouth pressed against her ear. She could still feel his warm breath on her neck and smell his woodsy aftershave lotion. That part of the day had been the most exciting thing of all. She wasn't about to share such a private moment with Donna—even if she was her best friend.

"What'd you do after you left Point Defiance?" Donna asked.

"We went to dinner at the Harbor Lights."

Donna let out a low whistle. "Wow! Things must be getting pretty serious between you two. The Harbor Lights costs big bucks!"

Tabby groaned. "It's not that expensive. Besides, going there doesn't mean anything special."

Donna gave her a knowing look. "Yeah, right."

"It's true," Tabby insisted. "I'm the queen of simplicity, so why would a great guy like Seth be attracted to someone like me?"

Donna clicked her tongue. "Are you ever going to see your true potential?"

Crossing her arms in front of her chest, Tabby shrugged. "I don't know. Maybe I do have some worth."

❧

After their day in Seattle, Tabby had hoped Seth might call and ask her out again. That would have let her know if he really was interested in seeing her on a personal level or not. However, the week went by without a single word from him. Today was Thursday, and she had another, previously scheduled ventriloquism lesson that evening. Thinking about it had very little appeal, though. If only Seth had called. If only. . .

As she drove across town, Tabby forced her thoughts away from Seth and onto the routine she'd been practicing with Rosie. She was determined to do her very best this time. Even if Seth never saw her as a desirable woman, at least she could dazzle the socks off him with her new talent.

When she arrived at Seth's, Tabby was relieved to see he had no customers. The thought of performing before an audience held no appeal whatsoever.

Seth greeted her with a warm smile. "I'll be with you in just a minute. I have to make a few phone calls."

Tabby nodded and took a seat, placing Rosie on her lap. Mentally, she began to rehearse the lines of her routine, hoping she had them memorized so well she wouldn't have to use her notes. Watching Seth as he stood across the room talking on the phone was a big enough distraction, but when the bell above the shop door rang, announcing a customer, Tabby froze.

In walked Cheryl Stone carrying her dummy, Oscar. She hurried past Tabby as though she hadn't even seen her and rushed up to Seth just as he was hanging up the phone. "Seth, you've got to help me!" she exclaimed.

"What do you need help with?" Seth asked.

"Oscar's mouth is stuck in the open position, and I can't get it to work." Cheryl handed him the dummy. "I'm supposed to do a vent routine at a family gathering tonight, and I was hoping you'd have time to fix Oscar for me."

Seth glanced at Tabby. "Actually, I was just about to begin teaching a lesson. Why don't you use your new dummy tonight—the one you recently bought from me?"

Cheryl shook her head. "I haven't gotten used to that one yet. Besides, Oscar's so cute, he's always a hit wherever I perform."

"Have a seat, then," Seth said, motioning toward the row of chairs along the wall where Tabby sat. "I'll take Oscar in the back room and see what I can do."

Cheryl smiled sweetly. "Thank you, Seth. You're the nicest man."

The chocolate bar Tabby had eaten on her drive over to Seth's suddenly felt like a lump of clay in her stomach. Cheryl obviously had her eye on Seth. For all Tabby knew, he might have more than a passing interest in the vibrant redhead, too.

Cheryl took a seat next to Tabby, opened her purse, withdrew a nail file, and began to shape her nails. The silence closing in around them was broken only by the steady ticking of the wall clock across the room and the irritating scrape of nail file against fingernails.

Should I say something to her? Tabby wondered. Just sitting here like this felt so awkward. Given her problem with stuttering, she decided that unless Cheryl spoke first, she would remain quiet.

Several minutes went by, and then Cheryl returned the nail file to her purse and turned toward Tabby. "Cute little dummy you've got there."

"Th–thanks."

"Are you here to see about getting it repaired?"

Tabby shook her head. "I–I'm t–taking l–lessons." She glanced toward the back room, hoping Seth would return soon. There was something about Cheryl's confidence and good looks that shattered any hope Tabby might have of ever becoming a successful ventriloquist, much less the object of Seth's affections.

Cheryl tapped her fingers along the arm of the chair. "I wonder what's taking so long? Seth must be having quite a time with Oscar's stubborn little mouth." She eyed Tabby curiously. "How long have you been taking ventriloquism lessons?"

"Not l–long."

"Guess you'll be at it for a while, what with your stuttering problem and all." Cheryl offered Tabby a sympathetic smile. "It must be difficult for you."

Hot tears stung Tabby's eyes as she squirmed in her seat then hunkered down as if succumbing to a predator. She bit her lower lip to stop the flow of tears that seemed insistent on spilling onto her flaming cheeks. She was used to her family making fun of her speech impediment, but seeing the pity on Cheryl's face was almost worse than reproach.

Dear Lord, she prayed silently, *please help me say something without stuttering.*

With newfound courage, Tabby stuck her hand into the opening at the back of Rosie's overalls, grabbed the control stick, opened her own mouth slightly, and said in a falsetto voice, "Tabby may have a problem with shyness, but I don't stutter at all." It was true, Tabby noted with satisfaction. Whenever she did ventriloquism, the voice she used for her dummy never missed a syllable.

Cheryl leaned forward, squinting her eyes and watching intently as Tabby continued to make her dummy talk.

"My name's Rosie; what's yours?"

"Cheryl Stone, and my dummy, Oscar, is in there getting his mouth worked on." Cheryl pointed toward the room where Seth had disappeared.

Tabby smiled. She could hardly believe it, but Cheryl was actually talking to her dummy like it was real. Of course, Cheryl was a ventriloquist, and people who talked for two did seem to have the childlike ability to get into the whole dummy scene.

"How long have you been doing ventriloquism?" little Rosie asked Cheryl.

Cheryl smiled in response. "I learned the basics on my own a few years ago. Since I met Seth, he's taught me several advanced techniques."

I wonder what else he's taught you. Tabby opened Rosie's mouth, actually planning to voice the question, but Seth entered the room in the nick of time.

"I think Oscar's good to go," he said, handing the dummy to Cheryl.

Cheryl jumped up. "How can I ever thank you, Seth?" She stood on tiptoes and planted a kiss right on Seth's lips!

Tabby wasn't sure who was more surprised—she or Seth. He stood there for several seconds, face red and mouth hanging open. Finally, he grinned, embarrassed-like, then mumbled, "I'll send you a bill."

Cheryl giggled and gave his arm a squeeze. "You're so cute." As she started for the door, she called over her shoulder, "See you on Saturday, Seth!" The door clicked shut, and Cheryl Stone was gone.

Tabby wished she had the courage to ask Seth why he'd be seeing Cheryl on Saturday, but it didn't seem appropriate. Besides, she had no claim on him, and if he chose to date someone else, who was she to ask questions?

"Sorry about the interruption," Seth said in a businesslike tone of voice. "We can begin now, if you're ready."

Tabby swallowed hard. Cheryl was gone, but the image of her lovely face rolled around in Tabby's mind. She'd been more than ready for a lesson when she came into Seth's shop, but now, after seeing the interchange between Seth and Cheryl, the only thing she was ready for was home!

Chapter 13

Seth eased into a chair and leaned forward until his head was resting in his hands. He couldn't believe how terrible Tabby's lesson had gone. Beside the fact that there had been an air of tension between them ever since Cheryl left, Tabby seemed unable to stay focused. What had gone wrong? Was he failing as a teacher, or was she simply losing interest in ventriloquism? Did she have any personal feelings for him, or had he read more into their Seattle trip than there actually was? Tabby seemed so relaxed that day, and when he'd held her hand, she hadn't pulled away. In fact, as near as he could tell, she'd enjoyed it as much as he had.

Seth groaned and stood up again. He wasn't sure how or even when it happened, but Tabitha Johnson definitely meant more to him than just someone to help. After seeing the way she was with her day care kids the other day, and after spending time with her in Seattle, he really was beginning to hope she was the woman he'd been waiting for. If he could only make Tabby see what potential she had. If she could just get past all that shyness and stuttering, he was sure she'd be perfect for him.

He moved toward the telephone. Tabby wouldn't be home yet. Maybe it was time for that talk with her friend.

Donna answered on the second ring. Seth quickly related the reason for his call, and a few minutes later he hung up the phone, happy in the knowledge that he'd be meeting Donna for lunch tomorrow. Between the two of them, maybe Tabby could become a confident woman who would use all her abilities to serve the Lord.

❧

"I am so glad this is Friday," Tabby murmured, as she prepared to eat her sack lunch at one of the small tables where the day care kids often sat.

"Me, too," Donna agreed. She grabbed her sweater and umbrella and started for the door. "See you later."

"Hey, wait a minute," Tabby called. "Where are you going?"

"Out to lunch, and I'd better hurry."

"Say, why don't I join you?"

"See you at one." Donna waved and disappeared out the door before Tabby could say another word and without even answering her question.

Tabby's forehead wrinkled. Donna hardly ever went out to lunch on a weekday. When she did, she always arranged for one of their helpers to take over the day care so Tabby could come along. What was up, anyway?

Tabby snapped her fingers. "Maybe Donna has a date and doesn't want me to know about it. I'll bet there's a mystery man in my friend's life."

"Who are you talking to, teacher?"

Tabby jerked her head at the sound of four-year-old Mary Steven's sweet voice.

"I—uh—was kind of talking to myself."

Mary grinned. "Like you do when you use Roscoe or little Rosie?"

Tabby nodded. "Something like that." She patted the child on top of her curly blond head. "What are you doing up, missy? It's nap time, you know."

The child nodded soberly. "I'm not sleepy."

"Maybe not, but you need to rest your eyes." Tabby placed her ham sandwich back inside its plastic wrapper and stood up. "Come on, sweetie, I'll walk you back to your sleeping mat."

❧

Seth tapped the edge of his water glass with the tip of his spoon, as he waited impatiently for Donna to show up. She'd promised to meet him at Garrison's Deli shortly after noon. It was only a few doors down from the church where she and Tabby ran their day care center. It shouldn't take her more than a few minutes to get here.

He glanced at his watch again. Twelve twenty. Where was she anyway? Maybe she'd forgotten. Maybe she'd changed her mind. He was just about to leave the table and go to the counter to place his order when he saw Donna come rushing into the deli.

She waved then hurried toward his table. Her face was flushed, and her dark curls looked windblown. "Sorry I'm late," she panted. "Just as I was leaving the day care, Tabby started plying me with all sorts of questions about where I was having lunch, and she even suggested she come along. I chose to ignore her and hurried out of the room. Then I got detained a few more minutes on my way out of the church."

Seth gave her a questioning look as she took the seat directly across from him.

"One of the kids' parents came to pick him up early. She stopped me on the steps to say Bobby had a dental appointment and she'd forgotten to tell us about it," Donna explained.

Seth nodded toward the counter. "I was about to order. Do you know what you want, or do you need a few minutes to look at the menu?"

"Chicken salad in pita bread and a glass of iced tea sounds good to me," she replied.

"I'll be right back," Seth said, pushing away from the table. He placed Donna's order first then ordered a turkey club sandwich on whole wheat with a glass of apple juice for himself. When he returned to the table, he found Donna staring out the window.

"Looks like it could rain again," he noted.

She held up the umbrella she'd placed on one end of the table. "I came prepared."

Seth decided there was no point in wasting time talking about the weather. "I was wondering if we could discuss Tabby," he blurted out. "That day you came into my shop to get the gift certificate for Tabby's dummy, we agreed that we'd work together to help her. I've really been trying, but to tell you the truth, I kind of feel like a salmon swimming upstream."

Donna giggled. "How can I help?"

"I have a few questions for you," he answered.

"What do you want to know?"

"I've never met anyone quite as shy as Tabby," he said. "Can you tell me why that is and what makes her stutter?"

Donna drew in a deep breath and exhaled it with such force that her napkin blew off the table. "Whew. . .that's kind of a long story." She bent down to retrieve the napkin then glanced at her watch. "This will have to be a scaled down version, because I have to be back at work by one."

Seth leaned forward with his elbows on the table. "I'm all ears."

"I've known Tabby ever since we were little tykes," Donna began. "Up until she turned six, Tabby was a fun-loving, outgoing child."

"What happened when she turned six?"

"Her sister was born." Donna grimaced. "Tabby's dad favored Lois right from the start. I can't explain why, but he started giving Tabby put-downs and harsh words. She turned inward, became introverted, and began to lack confidence in most areas of her life." She drummed her fingers along the edge of the table. "That's when she began stuttering."

Seth was about to reply, but their order was being called. He excused himself to pick up their food. When he returned to the table, Seth offered a word of prayer, and they both grabbed their sandwiches. "Do you think you can eat and talk at the same time?" he asked.

"Oh, sure, I've had lots of practice," Donna mumbled around her pita bread.

"I've noticed that Tabby stutters more at certain times, and other times she hardly stutters at all."

Donna nodded. "It has to do with how well she knows you, and how comfortable she feels in your presence."

"So, if Tabby felt more confident and had more self-esteem, she probably wouldn't stutter as much—or at all."

Donna shrugged. "Could be. Tabby's worst stuttering takes place when she's around her family. They intimidate her, and she's never learned to stand up for herself."

Seth took a swallow of apple juice, and his eyebrows furrowed. "Tabby doesn't stutter at all when she does ventriloquism. It's almost like she's a different person when she's speaking through her dummy."

Donna shrugged. "In a way, I guess she is."

"Just when I think I've got her figured out, she does something to muddle my brain."

"Like what?"

"Last night was a good example," Seth answered. "Tabby arrived at my shop for another lesson, and I thought she was in a good mood, ready to learn and all excited about it."

"She was excited," Donna agreed. "She's been enthusiastic about everything since the two of you went to Seattle."

Seth brightened some. "Really? I thought she'd had a good time, but I wasn't sure."

Donna grinned. "Tabby was on cloud nine when she came home that night." Her hand went quickly to her mouth. "Oops. . . Guess I wasn't supposed to tell you that."

Seth felt his face flush. That was the trouble with being fair skinned and redheaded. He flushed way too easily. *Tabby must have some feelings for me. At least she did until. . .*

"Tell me what happened last night to make you wonder about Tabby," Donna said, interrupting his thoughts.

He took a bite of his sandwich then washed it down with more juice before answering. "As I said before, Tabby was in a good mood when she first came in."

"And?"

"Then an unexpected customer showed up, and after she left, Tabby closed up like a razor clam."

"Hmm. . ."

"Hmm. . .what?"

Donna frowned. "Tabby was in kind of a sour mood when she came home last night. I asked her what was wrong, and she mumbled something about not being able to compete with Cheryl." She eyed Seth speculatively. "Cheryl wouldn't happen to be that unexpected customer, would she?"

"Afraid so. Cheryl Stone is a confident young woman with lots of talent as a ventriloquist."

"Is she pretty?"

He nodded. Cheryl was beautiful, vivacious, and talented. *That perfect woman you've been looking for,* a little voice taunted. *If Cheryl is perfect, then why do I think I need to remake Tabby?*

"Will you be seeing Tabby again?" Donna asked.

He swallowed hard, searching for the right words. Did he love her? Did she love him? He enjoyed being with her, that much he knew. Was it love he was feeling, though? It was probably too soon to tell.

"I—I don't know if we'll see each other again," he finally answered. "Guess that all depends on Tabby."

"On whether she wants more lessons?" Donna pried.

Seth shrugged. "That and a few other things."

Donna didn't pry, and he was glad. He wasn't in the mood to try and explain his feelings for Tabitha Johnson, or this compelling need he felt to make her into the woman he thought he needed.

"Well," Donna said a few minutes later, "I really do need to get back to work." She finished her iced tea and stood up. "Thanks for lunch, Seth. I hope some of the things we've talked about have been helpful. Tabby's my best friend, and I care a lot about her." She looked at him pointedly. "She carries a lot of pain from the past. I don't want to see her hurt anymore."

Seth stood up too. "My car's parked right out front. I'll walk you out," he said, making no reference to the possibility that he might add further hurt to Tabby's already battered mental state. He was so confused about everything right now, and some things were better left unsaid. Especially when he hadn't fully sorted out his feelings for her and didn't have a clue how she really felt about him.

❁

With a bag of trash in her arms, Tabby left Gail, their eighteen-year-old helper, in charge of the day care kids while she carried the garbage out to the curb. The garbage truck always came around three on Friday afternoons, which meant she still had enough time to get one more bag put out.

Tabby stepped up beside the two cans by the curb and had just opened the lid of one, when she heard voices coming from down the street. She turned her head to the right and froze in place, one hand holding the garbage can lid, the other clutching the plastic garbage bag.

She could see a man and woman standing outside Garrison's Deli. She'd have recognized them anywhere—Seth for his red hair; Donna for her high-pitched laugh. What were they doing together? Tabby's mouth dropped open like a broken hinge on a screen door. Her body began to sway. She blinked rapidly, hoping her eyes had deceived her. Seth was actually hugging her best friend!

Chapter 14

Tabby dropped the garbage sack into the can, slammed the lid down, whirled around, and bolted for the church. She didn't want Donna or Seth to see her. She had to think. . .to decide the best way to handle this little matter. Would it be better to come right out and ask Donna what she was doing with Seth, or should she merely ply her with a few questions, hoping the answers would come voluntarily?

Tabby returned to the day care center with a heavy heart. Were Seth and Donna seeing each other socially? Was he Donna's lunch date? Was he the mystery man in her best friend's life? As much as the truth might hurt, she had to know.

Tabby was setting out small tubs of modeling clay when Donna sauntered into the room humming "Jesus Loves Me." She looked about as blissful as a kitten with a ball of string, and not the least bit guilty, either.

"How was lunch?" Tabby asked after Donna had put her purse and umbrella in the desk drawer.

"It was good. I had pita bread stuffed with chicken salad."

"What did your date have?"

Donna spun around, and her eyebrows shot up. "My date?"

"Yeah, the person you met for lunch."

"Did I say I was meeting someone?"

Tabby shrugged. "Not in so many words, but you acted kind of secretive. Are you seeing some guy you don't want me to know about?"

Donna lowered herself into one of the kiddie chairs, keeping her eyes averted from Tabby's penetrating gaze. "Let's just say I'm checking him out. I need to see how well we get along. I want to find out what he's really like."

Tabby opened one of the clay lids and slapped it down on the table. "Why didn't you just ask me? I know exactly what he's like!"

Donna's forehead wrinkled, and she pursed her lips. "Since when do you have the inside scoop on our pastor's son?"

"Who?"

"Alex Hanson."

"Alex? What's Alex got to do with this?"

"I had lunch with Alex the Saturday you and Seth went to Seattle," Donna explained.

Tabby's insides began to quiver. What was going on here, anyway? "That's fine. I'm happy you finally agreed to go out with Alex, but what about today? Did you or did you not have lunch with someone over at Garrison's Deli?"

Donna's face grew red, and little beads of perspiration gathered on her forehead. "Well, I—"

"You don't have to hem and haw or beat around the bush with me," Tabby grunted. "I know perfectly well who you had lunch with today."

"You do?"

Tabby nodded. "I took some garbage outside a little while ago. I heard voices, and when I looked down the street, there stood Seth—with his arms around my best friend!" She flopped into a chair and buried her face in her hands.

Donna reached over and laid a hand on Tabby's trembling shoulder, but Tabby jerked it away. "How could you go behind my back like that?"

"You're wrong. Things aren't the way they appear."

Tabby snapped her head up. "Are you going to deny having had lunch with Seth?"

"No, but—"

"Was it you and Seth standing in front of the deli?"

"Yes, but—"

"You can't argue the fact that he was hugging you, either, can you?"

Donna shook her head. "No, I can't deny any of those things, but I'm not the least bit interested in Seth. We've been through all this before, Tabby, and—"

"Just how do you explain the secret lunch. . .or that tender little embrace?"

Donna's eyes filled with tears. "I didn't want you to know I was meeting Seth, because I didn't want you to think we were ganging up on you."

Tabby bit her bottom lip, sucking it inside her mouth when she tasted blood. "In what way are you ganging up on me?"

"Can't we talk about this later? The kids will be up from their naps soon," Donna said, glancing toward the adjoining room.

Tabby lifted her arm then held it so her watch was a few inches from Donna's face. "We still have three minutes. I think you can answer my question in that amount of time, don't you?"

Donna pulled a tissue from her skirt pocket and blew her nose. "Guess you don't leave me much choice."

Tabby's only response was a curt nod.

"It's like this. . .Seth was concerned about your actions last night. He said you didn't do well at your lesson, and that you seemed kinda remote. He's trying hard to help you overcome your shyness, and perfect your—"

"So the two of you are in cahoots, trying to fix poor, pitiful, timid Tabitha!" Tabby shouted. She could feel the pulse hammering in her neck, and her hands had begun to shake.

Donna's eyelids fluttered. "Calm down. You'll wake the kids."

Tabby pointed to her watch. "It's almost time for them to get up anyway."

"That may be true, but you don't want to scare the little tykes with your screeching, do you?"

Tabby sniffed deeply. "Of course not. But I'm really upset right now, and I'm not sure who I should be angrier with—you or Seth."

Donna grimaced. "Sorry. I didn't mean to get you all riled up. I just thought—"

Donna's sentence was interrupted when a group of children came trooping into the room, chattering and giggling all the way to the table.

Donna gave Tabby a look. For now, this conversation was over.

❀

Seth hung up the phone, wondering why he'd ever agreed to recruit another ventriloquist to perform with him at the Clearview Church Family Crusade. The female ventriloquist who'd originally been scheduled to perform had just canceled out. Now they were asking him to find a replacement.

Seth knew plenty of ventriloquists. The trouble was, it was so last minute. The crusade was set for next Friday night, and finding someone at this late date would be next to impossible. If only he could come up with. . .

The bell above his shop door rang sharply as a customer entered the shop. It was almost closing time, and the last thing Seth needed was one more problem he didn't know how to fix. He glanced up, and his heart seemed as though it had quit beating. It was Tabby, and she didn't look any too happy.

"Hi," Seth said cheerfully. "I'm glad to see you. You never called about having another lesson, and—"

Tabby held up one hand. "I've decided I don't need any more lessons."

"Then why are you here? You're not having a problem with Rosie, I hope."

She shook her head. "No, I w–wanted to talk about—"

Seth snapped his fingers, cutting her off in midsentence. "Say, you just might be the answer to my prayers!"

She furrowed her brows and turned her hands, palm up. "I d–don't get it."

He motioned toward a folding chair. "Have a seat, and I'll tell you about it."

When Tabby sat down, Seth took the chair next to her.

"Well, h–how am I an answer t–to your prayers?" she asked.

He reached for her hand. This was not going to be easy. Only a God-given miracle would make Tabby willing to do what he asked.

�</br>

Tabby was tempted to pull her hand from Seth's, but she didn't. It felt good. In fact, she wished she'd never have to let go. She stared up at him, searching his face for answers.

"I—uh—will be doing a vent routine at Clearview Community Church next Friday night," Seth began slowly.

"What's that got to do with me?"

"I'm getting to that." He smiled sheepishly. "The thing is, Sarah McDonald, the other ventriloquist who was originally scheduled, has had a family emergency and was forced to bow out." Seth ran his thumb along the inside of Tabby's palm, making it that much harder for her to concentrate on what he was saying. "I was hoping you might be willing to go with me next week—to fill in for Sarah."

Tabby's throat constricted, and she drew in a deep, unsteady breath. Did Seth actually think she could stand up in front of an audience and talk for two? He should be smart enough to realize she wasn't ready for something like that. The truth was, even though she had gained a bit more confidence, she might never be able to do ventriloquism for a large audience.

"I know it's short notice," Seth said, jerking her thoughts aside, "but we could begin practicing right now, then do more throughout the week. I'm sure—"

The rest of Seth's sentence was lost, as Tabby closed her eyes and tried to imagine what it would be like to perform before a crowd. She could visualize herself freezing up and not being able to utter a single word. Or worse yet, stuttering and stammering all over the place.

"Tabby, are you listening to me?" Seth's mellow voice pulled her out of the make-believe situation, and she popped her eyes open.

"I c–can't d–do it, Seth."

He pulled her to her feet then placed both his hands on her shoulders. "You can do it, so don't be discouraged because you believe you have no ability. Each of us has much to offer. It's what you do with your abilities that really matters. Now, repeat after me. . .'I can do everything through him who gives me strength.'"

In a trembling voice, Tabby repeated the verse of Scripture from Philippians 4:13. When she was done, Seth tipped her chin up slightly, so they were making direct eye contact. "I know you can do this, Tabby."

She merely shrugged in response.

"You're a talented ventriloquist, and it's time to let your light shine," Seth said with feeling. He leaned his head down until his lips were mere inches from hers. "Do this for me, please."

Tabby's eyelids fluttered then drifted shut. She felt the warmth of Seth's lips against her own. His kiss was gentle like a butterfly, but as intense as anything she'd ever felt. Of course, her inexperience in the kissing department didn't offer much for comparison. Tabby knew she was falling for Seth Beyers, and she wanted desperately to please him. She'd come over here this evening to give him a piece of her mind, but now all such thoughts had melted away, like spring's last snow. She reveled in the joy of being held in Seth's arms and delighted in the warmth of his lips caressing her own.

When they pulled apart moments later, Tabby felt as if all the breath had been squeezed out of her lungs.

"Kissing is good for you, did you know that?" Seth murmured against her ear.

Numbly she shook her head.

"Yep. It helps relieve stress and tension. Just think about it—when your mouth is kissing, you're almost smiling. Everyone knows it's impossible to smile and feel tense at the same time."

Tabby leaned her head against his shoulder. She did feel relaxed, happy, and almost confident. In a voice sounding much like her dummy's, she rasped, "Okay, I'll do it. Rosie and I will p–perform a vent routine."

He grinned and clasped his hands together. "Great! I know you'll be perfect."

Chapter 15

Tabby awoke the following morning wondering if she'd completely lost her mind. What in the world had come over her last night? Not only had she not told Seth what she thought about him trying to change her, but she'd actually agreed to do a vent routine next week—in front of a large audience, no less!

"It was that kiss," Tabby moaned as she threw back the covers and crawled out of bed. "If only he hadn't kissed me, I could have said no."

She winced, as though she'd been slapped. Would she really rather he hadn't kissed her? In all honesty, if Seth would offer another of his sweet kisses, she'd probably say yes all over again.

Feeling more like a dummy than a ventriloquist, Tabby padded in her bare feet over to the window and peered through the miniblinds. The sun was shining. The birds were singing. It was going to be a beautiful day. Too bad her heart felt no joy. She turned and headed for the kitchen, feeling as though she was part of a death march.

Discovering Donna sitting at the table, talking on the cordless phone, Tabby dropped into a chair. When Donna offered her a warm smile, she only grunted in response.

By the time Donna's conversation was over, Tabby had eaten an orange, along with a handful of grapes, and she was about to tackle a banana. "Good morning, sleepyhead. I thought you were never going to get up."

"I got in late last night," Tabby mumbled as she bit into the piece of fruit.

"Tell me about it!" Donna exclaimed. "I finally gave up waiting for you and went to bed. You said you had an errand to run after work. Where were you anyway?"

Tabby swallowed the chunk of banana and frowned. "I'm afraid my errand turned into more of an error."

Donna's eyebrows lifted in question.

"I went to Beyers' Ventriloquist Studio, planning to put Seth in his place for trying to run my life."

"And did you?"

Tabby sucked in her bottom lip and squared her shoulders. "Afraid not. I ended up promising to do a vent routine at the Clearview Church Family Crusade next Friday."

Donna slapped her hand down on the table, and Tabby's banana peel flew into the air, landing on the floor. "Awesome! That's the best news I've had all year. Maybe even in the last ten years!"

Tabby shook her head. "Don't get so excited. I haven't done it yet."

"Oh, but you will," Donna said excitedly. She pointed to the phone. "That call was from Alex Hanson. He asked me to go out with him again, and guess where we're going?"

"Please don't tell me it's the crusade," Tabby said, already knowing the answer.

"Okay, I won't tell you. I'll just let you be surprised when you look out into the audience and see your best friend and your pastor's son cheering you on."

Tabby gazed at the ceiling. "I think I need a doctor to examine my head more than I need a cheering section." She groaned. "I can't believe I let Seth talk me into such a thing!"

"You'll do just fine," Donna said with an assurance Tabby sure didn't feel. "I imagine you and Seth did some practicing last night?"

Yeah, that and a few other things. Tabby wasn't about to discuss Seth's kiss. Donna would probably go ballistic if she knew that had happened. "We had a bite of supper at the café near Seth's shop, then we worked on my routine till almost midnight." Tabby grimaced. "I'm lucky I even have any voice left after all that talking. Maybe I could get out of this if I had laryngitis or something. Seth asked me to do him a favor by filling in for someone else, and—"

"And you love the guy so much, you couldn't say no," Donna said, finishing Tabby's sentence.

Tabby's eyes filled with tears. "He wants me to be something I'm not."

"Which is?"

"Confident, talented, and ready to serve the Lord."

Donna reached across the table and patted Tabby's hand. "I've seen you do ventriloquism, so I know how talented you are. I also know you want to serve the Lord."

Tabby nodded and swiped at her face with the backs of her hands.

"The confident part will come if you give yourself half a chance," Donna assured her. "If you wallow around in self-pity the rest of your life, you'll never realize your full potential."

Tabby released a shuddering breath. "I know you're right, but I still stutter when I'm nervous or with people I don't know well. How can I become truly confident when I can't even talk right?"

"Philippians 4:13: 'I can do everything through him who gives me strength,'" Donna reminded.

Tabby sniffed. "Seth quoted that same verse last night."

"See," Donna said with a smile. "The Lord wants you to lean on Him. If you keep your focus on Jesus and not the audience, I know you can do that routine next week."

Tabby smiled weakly. "I hope so." Her eyes filled with fresh tears. "I owe you an apology for the other day. We've been friends a long time, and I should have known you'd never try to make a play for Seth behind my back."

Donna nodded. "You're right; I wouldn't. And you are forgiven."

Tabby and Seth met every evening for the next week to practice their routines for the crusade. Not only was it helpful for Tabby to memorize her lines and work on her fear of talking for two in public, but it was an opportunity to spend more time with Seth. Sometimes, after they were done for the night, he'd take her out for pie and coffee, and a few times they just sat and talked. They were drawing closer, there was no doubt in Tabby's mind, but much to her disappointment, Seth hadn't tried to kiss her again. Maybe he thought it best to keep things on a strictly business basis, since they were preparing to do a program and shouldn't be playing the game of romance when they needed to be working.

As she entered the Clearview Community Church that Friday night, carrying Rosie in a small suitcase, Tabby's heart thumped so hard she was sure everyone around could hear it. The driving force that enabled her to make the trip across town was the fact that Seth was counting on her, and she didn't want to let him down.

She spotted Seth talking to a man in the foyer. When he noticed Tabby, he motioned her to come over.

"Tabby, I'd like you to meet Pastor Tom Fletcher," Seth said, placing his arm around her waist. "He's heading up the program tonight."

"It's nice to meet you," the pastor said, reaching out to shake her hand.

She nodded and forced a smile. "N–nice to m–meet you, too."

"Seth was just telling me that you've graciously agreed to fill in for Sarah McDonald.

I sure do appreciate this."

Tabby cringed, wishing she could tell Pastor Fletcher the truth—she wasn't graciously filling in. She'd been coerced by Seth's honeyed words and his heart-melting kiss.

"Tabby's new at ventriloquism," Seth said to the preacher. "She's got lots of talent, though. Doesn't move her lips at all."

Right now I wish my lips were glued shut, she fretted. *I wish Seth would quit bragging about me. It'll only make the pastor expect more than I'm able to give.*

"Why don't we go backstage now?" Seth suggested, giving Tabby a little nudge.

She let herself be led along, feeling like a sheep heading straight for the slaughterhouse. If she lived through this ordeal, she'd be eternally grateful. She caught sight of Donna and her blond-haired date as they were entering the sanctuary. Donna waved, and Alex gave her a "thumbs-up." She managed a weak smile, but the truth was, she felt like crying.

As though he could read her mind, Seth bent down and whispered, "Relax. You'll do fine."

"I wish everyone would quit telling me that."

Seth offered her a reassuring smile. "Do you realize that your last sentence was spoken without one bit of stuttering?"

She shook her head. Right at this moment she could barely remember what her last sentence had been about, much less focus on the fact that she hadn't stuttered.

Seth led her through a door, and a few minutes later they were in a small room with several other performers. Tabby recognized a few of them who'd been part of the demonstration for Christian workers at her own church a few months ago. There were Mark Taylor, the magician from Portland, Oregon, and Gail Stevens, the chalk artist from Seattle. Tabby knew Donna would be glad to see her. She'd probably be practicing her chalk art in earnest after tonight's performance. Slow-Joe the Clown was busy practicing his animal twisting skills, and some puppeteers were lining up to do their puppet skit. Tabby envied them. . .partly because they were going first and could get their routine over with, but mostly because they had the advantage of a puppet box to hide behind. If only she didn't have to face that crowd out there in the sanctuary!

"Now remember," Seth said, pulling Tabby aside, "I'll go out first and do my routine with Rudy; then you'll come out with Rosie, and we'll do a little bantering with our dummies. By then your confidence should be bolstered, so I'll just bow out, and you'll be on your own."

She looked up at him with pleading eyes. "That's the part that has me so worried, Seth. Couldn't you stay by my side the whole time?"

He shrugged. "I suppose I could, but I think the audience will appreciate your talent more if they see you perform solo."

Who cares if the audience appreciates my talent? I just want to get through this ordeal and live to tell about it. Tabby's heart fluttered like a frightened baby bird, and she fidgeted with the bow on Rosie's new pink dress. Donna would be glad to see she'd taken her advice and dressed the dummy up a bit.

Seth reached for her hand and squeezed it. "Your fingers feel like icicles, Tabby. Take a deep breath, and try to relax."

"That's easy enough for you to say," she muttered. "You're an old pro at this."

It seemed like no time at all that Seth was being announced by Pastor Fletcher. He grabbed Rudy and his stand, blew Tabby a kiss, and walked confidently onto the stage.

Tabby stood as close to the stage door as she could without being seen. She didn't want to miss her cue and end up embarrassing both Seth and herself. Seth was doing a bang-up job with his routine, but she was too nervous to appreciate any of it. All too soon, Seth announced her.

Holding Rosie with one hand and balancing the metal stand Seth had given her with the other, Tabby swallowed the panic rising in her throat and moved slowly across the stage. Applause sounded from the audience, and she felt her face flame.

"Rudy and I both needed dates for tonight," Seth told the crowd. "This is my friend, Tabitha Johnson, and I'll let her introduce her little pal."

Tabby opened her mouth, but nothing came out. She just stood there, feeling like some kind of frozen snow woman, unable to remember her lines and too afraid to speak them if she had.

Coming quickly to her rescue, Seth opened Rudy's mouth. "I think Tabby's waiting for me to introduce her friend. After all, she is my date, so it's probably the right thing to do." The dummy's head swiveled to the left, and one of his doe eyes winked at Rosie. "This is Rosie Wrong, but someday I hope to right that wrong and make her my bride. Then she'll be Rosie Right, who's always right, because she married me—Rudy Right!"

The audience roared and clapped their approval. Tabby felt herself begin to relax a little, and she was even able to make her dummy say a few words.

"What makes you think I'd marry a dummy?" Rosie announced. "Do I look stupid?"

"No, but you sure are cute!" Rudy shot back.

More laughter from the audience. This was fun—almost. What was Tabby going to do once Seth and Rudy left the stage? So far, she'd only spoken for Rosie. How would things go when she was forced to speak herself?

Rudy and Rosie bantered back and forth a bit longer; then finally Seth said the words Tabby had been dreading. "Well, folks, I think it's time for Rudy and me to say good-bye. I'll leave you in the capable hands of Tabby and her friend, Rosie. I'm sure they have lots of fun up their sleeves." With that, Seth grabbed Rudy and his stand and marched off the stage. The audience clapped, and Tabby nearly panicked. She forgot to pray, and in her own strength, she tried to concentrate on her routine. Everything Seth had told her seemed like ancient history. She couldn't think of anything except trying to please the audience and the paralyzing fear that held her in its grip.

"Say, R–Rosie, h–have you h–heard any good elephant j–jokes lately?" she finally squeaked.

"Oh, sure. Would you like to hear them?" Rosie responded.

Tabby only nodded. One less sentence to stammer through.

"Why do elephants have wrinkles?" Rosie asked.

"I d–don't know."

"Well, for goodness' sake, have you ever tried to iron one?"

A few snickers came from the audience, but it was nothing compared to the belly laughs Seth had gotten. This did little to bolster Tabby's confidence, and she struggled to remember the rest of her performance.

"I sure wish I had enough money to buy an elephant," Rosie said.

"Why w–would you—you w–want an el–elephant?"

"I don't. I just want the money."

Tabby paused, hoping the audience would catch on to the little joke, but they didn't. Not even Donna laughed. Tabby felt like a deflated balloon. So much for the confidence she thought she might have gained. She was failing miserably at entertaining this audience, much less bringing any glory to God through her so-called talent. Then there was Seth. What must he think of his star pupil now? He was probably as mortified as she was, and she couldn't blame him one little bit.

"M–money isn't everything, R–Rosie," Tabby said.

"It's all I need."

"Do y–you know w–what the Bible says about m–money?"

"No, do you?"

Tabby did know what it said, but for the life of her, she couldn't remember. In fact, she had no idea what to say or do next. The audience looked bored with her routine, and she'd done nothing but tell stale jokes and stutter ever since Seth took his leave. Her hands were shaking so badly she could hardly hold Rosie still, and her legs felt like two sticks made of rubber. If she didn't get off this platform soon, she would probably pass out cold.

Tabby drew in a deep breath, grabbed Rosie up in one quick swoop, and darted off the stage.

Chapter 16

Tabby was sobbing hysterically by the time she reached the room offstage. With all Seth's encouragement, she'd almost begun to believe she did have some talent, but she'd blown it big-time. She had let God down, disappointed Seth, and made a complete fool of herself in front of nearly two hundred people! How could she have let this happen? Why hadn't she just told Seth no? All she wanted to do was go home, jump into bed, and bury her head under the covers.

She felt Seth's arms go around her waist. "It's okay, Tabby," he murmured against her ear. "This was your first time, and you were a little nervous, that's all. It's happened to everyone, and it will get easier with time and practice." He slid his hand up to her back and began patting it, as though that would somehow bring her comfort. "You'll do better next time, I'm sure of it."

Tabby pulled away sharply. "There won't be a next time, Seth! Except for the day care kids, I'll never have another audience."

"Yes, you will. You could be perfect if you'd give yourself half a chance. Please, let me help you. . . ."

It seemed as though Seth was asking her to be perfect at ventriloquism, but some of the things she'd heard him say to both Donna and herself made Tabby wonder if what Seth really wanted was for her to be perfect.

"You've helped me enough!" she cried. "Thanks to you, I made myself look like a total idiot out there!"

Before Seth could offer a rebuttal, Tabby jerked the door open. "Find someone else to help," she called over her shoulder. "I'll never be perfect, and I'm not the woman you need!" Slamming the door, she dashed down the hall. Despite the tears blinding her eyes, Tabby could see someone standing by the front door of the church. It was Donna.

Tabby shook her head. "Don't even say it. I don't want your pity or any kind of sappy pep talk about how things will go better next time."

Donna opened her mouth to say something, but Tabby yanked on the door handle, raced down the steps, and headed straight for her car. All she wanted was to be left alone.

🌼

The next few weeks were filled with mounting tension. Tabby barely spoke to anyone, and Donna kept trying to draw her into a conversation. Seth phoned several times, but Tabby wouldn't accept any of his calls. He even dropped by the day care on two occasions, but she refused to talk to him. It pained her to think she'd fallen in love with a man who couldn't accept her for the way she was. If he wanted "perfect," then he might be better off with someone like Cheryl Stone. Why hadn't he asked her to fill in for the ventriloquist who couldn't do the routine for the crusade? At least Cheryl wouldn't have humiliated herself or Seth in front of a church full of people.

A phone call from her parents, a week later, threw Tabby into deeper depression. On Friday night they would be hosting an engagement party for Lois. Tabby was expected to come, of course. She had always been obligated to attend family functions, even if no one seemed to notice she was there. If she didn't go, she'd probably never hear the end of it, but it irked her that they waited until the last minute to extend an invitation. There was hardly enough time to buy a suitable gift.

The party was set for six thirty, and it was a good forty-five-minute drive from Tacoma to Olympia. That was barring any unforeseen traffic jams on the freeway. Tabby knew she'd have to leave for Olympia by five thirty. The day care was open until six thirty, but Donna said she and their helper could manage alone for an hour.

❋

Seth was fit to be tied. His phone calls to Tabby and his trips to the day care had been for nothing. No matter how much he pleaded, she still refused to talk to him. He could understand her being upset about the routine she'd botched at the crusade. That didn't excuse her for staying mad at him, though.

Sitting at his workbench, mechanically sanding the arm of a new vent figure, Seth sulked. At first he'd only thought of Tabby as someone who needed his help. Then he began to see her as a friend. Finally, he realized he could love her, but she just didn't fit his mold for the "perfect" wife.

Even though they hadn't known each other very long, Seth cared a lot about Tabby and only wanted the best for her. She'd accused him of trying to change her. Maybe it was true. If he were being totally honest, he'd have to admit he did want her to be different—to fit into his special design and become the kind of person he wanted her to be. Tabby might be right. Perhaps he should find someone more suited to him. Maybe Cheryl Stone would be a better match. She had talent, confidence, and beauty. There was just one problem. . . . He wasn't in love with Cheryl. The truth of this revelation slammed into Seth with such force, it left him with a splitting headache. Until this very moment, he'd never really admitted it. He was actually in love with Tabby Johnson, and not for what she could be, but rather for who she was—gentle and sweet spirited with children, humble and never bragging, compassionate and helpful—all the qualities of a true Christian.

Seth left his seat and moved toward the front door of his shop. He put the CLOSED sign in the window then turned off the lights. What he really needed was a long talk with God, followed by a good night's sleep. Maybe he could think things through more clearly in the morning.

❋

"Are you sure you don't want me to go with you tonight?" Donna asked Tabby as she prepared to leave the day care center.

Tabby shook her head. "This shindig is for family members only—our side and the groom's. Besides, you've got another date with Alex, remember?"

Donna shrugged. "I know how much you dread being with your family. If I were there, it might buffer things a bit. I could call Alex and cancel."

"Not on your life! It's taken you forever to get past your fear of dating a PK. Don't ruin it by breaking a date when it's totally unnecessary." Tabby waved her hand. "Besides, I'm a grown woman. As you've pointed out many times, it's high time I learn to deal with my family without having someone there to hold my hand."

Donna squeezed Tabby's arm. "Okay, try to have fun tonight, and please, drive carefully."

Tabby wrinkled her nose. "Don't I always?"

"It's not your driving I'm worried about. It's all those maniacs who exceed the speed limit and act as if they own the whole road."

"I'll be careful," Tabby promised as she went out the door.

❋

Tabby was glad she'd left in plenty of time, because the freeway was terrible this night. She was tempted to take the next exit and travel the back roads, but the traffic was so congested, she wasn't sure she could even move over a lane in order to get off. By the time she finally pulled off at the Olympia exit, Tabby was a bundle of nerves.

She knew part of her apprehension was because she was about to enter the lions' den. At least, that's the way it always felt whenever she did anything that involved her family. If only Mom and Dad could love and accept her the way they did Lois. If only she was the kind of daughter they wanted. What exactly did they want? Beauty. . .brains. . .boldness? Lois had all three, and she'd been Dad's favorite ever since she was born. But what parent in their right mind would love one child more than another?

Tabby clenched her teeth. Everyone wanted her to change. Was there anyone willing to accept her just the way she was? Donna used to, but lately she'd been pressing Tabby to step out in faith and begin using her talents to serve the Lord. *If I ever have any children of my own, I'll love them all the same, no matter how different they might be.*

Then there was Seth. Tabby thought at first he just wanted to help her, but she was quite sure now he'd been trying to make her over ever since they first met. Was she really so unappealing the way she was? Must she become a whole new person in order for her family and friends to love and accept her?

A verse of scripture from Second Corinthians popped into her mind: *"Therefore, if anyone is in Christ, he is a new creation; the old has gone, the new has come!"*

Tabby had accepted the Lord at an early age. She knew she'd been cleansed of her sins, which made her a "new creation." Her stuttering problem and lack of confidence had made her unwilling to completely surrender her life to Christ and let Him use all her talents, though. If she were really a new creation, shouldn't she be praying and asking the Lord's help to become all she could be? She hadn't prayed or kept her focus on Jesus the other night at the church program. Instead, she'd been trying to impress the audience.

"I'll think about this later," Tabby murmured as she turned into her parents' driveway. Her primary concern right now was making it through Lois's engagement party.

❧

Seth was tired of dodging his problems. With Bible in hand and a glass of cold lemonade, he took a seat at the kitchen table, determined to relinquish his own selfish desires and seek God's will for his life.

The first passage of scripture he came to was in Matthew. Jesus was teaching the Beatitudes to a crowd of people. Seth read verse five aloud. " 'Blessed are the meek, for they will inherit the earth.' "

He propped his elbows on the table and leaned his chin against his palms. "Hmm. . . Tabby fits that category, all right."

He jumped down to verse eight. " 'Blessed are the pure in heart, for they will see God.' " How could he have been so blind? Purity seemed to emanate from Tabby. Morally, she seemed like a clear, crisp mountain stream, untouched by the world's pollution.

Seth turned to the book of Proverbs, knowing the thirty-first chapter addressed the subject of an honorable wife. "A wife of noble character who can find? She is worth far more than rubies." He scanned the rest of the chapter, stopping to read verse thirty. "Charm is deceptive, and beauty is fleeting; but a woman who fears the Lord is to be praised."

Praised. Not ridiculed, coerced, or changed into something other than what she was. Seth placed one hand on the open Bible. He knew he'd found a good thing when he met Tabitha Johnson. Even though she was shy and couldn't always speak without stuttering, she had a generous heart and loved the Lord. Wasn't that what he really wanted in a wife?

Seth bowed his head and closed his eyes. "Dear Lord, forgive me for wanting Tabby to change. You love her just as she is, and I should, too. Please give me the chance to make amends. If she's the woman You have in mind for me, then work out the details and make her heart receptive to my love. Amen."

Unexpected tears fell from Seth's eyes, and he sniffed. He had to talk to Tabby right away, while the truth of God's Word was still fresh on his heart. Praying as he dialed the telephone, Seth petitioned God to give him the right words.

When Donna answered, Seth asked for Tabby.

"She's not home," Donna said. She sounded as though she was either in a hurry or trying to put him off. Was Tabby still too angry to speak with him? Had she asked Donna to continue monitoring her phone calls?

"I really do need to speak with her," Seth said with a catch in his voice. "It's important."

"I'm not giving you the runaround, Seth. Tabby isn't home right now."

"Where is she?"

"She left work a little early and drove to Olympia."

"Why'd she go there?"

"It's where her parents live. They're having an engagement party for her sister, Lois."

"Oh." Seth blew out his breath. If Tabby was in Olympia, she probably wouldn't get home until late. There would be no chance of talking to her until tomorrow.

"I'd like to talk more, Seth, but my date just arrived," Donna said.

He groaned. "Yeah, okay. Tell Tabby I'll call her tomorrow." Seth hung up the phone and leaned his head on the table. Why was it that whenever he made a decision to do something, there always seemed to be some kind of roadblock? If only he'd committed this situation to God a bit sooner.

"Guess all I can do is put things in Your hands, Lord. . .which is exactly where they should have been in the first place."

Chapter 17

Tabby's mother greeted her at the door with a frown. "You're late. Everyone else is here already."

Tabby glanced at her watch. It was ten minutes to seven. She was only twenty minutes late. She chose not to make an issue of it, though, merely shrugging and handing her mother the small bag she was holding. "Here's my g–gift for L–Lois."

Mom took the gift and placed it on a table just inside the living room door. "Come in. Everyone's in the backyard, waiting for your father to finish barbecuing the sirloin steaks."

Tabby grimaced. Apparently Dad was going all out for his favorite daughter. *If I were engaged, I doubt I'd even be given an engagement party, much less one with all the trimmings. And even if there were a party in my honor, Dad would probably fix plain old hamburgers, instead of a select, choice cut of meat.*

"How was the freeway tonight?" Mom asked as she and Tabby made their way down the hallway, leading to the back of their modest but comfortable, split-level home.

"Bad. R–really bad. That's w–why I'm l–late," Tabby mumbled.

Mom didn't seem to be listening. She was scurrying about the kitchen, looking through every drawer and cupboard as if her life depended upon finding whatever it was she was searching for.

"C–can I help w–with anything?" Tabby asked.

"I suppose you can get the jug of iced tea from the refrigerator. I've got to find the long-handled fork for your father. He sent me in here five minutes ago to look for it."

Tabby crossed the room, opened the refrigerator, grabbed the iced tea, and started for the back door.

"Wait a minute," Mom called. "I found the fork. Would you take it out to Dad?"

"Aren't you c–coming?" Tabby took the fork from her mother and waited expectantly.

"I'll be out in a minute. I just need to check on my pan of baked beans."

Tabby shrugged and headed out the door, wishing she could be anywhere else but here.

About twenty people were milling around the Johnsons' backyard. Some she recognized as aunts, uncles, and cousins. Then there was Grandma Haskins, Dad, Lois, and her sister's wealthy fiancé, Michael Yehley. Some faces were new to her. She assumed those were people related to the groom.

"I see you finally decided to join us," Dad said gruffly, when Tabby handed him the barbecue fork. "Ever since you were a kid, you've been slow. Yep, slower than a turtle plowing through peanut butter. How come you're always late for everything?"

Peanut butter, Tabby mused. *That's what Seth has a fear of eating.* It seemed that lately everything made her think about Seth. She wouldn't even allow Dad's little put-down to rattle her as much as usual. She was too much in love. There, she'd finally admitted it—at least to herself. *For all the good it will do me. Seth doesn't have a clue how I feel, and even if he did, it wouldn't matter. He sees me only as a friend—someone to help out of her shell.* She frowned. *Besides, I'm still mad at him for coercing me into doing that dumb vent routine.*

"Are you just going to stand there like a dummy, or is there some justification for you being so late?" Dad bellowed, snapping Tabby out of her musings.

"I w–wasn't l–l–late on pur–pur–purpose," she stammered. She always stuttered worse around Dad. Maybe it was because he was the one person she wanted most to please. "Tr–traffic was r–really h–h–heavy."

"Why didn't you take off work early so you could get here on time?" Dad said, jerking the fork out of Tabby's hand.

She winced. "I—I d–did l–leave early." Tears hung on her lashes, but she refused to cry.

Dad turned back to the barbecue grill without saying anything more. Tabby pirouetted toward her grandmother, knowing she would at least have a kind word or two.

Grandma Haskins, cheerfully dressed in a long floral skirt and a pink ruffled blouse, greeted Tabby with a peck on the cheek. "It's good to see you, dear." She tipped her silver-gray head to one side. "You're looking kind of peaked. Are you eating right and getting plenty of sleep? You're not coming down with anything, I hope."

Tabby couldn't help but smile. Grandma was always worrying about something. Since she saw Tabby so seldom, it was only fitting that she'd be her target tonight. Tabby didn't really mind, though. It felt kind of nice to have someone fussing over her. Ever since she'd made a fool of herself at the crusade, she had been wallowing in self-pity. Maybe a few minutes with Grandma would make her feel better. "I'm f–fine, Grandma, r–really," she mumbled.

Tabby and Grandma were about to find a place to sit down, when Lois came rushing up. Her face was flushed, and she looked as though she might have been crying.

"What's wrong, Lois?" Grandma asked in a tone of obvious concern.

Lois sniffed deeply and motioned them toward one of the empty tables. As soon as they sat down, she began to cry.

Tabby gave her sister's arm a gentle squeeze. "C–can you t–tell us about it?"

Lois hiccuped loudly and wiped at her eyes, which only smudged her black mascara, making the tears look like little drops of mud rolling down her cheeks. "It's Mike!" she wailed.

"Is something wrong with Michael?" Grandma asked. "I saw him a little while ago, and he looked fine to me."

"Oh, he's fine all right," Lois ranted. "He's so fine that he's decided to take over the planning of our wedding."

"Isn't that the b–bride's job?" Tabby inquired.

"I thought so, until this evening." Lois blew her nose on a napkin and scowled. She didn't look nearly as beautiful tonight as she had the last time Tabby had seen her. That was the night of Tabby's birthday party. Lois didn't have little rivulets of coal-colored tears streaming down her face then.

"Tell us what happened," Grandma prompted.

Lois looked around the yard anxiously. Her gaze came to rest on her fiancé, sitting with some of his family at another table.

Tabby glanced that way as well. She was surprised when Mike looked over and scowled. At least she thought it was a scowl. Maybe he'd just eaten one of Mom's famous stuffed mushrooms. Tabby didn't know why, but those mushrooms always tasted like they'd been filled with toothpaste instead of cream cheese.

"Mike doesn't want us to get married the first Saturday in October after all," Lois whined, jerking Tabby's thoughts back to the situation at hand.

"He doesn't?" Grandma handed Lois another napkin. "Does he want to call the whole thing off?"

Lois drew in a shuddering breath. "He says not, but I have to wonder. Mike thinks we should have more time to get to know one another before we tie the knot. He wants to postpone the wedding until June, and he waited till tonight to drop the bomb."

"June?" Grandma exclaimed. "Why, that's ten months away!"

"That's not a b–bad idea," Tabby interjected. "I mean, s–sometimes you th–think you know a p–person, and then he g–goes and does something to r–really throw you a c–curve ball."

Grandma and Lois both turned their attention on Tabby. "Are you talking about anyone in particular?" Grandma asked.

Tabby shook her head. "No, n–not r–really." She had no intention of telling them about Seth. They'd never understand the way things were. Besides, they weren't supposed to be talking about her right now. This was Lois's engagement party, and apparently there wasn't going to be a wedding. . .at least not this year. "Do M–Mom and D–Dad know yet?" she asked.

Lois shook her head. "I only found out myself a few minutes ago." She reached for Tabby's hand and gripped it tightly. "What am I going to do?"

Tabby swallowed hard. She could hardly believe that her confident, all-knowing little sister was asking her advice. If only she had the right answers. Thinking back to the devotions she'd done that morning, Tabby quoted the following scripture: " 'Do not let your heart be troubled. Trust in God, trust also in me.' "

Lois's face was pinched, and her eyes were mere slits. "What on earth are you talking about? Why would I trust in you? What can you do to help my situation?"

Tabby bit back the laughter rising in her throat. Even though she and Lois had both gone to Sunday school when they were children, Lois had never shown much interest in the things of God. In fact, she'd quit going to church when she turned thirteen. "That verse from the book of John is saying you should trust God and not allow your troubles to overtake you. 'Trust in God; trust also in Me.' That was Jesus speaking, and He was telling His followers to trust in Him, as well as in God." Tabby smiled at her sister. "As I'm sure you already know, Jesus and God are one and the same. So, if you put your trust in God, you're trusting Jesus, too."

Lois's mouth was hanging wide open, and Grandma was looking at Tabby as though she'd never seen her before.

"What? What's wrong?" Tabby questioned.

"Do you realize you just quoted that Bible verse and gave me a little pep talk without missing a single word? No stuttering, no stammering, nothing," Lois announced. "I think that must be a first, don't you, Grandma?"

Grandma smiled. "I wouldn't say it was a first, because I can remember when Tabby was a little girl and didn't have a problem with stuttering." She reached over and gave Tabby's hand a gentle pat. "I think it's safe to say when Tabby feels convicted about something, she forgets her insecurities, so her words flow uninterrupted."

Tabby wasn't sure how to respond to Grandma's comment, but she never had a chance to, because Lois cut right in. "Well, be that as it may, it doesn't solve my problem with Mike. How am I going to convince him to marry me in two months? I'll just die if I have to wait until next summer."

Grandma's hand made an arc as it left Tabby's and landed on Lois's. "Everything will work out, dear. Just do as Tabby says, and put your trust in the Lord."

Tabby looked over at her grandmother, and her heart swelled with love. If Grandma was beginning to believe, maybe there was some hope for the rest of the family. With more prayer and reliance on God, there might even be some hope for her. Perhaps she just needed to trust the Lord a bit more.

Chapter 18

When rain started falling around eight o'clock, everyone went inside. Tabby decided to head for home, knowing the roads would probably be bad. Besides, she was anxious to be by herself. This had been some evening. First, her parents' little put-downs, then the news that Lois wasn't getting married in October, followed by that special time she, Grandma, and Lois had shared. For a few brief moments, Tabby had felt lifted out of her problems and experienced a sense of joy by offering support to her sister. If only Lois hadn't ended up throwing a temper tantrum right before the party ended. She and Mike had spent most of the evening arguing, and when they weren't quarreling, Lois was crying. Tabby couldn't help but feel sorry for her.

"No matter when the wedding is, you can keep the automatic two-cup coffeemaker I gave you tonight," Tabby told Lois just before she left. She said good-bye to the rest of the family and climbed into her car. It had been a long week, and she'd be so glad to get home and into bed. Maybe some reading in the Psalms would help, too. Despite his troubles, David had a way of searching his soul and looking to God for all the answers to his problems and frustrations. Tabby needed that daily reminder as well.

🌻

The freeway was still crowded, though it was not quite as bad as it had been earlier. To make matters worse, the rain was coming down so hard Tabby could barely see out her windshield. She gripped the steering wheel with determination and prayed for all she was worth.

By the time Tabby reached the Lakewood exit, she'd had enough. She turned on her right blinker and signaled to get off. Traveling the back roads through Lakewood, Fircrest, then into Tacoma would be easier than trying to navigate the freeway traffic and torrential rains. At least she could travel at a more leisurely pace, and she'd be able to pull off the road if necessary.

Tabby clicked on her car radio as she headed down the old highway. The local Christian station was playing a song by a new female artist. The words played over and over in Tabby's head. *Jesus is your strength, give to Him your all. . . . Jesus wants your talents, please listen to His call. . . .*

The lyrical tune soothed Tabby's soul and made her think about Seth again. For weeks he'd been telling her to use her talents for the Lord. "That's because he's trying to change me," she murmured. "Seth's more concerned about finding the perfect woman than he is about me using my talents for God."

Even as she said the words, Tabby wondered if they were true. Maybe Seth really did care about her. It could be that he only wanted her to succeed as a ventriloquist so she could serve the Lord better.

"But I am serving the Lord," Tabby moaned. "I bake cookies for shut-ins, take my turn in the church nursery, teach the day care kids about Jesus, tithe regularly, and pray for the missionaries. Shouldn't that be enough?"

As Tabby mulled all this over, she noticed the car in front of her begin to swerve. Was the driver of the small white vehicle drunk, or was it merely the slick road causing the problem? *Maybe the man or woman is driving too fast for these hazardous conditions,* she reasoned. Tabby eased up on the gas pedal, keeping a safe distance from the car ahead. If the driver decided to slam on his brakes unexpectedly, she wanted plenty of room to stop.

She was on a long stretch of road now, with no houses or places of business nearby. Only giant fir trees and bushy shrubs dotted the edge of the highway. The vehicle ahead was still swerving, and just as it rounded the next corner, the unthinkable happened. The little car lurched, spun around twice, then headed straight for an embankment. Tabby let out a piercing scream as she watched it disappear over the hill.

Tapping her brakes lightly, so they wouldn't lock, Tabby pulled to the side of the road. Her heart was thumping so hard she thought it might burst, and her palms were so sweaty she could barely open the car door. Stepping out into the rain, Tabby prayed, "Oh, Lord, please let the passengers in that car be okay."

Tabby stood on the edge of the muddy embankment, gazing at the gully below. She could see the white car, flipped upside down. She glanced up at the sky. Tree branches swayed overhead in a crazy green blur, mixed with pelting raindrops. She took a guarded step forward; then with no thought for her own safety, she scrambled down the hill, slipping and sliding with each step. Unmindful of the navy blue flats she wore on her feet or the fact that her long denim skirt was getting splattered with mud, she inched her way toward the overturned vehicle.

When she reached the site of the accident, Tabby noticed the wheels of the car were still spinning, and one tire had the rubber ripped away. Apparently there had been a blowout, which would account for the car's sudden swerving.

Tabby dashed to the driver's side. The window was broken, and she could see a young woman with short brown hair, lying on her stomach across the upside-down steering wheel. There was only a few inches between her head and the roof of the car. She could see from the rise and fall of the woman's back that she was breathing, but her eyes were closed, and she didn't respond when Tabby called out to her.

A pathetic whine drew Tabby's attention to the backseat. A young child, also on her stomach, called, "Mommy. . . Mommy, help me!"

Tabby's brain felt fuzzy, and her legs were weak and rubbery. She had no idea how to help the woman or her child. She certainly wouldn't be able to get them out by herself, and even if she could, she knew from the recent CPR training she'd taken, it wasn't a good idea to move an accident victim who might have serious injuries. What this woman and child needed was professional help. She'd have to go back to the car and call 911 on her cell phone. If only she'd thought to grab it before she made her spontaneous descent.

"D–don't be afraid, little g–girl," Tabby called to the child. "I'm g–going to my c–car and c–call for help. I'll b–be right b–back."

The blond-haired girl, who appeared to be about five years old, began to sob. "I don't know you, and you talk funny. Go away!"

A feeling of frustration, mixed with icy fingers of fear, held Tabby in its grip. She hated to leave but knew she had to. "I'll b–be right b–back," she promised.

As she scrambled up the hill, Tabby could still hear the child's panicked screams. They tore at her heart and made her move as quickly as possible. By the time she reached her car, Tabby was panting, and her fears were mounting. What if the car was leaking gas? What if it caught on fire and she couldn't get the passengers out in time? The stark terror that had inched its way into her head, was now fully in control. She felt paralyzed of both body and mind.

She offered up another quick prayer and slid into the car then reached into the glove box for her cell phone. With trembling fingers, she dialed 911. When an operator came on, Tabby stuttered and stammered so badly the woman had to ask her to repeat the information several times. Tabby was finally assured that help was on the way and was instructed to go back to the car and try to keep the occupants calm.

How in the world am I going to do that? she wondered. *The little girl didn't even want to talk to me.*

Suddenly, Tabby remembered Rosie, who was in the backseat. She'd taken the dummy to work that day, in order to put on a short routine for the day care kids. Maybe the child will feel less threatened talking to Rosie than she would me.

Tabby reached over the seat and grabbed the dummy. "Well, Rosie, you're really gonna be put to the test this time."

Back down the hill she went, feeling the squish of mud as it seeped inside her soft leather shoes and worked its way down to her toes. Her clothes were drenched, and her soggy hair hung limply on her shoulders. In the process of her descent, Tabby fell twice. The second time, Rosie flipped out of her arms and landed with a thud on an uprooted tree. Tabby picked her up, only to discover that Rosie's face was dirty and scratched, her head had come loose, and the control stick was jammed. Not only would Rosie's slot-jaw mouth no longer move, but the poor dummy looked a mess!

"Now what am I going to do?" Tabby lamented. "Rosie was my only hope of reaching that child."

"I can do everything through him who gives me strength." The scripture verse that popped into Tabby's mind offered some comfort and hope. She closed her eyes briefly and pictured the Lord gathering her into His strong arms. He loved her. He cared about her, as well as the two accident victims in that car down there. With His help, Tabby would step boldly out of her shell and serve Him in whatever way He showed her. She could do all things, because of His strength.

"Lord, I really do need Your strength right now. Please calm my heart and let me speak without stuttering, so I can help the little girl not be so afraid."

When Tabby hurried to the car, the child was still crying. She knelt next to the open window and turned Rosie upside down, hoping the sight of the small dummy might make the girl feel better. "This is my friend, Rosie. She wants to be your friend, too," Tabby said softly. "Can you tell me your name, sweetie?"

The child turned her head slightly, and her lips parted in a faint smile. "It's Katie, and I'm almost six."

Tabby released the breath she'd been holding. Progress. They were making a little bit of progress. "Rosie's been hurt, so she can't talk right now," she said. "Why don't the two of us talk, though? Rosie can just listen."

Katie squinted her blue eyes but finally nodded. "Okay."

Tabby's confidence was being handed over to her. She could feel it. She hadn't expected such a dramatic answer to her prayer, but the doors of timidity were finally swinging open. *Thank You, Lord.* Tabby tipped her head to one side and leaned closer to the window. Now Rosie's head was poking partway in. "Are you hurting anywhere?" she asked Katie.

"My arm's bleedin', and my head kinda hurts," the child said, her blue eyes filling with fresh tears.

"I used my cell phone to call for help," Tabby explained. "The paramedics should be here soon. Then they'll help you and your mommy get out of the car."

Katie choked on a sob. "Mommy won't wake up. I keep callin' her, but she don't answer."

Tabby wasn't sure how to respond. Even though Katie's mom was breathing, she could still be seriously hurt. She might even die. Katie had good reason to be scared.

"Listen, honey," she said with assurance, "I've been praying for you and your mommy. The Lord is here with us, and help is on the way. Let's talk about other things for now, okay?"

Katie nodded, but tears kept streaming down her bruised cheeks. It tore at Tabby's heartstrings, but she was thankful the child was willing to talk to her now. She was also grateful for answered prayer. Since she'd returned to the battered car, she hadn't stuttered even once.

"What's your last name, Katie?"

There was a long pause, then finally Katie smiled and said, "It's Duncan. My name's Katie Duncan."

"What's your mommy's name?"

"Mommy."

In spite of the stressful circumstances, Tabby had to bite back the laughter bubbling in her throat. Children were so precious. That's why she loved working with the kids at the day care. She'd probably never marry and have children of her own, and being around those little ones helped fill a void in her heart.

"I have a dolly, too, but she's not half as big as yours," Katie said, looking at Rosie.

Tabby chuckled. "Rosie's a ventriloquist dummy. Do you know what that means?"

Katie shook her head.

"She's kind of like a big puppet. I make her talk by pulling a lever inside her body."

"Can you make her talk right now?"

Tabby sucked in her bottom lip. "Rosie's control stick broke when she fell down the hill."

Katie's chin began to quiver, as a fresh set of tears started to seep from her eyes.

"I suppose I could make her talk," Tabby said quickly. "Her mouth won't move, though. Could you pretend Rosie's mouth is moving?"

"Uh-huh. I like to pretend. Mommy and I do pretend tea parties."

"That's good. I like to play make-believe, too." Tabby tipped Rosie's head, so Katie could see her better. Using her childlike ventriloquist voice, she said, "I'm Rosie Right, and I'm always right." *Now what made me say that? That's the line Seth always uses with his dummy, Rudy.*

"Nobody but God is always right. Mommy said so," Katie remarked.

Tabby nodded. "Your mommy's right. Rosie's just a puppet. She can't always be right, and neither can people. Only God has all the answers."

"Do you go to school, Rosie?" Katie asked the dummy.

"Sometimes I go to day care," Rosie answered. "Tabby works there."

The next few minutes were spent in friendly banter between Rosie, Tabby, and Katie. Tabby was glad she could keep the child's mind off the accident and her unconscious mother in the front seat, but when a low moan escaped the woman's lips, Tabby froze. Now she had two people to try and keep calm.

Chapter 19

Oh! Oh! I can't breathe," Katie's mother moaned. "My seat belt. . .it's too tight."
Tabby pulled Rosie quickly away from the window and placed one hand on the woman's outstretched arm. "Please, try to remain calm."

The woman moaned again. "Who are you?"

"I'm Tabitha Johnson. I was in the car behind you, and I saw your car swerve then run off the road. You ended up going over the embankment, and now the car's upside down."

"My name is Rachel Duncan, and I need to get this seat belt off. Do you have a knife?"

Tabby shook her head. "That's not a good idea. If we cut the belt loose, your head will hit the roof, and that might cause serious damage if there's a neck injury."

Rachel's eyelids closed, and she groaned. "Katie. . . Where's Katie?"

"Your little girl is still in the backseat," Tabby answered. "We've been visiting while we wait for the paramedics."

"Mommy, Mommy, I'm here!" Katie called.

Rachel's eyes shot open. "I'm so sorry about this, Katie. Mommy doesn't know what happened."

"From the looks of your right front tire, I'd say you had a blowout," Tabby said.

Rachel's swollen lips emitted a shuddering sob. "I told Rick we needed to buy a new set of tires."

"Rick?"

"Rick's my husband. He had to work late tonight, so Katie and I went to a movie in Lakewood. We were on our way home when it started raining really hard." She grimaced. "I hope someone gets us out of here real soon. I don't think I can stand being in this position much longer."

"Are you in pain?" Tabby asked with concern.

"My left leg feels like it might be broken, and my head's pounding something awful."

"Would you mind if I prayed for you?" Tabby didn't know where she'd gotten the courage to ask that question. It wasn't like her to be so bold.

"I'd really appreciate the prayer," Rachel answered. Tears were coursing down her cheeks, but she offered Tabby a weak smile. "I'm a Christian, I know how much prayer can help."

Tabby placed Rosie on the ground and leaned in as far as she could. "Heavenly Father," she prayed, "Rachel and Katie are in pain and need medical attention as soon as possible. I'm asking You to bring the paramedics here quickly. Please give them both a sense of peace and awareness that You are right here beside them."

Tabby had just said "amen" when she heard the piercing whine of sirens in the distance. "That must be the rescue vehicles," she told Rachel. "I think I should go back up the hill to be sure they know where we are. Will you be all right for a few minutes?"

"Jesus is with us," Katie squeaked.

"Yes, He's by our side," Rachel agreed.

"All right then, I'll be back as quick as I can." Tabby pulled away from the window and started up the hill as fast as she could, thankful the rain had finally eased up.

A police car, a fire truck, and the paramedics' rig were pulling off the road by her car

91

when she came over the hill. Gasping for breath, she dashed over to one of the firemen. "There's a car down there," she panted, pointing to the ravine. "It's upside down, and there's a woman and a little girl trapped inside."

"Could you tell if they were seriously injured?" one of the paramedics asked as he stepped up beside her.

"Rachel—she's the mother—said her head hurt real bad, and she thinks her leg might be broken. Katie's only five, and she complained of her head hurting, too. She also said her arm was bleeding."

He nodded then turned to his partner. "Let's grab our gear and get down there."

The rescue squad descended the hill much faster than Tabby had, but she figured they'd had a good deal more practice doing this kind of thing.

Tabby followed, keeping a safe distance once they were at the scene of the accident. She did move in to grab Rosie when a fireman stepped on one of the dummy's hands. Poor, dirty Rosie had enough injuries to keep her in Seth's shop for at least a month. Right now, Tabby's concerns were for Rachel and her precious daughter, though. She kept watching and praying as the rescuers struggled to free the trapped victims.

When they finally had Rachel and Katie loaded into the ambulance, Tabby breathed a sigh of relief. The paramedics said it didn't appear as though either of them had any life-threatening injuries, although there would be tests done at the hospital. Before the ambulance pulled away, Tabby promised Rachel she would call her husband and let him know what happened.

One of the policemen, who identified himself as Officer Jensen, asked Tabby a series of questions about the accident, since she'd been the only witness.

"You are one special young lady," the officer said. "Not only did you call for help, but you stayed to comfort that woman and her daughter." He glanced down at the bedraggled dummy Tabby was holding. "From the looks of your little friend, I'd say you went the extra mile, using your talent in a time of need."

Tabby smiled, although she felt like crying. For the first time in a long while, she'd forgotten her fears and self-consciousness, allowing God to speak through her in a way she never thought possible. Throughout the entire ordeal, she'd never stuttered once. It seemed like a miracle—one she hoped would last forever. Up until now, she believed that unless her family treated her with love and respect, she could never become confident. How wrong she'd been. How grateful to God she felt now.

When Tabby got into her car, she reached for the cell phone and called Rick Duncan at the number Rachel had given her. He was shocked to hear about the accident but thankful Tabby had called. He told her he'd leave work right away and head straight for Tacoma General Hospital. Tabby could finally go home, knowing Rachel, Katie, and Rick were in God's hands.

❀

Tabby awoke the following morning feeling as though she'd run a ten-mile marathon and hadn't been in shape for it. The emotional impact of the night before hit her hard. If she could get through something so frightening, she was sure the Lord would see her through anything—even dealing with her unfeeling parents and self-centered sister. Instead of shying away from family gatherings or letting someone's harsh words cut her to the quick, Tabby's plan was to stand behind the Lord's shield of protection. She could do all things through Him, and as soon as she had some breakfast, she planned to phone Tacoma General Hospital and check on Rachel's and Katie's conditions. Then her next order of business would be to visit Beyers' Ventriloquist Studio.

Seth had dialed Tabby's phone number four times in the last fifteen minutes, and it was always busy. "Who is on the phone, and who could she be talking to?" he muttered. "Maybe I should get in my car and drive on over there."

Seth figured Tabby was still mad at him, and he wondered if she'd even let him into her apartment. Well, he didn't care if she was mad. He'd made up his mind to see her today.

Seth left the red-nosed clown dummy he'd been working on and walked into the main part of his shop just as the bell on the front door jingled. In walked Cheryl Stone.

"Good morning, Seth," she purred. "How are you today?"

Seth's heart sank. The blue-eyed woman staring up at him with a hopeful smile was not the person he most wanted to see. "Hi, Cheryl. What brings you here this morning?"

"Does there have to be a reason?" Cheryl tipped her head to one side and offered him another coquettish smile.

Seth felt the force of her softly spoken words like a blow to the stomach. Cheryl was obviously interested in him. "Most people don't come to my shop without a good reason," he mumbled. "Are you having a problem with Oscar again?"

Cheryl gave the ends of her long red hair a little flick and moved slowly toward Seth. "Actually, I'm not here about either one of my dummies."

Seth swallowed hard and took a few steps back. *Now here's a perfect woman. She's talented, confident, poised, and beautiful. How come I don't go after her?* He groaned inwardly. *I'm in love with Tabby Johnson, that's why.* There was no denying it, either. Shy, stuttering Tabitha, with eyes that reminded him of a wounded deer, had stolen his heart, and he'd been powerless to stop it.

With determination, Seth pulled his thoughts away from Tabby and onto the matter at hand. "Why are you here, Cheryl?"

"I've been asked to be part of a talent contest sponsored by Valley Foods. My father works in the corporate office there," Cheryl explained.

"What's that got to do with me?"

"I was hoping you'd be willing to give me a few extra lessons." She giggled. "I know I'm already a good ventriloquist, but I think you're about the best around. Some more helpful tips from you might help me win that contest."

Seth cleared his throat, hoping to stall for time. At least long enough so he could come up with some legitimate excuse for not helping Cheryl. He had an inkling she had a bit more in mind than just ventriloquist lessons.

His suspicions were confirmed when she stepped forward and threw her arms around his neck. The smell of apricot shampoo filled his nostrils, as a wisp of her soft red hair brushed against his cheek.

"Please say you'll do this for me, Seth," Cheryl pleaded as she placed her arms around his neck. "Pretty please. . .with sugar and spice. . .now don't make me ask twice."

Seth moaned. Cheryl was mere inches from his face now, but all he could think about was Tabby. He opened his mouth to give Cheryl his answer, when the bell on the door jingled. Over the top of Cheryl's head, he saw the door swing wide open.

It was Tabitha Johnson.

Chapter 20

Seth expected Tabby to turn around and run out the door once she saw Cheryl in his arms. She didn't, though. Instead, she marched up to the counter and plunked her dummy down. "I'm sorry to interrupt," she said in a voice filled with surprising confidence, "but I need you to take a look at Rosie. Do you think you can spare a few minutes, Seth?"

Seth reached up to pull Cheryl's arms away from his neck. He was guilty of nothing, yet he felt like a kid who'd been caught with his hand inside a candy dish. He could only imagine what Tabby must be thinking, walking in and seeing what looked like a romantic interlude between him and Cheryl.

He studied Tabby for a few seconds. She looked different today—cute and kind of spunky. Her hair was curled, too, and it didn't hang in her face the way it usually did. Her blue jeans and yellow T-shirt were neatly pressed, and she stood straighter than normal.

"Do you have time to look at Rosie or not?" Tabby asked again.

Seth nodded, feeling as if he were in a daze. Tabby wasn't even stuttering. What happened to Timid Tabitha with the doe eyes? He glanced down at Cheryl and noticed she was frowning. "Excuse me, but I have to take care of business," he said, hoping she'd get the hint and leave.

Cheryl planted both hands on her slim hips and whirled around to face Tabby. "Can't you see that Seth and I are busy?"

"I'll only keep Seth a few minutes; then he's all yours," Tabby said through tight lips.

A muscle in Seth's jaw twitched. "I'll call you later, Cheryl," he said, turning toward the counter where the dummy lay.

"Yeah, okay," Cheryl mumbled.

When he heard the door close, Seth heaved a sigh of relief. At least one problem had been resolved.

❦

Tabby was trembling inwardly, but outwardly she was holding up quite well—thanks to the Lord and the prayer she'd uttered when she first walked into Seth's shop. Seeing Cheryl Stone in Seth's arms had nearly been her undoing. Only God's grace kept her from retreating into her old shell and allowing her tongue to run wild with a bunch of stuttering and stammering. It still amazed her that ever since the car accident last night she hadn't stuttered once. God really had changed her life.

"What in the world happened to Rosie?" Seth asked, breaking into Tabby's thoughts. "She looks like she got roped into a game of mud wrestling. I'd say she came out on the losing end of things."

Tabby snickered. "It was something like that." Then, feeling the need to talk about what happened last night, she opened up and shared the entire story of the accident she'd witnessed.

Seth listened intently as he examined the dummy. When Tabby finished talking, he looked up from his work and groaned softly. "I'm sure thankful you're okay. You were smart to keep a safe distance from that car when it began to swerve. It could have been your little hatchback rolling down the hill."

Tabby swallowed hard. Was Seth really concerned about her welfare? Was that frown he wore proof of his anxiety?

"Now about Rosie. . . ," Seth said, pulling her back to the immediate need.

"How bad is the damage? Will Rosie ever talk again?"

Seth's green eyes met Tabby's with a gaze that bore straight into her soul. "She will if you want her to."

Tabby blinked. "Of course, I do. Why wouldn't I?"

Seth cleared his throat a few times, as though searching for the right words. "After that program at the crusade, you didn't seem any too anxious to continue using your ventriloquistic talents."

She nodded. "You're right about that, but since last night I'm seeing things in a whole new light."

He raised his eyebrows. "You are? In what way?"

"For one thing, God showed me that I don't have to be afraid of people or circumstances that might seem a bit unusual or disturbing," she explained. "I was really scared when that car went over the embankment. When I found Rachel and her daughter trapped inside their overturned vehicle, I nearly panicked." Tabby drew in a deep breath and squeezed her lips together. "Little Katie wouldn't even respond to me at first. I was stuttering so much I scared her. Then I thought about Rosie in the backseat of my car, and I climbed back up the hill to get her."

Seth nodded. "Kids will react to a dummy much quicker than they will an adult." He smiled. "Guess we're a bit too intimidating."

"I dropped Rosie on the way down the hill, and by the time I got to the wreck, I realized her mouth control was broken." Tabby shrugged. "I had to talk on my own, and I asked God to help me do it without stuttering. I wanted Katie to be able to understand every word, so she wouldn't be afraid."

"So poor Rosie took a trip down the muddy incline for nothing?" Seth asked, giving the dummy's head a few taps with his knuckle.

Tabby shook her head. "Not really. After Katie and I talked awhile, I began to gain her confidence. Then I put Rosie up to the window and made her talk, without even moving her lips."

Seth tipped his head back and roared.

"What's so funny?"

"If Rosie's lips weren't moving, then who was the ventriloquist, and who was the dummy?"

Tabby giggled and reached out to poke Seth playfully in the ribs. "Ha! Very funny!" She wiggled her nose. "I'll have you know, Mr. Beyers, my dummy is so talented, she can talk for two without moving her lips!"

Seth grinned, and his eyes sparkled mischievously. "And you, Miss Tabitha Johnson, are speaking quite well on your own today."

Tabby felt herself blush. "I haven't stuttered once since last night." She placed her palms against her burning cheeks. "God gave me confidence I never thought I would have, and I'm so grateful."

"I think it was because you finally put yourself fully in His hands."

Tabby was tempted to ask Seth if he thought she was worthy of his love now. After all, he'd wanted her to change. Instead of voicing her thoughts, she nodded toward Rosie. "Is there any hope for her?"

Seth scratched the back of his head and smiled. "I think with a little help from some of my tools and a new coat of paint, Rosie will be up and around in no time at all."

Tabby smiled gratefully, but then she sobered. "Will the repairs be expensive?"

Seth winked, and she pressed a hand to a heart that was beating much too fast.

"Let's see now. . . . The price for parts will be reimbursed with two or three dinners out, and labor. . .well, I'm sure we can work something out for that as well," Seth said, never taking his gaze off her. "Something that will be agreeable to both of us." He moved slowly toward her, with both arms extended.

Tabby had an overwhelming desire to rush into those strong arms and declare her undying love, but she held herself in check, remembering the little scene she'd encountered when she first entered Seth's shop. It was obvious that Seth had more than a business relationship with Cheryl.

Seth kept moving closer, until she could feel his warm breath on her upturned face. She trembled, and her eyelids drifted shut. Tabby knew she shouldn't let Seth kiss her—not when he was seeing someone else. Her heart said something entirely different, though, and it was with her whole heart that Tabby offered her lips willingly to Seth's inviting kiss.

Tabby relished in the warmth of Seth's embrace, until the sharp ringing of the telephone pulled them apart.

"Uh, guess I'd better get that," Seth mumbled. He stepped away from Tabby and moved across the room toward the desk where the phone sat.

Tabby looked down at Rosie and muttered, "I think I was just saved by the bell."

🌼

As Seth answered the phone, his thoughts were focused on Tabby. He'd wanted to hold her longer and tell her everything that was tumbling around in his mind. He needed to express his feelings about the way he'd treated her in the past and share the scriptures the Lord had shown him. Maybe they'd be able to pick up where they left off when he hung up the phone. Maybe. . .

"Seth Beyers," he said numbly into the receiver. "Huh? Oh, yeah, I'd be happy to take a look at your dummy. I'm about to close shop for the day, but you can bring it by on Monday."

Relieved to be off the phone, Seth returned to Tabby. She was standing over Rosie, looking as though she'd lost her best friend. "She'll be okay, I promise," he said, reaching out to pull Tabby into his arms. He leaned over and placed a kiss on her forehead. Her hair felt feathery soft against his lips, and it smelled like sunshine.

She pulled sharply away, taking him by surprise. She'd seemed willing a few minutes ago. What had happened in the space of a few minutes to make her so cold?

"How long till she's done?" Tabby asked.

"I could probably get her ready to go home in about a week. How's that sound?"

She shrugged. "That'll be fine, I guess." She turned and started for the door.

"Hey, where are you going?" he called after her.

"Home. I left the apartment before Donna got up, and since I came home so late last night, I promised to fill her in on the accident details this morning."

Seth rushed to her side. "Don't tell me I'll be taking the day off for nothing."

She blinked several times. "I don't get it. What's your taking the day off got to do with me?"

"I'd really like to spend the day with you. That is, if you're not tied up."

"I just told you. . ."

"I know. You want to tell Donna about last night." Seth grabbed Tabby's arm and pulled her to his side again. "Can't that wait awhile? We have some important things to discuss, and I thought we could do it at the park."

"Point Defiance?"

He nodded.

Tabby hung her head. He knew she was weakening, because she'd told him before how much she loved going to Point Defiance Park.

"Wouldn't that be kind of like a date?" she murmured.

He laughed. "Not kind of, Tabby. . .it is a date."

"Oh. Well, I guess my answer has to be no."

His forehead creased. "Why, for goodness' sake? Are you still mad at me for coercing you into doing that vent routine?"

She shook her head. "No, I've done what the Bible says and forgiven you. Besides, what happened at the crusade was really my own fault. I could have said no when you asked me to perform. I could have prayed more and allowed God to speak through me, instead of letting myself get all tied up in knots, and ending up making my routine and me look completely ridiculous."

Seth gently touched her arm. "Neither you nor your routine was ridiculous, Tabby." He chewed on his lower lip, praying silently for the right words to express his true feelings. "Tabby, you're not the only one God's been working on lately."

"What do you mean?"

"Through the scriptures, He's showed me that I've been expecting too much. I wanted the perfect woman. . .one who'd fit into my preconceived mold. I thought I needed someone who would radiate with confidence and who'd have the same burning desire I do to share her talents with others by telling them about the Savior."

Tabby nodded. "I was pretty sure you felt that way, and I really couldn't blame you, but it did make me mad. I knew I could never be that perfect woman, so I was angry at you, myself, and even God."

Tears welled up in her dark eyes, and when they ran down her cheeks, Seth reached up to wipe them away with his thumb. "You don't have to be the perfect woman, Tabby. Not for me or anyone else. All God wants is for us to give Him our best." He kneaded the back of his neck, trying to work out the kinks. "I tried to call you last night. I wanted to tell you what God had revealed to me. I was planning to tell you that it didn't matter if you stuttered, had no confidence, or never did ventriloquism again. I just wanted you to know that I love you, and I accept you for the person you are. . .one full of love and compassion."

"Love?" Tabby looked up at him with questioning eyes.

He nodded. "I know we haven't known each other very long, but I really do love you, Tabby."

"But what about Cheryl Stone?"

His brows furrowed. "What about her?"

"After seeing the two of you together, I thought—"

"That we were in love?"

She only nodded in response.

Seth's lips curved into a smile, then he let out a loud whoop.

"What was that for?"

"I don't love Cheryl," Seth said sincerely. He dropped to one knee. "This might seem kind of sudden, and if you need time to think about it, I'll understand." He smiled up at her. "If you wouldn't mind being married to a dummy, I'd sure be honored to make you my wife. After we've had a bit more time to go on a few more dates and get better acquainted," he quickly added.

Tabby trembled slightly. "You—you w–want to marry me?"

Seth reached for her hand and kissed the palm of it. "You're stuttering again. I think maybe I'm a bad influence on you."

She blushed. "I'm just so surprised."

"That I could love you, or that I'd want to marry you?"

"Both." Tabby smiled through her tears. "I love you so much, Seth. I never thought I could be this happy."

"Is that a yes?" he asked hopefully.

She nodded as he stood up again. "Yes! Yes! A thousand times, yes!"

"How about a December wedding? Or is that too soon?"

"December? Why that month?"

"I can't think of a better Christmas present to give myself than you," he said.

She sighed deeply and leaned against his chest. "That only gives us four months to plan a wedding. Do you think we can choose our colors, pick out invitations, order a cake, and get everything else done by then?"

A dimple creased her cheek when he kissed it. "I'm sure we can." There was a long pause; then he whispered, "There is one little thing, though."

"What's that?"

"I don't want our wedding cake to have peanut butter filling."

Tabby pulled back and gave him a curious look.

"My peanut butter phobia, remember?"

She giggled. "Oh, yes. Now how could I forget something so important?"

Seth bent down and kissed her full on the mouth. When the kiss ended, he grinned.

"What?"

"I must be the most blessed man alive."

"Why's that?"

"If a man is lucky, he finds a wife who can communicate her needs to him. Me. . .well, I'll always know what my wife needs, because she can talk for two." He winked at her. "Now that we've had our little talk, do you still want to go to the park?"

She smiled. "Of course I do. I can't think of a better place for us to start making plans for our future."

Epilogue

Tabby had never been more nervous, yet she'd never felt such a sense of peace before. Next to the day she opened her heart to Christ, today was the most important day in her life.

Much to her sister's disappointment, Tabby had beaten her to the marriage altar. Tabby took no pleasure in this fact, but it did feel pretty wonderful to be married to the man she loved. Lois would find the same joy when it was her turn to walk down the aisle. By then, maybe she'd even be a Christian.

Tabby glanced at her younger sister, sitting beside Mike and her parents at a table near the front of the room. Thanks to Tabby's gentle prodding, Lois had recently started going to church. Now if they could just get her fiancé to attend.

The wedding reception was in full swing, and Tabby and Seth were about to do a joint ventriloquist routine. It was the first time she'd ever done ventriloquism in front of her family. Tabby gazed into her groom's sea-green eyes and smiled. If someone had told her a year ago she'd be standing in front of more than a hundred people, married to a terrific guy like Seth, she'd never have believed them. It still amazed her that she no longer stuttered or was hampered by her shyness. God was so good, and she was glad for the opportunity to serve Him with her new talent.

She felt the warmth of Seth's hand as he placed Rosie into her arms. He probably knew she was a bit nervous about this particular performance. He bent down and pulled Rudy from the trunk. With a reassuring smile, he quickly launched into their routine.

"How do you feel about me being a married man?" Seth asked his dummy.

Rudy's head swiveled toward Tabby. "I can see why you married her, but what's she doin' with a guy like you?"

Before Seth could respond, Rosie piped up with, "Don't talk about Seth that way, Rudy. I think he's real sweet."

"I think so, too," Tabby put in.

Rudy snorted. "He's not nearly as sweet as me." The dummy's head moved closer to Tabby. "How 'bout a little kiss to celebrate your wedding day?"

Tabby wiggled her eyebrows up and down. "Well. . ."

"Now, Rudy, what makes you think my wife would want to kiss a dummy?"

Rudy's wooden head snapped back to face Seth. "She kisses you, doesn't she?"

The audience roared, and Tabby felt herself begin to relax. Even Dad was laughing, and Mom was looking at her as though she was the most special person in the whole world. Maybe she wasn't such a disappointment to them after all. Maybe her newfound confidence could even help win her parents to the Lord.

"You know, Seth," Rudy drawled, "I hear tell that once a man ties the knot, his life is never the same."

"In what way?" Seth asked.

"Yeah, in what way?" Rosie echoed.

Rudy's eyes moved from side to side. "For one thing, some women talk too much. What if Tabby starts speaking for you, now that you're married?"

Tabby leaned over and planted a kiss on Rudy's cheek then did the same to Seth. "Yep," she quipped, "from now on, I'll definitely be talking for two!"

Clowning Around

by Wanda E. Brunstetter

Dedication

To Gordon, Kathy, Dell, and Bev—special friends who are great at clowning around.

Chapter 1

Lois Johnson slid her fingers across the polished surface of her desktop. *I love this job,* she told herself with a smile. She had been working as secretary for Bayview Christian Church only a few weeks, but she already felt at ease. She wasn't making as much money now, she reminded herself, but she had a lot less pressure than when she'd worked as a legal secretary in downtown Tacoma.

Lois hoped her job here would be a ministry, so she could do something meaningful while using her secretarial skills. She was a fairly new Christian, having accepted the Lord as her personal Savior during a recent evangelistic crusade. Now she had an opportunity to work in her home church where she felt comfortable.

Her older sister, Tabby, had told her about the position. Tabby worked in the day care center sponsored by Bayview Church and had heard that Mildred Thompson, the secretary then, was moving to California. Tabby had notified Lois right away, knowing she wasn't happy in her old job.

A vision of Tabby and her husband, Seth Beyers, performing their ventriloquist routine flashed into Lois's mind. The young couple worked well together, shared a love for Christ and the church, and were so much in love.

Lois stared at the blank computer screen in front of her then pushed the button to turn it on. *I hope I can find an area of service as Tabby and Seth have.* After attending the church for a year, she had signed up to teach a first-grade Sunday school class. She enjoyed working with children and felt she was helping to mold their young lives in some small way. But she wondered if she could be doing more.

As Lois waited for the computer to boot up, she let her mind wander. She'd come a long way in the last few months. The pain of breaking up with her ex-fiancé had diminished considerably. Since she'd become a Christian and started reading her Bible every day and spending time in prayer, her attitude toward many things had changed. No longer was she consumed with a desire for wealth and prestige. She knew money in itself wasn't a bad thing, but her yearning for more, simply for personal gain, had been wrong. Instead of being so self-centered and harsh—especially with her sister, who had been shy and had suffered with a problem of stuttering—with God's help, Lois was learning to be more patient and kind.

Thank You, Lord, for helping Tabby overcome her problems and for changing my heart. Show me the best way to serve You. She hesitated. *And if You have a man out there for me, please let me know he's the right one.*

Lois frowned and twirled her finger around a long blond curl. She'd been wounded deeply when Michael Yehley postponed their wedding. Then he broke things off completely once she started inviting him to go with her to church. He'd made it clear he had no interest in religious things, didn't need them, and could take care of himself.

Lois knew Michael hadn't been right for her. She also knew she could never love another man who wasn't a Christian or whose only goal in life was climbing the ladder of success. *Lord, if You have a man in mind for me, then he'll have to fall into my lap because I'm not planning to look for anyone. The chances of that are slim to none,* Lois told herself.

❧

Joe Richey was exhausted. He'd been on the road six weeks, doing a series of family crusades, Bible schools, and church camp meetings. He'd even managed to squeeze in a couple of kids' birthday parties. As much as he enjoyed clowning, he needed to rest. He'd just finished a five-day Bible school in Aberdeen, Washington, which had ended this morning at eleven o'clock. On his way home, he had stopped at the cemetery to visit his parents' graves. When Joe was eight years old, his father was killed in an accident involving the tour bus he drove around the Pacific Northwest. His mother had passed away last summer from lung cancer.

A knot formed in Joe's stomach when he opened the front door of his modest two-story home in Olympia. When his mother died, he hadn't shed a single tear, and he wasn't about to cry now. In fact, Joe hadn't cried since his father's death almost seventeen years ago. If today hadn't been the anniversary of his mother's death, he probably wouldn't have stopped at the cemetery. It was a painful reminder of his past.

Carrying his red-and-green-checkered clown costume in one hand and a battered suitcase in the other, Joe trudged up the steps to the second floor. He entered his bedroom and flung open the closet door. "Maybe I should take off for a few days and head to the beach," he said aloud, setting the suitcase on the floor and hanging up his costume. "But right now, I guess I'll settle for a hot bath and a long nap."

He yanked a red rubber clown nose out of his shirt pocket and stuffed it into the drawer where all his clown makeup and props were kept. "I'll be okay. Just need to keep a stiff upper lip and a smile plastered on my face." Joe glanced in the mirror attached to his closet door and forced his mouth to curve upward.

The phone rang sharply. He crossed the room and lifted the receiver from the nightstand by his bed. "Joe Richey here."

He listened to the woman on the other end of the line, nodding occasionally and writing the information she gave him on a notepad. "Uh-huh. Sure. My schedule's been as tight as a jar of pickles all summer, but things are slowing down some now. I'm sure I can work it in. Okay, thanks."

Joe hung up the phone and sank onto the bed with a moan. "One more crusade, and then I'll take a little vacation." He glanced over the notes he'd jotted down. "It's only a forty-five-minute drive from Olympia to Tacoma. It'll be a piece of cake."

❧

After discussing the church bulletin with Richard Smith, the associate pastor, Lois returned to her desk, and the phone rang. She smiled when she heard her sister's voice. "Hi, Tabby, what's up?"

"I was wondering if you could meet me for lunch today."

"Sure—sounds good. Should I come downstairs to the day care, or do you want to come up here?"

"Neither. I'd like to take you out for lunch. You've been cooped up in that office so much since you started working here, even eating lunch at your desk sometimes. Today's Friday, so I think we should celebrate. Let's go to Garrison's Deli."

Lois sighed. She didn't feel much like going out, even though the sun was shining brightly on this pleasant summer day and the fresh air would probably do her some good. She preferred to stay at her desk and eat the bag lunch she'd brought, but she didn't want to disappoint Tabby. She'd done plenty of that in the past. Now that Lois was trying to live her faith, she made every attempt to please rather than tease her sister.

"Sure—what time?" Lois asked.

"Donna's taking her lunch break at noon, so how does one o'clock sound?"

"Great. See you then." Lois hung up the phone and grabbed that day's mail. The first letter contained a flyer announcing a special service at another church in the north end of Tacoma. It listed all the people in the program, including Tabby and Seth. Lois noticed the program was a little over a week away, so she decided to make copies of the flyer and insert one into each bulletin to be handed out on Sunday.

By twelve thirty, Lois had finished the bulletins and was stuffing the flyers inside each one when Sam Hanson, the senior pastor, stepped into her office. "Have you had lunch yet, Lois?" he asked. Sam and his wife Norma were always concerned about her.

She shook her head but kept her eyes focused on the work she was doing. "I'm meeting Tabby at Garrison's Deli in half an hour."

"That's good to hear. I was afraid you planned to work through lunch again."

Lois looked up. "Not today."

The pastor smiled. "I'm glad you're taking your position seriously, Lois, but we don't want you to work too hard."

"I'm grateful for the opportunity to work here." Lois smiled, too. "I love my new job, and sometimes it's hard to tear myself away."

"Which is precisely why Norma and I think you should get out more," he said. "A lovely young woman like you needs an active social life."

She shrugged. "I do get out. I drive to Olympia to visit my folks at least twice a month."

"That's not quite what we meant."

"I know, but I'm okay, really."

Pastor Hanson nodded. "Anytime you need to talk, though, I'm a good listener. And so is Norma." He winked. "Since my office is right next door, you won't have far to go."

"Thanks, Pastor. I'll keep that in mind."

❀

Lois found Tabby waiting in a booth at the deli. "Sorry I'm a few minutes late," she said, dropping into the seat across from her sister.

Tabby smiled, her dark eyes gleaming. "No problem. I figured you probably had an important phone call or something. I've only been here a few minutes, but I took the liberty of ordering us each a veggie sandwich on whole-wheat bread, with cream cheese and lots of alfalfa sprouts."

Lois chuckled. "We may not look much like sisters, but we sure have the same taste in food." She nodded toward the counter. "What did you order us to drink?"

"Strawberry lemonade for you and an iced tea with a slice of lemon for me."

"Umm. Sounds good. An ice-cold lemonade on a hot day like this should hit the spot."

"It is pretty warm," Tabby agreed. "Kind of unusual weather for Tacoma, even if it is still summer."

"I heard on the news that it might reach ninety by the weekend," Lois commented.

Tabby's dark eyebrows raised. "Guess we'd better find a way to cool off, then."

Lois drew in a breath. Last year she'd been invited to use the Yehleys' swimming pool on several occasions. It was heated, so even when the weather was cool, the pool was a great place to exercise or simply relax. Lois wouldn't be swimming in Michael's pool this year, though. She didn't care. She could always go to one of the many fitness centers in town or, if she felt brave, take a dip in the chilly waters of Puget Sound Bay. Michael and his parents had no place in her life anymore, and neither did their pool!

"Lois. Earth to Lois."

Lois's eyelids fluttered. "Oh—you were talking to me, and I was daydreaming?"

Tabby laughed. "Something like that."

"What were you saying?"

"I was telling you about the special service Westside Community Church is having a week from Saturday night."

Lois nodded. "I already know. We received a flyer in the mail today."

Tabby frowned. "Kind of late notice, wouldn't you say?"

"That's what I thought, but I made copies and inserted them in the bulletins for this Sunday."

"Seth and I are doing a ventriloquist routine," Tabby said.

"Yes, I saw your names on the flyer."

They heard their order being announced, and Tabby slid out of the booth. "I'll be right back."

"Want some help?" Lois called after her.

"No, thanks. I can manage."

When Tabby returned a few minutes later, Lois offered up a prayer, and they started eating their sandwiches.

"I was hoping you would come to the service at Westside," Tabby said between bites. "You don't go out much anymore, and I thought—"

Lois held up her hand. "You thought you'd apply a little pressure." She clucked her tongue against the roof of her mouth. "You and the Hansons wouldn't be in cahoots, would you?"

Tabby flicked her shoulder-length chestnut-colored hair away from her face. "Whatever gave you such a notion?"

Lois lifted her gaze toward the ceiling. "I can't imagine."

"I really would like you to come," Tabby said. "Seth and I will do our routine, they'll have a gospel clown and an illusionist, and Donna's going to do one of her beautiful chalk art drawings." She leaned across the table and studied Lois intently. "If it weren't for a creative illusionist's testimony, you probably wouldn't be where you are today."

Lois narrowed her eyes. "You mean sitting here at Garrison's, drinking strawberry lemonade, and eating a delicious sandwich?"

Tabby grinned. "I meant that you wouldn't be working for our church. For that matter, if you hadn't committed your life to Christ during a crusade, you probably wouldn't be going to church."

"I know."

"So will you come to the program? I always feel better when I look out into the audience and see your beautiful face smiling back at me."

Lois grinned. How could she say no to the most wonderful sister in the world? "I'll be there—right in the front row."

Chapter 2

J oe stood in the small room near the main platform in the sanctuary of Westside Community Church, waiting his turn. He was dressed in a pair of baggy blue jeans, with a matching jacket, decorated with multicolored patches. He wore a bright orange shirt under his jacket, a polka-dot tie, and a bright red rubber nose. Attached to his hair was a red yarn wig, and a floppy blue hat perched on top. Black oversized shoes turning up at the toes completed his clown costume.

Joe peeked through the stage door window and saw Seth and Tabby Beyers on stage with their two dummies. He had watched the young couple perform on other programs and knew audiences loved them. Their unusual ventriloquist routine would be hard to follow.

I'm not doing this merely to entertain, Joe reminded himself. *It isn't important whom the audience likes best. What counts is whether we get across the message of salvation and Christian living.* Entertain, but have a positive impact on people's lives—that's what he'd been taught at the gospel clowning school where he'd received his training several years ago.

Joe reached inside the pocket of his clown suit, and his fingers curled around a stash of balloons. He knew one of the best things in his routine was the balloons he twisted into various animals. After every performance, a group of excited kids would surround him, wanting to talk to the goofy clown and to get a balloon animal.

Joe heard his name being called and grabbed the multicolored duffel bag that held his props. For some reason he felt edgy tonight. He didn't understand it because he had done hundreds of programs like this one. He figured it must be due to fatigue since he'd been on the road so much lately and needed a vacation.

Then "Slow-Joe the Clown" stepped onto the stage. Opening his bag of tricks, he withdrew a huge plastic hammer with a shackle attached. He held the mallet over his head. "I'm all set now to open my own hamburger chain," he announced.

The audience laughed, and Joe moved to the edge of the platform, holding his props toward the spectators. "If my hamburger chain doesn't work out, I'm thinking about raising rabbits." He pursed his lips. "Of course, I'm gonna have to keep 'em indoors, so they'll be ingrown hares."

Everyone laughed again, and Joe winked, dropped the hammer back into the bag, and pulled out a blue balloon. He blew into it, holding the end and stretching the latex as the balloon inflated. Tying a knot, he twisted two small bubbles in the center of the balloon and locked them together in one quick twist. Then he made five bubbles and formed the body of a baby seal. The lowest part of the balloon was the neck, and Joe added another bubble at the top, so the seal looked as if it were balancing a ball on the end of its nose.

Gripping his floppy hat, Joe tipped his head back and balanced the balloon seal on the end of his rubber nose. The crowd roared as he moved slowly about the stage, waving one hand and trying to keep the seal in place. When the seal toppled off, Joe explained how some people try to balance their lives between church, home, and extracurricular activities but don't always succeed.

Then he twisted more balloons into a blue whale, a humpback camel, and a lion with a mane. After each creation, Joe told a Bible story, including one about Daniel in the lions' den.

Next, Joe grabbed five red balls from his bag, tossing them one at a time into the air and juggling them. As he did so, he faced the audience. "I often get busy with my clowning schedule and have to juggle my time a bit. But I always feel closer to God when I take time out to read the Bible and pray. Just like juggling balls, our lives can get crazy and out of line with God's will."

Joe let one ball drop to the floor. "I took my eyes off the ball and messed up." He caught the other four balls in his hands and bent down to pick up the one he'd dropped. "The nice thing about juggling is, I can always start over again whenever I've made a mistake. The same is true of my spiritual life. God is always there, waiting for me to trust Him and accept His love and forgiveness for me."

Joe concluded his routine by creating a vibrant balloon bouquet that resembled a bunch of tulips. "I'd like to recognize someone special in the audience," he said, shading his eyes with his hand and staring out at the congregation. "Nope. I don't recognize a soul!"

Several people chuckled. Then he asked, "Has anyone recently had a birthday?"

Murmurs drifted through the crowd, but no one spoke up.

"Okay—let's do this another way. Anyone have a birthday today?" Silence greeted him. He waved the bouquet in the air. "How about last week?" Still no response. "Come now, folks—don't be shy. I'm sure at least one person in this group has had a birthday recently."

At last someone's hand went up in the front row. Joe grinned. "Ah-ha—a pretty lady with long blond hair has finally responded."

❧

Lois slid down in her seat. *What in the world possessed me to raise my hand?* She'd celebrated her twenty-second birthday two weeks ago, but she didn't need the whole audience looking at her now, which was exactly what they were doing!

The tall clown moved toward her. He wore a broad smile on his white-painted face, and his hand was outstretched. "A beautiful bouquet for the birthday gal," he said with a deep chuckle.

Lois forced herself to smile in return.

"Do you know what flowers grow between your nose and chin?"

She shook her head.

"Tulips!"

Everyone laughed, and the clown winked at Lois. "Would you like to tell us your name and when you celebrated your birthday?"

"My name is Lois Johnson, and my birthday was two weeks ago."

Slow-Joe shuffled his feet, lifted his floppy hat, then plopped it back down on his head. "Ta-da!" He held out the bouquet to her.

Suddenly, the young girl sitting beside Lois bounced up and down, crying, "I want a balloon! I want a balloon!" She leaped out of her seat and lunged forward, obviously hoping to grab a balloon out of Slow-Joe's hands. Instead she tripped and tumbled against his knees. He wobbled back and forth, and the audience laughed loudly.

Lois wondered if this were part of the act, but suddenly Joe fell forward and landed in her lap. She figured it had to be an accident and the child was just overexcited. Or was it? Hadn't she told God that if He wanted her to have a man, He'd have to drop him into her lap? She swallowed hard and stared into the clown's hazel eyes.

"Sorry," he mumbled. "Don't know how that happened." He handed Lois the balloon bouquet and stood up. He turned back to face the audience and wiggled his dark eyebrows. "Let's sing the birthday song to Lois, shall we?"

Lois felt the heat of embarrassment creep up her neck. *This is what I get for being dumb enough to raise my hand.*

The young girl who had been sitting next to her now stood beside the clown. Before anyone could say anything, she started singing at the top of her lungs: "Happy Birthday to you..."

The audience joined in, and Lois stared straight ahead, wishing she could make herself invisible. When the song was over, she leaned toward Slow-Joe and whispered, "Thanks for the flowers."

He nodded, took a bow, and dashed backstage.

Lois sat through the rest of the program feeling as if she were in a daze. Why had the clown singled her out? *Well, after all, I did raise my hand when he asked who'd had a birthday recently*, she reminded herself. *What else could he do?*

When the service was over, Lois made her way to the foyer, where she found Tabby and Seth standing by the front door. She tapped her sister on her shoulder. "You guys were great as usual."

Tabby turned and smiled. "Thanks. Your part of the program wasn't bad, either."

"Yeah, we were watching from off stage," Seth said, patting Lois on the back. "Maybe you should leave your secretarial job and become a clown. You had the audience in stitches."

Lois groaned. "It was that goofy clown who made everyone laugh." She shook her head. "It was bad enough that he fell into my lap, but he only embarrassed me more by having everyone sing to me."

"Aw, it was all in fun," Seth said with a chuckle.

"We're heading out for some pie and coffee. Want to join us?" Tabby asked, giving Lois a little nudge.

She shrugged. "Sure—why not? At least there I won't have any reason to hide my face."

Chapter 3

The all-night coffee shop Seth picked was bustling with activity. Lois slipped into a booth by the window, and Tabby and Seth took the other side.

"You ladies feel free to order anything you want," Seth said, offering Lois a wide smile. "This is my treat, so you may as well go overboard and order something really fattening if you feel so inclined."

Tabby snickered. "Does my little sister look as if she ever goes overboard when it comes to eating?" She wagged a finger toward Lois. "What I wouldn't give to have a figure like yours."

Lois shook her head. "My high metabolism and a half hour of aerobics every day might help keep me looking thin, but I have been known to indulge. Especially when chocolate is involved."

"Women and their addiction to chocolate!" Seth grabbed Tabby's hand and gave it a squeeze. "I guess if that's your worst sin, I can consider myself very blessed."

Tabby groaned. "You know I'm far from perfect, Seth."

"What's this about someone being perfect?"

The three young people turned toward the masculine voice. Even without his costume and clown makeup, Lois would have recognized that smile. Slow-Joe the Clown wiggled his eyebrows and gave her a crooked grin.

"Good to see you, Joe. I was just telling my beautiful wife how lucky I am to have her." Seth gestured toward the empty seat next to Lois. "Why don't you take a load off those big clown feet and join us for pie and coffee?"

"Don't mind if I do." Joe dropped down beside Lois. She squirmed uneasily and slid along the bench until her hip bumped the wall. "It's good to see you again, birthday girl." He extended his hand. "I don't think we've been formally introduced. I'm Joe Richey."

"I–I'm Lois Johnson," she said. "Tabby's my sister, and Seth is my brother-in-law."

As they shook hands, Joe's face broke into a broad smile. "Sure hope I didn't embarrass you too much during my performance tonight."

"Well—"

"So tell me, Seth—how'd you meet this perfect wife of yours?" Joe asked, changing the subject abruptly.

Lois felt a sense of irritation, but at the same time she was relieved Joe had interrupted her and taken the conversation in another direction. At least she wasn't the focus of their discussion anymore.

"Tabby took one of my ventriloquist classes, and I was drawn to her like a moth heading straight for a flame." Seth turned his head and gave Tabby a noisy kiss on her cheek.

Joe chuckled. "Since I'm not married, I don't consider myself an expert on the subject, but I recently heard about a man who met his wife at a travel bureau."

"Oh?" Seth said with obvious interest. "And what's so unusual about that?"

Joe grinned and turned to wink at Lois. "She was looking for a vacation, and he was the last resort."

Everyone laughed, and Lois felt herself begin to relax.

"Adam and Eve had the only perfect marriage," Joe continued, his eyes looking suddenly serious.

"What makes you say that?" asked Tabby.

Joe tapped his knuckles on the table. "Think about it. Adam didn't have to hear about all the men Eve could have married, and Eve wasn't forced to listen to a bunch of stories about the way Adam's mother cooked."

Seth howled, and Tabby slapped him playfully on the arm. He tickled her under the chin. "The other day I heard my wife telling our neighbors I was a model husband. I felt pretty good about that until I looked up the word in a dictionary."

"What did it say?" Lois asked, putting her elbows on the table and leaning forward.

"A model is a small imitation of the real thing."

Another gale of laughter went around the table, but the waitress came then to take their order. Lois figured it was time to get serious, so she ordered a cup of herbal tea and a brownie. Tabby settled for coffee and a maple bar. Both men asked for coffee and hot-apple pie, topped with vanilla ice cream. While they waited for their orders, the joke telling continued.

"I've heard that marriage is comparable to twirling a baton, turning handsprings, or eating with chopsticks," Joe said with a sly grin on his face. "It looks really easy till you try it."

"I wouldn't know. I'm an old maid of twenty-two," Lois interjected.

Joe bobbed his head up and down and chuckled. "Wow, that is pretty old."

Tabby wrinkled her nose. "Not to be outdone—when Seth and I got married, it was for better or worse. I couldn't do better, and he couldn't do worse."

Remembering the days of her sister's low self-esteem, Lois quickly jumped in. "That's not true, Tabby, and you know it."

Tabby raised her eyebrows and looked at Lois. "I was only kidding."

Joe nudged Lois gently in the ribs with his elbow. "Did you know this is National Clown Month?"

She shook her head.

"Yes, and as a clown I feel it's my duty to make as many people laugh as possible." Joe then tapped Lois on the shoulder. "Do you like to laugh?"

"Sure."

"And do you enjoy making other people laugh?"

She shrugged. "I suppose so."

"Then maybe you've got what it takes to be a clown." Joe grinned. "Don't mind me—I'm always trying to recruit others to become clowns."

Lois wasn't sure what to say in response, so she merely turned her head away and stared out the window. The idea of her becoming a clown seemed ridiculous. She studied her little green car sitting under the street light next to Seth's black Bronco. If she could only come up with a legitimate excuse, she'd forget about her chocolate treat and head straight for home. Joe Richey was cute and funny, but at the moment he was making her feel rather uncomfortable.

❊

Joe clenched his teeth and squished the napkin in his lap into a tight ball. *I think I've blown it with this woman. I had her laughing one minute, and the next minute she's giving me the silent treatment. What'd I say or do that turned her off?*

"When will your next performance be, Joe?" Seth asked.

"Tonight was my last one for a while."

"How come?" Tabby questioned. "I'd think a funny guy like you would be in high demand."

"I guess I am, because I've been doing back-to-back programs all summer," Joe said. "I'm in need of a break, though. Thought I might head for the beach or go up to Mt. Rainier to relax."

Seth nodded. "Makes sense to me. All work and no play—well, you know the rest of that saying. Even Jesus needed to get away from the crowds once in a while. If you don't take time for yourself, you'll burn out like a candle in the wind."

"How long have you been clowning?" Lois asked.

At least she's speaking to me again. Joe turned his head and offered her his best smile. "Ever since I was a kid, but professionally for about two years."

As Joe leaned even closer to Lois, his senses were assaulted by the subtle fragrance of peaches. *It must be her shampoo.* He wondered if her hair was as soft as it looked, and he fought the urge to reach out and touch the long golden tresses. "Do you live around here, Lois?" he asked.

"Tabby and I grew up in Olympia, and our folks still live there." Lois smiled. "We both settled in Tacoma when we found jobs here."

Joe tapped the edge of his water glass with one finger. "I'm from Olympia, too."

"Really? What part of town?" Lois asked.

"The north side."

"Lois drives to Olympia a couple of times a month," Tabby said, smiling at Joe. "Maybe you two should get together sometime."

❧

Lois nearly choked on the sip of water she'd just taken. She had the distinct feeling she was being set up. Maybe her well-meaning sister had planned it so Joe would meet them at the coffee shop. It might be that the little schemer was trying to play matchmaker. *Who knows? Tabby could have been behind that whole scenario at the church tonight. She may have asked Joe to single me out with the balloon bouquet and birthday song.*

Lois resolved to have a little heart-to-heart talk with her sister. If she ever had another man in her life, she needed to do the picking. Tabby might have her best interests at heart, but she wasn't Lois's keeper. Besides, Lois wasn't looking for a man now.

She gave Joe a sidelong glance, and he smiled, a slow, lazy grin that set her heart racing. *He sure is cute. And he did fall into my lap.* The waitress brought their desserts, which helped Lois force her thoughts off the man who was sitting much too close. She concentrated on the piece of chocolate decadence on her plate. A little sugar for her sweet tooth and some herbal tea to soothe her nerves, and she would be right as rain.

Chapter 4

"Don't keep me in suspense. Did he call or what?"

Lois glanced over her shoulder. Tabby had just entered the church office and was looking at her like an expectant child waiting to open her birthday presents. "Did who call?"

"Joe Richey."

"No, he didn't call," Lois answered as she shut down her computer for the day.

"You did give him your phone number, didn't you? I thought I saw you hand him a slip of paper the other night when we were at the coffee shop."

Lois slid her chair away from the desk and stood up. "Tabby Beyers, get a life!"

Tabby folded her arms across her chest and wrinkled her nose. "I have a life. I'm a wife, a day care worker, and a ventriloquist."

Lois puckered her lips. "Then that ought to keep you busy enough so you can manage to mind your own business and not mine."

Tabby stuck out her tongue. "For your information, I'm only interested in your welfare."

"I appreciate that." Lois smiled, her irritation lessening. "If you don't mind, though, I think I can worry about my own welfare."

Tabby shrugged. "Whatever you say. Starting next month I won't be around much to meddle in your life, anyway."

Lois drew her brows together. "What's that supposed to mean? You and Seth aren't planning to move, I hope."

Tabby shook her head. "We'd never intentionally move from Tacoma. We like it here too much." She fluttered her lashes. "It's all that liquid sunshine, you know."

Lois laughed and reached for her purse hanging on the coat tree by the door. "If you're not moving, then why won't you be around much?"

"We're going on an evangelistic tour with several other Christian workers," Tabby explained. "We'll be traveling around the state of Washington and to a few places in Oregon and Idaho. Probably be gone at least a month. Maybe longer if we get a good response."

"Is Slow-Joe the Clown going with you?" Lois asked. She didn't know why, but she hoped he wasn't. They'd only met a few nights ago, so she hardly knew the man. She'd never admit it to Tabby, but Joe had promised to call. She looked forward to it, because there was something about the goofy guy that stirred her interest, even if she had felt uncomfortable in his presence. She wasn't sure if it was his silly antics and wisecracks, his hazel eyes with the gold flecks, or his mop of curly brown hair that made him so appealing.

"Lois, are you listening to me?"

Lois whirled around to face her sister. "Huh?"

"You asked if Joe Richey was going on tour with us, and I said no. But you're standing there staring at your purse as if you're in a world of your own." Tabby wrinkled her nose. "I'm sure you didn't hear a word I said."

Lois laughed self-consciously. "I guess I was kind of in my own world."

Tabby's eyes narrowed. "Thinking about Joe, I'll bet."

Lois couldn't deny it, so she asked another question. "If you're going on tour for a month or longer, how will Donna manage the day care?"

Tabby waved her hand. "She already has that covered. Corrie, our helper, has a friend who has been taking some child development classes. Donna thought she'd give her a try." She shrugged. "Who knows? Maybe I'll quit the day care. Then Corrie can take my place."

"Quit the day care?" Lois could hardly believe it. "But you love working with the kids. I can't imagine your doing anything else."

Tabby started for the door. "How about becoming a full-time mother?"

Lois's mouth dropped open. "You're pregnant?"

"Not yet, but I'm hopeful. Seth and I have been married two years, you know. We both think it's time to start a family."

Sudden envy surged through Lois, and she blinked several times to hold back tears that threatened to spill over. She loved children. That was why she was teaching a Sunday school class. How ironic. *Tabby used to be jealous of me, and now I feel the same way toward her. Help me in this area, Lord.*

❀

Joe searched through his closet for the right clothes to take to the beach. It could be windy, cold, rainy, or sunny along the Washington coast, even during the month of August. He'd probably need to take a couple of sweatshirts, some shorts, one or two pairs of jeans and, of course, his most comfortable pair of sneakers.

His favorite thing to do at the ocean was beachcomb. The flower beds in his backyard gave evidence of that. Pieces of driftwood adorned nearly every bed, and scattered throughout the plants were shells of all sizes and shapes. Stationed beside his front door were two buoys he'd discovered after a winter storm one year, and a fishbowl full of beach agates was displayed on his fireplace mantel.

Joe wondered why he didn't sell the old house he'd grown up in and buy a small cabin near the beach. He knew it would be more peaceful there. But then he'd be farther from the cities where he found most of his work.

As he packed his clothes into his suitcase, Joe noticed one of his clown suits lying on the floor. He'd forgotten to put it in the hamper.

Joseph Andrew Richey, you're a slob! You need to learn to pick up after yourself. Joe could hear his mother's sharp words, as if she were standing right there in his room.

She had always been a neat freak, unless she was in one of her down moods. Then she didn't care what she or the house looked like. Joe could never understand how his mother could yell at her children one day to pick up their things and the next day sink into such despair that she'd need a bulldozer to clear the clutter off the kitchen table.

"No wonder Brian left home the day he turned eighteen," Joe mumbled. He bent down to pick up the clown suit and shook his head. "I wouldn't be surprised if my little brother isn't still running from job to job, trying to dodge his problems."

His brother had a hot temper and had been fired from several positions because he couldn't work well with others and didn't want to take orders from his boss. Joe prayed for Brian regularly, but he'd given up trying to talk to him; their last discussion had ended in a horrible argument, and Joe figured he might never hear from his brother again.

Pushing thoughts of his brother aside, Joe dropped the clown suit into the hamper. Without warning, another one of his mother's accusations pounded in his head.

You're not going to wash that without checking the pockets, I hope.

Joe chuckled. "No, Mom. I wouldn't dream of it."

He stuffed his hand inside one deep pocket and withdrew three red pencil balloons and one green apple balloon. "Whew! Wouldn't want to put these babies in the washing machine."

Joe plunged his hand into the other pocket and pulled out a slip of paper. "Hmm—what's this? Somebody's phone number?" He sank to the edge of his bed and stared at the paper. Who'd recently given him a number, and why hadn't he been smart enough to jot down a name to go with it?

Joe grimaced. He'd probably forget his own name if it weren't on his driver's license.

"Think hard, Joe. Whose number is on this piece of paper?"

Lord, if this phone number is important, help me remember.

Still nothing.

Joe stretched out across the bed, and within a matter of minutes he was asleep. Several hours later he awoke, feeling more refreshed than he had all day.

Sitting up, he noticed the slip of paper lying on the bed. He looked intently at the phone number, and a wide grin spread across his face. "Lois Johnson! Tabby's sister gave me her number when we met at the coffee shop the other night."

Feeling as if he'd been handed an Oscar, Joe grabbed the telephone off the small table by his bed. He punched in the numbers and waited for Lois to pick up, but only a recorded message answered. He hated talking to machines so he didn't leave a message.

"Guess there's no hurry," he assured himself. "I'll call her after I get back from the beach."

Chapter 5

Joe set his suitcase inside the front door, plodded to the living room, and sank wearily to the couch. Two weeks at the beach should have revived him. But they hadn't. His body felt rested, but he had a sense of unrest deep within his soul. Maybe he would feel better once he started working again. That's what he needed—a few more crusades or a couple of birthday parties to get him back on his feet.

Joe forced himself off the couch and headed for the kitchen. He hoped to find at least one job opportunity waiting for him on his answering machine. He didn't want to start hunting for programs. He had never been good at promoting himself, and so far he hadn't needed to. Word of mouth had served him well.

Among the messages, he heard five requests for his clown routine. Two were for church rallies, and the other three involved birthday parties. Even though the parties were mainly for entertainment, he still felt as if he were doing something worthwhile by providing children with good, clean fun. He usually gave some kind of moral lesson with his balloon animals, so at least the children were being exposed to admirable virtues and not merely being entertained.

Feeling a surge of energy, Joe returned the calls, lined up each program, and wrote the dates and times on his appointment calendar. The business end of Joe's clowning was important, and he tried to stay organized with his programs, even if he weren't always structured at home. It wouldn't do to forget or arrive late for an engagement. In fact, it could cost him jobs if he did it too often.

He was heading upstairs to unpack his suitcase when he spotted the slip of paper with Lois Johnson's number on it. He dialed but reached her answering machine, as he had two weeks ago.

"Isn't that woman ever at home?" Joe muttered. He hung up the phone without leaving a message. "I'll try again after I unpack and see if there's anything in the refrigerator to eat."

❀

Pastor Hanson had insisted Lois take off early from work today so she decided to explore some of the new stores at the Tacoma Mall. She didn't have a lot of money to spend, but she knew how to shop for bargains. If a store was having a good deal on something, she'd be sure to find it. Besides, Tabby and Seth had left the day before, and she was feeling lonely. A little shopping would help take her mind off her troubles. At least it would be a temporary diversion.

Lois parked her car in the lot on the north side of the mall then slipped off her navy blue pumps and replaced them with a pair of comfortable walking shoes. It might not look fashionable to shop in an ankle-length navy blue dress and a pair of black sneakers, but she didn't care. It wasn't likely she'd see anyone she knew at the mall.

Lois grabbed her purse, hopped out of the car, and jogged to the mall's closest entrance. Her first stop was a women's clothing store where she found two blouses for under ten dollars and a pair of shorts that had been marked down to five dollars because summer was nearly over.

Next she entered a bed and bath store in hopes of finding a new shower curtain. Her old one had water stains and was beginning to tear. The clerk showed her several, but they cost too much. Lois was about to give up when she noticed a man heading her way. She stood frozen in her tracks, her body trembling.

Lois glanced around for something to hide behind, but it was too late. Michael Yehley was striding toward her, an arrogant smile on his face. Feelings of the old hurt and humiliation knifed through her, and she fought to keep from dashing out of the store.

"Well, well, if it isn't my beautiful ex-fiancée," Michael drawled. He was dressed in a dark brown business suit, white shirt, and olive-green tie with tan pinstripes. He had never projected a flashy image, but he did carry about him an air of superiority. His dark hair, parted on the side, his aristocratic nose, and his metal-framed glasses gave him a distinguished appearance Lois had once found attractive.

She took a step back as he reached for her hand. "H–hello, Michael. I'm surprised to see you here."

"My mother's birthday is coming up, and I thought I'd get something for her newly redecorated bath." He grinned at her. "She's going with an oriental theme this time."

This time? How many other times has your mother redecorated her bathroom? Lois feigned a smile. "I'm sure she'll like whatever you choose. You always did have impeccable taste."

Michael looked directly at her. "I thought so when I chose you." He wrinkled his nose, as though some foul odor had suddenly permeated the room. "Of course, that was before you flipped out and went religious on me."

Lois swallowed hard. Michael first postponed their wedding because he thought she was too young and they hadn't known each other long enough. But later, after she became a Christian, he had forced her to choose between him and God. When she told him she wouldn't give up her relationship with Christ, he'd said some choice words and stormed out of her apartment. He had called a few weeks later, informing Lois she was acting like a confused little girl and that she should call if she ever came to her senses. That had been two years ago, but even now it hurt. Especially with Michael looking at her as if she'd been crazy for choosing God over him. She certainly didn't want the man back in her life. She had tried hard enough after her conversion to get him to attend church, but it always caused an argument. Michael had been adamant about not needing any kind of religious crutch, and he'd told her he wasn't going to church, no matter how many times she asked.

"How about joining me for a cup of coffee?" Michael asked. "We can try out that new place on the other side of the mall."

Lois opened her mouth, but he cut her off. "It'll be like old times, and you can fill me in on what you've been up to lately." He gave her a charming smile. "Besides, you look kind of down. Hot coffee and some time with me will surely cheer you up."

Lois shook her head. "You know I don't like coffee, Michael."

"You can have tea, soda, whatever you want." He took hold of Lois's arm and steered her toward the door.

"What about the gift you were planning to buy your mother?" she asked.

"It can wait."

Why was she letting him escort her along the mall corridor? Was she so lonely she'd allow him to lead her away like a sheep being led to slaughter?

When they reached the café, Michael found a table. He ordered a mocha-flavored coffee, and Lois asked for a glass of iced tea.

As they waited for their beverages, Michael leaned across the table and studied Lois intently. "Tell me why you quit working for Thorn and Thorn."

Her eyes narrowed. "News sure travels fast. When did you hear I'd quit?"

His lips curved into a smile. "I'm a lawyer, remember, sweetie? Ray Thorn and I had some business dealings a few weeks ago, and he filled me in."

"I'm working as a secretary for Bayview Christian Church."

He grimaced. "That must mean you're still on your religious soapbox."

Lois glanced down at her hands, folded in her lap. Her knuckles were white, and she was trembling again. Did Michael think it would help if he brought up her faith?

"I'm not on a religious soapbox," she said with clenched teeth. "I love the Lord, I'm enjoying my new job, and—"

He held up one hand. "And you obviously care more about all that than you do me."

She sucked in her bottom lip. "What we once had is over, Michael. You made it perfectly clear you weren't interested in marrying a religious fanatic. And from a scriptural point of view, I knew it would be wrong for us to get married if you weren't a Christian."

Michael's face grew red, and a vein on the side of his neck began to pulsate. "Are you saying I'm not good enough for you?"

"It's not that. With our religious views being so opposite, it wouldn't have worked out. We would always be arguing."

"As we are now?"

She nodded.

The waitress arrived then, and Lois and Michael sat in silence for a while, sipping their drinks. Lois wished she hadn't come here with him. Nothing good was resulting from this little meeting.

"I'm sorry things didn't work out for us, Michael," she murmured, "but, as I said before, I could never have married someone who didn't share my belief in God."

The waitress brought the bill and placed it next to Michael's cup. He gulped down the rest of his coffee and stood, knocking the receipt to the floor. "Some things never change, and you're obviously one of them!"

He bent down to pick up the bill. "Nice shoes," he said in a mocking tone, as he pointed to Lois's sneakers. "Real stylish."

Lois blinked back the burning tears threatening to spill over. So much for her afternoon shopping spree making her feel better. Michael had a knack for getting under her skin; he'd made her cry on more than one occasion, even when they were dating and supposed to be in love. Lois still found him physically attractive, but now she was even more convinced that he was not her type.

Michael stalked off, but a few seconds later he returned to the table with a grim expression on his face. "I just want you to know—I harbor no ill feelings toward you. I'm getting on with my life, and apparently you are, too."

Lois only nodded. Her throat was too clogged with tears, and she was afraid if she tried to speak she would break down. She didn't love Michael anymore, but seeing him again and hearing the way he talked about her faith made her know for certain she'd done the right thing. Her unshed tears were for the time she'd wasted in a relationship that had gone nowhere. She also ached for Michael, that he would discover the same joy she had in a personal relationship with God. Only then had she found freedom from the pursuit of wealth and power, and she wished the same for him. She thought of the people lost in their sin, refusing to acknowledge they'd done anything wrong and turning their backs on God and the salvation He offered through the shed blood of Christ. She sincerely hoped Michael would choose to receive this gift.

Suddenly Michael leaned close to her ear and whispered, "If you should ever come to your senses, give me a call." With that, he kissed her abruptly on the cheek, turned, and was gone.

Lois was too stunned to move. She could scarcely catch her breath.

❀

A half hour later Lois unlocked the door to her apartment and heard the phone ringing. She raced to grab it before the answering machine picked up. "Hello."

"Lois, is that you?"

"Yes. Who's this?"

"Joe Richey—the goofy gospel clown who fell into your lap a few weeks ago."

Lois's heart pounded, and she drew in a breath to steady her nerves. Since he hadn't called, she'd given up hope that he might.

"You still there, Lois?"

His mellow voice stopped her thoughts. "Yes, I'm here—just a little surprised to hear from you."

"I said I'd call, and you did give me your phone number," Joe reminded her.

"I know, but it's been over two weeks, and—"

"And you gave up on me."

"I—I guess I did."

"I've been to Ocean Shores, taking a much-needed vacation."

"Did you have a good time?"

"It was okay. I did a lot of walking on the beach and slept late every morning." Joe chuckled. "Something I hardly ever do when I'm at home."

Lois twirled the phone cord around her finger, wondering what to say next.

"Listen—the reason I'm calling is, I was wondering if you'd like to go bowling this Friday night."

Lois paused as she tried to absorb what Joe had said.

"You do know how to bowl, don't you?"

"Yes, but not very well."

"Maybe I can give you a few pointers. I've been bowling since I was a kid and have a pretty good hook with my ball."

Lois giggled. In her mind's eye she could picture Joe lining up his ball with the pins, snapping his wrist to the left, then acing a strike on the very first ball.

"So what do you say? Would you like to go bowling?"

"Sure—I'd love to."

Chapter 6

Lois paced between the living room window and the fireplace. Joe should have been here fifteen minutes ago. Had he encountered a lot of traffic on the freeway between Olympia and Tacoma? Had he forgotten the time he'd agreed to come? Maybe he'd stood her up. No, that wasn't likely. Joe seemed too nice a guy to do something so mean. He did appear to be a bit irresponsible, though. He'd said he would call her after they met at the coffee shop, but he'd gone on vacation and hadn't phoned until two weeks later.

"Sure hope I'm doing the right thing by going out with Joe," Lois murmured. "He's funny and cute, but not really my type." What exactly was her type? She'd once thought Michael fit the criteria—charming, good looking, smart, and financially well off. Weren't those the qualities she was looking for in a man?

"That was then, and this is now," Lois said as she checked her appearance in the hall mirror. She had a different set of ideals concerning men now. The most important thing was whether he was a Christian or not, and next came compatibility.

The doorbell rang, and Lois jumped. She peered through the peephole in her apartment door and saw one big hazel-colored eye staring back at her.

"Sorry I'm late," Joe apologized when she opened the door. "You gave me your address the other night, but I forgot where I laid it and spent fifteen minutes trying to locate it." Before she could reply, he pulled a bouquet of pink carnations from behind his back and handed them to her. Their hands touched briefly, and Lois was caught off guard by the feelings that stirred deep within.

"I hope these will make up for my forgetfulness," Joe said with a big smile.

Lois smiled, too, and inhaled the subtle fragrance of the bouquet. "Thanks for these. Carnations are my favorite. Come inside while I put them in water."

Joe followed her into the kitchen, and after she'd filled a vase with water and inserted the flowers, she turned to him and smiled. He was dressed in a black knit polo shirt and a pair of blue jeans. Nothing fancy, yet she thought he looked adorable. *It must be that crooked grin. Or maybe it's his curly brown hair. I wonder what it would feel like to run my fingers through those curls.* Lois halted her thoughts. She barely knew Joe, and after being hurt by Michael she hoped she was smart enough not to rush into another relationship.

"You look great tonight," Joe said. "In fact, we resemble a pair of matching bookends."

Lois glanced down at her black tank top and blue jeans. "Let's hope we match as well at the bowling alley."

"No big deal if we don't." Joe's eyebrows wiggled up and down. "That'll make it more interesting."

Joe sat on the bench, with his arms crossed and a big smile on his face, watching Lois line up her ball with the pins. Her golden hair, held back with two small barrettes, glistened under the bowling alley lights and made him wish he could touch it and feel its softness. He had no plans of becoming emotionally involved with anyone right now, but something about Lois drew him in a way he'd never experienced with other women. Was it merely her good looks, or did Lois have the kind of sweet spirit he desired in a wife? *Wife? Now where did that thought come from?*

Lois squealed with delight when she knocked down half the pins on her first throw, forcing Joe's thoughts back to the game. "Good job!" he exclaimed, pointing both thumbs up in the air.

She pivoted and smiled at him, revealing two dimples he hadn't noticed before. "Not too bad for an amateur, huh?" She grabbed her ball when it returned to the rack and positioned herself in front of the alley. This time her aim was a bit off, and the ball made it halfway down before it veered to the right and rolled into the gutter.

Lois returned to her seat, looking as if she'd lost her best friend. "That little boy a couple of lanes over bowls better than I do."

Joe patted her on the shoulder. "It's only a game, and you're doing your best."

She shrugged. "My best doesn't seem to be good enough."

"You know what they say about practice."

"I don't bowl often enough to get in much practice."

"Guess we'll have to remedy that."

She tipped her head to one side, and her blue eyes sparkled in the light. "Is that your way of asking me out again?"

He grinned. "Sure—if you're interested in dating a goofy guy like me."

Lois giggled and poked him on the arm. "You did look pretty silly a while ago when you were trying to bowl with your back to the alley."

He tweaked her nose. "Don't slam the technique. I knocked four pins down that time."

"Next I suppose you'll try to juggle three bowling balls at the same time."

"I think they might be a bit heavy," he answered with a smile. "I could see about juggling three or four pins, though."

She jabbed his arm again. "You would, wouldn't you?"

Joe stood up, retrieved his ball from the return rack, then turned back to face Lois. "Hang around me long enough, and you'll be surprised at what I can do."

🌼

After bowling three games, they walked over to the snack bar for hamburgers and french fries. Joe ordered a cherry soda and Lois a glass of lemonade before finding an empty booth.

Lois eyed Joe curiously as he poured ketchup on his fries. He looked like a little boy in a man's body, with eyes that twinkled like stars, a mouth turned up, and freckles spattered across the bridge of his nose.

He glanced up then. "A nickel for your thoughts," he said, smiling.

She could feel her cheeks grow warm. "Oh, uh, well, I was just wondering about something."

"What is it?"

"Well, I realized I don't know much about you. I know you're a gospel clown and you live in Olympia, but that's about all."

Joe shrugged. "There's not much to tell."

"What about your family?"

"What about them?"

"Do you have any brothers or sisters?"

"Just a brother who's a few years younger than I am."

"Where do your folks live?" she asked.

Joe stared at the table. "They're both dead."

"Oh, I'm sorry. What happened?"

"I'd rather not talk about it right now, if that's okay," he said, looking down at the table.

"Sure," Lois said, suddenly uncomfortable with the direction their conversation had taken. She hesitated before speaking, hoping she could find a better topic to discuss. "Do you work at any other job besides clowning?"

"I went to trade school right out of high school and learned how to be a mechanic," he answered. "I worked at a garage not far from home for a while, but after I started clowning, the job turned to part-time; finally I quit altogether."

"You mean you make enough money clowning to support yourself?"

He nodded. "Yes, but I'll never be rich. Besides crusades, Bible camps, and other church-related functions, I do birthday parties for kids of all ages. I've also entertained at some senior centers and have even landed a couple of summer jobs at the Enchanted Village near Seattle."

She nodded. "I know where that is. My dad used to take me there when I was a kid."

"What about your sister? Didn't she go, too?"

Lois swallowed hard. How could she tell Joe about her childhood and Tabby's without making him think she was a spoiled brat? The truth was that until she trusted the Lord with her life, she'd been exactly that. "Let's just say Tabby was afraid of most of the rides there, and our dad had no patience with her fears."

Joe shook his head slowly. "She sure doesn't seem afraid of much now. In fact, I've seen her do some routines that would rival anything the big-time ventriloquists have done. And she didn't act one bit nervous, either."

"Tabby has come a long way in the past few years. All she needed was to gain some confidence, and now she's using her talents to tell others about the Lord." Lois paused. "In the past we weren't very close. I was often critical of her. Things are much better between us now, and I can honestly say I love my sister to pieces. I owe that to the Lord."

Joe leaned across the table and took Lois's hand. A jolt of electricity shot up her arm. "I'm not trying to change the subject, but I've tried calling you a couple of times during the day, and I always get your answering machine. Do you work or go to school someplace in Tacoma?"

"For the past couple of weeks I've been working as the secretary at Bayview Christian Church in the north end of Tacoma," she said.

"And before that?"

"I was a lawyer's secretary."

Joe whistled and released her hand. "Wow! You must have been making some big bucks! What prompted you to give up such a job and take on a church secretary's position, which I'm sure doesn't pay half as much?"

Lois paused. Should she tell Joe about Michael and their broken engagement? It was part of the reason she'd decided to leave her job. The junior partner at the firm was a friend of Michael's, and Lois knew he kept her ex-fiancé updated on her comings and goings. Michael had said as much when they'd run into each other at the mall the other day.

"You're right," she replied. "My job at the church isn't very lucrative, but it does pay the bills, and I consider it to be a ministry of sorts."

His eyebrows lifted. "How so?"

"Many folks call or drop by the church, needing help with food, clothing, or spiritual matters. I'm not a trained counselor so I always send people with serious problems to one of the pastors, but I do pray for those who have a need."

"How long have you been a Christian?" he asked.

"Almost two years. Tabby and I went to church when we were kids, but I never took it seriously until shortly after she and Seth got married. I think seeing how my sister changed when she started using her talents to tell others about the Lord helped me see the emptiness in my own life." Lois lowered her gaze. "I wasn't a very nice person before I became a Christian. The truth is I was spoiled and self-centered and mean to my sister most of the time."

"But, as you said earlier, you and Tabby get along now, right?"

She nodded. "We're as close as any two siblings could be."

A strange look crossed Joe's face, and Lois wondered what he was thinking. Before she could voice the question, Joe said, "When I was eight years old, I went to Bible school. That's where I realized I had sinned and asked God to forgive me." He smiled. "Ever since then I've wanted to serve Him through some form of special ministry."

"Do you enjoy clowning?"

He chuckled. "Yep. I guess it's in my nature to make people laugh. I feel happier when I'm clowning around."

Lois was about to respond when Joe grabbed two straws from the plastic container sitting on their table and stuck one in each ear. "You think I could patent this?" he said in a teasing voice. "Hearing aids with no need for batteries." He shook his head from side to side, and the straws bounced up and down.

Lois stifled a giggle behind her hand. With his eyes crossed and two blue straws dangling from each ear, Joe looked hilarious. She was glad for those few minutes of finding out a little more about him. But she wondered if he ever stayed serious for long, and if so, would she find that side of him more appealing?

🌼

Joe tilted his head to one side and mentally replayed the questions she'd asked. She was not only beautiful but smart, and she'd laughed at his corny jokes and goofy antics. The only uncomfortable moment had come when she questioned him about his family.

He watched Lois drinking her lemonade. Her lips were pursed around the tip of the straw, and she drank in slow, delicate sips. *Wonder what it would feel like to kiss those rosy lips.* He gave his ear a sharp pull, hoping the gesture would get him thinking straight again. This was only their first date. He shouldn't be thinking about kissing Lois.

"You're staring at me."

He blinked then smiled. "Yeah, I guess I am."

"Do I have ketchup on my chin or something?"

"Nope. I was just thinking I'd like to get to know you better."

Lois nodded. "I'd like to know you better, too."

"How about coming to one of my programs?" Joe asked. "I'll be part of a revival service at one of the largest churches in Puyallup next Friday night. We'll have performers from all over the Pacific Northwest." He smiled at her. "After the program, maybe we can go out for pie and coffee."

"Sounds like fun."

"So will you come?"

"I'd love to."

Joe smiled again, feeling as if he'd been handed a birthday present when it wasn't even his birthday.

Chapter 7

Lois sat spellbound as the gospel illusionist on stage at Puyallup Christian Church performed a disappearing dove trick. "After the flood, Noah sent out first a raven, then a dove, in search of dry land," he told everyone. He placed a live dove inside a silver pan, covered it with a lid, and opened it again. The bird was gone. A few minutes later, it reappeared inside the illusionist's coat.

Lois applauded with the rest of the audience.

After that, she watched two clowns perform using mime. Neither of them held her interest the way Joe did, though. They were more sophisticated in their approach, and throughout their routine they never uttered a word, as was the custom with mimes.

A group of puppeteers followed the clowns, and an artist did a beautiful chalk drawing of the resurrection of Christ. Lois thought of Tabby's friend, Donna, who also did chalk art. She knew Donna hadn't gone on tour with Tabby and Seth, since she had the day care to run, but she'd expected to see her here tonight. She thought Donna's drawings were every bit as good as the one being done now.

When she heard Slow-Joe the Clown being announced, Lois smiled. He was the main reason she'd come tonight.

🌼

Joe was comfortable in the costume he'd chosen—a cowboy clown suit, complete with ten-gallon hat, chaps, and bright red leather boots. His red-and-white-striped shirt offset his baggy white pants with red fringe sewn to the pockets and side seams. He wore his usual white face paint and red rubber nose, but he'd added a fake mustache to give him a rugged cowboy look.

As Joe stepped onto the stage, he swung a rope over his head and hollered, "Yahoo! Ride 'em, cowboy!" Everyone cheered and clapped.

Joe threw the rope into the air, spun around as it fell to the ground, and shouted, "Now wait a minute! Where did that silly rope go? I had it in my hands a minute ago, and now it's disappeared."

When the laughter died down, Joe pivoted on his heels and tripped over the rope, which was lying a few inches in front of him. Next, he grabbed two folding chairs, draped the rope across the back of each one, then tied both ends in a knot. "Before I came out here, someone dared me to do this, so now I'm gonna walk the tightrope."

"Don't do it!" a child's voice shouted.

"Would you like to do it instead?" Joe called back.

"No, it's not safe!"

Joe eyed the rope. Then, slowly, deliberately, he lifted one foot, paused, and set his foot back down. "Anyone have an umbrella? I might need it for balance," he said to the audience.

"It's not safe!" the child yelled again.

Joe looked at the rope, tipped his head slightly, then bent to examine it more closely. "The rope looks strong, but the chairs might not hold my weight. Maybe I should do this the cautious way." With that, Joe quickly undid the rope, snapped it over his head, did a few fancy twirls, then flopped the rope onto the floor in a straight line. "Now it's safe!"

With exaggerated movements he stepped onto the rope, placing one boot in front of the other, and walked the tight rope. When he came to the end, he turned to the audience and bowed. He heard several snickers, but nobody clapped. Frowning, he tugged gently on his mustache. "You didn't think that trick was impressive?" he asked the audience, turning his hands palm up. A few more snickers filtered through the room.

"I'll tell you what's impressive," Joe continued. "Doing what you know is right, even when others try to get you to do something that could be bad for you. Someone dared me to walk this tightrope while it was connected to two chairs. If I'd taken that dare, it would have been pretty stupid."

"God gave each of us the ability to discern what's right and wrong," Joe continued. "Even if you want to be liked and think taking a dare is cool, you need to use your brain and decide what's best for you in any situation." He pointed to the rope at his feet. "I don't have an umbrella for balance, the folding chairs aren't very sturdy, and I've never walked a tightrope in my life, so I decided to do the sensible thing." He turned and went back across the rope. "I walked a tightrope that was lying safely on the ground."

Everyone clapped, and Joe reached into his pocket to retrieve a balloon. "I'm going to create my favorite balloon critter now—Buzzy the Bee."

He inflated the balloon to make the insect's body, twisted one-third of it off for the head, then withdrew and blew up a second balloon. After he'd tied a knot, he formed a circle with the balloon. He twisted it in half to make two smaller circles, which would become the bee's wings. These were attached to the body with another twist. Using a black marking pen, Joe drew a face on the bee and rings around its middle.

"Whenever I see a bee, I'm reminded that God wants me to bee a good witness, bee kind to others, and bee faithful about going to church," he said, holding up the balloon. Joe stepped off the stage and handed the bee to the child who had warned him about the unsafe tightrope.

He ended his routine by spinning the rope over his head and telling the audience each of them had talents they could use to serve the Lord in some way.

❀

Later that evening, at the restaurant where she and Joe had gone for dessert, Lois found herself once again enthralled with Slow-Joe the Clown's wit and goofy smile. "I could tell you were having fun during your performance tonight," she said.

"I always have fun when I'm onstage." Joe leaned across the table. "Speaking of fun, and changing the subject, I was at the mall the other day and stopped in to use the men's room."

Lois covered her ears with her hands. "Is this something I need to hear?"

Joe grinned. "When I was in the men's room, I noticed a sign on the wall, above a padded shelf. It read: 'Baby Changing Station.'" Joe shook his head slowly. "Can you imagine anyone wanting to leave their kid there, hoping it'll be changed when it comes out?" He chuckled and gave her a quick wink.

Lois groaned. "Don't you ever get tired of cracking jokes?"

"Nope." Joe reached for his cup of coffee. "So what do you do when you're not working?" he asked, changing the subject again.

She shrugged her shoulders. "I teach a first-grade Sunday school class, drive to Olympia to visit my folks a couple times a month, and read a lot."

"Nothing just for fun?"

"Reading a good book can be fun." Lois stared into her cup of tea for a moment then glanced up and saw Joe dangling his spoon with two fingers, directly in front of her face.

"Very funny," she murmured.

Joe dropped the spoon and reached for her hand, and at once Lois felt her face flame. Was Joe flirting with her? The way he kidded around all the time she couldn't be sure if he was serious or teasing.

"The Puyallup Fair starts next weekend," Joe said. "Would you be interested in tagging along with me, maybe sometime Saturday afternoon?"

Lois nodded and smiled. They could find lots of fun things to do at the fair, and it would give her another opportunity to get to know Joe better.

"Great! I have to warn you, though—I get a little carried away when I ride the roller coaster, especially after I've inhaled a couple of cotton candies."

She gulped. The roller coaster? Surely Joe didn't expect her to ride that horrible contraption!

Chapter 8

As Lois and Joe headed to the Puyallup Fair in his blue pickup truck, a surge of excitement coursed through her.

"Here we are," Joe announced when they pulled into the parking lot near the fairgrounds.

Lois focused on her surroundings. She saw people everywhere, which was nothing unusual for a fair this size. Today it seemed worse than any other time she could remember, though. Maybe it was because of the unseasonably warm weather they'd been having in the Pacific Northwest. Sunshine brought people out by the droves, and something as entertaining as the fair had a lot of appeal.

Joe turned and grinned at Lois after he'd placed his parking stub on the dash. "Ready for an awesome day?"

She smiled in return. "Ready as I'll ever be."

Hand in hand, they made their way to the entrance gates. Joe bought two admission tickets, and they pushed through the revolving gate.

"Where would you like to start?" Joe asked as he grabbed a map of the fairgrounds from a nearby stand.

Lois shrugged. The crisp aroma of early fall mingled with cotton candy, corn dogs, and curly fries, teasing her senses. "I don't know—there's so much to see."

"And do," Joe added. "Why don't we start with the rides? That way we won't be tilting, whirling, and somersaulting on full stomachs or with our arms loaded with stuffed animals."

"Stuffed animals?"

He chucked her under the chin and wiggled his eyebrows, a habit she was coming to enjoy. "Yeah, I'm pretty good at knocking down pins at my favorite arcade game. Last time I came here, I went home with two giraffes, a sheep, and a huge pink bear."

Lois giggled as she tried to envision Joe carrying that many stuffed animals back to his truck. Of course, she reminded herself, he might have been with a date. Why else would he have tried to win so many prizes?

"You don't think I'm capable of winning anything?" Joe said, inclining his head and presenting Lois with a look that reminded her of a puppy begging for a treat.

"It's not that. I just can't imagine how you ever carried them all out of here."

"I admit I did have a little help. I gave one giraffe and the bear to some kids who'd spent all their money trying to win a prize and had come up empty handed. The other giraffe and the sheep went home with me, and now they occupy a special place in one corner of my bedroom."

"So you have a circus theme in your room?"

"More like Noah's ark," he said, grabbing her hand again and pulling her through the crowd. "Which ride is your favorite?"

"Well—"

"Please don't tell me you like them all," he said in a teasing voice. "I don't think we have time or money enough to go on every one."

"Actually, the only rides I enjoy are the gondola, the Ferris wheel, and the merry-go-round."

Joe shook his finger at her and clicked his tongue. "All baby rides. If we're going to remember this day so we can tell our grandchildren about it, we need to do something really fun and exciting."

"Like what?" Lois asked, a knot forming in her throat.

"The roller coaster, of course!"

As they approached the midway, Lois grew more apprehensive. She hadn't ridden on the roller coaster since she was sixteen, and then she'd embarrassed herself in front of her friends. She could feel her fears mounting as she watched the cars climb the track, knowing they would zoom down and up again, and around the bend made her stomach lurch just thinking about it.

"You okay?" Joe asked with a note of concern. "You look a little green around the gills."

Lois swallowed hard, fighting down a wave of nausea. "I, uh, had a bad experience on the roller coaster one time."

"How long ago was that?"

"I was sixteen and had come here with a bunch of kids from my high school."

Joe nudged her in the ribs. "You're all grown up now, so riding the curvy monster should be easy as pie."

"Why don't you go on it alone, and I'll find a bench and watch from the ground below, where I'll be safe?" She nodded toward a mother and her two children who were walking by. "I'd much rather people watch, if that's okay."

"You can watch people from up there." Joe pointed to the climbing coaster, and Lois swallowed back another wave of nausea. "You'll be safe with me—I promise."

Before Lois could respond, Joe grabbed her around the waist and propelled her toward the ticket booth. "Two for the roller coaster," he announced to the woman behind the counter. Tickets in hand, he led Lois to the line where people stood waiting for the ride.

Lois wasn't sure what to do. She didn't want to make a scene in front of all these people, but if she rode on what Joe referred to as "the curvy monster," she was certain she would.

"Don't be nervous," Joe whispered in her ear. "Just hold my hand real tight, and when we're riding the wooden waves, scream like crazy. It wouldn't hurt to pray a little, either," he added with a chuckle.

Standing in line, Lois's fears abated some. Being with Joe made her feel carefree, and his jovial spirit and playful attitude kept her laughing. But when they were ushered to the first seat of the coaster, her throat tightened again. What if she got sick as she had when she was a teenager? Or, worse yet, what if she threw up on Joe's white polo shirt? She decided to turn her head away from him, just in case.

"Smile—you're on Candid Camera," Joe said, reaching for her trembling hand.

She moaned. "I hope not. I'd be mortified if the whole world saw me right now."

Joe nuzzled her ear with his nose. "You've never looked more beautiful."

"Yeah, right."

"I'm serious," he asserted. "I love your silky yellow hair, and those bonny blue eyes of yours dazzle my heart."

Lois's heart began to pound, and it wasn't just because the roller coaster had started up the incline. Did Joe think she was beautiful, and had she dazzled his heart? With his clowning around so much, she couldn't always tell if he was serious or not. She didn't have long to ponder the question, for they'd reached the top and were about to cascade down the first part of the track.

"Yowzie! Zowzie!" Joe hollered as they began their descent. "This is way cool!"

Lois braced herself against the seat and held on tight. She screamed—and screamed—and screamed some more, until they reached the bottom and began to climb the next hill.

"That wasn't so bad, was it?" Joe asked.

Lois shook her head quickly, too afraid to speak. The truth was that it hadn't been as awful as she'd remembered. At least this time she'd managed to keep her breakfast down—so far.

"Here we go again," Joe roared in her ear. "Hang on tight and yell like crazy!"

Lois complied. It felt good to holler and howl as the up-and-down motion of the coaster caught her off guard and threw her stomach into a frenzy. It was actually fun, and she was having the time of her life.

At the end of the ride Lois felt exhilarated, instead of weak and shaky as she'd expected. "Let's go again!" she shouted.

Joe chuckled. "Maybe later. Right now I'm ready to ride the Ferris wheel."

Lois sighed. After their wild ride on the roller coaster, the Ferris wheel would seem like a piece of cake. It would be mellow and relaxing, though, and that was probably a good thing. It had been a long time since Lois had been this keyed up, and she was a bit concerned that she might make a mistake and blurt out to Joe how much she liked him. *I don't want to scare him away. He's too good to be true, and I need to go slowly.* If she and Joe were going to have a relationship, she knew it was better not to push or reveal her feelings too soon.

The day sped by like a whirlwind. They moved from one ride to the next and even stopped to eat barbecued ribs, coleslaw, and a huge order of curly fries, with lemonade and, later, soft chocolate ice cream cones. Joe won Lois a fuzzy brown teddy bear and a huge spiral vase filled with gaudy pink feathered flowers. She loved it. The truth was that she would have been happy with a jar of old marbles if Joe had won them for her. Today had been like a fairy tale, and she wished it would never end. But it was getting late, and they both needed to be at church in the morning. She had a Sunday school class to teach, and Joe had told her he was scheduled to do a program at his home church in Olympia.

It was a little past ten when Joe walked Lois to her apartment door. She started to fidget. Would he kiss her good night? This was their third date, and so far he'd only held her hand, slipped his arm around her waist, and nuzzled her neck a few times. She didn't want him to see how nervous she was so she decided to ask him more questions about himself.

"You seem so naturally funny, Joe. I'm curious—did you get your humor from your dad or your mom?"

Joe stood there and stared at her while she waited for him to answer her question. She hoped he would tell her more about his family. Instead, he bent his head toward her and puckered his lips.

Lois held her breath then and closed her eyes. He was going to kiss her, and she was more than ready.

"Thanks for a great day." Joe gave her a quick peck on the cheek. "You were a good sport to ride that roller coaster with me." He squeezed her arm gently then turned to go. "See you, Lois."

Disappointment flooded Lois's soul as she watched him walk away. "So much for a perfect day," she muttered. Had she said or done something to turn him off? Maybe Joe didn't like her as much as she liked him. Would he call her again?

Chapter 9

Lois had given Joe her work phone number, hoping he might call during the day if he was busy doing programs at night. Four days had passed since their date to the fair, but still no word from him. The weekend would be here soon, and Lois was beginning to think she would have to spend it alone. Of course, she could make plans to visit her folks. They lived in Olympia, and so did Joe. Would that be a good enough excuse for her to drop by his house and say hello? Should she call first or stop by unannounced? What if that peck on the cheek and Joe's "See you, Lois" had been his way of letting her know he wouldn't be calling again? Even though he'd acted as if he enjoyed their day at the fair, he had made no promises to call.

She didn't want to scare him off. But if she didn't let him know she was interested in a relationship, he could slip through her fingers. She saw it as a no-win situation, and she felt frustrated.

As she prepared to leave the church after work on Friday afternoon, the pastor and his wife stopped her in the hallway. "Hi, Lois. How are things going?" Pastor Hanson asked.

"Good. Is there something I can do for you before I go?"

"No, but Norma just mentioned how you seemed a little down this week. We were wondering if you wanted to talk about anything before you head out for the weekend."

"Oh, well, I hate to bother you. You've both had a busy week."

"We're not in a hurry, Lois," the pastor's wife assured her. "We don't have any plans for the evening."

Lois studied the floral pattern in the carpet. Should she tell them why she was feeling so uptight? She felt sure they would hold in confidence whatever she told them. Besides, she knew they'd counseled several couples recently, some married and some about to be. No doubt they had good insights on men and dating and how to know God's will for finding that special person. Maybe she should get their opinions about Joe.

Lois looked up and smiled. "Actually, you might be able to help."

"Let's go to the study, then," Pastor Hanson suggested.

Once they were in the office, Lois took a seat across from the Hansons. "I've recently met a clown," she began.

The pastor chuckled. "You've just met a guy and already labeled him as a clown?"

Lois smiled. "No, he really is a clown." She leaned forward in the chair. "Joe Richey is a gospel clown, and I met him at a crusade at Westside Community Church a few weeks ago. He sort of fell into my lap."

The pastor's eyebrows shot up. "Oh?"

"You see—I told God that if He wanted me to find a man, He'd have to drop him into my lap." She paused then related the rest of the story, including the part about the little girl rolling into Joe and knocking him over.

The pastor and his wife laughed.

"That must have been quite a sight," Norma Hanson said.

"It was pretty embarrassing. Especially when Joe landed in my lap."

"I can imagine," she agreed kindly.

"After the program, Tabby and Seth invited me to join them for dessert at a nearby restaurant, and Joe showed up. I was wondering if Tabby planned the whole thing, but she said no when I asked her a few days later."

Pastor Hanson leaned forward on his desk. "Changing the subject for a minute—and we'll get back to it—I was wondering if you've heard anything from Tabby and Seth since they went on tour."

"Only once. Tabby called to say their group was in Baker City, Oregon, and they were having successful revival services. She said they might stay on the road a few more weeks."

"That's good news. I hope the rest of their trip goes as well," Pastor Hanson said.

"So do I."

"Now back to your clown. What's troubling you about him?" he asked.

Lois drew in a breath and let it out quickly. "Joe and I have gone out a few times since we met, and even though I don't know him well yet, I really like him."

"Well, that's good, Lois. You know we were hoping you would get out more. I'm sure you're talking with the Lord about this."

She nodded. "Oh, yes. I've done nothing but pray. The trouble is that I haven't received any answers, and I'm not sure whether Joe returns my feelings."

"What makes you think that?" Mrs. Hanson asked.

"He dropped me off after our date last Saturday and, after a quick kiss on the cheek, said, 'See you, Lois.'" She swallowed against the lump lodged in her throat. "He hasn't called all week, and I'm worried he won't."

"Because he didn't say he'd call, or you're just not sure he will?"

"A little of both," she admitted. "Anyway, I'm planning to drive to Olympia tomorrow, and since Joe lives in Olympia—"

"You thought you'd try to see him," the pastor said, finishing Lois's sentence.

She nodded.

"I'm not sure I believe it's always the man's place to pursue a relationship, though that's what worked best for Norma and me. And since I don't know Joe personally, I can't say how he would respond to your visiting him." He looked at her. "Did you plan to call first?"

"I don't have his phone number or address, so I'll need to get them from the Olympia phone book once I'm in town." Lois shrugged. "I'm not sure I should drop by without calling first." She looked down at her hands. "Besides, he may not want to see me anyway."

"Why do you think that, Lois?" Mrs. Hanson asked. "Didn't he enjoy your dates?"

"He seemed to, but then Joe always appears to be having a good time. He's a goofy guy who likes to laugh and make wisecracks and do silly things." Lois blinked against the burning at the back of her eyes. She didn't want to break down in front of the pastor and his wife. "Joe makes me laugh and feel carefree. It's something I've never felt with any other guy."

"Would you like our opinion, or do you feel better after talking about it?" the pastor asked.

"I'd like your opinion, if you wouldn't mind sharing it," Lois said.

"If it were me, I'd probably get Joe's phone number and call him. Tell him you're in town, and if he invites you to stop by, you'll know he wants to see you again."

"And I agree with Sam, Lois," Mrs. Hanson said. "I think that's a good idea."

Lois sighed with relief. That's what she had thought, too, but it helped hearing it from them. Calling first would be much better than barging in unannounced. If Joe didn't want to see her, at least she would be spared the humiliation of looking him in the face when he told her so.

Lois stood up, a smile on her face. "Thanks for taking the time to listen."

Pastor Hanson smiled. "We'll be praying for you, Lois."

His wife gave her a hug. "Everything will work out fine. You can be sure of that."

❧

Joe felt tired and out of sorts, although he never would have admitted it. On Monday he'd put on an hour-long program at a senior center, plus two kids' birthday parties the following day. This morning he had another party to do.

"Well, I'm glad people want me for my clowning and the balloon animals, especially for parties," he said aloud. "But I don't feel nearly as fulfilled as when I can present the gospel, too. Oh, well, it does help pay the bills," he reminded himself.

He zipped up his rainbow-colored clown suit, recalling the squeals of delight from the younger children when he'd worn it to a party. He put on a fuzzy wig with different shades of blue and a cone-shaped hat streaked with lots of colors. Joe had contrived many of his costumes, most of them from rummaging through thrift stores. A professional seamstress at his church had made the other ones, including the one he wore now.

Joe remembered asking his mother to make his first costume. He knew she could sew and thought she might enjoy taking part in his ministry, but she'd refused and then scolded him for expecting her to work her "fingers to the bones" and get nothing in return.

"Did your love always have to be conditional, Mom?" Joe murmured as he studied his reflection in the mirror on the back of his closet door. "Couldn't you have supported me and offered your love freely?"

Joe stuck out his tongue at the clown he saw staring back at him. At least he could hide behind the makeup, which had taken him nearly an hour to apply. His nonsensical costume took only five minutes to don, but it made him appear to be someone else. From the minute he dipped his finger into the jar of grease paint and slapped some of the goop onto his face, Joe was in character. Even though he knew deep inside that he would always be little Joey Richey, who could never please his mother, everyone seemed to love him when he was a clown.

"Forget about Mom and how she made you feel," Joe said, as if he were speaking to someone else. "She's gone now, and it's best for you to put on a happy face." He smiled at the image in the mirror then turned to leave when he heard the phone ring.

"Joe Richey here," he said.

"Hi, Joe. It's Lois."

Joe felt his heart slam into his chest at the sound of Lois's voice. He'd wanted to call her all week, but somehow he hadn't found the time. "Hey, Lois. What's up?"

"I'm in Olympia. I came to see my folks and thought if you weren't busy maybe we could get together while I'm here."

Joe frowned. He'd like nothing better than to be with Lois. If he'd had his way, they would find something fun to do and spend the whole day together. But he couldn't. He had a birthday party to do, and afterward he was supposed to meet with someone at the hospital about doing a special program for some of the staff next week.

"I'm busy today, Lois," Joe said. Did she know how much it pained him to turn her down?

"Oh, I see. Well, I thought it was worth a try. Guess I'll let you go, then. 'Bye, Joe."

"No, don't hang—" It was too late. The phone went dead. Lois hadn't given him a chance to explain. She probably thought he didn't want to see her.

"Oh, no! I can't call her back—I don't know where she was calling from." Joe snapped off his bedroom light. "I'll have to wait until next week when I can drive to Tacoma and try to straighten things out." He hurried out of the door, still wishing he could have explained.

❁

Lois left the phone booth and climbed back into her car. Feeling the weight of Joe's rejection, she let her head drop against the steering wheel. Each breath stung as she struggled to keep from dissolving into tears. It was exactly as she feared. Joe didn't want to see her anymore, and he was too polite to come right out and say so. If only he'd been more direct the other night when he'd taken her home from the Puyallup Fair, she wouldn't have called him at his home. He probably thought she was chasing after him.

She'd been foolish to let Joe steal her heart so soon. The happy clown's warm smile and carefree manner had captured her senses, but Lois knew she would have to be more careful from now on. She needed to guard her heart and her feelings.

Chapter 10

It was Monday morning, and Lois had been staring at her computer screen for the last five minutes, unable to type a single word. She needed to finish Pastor Hanson's sermon, since he'd given her his notes when she first arrived at work. She also had a stack of mail to go through, but Lois wasn't in the mood to do any of it. She was still feeling the pain of Joe's rejection. If only they could have met for a few minutes on Saturday, to talk and maybe share a meal. Would it have made any difference if they had? Tossing the question around in her mind brought no relief from Lois's frustrations. With sheer determination, she forced her thoughts off Joe and onto the work she needed to do.

By noon Lois had managed to catch up, and she decided to go out to lunch, hoping it would brighten her day. The deli was close to the church, and she could order her favorite veggie sandwich. She'd be glad when Tabby came back so she wouldn't have to eat alone.

❦

Joe hurried up the front steps of Bayview Christian Church. He hoped he wasn't too late. It was noon, and Lois might have already left for lunch. He drew in a breath as he opened the door, suddenly colliding with someone.

"Joe!"

"Lois!"

"What are you doing here?"

"I came to see you."

She took a step backward. "You did?"

He nodded. "I needed to explain about Saturday. You hung up before I had the chance to tell you why we couldn't get together." He looked at her. "Are you all right? I didn't mean to bump into you like that. I guess I was rushing too much."

"I'm okay. I'm on my way to lunch now," she said, turning away.

He touched her arm. "Mind if I join you?"

She shrugged. "I—I suppose we could talk at the deli down the street. That's where I was planning to eat."

Joe's stomach growled at the mention of lunch. He hadn't eaten a decent breakfast that morning because he'd been in such a hurry to get to Tacoma and see Lois. "That sounds good to me."

Lois led the way, and soon they were seated in a booth at the deli. Joe ordered a hamburger, fries, and a cola, while Lois asked for her favorite sandwich and a glass of iced tea.

They ate in silence for the first few minutes, and Joe used the time to study the young woman sitting across from him. A few pale freckles dappled her cute, upturned nose. Funny, he'd never noticed them before. *Maybe I should pay more attention to details.*

Joe knew he couldn't stall forever. It was time for him to explain about Saturday. If he didn't, they might spend the rest of their lunch without talking. He had a feeling Lois was pretty miffed at him. "I was on my way out to do a kid's birthday party when you called the other day. Later I had to see one of the men on the hospital board about doing a program at their staff meeting next week. That's why I didn't have time to get together with you when you were in Olympia." He winked and offered Lois what he hoped was his best smile. "Am

I forgiven for not explaining then and for not calling after our last date? I was really bogged down all week."

Was that a look of relief he saw on Lois's face? She'd seemed so tense only a moment ago, but now she was smiling.

"Thanks for explaining, Joe. I thought maybe you didn't want to see me anymore or that you'd rather I not come to your house." Her gaze dropped to the table. "I figured you might be afraid for me to meet your family."

He reached across the table and took her hand. "I live alone. I have ever since my mother died from lung cancer a year ago."

"I'm sorry about your mother. I should have remembered you said both of your parents were gone."

"Would you like to go out with me this Saturday?" he asked, abruptly changing the subject.

"What did you have in mind?" Her forehead wrinkled. "I hope you weren't planning to take me for another roller coaster ride."

He shook his head. "Not in the real sense of the word. Besides, I think our relationship has already had a few ups and downs."

He saw her throat constrict as she swallowed. "Does that mean we have a relationship?"

"I hope so." He grinned and wagged his finger. "About our Saturday date—"

"Yes?"

"It's a surprise, so you'll have to wait and see where I'm taking you."

"At least tell me how I'm supposed to dress."

"Wear something casual. Maybe a pair of blue jeans and a sweatshirt." He nodded toward the window. "As you can see by the falling leaves, autumn is here, so there's a good chance the weather will be chilly and rainy."

"What time will you pick me up?"

"How does eleven o'clock in the morning sound?"

"I'll be ready."

❀

An hour later, Lois was seated in front of her desk, feeling satisfied. Not only had she eaten a terrific lunch, but things were okay with her and Joe, and they were going out again. So much for her plan to guard her heart.

Lois tried to rein in her thoughts and concentrate on a list of names she needed to contact regarding church business, but an image of Joe's smiling face kept bobbing in front of her. She realized they had little in common, with his being a clown and her being Miss Serious. But he made her laugh, and she thought he could probably charm the birds right out of the trees.

Lois could feel the knots forming in her shoulders. She wondered if she'd be able to discard her fears and trust Joe not to hurt her. She hoped she could because she was beginning to care for him.

The telephone rang, halting Lois's thoughts. She needed to stay focused on her job. "Bayview Christian Church," she answered.

"Lois, is that you?"

"Tabby?"

"The one and only," her sister answered. "How are you doing?"

"Fine. How about you and Seth? Will you be coming back to Tacoma soon?"

"That's the reason I'm calling. We've decided to stay on tour awhile longer. I checked in with Donna earlier, and she says everything's fine at the day care."

"I've heard that, too."

"Seth's a little worried about his ventriloquist shop, but he was caught up on all repairs before we left, so I think it will be okay if he's gone another few weeks."

"I'm sure it will be fine," Lois agreed.

"What's new with you?" Tabby asked, changing the subject. "Did that cute, funny clown ever call?"

"Yes, and we've gone on a couple of dates. In fact, he's taking me out again this Saturday."

"That's great. Where are you going?"

"Joe said it was a surprise." Lois drew in a breath then released it in a contented sigh. "I don't see how he could top our last date."

"Where'd you go?"

"To the Puyallup Fair, and Joe talked me into riding the roller coaster."

Tabby's sharp intake of breath indicated her reaction. "And you lived to tell about it?"

"It turned out to be a lot of fun," Lois admitted. "I think I've finally overcome my fear of the crazy ride."

"That's wonderful. I'm glad you and Joe are getting along so well. You two should be good for each other."

"What's that supposed to mean?"

"You tend to be a bit solemn sometimes, and Joe's playfulness will help you see the humorous side of life. Joe's a big kidder, so your serious side should give him some new perspectives."

Lois nodded, not even caring that Tabby couldn't see her reaction. Her sister was right. Lois definitely could use more joy in her life, but Joe more serious? Was that even possible?

Chapter 11

A s Joe prepared for his date with Lois, he began to have second thoughts. He enjoyed her company. More than he had any other woman he'd ever dated, in fact. He knew she was a Christian, and he was physically attracted to her, but something was holding him back. Was it the serious side of Lois that bothered him, or the personal questions she'd asked him? Joe never talked to anyone about his mother's emotional problems, his brother's leaving home, or even the details of his parents dying. It was too painful, and he'd found his own way of dealing with it, so why dredge up the past? Yet several times, when he and Lois had gone out, she'd brought up his family. So far, he'd managed to distract her or change the subject, but how long could he put her curiosity on hold?

Joe hopped into his truck and slammed the door. "Guess I'll have to keep her too busy laughing to ask any serious questions today."

❀

Lois grabbed her sweater and an umbrella from the stand. She'd looked out her living room window and saw Joe pull up to the curb in front of the apartment complex. It was fifteen minutes after he'd said he would be there, so she hurried out the door, glad her apartment was on the ground floor and within easy reach of the street.

"I would have come to the door to get you," Joe said when she opened his truck door and slid into the passenger's seat.

"I was ready and figured it would save time."

"Looks like you came prepared." He nodded toward her umbrella.

Lois glanced out the window at the cloudy sky. "Even though it's not raining at the moment, it could be later on."

"You're probably right," he agreed.

"So where are we heading?"

"Remember? It's a surprise."

Lois glanced at her blue jeans and peach-colored knit top. Joe had told her to wear something casual for their date, so she hoped she looked okay. He was dressed in a pair of jeans and a pale blue sweatshirt, which probably meant they weren't going anywhere fancy. Relieved, she leaned against the headrest and decided to enjoy the ride. She had a habit of worrying over little things, but being around Joe was helping her relax.

By the time they turned onto the freeway and headed north, Lois's curiosity was piqued. Were they going to Seattle? Whidbey Island? Vancouver? She was about to ask, but Joe posed a question just then.

"Heard anything from your sister and brother-in-law lately?"

She nodded. "Tabby called me the other day. She said their evangelistic tour has been quite successful, so they've decided to keep on going for a couple of more weeks."

Joe tapped the steering wheel with both thumbs. "That's great. Maybe I should have gone with them. It's always rewarding to put on a gospel program and see folks turn their lives over to the Lord."

"I've heard Tabby say that many times," Lois agreed. "Sometimes I feel jealous when she tells me how many people accept Christ after one of their performances."

"Why would you feel jealous?"

She sighed deeply. "My sister is using her talents for the Lord and helping people find a personal relationship with Him. That's part of what she and Seth do. I, on the other hand, have no talents to share."

"You're a secretary for the church, right?"

"Yes," she said, nodding, "but it doesn't seem like much."

"Not everyone has the ability to type, file, organize, and keep an office running smoothly. I'd say that's a talent in itself."

"You may be right, but it's not the same thing as what you and Tabby and Seth are involved in." Lois paused a moment. "Sometimes I think I should pursue some kind of Christian ministry that could be part of a gospel presentation."

Joe reached across the seat for her hand. "How about becoming a gospel clown? There's always room for one more."

She giggled. "Me?"

"Yes, you."

"I don't know the first thing about clowning."

"You don't have to. There are plenty of classes you can take. In fact, I'll be teaching one at a seminar in Bremerton next month." He winked at her. "It might be fun to have someone enrolled in my class who likes to ride roller coasters and eat cotton candy."

She swatted his arm playfully. "You're the one who likes to do those things, silly. I was coerced into riding the roller coaster, and one bite of cotton candy was enough to last me all day."

"I stand corrected," he said with a chuckle. "Think about what I said, Lois. Even if you decide clowning isn't for you, I promise it'll be a fun class."

"I'll consider it. Thanks for telling me about it."

❧

Half an hour later, Joe exited the freeway and headed toward the Seattle Center. He was glad their conversation had been kept light and upbeat. Lois hadn't once mentioned his past. Of course, he'd kept her busy listening to his stories about the birthday parties he'd recently done, and then he'd told her several corny jokes.

"Ah-ha! So you're taking me to the Seattle Center!" Lois exclaimed.

"Yep. Sound like fun?" He glanced over to gauge her reaction.

She offered him a pleasant smile. "More carnival rides?"

"Nope—the Space Needle!"

Her mouth dropped open like a broken hinge. "You're kidding, right?"

He shook his head. "I thought we'd eat lunch in the restaurant up there. We can enjoy the magnificent view of Puget Sound."

Lois's face paled. "Uh, I really would rather eat at the food court, with my feet on solid ground."

Joe laughed. "Don't tell me you're afraid to go up in the Space Needle."

"Okay, I won't tell you that."

"Scared we might have an earthquake while we're in the elevator heading to the top?" he teased.

"I hadn't even thought about that prospect." Lois gripped the edge of the seat. "How about if I wait on the ground while you check out the beautiful sights?"

He shook his head. "No way! I planned to do something special for this date, and I aim to see it through to the finish."

When Lois didn't reply, he glanced her way again. She was leaning against the headrest with her eyes closed. "Lois, are you asleep?"

Her eyes snapped open, and she shot him a pleading look. "I don't want to go to the Space Needle for lunch. I'm not up to it today."

Not up to it? What exactly was Lois saying? "Want to explain?" he asked.

"I'm afraid of heights, Joe. I have been ever since I was a little girl and my dad took me to the top of the Space Needle."

"But you're all grown up now," he argued. "And I won't let anything happen to you—I promise. Besides, you went on the roller coaster at the Puyallup Fair, and that's pretty high off the ground."

She shot him an exasperated look. "That wasn't half as high as the Space Needle, and it was moving at such rapid speeds. I didn't have time to think about how high I was."

"How about this—we'll go up and see the sights then come right back down and have lunch at the food court. Does that sound okay?"

"Lunch at the food court would be great, but I'm still not sure about going up in that needle."

"It'll be a breeze."

"Anything like riding the roller coaster?"

"You said you had fun."

"I did, after I got over my initial fear," she admitted.

"This won't be any different. Once you take in the beautiful scenery below, you'll be begging me to bring you back for another ride to the top of the world."

"Okay. I'm not thrilled about it, but I'll give it a try," Lois said with a deep sigh.

They pulled into a parking lot near the Seattle Center, and Joe found a spot before she could change her mind. He felt confident that once they were on the observation deck she would relax and enjoy her surroundings.

❀

Lois fidgeted and pulled nervously on the straps of her purse as they stood inside the enclosed area, waiting for the next elevator to take them to the top. "The top of the world." Wasn't that what Joe had called it? *I only hope I don't do something stupid up there. What if I get dizzy when I look down? What if I don't look down and still feel faint? What if—?*

Joe slipped his arm around Lois and tickled her ribs. "It's going to be okay. Trust me."

She squirmed, giggled, and tickled him back. The distraction was helping her relax. Each time Lois was with Joe, she liked him more. He could make her laugh, and he'd convinced her to ride the roller coaster. Now she was standing at the foot of the Space Needle. Was there no end to this man's persuasions?

The elevator door zipped open, and the attendant ushered them in. Lois felt herself being crowded to the back of the elevator, as the elevator filled with people. Joe's arm tightened around her waist, and she leaned into him and whispered, "I hope I don't live to regret this."

He chucked her under the chin. "You'll be fine."

"I sure hope so."

Without warning, Joe bent his head and kissed Lois's lips, snatching her breath away and causing her arms to go limp at her sides. Before she had time to regain her bearings, they were at the top, and Joe had pulled away.

"Here we are," he announced.

Lois gulped and took a tentative step forward. Mount Rainier and everything in the distance radiated beauty beyond compare, but the things directly below resembled ants, toy cars, and tiny buildings that looked like children's blocks. A wave of dizziness hit her, and she inhaled deeply, hoping to squelch the dizzy feeling before she toppled over.

"You doing okay?" Joe asked as he pulled Lois closer to his side.

"I—I feel kind of strange."

"It's the gorgeous view. It takes your breath away, doesn't it?"

She pressed her lips together and stood there like a statue.

"Come on! Let's go to the railing and see what we can see."

Before Lois could respond, Joe grabbed her hand and pulled her away from the wall where she'd been hovering. A few seconds later they were standing on the edge of the world. At least that's how it felt to Lois. Joe was right. The roller coaster at the fair had been child's play compared to this. Even though the rails were enclosed, Lois felt as if she might tumble over the edge to her death. No way could she stay up here long enough to eat lunch in the revolving restaurant!

"Can we go back down now?"

Joe didn't seem to hear what Lois was saying, as he whistled some silly tune and studied the panorama below.

Lois stood slightly behind him, leaning into his back, and praying she wouldn't pass out. She closed her eyes, hoping it would make her feel better, but the knowledge of where she stood was enough to make her head spin.

After what seemed like an eternity, Joe turned to face her. "Have you seen enough?"

Lois had seen more than she cared to see. She headed toward the nearest elevator and was thankful they didn't have to wait as long as they had when they went up. She breathed a sigh of relief when the elevator door opened.

"That was awesome!" Joe announced as they stepped inside. "We were up so high I think I saw some of the passengers' faces looking out of the window in a jet that whizzed by."

Lois moaned. How could Joe make a joke at a time like this? Didn't he realize she'd nearly died of fright up there?

"Hey, you know what I think?"

She glared at him. "I can't imagine."

"Maybe we should go up in a plane for our next date."

"You have to be kidding!"

"I love being in the air. The only thing I don't like about plane travel is the waiting and, of course, having some airline personnel go through my belongings." Joe chuckled. "Airport security has been really tight lately. In fact, the last time I boarded a plane, they confiscated my most important possession."

"Really—what was that?" Lois asked, feeling a little better now that they were heading for solid ground again.

Joe's lips curved into a dopey little smile. "My sharp wit!"

Chapter 12

The rest of the day in Seattle passed swiftly. Joe bought Lois a souvenir replica of the Space Needle, to remind her she'd actually gone up in it, and they ate lunch at the food court, sharing a Mexican dish large enough for two. After walking around the entire Seattle Center and enjoying the sights and sounds, Joe suggested they go to the waterfront.

Lois loved the salty smell of the bay and eagerly agreed. The next several hours were spent browsing the various gift shops, touring the aquarium, and finally having fish and chips at Ivar's Fish Bar. Now they were on their way home, and Lois dreaded having to tell Joe good-bye. She enjoyed being with him and wondered if she could love him. It amazed her sometimes that he could see the humor in almost any situation.

Leaning her head against the window, Lois closed her eyes and relived the memory of Joe mimicking the seals they'd seen at the aquarium. He'd done everything but stand on his head to get them to bark and slap their fins against the wooden deck when they begged for food.

"What's that little smile about?" Joe asked, breaking into Lois's thoughts.

She opened her eyes and glanced over at him. "I was thinking about how much fun I had today."

Joe grinned like a Cheshire cat. "You mean you're not mad at me for dragging you into the Space Needle?"

Her lower lip protruded. "Well, maybe a little. . ."

"But I kept you well entertained the rest of the day, and you've decided to forgive me, right?"

She nodded and smiled.

"Maybe we can go to Snoqualmie Falls for our next date," he suggested. "We'd better do it soon, though, 'cause it's almost October, and the weather will be turning cold and damp soon."

Lois's heartbeat quickened. Joe wanted to see her again, and he was already talking about where they might go. "I haven't been up to the falls in ages. It's beautiful there, and we could take a picnic lunch."

His forehead wrinkled. "Since the weather is turning colder, and rain is a likely possibility, I'm not sure the picnic idea would fly, unless we eat in my truck."

She agreed. "A picnic lunch inside your truck sounds like a great idea."

"When would you like to go?" Joe asked.

"I'm pretty flexible. It's your hectic schedule we'll need to plan around. When will you have another free Saturday?"

He shrugged. "I'd better check my appointment book after I get home. I'll give you a call as soon as I know which day will work best."

"Sounds good to me," she said.

❋

Joe was glad they'd made it through the day without Lois's asking too many personal questions. Maybe she had given up on the idea of digging into his past and decided they could simply have a good time whenever they were together. That was all he wanted, wasn't it—just to enjoy Lois's company? No strings attached and no in-depth conversations about confidential things. It was too painful to talk about the past. Joe had managed fine all these years by clowning around, and he wasn't about to let his guard down now.

"Would you like to come in for a cup of coffee before you head back on the road?" Lois asked as they stopped in front of her apartment complex.

He smiled. "Sure, that would be great." Joe hopped out of the truck and sprinted around to the other side to help Lois down.

As they strolled up the front sidewalk, Joe noticed a broken beer bottle lying in the grass. "Looks like folks choose to litter no matter where they live," he muttered.

"I know," Lois said. "My apartment manager does his best to keep the yard free of debris, but it's almost a full-time job."

Joe bent down to pick up the shattered glass. "I'll carry this in and drop it in your garbage can, if that's all right."

"Sure. It will be one less thing for poor Mr. Richards to face in the morning."

In Joe's hurry to retrieve what was left of the bottle, he didn't notice the jagged edge and cut his hand. "Ouch!" He cringed and dropped the piece of glass as a sharp pain shot through his hand then continued up his arm. "Guess I should be more careful when I'm playing with glass."

Lois frowned. "Here—let me take a look at that." She reached for Joe's hand, and a stream of dark blood oozed between his fingers and landed on her palm. "Oh, my! That looks like a nasty cut. I think you may need stitches."

Joe shrugged it off as though it were no more than a pinprick. "Naw, it'll be fine once we get inside and I can wash my hand and slap on a bandage."

She gave him a dubious look, then handed over a clean handkerchief she'd taken from her purse. "Wrap this around the wound until we get indoors."

"What about the broken glass?"

"You'd better leave it for now. At the moment we have more pressing things to worry about."

Joe followed Lois to her apartment door. She unlocked the door and opened it for him to enter.

"I have antiseptic and bandages in the bathroom." Lois motioned to the kitchen table. "Have a seat and I'll get my first-aid kit."

"I can manage," Joe mumbled. "Just point the way to the bathroom."

"Are you sure you don't want my help? It's going to be difficult to work with only one hand."

He shook his head, although his hand was throbbing like crazy.

"The bathroom's the first door on the left," she said, nodding in that direction.

A few seconds later, Joe stepped into the bathroom, held his hand under the faucet, and turned on the cold water. A river of red poured from the wound. The room seemed to spin around him, and a wave of nausea rushed through his stomach. He leaned against the sink and moaned. "Guess I might need a couple of stitches after all."

"What was that?" Lois called from the other room.

"Could you come here a minute?"

She was at his side in a flash, concern etched on her face. "You look terrible, Joe. Maybe you should put your head between your legs, before you pass out."

"I can't stop the bleeding. I think you were right about my needing stitches." He smiled, but it took effort. "Guess we'll have to postpone our plans to go up to Snoqualmie Falls for a while."

She looked at his hand and shuddered. "It's bleeding badly. I'd better get a towel." Lois opened a small cabinet and withdrew a bath towel. She wrapped it tightly around his hand and led him toward the door. "I'm driving you to the hospital, and you'd better not argue."

"I wouldn't dream of it," he mumbled. Funny, he'd never felt this woozy when he'd seen blood before. Maybe he was getting soft in the head.

Lois slipped one arm around Joe's waist, and they headed outside. "Mind if we take your truck?" she asked. "My car's in the parking garage, and I don't want to take the time to get it."

"Sure—that's fine. The keys are in my left pocket," he said as she helped him into the passenger's seat.

Lois pulled out the keys, hooked Joe's seat belt in place, closed the door, and ran around to the driver's side.

"St. Joseph's Hospital is only a few miles from here," she told him.

"That's good." Joe leaned his head back and tried to conjure up some pleasant thoughts so he wouldn't have to think about the throbbing in his hand or the blood already soaking through the towel.

When Lois parked the truck in front of the emergency room, Joe breathed a sigh of relief. At last he would get some help.

✿

After they checked in at the emergency room desk and filled out forms, Joe and Lois took seats and waited. Apparently, an accident involving three vehicles had occurred across town, and those people were receiving treatment now. The woman at the desk had told Joe he would be examined as soon as possible.

Lois recognized one of the nurses on duty as her neighbor Bonnie McKenzie. She knew from the few conversations she'd had with Bonnie that she worked at St. Joseph's, was single, and dated often. Lois had seen more than a few men come to the apartment building to take out the vibrant redhead.

In a short time, Bonnie called Joe's name.

"I'll wait here, Joe," Lois told him. "You go on back."

"Oh, Lois—won't you come, too?" Joe asked. "I'd really like it if you would."

Before she knew it, Lois was sitting beside the table on which Joe was lying, wishing she could be anywhere else but there. Hospitals made her nervous. They smelled funny, and most of the people who came to the ER were in pain—including Joe. She could see by the pinched expression on his face that he was hurting, although he kept telling jokes while the nurse administered a local anesthetic and cleaned the wound.

"I still can't get over the fact that Tacoma would name one of their hospitals after me," Joe said with a wink.

"What do you mean?" asked Bonnie.

"St. Joseph." Joe chuckled. "You know, if hospitals are places to get well, then tell me this—why do they serve such awful food?"

Before the nurse could respond, a tall man with gray hair entered the room and introduced himself as Dr. Bradshaw. Lois could see by the stern expression on his face that he was strictly business.

The doctor examined Joe's hand and gave the nurse some instructions. "Now lie back and relax, Mr. Richey. This won't hurt."

Joe's head fell back onto the small pillow. "That's because Nurse Bonnie has numbed my hand."

Dr. Bradshaw made no reply but quickly set to work.

Lois turned her head away and studied the wall. She had no desire to watch the doctor put stitches in Joe's hand, even if she was fairly sure he wouldn't feel any pain.

"This is like an operation, isn't it, Nurse Bonnie?" Joe asked.

"I suppose it could be categorized as such," she replied with a chuckle.

"From what I hear, the definition of a minor operation is one that someone else has, so

I guess mine falls into the major operation category," Joe said with a loud guffaw.

Why is he doing this? Can't the man be serious about anything? Lois peeked at Joe, who was grinning from ear to ear. Nurse Bonnie was also smiling, but the doctor's face was a mask of austerity. *At least someone besides me sees the seriousness of all this.*

"We're nearly finished," the doctor said at last.

Lois breathed a sigh of relief, but Joe told another joke. "Does anyone here know what a specialist is?"

"Certainly," the nurse replied. "It's a doctor who devotes himself to some special branch of medicine."

"Not even close," Joe said. "A specialist is a doctor who has all his patients trained so they only get sick during his regular office hours."

Dr. Bradshaw groaned and shook his head, Bonnie chuckled, and Lois just sat there. *Maybe I'm too serious for my own good,* she thought, feeling her cheeks grow warm. *Bonnie obviously thinks Joe's funny, and maybe he's clowning around because it's the only way he knows how to deal with the pain. He could dislike hospitals as much as I do, but he sure does show it in a different way.*

The doctor cleared his throat. "Bandage this fellow's hand then give him a tetanus shot, Miss McKenzie. When I looked at Mr. Richey's chart, I noticed he's overdue for one." He turned and strode out of the room.

Lois noticed that Joe's face had turned white. He pressed his lips into a tight line as the nurse stuck the needle in his arm. Afterward, he plastered another silly grin on his face. "Say, did you hear about the guy who was always getting sick with a cold or the flu?"

Bonnie shrugged her shoulders. "That could be just about anyone."

He nodded. "True, but this guy was shot so full of antibiotics that every time he sneezed he cured half a dozen people."

Bonnie laughed and gave Joe's good hand a little pat. "Be sure to keep that wound clean and watch for infection. If you see anything suspicious, get right back in here."

Joe hopped down from the table. "Sure thing, but I live in Olympia. So if I have any problems the hospital there will probably get my business." He glanced over at Lois and winked. It was the first time he'd looked her way since they'd come into the examining room.

"Ready to go?" Lois asked.

"Ready as I'll ever be. Sure am glad you're driving, though. My left hand feels like it's ten sizes too big with this huge roll of bandage Nurse Bonnie has slapped on me."

"It's for your own good, Mr. Richey," the nurse said as she led them out of the room. "Take care now, and, Lois, I'll probably see you around our apartment complex."

Lois waved to Bonnie and hurried out the door. She was anxious to get outside and breathe some fresh air.

A short time later Lois drove away from the hospital and headed for the freeway. "Hey—where are we going?" Joe asked. "Your place is that way." He pointed with his right hand.

"I'm taking you to Olympia."

His eyebrows shot up. "You're driving my truck—remember?"

"I know that."

"How will you get back to Tacoma? And where will you stay tonight?"

"My dad can pick me up at your house, as soon as I make sure you're okay, and then drive me back tomorrow. I'll stay at their house tonight."

"Why didn't I think of that?" Joe laughed.

Lois smiled. "You just had stitches—remember?"

Chapter 13

Lois woke up feeling groggy and disoriented. It took her a few minutes to realize she was in her old bedroom at her parents' home in Olympia. She yawned, sat up, and glanced at the clock on the table by her bed. It was almost eight o'clock. There was no way she and Dad could drive to Tacoma for her to shower, change, and still make it in time for Sunday school. She would have to call the superintendent and ask him to find a substitute for her class. If she left right away, she might make it for the morning worship service.

Maybe I should call Joe and see if he'd like me to go with him to his church this morning. Then Lois remembered she didn't have a change of clothes since she hadn't planned to stay all night at her parents' home. *The least I can do is give him a call and see how he's doing this morning.*

Lois reached for the telephone and dialed Joe's number.

"Joe Richey here." Joe's deep voice sounded sleepy, and Lois figured she had probably awakened him.

"Hi, it's Lois. I was wondering how your hand is this morning."

"It's still pretty sore, though I think I'll live." He laughed, but it sounded forced. "Thanks for coming to my rescue last night."

"You'd have done the same for me."

"You have that right."

There was a long pause. "Well, I should let you go. I need to spend a few minutes with my parents then hurry back to Tacoma if I'm going to make it in time for church."

"I'd invite you to visit my church with me, but I think it might be best if I lie low today. The doctor said I should ice my hand if there's swelling and try to rest it for the next twenty-four hours."

"That makes sense to me," Lois said. "Is there anything I can do for you before I head home?"

"No, I think I can manage. Thanks for offering, though."

"Guess I'll be seeing you, then."

"Have a safe trip back to Tacoma."

"Thanks. Take care now."

"You too. 'Bye, Lois."

Lois hung up the phone and went down to the kitchen, where she found her parents sitting at the table, drinking coffee.

"There's more in the pot." Dad lifted his mug as she entered the room. Even with his paunchy stomach and thinning blond hair, she still thought her father was attractive.

She smiled and shook her head. "Thanks, Dad. I'd rather have tea."

"There's some in the cupboard above the refrigerator," her mother said. "What would you like me to fix for breakfast?"

"I'll just grab a piece of fruit," Lois replied. "Dad, can you drive me to Tacoma right away?"

His eyebrows lifted. "So soon? What's the rush?"

She took a seat at the table. "I've already missed Sunday school, and I'd like to at least get there in time for church."

Her mother sighed. "Church—church—church. Is that all my two daughters ever think about anymore?"

Lois held back a retort. Instead she smiled and said, "Have you heard from Tabby recently?"

"She sent us a postcard from Moscow, Idaho, a few weeks ago," her mother answered. "Her note said she and Seth were extending their time on the road."

"I'm glad Tabby finally got over her shyness," her dad interjected, "but I don't see why she has to run around the countryside preaching hellfire and damnation."

Lois felt her face flame. Not too many years ago she'd have felt the same way about her sister. But now that she was a Christian, she understood why Tabby wanted to share the good news. "Tabby and Seth don't preach hellfire and damnation, Dad. They share God's love and how people can know Him personally through His Son, Jesus Christ."

Her dad shrugged and rubbed a hand across his chin. "Whatever."

Lois grabbed a banana from the fruit bowl and stood up. "Will you drive me back to Tacoma?"

He nodded curtly. "If that's what you want. You know me—always aim to please."

🌼

It was harder to do things with one hand than Joe had expected. *Maybe I should've asked Lois to come by this morning and fix me a decent breakfast.* He shook his head as he struggled to butter a piece of toast. He hadn't realized until now how dependent he was on using both hands to do simple, basic things. "Guess it wouldn't have been fair to expect her to give up going to church and play nursemaid to me."

Joe dropped into a chair and stared blankly at the Sunday morning newspaper. He'd come to care for Lois. But did he have anything to offer a woman like her? She was sophisticated and beautiful and blessed with a sweet, Christian spirit. She didn't seem prone to mood swings, which probably meant she was nothing like his mother. Still, Joe was holding back from any kind of commitment. What bothered him most was that he had no secure job, never knowing from week to week, month to month, where, when, or even *if* he would be called to do another program. What kind of future did he have to offer a wife?

"A wife?" Joe moaned. "Why am I even thinking about marriage?" After his mother died, he'd told himself he would never marry. Even though he'd been concerned about finding a woman whose emotions were stable, he was even more worried about his inability to support a family. Like Jesus' disciples, Joe lived from month to month on what others gave in payment for the services he rendered as a clown.

He glanced at his Bible, lying beside the newspaper. "I don't need to waste my time on these negative thoughts," he muttered. "I can look in my Bible for verses that remind me to have a merry heart."

🌼

Lois slipped into the pew, realizing she was ten minutes late, but glad she'd made it to church at all. Her dad hadn't been happy about driving her home before he'd read the Sunday newspaper. But at least they'd enjoyed a good visit in the car, though Lois was careful to keep the conversation light and away from religious things. It troubled her the way her parents were so opposed to church and faith in God and even talking about spiritual matters. She wanted them to see their need for Christ's forgiveness of their sins.

If Tabby and I keep praying and showing Mom and Dad we love them, maybe someday it will happen.

Lois opened her hymnbook and joined the congregation in singing "Love Lifted Me."

After a few lines, she felt her burdens become lighter as she thought about how much God loved her. Enough to send His Son to die in her place.

When the service was over, Lois spotted Tabby's friend, Donna, talking to the senior pastor and his wife. Lois waited patiently until they were finished, then she stepped up to Donna and gave her a little nudge. "How's everything with you?"

Donna shrugged. "Okay, but I'll sure be glad when Tabby's back. Things aren't the same without her, and the day care kids miss her something awful."

Lois was about to comment, but Donna cut her off. "Tabby really has a way with children. I think she'll make a good mother someday, don't you?"

Lois nodded. "I agree."

Donna motioned for Lois to move away from the crowd, and the two of them found a spot in one corner of the room. "So what's new in your life?"

"Well, I—"

"Hey, Lois, I'm glad to see you made it to church."

Lois turned and smiled at Dan Gleason, the Sunday school superintendent.

"I asked one of our older teens to take your class, and she said everything went fine," he told her.

"That's great. Thanks for taking care of things on such short notice," Lois responded.

"No problem." Dan grinned and reached up to scratch his head. "Say, I was wondering if you'd be interested in having Carla Sweeney help you every week. She'll graduate from high school in June and wants to find some kind of ministry within the church."

Lois smiled. She would love to have some help with her class. Sometimes she felt she had more kids than she could handle. An extra pair of hands would be helpful when it came to craft time as well. "Sure! Tell Carla I'd be happy to have her as my assistant."

Dan nodded, said good-bye, and walked off. Lois turned back to Donna, but she was gone.

Lois shrugged and headed for the nearest exit. It would be good to get home where she could relax for the rest of the day.

Chapter 14

Lois was sitting in front of her computer at work on Monday morning when she felt someone's hand touch her shoulder. She whirled around and was surprised to see her sister standing there.

"Tabby! When did you get back? Why didn't you call?"

Tabby held up one hand. "Whoa! One question at a time, please."

Lois stood and gave her sister a hug. "It's so good to see you."

"It's great to see you, too. Seth and I got in late last night, which is why I didn't call. I decided to surprise you instead."

"You did that all right." Lois nodded toward the chair next to her desk. "Have a seat and tell me about your trip."

Tabby dropped into the chair and smiled. "It was awesome, Lois. Everywhere we went there were spiritual conversions. I feel so energized—I think I could hike up Mt. Rainier and not even feel winded."

Lois chuckled and gave her sister's arm a gentle squeeze. "Now that I'd like to see."

"Seriously, though, I wish you could have been there to see people asking Jesus into their hearts." Tabby's eyes misted.

"I wish that, too," Lois murmured.

Tabby grinned. "What's new in your life? Are you still seeing Joe Richey?"

Lois nodded. "Up until last Saturday I was. I'm not sure about the future, though."

Tabby's eyebrows furrowed. "Why not?"

"I'm worried that Joe and I might not be suited for one another. He probably needs someone more carefree and fun loving than I am. Maybe I should bow out, before one of us gets hurt."

"Bow out? You have to be kidding! I can see how much you care about Joe. It's written all over your face."

Lois hated to admit it, but Tabby was right. In spite of Joe's refusal to see the serious side of things, she was falling headlong into the tunnel of love.

"Did something happen between you and Joe to make you question your relationship?" Tabby asked.

"Sort of."

"Want to talk about it?"

"I—I guess so." Lois nodded toward her computer screen. "I really should get back to work right now. And you're probably expected in the day care center. Why don't we meet at our favorite spot for lunch, and I'll tell you about it then?"

Tabby stood up. "Sounds good to me." She smiled. "I'll meet you at Garrison's at noon."

Lois watched as Tabby left the room. Her sister walked with a bounce to her step and an assurance she'd never had before she started using her talents to serve the Lord. Talents. There was that word again. Lois couldn't help but envy others like Tabby and Seth who were both ventriloquists, Donna and her beautiful chalk art drawings, and Joe with his gospel clown routines. What could Lois do that would have an impact on people's lives? Were being the church secretary and teaching a Sunday school class enough for her?

You could take the clowning class Joe is scheduled to teach next month, a little voice reminded her. *You won't know if you'd enjoy clowning until you give it a try.*

Lois grabbed her desk calendar and studied the month of October. She didn't have anything penciled in, except a dental appointment, and the church harvest party. "I have the time," she murmured. "The question is, do I have the talent?"

❀

Garrison's Deli was crowded, but Lois and Tabby found a small table in the corner. They both ordered veggie sandwiches and ate as they chatted.

"Tell me what the problem is with you and Joe," Tabby prompted her. "I thought you'd decided it didn't matter whether you and he were equally matched."

Lois shrugged. "I did think that for a while, but the other night Joe cut his hand, and—"

"What happened? Was he hurt bad?"

"He was dropping me off at my apartment, and a bottle was lying in the front yard. When he picked it up, he cut his hand."

Tabby grimaced. "That's terrible. Did he need stitches?"

"Yes, and all during the process he kept cracking jokes." Lois wrinkled her forehead. "I could see by the look on his face that he was pretty stressed out; yet he kept making small talk and telling one joke after another." She sighed. "I guess he was trying to cover up his real feelings, but it made me wonder if he even knows how to be serious."

"Have you ever thought maybe Joe is so used to clowning he doesn't know when to quit? It could be that once you know him better, you'll see another side of the man."

"You think I should keep seeing him?"

"Of course. In the months since you and Michael Yehley broke up, I haven't seen you look so content." Tabby patted Lois's hand. "Instead of hoping Joe will become more serious, why not try to be more lighthearted yourself?"

Lois contemplated her sister's last statement. "You could be right. Maybe I'll take one of Joe's clowning classes and find out how much humor I have inside of me."

❀

It had been a little over a week since Joe had cut his hand. The pain had subsided, and he was finally able to use it again. He'd had only one program in the last week, so that gave him time to allow the injury to heal—and the opportunity to think about his friendship with Lois.

Joe stared at his morning cup of coffee. Was their relationship going anywhere? He thought they'd had a great time at the Seattle Center last Saturday, but after he'd cut his hand and she'd taken him to the hospital, Lois seemed kind of distant. He hoped she wasn't prone to mood swings after all.

An uninvited image flashed onto the screen of Joe's mind, and a hard knot formed in his stomach. He could see himself and his little brother, Brian, sitting on the steps of their front porch. They were blowing bubbles and having a great time. Mom was seated in a wicker chair nearby, doing some kind of needlework. One minute she was laughing and sharing in the joy Joe felt as each bubble formed. But the next minute she was shouting at him. "Do you plan to sit there all day blowing bubbles, Joe, or are you going to weed those flower beds?"

Joe's throat constricted as the vision of his mother became clearer. She was wearing a pair of men's faded blue overalls, and her long, dark hair hung in a braid down her back. Her brown eyes flashed with anger as she jumped up from her seat, marched across the porch and grabbed hold of Joe's ear. "Do you hear me, boy? Why are you wasting the day with those stupid bubbles?"

Tears stung the back of young Joe's eyes as he rose to his feet. "I—I didn't even know you wanted the flower beds weeded."

"Speak up! I can't understand when you mumble!"

"I didn't know you wanted me to do any weeding today," Joe said, much louder this time.

"Of course you knew. I told you that yesterday."

Joe handed his bottle of bubbles to Brian. "You might as well have some fun, even if I have to work all afternoon."

Brian's expression was one of pity, but he took the bubbles and looked away. Joe sauntered down the steps, as though nothing unusual had happened. In fact, by the time he reached the shed where the gardening tools were kept, Joe was whistling a tune.

The sharp ringing of the telephone jolted him back to the present. He was glad for the interruption. It always hurt when he thought about the past. It was difficult to deal with his pain over the way Mom used to be, but at least she'd committed her life to the Lord the night before she died. That was comforting, even though it hadn't erased the agony of the past.

The phone kept on ringing, and Joe finally grabbed the receiver. "Joe Richey here."

"Hi, Joe. It's Lois."

Joe's lips twitched, as he tried to gather his whirling thoughts into some kind of order. "What's up, Lois?"

"I called to see how your hand is doing."

"Much better, thanks," he said, flexing the fingers of the hand that had been cut.

"I'm glad to hear it." There was a long pause. "I also wanted to tell you, Joe, that I've made a decision."

A feeling of apprehension crept up Joe's spine. Was she going to say she didn't want to see him anymore? "What decision is that?"

"It's about that clowning class you'll be teaching in Bremerton next month."

Joe expelled the breath he'd been holding. "What about it?"

"I've decided to take you up on your offer. I want to learn how to be a clown."

Chapter 15

L ois sat in the front row of a classroom with about fifty other people. She held a pen and notebook in her hands and was ready for Slow-Joe the Clown to begin his presentation. Joe swaggered into the room, dressed in a green-and-white-checkered clown costume and wearing white face paint with a red nose. "Good mornin', folks! Glad you could be here today." He spotted Lois, waved, and gave her a quick wink.

She smiled at him but wished he hadn't singled her out.

"The first thing you should know about clowning is that clowns aren't just silly comedians who dress up in goofy costumes to entertain kids." Joe shook his head. "No, clowns are performing artists, and to be a successful clown you need to possess certain skills."

Lois stared down at her hands, now folded in her lap across the notebook. What skills did she have, other than being able to type eighty words a minute, answer the phone with a pleasant voice, and keep the church office running as smoothly as possible? She couldn't juggle balls, twist balloons into cute little animals, or think of anything funny to say. Did she have any business taking this class?

"The first recorded reference to clowning dates back to about 2270 BC," Joe stated. "A nine-year-old reportedly said, 'A jester came to rejoice and delight the heart!' Until the mid-1800s, most clowns wore very little makeup. Many clowns today do wear makeup, and each type of face paint can have some kind of meaning." Joe pointed to his cheek. "Take the white-faced look I'm wearing. Clowns who wear this type of makeup are usually the reserved, refined kind of clown." He offered the audience a lopsided grin. "Of course, there are exceptions to every rule."

Lois's hope began to soar. *Maybe I'm an exception. Maybe I can pretend to be sappy and happy.*

Joe moved over to the board and picked up a piece of chalk. He wrote in bold letters, "What Is a Clown Character?"

Lois smiled to herself. *You. You're a clown character, Joe Richey.*

"Each clown must somehow be different from all the other clowns," Joe said with a note of conviction. "Your unique personality is what will make you stand out from the rest. The makeup and clothes you choose to wear will enhance this creation. Your clown's appearance, way of moving, actions, and reactions are all influenced by your character's personality."

Joe seemed so confident and in his element talking about clowning. Lois picked up her notebook and pen again to take some serious notes.

"Next," Joe said, writing on the board, "ask yourself this question: What do I need to be a great clown? You could add some balloon animals to your routine. Or how about a bright orange vest? A few tricks? Juggling? A pet bird?" He shook his head. "While those are all good props and fun additions to your routines, the things you'll probably need more than anything else are improvisational skills, character development and, most important, a knowledge of the elements of humor."

Lois sighed and placed her notebook back in her lap. *Elements of humor. Sure hope I learn some of those today.*

"Have you ever noticed how we often make assumptions about people based on what they are wearing?" Joe asked. "For instance, picture a man dressed in a pair of faded blue jeans with holes in the knees and a sweatshirt with a college logo on the front. He's wearing paint-stained tennis shoes and a wedding ring on his left hand, and he's holding a cup of coffee in one hand. What do we know about this person?"

"The guy's married and has a college degree, but he's too poor to buy new clothes," a young man in the audience called out.

"Could be," Joe said with a nod. "Anybody else have an idea?"

"The gentleman could be an educated, hard worker who likes to putter around the house," the older woman sitting beside Lois suggested.

Joe smiled. "You may be right. The point is, we can't always judge someone by the clothes he wears. His actions play a major role in defining who he is." Joe turned to the board and wrote, "Your character's appearance and personality must be consistent to seem real." He pivoted back to the audience. "If you dress in black, the audience will expect you to be an elegant or somber character, because clothing conveys a meaning. If you wear a baggy, torn costume, people will get the idea you're a hobo clown." He winked at the audience. "Since most clowns don't make a lot of money, this particular costume would be kind of appropriate."

Lois laughed along with everyone else. The concept of clowning was more complicated than she'd imagined it to be. If she was going to become a gospel clown, she'd have to come up with the kind of character she wanted to be. Next, she would need to find or make a suitable costume—one that would affirm the personality of her clown character. And that was only the beginning. She would still need to find a gimmick like balloon twisting or juggling—and be humorous.

Lois turned and glanced at the clock on the back wall. In fifteen minutes the class would be dismissed for a break. She wondered if she should head back to Tacoma or force herself to sit through the rest of Joe's class, hoping she might find some sense of direction.

"The more outrageous your personality, the more outlandish your costume should be," Joe said. "Contrary to popular belief, a good clown outfit is not a mixture of mismatched, odd-sized clothes. A costume you design, using your own choice of colors and prints, becomes your trademark."

Joe moved to the front of the room. "Here's an example of what I mean." He withdrew several balloons from his pocket, quickly blew up each one, and twisted them until he'd made something that resembled a hat. He then proceeded to add several curled balloons, sticking them straight up. He placed the hat on his head. The audience laughed, and Joe looked at the end of his nose so his eyes were crossed. "I'm so thankful I'm not bald anymore. Now I can change my name from Joe to Harry."

Joe Richey was not only a clown by profession, but he was also the funniest man Lois had ever known. Not that she knew him all that well, she reminded herself. In the short time they'd been dating, he'd told her very little about himself. She wondered why.

When the class was dismissed at the break, several people surrounded Joe, pelting him with questions. Lois knew this was her chance to escape. Joe wouldn't know she was gone until the next session began. She left the room, headed for the front door of the church then stopped. Did she want to leave? How would she know if she had the ability to become a clown if she didn't stay and learn more?

She turned and headed for the snack bar. She would grab a cup of tea and a cookie and march back into that classroom and soak up all the information she could.

The class was over at five o'clock, and Lois was tempted to linger. She wanted to spend a few minutes alone with Joe, but he was busy answering more questions and demonstrating some of his balloon techniques. She decided to head for home, knowing it would take almost an hour to get back to Tacoma. Tomorrow was Sunday, and she still had a little preparing to do for her Sunday school class craft. She would have to talk to Joe some other time.

❧

Joe thought Lois would wait after class, but when he finished talking to the last student he discovered she was gone. Had she been in such a hurry to get back to Tacoma that she couldn't even say good-bye?

He shrugged and grabbed up his notes. *Maybe it's my fault. I should have told her earlier that I wanted to take her to dinner.*

Joe was fairly certain Lois had enjoyed his class; he'd caught her laughing whenever he looked her way. He'd also seen her taking notes. Was she interested in pursuing a career in gospel clowning, or had she taken the class only out of curiosity?

Maybe she did it for a lark. Could be Lois has no more interest in clowning than she does me. Joe slapped the side of his hand with his palm. "Oh, man! You shouldn't have made any reference to clowns being poor. That's probably what turned her off."

Joe pulled himself to his full height and plastered a smile on his face. *Get a grip. It's not like Lois said she doesn't want to see you anymore. Besides, I'm supposed to be happy, not sad. Isn't that what clowns do best?*

Chapter 16

For the next two weeks, Lois studied her notes from Joe's clowning class, in hopes of doing a short skit for her Sunday school class. Joe had called her a few times, but he hadn't asked her out; he said he was swamped with gospel programs and kids' birthday parties.

Lois missed not seeing him, but she kept busy practicing her clowning routine and had even made a simple costume to wear. The outfit consisted of a pair of baggy overalls, a straw hat with a torn edge, a bright red blouse, and a pair of black rubber boots, all of which gave her a hillbilly look.

Finally, Sunday morning arrived, and Lois stood in the first-grade classroom, dressed in her costume, waiting for the children and her helper to arrive. She'd worn her hair in two ponytails with red ribbons tied at the ends, and had pencilled in a cluster of dark freckles on her cheeks and nose. In an attempt to make her mouth appear larger, she had taken bright red lipstick and filled in her lips then gone an inch outside with color. She also wore a red rubber clown nose.

Lois's main concern was the skit she'd prepared. Had she memorized it well enough? Could she ad-lib if necessary? Would the kids think it was funny, yet still grasp the gospel message?

Feeling a trickle of sweat roll down her forehead, she reached into her back pocket and withdrew a man-sized handkerchief. She wiped the perspiration away and was stuffing the cloth into her pocket when the children started pouring into the room. "Look! Miss Lois is dressed like a clown!" one girl squealed.

"Yeah! A clown is here!" another child called out.

"Are you gonna make us a balloon animal?"

"Can you juggle any balls?"

"How about some tricks?"

The questions came faster than Lois could answer. She held up her hand to silence the group, looking around frantically for Carla Sweeney, the teenager who had promised to help. "If you'll all take a seat, I'll answer each of your questions one at a time."

The children clambered to the tables, and as soon as they were seated, their little hands shot up. Lois answered each child, letting them know she couldn't juggle, didn't know how to make balloon animals, and had no tricks up her sleeve. She did, however, have a skit to present. Relief flooded her when Carla slipped into the room, and before the children could fire more questions at her, Lois launched into her routine.

Using an artificial flower and a child's doctor kit, she did a pantomime, showing how the flower was sick and needed healing. She then explained out loud how the idea was compared to people who have things in their lives that make them sin-sick. "Jesus is the Great Physician," she said. "He will take away our sins if we ask Him to forgive us."

The children seemed to grasp the message, but they weren't spellbound, as the audience was when she'd seen Joe perform.

After class Lois washed her face, changed out of her costume, and slipped into a dress to wear to church. *Maybe I need to take another clowning class. I could learn how to juggle or maybe do some tricks. . .anything to leave a better impression.*

After church, Lois went with Tabby and Seth to dinner at a restaurant along the waterfront. As soon as they were seated, Seth informed Lois that this was the place he and Tabby had eaten after returning from their first date in Seattle.

Sitting at the table overlooking the beautiful bay, Lois couldn't help but feel a little jealous of her sister. She was married to her soul mate and glowed like a sunbeam. Lois knew she was still young and had plenty of time to find the right guy, but she didn't want to wait. She'd met a Christian man—one who made her laugh and feel accepted and who didn't seem to care about wealth, power, or prestige. She saw only one problem: Joe kidded around so much that she didn't think he'd ever take their relationship seriously.

"Lois, did you hear what I said?"

Tabby's pleasant voice halted Lois's disconcerting thoughts. She turned away from the window and offered her sister a halfhearted smile. "Sorry. I guess I was deep in thought."

"Tabby and I have an announcement to make," Seth declared.

Lois lifted her eyebrows. "I hope you're not leaving on another trip. I really missed you guys while you were gone."

Tabby shook her head. "I think we'll be sticking close to home for the next several months."

"Yeah—seven to be exact," Seth put in. He slipped his arm around Tabby and drew her close.

Lois narrowed her eyes. "I don't get it. Why will you be staying close to home for the next seven months?"

Before Tabby could reply, the light suddenly dawned. "Are you expecting a baby?"

Her sister nodded, and tears welled up in her eyes. "The baby's due in the spring."

With mixed emotions, Lois reached across the table and grasped Tabby's hand. "Congratulations!" She glanced over at Seth. "I'm happy for both of you."

Lois was delighted to hear her sister's good news. It meant she would soon be an aunt, and Tabby deserved the opportunity to be a mother. But somewhere inside was her own desire to be married and have a family. She only hoped it would happen someday. "You'll both make good parents," she said sincerely.

"Sure hope so, 'cause we're really excited about this," Tabby said.

The waitress came to take their order, interrupting the conversation.

"I put on a little clowning skit for my Sunday school class this morning," Lois said, after the waitress left the table.

Tabby's eyebrows shot up. "Really? What prompted that?"

"I took one of Joe's clowning classes a few weeks ago."

"You never said a word about it," Tabby said, shaking her finger at her sister.

"I wanted to see if I could do it before saying anything."

"So how'd it go?" Seth asked.

Lois shrugged. "Okay, I guess. The kids seemed to get the message, but I think they were disappointed because I didn't do anything exciting, like balloon twisting, juggling, or some kind of trick."

"If you think clowning is something you want to pursue, maybe you should take another class or two," Tabby suggested.

"I hear there's going to be a workshop in Portland next weekend," Seth said. "A clown from Salem will be teaching the class. He has a bubble-blowing specialty he's added to his routines. Should be interesting."

Lois leaned forward, smiling. "I might look into that one. I think blowing bubbles would be a whole lot easier than creating balloon animals."

Tabby snickered. "As I recall, you always did enjoy waving your wand around the backyard and seeing how many bubbles you could make at one time."

Lois laughed. "And you liked to see how many you could pop!"

❀

Joe hung up the phone and sank to the couch. Still no answer at Lois's place. She should have been home from church by now.

Just then the phone rang, causing Joe to jump. He grabbed the receiver. "Joe Richey here."

"Hey, big brother! Long time no talk to."

Joe's mouth fell open. He hadn't heard from Brian in nearly a year. Not since he'd called asking to borrow money to pay his overdue rent.

"Joe. You still there, buddy?"

Joe inhaled sharply and reached up to rub the back of his neck. He could almost see his brother's baby face, long, scraggly blond hair, and pale blue eyes. "Yeah, I'm here, Brian. What have you been up to?"

"Keepin' busy. And you?"

"Oh, about six feet two." Joe chuckled at his own wisecrack, but Brian's silence proved he wasn't impressed. "You still living in Boise?"

"Not anymore. I needed a new start."

Joe shook his head. *A new start, or are you leaving another string of bad debts?* He could only imagine how much his kid brother had probably messed up this time.

"I call Seattle my home these days, so we're practically neighbors."

"Seattle? How long have you been living there?"

"A couple of months." Brian cleared his throat. "I'm driving a taxicab."

Joe wrinkled his brows. "You're a taxi driver? What happened to the sporting goods store you were managing in Boise?"

"I, uh, got tired of it."

Joe flexed his fingers. He thought his brother's voice sounded strained. No doubt Brian's previous employer had asked him to leave. It had happened before, and unless Brian learned to control his tongue it would no doubt happen again.

"If you've been in Seattle for a while, why is this the first time I've heard from you? I was in that neck of the woods a couple of weeks ago and could have looked you up."

"Well, I've—"

"Been busy?"

"Yeah. Seattle's a jungle, you know."

"I can't argue with that." Joe's thoughts took him back to the date he'd had with Lois at the Seattle Center. He'd seen more cars on the road that day than he had for a long time, and people milled about the center like cattle in a pen. He didn't envy Brian's having to weave his way in and out of traffic all day, transporting irate customers to their destination.

"Listen, Joe. The reason I'm calling is, well, I was wanting to—"

"I don't have any extra money, Brian," Joe interrupted. "I can barely manage to pay my own bills these days."

"What bills?" Brian shouted. "Mom left you the house and the money from her insurance policy, so I would think you'd be pretty well set."

Joe felt a trail of heat creep up the back of his neck. If Brian hadn't run off to do his own thing, leaving Joe to deal with their mother's emotional problems, maybe he would have inherited more from the will. As it was, Mom was crushed when her youngest son left home and seldom called or visited them.

Forcing his ragged breathing to return to normal, Joe plastered a smile on his face. He didn't know why, since his brother couldn't see him through the phone. Whenever Joe was riled, putting on a happy face seemed to help. It was the only way he knew how to handle stress. Besides, he wasn't about to let Brian push his buttons. One emotional son in the family was enough. Joe would keep his cool no matter how hard his brother tried to goad him. "Let's change the subject, shall we, Brian?"

"Did you ever stop to think I might have called for some other reason than to ask for money?" Brian's tone had a definite edge.

Joe snorted. "You never have before."

"You know what they say—there's a first time for everything."

Joe's patience was waning, and he knew if he didn't end this conversation soon, he might lose control. He couldn't let that happen. It would be a sign of weakness. He drew in a breath and let it out slowly. "Why did you call, Brian?"

"To wish you a happy birthday."

Joe leaned his head against the sofa cushion and chuckled. "My birthday's almost two weeks away, little brother. It's next Friday, to be exact."

"Next Friday, huh? Guess I forgot."

"It's no big deal." *Mom used to make a big deal out of her birthday,* Joe thought ruefully. *But she usually ignored Brian's and my birthdays.*

"Doin' anything special to celebrate?"

"Well, I'm hoping Lois and I might—"

"Lois? Who's she?"

"A friend." *A very special friend. But I'm not about to tell you that.*

"Where's the party going to be? Maybe I'll drive down to Olympia and join you."

"I'm not planning any big wingding to celebrate my twenty-fifth birthday. If I do anything at all, it'll just be a quiet dinner someplace nice."

"Okay. I get the picture. You don't want your loudmouthed, hot-tempered little brother crashing your party. I can live with that. After all, it's nothing new for you to give me the brush-off."

Joe opened his mouth to refute his brother's last statement, but he heard a click, and the phone went dead. "Now what I have done?" he moaned.

With a firm resolve not to dwell on the unpleasant encounter he'd had with Brian, Joe dialed Lois's number again. Her answering machine came on, and this time he left a message.

"Lois, this is Joe. I'm still pretty busy this week. I have two more birthday parties to do, not to mention a visit to a nursing home and a spot on a local kids' TV show. Things are looking better for the following week, though, and next Friday is my twenty-fifth birthday." He paused. "I, uh, was hoping you might be free to help me celebrate. Please give me a call when you get in—okay? Talk to you soon. 'Bye."

Chapter 17

It was close to six o'clock when Lois returned to her apartment Sunday evening. After dinner with Tabby and Seth, she had driven through Point Defiance Park then stayed for a little while at Owen's Beach.

Dropping her purse on the coffee table, she noticed her answering machine was blinking. She clicked the button then smiled when she heard Joe's message asking her to help him celebrate his birthday. "I wonder what I can do to make it special," she murmured.

She reached for the phone and dialed Joe's number. She was relieved when he answered on the second ring. "Hi, Joe. It's Lois."

"Hey, it's good to hear your voice. Did you get my message?"

"Yes, I did. I just got in."

"What do you think about next Friday night?"

"So you need someone to help you celebrate your birthday?"

"Yeah, and I can't think of anyone I'd rather spend it with than you."

Lois grinned. Joe sounded sincere, and she was beginning to think he really did care for her.

He cleared his throat. "We'll get back to my birthday plans in a minute, but I've been meaning to ask you something, Lois."

"What's that?"

"I was wondering why you hightailed it out of my clowning class two weeks ago."

"I could see you were busy, and I didn't want to cut in on your time with the people who stayed to ask questions."

"I thought you might not have enjoyed the class," he said. "I was planning to ask you to dinner, but when I realized you'd left I figured the worst."

"The worst?"

"Yeah. I thought maybe you hated my class and didn't have the heart to say so."

Lois's heartbeat quickened. Joe had wanted to ask her out, and he thought she didn't like the class? She felt terrible about leaving him with the wrong impression. "I did enjoy your clowning presentation."

"Is it about the money, then?"

"What? What money?"

"The fact that most gospel clowns aren't rich."

"Money's not an issue with me, Joe," Lois said, smiling. "It used to be, but not anymore. I realized it wasn't so important when I broke up with a man who had money but wasn't a Christian."

She heard Joe release his breath. "I'm glad we settled that." He groaned softly then followed it with a chuckle. "I've had enough unpleasantness for one day."

"What happened today that was unpleasant?"

"I had a phone call from my kid brother, Brian," he replied. "It seems he's left his job in Boise, Idaho, and lives in Seattle now."

Lois held her breath. Was Joe finally going to open up and talk about his family?

"He called under the guise of wishing me a happy birthday, but I think he really wanted money," Joe continued.

"Is Brian unemployed?"

"He said he's driving a cab, but from past experience. . ." Joe's voice trailed off, and he was silent for a moment. "Let's not talk about my renegade brother—okay? I'd much rather discuss our dinner plans for next Friday."

Lois smiled. "I'd love to help celebrate your birthday, Joe. How about letting me pick the place? I'll even drive to Olympia to get you."

"You're going to be my chauffeur?"

"Yes."

"Oh, boy! Does a white stretch limo come with the deal?"

She giggled. "I'm afraid you'll have to settle for my little green clunker."

He moaned. "Well, if I must."

"I'll be by to pick you up at six o'clock sharp, so you'd better be ready and waiting."

"Yes, ma'am."

Lois hung up the phone, feeling happier than she had all day. Joe wanted her to help celebrate his birthday, and now she could plan to do something special.

❀

On the drive to Portland Saturday morning, Lois was a ball of nerves. What if she took the second clowning class and still had no audience appeal? What if she lacked the courage to do a program in front of anyone besides her Sunday school kids? She knew she was probably expecting too much. After all, this would only be her second course in clowning, and Rome wasn't built in a day. She didn't have much time though. Joe's birthday was a week away, and she was determined to give him a surprise he'd never forget.

When Lois pulled into the parking lot of First Christian Church, she was amazed at all the cars. "There must be a lot of people interested in clowning," she murmured, turning off the engine.

Stepping inside the foyer of the large brick building, she realized why so many cars were parked outside. She saw that not only were classes in clowning being offered, but also ones in puppetry, ventriloquism, illusions, and chalk art. It reminded her of the story Tabby had told of her first encounter with ventriloquism and meeting Seth Beyers.

Lois stopped in front of the table marked CLOWNING BY BENNY THE BUBBLE MAN and registered for the class. A young woman dressed as a Raggedy Ann type of clown handed Lois a small notebook and a name tag.

A short time later, Lois was seated at the front of the class. *Joe would sure be surprised if he knew I was taking another clowning class. I'm glad he's not teaching at this seminar, or else he would have discovered my little secret by now.*

She forced her thoughts off Joe and onto Benny the Bubble Man, who with the help of his assistant, Raggedy Ruth, was demonstrating the art of making bubbles in different sizes and shapes. The pair expertly used a variety of wands and even a straw.

Lois thought it looked pretty simple until everyone in the class was given a jar of soapy liquid and instructed to make a bubble chain. She'd always prided herself on being adept at blowing bubbles, but her childhood tricks had involved making only one, two, or maybe three effervescent balls at one time. Making a string of six to eight bubbles was difficult, if not impossible. Even with Raggedy Ruth's help, Lois fumbled her way through the procedure. Something as tedious as this would take weeks, maybe months of practice, and she had only until next Friday.

"Maybe I should have taken one of the other clowning classes," she muttered.

"You're doing fine. Just keep practicing," Ruth assured her.

Lois was the last student to leave the classroom; she was determined to learn at least one bubble maneuver that might impress Joe and show him she could act as goofy as he did. If she could learn to be a clown, maybe Joe would start to show his serious side. It seemed like a fair trade to Lois.

Chapter 18

Lois leaned back in her office chair and yawned. How could she ever stay awake the rest of the day? For the last four nights she'd been up late, practicing her clown routine and blowing bubbles until her lips turned numb. She'd finally managed to make a chain of eight small bubbles and a bubble within a bubble, but she didn't think either trick was too exciting. Neither was her hillbilly clown costume.

Maybe I should forget the whole idea and take Joe to dinner as he's expecting. At least then I won't be as likely to embarrass myself.

Lois grabbed the stack of bulletins in front of her and started folding them. On the front cover was a picture of a nurse taking a child's temperature. Suddenly, an idea popped into her head. A new outfit—that's what she needed. A costume and some props. A small shop on the other side of town sold tricks, costumes, and other clowning aids. She would go there as soon as she got off work.

❁

Joe stared out his living room window. It was raining, which was nothing unusual for fall weather in the Pacific Northwest. He wasn't going to let it dampen his spirits, though. Today was his birthday, and he was going to dinner with Lois. *Sure hope she drives carefully on the freeway. It's bound to be slick with all this liquid sunshine. She should have let me drive to Tacoma and pick her up.* He glanced at the clock on the wall. *Five minutes to six. She should be here any minute.*

Joe sat on the couch to wait and turned his thoughts in another direction. He'd been presenting a program at a nearby nursing home the previous week when the son of one of the patients offered him a job. The man owned a hotel and needed several full-time entertainers. The position paid well and had some fringe benefits, but it involved secular clowning and would leave little time to minister as a gospel clown. He pulled out the man's business card and studied it for a minute. He'd told him he would think about it, but Joe knew he couldn't accept the position no matter how well it paid. He always seemed to need money, but his primary goal as a clown was to see people's lives changed through faith in Christ. If he spent most of his time entertaining, simply to amuse others, he'd lose precious opportunities to witness about God.

I'll call him in the morning and let him know I've decided not to take the job.

The doorbell rang then. He grinned. It must be Lois.

❁

Lois smiled when Joe opened the door. He looked so nice, dressed in a tan shirt, dark brown blazer, and matching slacks. He'd worn a tie, too—a silly cartoon character standing on its head. "Happy birthday, Joe. You ready to go?" she said, reaching up and kissing him on the cheek.

Joe nodded enthusiastically. "Yes! I've been waiting all day for this." He drew her into his arms and kissed her upturned mouth.

"Are you having your dessert first?" she asked, tipping her head to one side.

He nodded and gave her a playful wink. "Absolutely! I may have more dessert after dinner, though."

Lois felt her cheeks grow warm. She hoped the rest of the evening went as well as these first few minutes.

"Where are we off to?" Joe asked as he followed Lois to her car. "Are we finally going to Snoqualmie Falls for that picnic?"

"Not tonight." Lois opened the door on the passenger's side and motioned for Joe to get in. "Don't ask me any more questions. My lips are sealed."

"You're going to chauffeur me, aren't you?"

"Yes, and you'd better get in before the rain turns us into a couple of drowned rats."

"It seems like ages since we last saw each other," Joe said as they started for the freeway. "I've missed you, Lois."

She glanced at him out of the corner of her eye. "Ditto."

"Anything new in your life since we last talked?"

"Nothing much. How's your busy schedule? Anything exciting happening in the life of Slow-Joe the Clown?"

"I was offered a job last week," he answered. "It pays really well, but I'm going to call the guy tomorrow and turn it down."

"Why?"

"It's a secular position that would take a lot of my time. I wouldn't be able to do nearly as many gospel presentations."

"I'm sure you've prayed about it," Lois said.

"I have." He reached for her hand. "Do you think I'm dumb for giving up the money?"

She shook her head. "Not at all."

Joe squeezed her fingers. "I'm glad you feel that way."

They drove in silence for a while, listening to the Christian radio station Lois had turned on. When they left the freeway, Lois headed across town to the north end. Soon she pulled up in front of a quaint three-story house with gray siding.

Joe gave her a strange look. "Where are we? This doesn't look like a restaurant to me."

She smiled and turned off the engine. "It's not. This is where Tabby and Seth live."

"He has his ventriloquist shop in the basement, right?"

Lois nodded. "Have you ever been here?"

"No, but Seth told me about it. He said the place used to belong to his grandparents."

"Right again," she said as she unbuckled her seat belt.

"So what are we doing here? Are Seth and Tabby joining us for dinner?"

"Yes, they are." Lois turned in her seat to face Joe. "I hope you don't mind."

He shrugged and smiled. "Sure—whatever."

"Let's go inside and see if they're ready."

"Why don't I wait here and you get them?"

Lois knew her surprise wouldn't work if Joe didn't go inside the house. "Their place is really neat. I'd like you to see it," she insisted.

Joe was quiet.

"They have lots of antiques," Lois added, "and Seth has an old ventriloquist dummy he's dressed as a clown."

Joe undid his seat belt and opened the car door. "Okay, you win. Let's go inside."

They walked up to the Beyers' front porch, and Lois was about to turn the knob on the door. "Wait, Lois," Joe said, reaching for her hand. "There aren't any lights in the windows. Maybe they're not home."

"They're probably at the back of the house." Lois grasped the knob and opened the door.

It was dark inside, and she grabbed Joe's hand then led him along the hallway, feeling her way as she went.

"Are you sure they're home?" Joe asked. "I don't hear a sound."

"Just hush and stay close to me."

They stepped into the living room, and in the next moment the lights snapped on. "Surprise!" a chorus of voices shouted. "Happy birthday, Joe!"

※

At once Joe painted on a happy face and backed away from the exuberant people who had greeted him. This was a surprise party, and it didn't take a genius to realize Lois was behind the whole thing. Besides Seth and Tabby, he recognized several other people with whom he'd done gospel presentations. His biggest surprise was seeing his brother. Joe didn't know how it was possible, since none of his friends knew Brian. Other than Lois, he'd never mentioned him to his associates.

Joe leaned close to Lois and whispered, "How did my brother get here?"

She opened her mouth to reply, but Brian cut her off. "I'm here because she called around until she located the cab company I work for. I guess she thought you'd be happy to see me."

Joe swallowed hard and forced his smile to remain in place. "Of course I'm glad to see you. I'm just surprised." He gave Brian a quick hug then turned to face Lois. "I thought we were going out to dinner."

Her face turned pink, and she squeezed his hand. "I wanted to do something different for your birthday."

Seth stepped forward and grasped Joe's shoulder. "You're lucky to have someone as special as my wife's sister looking out for you. Lois has worked hard planning this shindig in your honor."

Joe felt like a heel. He should be grateful Lois cared so much about him. He couldn't let her know how disappointed he was at not spending the evening alone with her. He reached over and hugged her. "Thanks for the surprise."

"There's more to come!" Lois said excitedly. "Besides the pizza, cake, and other goodies, I've planned a special program in your honor."

Joe raised his eyebrows. "A program? Now that does sound interesting."

※

Lois breathed a sigh of relief when she realized Joe seemed okay with her change of plans. She hoped he would enjoy the festivities, especially since he always seemed to be the life of the party. She led him across the room and pointed to the recliner. "You sit here and visit with your friends while I go change into my party clothes."

He wrinkled his forehead. "I think you look fine in what you're wearing."

Lois glanced down at her beige slacks and rose-colored knit top. "I won't be long, and I hope you won't be disappointed." She leaned over and gave him a light kiss on the cheek then hurried out of the room. Tabby was behind her, and they both giggled as they started up the stairs leading to the bedrooms.

"I can't believe you're going through with this," Tabby said as she pulled Lois into her room.

Lois nodded soberly. "I hope I'm not making a mistake."

Tabby shook her head. "I don't think so. In fact, it might be just the thing that will bring Joe Richey to his knees."

"I don't get it."

"Knees. . .marriage. . .proposal. . ."

Lois waved her hand. "Get real, Tabby. Joe and I have been dating only since August. We barely know each other."

"But you're a couple of lovesick puppies," Tabby asserted. "I can see it all over your faces."

Lois shrugged. "Let's get my costume on and forget about love, shall we?"

A half hour later, the sisters emerged from the bedroom. Tabby went down the steps first, and Lois followed, wearing a nurse's uniform and carrying a satchel full of props.

She stood in the hallway while Tabby stepped into the living room. "Ladies and gentlemen, it's my privilege to introduce our special guest tonight—the lovely nurse, Lois Johnson!"

Lois skipped into the room. "Is there a patient in the house? Somebody please provide me with a sick patient!"

On cue, Seth jumped up from his seat and grabbed hold of Joe's hand. "Here's your patient, Nurse Lois, and he's one sick fellow!"

Lois placed a chair in the middle of the room and asked Joe to sit down. Then she opened her satchel, drew out an oversized pair of fake glasses, and put them on. Next she removed a rubber chicken and threw it into the air. "Oops! No dead birds around here!" she exclaimed. "It's my job to make people well."

She pulled a can of peanuts out of the bag and grinned at Joe. "I hear you've been feeling under the weather lately." Before he could respond, she tossed him the can. "Remove the lid, please."

Joe lifted the top, and a paper snake sailed into the air, almost hitting him in the nose. He stared at Lois for a second then burst into gales of laughter.

Lois dipped her hand into the satchel again and retrieved an oversized toothbrush. "Open real wide," she said, tipping Joe's head back. He opened his mouth, and she pretended to brush his teeth while she blew on the end of the toothbrush. A stream of bubbles drifted toward the ceiling. Joe laughed so hard his face turned cherry red. He thought she was funny, and apparently so did everyone else, for they were all laughing, clapping, and shouting for more.

"Now, sick patient, I'd like you to lie on the floor," Lois instructed. As Joe complied, she turned to face Tabby. "May I have the sheet, please?"

Tabby reached into a basket that was sitting on the floor and pulled out a white sheet. Lois threw the sheet over Joe, leaving only his head and feet exposed.

"I understand you're having some trouble with your left arm these days," Lois said, as she grabbed Joe's arm and raised it a few inches off the floor. Suddenly Joe's left leg came up, and everyone howled. She couldn't believe it; Joe was playing along with her routine.

Lois pushed on his leg, and up came the right arm. She shoved that down, and Joe's other arm shot up. They continued the game a few more minutes, until Lois announced, "I think this patient is well enough for some pizza. But before that I'd like to present him with a beautiful flower."

Lois drew a fake flower from her bag. Joe sat up, and she handed it to him. "Take a whiff and tell me what you smell."

Joe held the flower up to his nose and inhaled deeply. Lois squeezed the stem, and a stream of water shot out and hit Joe in the face. He yelped then jumped up and began chasing Lois around the room. "I've always wondered what it would be like to catch a nurse!" he cried.

By the time Joe caught Lois, they were both laughing so hard tears were running down their cheeks. Lois had planned a few other things for her routine, but she knew she couldn't go on with the rest of the show. She didn't think she needed to anyway, since she had shown Joe what she'd learned about clowning and helped to make his birthday one to remember.

❧

Joe couldn't believe how much he was enjoying the party. Lois was very funny when she decided to let her hair down.

"I didn't realize you'd learned so much about clowning during my short class," Joe said to Lois. They were all sitting around the table eating chocolate cake and strawberry ice cream.

She gave him a sheepish grin. "I took another class last Saturday in Portland."

"Ah-ha! I wondered where you were when I tried to call that afternoon." Joe needled her in the ribs. "Now the two of us can team up and do all sorts of routines at church functions."

"Speaking of church—have you found a church home in Seattle yet, Brian?" Seth asked, turning to Joe's brother.

Brian scrunched up his nose. "I'm religious enough. I don't need an hour of boring church every Sunday to make me a better person."

"Since when did you get religious?" Joe asked his brother.

"It's like this—when I drive my cab around the city, people pray a lot!"

"Yeah, I'm sure your passengers do pray," Joe said, forcing a smile. "As I recall, you always had a lead foot."

Brian frowned. "To be a cabby, you have to know how to move in and out of traffic."

"If you want my opinion—"

"I respect your opinion," Brian interrupted, "but I'd respect it even more if you kept it to yourself."

Joe opened his mouth to offer a comeback, but he felt Lois's hand touch his under the table. He wondered if she was trying to signal him to change the subject, so he squeezed her fingers in response. "This cake is delicious. Did you make it, Lois?"

She shook her head. "Tabby did the honors. I was too busy trying to come up with some kind of goofy clown skit."

"That nurse routine you did was pretty impressive," Seth interjected. "You and Joe work well together."

Joe draped his arm across Lois's shoulder and whispered in her ear, "We do, don't we?"

Chapter 19

Over the next few weeks Joe and Lois saw each other often. They visited Snoqualmie Falls and had a picnic in Joe's truck, drove up to Mount Rainier for a day of skiing, and got together at Lois's place to practice some joint clowning routines. On the night of Joe's birthday, he'd convinced Lois she had talent and suggested she use it to help him evangelize. Lois thought that after more practice she might be able to do some kind of routine with him.

She was still concerned about his inability to be serious, as well as his refusal to talk about his brother or other family members. She had noticed the way Joe and Brian related at the party and knew a problem existed between them. She kept hoping and praying he would open up to her as they drew closer to one another, but so far he'd remained the jokester. Her own clowning around didn't deter him, either. If anything, Joe seemed to be even goofier. She worried that he might have something to hide, some family skeletons buried beneath his lighthearted exterior. She was concerned that those things, whatever they were, might put a wedge between them, either now or in the future.

Today was Thanksgiving, and Lois had invited Joe, Brian, Seth, and Tabby for dinner. Her sister had volunteered to bring the pies, but Lois insisted on doing the rest. She was eager for Joe to sample her cooking, and she hoped Brian's presence would help him relax and talk about his family.

By one o'clock, the turkey was almost cooked. Lois boiled the potatoes then finished setting the table in her small dining room with her best china. The guests would be here any minute, and she was looking forward to the day ahead.

Seth and Tabby arrived first, bringing two pumpkin pies and one apple, along with a carton of whipping cream. "It looks like you've outdone yourself," Tabby said as she studied the table.

Lois smiled and took one of the pies from her sister. "It's my first attempt at holiday entertaining, and I wanted everything to be perfect."

Seth whistled. "If the smell of that bird is any indication of what dinner's going to taste like, then I'd say everything will be more than perfect."

Lois winked at her brother-in-law and motioned toward the couch. "Have a seat, and when Joe and his brother arrive you can keep them entertained." She nodded at Tabby. "The two of us have some work to do in the other room."

Tabby set her pies on the countertop and grabbed one of Lois's aprons from a drawer. "What would you like me to do first?"

"How about mashing the potatoes while I make some gravy?"

"I think I can manage that."

Lois noticed that Tabby's stomach was protruding slightly, and a pang of jealousy stabbed her heart. What if she never married or had any children? Could she learn to be content with being an aunt? *I don't need to think about this now,* she chided herself. *There's too much to do.* She focused her thoughts on stirring the gravy.

By the time Lois and Tabby were ready to serve dinner, Joe and Brian arrived. They hadn't come together, but Lois figured that was because Joe had been driving from Olympia and his brother from Seattle, which was in the opposite direction.

Joe greeted Lois with a kiss on the cheek, and soon everyone was seated at the table. Lois asked Seth to say the blessing then excused herself to bring in the turkey. Moments later she placed the platter in front of Joe amidst everyone's oohs and ahhs and asked if he would carve the bird.

"You picked the right guy for the job," he said with a grin. "When Brian and I were growing up, carving the bird was always my responsibility."

"Did your dad teach you how?" Tabby inquired.

"He was killed in an accident involving the tour bus Dad drove. Joe and I were both kids," Brian answered before his brother could open his mouth. "I hardly remember our father."

"My folks died when I was pretty young, too," Seth said. "Grandma and Grandpa Beyers raised me after Mom and Dad were killed. Then later, when they decided to move to a retirement center, they gave me their home."

"After Dad's death, our mother raised us." Brian frowned. "At least that's what she thought she was doing."

Lois's interest was piqued. What did Brian mean by saying his mother *thought* she was raising them? She turned to him. "It must have been hard for your mother to raise two boys without a father. I'm sure she did the best she could."

Brian snorted and reached for a biscuit from the basket in the center of the table. "If Mom had done the best she could, she would have admitted she was sick and taken the medicine the doctor prescribed. Now she's dead, and we're left with only each other and a lot of bad memories."

Lois glanced at Joe, sitting on the other side of her, and hoped he would add something to Brian's comment.

Joe was silent. With a silly grin plastered on his face, he reached for the tray of fresh vegetables, grabbed a cherry tomato, poked a hole in one end, then stuck the whole thing on the tip of his nose. "How's this for a new clown face?" he asked with a chuckle. He reached into the tray again and withdrew two cucumber slices. He cut a hole in each one then placed them over his ears. Next he grabbed a carrot and stuck that in his mouth. "What'd ya think ub this?" he mumbled.

Everyone but Brian laughed at Joe's silly antics. "If you don't want to discuss our mother's problems, that's fine—but let's not make these folks think you're ready for the loony bin as well," Brian said.

The carrot dropped to his plate as Joe opened his mouth. "I don't think we should be having this discussion right now. Today's Thanksgiving, and we ought to be concentrating on having a good time and being thankful for all we have, instead of talking about someone who made her peace with God and isn't here to defend herself."

Joe's face was as red as the tomato still dangling from his nose, and Lois wondered what she could do to help ease the tension. She offered up a quick prayer then reached over and took his hand. "Maybe after dinner you can do one of your juggling routines. In the meantime, how about slicing that turkey before we all starve?"

Joe snatched both cucumbers off his ears and the tomato from his nose and placed them on the edge of his plate. Without another word, he grabbed the knife and stuck it into the bird.

❀

Joe's insides were churning like a blender running on full speed. How dare his brother air their family's dirty laundry in front of Lois and her relatives! If he hadn't been trying so hard to keep his emotions in check, he might have shouted at Brian to shut up and eat, rather than make himself look foolish by putting on a vegetable clown face. Lois probably thought he was the one with a mental problem. Keeping control of his emotions was important to Joe. If he acted on his feelings, he might flip out, the way Mom had on more than one occasion.

Joe found himself beginning to care more and more for Lois, and he didn't want to turn her off by losing his cool—or by revealing too much about his family. Making a joke out of things was the only way he knew how to cope with the unpleasant things in life. It was better than turning to drugs or alcohol, as Brian had when he was a teenager. Joe hoped his brother had given up those bad habits, but after today it was obvious he still hadn't learned to control his tongue.

Many times when they were growing up Brian had blurted out something to someone about their mother and her mood swings. Joe had tried then to talk to him about keeping their family affairs quiet, but his little brother seemed to take pleasure in letting everyone know their mother had a serious problem. When Brian finally graduated from high school and left home, Joe hated to admit he was relieved. At least his brother could no longer talk about their personal lives. Joe felt a sense of duty to Mom and had continued to live with her until she died. In all that time, he'd never told anyone about her problem with extreme mood swings or discussed the way it had made him feel.

"When's your next performance, Joe?"

Seth's question drew Joe out of his reflections, and he smiled and passed him the plate of turkey. "I'm scheduled to do one tomorrow at the Tacoma Mall. It's part of the pre-Christmas festivities, and I'll be making some balloon animals to give out to the children who visit Santa."

"Sounds pretty corny if you ask me," Brian muttered. "If I had a choice, I'd choose driving in and out of traffic all day rather than spend five minutes with a bunch of runny-nosed, rowdy kids."

All eyes were focused on Brian. Joe knew Tabby and Seth were expecting a baby in the spring and that Lois loved kids. He could only imagine what Lois and her family must think of his self-centered brother.

"Kids and laughter are what makes the world go around," Joe said. "I love working with the little tykes because they spread happiness, peanut butter, and chicken pox."

Brian frowned. "Humph! And that coming from someone who's a big kid himself! You were always Mom's funny little boy, full of jokes and wisecracks, and never wanting to rock the boat or make any waves."

Joe inhaled sharply. He thought about telling Brian he'd made up a new beatitude: "Blessed are they who have nothing nice to say and can't be persuaded to say it."

Just then Seth spoke up.

"The turkey is great, Lois. You really outdid yourself."

"Yes, everything tastes wonderful," Tabby agreed.

Lois smiled, and her face turned pink. "Thanks."

Joe patted his stomach. "They're right; the meal was terrific. In fact, tomorrow I'll probably have to go on a diet." He winked at Lois. "Whenever I have to start applying my clown makeup with a paint roller, I know it's time to lose weight."

Everyone, except Brian, laughed at Joe's joke. He was eating mashed potatoes at lightning speed. *That's okay,* Joe mused. *Brian never did appreciate a good pun. Maybe I should try another one and see if that gets any response.*

"You look kind of stressed out, Brian. Must be ready for those tasty desserts Tabby brought, huh?"

His brother's forehead wrinkled, but he remained silent.

Joe chuckled. "Stressed spelled backwards is desserts."

Again, everyone but Brian laughed. Instead he narrowed his eyes at Joe. "You're really sick, you know that? I don't see how anyone as beautiful and intelligent as Lois could put up with you clowning around all the time."

Brian's words pierced Joe. He wondered if Lois felt the same way about his silliness. If she did, she'd never said anything. In fact, she was learning to be a clown herself, so that must mean she liked his goofy ways and wanted to be more like him—didn't it?

Chapter 20

A s Lois put away the last of the clean dishes from their Thanksgiving meal, her mind wandered. Joe's brother had revealed some important things about their past, including that their mother had suffered with a mental illness. Could that be why Joe was reluctant to talk about his family? Maybe it was also why Joe showed only his silly side. Lois had a hunch Joe had a lot of pain bottled up inside and for some reason was afraid to let it out. She wondered what it would take to break down the walls he'd built up. She wished he'd stayed around after the others left, but he was the first person to say he needed to leave.

Lois had no idea why Joe needed to go home, since today was a holiday and he had no clowning engagements scheduled. She'd tried to talk to him for a few minutes in front of her apartment building, but he'd hurried away, mumbling something about the ocean calling to him.

She sank into a chair at the kitchen table and closed her eyes. She could still picture Joe sitting at her dining room table during dinner, leaning slightly forward. His pinched face and forced smile betrayed the tension he must have felt when Brian began talking about their mother's condition.

"Dear Lord," Lois prayed, "I think Joe is deeply troubled and needs Your help. Please show me if there's something I can do."

❁

Joe had intended to go home after he left Lois's, but he couldn't face his empty house tonight. Not when he had Mom on his mind. He drove past the Olympia exit and headed toward the coast. Maybe he would feel better after some time at the beach. A blast of salt sea air and the cold sand sifting into his sneakers would get him thinking straight again. So what if he only had the clothes on his back and no toothbrush? If he stayed more than a day he could buy what he needed.

"Lord, I've blown it with Lois," Joe prayed. "I could see by the look on her face during dinner that she's fed up with me. Did hearing about Mom's problems turn her off, or was she irritated because I wouldn't hang around and talk?"

Joe's stomach ached from holding back his feelings. He wanted to pull his truck to the side of the road, drop his head onto the steering wheel, and let the tears that had built up through the years spill over like water released from a dam. He couldn't, though. He had to keep driving until the Pacific Ocean came into view. He needed to drown out the past. Joe didn't care that by leaving town he'd have to cancel the performance he was scheduled to give at the Tacoma Mall the next afternoon. So what if they never asked him to do another clowning routine? Right now he didn't care if he ever worked again.

❁

Lois hadn't heard anything from Joe since Thanksgiving, and now it was Friday of the following week. She'd been tempted to call several times but decided she should give him more time to make the first move.

She turned off her computer and was about to call it a day when the pastor's wife entered her office.

"How are things going, Lois?" she asked. "Do you and your clown friend have big plans for the weekend?"

"It's going okay here at work." Lois swallowed against the knot in her throat. "I haven't heard from Joe all week, and frankly I wonder if he will ever call again."

Norma Hanson slipped into the chair beside Lois's desk. "Would you like to talk about it?"

Lois hesitated then took a deep breath. "I found out Thanksgiving that his mother had severe mood swings, and he acted strange after his brother blurted out the information." She sighed. "I think Joe's past might have something to do with the way he makes light of everything."

The pastor's wife handed Lois a tissue from the box on her desk. "Does Joe's humor bother you?"

Lois smiled through her tears. "Actually, I think he's been good for me, and his joking has helped me learn to relax and have a good time." She paused. "I just wish he could show his serious side, too. If he even has one, that is."

The older woman nodded. "I'm sure he does. Maybe he needs more time. Perhaps as your friendship grows, he'll open up to you more."

"I hope so, Mrs. Hanson." Lois reached for her purse. "Well, I mustn't take up any more of your time."

"I'm glad to listen anytime and even offer an opinion if you ask," she said, smiling. "Before you go, though, let's have a word of prayer."

A whole week at the beach, and Joe still felt as if his world were tilting precariously. He couldn't afford to spend any more nights in a hotel, and it wasn't warm enough to pitch a tent on the sand. Besides, he was expected to perform at his home church on Sunday morning. It was bad enough he'd missed the mall program right after Thanksgiving. He certainly wouldn't feel right about leaving Pastor Cummings in the lurch. Especially when his clowning skit was supposed to be the children's sermon for the day and coincide with the pastor's message.

With his mood matching that of the overcast sky, Joe climbed into his pickup on Saturday morning and headed home.

On Sunday morning, he was still struggling with feelings he kept pushing down. He was determined to put on a happy face and act as if nothing were wrong.

Checking to see that his chaps were in place and donning his floppy red cowboy hat, he entered the sanctuary through a side door near the pulpit.

"Howdy, pardners!" Joe shouted as he sprinted onto the platform, twirling a rope over his head. "Anyone know what the rope said to the knot?"

When no one responded, Joe said, "You're naughty!"

Several children in the front row giggled, and Joe winked at them. "Today we'll be talking about witnessing and inviting our friends to church," he announced. "I'll need a helper, though. Any volunteers?"

A few hands shot up, and Joe pointed to a young boy. "What's your name?"

"Billy," the boy told him.

"Well, come on up, Billy, and stand right over there." Joe pointed to the spot where he wanted Billy to stand then took several steps backward. "Now let's think of some ways we can witness to our friends about Jesus." In one quick motion, Joe twirled his rope, flung it over the boy's head, and cinched it around his waist. "There! I've roped you real good, and now you've gotta listen to the pastor's message."

Billy looked at Joe as if he'd taken leave of his senses. "Guess ropin' your friends isn't the best way to invite them to church." He undid the rope. "Hmm. . .what else could I do to get someone to come to church?"

Joe tipped his head to one side, pressed his lips together, then snapped his fingers. "I know! I'll handcuff this young man and force him to come to church." Joe reached into his back pocket and pulled out a pair of plastic handcuffs. He dangled them above Billy's head, and several children laughed. "You don't think that's a good idea?"

"That wouldn't be nice!" a little girl shouted.

Joe nodded. "You're right. It wouldn't be." He tapped the toe of his cowboy boot against the floor. "Let's see now." Joe bent down so he was on the same level with the boy. "If you're not willing to go to Sunday school with me, I won't be your friend anymore."

Billy raised his eyebrows. Joe chuckled then ruffled the child's hair. "Guess that's not the way to witness, either."

Joe began to pace the length of the platform. "What's the best way to witness? What's the best way to witness?" He stopped suddenly, nearly running into the boy. "Hey! You still here?"

Billy nodded. "Do you want me to sit down?"

Joe shook his head. "No way! We still haven't shown these kids the best way to witness."

Billy tapped Joe on the arm, and Joe bent down so the boy could whisper something in his ear. When he lifted his head again, Joe was smiling. He turned to face the audience. "This young man thinks I should offer him something so he'll agree to come to Sunday school with me." He winked. "And I think I have the perfect gift."

Joe reached into another pocket of his baggy jeans and grabbed a couple of pencil balloons. The first one he inflated flew across the room, and everyone howled. When he blew up the next one, he twisted it quickly into an animal. "Here you go, son—your very own pony." He handed Billy the balloon creation then told him he could return to his seat.

Next Joe pulled a small New Testament from his shirt pocket. He opened it and turned a few pages. "In Mark, chapter 16, verse 15, Jesus commanded His disciples to go into the world and preach the good news to all creation." He held up the book. "That means we should do the same. We need to tell others about Jesus, and one of the ways we can do that is by inviting our friends and relatives to Sunday school and church where they can hear Bible stories about Him."

Joe moved to the end of the platform and held up the rope and handcuffs. "Forcing them to come isn't the answer." He drew a fake flower from his vest pocket and showed the audience. "If you use some form of bribery, it might get them here—but will it keep them?" He shook his head. "I doubt it, and I don't think that's the way Jesus meant for us to preach the good news. We need to live the Christian life so others will see Jesus shining through us. Then, when we invite our friends and family to church, they'll want to come and see what's it all about." He shook his head slowly. "Shame on me for trying to make you think otherwise."

Joe held the flower in front of his own face and squeezed the attached bulb. A stream of water squirted on his nose, and the audience clapped heartily. Joe took a bow and dashed out of the room.

Joe didn't wish to disturb the church service, so he stayed in the small room outside the sanctuary, listening to the pastor's message from his seat near the door. After the congregation was dismissed, Joe stepped over to the pastor. "If you're not too busy, may I speak with you for a few minutes?"

"Sure, Joe. I have time to talk now."

Joe followed Pastor Cummings down the hall to his office where they sat down in easy chairs.

The pastor leaned forward. "You're an excellent clown, Joe. God's given you a special talent, and it's good to see you using it for Him."

Joe folded his arms. "If I can bring a smile to someone's heart, it's a ministry worth doing."

Pastor Cummings nodded. "Most people seem to open up to a clown. I've noticed that the barriers seem to come down the minute you step into a room."

"You're right, but I've seen a few exceptions," Joe said. "I remember being in a restaurant one time to do a kid's birthday party, and an older man was sitting at a nearby table. He seemed nervous by my presence and stayed hidden behind his newspaper until I left."

"Guess he forgot what it was like to be a child."

Joe shrugged. "Could be."

Pastor Cummings wrinkled his forehead. "Maybe the man was afraid to laugh. Some people have a hard time getting in touch with their emotions—especially if they've been hindered during their growing-up years."

Joe shifted uneasily in his chair. Could the pastor see inside his heart and know how discouraged he'd been as a child? Did he know how hard it was for him to get in touch with his feelings?

"What did you wish to speak with me about, Joe?"

Joe's nerves were as taut as a rubber band. This was going to be harder than he thought. "I'm. . .dating a woman now who is. . .well, Lois tends to be kind of serious."

"Does that bother you?" the pastor asked.

"Not really, because she's recently taken a couple of clowning classes and is learning to relax and joke around."

"Then what's the problem?"

"I think I'm the problem," Joe said.

"How so?"

"Lois wants to know about my family and what went on in my past."

"And I take it you'd rather not talk about that part of your life?"

Joe nodded. "The truth is, I don't even want to think about the past, much less discuss it."

He took a few deep breaths and tried to relax. The only sound was the soft ticking of the clock on the wall behind the pastor's desk.

Suddenly an image of Joe's mother popped into his mind. He could see her shaking her finger at him. He could hear her shouting, "You're a slob, Joseph Andrew Richey! Why can't you do anything right?" She slapped his face then ran from his room, sobbing and shouting obscenities.

"Why was she always so critical?" Joe mumbled to himself. "Why was everything I did never good enough?" His voice lowered even more. "Why couldn't she at least say something positive about me?"

"Who was critical of you, Joe?"

Joe raised his head. Pastor Cummings was staring at him. "Oh. I guess I was sort of daydreaming. All of a sudden I could see my mother and hear her shouting at me."

"Both of your parents are dead, as I recall from what you told me when you first started coming here. Is that right?" the pastor asked.

Joe nodded.

"Were you and your mother close?"

"I—I guess so. I did everything she asked, even when she wouldn't take her medicine and sort of flipped out."

"Was your mother ill?"

Joe swallowed past the lump wedged in his throat. How could he explain about Mom? Would Pastor Cummings understand, or would he be judgmental, the way Joe's childhood friends had been when they'd seen his mother in one of her moods?

"Being able to talk about your feelings will help you get in touch with them," the pastor prompted.

"My mother was mentally ill," Joe blurted out. "She was diagnosed with manic depression, but she never acknowledged it or took the medicine the doctor prescribed."

"I see. And how did her illness affect you, Joe?"

Joe stood suddenly. "I've spent the last week alone, wrestling with my past, and I thought I was ready to talk about it—but now I don't think I am."

The older man nodded. "It's okay. We can talk more when you're ready."

Joe was almost to the door when he felt the pastor's hand touch his shoulder.

"I want you to know, Joe, that I'm here for you. Anytime you need to talk, I'm available," Pastor Cummings said in a sincere tone.

Joe nodded and forced a smile on his face. "Thanks. I'll remember that."

Chapter 21

Lois stared at the telephone, praying it would ring. If only she would hear from Joe. It had been two weeks, and she was getting more worried. She was reaching for the phone when it rang.

Startled, she grabbed the receiver. "Hello."

"Hi, Lois. It's Joe."

Lois felt as though the air had been squeezed from her lungs. She hadn't talked to Joe since Thanksgiving and had almost given up hope of ever hearing from him again.

"Are you still there, Lois?"

"Yes, I'm here."

"How have you been?"

"Fine. And you?" Lois knew they were making small talk, but she didn't know what else to say. Things seemed strained between them.

"Well, the reason I'm calling is, I was wondering if you're still mad at me."

"I was never mad, Joe."

"Okay. Irritated, then."

"Not even that. I was a bit disappointed because you left so abruptly on Thanksgiving and wouldn't tell me what was bothering you."

"I'm sorry, but my brother had me pretty upset," Joe said. "I took off for Ocean Shores and stayed a whole week."

"An impromptu vacation?" Lois asked.

"I needed time to think. I've been doing a lot of that lately."

"What have you been thinking about?"

"You. Me. My past."

"Want to talk about it?"

"I'd like to talk about you and how you make me feel," he replied.

"Oh. How's that?"

Joe paused. Then in a high voice he sang, "Some might think I'm a clown who laughs and doesn't like to frown. But I'm really a lovesick fellow who's too scared to say so 'cause he's yellow."

Lois laughed, in spite of her confused feelings. "Did you make up that little ditty?"

"Guilty as charged."

Lois wondered if Joe really did love her. In a roundabout way he'd said he did, if his silly tune proved how he felt. She chuckled as she played the words of Joe's song over in her head.

"You're laughing at my love tune?" Joe asked.

"Not really. It's just—"

"I'll be the first to admit I can't carry a tune in a bucket."

Before she could reply, he asked another question. "Are you doing anything special for Christmas?"

Lois hesitated. Was he hinting at spending the holiday together, or was he trying to change the subject? "I'll be spending Christmas Eve with Tabby and Seth and his grandparents, at their retirement home. On Christmas Day we'll be in Olympia with Mom, Dad, and my grandmother."

175

"If you're coming to Olympia, why don't you stop by my house for a while? You could make it either before or after your visit with your folks."

Lois considered Joe's offer then asked, "Don't you have any plans for Christmas?"

"Brian said he might stop by sometime on Christmas Eve, but other than that I'm on my own."

Lois's heart sank at the thought of Joe spending the holiday by himself. It wasn't right for anyone to be alone on Christmas Day. "Why don't you come over to my parents' place for Christmas dinner? They aren't Christians, but they're very hospitable, and I'm sure they'd enjoy meeting you."

"Will Seth and Tabby be there?"

"As far as I know."

Joe was silent for a moment, and then he chuckled.

"What's so funny?"

"Nothing. I'd like to join you for dinner. Just give me your parents' address, tell me what to bring, and I'll be there with my Christmas bells on."

❦

Lois groped for her slippers and padded to the bedroom window. She had been hoping for a white Christmas, but the brilliant blue sky that greeted her on Christmas morning was filled with sunshine and fluffy white clouds. She studied the thermometer stuck to the outside of the glass. Ten degrees above freezing, so there was no snow on the horizon. At least it wasn't raining. Lois would be driving the freeway from Tacoma to Olympia on bare, dry roads, and for that she was thankful.

She had spent Christmas Eve in pleasant company with Tabby and Seth and his dear Christian grandparents. Today would be a sharp contrast. Although her grandmother had recently become a Christian, her parents still refused to see their need for the Lord. Lois hoped her light would shine so they could see how God had changed her life for the better. Tabby and Seth felt the same way. And with Joe there for Christmas dinner, her parents would be surrounded by Christians. She hoped it would make a difference in their attitude toward spiritual things.

❦

Whistling "Jingle Bells," Joe sauntered up the sidewalk toward the Johnsons' brick home. He was in better spirits this Christmas than he had been in many years. Brian had come by his home the night before and told him he'd found a tract someone had left in his cab. He'd been civil and even said he was thinking about going to church. That was an answer to prayer, and if Brian did start attending church, maybe he would finally see his need for Christ. Joe had witnessed to his brother several times over the years, but Brian always refused to talk about it. Now Joe felt as if there might be hope. He would continue to pray for his younger brother and with God's help try to understand him and work toward a better relationship.

Joe glanced down at the Christmas present he'd brought for Lois. He was also carrying a box of cream-filled chocolates he planned to give her folks. He was eager to meet them and hoped they liked candy.

He hesitated a second then rang the bell. Almost at once Lois opened the front door, and the sight of her took his breath away. She was wearing a blue velvet dress that matched her eyes and almost reached to her ankles. Her hair hung down her back, held away from her face with two pearl combs. He thought she looked like an angel.

"Come in," Lois said, warming Joe's heart with her smile. The sparkle in her eyes told him she was glad to see him.

He handed her the wrapped package, along with the chocolates. "The gift's for you, and the candy is for your folks."

"That's so sweet. I have something under the tree for you, too."

Joe followed Lois down the hall and into a cozy living room, where Seth and Tabby sat on the couch beside a middle-aged woman he assumed was Lois and Tabby's mother. She had brown hair and eyes like Tabby's, and her smile reminded him of Lois. Across the room sat an older woman with short, silver-gray hair and pale blue eyes. Lois's grandmother, he guessed. A man with thinning blond hair, a paunchy stomach and eyes the same color as Lois's was relaxing in a recliner near the fireplace. He stood when Joe entered the room. To complete the picture, a fir tree decorated with gold balls and white twinkle lights took up one corner of the room. Joe inhaled the woodsy scent and smiled. It was a pleasant scene, and he was glad he'd come.

"Mom, Dad, Grandma," Lois said with a sweep of her hand, "I'd like you to meet Joe Richey." She turned to Joe and smiled, then nodded toward the woman sitting beside Tabby. "This is my mother, Marsha Johnson."

Mrs. Johnson offered Joe a tentative smile. "Welcome, and Merry Christmas."

Lois gestured toward the older woman sitting in the rocking chair. "I'd like you to meet my grandma, Dottie Haskins."

Grandma Haskins winked at Joe. "It's so nice we're finally able to meet. We've heard a lot about you, young man."

Joe grinned when he noticed Lois was blushing. Apparently she'd been talking about him to her family. "Thanks. It's great to be here."

Lois's father came forward, his hand extended. "And I'm Earl Johnson." He scrutinized Joe a few seconds then his face broke into a broad smile. "I understand you're a clown."

Joe nodded, reaching for his hand.

"I remember seeing some hilarious clown routines when I was a kid and went to the circus. Have you ever worked in a circus?"

"No, I'm a gospel clown, but I also do kids' birthday parties and some other events."

"Well, I'm pleased to meet you, Joe."

"Likewise, Mr. Johnson."

"Earl. Please call me Earl."

Joe pumped his hand. He liked Lois's dad. The man had a firm handshake, and he seemed taken with the idea that Joe was a clown.

"Look what Joe brought," Lois said, handing the box of chocolates to her mother.

Mrs. Johnson looked at Joe and smiled warmly. "Thank you. I'll pass the candy around after dinner so everyone can have some."

"Unless Tabby gets one of her pregnancy cravings and can't resist the temptation to dive into the box before then," Seth said with a deep chuckle. He winked at Joe and nudged his wife gently in the ribs.

"How would you like to sleep on the couch tonight?" Tabby asked, wrinkling her nose at Seth.

He held up one hand. "Not on Christmas Day. It wouldn't be right to kick a man out of his warm bed on Christmas."

Everyone laughed, and Joe took a seat on the floor in front of the fireplace. It felt good to be here with Lois and her family. It had been a year since he'd spent Christmas with anyone, and that had been just him and Mom.

Lois placed the gift Joe had given her under the tree and dropped down beside him, settling against a couple of throw pillows. "Dinner should be ready soon, but if you're hungry we put some cut-up veggies and dip on the coffee table."

Joe glanced at the tray on the table, and his stomach rumbled. He was hungry, but he thought he'd better not fill up on munchies, since the real thing would be served soon.

Everyone engaged in small talk for a while then Mrs. Johnson stood up. "I'd better check on the turkey."

"Would you like some help, Mom?" Tabby asked.

"That's okay, honey. You look kind of tired today, so stay put and rest."

Mrs. Johnson's gaze swung to her younger daughter, and immediately Lois stood to her feet. She looked down at Joe. "Keep the fire warm. I'll be back soon."

❧

Lois helped take the turkey out of the oven then mashed the potatoes while her mom made gravy. She hoped everything was going okay in the living room. Joe appeared to be well received by her family and at ease with everyone.

"Dad seems to have taken a liking to your clown friend," her mother said.

Lois smiled. "Joe's an easy guy to like."

"Like or love?"

Lois's head came up at her mother's direct question. "Who said anything about love?" She searched for words that wouldn't be a lie. "Joe and I are good friends, and even though I care deeply for him, we do have a few problems."

Her mother stirred the gravy. "What kind of problems?"

"Joe's very reserved when it comes to talking about his past, and he doesn't show any emotion but laughter."

"But don't you think being around someone who looks at the bright side of life would be better than having a friend who's full of doom and gloom?"

Lois nodded. "Yes, you're right about that. But too much laughter and clowning around could get to be annoying at times. It seems as if it would be better to have something in between, more of a balance, for a relationship to work."

"You have a point, dear, but keep an open mind. A man can have much worse traits than being a funny guy."

"I know, Mom, and I'm trying to stay open minded."

Her mother moved away from the stove and went to the sink. "This gravy is still a bit too thick. I'd better add more water to the flour mixture."

"I imagine you're looking forward to becoming a grandmother in the spring," Lois said then.

Her mother groaned softly. "I'll say, but it's kind of scary to think about being a grandma. It's been a long time since I held a baby, much less changed diapers or tried my hand at burping."

Lois dropped butter into the potatoes. "It will come back to you." She chuckled. "It's probably like riding a bike. Once you learn, no matter how long it's been between rides, you still remember how to hold on to the handle bars and steer the silly thing."

"I hope you're right. I don't want to mess up my role of grandma as badly as I did mothering."

Lois whirled around to face her mother. "What are you talking about? You were a good mother. You always saw that our needs were met."

Her mother's eyes filled with tears. "I did my best to see to your material needs, but I'm afraid I failed miserably at meeting your emotional needs." She blinked several times.

"Especially Tabby's. I should never have let your father make fun of her the way he did."

Lois wiped her hands on a dish towel and hurried to her mother's side. She put her arms around her shoulders and hugged her. "I'm afraid Dad wasn't the only one guilty of tormenting Tabby. I did plenty of that myself."

"Another area where I failed," the older woman said tearfully. "I should have prevented it from happening. Instead, I watched you and your father become close while Tabby stood on the sidelines feeling insecure and ugly." She gave Lois's arm a gentle pat. "I'm glad the two of you have mended your fences. Even Dad and Tabby are getting along better these days." She stepped back then looked at Lois. "I. . .went to church with your grandmother last week. Did she tell you?"

Lois's mouth dropped open. "She never said a word, but I'm glad to hear it."

"We asked Dad to join us, but he wouldn't budge out of that recliner of his. He said a game was playing on TV, and he wasn't about to miss it."

Lois smiled to herself. She was so grateful her grandmother had made a commitment to the Lord, and now her mom had attended church. Hope for her dad, for both of her parents, welled up inside her.

🌺

Joe sat at the Johnsons' dining room table, enjoying each bite of food he ate. Lois's mother was a good cook, and she also seemed quiet and steady. *Nothing like my mom,* he thought. Being around Lois's father was a pleasure for him, too. Since his own dad died when he was young, he'd grown up without a father. *Maybe if Dad hadn't been killed, Mom would have been easier to live with. At least she'd have had a husband to lean on, and Dad might have persuaded her to take the medicine the doctor prescribed. Maybe if she'd become a Christian sooner—*

"Lois mentioned you use balloon animals and some juggling in your clown routines."

Grandma Haskins's pleasant voice pulled Joe abruptly from his thoughts.

"Oh—yes, I do," he said, blinking.

"Maybe you could give us a demonstration after we've finished dinner and opened our gifts," Lois's mother suggested.

Joe looked at her and smiled. "I suppose I could put on a little skit."

"When I was a boy I used to dream about running away from home and joining the circus," Lois's dad put in. "I either wanted to be a clown or a lion tamer." His stomach jiggled when he laughed.

Joe chuckled. "Now that's quite a contrast, Mr. Johnson—I mean, Earl. Did Lois tell you she's learned some clowning tricks?"

He felt an elbow connect to his ribs and knew Lois wasn't thrilled with his question.

"She's never mentioned it," her mother said, raising her eyebrows. "Lois, maybe you and Joe could perform a routine together, the way Tabby and Seth do."

"That would be fun to watch," Tabby agreed.

Joe glanced at Lois and saw her frown. He knew she wasn't happy about doing a clown routine with him. He reached for her hand under the table. "Lois has taken only a couple of clowning classes, and she's still practicing. Maybe it would be best if I went solo this time."

Lois let out her breath. "Joe's right—he will do much better without me."

Chapter 22

During the rest of dinner, Joe remained quiet, answering questions only when they were directed to him. He was reviewing in his mind the clown routine he planned to do, as well as thinking about what he wanted to say to Lois before he went home.

After they finished eating and the table was cleared, everyone moved to the living room to open Christmas presents. Joe felt out of place, as each member of Lois's family exchanged gifts. Besides the candy, he'd brought only one gift, and that was for Lois. Joe had hoped to give it to her in private, but it didn't look as if that would happen.

"Only two presents are left," Tabby said, as she stacked the items she'd received onto the coffee table.

"One's mine to give Joe, and the other he brought for me," Lois said. She went to the tree and picked up Joe's gift. Joe followed, and they handed each other their presents.

"Should we open them at the same time or take turns?" Joe asked.

Lois shrugged. "Whatever you'd like to do is fine with me."

"Let's open them together," he suggested. "On the count of three. One—two—three!" Joe reached into the green gift bag and pulled out a necktie with a painting of Noah's ark and a rainbow on the front.

"Thanks, Lois. This is great," he said with sincerity.

"You're welcome." Lois tore the wrapping off her gift and peered inside. Then she looked at Joe.

"What is it?" Tabby asked, craning her neck to see around Seth, who sat beside her on the couch.

Lois held up a bright orange construction worker's hat with a bunch of gizmos attached. Even to Joe it looked weird.

"What in the world is that?" Lois's father asked from his chair across the room.

"It looks like something from outer space," Seth said, laughing. "Why don't you model it for us, Lois?"

✿

Lois stared numbly at the so-called "hat" Joe had given her. Two empty cans of soda pop were attached to either side, each connected to a giant plastic straw that trailed over the top of the hat. A third straw came up the back then down over the bill. Hooked to one corner of the helmet was a microphone cord, which was attached to a small metal box with a red lever on the side. Lois had no idea what Joe expected her to do with it.

"I—I thought it would be a nice addition to your clown outfit," Joe said, his face flushed. "Why don't you try it on and show us what it can do?"

Lois stood there, her gaze shifting from Joe to the gruesome hat and back again. She would never wear such a hideous thing! What had possessed the man to give her this ridiculous Christmas present? She handed the hat to Joe. "Here—you wear it."

He shrugged and set it on top of his head. "I might as well show you how it works while I do my clown routine."

Lois sat down on the couch beside Tabby, folded her arms across her chest, and watched. Joe flicked the red button on the small box attached to the microphone, and suddenly a

180

high-pitched noise pierced the air.

Lois cupped both hands over her ears and grimaced. She noticed Mom and Grandma had done the same. Tabby, Seth, and Dad were all smiling as if Joe had done something great.

Joe switched the red lever to the right this time, and bells started ringing. He jumped up and down. "Are those Christmas bells, or is the fire alarm going off?" he shouted.

Before anyone could respond, he bent down and grabbed an orange and two apples from the glass bowl sitting on the coffee table. One at a time he tossed the pieces of fruit into the air, and he soon had them going up and down simultaneously.

Lois had to admit that Joe was good at juggling—and all other phases of clowning for that matter. In minutes he could captivate an audience, as he apparently had her family.

"What goes up must come down!" Joe shouted into the makeshift microphone. "Anyone thirsty?" He continued to juggle the fruit as he pretended to drink from the straw connected to the cans. As if that weren't enough of a show, Joe did it while he hopped on one foot.

Everyone cheered, and Lois noticed her father was laughing so hard tears were streaming down his cheeks. Joe's goofy antics had sure made an impression on him. *If Slow-Joe the Clown comes around more often, Dad's interest in spiritual things might even be sparked.*

As he juggled the fruit, Joe talked about Christianity and how people often juggle their routines to squeeze in time for God. When he was finished, he dropped the fruit back in the bowl then bowed. Everyone clapped, including Lois. Joe had done a good job of presenting the good news, and he'd made her family laugh. Not only was Slow-Joe a great entertainer, but he was a lot of fun. Was that enough? she wondered.

🌼

As the day wore on, Joe began to feel nervous. He liked Lois's family, and he had finally admitted to himself that he was in love with Lois. During the first part of the day she'd been warm and friendly, but since he'd given her that dumb hat and done his impromptu routine, she'd been aloof. He wondered if she was sorry she'd invited him today. It might be his first and last meal at the Johnsons' home, and in his book that would be a real shame.

When Lois excused herself to clear away the dessert dishes, Joe jumped up and followed. "Need some help?" he asked, stepping into the kitchen behind her.

Lois placed the pie plates in the sink. "You rinse, and I'll put the dishes in the dishwasher."

"I think I can handle that." Joe went to the sink and turned on the faucet. He waited for Lois to say something, but she remained quiet as he rinsed the plates and handed them to her.

When the last dish was in place and the dishwasher turned on, Joe reached for Lois's hand. "I had a good time today. Thanks for inviting me to share your Christmas."

She nodded. "You're welcome."

Joe leaned forward, cupped Lois's chin with his hand, and bent to kiss her.

She pulled away abruptly. "We should get back to the others."

"I blew it with that dumb gift I gave you, didn't I?"

She looked at Joe, tears gathering in her blue eyes. "You made a hit with my dad."

"But not you?"

She pressed her lips together.

The tears in Lois's eyes were almost Joe's undoing, and he was tempted to pull her into his arms and say something funny so she would laugh. He hated tears. They were for weak people who couldn't control their emotions.

"I'm in love with you, Lois," he whispered.

Lois stared at him, her eyes wide.

"Aren't you going to say something?" he asked, tipping her chin.

"I–I'm speechless."

Joe chuckled and kissed her forehead. When she didn't resist, his lips traveled down her nose and across her cheek then found her lips.

She wrapped her arms around his neck and returned his kiss. Finally, Lois pulled back and sighed, leaning her head against Joe's chest. "I love you, too, but I think you might need a woman who's more like you."

Joe took a step backward. "What's that supposed to mean?"

She shook her head slowly. "You're a clown, Joe. You clown through the day and into the night."

"That's my job, and I hope I'm good at what I do."

"You are," she assured him.

"Is it because I don't make a lot of money clowning? Is that the problem?"

Lois shook her head. "I've told you before that I'm not hung up on money. But the thing is, all you ever do is clown around. You make jokes when other people would be saying something serious. You don't show any other emotion besides happiness. I suspect you do it to avoid revealing your true feelings." She paused. "After that scene with your brother on Thanksgiving, I think there's a lot you haven't wanted to share with me. I respect your privacy, Joe. But if we're going to continue our relationship, don't you think you need to trust me by sharing what happened in your past that has upset you so much?"

Joe looked at his feet. Lois was right; he needed to be up front with her and stop hiding behind his clown mask to keep from facing his true feelings. But he wasn't sure he could do either yet. Maybe he needed a few more sessions with Pastor Cummings.

"I'm not ready to discuss my family's problems at the moment," he said, offering her what he hoped was a reassuring smile. "But if you'll be patient with me, I hope maybe someday...."

She squeezed his hand. "Let's both be praying about this, okay?"

He nodded and brought Lois's fingers to his lips. "I'd better be going. It's been a great day, and no matter what happens down the road, always remember I love you."

Chapter 23

J oe sat in the chair across from Pastor Cummings's desk, his left leg propped on top of his right knee. Today was his fourth counseling session, and each time he entered this office he became more uncomfortable. The pastor had a way of probing into Joe's subconscious, and some of the things he'd found there scared Joe.

"Tell me more about your mother," the older man said.

Joe released his breath and with it a deep moan. "Well, I've told you she was very depressed one minute and happy the next, and she only got worse after Dad was killed. Her moods were so unpredictable and her expectations ridiculous." He dug his fingers into the sides of the chair and fought against the urge to express his anger. "It was because of Mom's actions that Brian left home shortly after high school. She made our lives miserable when she was alive, but I still loved her."

"Of course you did, Joe." Pastor Cummings leaned forward, resting his elbows on the desk. "What did you do about your mother's actions?"

Joe shrugged his shoulders. "To avoid her anger, I gave in and let her have her way on things—even stuff I felt was wrong." He looked at the pastor. "It was easier than fighting back and suffering the consequences of her frequent outbursts."

"If I've been hearing you right, you felt as though your mother wanted something you weren't able to give."

Joe moved in the chair, putting both feet on the floor. "That's correct. Sometimes I just wanted to shout, 'Go away, Mom, and leave me alone!'"

"But you thought by your mother's actions that your feelings didn't matter?"

Joe nodded again.

"The truth is, they do matter. Because you didn't want to be like your mother, you've chosen to stuff your feelings down deep inside." Pastor Cummings picked up his Bible. "Part of the healing process is being able to accept the pain. God made our feelings, and He uses them to help guide us."

Joe only shrugged.

"Do you let yourself cry when you're hurting, Joe?"

Joe shook his head. "Tears are a sign of weakness. Mom was weak, and she cried a lot. Brian was weak, and he ran away from home." Joe pointed to himself. "I chose to stay and take care of Mom, even though she never showed any appreciation." He frowned. "When she was nice, I felt myself being drawn into her world, like a vacuum sucks lint from the carpet. When she was hateful, though, I wanted to hide my head in the sand and cry until no more tears would come. But I didn't."

"It's not a weakness to cry or hurt, son. Tears can be a key element to strength."

Joe blinked. He'd never thought of tears being related to strength.

Pastor Cummings held the Bible out to Joe. "Here—open to Ecclesiastes, chapter three. Then read verses one to four."

It took a few seconds for Joe to locate Ecclesiastes. He read the passage aloud:

" 'To every thing there is a season, and a time to every purpose under the heaven. . . . A time to weep, and a time to laugh; a time to mourn, and a time to dance.' " He paused and looked at the pastor. "I guess I've never read those verses before, or if I have they never hit home."

"The Lord reveals the meaning of His Word when the need arises. Perhaps you weren't ready to accept the truth before today."

Joe swallowed hard. Pastor Cummings was right; he hadn't been ready. Even now, when he'd been hit with the truth, he was having a difficult time dealing with it. He'd spent so many years hiding behind his clown mask, refusing to show any emotion other than laughter, and even that was forced at times. He felt like a phony, realizing how often he'd clowned around or cracked jokes when deep inside he felt like weeping. Part of him wanted to give in to his tears. Another part was afraid if he did he might never stop crying.

"Mom asked the Lord to forgive her and committed her life to Him shortly before she died," Joe said. "Even though I knew God had forgiven her for treating me so badly, I guess I never forgave her." Joe lowered his head. "I've always felt guilty about it, so maybe that's part of the reason I've been hiding behind humor."

"You've discovered a lot in our last few sessions," the pastor said softly. "It will take time for you to put it into the proper perspective. For now, though, pat yourself on the back and rest in the Lord. He will show you how and when to cry if you need to."

Joe nodded, feeling as if his burden was much lighter than when he'd entered the pastor's study. Maybe someday he would even be ready to discuss his feelings with Lois.

❀

The month of January and the first days of February drifted by like a feather floating in the breeze. Lois kept busy with her secretarial duties at the church during the week, and she spent most weekends helping Tabby redecorate their guest room, turning it into a nursery for the soon-coming baby. It kept her hands busy and her mind off Joe Richey. Since they'd said good-bye on Christmas Day, she'd heard from him only twice. Once he'd called to tell her how much he liked the cute tie she'd given him, and today she'd received a Valentine's card from him in the mail.

"Hey, sis. You look as if you're a thousand miles away."

Tabby's sweet voice pulled Lois out of her musings, and she swiveled her chair around to face her sister.

"You're good at sneaking up on me," Lois said with a grin.

Tabby ambled across the room and lowered herself into the chair beside Lois's desk. She patted her stomach. "I'm practicing for motherhood. Aren't moms supposed to be good at sneaking up on their children and catching them red-handed?"

Lois chuckled. "You're right, but I was only typing a memo for Pastor Hanson. So you didn't catch me with any red color on my hands," she added, smiling.

"It looked more like you were daydreaming to me," Tabby said in a teasing tone. "Unless you've learned how to make that computer keyboard work without touching the keys."

"I guess I *was* caught red-handed," Lois admitted with a sigh.

"What, or shall I say whom, were you thinking about?"

Lois handed the Valentine to her sister. "This came in today's mail."

Tabby's eyes opened wide as she read the verse inside the card. "Sounds like the guy's got it bad, and it's a far cry from the funny clown hat he gave you for Christmas."

Lois lifted her gaze to the ceiling. "Sure—that's why he never calls or comes around anymore."

"Maybe he's been busy with performances. Entertaining is what he does for a living, you know." With her finger, Tabby traced the outline of the red heart on the card. "This Valentine could be a foreshadow of something to come, you know."

Lois was silent then finally said, "Yes, it could be."

Tabby stepped over to Lois's chair. "There are only two ways to handle a man." She laughed. "Since nobody knows what either of them is, I suggest you give the guy a call and thank him for the beautiful card."

"I'll think about it," Lois murmured. "But I've called him a lot over the last few months, and I don't want to seem pushy."

Tabby hugged her sister. "There's nothing pushy about a thank-you."

"True." Lois smiled. "Okay, I'll call him tonight."

"Good for you." Tabby started toward the door. "I need to get back to the day care. I've taken a longer break than I'd planned." She stopped suddenly and sniffed the air. "Say! Do you smell something?"

Lois drew in a breath. "Smoke. It smells like there's a fire somewhere in the building!"

Chapter 24

Joe had battled the desire to see Lois for several weeks. But today was Valentine's Day, and he'd decided to take action. She would no doubt have received his card by now, so he hoped the sentimental verse might pave the way.

As he headed toward Tacoma on the freeway, all he could think about was the need to make things right with Lois. Through counseling with Pastor Cummings and studying the scriptures, he'd finally forgiven his mother and come to grips with his past. Now he wanted to share everything with Lois. He hoped she would be receptive.

A short while later, Joe drove down the street toward Lois's church. His heart lurched when he saw two fire trucks parked in front of the building. As he pulled his pickup to the curb, he could see firemen scurrying about with hoses and other pieces of equipment. Billows of acrid smoke poured from the church.

Joe sprinted from his truck across the lawn, only to be stopped by a fireman. "You can't go in there, sir. A fire started in the janitor's closet, and it's spread throughout most of the building."

"My girlfriend—she works here," Joe said between breaths. He would do anything to find Lois. "I have to get inside!"

The fireman put his hand on Joe's arm. "It's not safe. We're doing everything possible to put the fire out, so please stay out of the way."

Joe dashed to the back of the church, thinking he could slip in that door unnoticed. He had to find Lois and see if she was all right. Others might also be trapped in the church.

He had almost reached the door when two firemen stepped between him and the building. "Where do you think you're going?" one of the men asked.

"I need to get inside. My girlfriend—"

"Oh, no, you don't!" the other fireman shouted. "There's been a lot of damage to the structure. Most of the fire is out, but it's not safe in there."

Joe looked around helplessly, wondering if he could get inside another way. "What about the people inside?" he asked, feeling his sense of panic taking control.

He filled his lungs with air and prayed. *Dear Lord, please let Lois and everyone else be okay.*

Joe felt someone touch his arm. "I thought I saw your truck parked out front. What are you doing here?"

He spun around at the sound of Lois's voice, and the sight of her caused tears to flood Joe's eyes. His stomach knotted as he fought to hold back the tide of emotions threatening to wash over him. He didn't want to cry, but the tears came anyway. He was so relieved to see that Lois wasn't inside the church and appeared to be okay. "Thank God you're not hurt!" he exclaimed.

She smiled at him and reached up to wipe away the tears that had fallen onto his cheeks. "Joe, you're crying."

He nodded and grinned at her. "Yeah, I guess I am." He grabbed Lois around the waist and lifted her up, whirling them both around. "Thank You, Lord!" he shouted. "Thank You a thousand times over!"

"Put me down, you silly man! I'm getting dizzy," Lois said breathlessly.

Joe set her on the ground then placed both hands on her shoulders and stared into the depths of her indigo eyes. "Are you really all right, and did they get everyone out in time?"

She nodded, and her eyes pooled with tears. "Everyone is fine, but the building isn't. I'm afraid what's left of it may have to be torn down."

"The church can be rebuilt," Joe said, "but human life is not replaceable."

"You're so right," Lois agreed. "When the fire broke out, Tabby and I were in my office. Our first thought was about the day care kids who were in the basement."

Joe felt immediate concern. "Were they hurt?"

She shook her head. "Not a single child. Almost everyone was out of the building before the fire trucks even arrived."

"When I got here and saw all the commotion, then looked around and didn't see you, I was afraid you were trapped inside the church," Joe said, feeling as if he might cry again.

Lois smiled up at him. "It's nice to know you care so much."

Joe clasped her hand and gave it a gentle squeeze. "Thanks to my pastor's wise counsel and God's Word, I'm learning to put the past behind and show my emotions. That's why I drove over here, Lois. I wanted to tell you about it." He pulled a bunch of balloons from his jacket pocket and held them up. "I also wanted to give you these."

She tipped her head to one side. "Some deflated balloons?"

He chuckled and wiped his sweaty palms on the side of his blue jeans. "Well, I'd planned to show up at your office with a bouquet of balloon flowers—like the ones I made you the night we first met." Joe cleared his throat. "I, well, I came here to ask you a question."

"What question?"

Joe felt jittery all of a sudden. If he weren't careful, he would slip into the old Joe—the clown who didn't know how to show his real feelings.

He stuffed all but one balloon back in his pocket then blew up that one and twisted it into a wiener dog. He handed the pooch to Lois, bowed low at the waist, and said, "Lois Johnson, will you be my housewife—I mean, maid—I mean—"

Lois stepped away, a puzzled look on her face. "You're such a big kidder, Joe."

❀

Joe watched Lois walk next door to the senior pastor's house. She'd thought he was clowning around when he tried to propose, and now she was probably mad at him.

Tears welled up in his eyes at the thought of losing her. He had meant for the proposal to be sweet and tender, and he'd botched it up but good, giving her a balloon dog then asking her to be his housewife. "What a jerk she must think I am," Joe mumbled, staring down at his feet. "What can I do now?"

"Go after her," he heard a voice whisper behind him. He turned to find Tabby standing near him. "Tell her you weren't kidding but just got nervous and messed up your presentation."

"Yeah, I guess you're right. I hope she'll believe me."

Tabby patted Joe on the back and started across the lawn toward the parsonage.

Joe sucked in a breath and offered up a quick prayer. Tabby was right; he did need to do something—quickly.

❀

Lois couldn't believe Joe was crying one minute, telling her he'd been in counseling and was learning to express his feelings, and the next minute he was joking about something as solemn as marriage. In light of the seriousness of the church fire, he was probably just trying to get her to chuckle. She shouldn't have been so sensitive. She wished she hadn't walked away so abruptly without letting him explain.

Tabby had entered the parsonage a few minutes earlier and gone inside with the others. Rather than talking about the fire with everyone, Lois was sitting on the front porch, trying to sort things out. She closed her eyes and was about to pray when she heard a familiar voice.

"Lois, I need to talk to you."

She opened her eyes as Joe took a seat beside her. He was smiling, but she saw the tension in his jaw. His smile seemed fake, like the one he painted on when he dressed as a clown.

He leaned closer, his face inches from hers, and Lois let out a sigh.

"I'm sorry about the dumb proposal and balloon dog," he murmured. "Would you take a walk with me so we can talk?"

She hesitated for a moment, uncertain what to say.

Joe grabbed Lois's hand and pulled her gently to a standing position.

She looked up at him. "What's going on?"

"I'm taking you someplace special."

Lois was tempted to resist. She couldn't explain the funny feeling she got every time she saw Joe. At some moments, like now, she had to fight the urge to throw herself into his arms.

They left the pastor's yard and walked in silence, until the small chapel behind the church came into view. It was used for intimate weddings, baptisms, and foot washing. "At least this building didn't catch on fire," Lois said as Joe opened the door and led her inside.

Joe nodded and motioned her to take a seat on the front pew. Then he knelt on one knee in front of her.

She squirmed uneasily and held her breath. What was he up to now?

"I love you, Lois," he whispered. "I know I'm not the ideal catch, and I'll probably never make a lot of money, but if you'll have me as your husband, I promise to love you for the rest of my life. Will you please marry me?"

Lois's vision clouded with tears as she smiled at Joe. "Yes. A thousand times, yes!"

His face broke into a huge grin. "Can I take that as a yes?"

She chuckled and winked at him. "It's a definite yes."

Joe stood and helped Lois to her feet then pulled her into his arms. "From now on we can clown around together, but I promise to get serious sometimes, too."

She laid her head against his chest and sighed contentedly. "I'd like that, Joe. I want to spend the rest of my life telling others about God's love, and I want to be the kind of wife who loves you no matter how much you clown around."

Secret Admirer

by Gail Sattler

Chapter 1

S hannon, I'd like you to meet the new dispatcher, Todd Sanders. Todd, this is Shannon
Andrews, our payroll clerk."

Shannon squeezed her eyes shut at the sound of the name. It couldn't be. It just couldn't.

"Hey, Shan-nooze. Long time no see."

That voice. The hated nickname. It could be, and it was.

"Todd," she muttered. "Long time no see." Shannon forced her eyes open and gave him a welcoming smile, even though it was almost painful. She wanted to pinch herself to wake up but knew it wouldn't help her present nightmare. Gary, the operations manager, smiled first at her then at Todd. "You two know each other? It's a small world, isn't it? Come on, Todd. I'll introduce you to the rest of the staff, then we'll get you set up at your station."

All thoughts of the coming payroll deadline deserted Shannon as she watched Gary introduce Todd around the office. She hadn't seen Todd for a long time, and it was no loss. Briefly she considered turning in her resignation then banished the thought. She would be strong and show him he no longer affected her.

Unpleasant memories flashed through her mind. From the time she was eight, Todd and her eleven-year-old brother Craig had been best friends. The day she moved out was the day she finally stopped having to bear the brunt of Todd's teasing.

During the time leading up to her high school graduation, she'd foolishly thought she was in love with Todd. However, the painful, constant jabs about being nothing more than his friend's bratty kid sister cured her. Thankfully, she got over her high school crush before he discovered how she felt. If he had, she never would have lived it down.

Over the past two years, Shannon had avoided Todd, seeing him only when Craig dragged him to one of their church functions. Despite the safe atmosphere of the church she'd grown up in, those occasions always affected her, bringing back the memories of past hurts, even after all that time. Fortunately, it didn't happen often. In the past year she hadn't seen him at all. Maybe that was why seeing him now at work, it hit her with a double whammy.

She thought she had put Todd and his idiocy behind her. Obviously, she was wrong.

Shannon forced herself to return her attention to her work. She'd almost completed the warehouse payroll when she felt someone poking her arm.

"Shan! I'm talking to you! Have you met that new dispatcher? He sure is a sweetheart, isn't he? Wouldn't you love to meet him in a dark corner one night?"

In the light or dark, despite his good looks and charming ways, which he used when it suited him, she'd already seen enough of Todd Sanders to last a lifetime. "No," she muttered through gritted teeth. The last time she met Todd in a dark corner she hadn't known he was there until too late. That time, he had scared her half to death with some furry monster toy. She didn't hear the end of it for months.

Without fail, every time she went to her parents' home for a family occasion, her brother regaled her with never-ending tales of Todd that she didn't want to hear. According to Craig, Todd had turned his life over to Christ about a year ago. He claimed Todd had changed and grown up a lot since then. Regardless, even though his faith would make a lot of changes in him, deep down, Shannon knew he was still the same old Todd. She was sick to death of his immature pranks. Out of self-preservation, she intended to avoid him as much as possible.

"Hey, Shan. Aren't you coming for lunch?"

Shannon shook her head. "No. I'm going to work through my break and catch up on a few things. I have a three o'clock cutoff deadline on this, and it's going to be close."

❀

Todd walked into the lunchroom, but Shannon wasn't there, leaving him strangely disappointed. He'd always enjoyed their verbal banter over the years. Even though the sharp repartee didn't belong in the work environment, that didn't mean they couldn't talk civilly to each other during break time.

He hadn't seen much of Shannon since she'd moved into her own apartment. In fact, the last time was probably at least a year ago. He thought of her often, and seeing her now only emphasized how much he'd missed her. Todd found it amusing that she hadn't noticed him when he came in to apply for the job, but he'd seen her. At the time, she'd been concentrating on the computer screen at her desk, oblivious to all else around her. Either she had grown prettier in the last year, or the old saying about absence making the heart grow fonder was true after all.

He'd liked Shannon for years. Since she was his best friend's kid sister, though, he didn't want to damage his friendship with Craig. Most of all, he didn't want to get beaten to a pulp if any relationship between them went sour. He'd done whatever he had to in order to keep everything the same as it had always been, maintaining a safe emotional distance. Sometimes, he'd even deliberately done things to push her away, rather than risk getting too close.

Gary and one of the other dispatchers joined him at the table, spread their lunches out in front of them, and began to talk about the events of the day. Todd responded to a few comments, but his thoughts kept drifting back to Shannon.

He remembered the crush she'd had on him when she was in high school. He'd never been so flattered in his life. But, while Shannon had graduated with honors, he'd been working two jobs to pay off a major debt not of his own making. Plus, he'd been going through a rough time at home with his mother, which had become increasingly worse since his father left. Instead of dealing with his problems, he'd taken out most of his frustrations on Shannon, over and above the usual jokes he played on her as Craig's kid sister. She hadn't deserved it. Memories of his behavior still filled him with guilt, even after all this time.

In hindsight he realized life would have been easier if he'd shared his troubles with Craig sooner, but he'd been too proud and too overwhelmed to ask for help.

But that was years ago. Todd pushed a past he couldn't change to the back of his mind and concentrated on things as they were today. Over the years, Shannon had grown from an awkward, mouthy kid into a witty, attractive woman. Todd tried not to smile as he thought of his last view of Shannon, typing away at her computer. He'd always teased her about being nerdy with her aptitude for figures; he hadn't wanted to admit how proud of her he'd been since mathematics was never his strong suit.

Now, after much hard work, at the young age of twenty-five, Shannon had become the chief payroll administrator for a multinational courier corporation. Through Craig, Todd knew the extent and responsibilities of her job, and it bothered him that Gary had referred to her as only a clerk. She deserved more respect than that.

He couldn't erase the past, but Todd figured that since they would now be working together, it would be a good time to make a new future. Her graciousness in the face of defeat had always impressed him. Even though she didn't know it, she'd always held a piece of his heart in the palm of her hand.

The timing may not have been right to start a relationship with Shannon Andrews before this, but things were about to change. He hadn't been a Christian long in the overall scheme of life, but he didn't think it a coincidence that God had placed him at Kwiki Kouriers for a good reason; he felt sure that reason was Shannon.

First he'd catch up on old times and tell her all that had changed in the last year or so. He imagined the two of them, walking down the beach, barefoot, hand in hand, the water lapping around their ankles as they talked. Of course, it would be different without Craig present. Todd couldn't remember ever being alone with Shannon for more than a few minutes at a time. That, too, was about to change.

Since the beach wasn't very realistic, Todd thought of other places to be alone with Shannon and where the best spot for that kind of conversation would be. He imagined them sitting side by side in a dimly lit restaurant, romantic music playing in the background, where they could have a special quiet time, just the two of them.

Todd shook his head. They were nowhere near that stage in their relationship. The most likely place for them to spend time together without the encumbrance of work would be after church on Sunday morning, although he didn't want to wait a week just to talk. He'd been attending Craig's church recently, and he missed not seeing Shannon there. Craig had told him Shannon now attended a small church close to her apartment, along with some of her friends who lived nearby. She attended church with her family only when something special was going on. However, those occasions seemed to be when Todd was unable to attend. It was almost as if she planned it that way.

Todd frowned as he checked his watch. The lunch break was nearly up, and Shannon still had not appeared. He wanted to detour past her desk to talk but decided against it since it was his first day at the new job. Instead, he would leave it up to her to approach him.

She didn't approach him all week. She worked through her lunch every day, and he heard talk that the rest of the staff was starting to wonder why she suddenly had so much extra work to do. He had a nagging suspicion her work wasn't the reason for her absence at lunchtime—he was.

By Friday, Todd couldn't stand it any longer. He didn't want to risk a confrontation in the middle of the office, so at the end of the day when he left the building, he didn't leave the parking lot. He leaned against the fender of her car, crossed his arms, and waited.

He didn't wait long. Soon Shannon rushed out the back door at a near run, straight for her car, and straight for him.

Her feet froze on the spot as soon as she saw him. "What are you doing here?"

"I've wanted to talk to you all week, but you seem to be avoiding me."

"Me?" She laughed a very humorless laugh. "Why would *I* avoid *you*?"

Todd covered his heart with his hands. "I detect a hint of sarcasm in your voice, Shannon. If I were the sensitive type, which I am, by the way, you could hurt my feelings."

She snorted. "Move over, Todd. I have places to go. I don't want to run you over, but I will if I have to."

"The only thing you've run over is my poor heart."

She snorted again. "Give me a break."

"Come on, Shannon. Seriously. I think we should go somewhere and talk. We can go out for supper. I'll even pay."

Rather than the enthusiastic response Todd would have preferred to see, she stared at him in open astonishment. He couldn't help but feel stung.

"Is this some kind of joke? You wouldn't take me to some place that serves frog legs, would you?"

"Frog legs?" He watched her cross her arms and tap her foot while his mind raced, trying to figure out the significance of her remark. "Oh! Frog legs! That was just a joke!"

She wagged her finger in the air at him then stabbed him in the chest with it. "I have never been so embarrassed in my life. Imagine when I got to work, opened my lunch bag, reached in for my sandwich and touched a cold, slimy frog instead! When I screamed and nearly fainted, they were ready to call either the funny farm or an ambulance."

"You mean you didn't look in the bag before you left the house? You took the frog to work? It was my idea, but it was Craig who took out your sandwich and put in the frog before you left."

Instead of replying, she lifted her purse. Todd ducked and raised his hands to protect himself, but she wound back and whacked him anyway.

"Not only did I take the frog to work, but it took my entire lunch break to drive around and find a park with a running stream so I could let the poor thing go. No pet store would take it, and I couldn't wet it with chlorinated tap water! And then I had to face everyone's jokes for weeks."

"I'm sorry. I really am."

"Get out of my way. I'm going home. Alone."

Dazed, Todd stepped aside and watched as Shannon jabbed the key into the lock. She swung the door open, hopped in, slammed the door, and took off with a squeal of rubber.

The woman used up her entire lunch break to save a frog he'd found in a ditch? Todd was suddenly hit by what he should have realized years ago. He was in love with his best friend's sister.

Todd frowned as her taillights disappeared around the corner. Over the years, he'd been less than kind to her, but in the end, she always forgave him, which he now saw made him love her even more. This time, however, it looked as if he'd gone too far. He recalled that not long after he convinced Craig to put the frog in her lunch bag she moved away from home. The Bible spoke of forgiving someone seventy times seven, but the frog might have made seventy times seven plus one.

It would be the hardest thing he'd ever had to do, but he had to show Shannon how sorry he was—and somehow convince her to take him seriously as her Mr. Right for the rest of her life.

He knew she didn't like frogs, but he knew her well enough to know what she did like.

All he had to do was figure out what to do about it.

Chapter 2

Shannon ran from her parking space into the office then stiffened in an effort to appear dignified as she walked to her desk, past everyone else who was already hard at work. In four years, she'd never been late, until today. All night, she'd tossed and turned and hadn't fallen asleep until almost dawn. Then she slept through her alarm.

It was Todd's fault.

On Friday night, she thought she made it clear when she told him to leave her alone, but as usual he didn't listen. On Sunday morning, she'd gone to church with her family to see her brother sing a solo, and Todd had arrived. When she realized he was going to sit beside her, Shannon moved to the end of the row. Todd had never been one to take hints. To her dismay he sat beside her again. To show him she had no intention of being near him and that she wouldn't let him manipulate her, she moved again. She squeezed herself between her parents, which she hadn't done since she was five years old. Both of them had been shocked but said nothing at her childish behavior.

Todd had driven her to it.

She busied herself in her work then nearly snapped her pencil in half at the sound of a familiar, deep male voice beside her.

"Good morning, Shannon."

She refused to look up. She began adding a row of figures, pushing the keys on her calculator much harder than necessary. "Good morning, Todd."

"Ah. You said good morning rather than grunting at me. I'm making progress."

Shannon hit TOTAL, clasped her hands on the desk in front of her, and turned her head to look up at him. "May I help you with something, or are you here just to torture me?"

At her words, he sighed, his playful grin dropped, and he rammed his hands into his pockets. If she didn't know him so well, she might have felt guilty for bruising his feelings. Even when he didn't try, Todd exuded a unique charm. Fortunately, she was immune. After one agonizing week, though, at least half the female staff was infatuated with him. His sparkling brown eyes were exactly the same color as his hair, except in the peak of summer, when the sun bleached it almost blond. People always counted on him to liven up any situation, which he always did. Except for when she bore the brunt of it, which was most of the time, Shannon hated to admit she also enjoyed his sense of humor.

"All I wanted to do was ask if you would be as busy this week as you were last and if you were going to start taking your lunch break again."

She couldn't lie. She expected he would eventually figure out she was avoiding him. This week she refused to play mind games with herself. If Todd was in the lunchroom at the same time, it didn't matter. He wasn't going to stop her from eating. She refused to give him control of her life or let him intimidate her anymore. "I'll be taking my lunch break at the regular time."

His grin returned, and his brown eyes lit up. Eyes a woman could get lost in. Shannon forced herself to remember this was Todd Sanders.

He leaned forward and covered her hands with one of his. "Would you give me the honor of sitting with me?"

Shannon yanked her hands away. "Never."

He snapped his fingers. "Can't blame a guy for trying."

Why he wanted to sit with her, she would never know. A week had passed, and everything was normal except for the constant reminders of his presence. Shannon wondered if perhaps she might have misjudged him by expecting that he would still play foolish pranks or bring up embarrassing moments in front of their workmates. But just because he was behaving himself at work didn't mean she could trust him to be the same when they were alone. Even if she could eventually trust him, that didn't mean she wanted to spend her breaks with him.

Over the weekend, she'd spent much time in prayer, trying to convince herself to forgive and forget. When she'd done the same over the years he had disappointed her again and again. After his little performance Sunday morning, Shannon decided to err on the side of caution.

"If you'll excuse me, I have work to do." She picked up her pencil and continued with her calculations.

❧

Todd returned to his station. He tried to be happy but couldn't. He still felt guilty knowing she had avoided going into the lunchroom the previous week because of him. It gave him some relief to know she had progressed to sitting voluntarily in the same room with him. But Todd wanted more.

He wanted to sit at the same table with her and start fresh. He wanted her to like the new, slightly improved Todd Sanders.

It had been over a year since he'd left the old Todd behind. At the time, he'd had a serious heart-to-heart talk with Craig, and in that one day, his life changed forever. Craig had always been a steadying influence, especially throughout the years leading up to his parents' divorce. While growing up, he spent more time at Craig's house than his own. There he'd seen the way a normal family lived, compared to the constant fighting, bickering, and even violence he was used to.

Craig had taken him to his church's youth group meetings a number of times and talked to him often about the love of Jesus, but Todd had always shrugged it off, not feeling very lovable. Then one day, when he was talking to Craig, years after he'd become an adult and stopped going to youth group, something inside him snapped. He thought he'd been handling things just fine, but suddenly, everything came spilling out. He surrendered control of his life to Jesus, and in finding Jesus he found himself.

It was time to move forward and correct some past mistakes, and Shannon was one of them. Not just one—Shannon was the most important.

He watched from a distance until Shannon was settled in the lunchroom with her lunch spread in front of her so she couldn't move then to another table without looking odd to her friends. Todd sucked in a deep breath and gathered his courage. He cleared his throat, marched to her table, and sat in the empty chair beside her.

"Hi, Shannon. Mind if I join you?"

She nearly choked on her food, but he pretended not to notice.

He wanted to slide his chair closer to hers, but everyone else at the table, all women, was staring. He gave them his best smile then winked at the youngest, whom he recognized as the file clerk. She giggled, making him wish a certain someone else would be as enthusiastic about his presence.

"Yes, Todd? Did you forget to turn in some of the drivers' time cards?"

He pretended to shiver at her cold response, knowing she would pick up his meaning from past experience, but none of the other women would.

She had the grace to blush.

He plunked his lunch tote on the tabletop and proceeded to empty the contents. The women stared as he pulled out the individual containers one at a time, moving aside their own lunches to make room on the table.

"You're going to eat all that? Well, some things never change."

Todd patted his flat stomach and grinned. "I'm a growing boy. But I'll make a sacrifice for you. I'll share." He picked up the chocolate bar, which he knew was her favorite kind, waved it in front of her, then held it out to her, inviting her to take it from his hand.

She shook her head. "I'm on a diet. Thanks anyway."

His eyes narrowed. While Shannon had never been thin, she certainly wasn't fat. If he had learned one thing over the years, it was never to make comments about a woman's weight, except to ask if they'd lost some. He'd bought the chocolate bar especially for her as a peace offering, but apparently, she wasn't going to make it easy for him, not that he deserved easy. "Take it. If you feel you need to work it off we can go jogging, or I'll challenge you to a game of tennis after work. I promise I'll let you win."

She rolled her eyes then took a sip of her tea, some herbal blend he absolutely hated but couldn't recall the name. He knew the box was green. And a box of it just happened to be in his cupboard, in case he could ever convince her to set foot in his door.

"I don't think so."

The young clerk piped up. "I'll go jogging or play tennis with you after work, Todd."

Todd cleared his throat. He didn't really want to do either. After work, he wanted only to go home, sit back on the couch, and put his feet up, especially if he could get Shannon to relax with him. He'd even make her a cup of that horrid tea.

He turned and smiled at the girl, wishing he could remember her name. "Sorry. I was just kidding. I'm going straight home after work."

Todd thought it best to be quiet as he ate his sandwich, then the carrots, the muffin, and the apple, while the ladies around him nibbled at their salads. They sipped their coffee and tea, and Todd chugged down a pint of chocolate milk.

When lunchtime was over, the others gathered their belongings, and Todd tossed his empty containers into his lunch tote.

The sound of Shannon's voice beside him almost made him miss his last shot before he snapped the lid shut.

"Honestly, Todd—I don't know where you put all that food."

He grinned and patted his stomach again. "I told you I'm a growing boy."

She rolled her eyes. "That's for sure."

Without another word, she returned to her desk.

Todd lowered his chin so no one could see him smiling. She spoke to him without his initiating it. He was making progress.

✾

It had taken two weeks, and his only improvement was that when he smiled or said hello she would smile back.

Two long weeks. Todd didn't want to calculate how long it would take to get a warm response. What he wanted most was for her to see he'd changed. He wanted to ask her out. He wanted to share his joys and his sorrows with her, and for her to do the same. He wanted to be close enough to pray with her. Not the general prayer and praise items he heard at the large Bible study he attended weekly. He wanted to know the things near her heart. And when they had nothing to say, he wanted to be able to enjoy a companionable silence, to be comfortable together without the need for words.

He wanted to touch her without her cringing, thinking he was going to tickle or jab her. He wanted to hold her the way a man holds a woman, to hold her tight and bury his face in her hair and tell her he loved her and hear she loved him, too.

He wanted to win her confidence and earn her trust, something he hadn't done before.

He needed advice.

Usually, he asked Craig for help, especially lately. This time, however, he deemed it wise not to talk to Craig about how to get close to his sister. Todd valued his life.

He went home and prayed for an answer.

Chapter 3

Good morning, Shannon."

"Good morning, Todd."

To Shannon's surprise, Todd didn't stop to linger as they crossed paths on the way to their desks. He merely smiled and continued on his way into the dispatch office, coffee mug in hand. Shannon couldn't decide if she was disappointed or not. It was the start of the third week of being in close proximity for eight hours a day, and so far, to the untrained eye, all had appeared normal. Todd had not brought up past experiences, nor had he been overly familiar with her in front of the rest of the staff. He treated her exactly the same as everyone else. And she didn't know what to make of it.

Shannon rested her mug of hot tea on the corner of her desk as she sat down then opened the drawer to get her pencil. Instead of the pencil, she found a roll of white paper tied with a bright red ribbon. What looked like a chocolate kiss wrapped in foil was knotted to the ribbon. Shannon glanced from side to side, and when she was certain no one was looking, she untied the ribbon and read the note.

Dearest Shannon,
Roses are red,
Violets are blue.
Chocolate is sweet,
And so are you.
Your Secret Admirer

Shannon reread the note then dropped it, along with the ribbon and the candy, back into the drawer. She slammed the drawer shut.

Dearest Shannon? Secret Admirer?

She couldn't imagine who would do such a thing. Whoever the joker was, Shannon didn't consider it very funny. Her first suspect was Todd, but this wasn't his style. There was no obvious punch line. Anonymous frogs were his style, not sweet little personal notes presented with candy. Besides she had just walked in with him. Todd received great satisfaction from watching the recipients of his little jokes, but he had stepped right past her, straight into the dispatch area, just as he had every other day in the past two weeks.

As discreetly as she could, without moving her head, Shannon once more studied the office. Still no one was watching, so she slowly opened the drawer and delicately picked off the foil wrapping.

It looked like chocolate.

She picked it up.

It felt like chocolate. It smelled like chocolate. She cautiously bit the tip off. It even tasted like chocolate. In fact she recognized the chocolate. This was not from the bulk bin at the grocery store. This was from her favorite specialty shop. At first, she thought it had to be from someone who knew her fairly well but then decided it was just a coincidence. Lots of people loved this particular brand; that was how the store stayed in business.

All day, not a soul acted any differently toward her, nor did anyone exhibit any suspicious behavior. By the end of the day, Shannon managed to shrug it off, chalking it up to one of life's little mysteries.

❀

Tuesday morning, after relaxing with an early cup of tea in the lunchroom with a few of the other women, Shannon headed for her desk. She sat down, set her mug on the corner of the desk as she had every other morning; but when she reached to open her drawer, she hesitated.

Shannon bit back a smile. Yesterday was an isolated incident. She just hadn't figured out the person or the punch line.

Shannon opened the drawer and caught her breath. Another note lay in her pencil tray. White paper tied with a red ribbon, chocolate kiss attached. Before she touched it, not bothering to be discreet, she spun around in her chair and blatantly studied everyone in the office. Fewer people were in the office than yesterday this early, and all of them were women. Faye lifted her head, made eye contact, then returned to her work.

Shannon concentrated on the little white piece of paper. Quickly, she pulled the ribbon off, left the chocolate kiss in the tray, and unrolled the paper.

Dearest Shannon,
 A chocolate kiss
 Makes me think of you.
 I hope that now
 This will remind you of me, too.
     Your Secret Admirer

Shannon's heart raced as she scrunched the paper in her hand and glanced around the room. The words *Dearest Shannon* echoed in her head as sharply as if she'd heard them out loud. She contemplated the possibility of another woman named Shannon being hidden somewhere in the building. Whoever the man was, his sentiments were romantic, even if his pentameter wasn't quite right.

"Hey, Shan-nooze. Did you see the hockey game on TV last night? The Leafs won." Todd approached from the lunchroom, holding his coffee mug.

Shannon fumbled with the note, shoved it back in the pencil tray, and slammed the drawer shut. Here was one man who knew better than to call her sweet. Over the years, one of the few activities she had managed to participate in with her brother and his friends, Todd included, was to play hockey with them. She was the best forward among them, and she never let them forget it.

"Yes, it was a good game," she mumbled.

The same as the day before, Todd didn't stop to chat. Once again, he simply disappeared through the doorway into the dispatch office. The man was going to drive her crazy.

Last night, she'd had a long talk with Craig. She didn't know how it happened, but a major portion of their conversation centered around Todd.

Craig had been accompanying Todd to the Bible study she used to attend when she lived at home. Shannon wanted to hear more, but Craig didn't tell her anything she hadn't heard before. Craig said Todd took his faith seriously and was now living a good Christian life, which meant both in and out of church.

She tried to prod Craig for information on what Todd thought of the two of them working together, but Craig didn't know. He said Todd deliberately avoided that topic.

Shannon found it difficult to focus on her work. Out of the corner of her eye, she watched everyone around her, testing their reactions as she purposely mentioned her favorite brand of chocolate kisses in every conversation. No one acted any different than any other day.

She tried to limit the possibilities of who the note writer could be; but when she counted the single male members of the office staff, the dispatch office, the foremen, warehousemen, and drivers, the list seemed endless. She didn't think most of them even knew her name; they only knew her as the payroll clerk. But all it took was one.

By the time she went home for the evening, she was still no closer to a solution.

❧

Wednesday morning, Shannon deliberately arrived at work early. She didn't linger in the lunchroom. She didn't take time to make a cup of tea.

Shannon hustled to her desk and opened the drawer.

Another white paper lay rolled up in her pencil tray, again tied with a red ribbon and accompanied by a chocolate kiss. Her hands shook as she tugged the ribbon open.

Dearest Shannon,
　　Your happy smile
　　Shines every day.
　　You are more special
　　Than words can say.
　　　　Your Secret Admirer

Shannon nearly choked. She wasn't special. She was ordinary. Very ordinary. Nor could she figure out who in the world would think she was special, except her parents, who didn't count in this instance.

She tried to determine who had access to her desk, and the answer was everyone.

Apparently, some detective work was in order. The first and most logical step would be to ask, without giving away details, if other office staff had seen anyone lingering around her desk. It would take only two seconds, though, to open her drawer, slip something in and close it. A person wouldn't have to slow down very much when walking past. Employees dropped time cards and medical forms on her desk all the time. Some even opened her drawer freely to borrow her pens if she wasn't there and they needed to leave her a note.

She decided not to ask questions of the men, in case she asked the person who had actually left the note. Most of all she didn't want people talking. She only wanted to find out who was doing this.

Footsteps sounded behind her. Todd, with his usual morning coffee in hand, was on his way to the dispatch office.

"Todd, may I ask you something?"

He shuffled the mug from one hand to the other. "Ouch, ouch! I can't stop now. I overfilled my coffee, and it's spilling on my fingers. Maybe later."

Muttering under his breath and leaving a trail of coffee dribbles on the floor, Todd disappeared through the dispatch office doorway.

For a moment, Shannon had considered that Todd could be on her list of suspects, but she now mentally crossed him off. He could have saved his fingers from further harm by resting the coffee mug on her desk and talking to her for a minute or two before resuming his journey. But he didn't. He'd kept right on going, not even looking at her as he balanced his too-full coffee mug.

Oddly, his actions gave Shannon a strange sensation in the pit of her stomach. She wondered if he had intended to give her a taste of her own medicine by virtually ignoring her. He'd done exactly to her what she'd been doing to him since they had begun working together. Intentional or not, it gave her a stab of guilt, now knowing what it felt like to be passed by.

Shannon continued to stare at the doorway long after Todd disappeared from sight. He hadn't deserved to be treated the way she'd been treating him. Since they had been working together, he had been friendly and courteous. No one who saw them together would know of their shaky past relationship. For once, he was acting mature, which made her wonder if perhaps Craig could be right. Perhaps Todd had changed.

Shannon blinked hard a couple of times and shifted her gaze to a blank spot on the wall. What was she thinking? Just as in the past, no matter how much she hoped and prayed he would change, Todd was still Todd.

The warehouse supervisor thunked a pile of time cards on the corner of her desk, interrupting her mental meanderings. Shannon returned her thoughts to her job.

The whole day, she didn't venture far from her desk. Whenever she did leave, she watched it out of the corner of her eye. To her dismay, no one came within touching distance of it when she was nearby, except to drop off more time cards or mail. Short of video surveillance, she didn't know what else to do.

Not wanting to waste any more time, she gave up trying and buried herself in the stacks of papers and time cards.

✿

Shannon flipped the page on her desk calendar. Today was Thursday. She didn't want to know what was inside her drawer. But before she could begin her work she had to get her pencil. She couldn't sit and stare at the closed drawer all day.

Taking in a deep breath for courage, Shannon yanked the drawer open. Sure enough, another note awaited her. With trembling fingers, she pulled open the ribbon.

Dearest Shannon,
You're sweet, you're kind,
You're very smart.
Just by being you,
You've won my heart.
   Your Secret Admirer

A sick feeling rolled through Shannon's stomach. Whoever this Secret Admirer was, she worried in earnest that he was serious. What scared her more than anything was that she had no idea who he might be.

She needed help. Except she didn't know whom to ask. She had already figured out she couldn't ask any of the men. Nor did she want to ask the women in her immediate vicinity. She was too embarrassed to tell anyone what was happening and too afraid they would start to gossip.

The only person she could trust was good ol' Todd. Being a man, Todd might overhear talk amongst the other men. If she was lucky, Mr. Secret Admirer might let a few things slip—if someone knew what to listen for.

The key would be Todd. Once she told him what was going on, she knew he'd keep her secret. Shannon could weasel almost any information out of Craig. But she'd never stood a chance with Todd, which was probably one of the reasons he was so successful at his many escapades.

For the first time since Todd started working at Kwiki Kouriers, Shannon could hardly wait for his arrival.

This time, however, when Todd walked through the main office on his way to the dispatch area, he wasn't alone; he was deep in conversation with Gary, his supervisor. Shannon couldn't interrupt, especially with such a delicate personal matter. It would have been bad enough if any of her female coworkers found out, but she certainly didn't want any of the men to know, least of all, Gary. Gary had asked her out a few times, and she'd turned him down, so she didn't want him to suspect a potential romance was growing right under his nose, even if it was one sided.

By the time Shannon had an opportunity to talk to Todd alone, she'd lost her courage. Years ago, she knew he would have laughed at her trepidation about an unknown suitor attempting to woo her from a distance, since she wasn't the romantic type.

Still, the notes and the effort the Secret Admirer was making touched her heart in a strange way. She didn't want to hurt the man; she only wanted him to stop.

She wanted to think Todd would understand why she felt that way, but she wasn't sure he would. Not that Todd was completely insensitive; she had seen occasional flickers of a gentle side, especially since he'd been working there. She simply decided he wouldn't understand why she couldn't let it run its course and stop.

She figured he'd tell her to enjoy it, too. Todd had always had an insatiable need for attention. He didn't know when to quit, and he often created a scene when he knew people were watching him. Shannon didn't like to be the center of attention. She just wanted to be left alone, and that included anonymous romantic notes.

❧

Shannon flipped the page on her desk calendar. It was Friday. Only one more day until the weekend when she could either put this foolishness behind her or spend some serious time trying to figure out the identity of her mysterious admirer. For a second, she considered coming in over the weekend and dusting for fingerprints.

Sure enough, Shannon found another note in her drawer, as she had the previous four days.

After she made a cursory check to see if anyone was watching, she untied the bow, popped the chocolate kiss into her mouth, and opened the roll of paper.

This time the note wasn't a poem at all; it was a message, and it was longer. Rather than take the chance that someone would see it in walking by, she quickly folded it, stuck it in her pocket, ran into the ladies' washroom, and shut the door. She dug the note out of her pocket.

Dearest Shannon,

As you can tell by now, I'm not very good at writing poetry, so I will simply tell you what is in my heart. You are sweet and wonderful, and your laugh warms my soul like the spring sunshine, filling me with hope and happiness. Please keep smiling.

Your Secret Admirer

Shannon's lower lip quivered, and she brushed a tear away from her eye. Who was this man, and why was he doing this? Did he think she might scorn him if he asked her out? A couple of the men besides Gary had asked her for a date, and it was true she had turned them down, but she had done it kindly. She didn't want to be yoked with an unbeliever, so she didn't open the potential for heartbreak by dating someone who didn't share her faith.

She read the note again then refolded it and tucked it in her pocket.

She would have to dig seriously for clues.

The first would be handwriting comparisons. Monday morning she would come in early. Not only did she have access to people's payroll forms and files, but she also had access to all the time cards. She could start by comparing signatures and see if that would give her some indication of who this could be.

She would solve this mystery, and when she found out who was behind it she would—

Shannon shook her head. The first few notes were kind of silly, but the last note had touched her heart. It exuded a simple honesty that told her the sender was, indeed, serious. It was flattering beyond belief that someone thought so much of her yet was so shy he would resort to this.

For the rest of the day, Shannon buried herself in her work. Over the weekend, she would devise a plan to discover the sender of the notes, as well as figure out what she would say to this person. But for now, she had a payroll deadline to meet.

※

Todd walked to his car ahead of Shannon, waved at her as they started their engines, and waved again to signal her to go ahead of him. When she was out of the parking lot, Todd shut off his engine and returned to the building.

The only remaining employees at this hour were in the dispatch office and warehouse, and everyone was running around at what was always the busiest time of the day. The drivers were lined up at the bay doors, bringing everything in for distribution to be organized for delivery the next business day. As usual, Friday night was the busiest of all.

He could have danced in with colored spotlights, wearing a clown suit, and whistling Dixie. No one would have given him a second glance. And that was just the way he wanted it.

Todd walked to Shannon's desk, opened her drawer, dropped in another note, chocolate kiss attached, and left the building.

Chapter 4

"Excuse me. I was supposed to be in early today."

Faye stepped back for Todd, allowing him to stand beside Shannon while he filled his mug with coffee and Shannon poured boiled water from the kettle into her mug.

Todd winked at Faye over his shoulder then turned to smile at Shannon while he deliberately overfilled his coffee mug. Balancing it carefully, he slowly began his trek through the office on the way to his station. Mentally, he counted out the time Shannon would take to dunk her tea bag in the water until it was the right color and toss the tea bag into the garbage pail.

Picturing her task completed, he sloshed coffee over the edge of his mug to make a large splash on the floor. He grumbled loud enough for everyone in the vicinity to hear, set his cup down on the nearest desk, and returned to the lunchroom. His timing was perfect. He met Shannon in the doorway as she was on her way out, and he was on the way in.

He stepped to the side to allow her to pass. "I spilled some coffee on the floor. Don't trip. I need a paper towel."

"Serves you right for cutting in front of Faye."

He winked at her, enjoying the slight blush. "She didn't mind." He dropped his voice to a whisper. "I think she likes me."

Shannon mumbled something under her breath he didn't think he wanted to hear and headed across the room to her desk.

Todd hurried back into the lunchroom. While he tugged a few paper towels from the holder, he calculated the seconds Shannon would take to set her mug on the corner of her desk and walk around it as she always did. Once back in the office area, he smiled at the ladies who were nearby as he returned to the splotch on the floor. He squatted down to wipe it at the same time Shannon sat in her chair. He had deliberately spilled his coffee where he would have an unencumbered view of her as she opened her drawer.

From his vantage point near the floor he watched as she hesitated. She turned her head ever so slightly from side to side to see if anyone was watching, which fortunately didn't include him, even though she was aware he was there. She pulled the drawer open.

He heard her soft intake of breath when she saw the note. Again, her head moved from side to side. She paused and gently pulled the ribbon open. Todd's heart pounded as he mentally recited the words he'd worked so hard to write.

Dearest Shannon,
Monday is here, the weekend is gone.
Which is good, because Saturday and Sunday were much too long.
My heart ached with loss. I didn't know what to do.
I couldn't see your smile from home, and I missed you.

Your Secret Admirer

Moving ever so slowly, she tucked the note back into the drawer.

Todd lowered his head and smiled to himself as he swiped the paper towel over the floor one last time. She didn't throw the note in the garbage can, and she was eating the chocolate kiss, meaning that so far all was well.

He stood, tossed the paper towel into the nearest wastepaper basket, and picked up his mug. He slurped some coffee off the top then began walking toward the dispatch office.

Shannon raised her head and looked straight at him. "Todd, may I ask you something?"

His heart stopped then started up in double time. The only reason she would want to talk to him would be to ask him about the note she had just read. He wasn't ready to talk about the note or any of the others before it. He hadn't even completely figured out what he was going to say, day after day. He simply wanted to keep telling Shannon how special she was and that she held his heart in the palm of her hand. Not that she would fall in love with him just because he wrote bad poetry. His goal was to prove he was serious and really did love her, despite the rotten and immature things he'd done to her in the past. Hopefully, when the time came for him to reveal himself, they could put the past behind them and move forward into a real relationship.

But he couldn't talk about any of that now. He was already nervous about what he was doing and still not confident it would work. In fact, he was afraid he might blurt out how he felt if she confronted him. He didn't want that to happen in the middle of the office. Most of all, he didn't know if he could handle her rejection.

He wrapped his fingers around his mug, glanced at the door to the dispatch area, then turned back to Shannon. "Gary wanted me here early today to go over some special requests for a new customer. How about if I catch you at lunchtime?"

Her posture sagged, not much, but just enough to note her disappointment. "I guess. I'll see you later, then."

Todd walked to his station as quickly as he could with his full coffee mug. He almost had to push the image of Shannon reading his latest note out of his mind so he could begin his perusal of the paperwork Gary had already spread out over the counter.

He was now starting the fourth week of his job. He was familiar with procedures, better acquainted with the rest of the staff, and confident enough in his abilities that he was comfortable working there.

The words on the papers blurred before him. After seeing Shannon every day, he was also more in love with her than ever before.

But, before he could think any more about Shannon, Gary appeared beside him. He rested his finger on one of the requests their new customer had stipulated before signing the contract. During their last meeting, they had been trying to determine if the expense of paying the overtime needed to fulfill the request would be worth it to secure the new business. "We've got everything covered except for this. What do you think?"

Todd cleared his throat, which helped clear his thoughts. "If we can convince Charlie to take his coffee break half an hour later, then we can send him here"—he pointed on the map to an area on one of the other drivers' runs—"and send Tyler in the other direction. With the slight delay, we can send Charlie to the industrial park, then to their new warehouse in the new development. That way, we can meet their schedule without compromising the other appointments. We can get Bob and Hank to do the rest of Charlie's run and use hired cartage or a part-timer to do what Bob and Hank leave behind. That would eliminate the need for any overtime."

Gary rubbed his chin. "I never thought of that. That would work. Great idea."

Todd suppressed his smile. "Thanks," he mumbled, trying not to look like a child receiving praise from his favorite teacher.

Gary gathered the papers and began sorting them back into order. "I see you're friendly with Shannon," he said, without looking at Todd. He paused, letting the silence hang.

Todd's satisfaction for a job well done dropped as heavily as a lead balloon. He didn't know why the relationship he had with Shannon was any of his supervisor's concern, but Gary's continued silence told him he was waiting for clarification.

Todd turned to study the man. He didn't know what Shannon thought of him. He only knew Gary and Shannon appeared to share nothing more than a companionable working relationship. But Todd wasn't stupid or blind. Even though Gary, as the operations manager, spent much of his time in his office, he also worked with Todd and the other two dispatchers. While the men worked, they talked.

Bryan was happily married with a baby on the way, but Gary and Rick were both single. Being single, and not Christians, they talked a lot about women, not all of which Todd wanted to hear. So far, he'd heard a few of their opinions of the women who worked in the office, some complimentary, some not. Fortunately, not much had been said about Shannon, probably because it was obvious he knew her prior to working there. He had a bad feeling that was about to change.

"Yeah, I've known her for years. Why?"

"Just wondering. I saw you talking to her again this morning. I was wondering if you two had anything going—that's all."

The short conversation he'd had with Shannon raced through his head. They'd said nothing of significance, only that they would talk again at lunchtime.

Todd continued to watch Gary, who was still fiddling with the papers in the folder. After listening to Rick and Gary for the past three weeks, Todd knew Rick made it a policy never to date women at work, just in case things ended badly and they had to see each other every day. But Gary had no such standards or considerations. He had dated Jody, a woman in the credit department, for a while. Every time Jody and Gary were in the lunchroom at the same time, Jody began acting strange. Gary, on the other hand, showed no signs of awkwardness, aversion, or regret. He didn't know Gary well enough yet to know if that was good or bad.

As much as he wanted to know why Gary was asking, unless Todd could claim something more positive than Shannon's finally being able to stay in the same room with him without wanting to run after three minutes, he had no grounds to suggest a relationship that wasn't there.

He tried to make it sound as good as he could without lying. "We're old friends from back when we were kids." At least Shannon had been a kid and just part of the package of his friendship with Craig. But now, he kicked himself for not appreciating what could have developed between them, if he had treated her with the respect she deserved.

He fought back a grin at the last time he'd teased her about playing hockey with the big boys. She'd defiantly given him a hip check as potent as any of the guys. He'd had a bruise for a week to remind him she didn't just deserve the respect; she demanded it.

Todd became serious as he turned his thoughts back to his supervisor. Gary's sudden questions were starting to worry him.

"So you know her pretty well, then?"

Todd tried to keep his expression casual. He knew Shannon well enough that he would marry her tomorrow, if she'd have him, which at this point she wouldn't. But if his words on paper could open her heart to accept the new man he had become, then, sometime in the future, living with her forever as man and wife might be a real possibility. He knew what she liked and didn't like, and he loved her more than life itself.

He cleared his throat. "I know her very well, actually."

"Anything else?"

Todd opened his mouth, but no words came out. He wanted to tell Gary that he and Shannon were going to be bound together until the end of time, except that Shannon had only recently began speaking to him again. He was stuck—for the time being.

"By the way," Gary added before Todd could answer, "if you're not, you know, doing anything with Shan, I think Faye's pretty interested in you."

Inwardly, Todd cringed. He knew Faye had a crush on him. He also knew she wasn't a Christian. Shannon's faith through the years, in good times and bad, was one of the many things he loved about her. Even if she never returned his feelings, he wouldn't go out with someone who didn't share his faith. He tried to be kind to Faye without encouraging her. While he was flattered by her attentions, he wasn't interested. He was interested only in Shannon.

He didn't quite know how to handle Gary yet, but he did know that humor had always worked for him. Todd splayed both hands over his heart and sighed melodramatically. "I know about Faye, but my heart belongs to another."

Gary rolled his eyes. "You've been watching too many cheap chick flicks. I think you have some work to do."

Todd gladly picked up his book of notes to follow up on, sat at his station, and lifted the phone to dial. He had never been so glad to get to work.

By the time the lunch hour arrived, Todd was more than ready. Like every other day, he was alone in the dispatch office for half an hour while Rick and Bryan went for lunch. Gary was in his office catching up on the morning's happenings, but he was prepared to come into the dispatch area if the phones went wild while Todd was alone.

Fortunately for Todd, everything remained quiet, and for now, his paperwork was done. He'd finished the routing for the pickup requests received so far. Even most of the drivers were now officially off for their break.

Line 3 was lit up. He glanced over his shoulder to see that Gary was on the phone. As long as the light was on, Gary would remain in his office.

As usual at this time, Todd had nothing to do but watch the wall. He began to write the note Shannon would read on Tuesday morning.

Dearest Shannon,

The pen froze. He knew she had become more curious about the sender of the notes because she was going to talk to him about it, until he put her off.

Todd looked down at his own handwriting. He didn't want the notes to be perceived as threatening in any way so he had decided to handwrite them, to give them a friendly and personal touch, instead of typing them on his computer and printing them. But now, staying anonymous had become more of an issue. As far as he knew, Shannon had never seen his handwriting. Since he was salaried and not hourly, he didn't fill out a time sheet at the end of the week. When the drivers had overtime, he initialed their time cards, but that was only a scribbled *TS*, which he usually did standing, without a solid surface behind them. His initials were not even close to use as a comparable handwriting sample.

The only official documents on file with his handwriting written legibly were the job application he had filled out and the IRS form. Shannon was the payroll administrator, but he didn't think she had access to those files. Even if she did, she had too much honor to search through personnel files for handwriting samples.

He looked at the customers' routing cards sorted neatly in the various drivers' route slots. The names of their customers were written in, but he wasn't the only one doing it. Gary and the other dispatchers wrote in the names, and sometimes people in the office wrote an occasional pickup request. As well, the times the calls were given to the drivers were noted by whoever was on the radio to that driver at the time, which was any one of the four of them. At the end of the day, all the cards were gathered into a bundle, labeled by date, and tossed into a box, never to be looked at again unless there was a problem. It wasn't likely Shannon would ever look there. Even if she did dig through the box and match the handwriting, nothing was identifiable as his.

Todd smiled and continued writing.

> *Every day while we're at work,*

Todd stopped writing. His brain stalled while he tried to think of a word that rhymed with "work." Since nothing came, he mentally ran through the alphabet starting with A, taking each letter and ending it with the "erk" sound. The first combination he made that was really a word was "jerk," so he kept going. The next word started with the letter L, but he didn't think it was a good idea to mention the word "lurk" in a note. He was already leaving anonymous notes, and he didn't want to frighten Shannon or hint that he was following her around. He wasn't a stalker. He only wanted to tell her he recognized the special Christian woman she'd become and how much he loved her.

He crumpled the paper and shoved it in his pocket to put through the shredder then started again.

> *Dearest Shannon,*
> *Thinking of you makes me smile,*
> *Like. . .*

The pen froze again. What happy thing rhymed with smile? He started to run through the alphabet again, mentally choked on the word "bile," shook his head and kept going with the alphabet.

> *Like an alligator in the lazy Nile.*

Or was it crocodiles in the Nile? He knew alligators lived in Florida and crocodiles lived in Australia, but he didn't know which ones lived in Egypt.

Todd scribbled out the words and shoved that piece of paper in his pocket, too. He didn't want her to think he was a predatory animal. He'd already nixed another predatory word.

Todd started again.

> *Dearest Shannon,*

The phone rang before he could think of another opening sentence. He chatted with the caller for a few minutes while noting some special requests for a pickup of a priority parcel then resumed his quest.

The light went out for line 3. The scrape of Gary's chair along the tile floor was followed by the metallic grind of his filing-cabinet drawer opening. "Almost ready?" Gary called out. "Those guys should be back soon."

Todd looked up at the clock. He had five minutes left in which to write the note he would leave tomorrow.

He gritted his teeth. Writing poetry was hard enough, but writing good, meaningful, sincere poetry was even harder, especially when he had to do it while watching the clock.

> *Dearest Shannon,*
> *I love you more every day*
> *You are more special than words can say*

He stopped writing, fighting for the words as every tick of the clock echoed loudly through his head, reminding him time was running short.

Nothing came. Bryan's and Rick's voices drifted through the doorway, signaling their imminent arrival.

Todd folded the paper carefully and shoved it in his pocket. His only option to finish the note in private would be to do it in the washroom before he left. He told himself this was what he deserved for not writing the note at home, when he had more time and the privacy he needed. His struggles also served as a reminder that the more notes he wrote, the harder it was becoming to find different wording and more rhymes he hadn't used before.

It was a lot of work, and he knew he had to be diligent, but this was the only way he could think of to tell Shannon how he felt. When the time was right to reveal himself, he hoped she would see that for once in his life his actions toward her were sincere and she would take him seriously.

🌸

Shannon set her mug on the corner of her desk, walked around to her chair, and slid in.

When she reached for the drawer handle, she realized she would be disappointed if she didn't find a new note.

She held her breath, wrapped her fingers around the cold metal, and pulled. Sure enough, another note lay in the pencil tray.

As she picked up the small piece of notepaper, again bound by a red ribbon with a chocolate kiss tied to the end, she paused. This note wasn't as pristine as the other notes. For the first time, the paper was crinkled.

She shrugged her shoulders, tugged the bow on the ribbon to open it, set the chocolate kiss aside, and began to read.

> *Dearest Shannon,*
> *I love you more every day*
> *You are more special than words can say.*
> *These words I write are to say to you*
> *That I think of you in all I do.*
> > *Your Secret Admirer*

Shannon smiled. The Secret Admirer's poetry was still bad, but his sentiments continued to be just as sweet.

She put the paper down in front of her and picked up the chocolate kiss. As she picked off the colored foil wrapping, she reread the note, trying to figure out if the word patterns were familiar or if any expressions might be unique to one person. She had almost finished the last line when she heard footsteps behind her chair. She quickly whipped the note into her drawer, grabbed her pencil, and popped the chocolate kiss into her mouth.

"I saw that," Faye said as she appeared beside Shannon.

Shannon's heart pounded. She had thought she'd tucked the note away soon enough, but she'd become careless. She turned to the side and looked up at Faye, who was standing beside her chair and holding a mug of steaming coffee in one hand. Shannon's voice dropped to a whisper. "Please don't tell anyone."

Faye's eyebrows raised. "Why? Are you on a diet? You of all people, too." She rested her free hand on her stomach. "I'm the one who could probably lose ten pounds, but not you."

Shannon tried not to sag with relief that it was only the chocolate Faye had seen. She said the first thing that came to her mind. "I guess it's just a girl thing. Next weekend I'm going to an anniversary celebration at my old church, and I want to be able to fit into my dress."

Faye picked up the foil wrapping. "It was just a chocolate kiss, not a whole bar. How many calories can it have?" She glanced around Shannon's desktop, then to the drawer, which was tightly closed. "Got any more? Do you share?"

"Sorry. I only got one."

Faye turned and looked at her own desk, beside Shannon's, which was bare except for her in and out baskets and computer. "Got? You mean someone around here has good chocolate kisses and skipped me? I'm going to have to wring someone's neck. Who's giving them out?"

Shannon nearly choked, even though the last of the kiss had already dissolved in her mouth. Her mind raced to think of what she could say that wouldn't be lying but yet wouldn't be spilling the beans about what had been happening for over a week now. "I don't know. Someone left it for me." She deliberately didn't mention the notes that came with the kisses and hoped and prayed Faye wouldn't ask for more details.

"Wow. Someone has a crush on you, I'll bet."

Shannon had a bad feeling it was more than a crush, since someone was going to a lot of trouble and for so long. "Naw. It's probably just someone who knows I like this kind of chocolate. I'll bet they're even wondering why I haven't thanked them. I should probably know who it is, but I can't figure it out."

Faye sighed, her eyes drifted shut, and she pressed her free hand over her heart. "I wish some handsome knight would woo me with chocolate kisses. He'd have my heart for sure." Her eyes opened, and she grinned at Shannon. "I'd really like it if Todd would leave me romantic stuff like that."

"Todd?" Shannon blinked. The only thing he'd ever left her was a cold, slimy live frog. "That man doesn't have a romantic bone in his body. Don't tell me you have a crush on him." His remark from the previous day—that he thought Faye liked him—repeated in her head. It appeared he was right.

"He's so-o-o handsome. And so funny!"

"He's also. . ." Shannon's voice trailed off. Todd was funny, when a person wasn't the target of his jokes. And she couldn't argue that he wasn't handsome, because he was. The biggest problem was he knew it.

She tried to think of something else to say about Todd to discourage Faye, to tell her what he was really like, but again, she had to be fair. They'd worked together for nearly a month, and he'd done nothing untoward. He hadn't played a single practical joke on anyone. He was polite, helpful, and appeared to be doing a good job. If she had to draw a dotted line in time, from the day he started working there, she couldn't think of anything bad to say about him.

As well, Todd continued to be her brother's best friend after fifteen years. Craig always chose his friends carefully. He had many acquaintances but only a select group of people he would call close friends. Craig said repeatedly that Todd had turned his life around and changed into a decent human being.

Faye waited expectantly beside her. "Todd's also. . . ?"

"Nothing," Shannon mumbled as she typed in her password and opened her e-mail. "I forgot what I was going to say. Just remember that even though Todd isn't bad looking, beauty is only skin deep."

Faye nodded. She began to walk the three steps to her desk but stopped after only two steps. She turned her head to look over her shoulder at Shannon. "That may be so, but beauty is also in the eye of the beholder."

Chapter 5

Todd walked into the bookstore, trying to make it look as if he were comfortable in such a place. He stared up and down one aisle, then another, unable to believe there could be so many books under one roof. They even had a coffee shop in the back. The public library hadn't been as large as this store.

The book he'd wanted had been marked "library use only," and he couldn't go into the library every few days. Therefore, he had come to buy the book.

If he could find it.

A young lady wearing a green polo shirt with a pin-on badge showing the logo of the store and the name "Staci" approached him, proving he looked as lost as he felt.

"May I help you?" she asked.

He didn't know if he should admit he'd just been to the library, where he didn't have to pay for anything. "I'm looking for one of those books that has rhyming words in it. For writing stuff."

She smiled politely. "You mean a rhyming dictionary? We have a number of different kinds. There are rhyming dictionaries for both children and adults. Some are geared for poets. We have a nice one for musicians—and a few in more of a dictionary format. We have them in paperback or hardcover."

Todd's head swam. If it wasn't hard enough to pick meaningful words that rhymed and still get his point across, now he had to decide which reference book was the best kind to suit his needs. The one he'd found at the library seemed good, but he hadn't realized it was any specific kind. He only knew he couldn't leave the building with it. "Yeah," he mumbled. "That's what I want."

She pointed across the room. "In the nonfiction section, in 18B."

"Thanks," he mumbled again and began walking.

When he finally found the right shelf, he gritted his teeth and went through all of the books, one by one, until he found one that looked as if it had the biggest selection of words per page. He cringed at the price, now realizing why the library wouldn't let their copy out of the building, then picked a smaller paperback version instead. For what he was doing, he didn't need every word in the English language. He only needed lists of words that rhymed.

With his selection in hand, Todd headed toward the front of the store to check out. While he walked, he continued to survey the building and its contents, feeling more in awe with every table and shelf he passed. Finally, when he came to a table displaying a big yellow sign that announced everything on it was marked 70 percent off, his curiosity got the better of him. He stopped.

The subject of most of the books centered on past holiday seasons. Some were works of fiction by authors he had never heard of before. When he saw one title that contained the word *Bible* he picked it up. He turned it over and started reading the back cover to discover the book was a work of fiction based on the life of one of the Old Testament prophets.

Todd couldn't remember the last time he read anything that wasn't nonfiction or was longer than a magazine article. He opened the book and started to read the first page to see if he might like it when a voice piped up beside him.

"Todd? What are you doing here?"

He fumbled with the book, snapped it shut, and slipped it over the rhyming dictionary to hide the title.

"Shannon," he muttered, trying to keep his voice from cracking. "What are you doing here?"

She glanced at the table, then at the two books in his hand. "The same thing as you, apparently."

Shannon, too, held a couple of books. From as far back as he knew her, he remembered her reading something. He shouldn't have been surprised to find her in a bookstore.

She lowered her head to look at his two books and tipped her head slightly. "What do you have? Anything interesting?"

He pressed the two books tightly together, not offering her either one. "I guess. Maybe. I'm not sure. What do you have?" Not that he wanted to know specifically what she was reading. He only wanted to distract her from the books in his own hand. Especially the one on the bottom.

Shannon had no such hesitations. She held out both books to him so he could plainly see the covers. "I have a couple of inspirational romance anthologies. I just love Christian fiction, and we have more to choose from now. It's especially great to find them in a store like this. You know how much I love to read. I have to admit I'm a little surprised to see you here. I can't say I've ever seen you with a book in your hand."

He grinned. For years, he'd teased her about being a bookworm. He'd only meant it as a compliment. He considered her diligence in reading to be a sign of intelligence. She always countered his teasing by calling him illiterate.

Todd cleared his throat and straightened his smile. He pressed his hand to his chest, over his heart, and did his best to appear serious. "There're a lot of things about me you don't know. How about if I treat you to a coffee, and I'll tell you about them?"

She glanced at the coffee shop in the back of the store. "I don't know."

"Come on. It'll be fun."

She shrugged her shoulders. "Sure. Why not? I don't have anything better to do or anywhere else to go."

He tried not to let her comment sting, but after the things he'd said to her in the past, he probably had it coming. The important thing was that she had accepted his invitation. For that he had to be happy or at least relieved she wasn't holding a grudge. "How about if you get us a nice table, and I'll be right back. I want to pay for these first."

"Pay? But—" Once again, she glanced over her shoulder to the coffee shop then back to him. "You don't need to pay first. You're allowed to take unpaid-for books to the tables. That's how lots of people decide whether or not they're going to buy the book."

"I've already decided, so I want to pay for them first. Then I won't have to worry about forgetting." Even if he kept the sale book on top of the rhyming dictionary, she might read the title from the spine. After he paid, the dictionary would be tucked inside the bag.

She shrugged her shoulders again. "That doesn't make sense, but if that's what you want, I guess I can pay for mine, too."

He shook his head frantically. "No, I don't want to rush you. How about if you go look at the desserts and pick something good for both of us. I'll be right back." Before she could protest, he turned and walked quickly to the checkout, leaving Shannon standing beside the sale table.

Fortunately, there weren't any lines. He soon joined Shannon at the coffee shop, where she was standing in front of the display with the desserts, eyeing a selection labeled TRIPLE CHOCOLATE DREAM. That didn't surprise him. He almost commented on her choice but bit his tongue. He had promised himself he'd treat her with the respect she deserved and never tease her again. Besides, he didn't want to do anything to associate his knowledge for her love of chocolate to the chocolate kisses he left her every day. One day he would tell her, but only when the time was right, which wasn't now.

Todd selected something else for himself and remained silent when the clerk put their order on a tray. He paid for everything, and they moved to a table.

Shannon sipped her coffee then nibbled the chocolate piece off the top of her dessert. Todd knew the chocolate wasn't as good a quality as the specialty kisses he'd been buying and wondered if she was comparing them. He held back his smile and drank his coffee slowly so she wouldn't notice.

After she finished the piece, she spoke. "I can't believe we've been working together for nearly a month. The time sure has gone fast, hasn't it?"

Todd nodded. "It sure has. Do you know this is the first time we've had just to sit and talk? It's almost funny we're not at work."

"I know. But you've seen by now how busy it gets in that lunchroom."

"Yeah. It's sometimes crowded in there." He smiled wryly. Even though he didn't sit with her during lunch, they often sat at the same table at coffee time, as part of a group. It wasn't what he wanted, but it was an improvement over his first week, when she wouldn't go into the lunchroom at all when he was in there.

He had to take comfort in how far they'd come since then. She was now willingly sitting with him, alone, in a friendly, semiprivate atmosphere, although he wished it could have been from something more intimate than bumping into each other at the bookstore.

"I'm actually glad to see you. I've been meaning to talk to you about something. Do you mind?"

Inwardly, he cringed. He had a bad feeling he knew what she was going to ask; only this time he couldn't run away, since sitting together for coffee was his idea. He forced himself to smile. "No, go ahead."

She leaned closer across the table. Her eyes widened, and Todd immediately became lost in their depths. The mixture of olive green and brown in her hazel eyes always fascinated him, although up until now he would never have admitted it.

"Please don't take this the wrong way, but do you know if anyone at work has a crush on me?"

His brain stalled. A little voice called for evasive maneuvers. "You mean, have I heard any of the guys talking?"

She smiled. His heart went into overdrive. "Yes. I know you're fairly new, but, well, you certainly must hear the men talk."

"I haven't heard anyone say anything about you that isn't work related, but I can try to listen if you want."

She reached toward him and rested her hand on his forearm. Her touch was gentle, even affectionate, although he knew his interpretation was probably only wishful thinking. Still, the warm contact made him hope he wouldn't break out into a cold sweat.

"That would be great. I know you think it's a strange question, but I have to know."

He blinked to clear his mind. He didn't think it was strange at all. What he did think strange was that no one else had managed to win her heart already. "Has somebody been making you nervous?"

Shannon shook her head and withdrew her hand. He almost begged her to put it back. "No. Nothing like that." She grinned and took a sip of her coffee then spoke over the top of the cup. "Actually, someone is being very sweet. I just wish I knew who it was."

He opened his mouth, about to blurt out he was the one, but she started talking before he could formulate the words.

"In a way, it reminds me of when I was a kid and Tommy Banks had a crush on me. We were seven years old, and he bought me a chocolate bar out of his allowance; but he ate it on the way to school. Instead he made me a bookmark. I haven't received a special gift from a guy since, except for my birthday and Christmas, of course. But I still have the bookmark. He drew little red and purple hearts all over it. Do you remember Tommy?"

"Can't say that I do." What stuck in his mind, though, was not the bookmark, but her wistful comment that over the years no one else had given her anything she considered special. He'd met a few of the boys and young men she'd gone out with. He'd openly insulted every one of them, although not to their faces. She'd been angry with him every time, but he did notice that soon after he told her what he thought of her various dates and boyfriends, she broke up with them, probably because he was right. She deserved better.

But the important thing was that not one of them had given her anything she considered special that wasn't also attached to an obligatory occasion. Since she thought receiving the notes and chocolate kisses was sweet, that was reason enough for him to put his own desires aside and keep giving them to her instead of revealing himself so soon.

Before they crossed the line into dangerous territory, where being evasive might transcend into actual lying, Todd changed the subject to the upcoming twenty-fifth anniversary celebration of his church. Craig had told him Shannon would be attending both the open house on Saturday and the service on Sunday, since she'd grown up in that church. He always went to church Sunday morning, but he hadn't made up his mind about the open house Saturday night until he heard she was going. His clothes were already picked out, and he'd even ironed the pants.

He hadn't realized how much time had passed until an announcement echoed over the speakers asking shoppers to take their purchases to the checkout because the store was closing in five minutes.

Todd stood in line with Shannon so she could pay for her books. He didn't feel the least bit contrite when she teased him that he should have waited with his own purchase, since he was now standing in line a second time. In a way he found it oddly satisfying that for once she was teasing him instead of the other way around.

In fact, he couldn't remember the last time he'd enjoyed himself so much or felt so relaxed—once they stopped talking about work.

Outside, he wished he could ask her to do something so they could spend more time together, but he couldn't think of anything open at that hour on a weeknight except for the fast-food restaurants. They'd just spent the last two hours together over coffee and dessert, so she would think he was up to something if he suggested more food. Instead, he could only accompany her to her car, which was across the almost empty parking lot from his car.

He watched as she inserted the key into the lock. The time they'd spent together was the closest thing to a date he'd ever had with Shannon. Every other time they'd been together outside work, they'd traded constant banter, even insults, and were always part of a threesome, with her brother, Craig, present.

She swung the door open, tossed her purse and the bag containing the books onto the passenger seat, and started to step into the car. "I guess I'll see you at work tomorrow. 'Bye, Todd."

Todd stepped closer as she bent more to get into the car. He didn't know what they could do, but he didn't want to part ways. "Shan! Wait!"

At his words, Shannon retracted her foot, which had not yet touched the floor of the car, and backed up. "What?" she asked as she straightened. She obviously hadn't known he had moved so close to the car, because when she turned around her eyes widened when she discovered they were now only inches apart.

With the car behind her, Shannon couldn't back up. Todd didn't move. They were so close he could have simply lowered his head—and kissed her. He suddenly wanted to kiss her more than anything he'd ever wanted in his life.

"Well? Did you want something?"

"I. . .uh. . ." Todd's brain backfired. He couldn't do it. Not only would she not have expected such a thing from him, but they were in the middle of an almost deserted parking lot. He stood there with his mouth hanging open.

Shannon giggled. "What's the matter? Does calling me Shan instead of Shan-nooze when we're out of work short-circuit your vocal chords?" She raised her hands, rested her palms on his chest, and gave him a gentle nudge backward. "While I appreciate your not calling me that anymore, you're standing so close I can't focus properly. Was there something you wanted to tell me?"

He wanted to tell her he loved her. He shook his head. "It's not important. I'll see you in the morning."

Todd waited while Shannon got into her car and drove away, not moving until she'd left the lot.

He could hardly wait for morning and the start of a new day at work.

❀

Todd walked slowly into the office and looked around. Since he was earlier than usual, none of the office staff had arrived, which was what he needed. He hurried to Shannon's desk, picked up the note he'd left from the day before that was meant for her to read this morning, and replaced it with a new one. He rammed the old one into his pocket, hurried into the lunchroom, and began making a pot of coffee to be ready when everyone else arrived.

Just as the last drop dripped into the pot, Todd heard footsteps in the doorway. He peeked over his shoulder, hoping it was Shannon, but it was only Gary.

"Good morning, Todd. You're in early."

"Yeah. I left a little earlier than usual, and traffic was light."

"You have good timing. You know I've given Bryan the day off. Rick called me on my cell—he's sick and won't be in. I have to go out for a meeting with a couple of new accounts in an hour. I want you to pull one of the drivers in to help with the phones and reshuffle his route. I'll see if I can get someone off the casual list to come in on short notice. Do you know where it is?"

Todd glanced up at the clock. If he was to endure a testing period to see if he was worth his salary, today would be the day. He only hoped he'd learned enough in a month to meet Gary's expectations. "I don't know. Last I saw the list, Bryan had it. I don't understand his filing system, but I can try to find it."

"Never mind. Shannon has a copy. I'll use that one," Gary said as he left the lunchroom.

Todd poured his coffee then froze, nearly overflowing it until he realized what he was doing.

Gary was going to get the list from Shannon. But Shannon wasn't in yet.

217

That meant Gary was going to get into Shannon's desk.

He couldn't stop his supervisor from looking for something he legitimately needed, but Todd had his own good reasons for not wanting Gary to open her top drawer. Maybe he would only go through the bottom drawer where Shannon kept her files and nowhere else.

But Todd couldn't take the chance.

He left his mug on the counter and dashed across the lunchroom to the office. "Hey, Gary," he said, trying his best to quell the panic and sound casual as he entered the main office area. "I think I know where it is. I'll be right back."

Just as Gary straightened, Todd heard the thud of a drawer closing. Because he was looking at the front of the desk, he couldn't tell which drawer Gary had been in.

"It's okay," Gary said, holding a paper in his hand. "Shannon is very organized. I found it. Let's get busy. I have to be out of here soon."

Todd swallowed hard and returned to the lunchroom for his coffee. He had to tell himself that since Gary's expression had been neutral, he hadn't seen the new note Todd had left for Shannon this morning. If Gary had opened the top drawer, the stark white paper with the red ribbon and red foil wrapping of the chocolate kiss would have been impossible to miss.

The phone started ringing at the same time he set his mug on the counter. He handled the call quickly then chose a driver to help him. While Gary made a few phone calls from his office, Todd called the foreman and talked to him about pulling the priority deliveries out of Bill's truck and loading them into another. By the time Gary found a driver to replace Bill, Todd had everything under control. Or at least everything would be under control until the phones started ringing.

Gary stood beside Todd at the counter, checked the changes he'd made to the routing, and nodded. "Looks good. I have to go. Call my cell if you need me, but everything looks fine."

Todd forced himself to smile. "Yeah. See you sometime after lunch."

Chapter 6

Shannon gritted her teeth as she watched a couple of the ladies from the accounts department yakking incessantly while standing in front of the lunchroom counter. She didn't want to be rude, but the kettle had boiled, and she could now make her tea. Or at least she could if she barged between them and elbowed them out of the way, which was almost what Todd had done to poor Faye the other day. Normally, she wouldn't even consider being so rude, but Shannon wanted to get to her desk.

Not that she wanted to get to work so fast. She wanted to open her drawer to see the new note of the day.

Finally, she couldn't stand it any longer. She walked forward and stepped between them to reach for the kettle, smiling politely while they stared at her in silence for interrupting them.

She dunked and redunked her tea bag, wondering if it took this long every day or if she'd somehow picked a low-quality tea bag this morning.

Even though the tea wasn't as dark as she normally liked it, Shannon tossed the bag into the trash and walked to her desk as quickly as she could without spilling anything or making it look as if she was rushing. Todd had spilled his coffee the same day he'd barged in front of Faye, and she didn't want to do the same. She had been impressed that he'd immediately wiped up his mess. Whenever the other dispatchers slopped coffee onto the floor, they let it dry, and the janitors got it when they washed the floor at night. Mostly, she didn't want anyone to notice her.

Shannon's stomach fluttered as she opened the drawer. The same as every other day for over two weeks, a little white note, fastened with a red ribbon tied to a chocolate kiss, lay in the center of her pencil tray. Keeping the note low so no one could see what she was doing, Shannon pulled the ribbon off and set the kiss aside.

Dearest Shannon,
> When I think of you I don't know where to begin
> Your magical voice is like a sweet violin.
> My heart beats with joy at the sound of your laughter,
> And your happy smile fills me with joy ever after.

> Your Secret Admirer

Shannon smiled. The note was tender and sweet and oddly flattering, even though the poetry itself hadn't improved. Today, though, something was different, but she couldn't quite figure out what it was.

She tucked the note into the envelope containing the other notes, unwrapped the kiss, and popped it into her mouth. While she savored the rich chocolate, Shannon turned her head toward the opening for the lunchroom. Any second now, Todd would be walking through the doorway.

She hadn't told him about the notes, but he'd promised to keep his ears open to any conversation concerning her. Of course, it was too early to hear anything. Once he arrived, she would simply remind him.

Instead of Todd, Faye walked into the office. Shannon found herself strangely disappointed.

She couldn't stop thinking about Todd. Not only had she spent the evening with him, she'd actually enjoyed herself. In many ways, he was the same old Todd she'd known since she was a kid. Yet it was the first time she'd talked to him as a single man and not as her brother's annoying friend.

Then, when they were leaving, he'd acted so strange. Todd always radiated confidence and control; yet he was at a loss for words. He'd even stammered. She didn't know what was going through his mind, but with Todd Sanders, it could have been anything. He couldn't have realized how charming his momentary lapse had been, but it showed her a side of him she didn't know existed. At the time, she'd almost been inclined to give him a hug, but since it was Todd, she'd erased the thought from her mind.

"Hi, Shan."

"Good morning, Faye. Is Todd in the lunchroom?"

"Nope. Haven't seen him yet."

Shannon checked her watch. Most days they arrived about the same time. Today she'd come in a few minutes early to be sure she could read the Secret Admirer's note in private. With the clock now showing ten minutes after Todd's usual arrival time, a niggling worry started to prod Shannon. She rose and unlocked the filing cabinet so she could get his phone number out of his personnel file; but just as she touched the folder with his name on it, the familiar sound of Todd's laughter echoed from the dispatch office.

With a quick push, she closed the drawer and engaged the locking button then walked to the dispatch office. She found Todd and one of the drivers in the small room, talking with someone she'd never seen before through the window opening into the drivers' area. Bryan, Rick, and Gary were nowhere to be seen.

"Todd? What time did you get here? I wanted to talk to you."

"About what?" When he turned to face her, he was still winding down his laughter. His eyes were moist, and he swiped over them with his sleeve. "Did you need a form for Terry? He's been here once before, about four months ago, Gary says."

"No, it isn't that. I just wanted to remind you about what we talked about yesterday."

He grinned, and Faye's words echoed through Shannon's head. Todd truly was even more handsome when he smiled. In the throes of his laughter, his smile was almost magnetic. It was the same smile she remembered from her high school days, when she briefly had a mad crush on him; only now the years and alleged maturity added attractive little crow's-feet to the corners of his big brown eyes. "I haven't forgotten. I'll keep my ears open and let you know if something comes up." With the other men standing behind Todd, neither one could see his face. Using that advantage, Todd placed his hand over his heart and gave her an exaggerated wink. "Promise."

Shannon opened her mouth, but no words came out. Her heart started pounding, just as it had back in those foolish high school days.

Before she said something stupid, Shannon spun around and strode out of the room. She busied herself with her work, ignoring all around her until Faye appeared at the front of her desk to announce it was time for coffee break.

They had barely sat down before Faye started talking. "Have you been in the dispatch area today? It's nuts in there."

Shannon nodded. "I know. Where's Gary? He should be in there with both Rick and Bryan off."

"Gary had a bunch of meetings lined up this morning, and he couldn't cancel. Todd seems to be doing okay in there, considering."

"I noticed you checked on him fairly often."

Faye smiled. "Yeah. I got him coffee a couple of times. I thought he could use it. He said he really appreciated it."

Shannon sighed. "You've got it bad. Maybe there's medication for that."

Faye grinned. "Get serious, Shan. Todd's different from anyone else I've ever met."

Shannon nearly choked on her tea. "You can say that again."

Faye's smile disappeared. "I don't know what you have against him."

Shannon looked down into her mug, not able to face Faye as she spoke. "I already told you Todd is my brother's friend. Let's just say we haven't always gotten along that great over the years. I guess I'm finding it a bit strange to see him so normal, for lack of a better word. I can't help but expect this is a bad dream and I'm waiting for the punch line. Any moment, I feel as if I'm going to wake up, and he'll do something to embarrass or insult me the way he did when we were kids. I know I shouldn't feel that way. After all, it's been over a month now, and he's been nice to me and everything's been fine."

In fact, things were more than fine, even outside of work when no one was around he'd have to answer to or see the next day. When the bookstore closed, she'd enjoyed their time together so much that for a moment she'd wished the store was open until midnight, just so she could have stayed to talk with Todd longer.

Faye smiled dreamily. "Yeah. He's mighty fine."

Shannon rolled her eyes. "Oh, puh-leeze."

"I can dream, can't I?"

"He's not some movie star or idol in one of those teen magazines. He's just Todd."

"If you've known him for years, haven't you ever thought of what it would be like if something developed between you?"

Briefly, when she was going through a period of teenage insanity. She wondered if Faye had heard a word she just said about how sometimes she didn't know whether to scream or cry after yet another unpleasant day spent with Todd and her brother. Before she could answer, Faye continued her questioning.

"Haven't you ever considered what it would be like to be alone with him, like on a romantic date?"

Actually, she had been alone with him prior to last night, but it wasn't on a date. Craig and Todd were in the garage at her parents' home. She'd gone to tell Craig their mother wanted him for something, so Craig went into the house, leaving her alone in the garage with Todd for a few minutes. For entertainment, Todd asked her to hold some kind of auto part she hadn't known was greasy until it was too late. It took ten solid minutes of scrubbing to get the slime and oily stink off her hands, then a whole day to get the grime out from under her fingernails.

She set her empty mug down on the table with a thud. "I'm sorry, Faye, but I have enough problems with men without adding Todd to the mix."

Faye's eyebrows quirked. "Oh? Is there something you're not telling me?" She leaned closer over the top of the table. "Is it someone here? What's happening? Did you find out who gave you the chocolate kiss? I couldn't find who was giving them out. In fact, no one knew anything about chocolate kisses."

Shannon sucked in a deep breath. "Oh, Faye. . .you didn't go around asking, did you?"

"I asked a couple of people where they came from, but not many. Why?"

"Because it was just meant for me. There was a note attached." Shannon leaned toward Faye then straightened, not wanting anyone to see they obviously wanted to keep their conversation confidential, as that would attract attention. "I'm afraid I have a Secret Admirer."

Faye's eyes widened. "Wow! That's so exciting!"

"Shh!" Shannon fanned one hand in the air then hunched in the chair. "Don't tell anyone. I have no idea who it could be. Think. If you were asking around about the chocolate kiss, then that makes at least a couple of people I can eliminate from my list. Who did you talk to?"

"Nanci and Brenda."

Shannon's heart sank.

"Sorry. I didn't ask any of the guys. I didn't think any of them would be bringing stuff like that to work. That's why I just asked women. I didn't specifically say you had one. I just walked up to them and asked if they had chocolate, and both said no."

"I guess that's okay, then. Whoever he is, he has to know I'm trying to figure it out. I just don't want him to think I have an investigative team out looking for him, or he'll stop doing it, then I'll never know." She didn't want to tell Faye that Todd was already helping her. From past experience, she knew Todd could be very tight lipped when it suited him. No one would ever know Todd knew about the Secret Admirer or that he was helping her discover the man's identity.

Faye, on the other hand, was not known for being discreet.

"Just keep your ears and eyes open, but please don't say anything to anyone, and especially don't ask questions. If you hear something, tell me, and I'll take it from there, okay?"

Faye nodded, the personification of seriousness. "Okay."

Shannon pushed the chair back and stood. "We had better get back to work. I have a million things to do."

Shannon couldn't stop thinking about Todd, even though she didn't see him. His absence in the lunchroom during break times only served to show she'd come to expect his presence. He was buried in work, dealing with a system he wasn't entirely proficient at yet, while doing the volume of at least two people. He only came out of the dispatch office a couple of times, when he ran for the washroom, then right back.

By the time Gary finally returned, it was half an hour before quitting time. Bill left the room, but she still didn't see Todd.

When it was time to go home for the day, Shannon hadn't completed all she'd wanted to do to meet her payroll deadline for the next day. Rather than leave it for the last minute, she took advantage of the quiet office to work undisturbed.

Twenty minutes after everyone else left, Todd emerged from the dispatch room at a slow pace, the wear and tear of a stress-filled day apparent on his face and in his posture.

She couldn't help but feel sorry for him.

"Hey, Todd. How did things go in there?"

"Okay, I guess, but I can't remember ever being so tired." He turned and looked at Faye's empty desk. He pulled her chair out and sank down into it. "Since it's just you and me here, do you mind if I talk to you about something?"

Shannon had a feeling she knew what he was going to say. She'd seen Faye going in and out of the dispatch office a number of times, sometimes with Todd's coffee mug in her hand; other times, Faye was empty handed. Shannon didn't mind helping him out or giving him a bit of womanly perspective, but she didn't want to do it in the middle of the office. Even though the other regular day staff had left, Gary was still in his office and could appear at any time. Also, not all the drivers were in, and the afternoon-shift warehouse staff members were just beginning their day. Any one of them could walk in at any time, and often did, once they realized she was still there.

Shannon stood. "I have a better idea. You look so tired. Let's go to my place. I just happen to have a great lasagna left over in the fridge from yesterday. All I have to do is heat it up and make a salad, and we'll have a ready-made dinner. We can talk then, without any worry about being disturbed."

"You're inviting me over to your place? And you're also going to feed me?"

"I guess. I just thought it would be a better place to talk."

"That sounds great. I appreciate it."

"I only have to finish what I'm doing."

Todd lounged in Faye's chair until Shannon was ready then followed her out and into the parking lot. Shannon unlocked her car door but didn't get in. Instead, she stood watching Todd, who was standing beside his car and pressing his hands to every pocket in his jacket, jeans, then shirt.

"I don't believe this," he called out. "I must have forgotten my car keys in the office. I'll be right back, unless Gary sees me. Don't leave without me, because I've never been to your place before. I'm not exactly sure where it is."

"No problem."

As Todd jogged back into the building, Shannon had time to think about what she'd just done.

Surely, she was losing her mind. She'd just invited Todd Sanders to her apartment. The apartment she moved into so she could get away from him.

That she felt sorry for him further confirmed she was losing her mind. She justified it by telling herself she was doing it to talk to him for Faye's benefit and was making the sacrifice for a friend.

Todd was back within minutes, and she was soon on her way, with him following. She pointed him to the visitor parking area then entered the residents' underground parking area. She was about to push the button in the elevator when she realized she'd left Todd outside. Not only did he not have a key to get in, but he didn't know which was her apartment, although he certainly could find it from the listing by the door.

Instead of hitting the button for the fifth floor, Shannon rode the elevator to the lobby, where she walked to the main door to let Todd in then took him to her apartment.

"This seems like a nice place. You like living here?"

"Yes. For an apartment, it's pretty peaceful."

Having known him for years, she was comfortable with Todd's help in getting their dinner together. They only chatted about inconsequential things until it was ready and on the table.

For a second, Shannon hesitated. Even when she was alone, which was most of the time, she always bowed her head and gave God thanks for her meal and her day. She didn't know if Todd did the same.

She'd seen him in church, and Craig had told her about Todd's turning his life over to Jesus. She'd also seen him in action at work. All these showed a man living his faith. But this was the first time she was alone with Todd in a private setting. No one was there with him except her, and God, of course.

After knowing Todd for so long, there was no pretense between them. Sometimes she felt that Todd didn't consider her any differently than an annoying piece of furniture. He never pretended to be anything he was not, and he never changed his behavior because she was there.

She'd seen him happy and sad. She'd seen him at his best, and definitely at his worst.

Todd smiled at her, clasped his hands, bowed his head, and waited for a few seconds for her to do the same. "Dear heavenly Father, thank You for the food we're about to eat. Thank You for Shannon and her willingness to open her home and share it with me. Thanks, too, for the good jobs You've given both of us, and I pray we'll be able to show Your glory to all who work there. Amen!"

"Amen," Shannon murmured, unable to believe the tightness that formed in her throat from his heartfelt words.

Todd didn't wait for her to respond or start talking. He began eating right away. "This is great," he said, speaking through his mouthful. "I didn't realize how hungry I was until we started heating this up. I didn't have time to stop for lunch. All I've had today was a bag of chips out of the machine and a few dozen cups of coffee."

Shannon cleared her throat and reached for the salad dressing. "Yes, I had a feeling."

After a few more hearty mouthfuls, Todd slowed down. "Actually, that's what I have to talk to you about."

"You want to talk to me about your bad eating habits?"

He sighed while he rose and helped himself to another piece of lasagna from the pan. "No. About Faye and the coffee. She came in more times than I could count to bring me coffee. While I appreciated it, I think it's getting out of hand."

"You admit you've been drinking too much coffee?"

He sat down at the table with his refilled plate but didn't continue eating. "Get serious, Shan. I think I'm starting to see what it's like when I did this kind of thing to you, and I'm sorry I used to do that. I wanted to talk to you about Faye."

Shannon nodded. Of course she'd known what he was going to say. She'd already heard Faye's side of the story. Faye had made her feelings toward Todd rather obvious. Shannon knew him well enough to realize that if he returned her feelings, even in the slightest, he would already have asked her out. Still, she had to give him a chance to say the reason he was seeking her out. "Sorry. I didn't mean to be like that. What did you want to ask me?"

"I don't know what to do about Faye."

"You know she likes you."

"I know that. I think everyone in the office knows. And probably half the drivers, too."

"Why don't you take her out a few times and see what happens? Faye is really nice. After a while, it'll either work, or it won't."

"It wouldn't be right to do that. I'm old enough now that I have to be realistic. Any relationship I enter into could develop into marriage, and I can't marry Faye. I don't know her that well, but I don't think she's a believer. I don't want to get into something like that."

Shannon nodded. "I know what you mean. But I think Faye is a Christian. She's even been to church with me a couple of times. I get the impression that something in the church has hurt her, and she's stepped back. She doesn't want to talk about it, but I think she just needs some time to work things out, and she'll be fine."

"I can understand her situation, but that doesn't change the way I feel. I have to figure out a way to tell her gently I'm not interested. It wouldn't be fair to go out with her when I know nothing would come of it."

"You don't know that."

"But I *do* know that." Todd raised his fork in the air with his right hand and placed his left hand over his chest. "Because my heart already belongs to someone else."

Shannon nearly choked on her food. Despite how ridiculous he looked, she knew he was serious. Todd may have been a lot of things, but he had never been a liar. The more she was getting to know the new Todd, the more she knew he wasn't a liar now. "I didn't know. Aren't you going to tell me about it?"

With his hand still over his heart, Todd shook his head. "Nope. It's a secret."

"I think there are too many secrets around here," Shannon grumbled as she stuffed the last bite of lasagna into her mouth. First she had a Secret Admirer, and now Todd had secrets, too. All those secrets were going to drive her insane.

Todd settled back into position and began eating again. "By the way, Craig tells me you're coming to the open house at church on Saturday."

"Yes, I am. Are you going?"

He grinned. "Wouldn't miss it for the world."

Chapter 7

Todd straightened his tie, fixed the knot, and stood back to look at himself in the mirror, trying to get some satisfaction from his pristine appearance.

He yanked off the tie. It was his face, but he wasn't the man in the mirror.

The man in the mirror was dressed up in a neatly ironed shirt and black dress slacks, now minus the perfectly matched tie. He had just had a haircut and was freshly shaved.

He didn't know why he was trying so hard. Nothing he changed on the outside was going to make a difference to Shannon. She was never swayed by outward appearances. When she looked at him, she saw only a man who used to taunt and tease her when she was dressed up in her finest to go on a date. A man who frequently rummaged through her parents' refrigerator and ate the leftovers she had intended to take for her lunch at work. A man who made rude remarks to her in any situation.

In her position, he wouldn't have liked that guy, either.

He had to make up for every ignorant and stupid thing he'd ever done to her, and clothing and a haircut weren't going to do it. More than anything, he wanted to tell her how sorry he was, but he'd learned the hard way that talk was cheap.

Todd covered his face with his hands. "Lord God, I don't know what to do," he mumbled between his fingers. A million thoughts roared through his mind, none of which would be helpful.

He walked into the kitchen to sit at the table where he had the rhyming dictionary, a pen, and a piece of paper handy.

Soon he had to leave for church, but he had enough time to write down his thoughts.

Dearest Shannon,
> *My heart longs for the day we can be together*
> *In either fine or stormy weather.*
> *In every way it's you I adore,*
> *Because every day I love you more.*

Your Secret Admirer

Without analyzing his words, Todd rolled the note, tied it with a ribbon, and attached a chocolate kiss. He'd already left the note she would find Monday, but this one he would leave for her Tuesday.

He didn't know if she could ever love him as much as he loved her, but so far, the fact that she was tolerating him gave him hope. He hadn't considered how he'd feel about writing the notes every day, but it made him feel good to know she appeared to enjoy reading them. But there was a benefit he hadn't thought of. Not that he would ever regard himself as the creative or artistic type, but pouring out his heart onto paper, even if she didn't know who was creating the words, was therapeutic. Since he couldn't tell her in person how he felt, writing the notes was the next best thing.

Never in his life had Todd waxed poetic, but now he was doing so—literally. He found it ironic, since back in high school he'd passed English only by the grace of his teachers.

On his drive to church, he tried to compose more verses in his head. He wasn't having much success, except he knew what he wanted to say. For the actual writing of the words, the rhyming dictionary was probably the best purchase he'd ever made.

The parking lot was nearly full when he pulled in. The spot he found was farther from the building than ever before, giving him a slightly different perspective of the building and grounds from the usual.

The church wasn't big or grand, but the building was solid and well cared for. Since the board had been preparing for the anniversary celebration for months, some of the church's history had crept into the Sunday sermons. He'd learned the building had been constructed a year after the church was planted twenty-five years ago, due to the generosity of the parent church and a member of the missions conference. Even though he'd attended for only a year and a half, he knew both Craig and Shannon had grown up there, attending almost every Sunday. Everyone knew the Andrews family and loved them.

In comparing his own home life to theirs, he'd seen what he'd missed by not growing up in a stable environment. After experiencing the added love of extended family through other church members, he missed even more not having a network of people and programs to fall back on when he needed them. For a few years, however, that had been his own fault. Ever since he met Craig, Craig had given him an open invitation to go to church or even church activities if he didn't want to attend Sunday morning, which he hadn't. Todd had rejected Craig's offers of help, telling himself he could handle his life on his own. In so many ways, he'd been a fool. Ever since he had experienced the grace of God's love, he joined in freely, although for now the best he could do was help Craig supervise and provide transportation for the youth group's activities. He bit back a wry smile, thinking that most of the kids knew the Bible better than he did. But he was working on it, and Craig assured him that was what mattered.

As he walked closer to the building, he recognized Shannon's car. Judging from her good parking spot, close to the building, she'd arrived much sooner than he had.

Fortunately, the weather was warm for an early spring day. The committee had been prepared for rain, but the weather was cooperating, ensuring the Saturday open house would be a success. The aroma of the barbecue already enticed him before he reached the crowd milling on the grass. The people gathered outside already exceeded the usual number present for a normal Sunday service. Judging from the cars, which were being parked on the street, the people inside would be almost equal to those outside.

He only waved a friendly greeting at Craig and Shannon's parents in passing, since he saw them every Sunday and a few days during the week, and continued on his quest to find Shannon. He found her with Craig, talking to some people he already knew, making it easy to slip in beside her and not raise any eyebrows.

After sharing a few comments about the number of people present, the conversation continued as it had prior to his arrival. Instead of joking around as he usually did with those same people, Todd kept silent. He listened and watched everyone else.

As conversation continued, each one of them occasionally glanced at him, probably wondering why he wasn't making jokes. Either that or they didn't recognize him since he was all dressed up.

Craig looked at him frequently, but Shannon didn't look at him at all. He had a feeling she was waiting for him to tease her about something and embarrass her in front of their mutual friends. It made him more aware of what a jerk he'd been to her in the past. It had been a year since the last time they'd been in church together, with the exception of a few weeks ago, when he'd tried to be with her and she'd pointedly ignored him. Before that, though, he'd embarrassed her often enough that she would have no reason now to think things had changed.

After the threads of talk about the anniversary celebration were exhausted, Brittany turned to Todd. She then looked at Shannon and back to Todd, as if she couldn't decide which one of them to speak to.

She turned again to Shannon. "I couldn't believe it when I heard you two were actually working together. How's it going?"

Shannon drew in a short breath. "Fine."

A silence hung in the air within their circle, while Brittany waited for Shannon to say more, but she didn't. Brittany turned to face Todd. Since she appeared to be waiting for something, Todd thought he should answer, even though he considered her question intrusive.

"It's been fine, although we don't see each other all that much. It's a very busy place."

Brittany turned back to Shannon with one eyebrow raised.

Shannon nodded. "It's the same building, but we work in different areas."

Brittany's eyes widened. "Surely you must bump into each other sometime. What about your breaks?"

All eyes remained fixed on them. Todd felt strange with everyone staring at them. He was accustomed to being the center of attention, but this time, he wasn't trying to entertain. Instead, he felt like a bug under a microscope. And to have Shannon under the microscope with him made him angry.

He stiffened from head to toe. "I take my first coffee break at 10:15, my lunch at 12:30, then my second coffee break around 3:00, if I have time. Would you like to know Shannon's schedule, too? Is there anything else you want to know?"

Brittany's face turned beet red. "Sorry. I was just curious because you and Shannon always, uh, never mind—I think I'm going to get a hamburger."

Everyone else mumbled their agreement under their breath, and the group broke up. They headed outside, including Craig, which left Todd as alone with Shannon as he could be in a crowd of people.

He rammed his hands into his pockets. He knew he'd been relentless at times with Shannon, using her as an easy target. She'd always been so graceful to put up with him that he hadn't considered what everyone else around them saw. He hadn't realized he'd been so bad that everyone would want to know how they could function in the same room together. "I didn't know we were going to be such a topic of interest. This is my fault for teasing you all the time. I'm really sorry."

She tipped her head down, studying some spot on the floor as she spoke. "It's okay. I'm a big girl now. I can handle it."

His heart hammered in his chest. "You shouldn't have to handle it. I wish I could take it all back, but I can't. Saying I'm sorry somehow isn't enough."

She still wouldn't look up at him. "It's okay. I know you weren't that way on purpose. I guess everyone else who didn't know you as well as I did thought we were fighting all the time."

Todd's stomach flipped over. The last thing he wanted to do was fight with Shannon, but he had openly taken out his frustrations on her. Guilt roared through him. He knew he should say something, but he didn't know what. The words spilled out of his mouth before he could think about what he was saying or stop himself. "I don't want to fight with you, Shan. But if it looked as if we were fighting, then we can always kiss and make up."

Her head snapped up, and she stared straight into his eyes. All he could do was grin like an idiot.

"Get real, Todd. Honestly—sometimes I just don't know what goes on inside your brain."

He lost the grin and shrugged his shoulders. "If you won't kiss me, then how about if I get us a couple of burgers?"

"I'll get my own," she muttered.

She turned and walked away, but Todd caught up quickly and walked beside her to the barbecue then stood directly behind her in the line.

"Are you coming back tomorrow for the service?"

She didn't look at him as she replied. "Yes, I had planned on it."

"Are you staying for the speeches and stuff tonight?"

"Yes. Actually, I've been asked to say a few words, since I was the first baby born and dedicated here. In a way I'm almost dreading it, because lots of people here still remember that. I'm going to hear choruses of 'I can't believe how you've grown up' for the next year, I think."

Todd smiled. He also could say how much she'd grown up. The age difference of three years was nothing now, but he remembered what she was like when he first became friends with Craig. One reason he'd paid so much attention to Shannon then was because he was jealous that Craig had a little sister who loved and adored him, while Todd had felt alone.

He touched Shannon's arm gently with one finger then ran his finger up to her shoulder. While he cupped her shoulder, he rubbed soothing little circles into her shoulder blade with his thumb, as he knew she liked. He dropped his voice to a low whisper so only Shannon could hear him. To further ensure he wouldn't be overheard, he leaned closer to her so his mouth was nearly at her ear. "I can tell you how much you've grown up, but then you could say the same about me, since we met when we were both kids. I won't talk if you don't."

A few strands of her hair tickled his nose, but Todd didn't move. He'd never been so close to Shannon, touching her gently, when she wasn't backing away or screaming because he was tickling or poking her with something. His eyes drifted shut as he blocked out the smell of the meat on the grill and inhaled the heady aroma of her apple-scented shampoo.

"Todd?"

He nuzzled in closer. "Mmm. . .you smell so nice."

Suddenly, she stepped forward. Even though the spring air was warm, the abrupt separation felt like an arctic front had fallen between them. "What are you doing? What's gotten into you?"

He felt his ears heat up as he became aware of their surroundings and the people around them, even though no one was looking at them. "Sorry. Is it almost our turn?"

As they filled their plates and found a place to sit and eat, Todd kept the conversation light. The closer they came to the start of the evening service, the more nervous Shannon became. Fortunately, it was easy for Todd to slip into his old behavior patterns. He made jokes and wisecracks and soon had her laughing, and with her laughter time passed quickly.

When the service began, he had convinced her everyone else who had been called on to speak was as nervous as she was. They listened to other people tell their stories of being with the church body in the last twenty-five years, some giving testimonies and some history lessons on the church's founding. Others talked of the transition from a home group to constructing and moving into a dedicated building. Most people simply shared times that were special to them.

Todd had never thought of what Shannon would be like in front of a large group;

but once she overcame her fear of the microphone, she was a good speaker—clear, easy to understand, and entertaining. By the time she finished her short speech on growing up from birth to adulthood in the same congregation, he heard a few elderly ladies sniffling, none of whom was Shannon's grandmother.

"You were great," he said as she returned to her seat and shuffled in beside him.

"Thanks." Joy radiated from Shannon as she smiled ear to ear. It made Todd hope that one day she would smile like that for him.

They sat quietly for the rest of the service. At the close, everyone stood and joined with the choir in a rousing rendition of the "Hallelujah Chorus."

They talked with several people as they all made their way out of the building.

When one of the elderly ladies who had been sniffling in the back row stopped Shannon at the door, Todd said good-bye and walked out to the parking lot to his car.

As he pointed the key toward the lock, he paused. Something felt wrong—as if he were too high.

He looked at the front tire. It was completely flat and sitting on the rim. The back tire was the same. He noticed that the car beside his had a flattened tire as well, but at least it was only one. Todd walked around to the other side of his car. Fortunately, that side was untouched.

He sucked in a deep breath and checked inside, making sure his stereo was still intact, which it was.

He walked back to the driver's side and rested his fists on his hips. He couldn't tell if someone had let the air out of the tires or if the tires had been punctured. He certainly wasn't going to have the car towed, if all he had to do was reinflate the tires. He had a spare, but with two tires flattened, one spare wouldn't do him a lot of good.

A few unkind words tumbled through his mind, but he stopped himself before he said them out loud. He returned to the church, where he found Shannon still talking to the same lady. She looked as if she wanted to get away, and fortunately, Todd could help her.

"Excuse me, Shan—may I talk to you? There's something wrong with my car."

The lady, whose name he couldn't remember, waved her hand, smiled, and walked away to stop some other people who also looked as if they were trying to leave.

"What's wrong? Or were you just being a hero and rescuing me?"

He ran his fingers through his hair. "I wish I were being gallant, but it looks as if someone let the air out of a couple of my tires. I have a portable compressor, but it's at home. Can you give me a ride? You have to go sort of past my place anyway."

"Someone flattened your tires!?" She raised her hands to cover her mouth. "Here? At church?"

"It's a sick world we live in, Shan. Nothing is safe." That was an early lesson he learned. Nowhere was a safe haven, not even home, which should have been one of the first places a person could go.

"Of course I'll give you a ride home. Let's go."

He followed Shannon to her car, and soon, they were on the way to his apartment.

"I really appreciate this. Would you mind picking me up on the way to church, too? I can leave the car in the lot overnight and then pump the tires back up after the service is over."

"No problem. But if you want to go back and do it now, I don't mind. It's still earl—"

Shannon gasped and slammed on the brakes. The tires screeched. Todd lurched forward but avoided smacking his face into the windshield only by the seat belt locking and holding him in place. The car jerked with the bump of a small impact. A big black dog bounced slightly off the front right fender and landed on the road beside the car. Before Todd could think of what to do, the dog scrambled up and bounded away.

"I hit him," Shannon whimpered. "I just hit a dog."

Todd watched the dog disappear between a couple of houses. "Yeah, but he couldn't be hurt too bad. He's running away."

A horn honked behind them. Shannon started moving forward but far below the speed limit.

He turned toward her. All the color had drained from her face. She was gripping the steering wheel so tight her knuckles had turned white. Even from the side, he could see her eyes were glassy.

"Maybe you should pull over."

She shook her head. "I can't. There's nowhere to stop here."

"We're only a few blocks from my place. Maybe you should come inside with me and settle down a bit before you go home."

She nodded tightly. "Maybe I will."

He directed her to the visitor parking, since the control for the underground security parking area was still attached to the visor of his own car.

"I'm sure the dog is okay," he said as he punched in the code to open the front door. "After all, it ran away. But I know it's a shock to hit something. I once hit a deer when I was in the mountains. It was pretty scary. The deer ran away, too, but I had to pull over for a while."

All she did was nod.

Todd guided her up the elevator and to his apartment. Once inside, he left her at the door and hurried into the kitchen ahead of her. He picked up the rhyming dictionary from the table and shoved it into the nearest drawer. Shannon appeared behind him just as he opened the cupboard above the stove. After he started working at Kwiki Kouriers, he'd bought a box of Shannon's favorite tea in the faint hope that one day she would come for a visit. He was happy to have it on hand, although these weren't the circumstances under which he had wanted to give it to her.

He started pouring water into the kettle. "If you want, I can ask around the neighborhood and see if anyone knows who owns the dog and maybe check up on it for you."

Shannon's voice wavered as she spoke. "Yes, that would be nice." Her lower lip quivered. Tears started to stream down her cheeks. Todd set the kettle aside, took a few steps toward her, and extended his arms. "Come here," he said softly.

Without saying a word, Shannon stepped into the cradle of his arms. As he closed his arms around her, she cried even more. Her whole body shook.

"It's okay," he murmured as he stroked her hair with one hand. "He didn't appear to be limping. I watched him run away." Despite his words, he knew that as soon as Shannon left, he was going to take a flashlight and walk to the spot and check to make sure there was no blood. Only then would he be satisfied the dog probably wasn't seriously hurt, but he wasn't going to tell her that until after he'd confirmed it.

After a few minutes, she stopped crying, but Todd didn't let her go. Since she made no effort to move away from him, he kept his arms around her, holding her close to his heart.

In the car, he had considered hinting to her that he was the writer of the notes. He'd been praying for a sign to show him when the time was right to tell her he was her Secret Admirer. Even though he didn't appreciate the flat tires, it did create a situation he could have used to his advantage.

That had now changed, though. He couldn't tell her he loved her when she was so upset over hitting a dog. But, in holding her, he was more certain he wanted to do this forever. He wanted to be there for Shannon when she needed someone. He wanted her trust, and he wanted her to know he would do anything for her.

With her leaning into his hug with no hesitation, he wanted to know the same thing could happen again, only next time not in trying circumstances. He wanted to be able to hold her in good times and in bad. In sickness and in health, until death parted them.

He loved her so much he wanted to marry her.

But he couldn't ask her such a thing yet. He didn't know how she would respond when he told her he was her Secret Admirer.

She shuffled in his arms but didn't back up or indicate she wanted him to release her. Her words sounded muffled as she spoke against his chest. In a way, he liked the vibration of her voice against him. It was a tangible reminder of how close she was and that she wasn't backing away. "I'm so sorry for acting like such a ninny and crying like that. I know the dog ran away, but I couldn't stop myself."

Todd lowered his head so his cheek pressed against her temple. Her skin was soft, and her hair smelled almost as good as it had earlier. He meant to speak clearly, but his voice came out in only a hoarse croak. "It's okay. Don't worry about it."

Slowly, Todd lowered his head a little more, just enough to brush his lips against the soft skin of her cheek. He could taste the saltiness of her tears against his lips.

The sensation drove him over the edge. He couldn't stop himself. Or rather, he probably could have stopped, but he didn't want to. Ever so gently, he brushed a light kiss on her cheek in that spot. He brushed another soft kiss a little farther down, closer to her mouth. When she sighed, he stopped. His cheek was against hers, and their lips so close he could almost taste her. In slow motion, Todd slid one hand up her back then over her shoulders, until he touched her chin with the tip of his index finger. He guided her chin up, closed his eyes, and kissed her mouth—lightly, gently, and only for a second.

His heart raced. He wanted to kiss her again, only longer and fully.

Again, he guided her chin with his finger, just to tip her chin up a little more.

Suddenly, Shannon stiffened and stepped backward.

Todd let his arms drop. He would never hold her against her will. He knew she would never have expected him to kiss her, but he hadn't thought about her reaction until it happened. All he knew was that he wanted to do it again and do it right—he wanted to kiss her well and good, only stopping for breath long enough to tell her he loved her and to hear she loved him, too.

"I think I should go. I'll see you tomorrow morning. 'Bye."

The door closed before he had a chance to say a word.

Chapter 8

Shannon set her mug on the corner of her desk then slid into her chair. She grasped the handle of her drawer but didn't open it.

If the Secret Admirer wasn't perplexing enough, now she had Todd to think about, too.

Todd.

Because she was at work, Shannon fought the urge to cover her face with her hands.

Again Todd Sanders was driving her insane.

When she picked him up for church Sunday morning, it was as if everything were normal, but things would never be normal again. Actually, where Todd was concerned, she didn't know what normal was.

He'd been his usual bright, cheery self on the way to church. When they arrived, he tossed a black case into the trunk of his car, and they went into the service together. To be safe, she'd immediately gone to sit with her parents. Taking it for granted he was welcome, Todd had followed right along with her, and they'd all sat together.

To make matters worse, her parents invited her for lunch at the close of the service. After she accepted, they also invited Todd. Of course, he accepted, too.

The last time she'd stayed for a meal at her parents' house when Todd was present had been two years ago, before she moved out. Todd and Craig had been in rare form that day. They'd been out fishing together, and neither of them had taken a shower before coming to the table. The stench of sweaty men, fish, and diesel fuel turned her stomach so bad she asked them to move and sit near an open window. Neither Todd nor Craig moved, but Todd teased her relentlessly for making the request.

Then, while they were eating, Todd expressed his frustration to her mother about the problems he had gutting the fish he'd caught that morning, including a detailed portrayal of the procedure he'd used. Her mother had listened intently, giving Todd some suggestions on how to get a clean cut next time, including another vivid description of the various body parts of a dead fish, while Shannon struggled to keep her stomach settled.

The final straw came when Todd pulled some kind of huge dead bug out of his pocket, claiming he was going to make a fishing lure to look exactly like it.

Everyone had thought he was funny. Except Shannon. She thought he'd been rude and obnoxious, which was typical for Todd.

On Sunday, he'd been so polite and well mannered the whole day, she wouldn't have known he was the same man. Since she hadn't known what to do or say, she'd said little and listened to Todd talk. Even if he wasn't a scholar, he had certainly been a gentleman.

Something was wrong, but she couldn't figure out what.

At the sound of a thud echoing from the lunchroom, Shannon returned her thoughts to where she was and opened the drawer. She pulled out the note of the day, but instead of reading it, she held it in her hand.

So far she could handle the Secret Admirer. The notes were flattering and sweet, even sensitive and kind. No one had ever told her she was special before, and especially not in such an old-fashioned and romantic manner. If she allowed herself the fantasy, she could have called the writing love sonnets, rather than bad poetry. She was enjoying the attention and anticipated coming to work so she could read the new note.

She grasped the end of the ribbon, about to tug it open, when Todd's laughter rang out from the lunchroom.

Her hand froze, and she shut her eyes.

Todd.

He'd been so sweet to her Saturday night that it seemed almost natural when he kissed her.

Shannon had to force herself to breathe. Todd Sanders had kissed her.

He'd kissed her once before. She'd been seventeen, and it had been the day of her high school graduation. When she arrived home from the ceremony, diploma in hand, ready to change for the dinner celebration, she'd found Todd and Craig in the living room. Todd had smiled and held his arms open, and she'd gone to him with stars in her eyes. When he asked if he could give her a celebratory kiss, she thought she had died and gone to heaven. Just like a schoolgirl, which of course she was at the time, her heart pounded out of control, and she could barely breathe as he bent down. His lips brushed her ear, setting her all aquiver. Then he whispered "woof" in her ear and licked up the side of her face. He was across the room before she could lift her arm fast enough to smack him.

But on Saturday, when he kissed her so gently and sweetly, she'd stood very still. She had even wanted him to kiss her again. He'd definitely improved on his kissing skills, which wasn't what she should have been thinking about.

Surely she was going insane.

Just as she had told Todd before, she was a big girl now. And Todd was now a grown man. He'd been a great comfort to her and done the right things while she cried so much after the shock of hitting the dog, who may not have been hurt after all. She supposed she'd even made it easy for him. Any man in that situation probably would have done the same.

But this wasn't any man. It was Todd Sanders. She shouldn't have wanted more.

So she'd acted like the grown-up woman she was. She ran away. And now she was simply going to pretend it hadn't happened.

"Hey, Shan. Top o' the morning to ya," Todd quipped in a bad, fake Irish accent as he passed by, coffee in hand, before he disappeared into the dispatch office.

Behind him, Faye giggled.

Shannon gagged.

When Todd disappeared from sight, Faye sighed. "Are you coming tonight? I have a seat reserved for you."

"Tonight?"

"Did you forget? We're all going out for Rick's birthday. To that steak place a few blocks away."

"I remember, now that you mention it. Yes, of course I'm going."

Faye nodded and sat down at her desk. Shannon didn't want to think about the fact that Todd might go, but she wouldn't stay away just because he would be there. She refused to let him control her life, even if it was in an indirect way.

For now, Shannon wanted to read the newest note. Faye already knew about them, and so did Todd, but he didn't count. She'd waited too long, though, and other staff had started to arrive in the office. She didn't want to wait until the end of the day when the office would once again be empty, so she picked up the note, shoved it into her pocket, and ran into the washroom.

She tried to tell herself that reading it in the washroom didn't lessen the romanticism of the situation.

Dearest Shannon,
Again I am glad the weekend is finished
Because my love for you has not diminished.
Monday has come, and I get to see you once more
And tuck another note and a kiss in your drawer.

Your Secret Admirer

Shannon smiled as she reread the note. The poetry might be getting worse, but the words still warmed her heart. She popped the kiss into her mouth, savoring it until the last morsel had dissolved, then returned to her desk and began her work for the day.

The whole day, she eagerly anticipated the coming dinner, not that the occasion was extraordinary.

But maybe, just maybe, *he* would be there.

🌸

Todd walked into the dimly lit restaurant. He was with Rick and Bryan, but soon he would be with Shannon.

The atmosphere was happy and informal, just a bunch of people who didn't necessarily know each other well getting together for a fun evening. Since more than twenty-five people were attending, a small room had been reserved for their group. It was a private gathering so everyone would be free to sit down, eat, or mingle as they wished. It would be more of a party atmosphere than a formal dinner gathering, and people could leave early or stay until the restaurant closed.

The scenario was perfect for Todd. If he spent most of his time with Shannon, no one would notice or care.

Shannon stood near the front of the room, talking to Faye. Just as Todd was about to join Shannon, Gary appeared beside Rick.

Without preamble, Rick elbowed Gary in the ribs and made a crude comment about Shannon's figure. Gary responded in like manner. Todd's mouth nearly dropped open in shock, but he struggled to compose himself. What they were saying was nothing he hadn't thought himself before he became a Christian. He'd even said a few of the same things out loud to Shannon years ago. Suddenly, he felt ashamed.

He had an almost uncontrollable urge to go and stand between the men and Shannon, so they wouldn't be able to look at her. Of course, that would provide only a temporary solution. His actions would simply stall their observations and discussion for a short time.

But any time was better than no time.

He turned to Gary. "Excuse me. I just remembered something."

Todd forced himself to walk, not run, as he crossed the room to join Shannon and Faye.

"Good evening, ladies." He smiled first at Faye, then more at Shannon, hoping he wasn't being too obvious. "Mind if I join you?"

Faye wrapped her fingers around his arm. "Please do! We could use some manly company, right, Shan?"

Shannon glanced from side to side, then back to Todd. "I guess."

Todd shuffled a few inches to block Gary's view of Shannon. "This is a great idea. By the way, who's collecting the money?"

Faye stuck out her hand. "Me. This month only Rick is having a birthday, so everyone else pays for just one meal. One dollar, please."

Todd gave her the dollar. For the person or persons having a birthday that month, everyone else contributed enough money to cover their meals. Between so many people, it wasn't a large expense, and everyone always had a good time. This was his first dinner since he'd started, and he'd been looking forward to it.

Todd grinned and leaned closer to Faye, but he still spoke loud enough for Shannon to hear. "My birthday is coming up, you know. My last birthday. I'm going to be twenty-nine forevermore."

Shannon rolled her eyes. "Then we'll only have to pay for one dinner—and no more for the rest of your life. It would serve you right. I think I'm going to sit down. Everyone's here, so we're going to get settled and order soon."

"I have a few more people to collect from. I'll catch you guys later," Faye said and headed across the room.

Todd followed Shannon to one of the tables and sat beside her. She glanced to the other dispatchers and Gary, then back to Todd. She raised an eyebrow. She didn't say a word, but her question was obvious.

"It's okay if I sit with you, isn't it?" Todd tried to calm his heart from going into overdrive as he asked his next question. "We can be friends, can't we?"

She paused, as if she had to think about it. "Yes, I guess so. It just feels strange, that's all."

His gut clenched. The room was filled with people milling about, but for a limited time, they were alone in their own small corner. It wasn't exactly ideal, but he'd made a bit of progress, and he couldn't let the opportunity lapse. He had too much he wanted to say.

"I can only guess how you feel about sitting with me, and I can't blame you. I know words are inadequate, but I don't know what I can do except say I'm sorry for everything I've done to you." For all the good being sorry did. His mother had been sorry for twenty years. She continued to be sorry, but still nothing had changed except he'd become smarter and wiser, he hoped.

"It's okay, Todd. I've been thinking a lot about stuff lately. It's really okay. Since we've been working together, you've been different. I'm working to put everything behind me."

Once again, her unselfish grace washed over him like a cleansing balm. He'd never felt so unworthy beside another person or so undeserving. And he'd never loved her more. "Shan, I know this is going to sound strange, but would you like to go—"

"Hi, Shannon. Todd." Gary's voice interrupted Todd's words.

Todd gritted his teeth. He was about to ask Shannon if she would go out to dinner with him the next day, just the two of them, so they could talk, like a real date. He wasn't going to tell her how much he cared in the middle of a work-related outing. He wanted to show her, in private, away from the hustle and bustle of anything work or church related.

Gary and Rick pulled out chairs and joined them at their table for four. "I brought the birthday boy."

Todd smiled politely, but the last people he felt like sitting with were Gary and Rick, especially after what he'd heard them say. However, since Shannon had no idea what they'd said behind her back, he had no good reason to suggest they move.

Todd nodded and responded when appropriate as they ordered their food. When they received their meals, he did the same as Shannon and bowed his head in silence for a couple of seconds to give thanks to the Lord. He thanked God first for the meal, then for the reason for being with everyone out in a restaurant—his good job.

To enjoy the evening, Todd pushed the crude comments out of his head. When they finished eating, he stood and mingled, as did everyone else. He wanted to spend every minute he could with Shannon, but he knew it would look strange if he never left her side.

Still, the second the dessert tray arrived, he made a beeline for his seat before anyone else could sit beside Shannon. As he knew she would, she selected a slice of triple chocolate cake while he chose a hearty piece of peach pie.

He hadn't finished his first bite when Gary reappeared, this time without Rick, but with a chocolate dessert.

Gary lowered himself into the chair. "I see you also picked chocolate. A woman after my own heart."

Todd stiffened.

Shannon smiled at Gary. "I've had this here before. It's the best I've ever had." She turned back to Todd. "There's one at the bookstore that runs a close second, though."

Gary continued to look solely at Shannon, ignoring Todd. "That may be so. But nothing beats pure chocolate. Like, for example, a chocolate kiss."

Shannon dropped her fork.

Todd nearly choked at Gary's mention of a chocolate kiss. He'd wondered if Gary had seen the note with the kiss attached the day he went into Shannon's drawer. Now, after hearing his roundabout reference to it, he knew he had.

Gary smiled and leaned slightly closer to Shannon. "I love chocolate, too."

Todd's stomach took a nosedive into his shoes. Unless he was mistaken, Gary had just intimated he was somehow connected to the chocolate kisses Todd had been leaving for Shannon every day.

Todd cleared his throat, hoping his voice would come out sounding casual. "I think most people like chocolate, Gary."

Gary's expression turned smug as he watched Shannon take a shaky sip of her coffee. "Probably. Just some people think chocolate is more special than others. Sometimes it even carries a message."

Shannon started coughing in the middle of her sip. She set the cup down in the saucer so fast she spilled some, while she pressed her other fist into the center of her chest.

Todd narrowed his eyes. Gary was slick; there was no doubt about it. He'd seen hints of that characteristic while working with him. Now he saw the trait extended into Gary's personal life and thoughts as well, which shouldn't have been a surprise.

He opened his mouth to counter, even though he hadn't yet put his thoughts together to make a coherent sentence. Before he could get a word out, Faye slid into the empty chair.

"Hi, Gary. You still owe me a dollar."

Gary leaned sideways in the chair to retrieve his wallet from his back pocket. "Of course. Is everyone having fun?"

Faye nodded. "As always. What about you, Todd? This is your first time."

All he could think about was the new complication to his Secret Admirer plan. Shannon had asked him to listen to the talk around him, to see if he could help her discover who was leaving the kisses. She never actually told him about the notes, and he didn't know if she'd done that on purpose or by simple omission. Even though Gary wouldn't know what was in the notes, it would have been an easy guess. The point was that he knew, and he'd mentioned the kisses to Shannon.

Todd didn't know if Shannon had told any of the other women, but he did know he was the only male she'd confided in. The only reason for that was his unique position in what he could now call, with caution, an old friend.

Being in transition from nemesis to friend wasn't the time to tell Shannon he was her Secret Admirer. Despite her forgiveness, he had to prove himself. He could tell she was still being cautious around him. He had to earn her trust and, if he could, a little affection, before it was time to reveal himself to her.

Gary's sudden appearance in the scenario complicated things. He couldn't tell Shannon that Gary wasn't her Secret Admirer. To know he wasn't, Todd would have to know who was, and he couldn't say so yet.

But just as Shannon didn't know the Secret Admirer was Todd, neither did Gary. He also didn't realize Todd knew there was a Secret Admirer, which probably explained why Gary had the nerve to mention "a message" in front of him.

Todd didn't know what Gary had in mind, but he planned to find out.

He turned to smile at Faye. "I'm having a great time. This is a good way to get to know people away from work."

Faye rested her hand on his arm, and her smile turned sappy. "I'm so glad you feel that way."

Todd patted her hand, while desperately thinking of a way to remove it without being too obvious. He knew Faye had a crush on him. He hoped that, like the other women who had developed a fast crush on him because of his smile and his ability to tell a good joke, her crush would fade as quickly as it started. He didn't want to hurt Faye. He liked her, but only as a friend at work.

He turned toward Faye's plate, which contained a half-eaten piece of cake. "That looks good. I got the peach pie. It tastes good, too."

Faye looked at his dessert then and saw he'd eaten only one bite. She blushed and released his arm. He immediately began to eat, openly savoring every bite. His acting caused everyone at the table to smile, including Shannon, and they all resumed eating their own desserts.

With Faye's arrival, Gary made no more personal references.

Since it was only Monday evening, no one stayed much longer after the desserts were finished. Todd became caught up in a conversation with one of his coworkers, so he stayed longer than he had intended. In so doing, he found himself walking out to the parking lot at the same time as Gary.

"You said before that you've known Shannon for a long time."

Todd stiffened. "Yes. I'm good friends with her brother."

"I know you don't have anything on now, but have you ever gone out with her?"

Todd didn't know what to say. He didn't know Gary well, but he did know he had a reputation as a playboy and was proud of it.

Todd considered the time he'd spent with Shannon at the bookstore the closest thing to a date he'd ever had with her. The way things were going now, it would be the closest he'd get for a long time. "No," he mumbled. "Never did."

Gary jingled his keys in his pocket as they walked. "But you've known her for a long time, so that's close enough. Tell me what she likes and doesn't like."

A list of Shannon's favorite things flooded his mind. Books, especially Christian romance fiction. Apple-scented shampoo. The emergence of spring. Animals in general, but especially big dogs of no particular heritage. The color green. Classical music with lots of strings. Tall trees.

He shook his head. He had no intention of helping Gary date Shannon. Since he didn't know what Gary expected to hear, he decided to be vague.

"She likes chocolate," he muttered.

"Anything else? I need more. I want to see what progress I can make with her. You can help your boss, can't you?"

Todd nearly tripped over his own feet. He didn't want to think Gary would use his authority to hire and fire to obtain the information he wanted, in something that had nothing to do with work—and everything to do with Todd's heart.

Fortunately, they had arrived at Todd's car, saving him from having to say too much, but Gary stopped beside him.

Todd opened the door and slid in. He reached to close the door, but Gary stepped forward, preventing Todd from moving it without hitting him and forcing him to reply. Todd remained with his arm outstretched, his hand gripping the handle. "Do you have a cat?"

"No, but my sister does. Does she like cats?"

"Not particularly. Focus on that."

"Great. I trust you'll tell me what I need to know?"

"Sure."

Gary stepped back, finally allowing Todd to close the door.

The dinner Todd had paid good money for threatened to surface. He didn't like the position Gary was putting him in with Shannon. He had no intention of helping Gary try to seduce Shannon. But Gary's veiled threat hung over him. He expected him to provide insider information on Shannon.

If Todd didn't need the job so bad, he would have quit right there. But he couldn't do that. Not only did he need the job, but for years, he'd wanted this particular job. Being a city dispatcher was the dream of a lifetime for him. He didn't have enough experience, but Gary told him when he was hired that he would take the chance, hire him anyway, and let him prove himself. So far, he was exceeding expectations, but he hadn't passed his initial three-month probationary period yet.

The job also paid decent money, something else Todd couldn't make light of. Along with supporting himself, he still had to pay off a few of his mother's debts plus a number of ongoing expenses for her.

He couldn't jeopardize the job, or he'd be out on the street. But he refused to let Gary seduce Shannon or be any part of the man's efforts.

Shannon's faith was solid. He knew she wouldn't date someone like Gary. At least, he hoped she wouldn't.

The first thing Todd did when he arrived at home was to go into the kitchen and page through his rhyming dictionary.

Somehow he had to show Shannon that Gary was not the man behind the notes, but he didn't know what to say that wouldn't also show he was the one. For lack of anything to say, Todd simply wrote from his heart.

Dearest Shannon,
> *Your words are kind, and your thoughts are tender.*
> *My love to you I completely surrender.*
> *When comes the day I can reveal my name*
> *I hope and pray you will feel the same.*

Your Secret Admirer

Once he had rolled and tied the note and attached a kiss, Todd changed into his pajamas. It wasn't his bedtime for hours, but he had a lot of praying to do, and he was going to do it in the dark, where he would have no distractions.

Then maybe tomorrow would be a better day.

Chapter 9

S hannon read the newest note a third time. Something was different, but she couldn't figure out what. Finally she told herself it was that the pentameter matched this time. She rose, unlocked her filing cabinet, and tucked the note into the newest envelope.

She smiled as she closed the drawer and pushed in the locking button. Rather than leaving the notes where anyone could gain access to them when she wasn't at her desk, she had been storing them in a safe and secure location. She took each envelope home on Friday, then spent a good portion of every Friday night reading the notes, studying them, and trying to figure out who wrote them.

Her smile faded when she realized she was no closer to discovering the identity of the man than when the notes started appearing. Trying to analyze and compare the handwriting had turned up nothing. No one wrote anything by hand anymore. Everything was sent via the company computer, either e-mailed or printed out for everyone to initial if necessary. She'd used a few signatures to eliminate some people, but the signatures weren't enough to determine a match, as most people's didn't correspond with their normal handwriting.

Her only lead was Gary's mention of the chocolate kisses, but his words were by no means conclusive. She'd been working at Kwiki Kouriers enough years with the same people that it was no surprise for someone to know she loved chocolate, especially chocolate that wasn't mixed with caramel or nuts or common fillers. Still, Gary's reference to chocolate kisses had been bugging her for days. She'd prayed about the Secret Admirer more times than she could count. Over the last couple of days, she'd also prayed about Gary, not that he would be the Secret Admirer—she just wanted to know if he was or wasn't. She hadn't received an answer.

A thud echoed from the kitchen, followed by a grumble.

Shannon smiled. Todd arrived his usual ten minutes after she did. His first stop was the lunchroom. He would pour his coffee then begin his trek through the office toward the dispatch area. At least twice a week, he overfilled his mug, causing him to spill some coffee on the floor. He then had to go back into the lunchroom for a paper towel to wipe up his mess. She had his routine clocked almost to the minute.

This time she stopped him.

"Todd, I need to talk to you."

He smiled so vividly she could see the little crow's-feet at the corners of his eyes from where he stood. He lowered his voice. "By the way, I meant to tell you—that dog was all right. I went back and checked. No sign of anything."

She let out her breath. "Thanks for doing that."

"So, what's up?"

"This Secret Admirer thing has me completely stumped. I've studied the handwriting, I've listened around, I've asked questions, and I've watched to see if anyone looks at me a little more than they should. Everything comes up blank. Have you heard anything?"

"No, Shan, I haven't heard a thing. Sorry."

She glanced from side to side, to be sure they were alone in the office. "What about Gary? You heard what he said at the restaurant."

"You mean about the chocolate kiss? I think he heard that from Kathy."

Shannon's stomach clenched. She'd tried so hard to keep the Secret Admirer secret. She didn't know word was floating around the office. "You mean Kathy knows? Who else knows?"

"I don't think anyone knows anything specific. The same day you asked me if I'd heard anything, Kathy came into the dispatch office and asked Bryan if he had chocolate kisses. Kathy said Nanci had asked her for one because Faye asked Nanci, and she was wondering if someone had given them out and she'd missed one."

Shannon gritted her teeth. Faye knowing something was going on would be her downfall, but it was too late to do anything about it now. "I guess it's a relief then that I know the source of the information. I won't have to take Gary seriously."

Todd shrugged his shoulders. "I wouldn't. Besides, you know what he's like. He's broken a few hearts around here. Jody, for one. Gary eats women like you for breakfast. He's not your type anyway."

She folded her hands in front of her on the desk. "And how do you know what my type is?"

He grinned and winked. "I just know. He's not your type."

She tipped her head to study Todd. Over the years he'd seen every male she'd dated. She wouldn't have wanted Todd to pick what kind of man would be her type for her life's mate; yet, she could certainly trust his judgment on who wasn't. From the time she was old enough to date, whenever she started to get serious about a boyfriend, along came Todd, telling her at least one major character flaw, usually in a belittling manner and at the worst possible moment. The trouble was, even though it hurt, Todd was always right in his assessment.

This time, though, Todd hadn't put her in a state of emotional upheaval, telling her what a loser her current boyfriend was. She knew Gary was a charmer and not a Christian. Of course, he was likable and intelligent, but that didn't make him suitable, at least not for her. But she wasn't going to tell Todd that once again he was right.

She shrugged. "I'll be the judge of that. By the way, I was talking to Mom last night. Since she knows we see each other every day, she asked me how your mother was doing."

All traces of Todd's grin disappeared. "About the same," he mumbled. "I should get in there before the phones start going crazy."

Before she had a chance to say another word, Todd hustled into the dispatch office.

Shannon suddenly regretted bringing up a tender subject. She didn't know what the problem was between Todd and his mother; she only knew it had existed before she met him. When she'd asked Craig, Craig wouldn't tell her anything. At first it annoyed her, because they never kept any secrets from one another until Todd came along. But, when she became a teen, she realized she didn't have to be privy to all Craig's inner thoughts and knowledge, especially about his friends. Nor had she wanted to share all her thoughts with Craig anymore.

Just before she moved out, at the height of her frustration with Todd, she'd seen him come over for a visit. Because she didn't want Todd to drive her to the edge of insanity, she'd ducked into the kitchen, meaning to go out the back door instead of the front. Before she left, she'd overheard Craig ask Todd if his mother did "it" again. But all she heard in reply was muffled sobs.

She didn't know men did that. She'd heard women cry, but never a man. Until that day, she hadn't considered that Todd's problems at home could be so serious. She knew a social worker was involved with the family, but she'd always assumed it had something to do with social assistance, since he had no father and his mother never seemed to hold down a job.

Regardless of his mother's employment history, Shannon figured out then that Todd must have been living in a dysfunctional environment if one question about his mother could cause him to break down like that. From that day on, whenever Todd did something to hurt or embarrass her, she told herself he was acting like a wounded puppy, striking back at her for whatever was striking at him. It didn't make it any less painful for her, nor did it make it right, but it did provide an excuse.

That was also the day that despite how much he tormented her, Shannon had begun to pray for Todd, although not as regularly as she felt she should have.

Faye and Brenda's arrival in the office turned Shannon's thoughts to her upcoming payroll deadline. Right on schedule, Gary appeared with the drivers' time sheets.

"Hi, Shannon," he said, dropping them in her basket.

"Thanks, Gary," she muttered as she finished her current calculation.

He leaned forward. "Anything else I can do for you?"

Shannon slid a piece of paper across the desk and handed him her pencil. "Yes. Can you write something for me?"

He grinned and returned the pencil. "Sorry. I won't let you catch me. Nice try, though. Maybe we can go out for coffee or dinner one night and discuss what's going on."

In your dreams, she thought. "Maybe," she said.

"Great. It's a date, then."

Before she could refute him, he turned around.

Shannon sighed as Gary walked away. She'd done a lot of thinking about every man she came in close contact with at work, Gary included. Not only was Gary intelligent, he had control issues, and he was also cagey. Being second only to the terminal manager, Gary had access to the building any time he pleased—days, nights, and weekends. Even if Gary wasn't the Secret Admirer, he had access to her desk when no one else was around, and he could easily have seen a note left for her, even if he didn't put it there. She could see him trying to lead her on, to get what he thought he could from another man's work. She'd seen him do such things professionally; she had no doubts he would do them personally.

But she wasn't positive he wasn't the Secret Admirer. If he was, she thought she might faint.

She doubted he was, though. The notes had an emotional flare she couldn't pin down. She was sure they sometimes didn't come out quite right because the Secret Admirer was working so hard at rhyming, but the message was clear. Someone had a crush on her, and he meant every word he said.

Gary wasn't the type to be poetic. He had a sharp wit and an analytical mind. If he turned to poetry, she was sure Gary's poetry would be more trendy and stylish, and he would certainly use more flare and alliteration in his choice of words.

Todd, on the other hand, might write like this, except she knew he wasn't capable of rhyming any words with more than a single syllable. The Secret Admirer used words she would never have dreamed of rhyming; yet they did.

Shannon looked toward the dispatch office.

She was sorry she'd put Todd in an awkward position, bringing up something that disturbed him when he should have been concentrating on his work. She knew he had some kind of difficulty with his mother, even as an adult. Craig told her Todd had started to change after he'd moved out and into his own place, just before Shannon moved out on her own. According to Craig, Todd became a Christian shortly after that. Now that she'd been working with him for a few months, she could see he was a changed man, not just because of his Christianity, but something else, too. She would never have thought Todd would mature, but he had.

But becoming a Christian didn't mean his struggles with his family would end. She'd known it was a sensitive subject, and she never should have asked him such a thing at work. For the first time, Shannon owed Todd an apology.

Until the opportunity arose to talk to him, Shannon resumed her work. Before she knew it, Faye was standing in front of her desk, and her stomach was starting to rumble.

"Faye, if you don't mind, I'm going to wait for half an hour and take my lunch break with Todd. There's something I have to talk to him about. Do you mind?"

Faye's eyes widened. "What did he do?"

Shannon smiled. "He didn't do anything. I just have to talk to him about something."

Faye's cheerful demeanor sagged. "Oh. Well, have fun."

Shannon couldn't help but feel sorry for Faye. She knew Faye had a crush on Todd, and it was a big one. But the more she thought about Todd—and Faye—the more she thought Faye needed someone more solid and grounded in his faith.

Like her brother Craig. . .

Shannon brightened. "I'm not going to have fun. It's something I have to talk to him about. I'll catch you at coffee time."

The next half hour was the slowest of her life, second only to the half hour she once spent trying to find a clear stream as a suitable habitat for a poor, displaced frog on death's doorstep.

As soon as Todd exited the dispatch room, Shannon hit SAVE on her computer and followed him into the lunchroom.

He walked straight for the fridge and removed his lunch. When he turned around and saw her, his eyes widened. "What are you doing here?"

Shannon grinned, reached around him, and removed her own lunch. "I work here, and it's lunchtime. Mind if I share your table?"

His eyes widened even more. "Not at all."

Before they ate, they paused for a word of thanks. Shannon thought it special that for once, she wasn't the only one to pray out loud softly at work, as she always did with Faye. Today Todd prayed. He wasn't eloquent, and his words didn't flow smoothly, but they came from his heart, and that was what counted.

While Shannon sprinkled dressing on her salad, she replayed his prayer in her mind. The more time she spent with Todd, the more she saw that Craig was right. Todd had changed, in many ways. She hadn't given him enough credit, and she felt guilty.

"I was wondering—have you ever been to any other church besides the one you attend now?"

Todd took a big bite of his sandwich. "Nope."

She started to nibble her carrot sticks. "You might enjoy going to a smaller service, one where there's more interaction and more opportunity to ask questions. I have an idea. Why don't you come to my church with me next Sunday? I think you'll like it."

"You're asking me to go to church with you?"

Suddenly, Shannon realized that was what she had done. "I guess I am."

His whole face brightened. "Sure. I think I'd like that. Is that why you wanted to have lunch with me?"

Shannon felt her cheeks heat up. "Not really. I think that was a spur-of-the-moment thing. Not that I'm going to change my mind. I wanted to apologize for this morning."

Todd started to cough and gulped down his mouthful, almost choking. "Apologize? To me? For what?"

"For bringing up a touchy subject here, where it had no place. That was poor timing on my part, and I apologize."

His cheeks reddened. "I appreciate it, but I think I'm the king of bad timing. Please don't think you ever owe me an apology for anything."

Shannon grinned at him. "Too late. I already apologized, and it's too late to take it back. By the way, I heard you did a great job in calming down one of the customers today."

"And I hear you cleared up a big muddle after Bryan messed up Jason's time sheet."

In contrast to the previous half hour, the lunch break flew by so fast Shannon didn't know where the time went.

She also had a feeling the week would be short, too. She didn't know if it was smart to invite Todd to her church, but she couldn't rescind her invitation. So she would make the best of it.

❁

Todd smiled as he worked. It still wasn't a date, but going to church with Shannon was the next best thing. Especially since she was the one who invited him.

He began entering a new pickup into the computer when he heard Shannon's name come up in Gary and Rick's conversation behind him.

Todd made a typo, backspaced, and kept typing, slowly, paying more attention to their words than to the pickup instructions. He didn't want to hear Gary telling Rick what he would like to do on a date with Shannon, but he couldn't stop listening. Something about his words gave Todd the impression it sounded less like a fantasy and more as if Gary thought it was a real possibility Shannon would participate.

In fact, the more he listened, the more it sounded as if Gary and Shannon had a date planned.

Todd's stomach churned. They'd just shared their lunch break, and Shannon hadn't told him she was going out on a date with Gary. If she had, he'd have told her a few of the things Gary said behind her back.

As Todd finished typing the entry, Gary appeared beside him.

"I thought you'd like to know Shannon's falling for it. One day soon, I'll have her."

Todd spun around to face Gary. "I don't think so. Shannon's not that way." He opened his mouth, wanting dearly to snap at Gary that Shannon had high moral standards, something Gary didn't, but self-preservation stopped him. He was still in his initial probation period, Gary was his boss, and Todd desperately needed the job. He scrambled to reword his statement, without pointing fingers. "You do know Shannon goes to church every Sunday?"

Gary's eyebrows rose; then he made a sly smirk. "You never know, but maybe one day I'll be going to church, too."

Gary spun on his toes, laughed heartily, walked into his office, and closed the door.

Todd's mind raced. From what he'd seen so far, Gary would never set foot in a church. But he'd also seen that Gary was wily. He didn't know what was so funny, but he had a feeling he had to find out. While he would have liked to see Gary open his heart to spiritual things, he wouldn't put it past him to attend church solely to impress Shannon. Gary had already used his position and authority to threaten him, without saying so directly. Todd feared he would also try to pressure Shannon in the same way, and he didn't want to see that happen. Gary's decisions carried a lot of weight. He worried Shannon might weaken if Gary turned on the charm; but he also feared what might happen if Shannon didn't do what the man wanted and he didn't take it well.

What made the situation worse was that Gary wouldn't have tried to get Shannon now if it hadn't been for his seeing Todd's Secret Admirer note. The whole thing was his fault.

Somehow, Todd had to find out what Gary was planning and warn Shannon.

He hoped she would listen and take him seriously. He'd told her so often why all her dates and boyfriends were wrong; he wasn't sure she would listen to him anymore.

Until he could find out a way to get Gary to confide in him so he could tell Shannon, he could only advise her to be careful. Then, on Sunday, he could take her out for lunch after church, and finally, they could have their first date. Maybe, if the time was right, he could tell her how he felt, and he wouldn't have to worry about Gary anymore.

Todd smiled. He could hardly wait until Sunday.

Chapter 10

H
ey, Shan. It's me. Todd. Let me in."

The buzzer sounded. Todd hurried to catch the elevator and was soon standing in front of Shannon's apartment door.

The door opened. Shannon stood in front of him wearing jeans and a T-shirt. A towel was wrapped around her hair. He smiled as he inhaled the heady aroma of her apple-scented shampoo, stronger than ever because her hair was still wet. As if he didn't think enough of Shannon, now every time he smelled apples, he'd think of her even more.

"I was getting ready to go out. What are you doing here?"

His smile disappeared. "Where are you going?"

Her brow creased. "It's Thursday night. I'm going to Bible study."

"Oh. Sorry."

"Do you go at your church? I know there are several groups to choose from."

"Yes. But I go Wednesday. Craig and I went last night." He had come because he didn't want to wait for Sunday and had wrongly assumed she also attended her home group on Wednesday night.

"Since you're here, do you want to come with me?"

Todd followed her as she returned to her room and started blow-drying her hair. "Sure. I'd like that. If I'm invited."

"Anyone is invited."

He didn't want to contemplate the impersonal nature of her invitation. He only wanted to talk to her in private.

But since he couldn't talk while she dried her hair, Todd sauntered into the living room and sat down on the couch. Accompanying her tonight wasn't what he had planned, but it wasn't a bad thing. He would still be alone with her for part of the evening, and in that time, they could still talk. A few days ago, when they'd taken a late lunch break and were alone together, he'd had a very enjoyable time, and unless he was mistaken she had, too.

He could see the start of a beautiful relationship, and he wanted to start it today.

Shannon emerged from her room, her hair fluffy and bouncing with the natural wave he liked so much. "We have to leave in ten minutes. I hope you had something to eat before you got here."

"Yes, I did. You don't have to worry about feeding me. I just thought—"

The buzzer for the door cut off his words.

Shannon picked up the telephone. "Come on up," she said as she pushed the button.

"Who's that?"

"It's Craig. I have to talk to him about something, and he said he'd come with me. Now you're coming, too. This is going to be a regular party, isn't it?"

He tried to smile. "Yeah. A party."

Until they started working together, every time he'd been out with Shannon, it was because she'd tagged along with Craig. While he hadn't minded being a threesome before, today he wasn't in the mood to share her with her brother.

Shannon opened the door to let Craig in. Immediately, Craig turned to Todd.

"I thought I recognized your car in the visitor parking. Long time no see, huh?"

"Yeah," Todd muttered. "Since about this time yesterday."

"Look at this—the three of us together. Just like old times."

Todd didn't comment. He didn't want old times. He wanted to make new times. Without Shannon's brother hanging over his head, watching him, protecting his little sister.

"Do you remember the last time the three of us were together?"

"Yeah. We were at church."

Craig shook his head. "That's different. I was thinking about that time just before Shan moved out. We were at the mall."

As best he could recall, the last time they were together in public they had been shopping and bumped into Shannon and her friends. It was so long ago he couldn't remember anything about the day, except that it had been good for their male egos to spend the afternoon with Shannon and five or six of her friends.

Shannon's eyes narrowed as she turned to stare at Todd. "I remember that. We all went into the coffee shop together for lunch."

Todd tried to remember why that detail would have been important.

Her eyes narrowed even more. "You went into the aisle, got down on one knee with a drink in your hand, and started singing Happy Birthday at the top of your lungs. That would have been bad enough, but it wasn't my birthday, and you knew it."

Suddenly, it all came back. Shannon had wanted a piece of chocolate cake, and she hadn't had enough money in her wallet to cover both lunch and dessert.

He pasted on a grin that he hoped wasn't as phony as it felt. "I was just trying to get you a free piece of cake."

"I can't remember the last time I'd been so embarrassed. But of course, the last time would also have had something to do with you."

All thoughts of how much progress he'd made in obtaining a wee bit of forgiveness evaporated.

Craig laughed out loud. "That was so funny! You should have seen your face!"

Todd smiled sheepishly. Back then, her face hadn't looked too cheery, nor did it now. In fact, Todd was glad they were going to a Bible study, where he hoped it would be stressed that God desired people to forgive those who hurt them.

Todd cleared his throat. "I think it's time to leave. Whose car are we taking?"

"Yours. I'm almost out of gas."

During their ride down the elevator, Todd wished Craig would run out of gas. Craig, in his wisdom, brought up another "amusing" trip down memory lane. Then he detoured on yet another memory in the car. Before Craig retold a fourth instance which involved Todd's humiliating poor Shannon, Todd managed to change the subject. However, he feared his efforts were too little, too late.

Throughout the lesson, Todd sat beside Shannon because he was the only one present who had not brought a Bible. He remained cautious in his comments and questions and tried to honor Shannon in his behavior.

When they returned to her apartment, Craig sat down on the couch, ready to talk about whatever it was Shannon had called him for in the first place. Todd took that as his cue to leave.

She walked Todd to the door.

"Before I go, I wanted to talk to you about something."

She glanced back at the opening to the living room, then back at him. "Go ahead, but remember Craig is waiting for me. I have to talk to him, and we all have to get up early for work tomorrow."

He stepped closer and picked up her hands, holding them gently while he spoke. "I just want you to be careful about Gary. Make sure you pray about it before you do anything. I really don't think he's your Secret Admirer. Be careful with him."

Her voice skipped. "Of course..."

"I'll see you tomorrow, and I can hardly wait until Sunday when I go to your church with you."

Before she could tell him she changed her mind, Todd turned and left.

✿

"Hi, Shannon."

Shannon laid her pencil down and folded her hands on the desk in front of her. "Hi, Gary. Is there something I can do for you?"

Gary crossed his arms, leaned on the edge of her desk, and grinned. "Yes. You can join me for dinner tonight."

Shannon studied Gary. Within the company, he was above her on the corporate ladder, second in command at their branch. While he didn't have any direct authority over her, she knew he was in a position of influence with the company. On the personal side, she knew Gary was young to be in his position, which was a good testimony to his management skills. While she didn't know his exact age, she guessed he was eight years older than she was.

Being a non-Christian, that also meant he had much more worldly experience than she did, both in the dating arena and in dealing with people in general. Gary's reputation preceded him, and his reputation told her this was a situation she didn't want to get involved with. Shannon tended to keep to herself and stayed within her church circles. She wasn't unhappy doing that. Instead, she felt safe and comfortable in her protected circle of friends and Christian family.

Secret Admirer or not, she made her decision.

"I don't know if going out for dinner with you is a good idea. We have to work together, regardless of what happens, if you know what I mean."

He leaned closer. "I know that, but I've been doing a lot of thinking lately. I know you go to church faithfully, and I was wondering if I could go with you on Sunday. But first I have a few questions."

Shannon's eyes widened. "You do?"

Gary nodded. "Yes. I thought you'd be the best person to ask."

Shannon often prayed she could be a good witness at her workplace, to be able to live in a way that people wouldn't write her off as a religious fanatic, yet still live her life to God's glory. She thanked God she could see the fruit of her efforts when someone like Gary could be interested in learning more about Jesus Christ as his Savior.

"I'd be happy to answer any questions you have, although here in the middle of the office isn't the best place."

"I know. That's why I thought we could go out for dinner."

Shannon checked the page on her calendar to be sure. "I actually have plans for tonight. Saturday, too. But I can still pick you up on Sunday morning."

Gary's smile dropped. "I don't know...."

Shannon smiled. "Don't be shy. There's nothing to be afraid of. Give me your address, and I'll pick you up about a quarter to ten."

"I would prefer to pick you up."

Shannon forced herself to keep smiling. She thought it would be a good idea for her to be the one providing transportation, because if she were transporting him, it would be harder for Gary to change his mind at the last minute. But for now, she had to take any opportunity she could find to get Gary to church.

She scribbled her address on a piece of paper and slid it across the desk. "Okay. You can pick me up at a quarter to ten."

Gary grinned, winked, and tucked the note into his pocket. "See you then," he said as he returned to his office.

Shannon glanced to the dispatch area where Todd was. While it was good to bring a newcomer to church, this did present a complication. She had already arranged to pick up Todd for church on Sunday; but now she wouldn't have her car, and she'd also be with Gary. She thought Todd, a fairly new Christian, would understand. In fact, Shannon was certain Todd could relate to where Gary was now, since it wasn't that long ago Todd was searching for answers and found them.

She returned to her work. Tonight she planned to have dinner with Craig and some friends from her old church. She figured she'd see Todd there also, so she could talk to him tonight. She was sure Todd would be as happy as she was to know Gary would be at church on Sunday.

❀

"Pardon me? Did I hear you right?"

Shannon leaned closer to Todd so the rest of the people at the table wouldn't hear. "Yes, you heard me right. Isn't that exciting? He even said he has questions."

She backed up to gauge Todd's reaction, but instead of the smile she'd expected when she told him Gary would be coming to church with her, Todd's face turned to stone.

"I'll believe that when I see it."

All the joy seeped out of her. "I can't believe you aren't excited. The only thing is that he wants to take his own car, so I can't pick you up as we agreed. I hope that's okay."

Todd blinked, laid his fork down, and stared at her. "I can't believe you've suddenly turned gullible. He doesn't want to learn about God. He wants to learn about you."

"You don't know that."

Todd's eyes narrowed. "Yes, I do."

"Don't you think it's possible for him to listen if God is poking him and telling him to check out his options? Even murderers and people in jail can have a change of heart."

"I suppose."

"Then it's possible for Gary to want to discover God, too, don't you think?"

Shannon waited for Todd to say something. She didn't think she'd asked him a hard question. She'd prayed for Todd fairly often after overhearing about his mother, but she'd also prayed for him over the years because God told everyone to pray for their enemies. She wouldn't have thought it possible for him to open his hardened heart and become the man he was today, unless she'd witnessed the change herself. If it was possible for Todd, then it could happen with Gary.

Other people in their group chatted gaily, and the quiet murmur of voices echoed through the restaurant. But between her and Todd, the silence was so thick it shouted. When Todd was silent too long, Shannon crossed her arms and glared at him.

His voice dropped to a disgruntled whisper. "I guess," he muttered, barely loud enough for her to make out his words.

Before she could rebuke him for his bad attitude, Craig leaned forward from across the table. "What's going on?" He turned to Todd. "If you're doing something to upset my little sister, I'll have to take you outside."

Both of them stared at Craig.

"I'm not your little sister anymore, Craig."

He smiled. "Until we're both old and gray, you'll always be my little sister. All I know is that you two seem to be spending a lot of time together lately, and I don't mean just at work. If he's causing you trouble, I can take him outside and beat him up for you."

Shannon continued to stare at her brother. When she talked to Craig about her job and the possibility of his meeting Faye, Todd had come up in the conversation. She'd let it slip that she'd bumped into him at the bookstore, then again, mentioned being together when all her workmates went out for dinner. Plus Craig had seen Todd at her apartment yesterday.

Of course she didn't tell him about the time she hit the dog with her car and Todd kissed her. She knew Craig was only kidding about beating up Todd. However, she had a feeling that if she told Craig he'd kissed her, it would come to blows between them, friends or not.

She narrowed her eyes, trying to look stern when really her insides were trembling. "I think I can handle Todd by myself."

"Are you sure?" He glanced back and forth between her and Todd, who remained silent. "It's just that in the past getting you two together in the same room was, well, not altogether pleasant." He leaned back in the chair and grinned. "Did Mom and Dad tell you? I'm thinking of trading in my car and getting a new one. Brand new."

Shannon sat back and listened to Craig prattle on about the car he was looking at, along with a lengthy list of all its features. She noticed Todd still didn't say anything.

He truly was a mystery. Shannon had seen only his comic side, and most of that from the receiving end. Lately, she'd seen so much else. When she'd asked him about his mother, it was as if a brick wall had gone up around him. Now he sat in brooding silence. If she didn't know better, she would have thought he was angry that she was planning to spend time with Gary. But that was ridiculous. For Todd to be angry would indicate he was jealous, and that idea was so far fetched it didn't deserve any further consideration.

After everyone was finished and the group had broken up, she found herself leaving at the same time as still-brooding Todd. To her surprise, he followed her to her car and stood beside her while she fished her keys out of her purse.

Finally, Todd broke the strained silence. "I don't know why you won't listen to me. Gary isn't the least bit interested in learning about God. He's using this as a way to earn points. He's just picking something he feels is close to your heart and taking advantage of it. I hope you don't trust him, because if I were a woman, I sure wouldn't. He doesn't want to change. He just wants to have a little fun with you and nothing more."

Shannon's hand froze with the key inserted in the lock. She turned to face Todd. "Don't you think you're being rather harsh? And *very* judgmental."

"I'm being realistic."

"You haven't worked with him as long as I have, and you've been with him outside of work only once. How can you make that kind of accusation?"

"Stuff I've heard."

She crossed her arms. She knew Gary's reputation with the ladies, but that wasn't the issue. They had mentioned that regardless of what happened between them they would have to work together every day. She didn't agree to date Gary. In fact, she'd told him the opposite. She'd told him she was busy, but she still was happy to take him to church and answer any questions he had. "I wish you wouldn't be so quick to think the worst of Gary. I know he has his faults, but he's dedicated and intelligent. You should give him some credit."

"Credit for what? His good looks? The good job? Money? His fancy car?"

Shannon turned around and yanked the door open. "That's enough. I don't have to listen to you and your bad attitude."

"The only reason he's talking about going to church is that you have a reputation for not going out with anyone, even once, who doesn't go to church. That's it."

She slid inside the car. "I don't believe you."

She tried to close the door, but Todd grabbed it, preventing her from moving it. "It's the truth. I don't want him to take advantage of you. He's only looking for a good time."

Her blood boiled. "I know what I'm doing, Todd," she said harshly. She sucked in a deep breath and pulled the door, forcing him to release it or catch his fingers as it slammed. She turned the key in the ignition, rolled down the window, and leaned her head out for one last parting comment as she drove away.

"Besides, for your information, he just might be my Secret Admirer."

Chapter 11

Todd stood in front of the mirror and straightened his tie. His hand froze on the knot as he gave it a final tug. He closed his eyes.

He'd had a fight with Shannon. That was Friday night. He hadn't spoken to her since.

He'd let the sun go down on his anger. He'd also let Saturday's sun, a second night, go down on his anger.

He didn't know if he'd ever been so angry or so disappointed in himself.

Shannon hadn't listened to a thing he said; yet he'd been speaking the truth. Still, he had no right to be so angry. He'd had all night Friday, all of Saturday, and the early part of Sunday morning to think, giving him plenty of opportunity to sort things out.

Of course, Shannon would give Gary the benefit of the doubt if he said he was interested in learning about God. Her gentle and forgiving spirit was a big part of what made Shannon who she was. She was starting to open up at least to be friends. She'd put aside all the bad things he'd done to her and forgiven him. If she did that for Todd, she would do the same for Gary, who had never personally done anything to hurt or embarrass her, as Todd had.

In many ways, Gary deserved more of a chance than Todd did. And she was giving Gary the chance, too.

Todd was jealous, and he knew it. And that was another thing that hurt.

He knew what the man was like. Shannon had worked with Gary for longer than he had. Years. She knew Gary far better than he did, which made it even worse that she would consider spending personal time with him. The thought of her hanging around with him and liking him was too much for Todd to bear.

What if she liked Gary more than she liked him. . . .

Todd opened his eyes and studied his reflection in the mirror. He'd just showered and shaved, and he'd gelled his hair meticulously into place. He'd bought some new toothpaste; his teeth hadn't been so white since his last trip to the dentist. His shirt and pants were clean and pressed. His tie was a perfect match, the most expensive one he owned, and it didn't even have a sound chip or flashing lights. He didn't get any better than this.

But this time, he needed more. If he wanted to look better than Gary, there was no competition. Gary was taller than he was and had one of those handsome faces that turned women's heads. He was in better physical condition because he worked out at the gym three times a week, since he had the money for it. If Todd were honest with himself, Gary was probably smarter than he was, too. When Todd became uncomfortable, he made jokes and displayed ridiculous behavior—anything to get a laugh to ease a difficult moment. Gary, on the other hand, oozed confidence and poise in everything he said and did.

On the surface, Gary had everything going for him. But beneath the trendy clothes and perfect hair and movie-star-handsome face, Gary was pond scum. And Shannon was right. Todd knew he was being judgmental, but that didn't make him wrong. While everyone knew beauty was only skin deep, Shannon had to get past Gary's skin layer to see the real man. In doing so, he hoped Gary didn't do something to hurt her, either physically or emotionally.

After Gary's comment the other day, Todd should have figured out he would try to motivate Shannon to see him outside of work. Shannon was right; he was intelligent. The only reason she would see him would be to minister to him, so that was what Gary zeroed in on.

Despite what Todd thought was the reality of the situation, there was still a one-tenth-of-one-percent chance Gary might be sincere in his quest to know God. If that were so, then Todd was being worse than judgmental. He was being unfair. God had touched him when he had no thoughts of Him. Craig had tried to show him God's love ever since they'd been in their teens and often told Todd he'd been praying for him. Every time, Todd had scoffed and told him not to bother. Looking back, he had a feeling Shannon might have been praying for him, too.

If the two of them had been praying for him for ten years before he allowed God to touch him, then it happened, the same could happen with Gary. Todd was a sinner, just as Gary, and God loved Gary, too.

Todd looked around. He figured Shannon would be ten minutes early for the church service, as she was at work, regardless of whether she was driving or if Gary was picking her up.

Todd said a short prayer for wisdom and made his way to Shannon's church, not caring if she wanted him there or not.

He recognized Gary's car in the parking lot and parked nearby.

Once inside the building, he found them easily. Of course, Gary was dressed perfectly, in clothes Todd could never afford. Shannon wore a pretty skirt and blouse, with shoes the same color as the skirt. Over her top, she wore a sweater Todd knew her mother had knitted for her. Todd smiled. She wasn't fancy. She was just Shannon.

He wiggled the knot on his tie and approached them.

"Hey, Shannon, Gary. Good morning."

Shannon spun around in the blink of an eye. Gary turned more slowly.

"Todd!" Shannon gasped. "What are you doing here?"

He raised his hand and pressed his Bible to his chest. "It's Sunday. I came to church—which is where I go every Sunday morning. Your invitation to join you this morning still stands, doesn't it?"

Her face turned ten shades of red. "Of course," she muttered. "I just didn't expect you to come by yourself."

Todd smiled at her. "I'm not alone. I'm with friends now." He turned to Gary. "It's good to see you here in God's house." He forced himself to keep smiling, trying to tell himself he really meant his words. "Shall we find a seat?"

The three of them walked toward the sanctuary together. When they came to the entranceway, Gary stepped in front of Todd, forcing him to enter behind Gary. Before he could catch up to Shannon, Gary guided her into the nearest pew. He slipped in beside her, leaving enough room for Todd at the end.

Todd narrowed his eyes. He didn't want to sit beside Gary; he wanted to sit beside Shannon, and Gary knew it.

Once again, he forced himself to smile and stepped toward Gary. "Excuse me," he said. Not giving Gary a choice, he stepped in front of him, forcing him to tuck his legs to the side so Todd could get by. He then stepped gently past Shannon, as she also tucked her legs to the side, then sat beside her. Once seated, he turned to address them both at the same time. "I like to leave the aisle seat open. For elderly ladies."

Shannon smiled tenderly and rested her fingers on his forearm. "Oh, Todd, that's so sweet." She sighed.

Gary's ever-present friendly expression faltered for just a second. "That's a good idea. I'll have to remember that for next time."

Todd hoped there wouldn't be a next time, then mentally kicked himself, in case this was the one-tenth-of-one-percent chance that Gary was here for good and honest reasons that had to do with God and not specifically with Shannon.

When the service started, Todd noted the routine was similar to his own church's but not identical. Shannon's church was much smaller and geared more to a younger congregation than his own, which was the only church he'd ever attended. With the difference in mind, he was relieved to know all the songs except one. Even though singing wasn't one of his greatest strengths, he worshipped from his heart, trying not to notice Gary caught on quickly to the songs and sang better than he did.

Shannon's pastor preached a good message with a little more fire and brimstone than he was used to, about the parable of the man sowing his seed. Once Todd became accustomed to the pastor's animated speech and the shout of the occasional "Amen" from various members of the congregation, the enthusiasm of the pastor and the congregation became infectious. Todd almost called out an "Amen" to a point that hit home with him but held himself back because he didn't want to startle Shannon. Sitting between him and Gary, she didn't appear completely comfortable, and he couldn't blame her. He didn't want to make it worse for her.

Throughout the entire service, in between being enthralled with the pastor's words and writing notes on the back of the bulletin, Todd snuck a few sideways glances over Shannon at Gary. In a way, Todd hoped the pastor would have been more calm and sedate, allowing Gary to fall asleep. Instead he'd caught Gary sneaking sideways glances at him, probably hoping the same thing.

At the close of the service, Todd forced all thoughts of Gary out of his head and followed in his heart with the pastor's prayer and benediction. When most of the congregation called out an "Amen," he did, too, which caused Shannon to jump and Gary to stare at him, but he didn't care. The service had been great, with the possible exception of Gary being there.

As they filed toward the sanctuary's exit, he tried to push away the guilt he felt about being annoyed by Gary's presence. If the man truly was searching, the sermon had been great for him. If not, it wasn't Todd's place to judge, as Shannon had reminded him.

Todd gritted his teeth as Gary deliberately stepped in front of him at the doorway between the sanctuary and the foyer, nearly landing on his foot. He decided his guilt was again misplaced. From the way Gary kept trying to put distance between Todd and Shannon and the fact he was becoming more aggressive about it, the one-tenth-of-one-percent chance Gary was there for legitimate reasons was becoming exponentially smaller.

Back in the foyer, Shannon introduced both Todd and Gary to other members of the congregation. After a bit of small talk and people welcoming them to the church, Gary suggested he and Shannon go for lunch.

Todd chose to ignore that Gary's invitation had been worded not to include him. He grinned enthusiastically so Gary would look like a schmuck in front of Shannon if he said anything about Todd's not being invited. "That sounds great." He turned to Shannon. "I think you were saying that most of your congregation goes to that pancake place across from the skating rink. But I also remember your saying parking was pretty tight. Maybe I should go with you guys, then you can just drop me off back here when we're finished so I can pick up my car."

Gary's eyes narrowed. In response, Todd widened his smile.

Shannon tapped one finger to her chin. "You know, that's a pretty good idea. Some people park their cars in the rink's lot; but there are signs warning people that if they're not there to skate, they could get towed."

Todd nodded. "I think I've had enough problems with my car lately. I'll leave it here. Let's go."

Gary didn't say much as they walked out to the parking lot. Once at the car, Todd slid into the back, which he didn't mind. He knew Gary wasn't going to make any efforts to include him in the conversation, but this way he could keep an eye on what was happening in the front, with Gary very aware he was being watched.

While they waited for a table, Todd could tell Gary was pushing himself to make polite conversation with him there. After they were seated and their orders taken, Todd decided it was time to show Shannon the level of Gary's sincerity about learning about God.

He tried to ignore that Gary was sitting beside Shannon in the booth and he wasn't. But this way gave him a better opportunity to watch what Gary was doing. Todd could see him eye-to-eye instead of peeking up from between the bucket seats as he had in the car.

With his elbows on the table, Todd cradled his coffee cup in both hands and made deliberate eye contact with Gary over the top of the steaming coffee.

"Shannon tells me this is the first time you've been to church. What did you think of the service?"

"It was interesting," Gary replied, smiling politely.

Todd nodded. "Yes. He really made me think. I thought it was an interesting question, asking what kind of ground we were, as an individual."

"Yes. He allowed for a lot of introspection."

Todd stared right into Gary's eyes. "Do you remember the four types of ground?"

"Not really. Although I saw you writing notes, so you have more likelihood of remembering."

"That may be true, but that's not what I was writing down. The four different types of ground are"—Todd set the cup back into the saucer and counted off on his fingers as he spoke—"on the path, in the rocks, among the thorns, and on good soil."

Gary's expression glazed over for a few seconds, indicating to Todd that Gary hadn't been paying attention and didn't want to be paying attention now. "Yes, that's right," he said.

The more Todd thought about it, and watching Gary's face now, Todd suddenly understood why Gary hadn't paid attention. According to the parable, the ground accepted the seed initially, and all but one type fell away for various reasons. Gary's situation didn't apply to this because he had no desire to sample the seed in the first place. He only wanted to sample Shannon.

Todd picked up his cup again, suddenly needing something to do with his hands, rather than reaching across the table and wringing Gary's neck.

He smiled nicely, hoping his face wouldn't crack. He opened his mouth, about to comment on the possibility of giving Gary a Bible, when Shannon clinked her cup down into her saucer.

"I think that's enough talk about the sermon. This isn't a question-and-answer period." She glared at him from across the table. "Todd," she said firmly. She turned her head slightly toward Gary. "Did you see the construction at the mall on the way here? It looks as if they're expanding the building. I wonder where everyone is going to park."

They spent the remainder of lunch making small talk about nothing in particular. Gary insisted on paying for all three lunches, which griped Todd but looked good to Shannon.

To Todd's surprise, Gary dropped off Shannon first, instead of returning to the church parking lot so Todd could get his car. Because Todd didn't want it to look as if he was following them, which he was, he stayed in the car while Gary walked Shannon to the door. Part of him was glad he was taking Shannon home first. This way, good manners dictated that Shannon not invite Gary in and that Gary didn't take too long saying good-bye, since Todd was waiting in the car.

But this also meant he would be alone with Gary traveling from Shannon's apartment to the church parking lot.

The thought made Todd break out into a cold sweat.

He looked at the empty front seats, thinking he should have the grace to move from the backseat into the front. But the last thing he wanted to do was sit beside Gary because that meant he would have to talk to him.

By the time Gary returned, Todd was settled in the front seat, buckled in, ready to go, and praying they caught every light green.

The second Gary started the engine, Todd leaned forward and turned the radio up, not caring what kind of station it was or what was playing.

Even though the music was loud, the lack of conversation hung in the air between them like a cold, looming black cloud. When they were a block from the church, Gary reached forward and turned the radio down. The lightness of Gary's tone was completely negated by his words. "You know, Sanders—I don't know if you think you're trying to be funny, but you might notice I'm not laughing."

Steeling his courage, Todd turned to Gary. "You know, for once, I wasn't trying to be funny."

Gary kept his face forward, not looking at Todd as he spoke, which only seemed to accent his words. "I think it would be in your best interests if you kept out of this and started minding your own business. What I do with Shannon is none of your concern. I like the way you do your job, and I enjoy working with you, but I would hate to suddenly start finding too many mistakes while you're still on probation."

Todd's head spun. He had expected Gary to confront him, but he hadn't expected this.

Before he could put two thoughts together to respond, the car stopped in the parking lot beside his car, the only one in the entire lot.

Gary still didn't turn his head but kept his face forward, watching ahead of him through the windshield. "I'll see you tomorrow at work, Sanders. Good day."

Todd exited Gary's car quickly.

He stabbed the key into the lock, slid in, and slammed the door. Instead of starting the car, he whacked the steering wheel with his fist and muttered under his breath.

He was only trying to protect Shannon—from Gary and from herself. He hadn't considered that his actions could mean losing his job. He needed the job. If he lost it, he wouldn't be the only one to suffer, and he couldn't let that happen.

And if Gary would stoop so low as to threaten Todd, then he wondered if the man would use his power and authority at work on Shannon. While Gary wasn't her supervisor, as he was Todd's, he was still second in command over the branch. As such, he had some degree of authority over every department, even if only by influencing the one person higher than Gary in the corporate ladder.

Todd clenched his teeth as he started the car. Shannon didn't know who she was getting herself involved with. He doubted she had the slightest idea of what the man who said he wanted to learn about God really wanted. Or what he was willing to do to get it.

But Todd intended to tell her.

It took every ounce of Todd's self-control to drive within the posted speed limit to Shannon's apartment.

The time it took for him to park the car, walk to the main door, press the button, and wait for her to respond gave Todd time to calm down and think more clearly.

He was angry with Gary, but he couldn't be angry with Shannon. She was only doing what she thought was best. He couldn't belie her efforts in what she saw as the right and noble thing, even though she was wrong.

Shannon's voice crackled through the intercom. "Hello?"

He cleared his throat and tried to sound cheerful. "Hi, Shan. It's me. Todd. Want to do dinner?"

"Todd?" For a few seconds, he heard static sparking through the metal grating. "Uh—it's kind of early for dinner; we just had lunch. But come up. I guess."

When the elevator door swooshed open on Shannon's floor, he found her waiting in the hallway outside her door. She stood with her arms crossed, and she wasn't smiling. "What are you really doing here? Even you can't be thinking about eating again."

"I wanted to talk to you about something." He glanced both ways down the hall. He was prone to public displays and appreciated when he had an audience that was amused by his antics, but that was when nothing important was at stake. This time he wanted everything he said kept between him and Shannon and not her neighbors. "Can we go inside?"

Shannon stepped back and extended one arm but said nothing.

The second the door closed, Todd could no longer hold back. "I don't think you have any idea what you're dealing with. I came here to tell you to be very careful with Gary. You're in way over your head."

Her eyes narrowed. "I thought I knew what he was like, but I'm wondering if I've been wrong. On the way to church, he talked to me about how he has to put on a tough, hard-edged facade in front of the men at work to earn and keep their respect. He says part of that includes acting like a ladies' man."

Todd crossed his arms. "He's only telling you what you want to hear."

Her voice lowered. "I'm not stupid, Todd. I've seen him in action at work. I'm only saying we talked, and I think I have to make some allowances for him. I at least have to think about it."

"You don't need to think about it. I wanted to give him the benefit of the doubt, too. He said something in the car, though, that made me realize not only have I been right, but he's even worse. And you can forget any romantic notions he has for you. He's only trying to mislead you. He has nothing good or noble in mind for you. You shouldn't be seeing him outside work. And that includes church. You think you're safe on Sunday morning, but you're not. Not with him."

"What did he tell you in the car?"

"I'd rather not say now."

Shannon tipped her head and studied him, not saying anything while the seconds dragged on like hours. "Why are you doing this? What do you have against Gary?"

"I have nothing against him."

Her posture stiffened even more. "It sure sounds like it to me. And besides his interest in learning more about God and Jesus Christ, he said he wanted to be sure I liked chocolate kisses. It looks as if he might be my Secret Admirer after all. He's hinting, trying to build the suspense. He's waiting for the right moment to tell me."

Todd's restraint exploded in a puff of smoke. He waved one hand in the air, barely able to keep from yelling. "Can't you see he's lying to you? He's just using that because he knows it's a soft spot with you. Just like going to church is a soft spot with you."

"How dare you!"

He stepped closer and lowered his voice. "Shannon, I'm not saying these things to make you angry. I'm only saying this out of concern because I, uh"—he swallowed hard and cleared his throat—"I like you a lot. I don't want to see you get hurt, and I think your spending time with Gary is a bad idea. I only want to help you."

"I have to finish what I started, with or without you. Surely you agree that Gary needs someone to walk through this with him. Maybe next week you should go to your own church."

Todd's heart sank. "What?"

She checked her watch. "And I can't go out to dinner with you. I had already made plans to go out with a friend for dinner. In fact, I think you should leave now."

Todd felt as if he'd been smacked in the chest with a two-by-four. He wanted so much to reveal his proof that Gary was lying to her, but he couldn't tell her he was her Secret Admirer now. He'd had dreams of the right moment—in a romantic atmosphere, wrapped in each other's arms, soft music playing in the background. Maybe even feeding her chocolate kisses by hand or sharing chocolate kisses between real ones. Not only was there nothing romantic about this moment, but she was throwing him out of her home. She was so angry with him that he had a feeling she'd never believe him.

"Fine," he muttered, trying to take her rejection like a man. "I guess I'll see you at work tomorrow." He turned on his heel and stomped to the door.

As he stepped into the hallway, he felt Shannon's fingers touch his arm, stopping him in his tracks.

"Todd, wait. I want you to understand why I'm doing this. I have to give him a chance. God gives us all a chance, regardless of whether we deserve it or not. I have to do the same."

Todd's head spun. His thoughts and emotions had ricocheted in his head and heart in so many directions and on so many levels that he didn't know what to think anymore. He felt himself going into autopilot mode with his reaction.

He turned around. "So in other words you're telling me don't go away mad; just go away."

She smiled. He felt himself melting into a puddle on the floor.

"Yes, something like that. Good-bye, Todd."

The door closed.

Todd's brain was so numb he didn't remember the drive home, only that he was there.

He sat at the kitchen table and did the same thing he did every day when he couldn't get Shannon out of his mind. He tore a piece of paper out of the pad, opened the rhyming dictionary, and began to compose his newest poem.

Dearest Shannon,
Your merciful spirit soothes my tortured soul

Todd grimaced and crumpled up the paper. He didn't want to acknowledge her anger or her forgiveness or that he was feeling rotten from arguing with her. Shannon was intelligent and perceptive. If he mentioned anything even remotely related to what had just happened, she might figure out why her Secret Admirer would say such things, then know who he was. He couldn't afford for that to happen. Not now. Not until everything was perfect between them.

He tore off a sheet of fresh paper and tried again.

Dearest Shannon,
Your shining smile fills me with happiness

Todd flipped through the book and harrumphed when he discovered there was no exact rhyme for happiness. He wadded up the paper and closed his eyes to picture Shannon in his mind before he started again.

Dearest Shannon,
Like the sweet, clean scent of a tangy apple

Todd buried his face in his hands. That apple shampoo was affecting him more than he thought. This time he ripped the paper into multiple pieces and pushed them to the center of the table.

Dearest Shannon,
Like the sparkling spring sunshine in the month of May,
Like the sweet, clean scent of a fresh bouquet,
Like the beauty and fullness of a rose when it's blooming,
My love for you is all consuming.

Your Secret Admirer

Todd smiled. This was one of his best. In fact, it was so good he thought when the day came to reveal himself to Shannon, he would share a case of chocolate kisses and go to the florist and pick out a nice red rose. Or maybe one of those two-toned ones, because he knew she liked them.

As Todd tied the ribbon and attached the kiss, his thoughts drifted back to the situation with Gary. Of course, Shannon was right. God had given Todd more chances than he could count, when he was nowhere near looking for God's heart. He had to step back and let Shannon handle Gary in whatever way she thought best. Even though it hurt, Todd knew he would have to pray for Gary, even if it took ten years or more, just as Craig and Shannon had prayed for him.

The events of the day also proved to him he never wanted to fight with Shannon over Gary again. He didn't want to fight with her about anything. It was too painful. He'd put her through enough over the years without adding more tension. When he thought of what could have happened by fighting over Gary, he felt sick. He didn't want to lose her over something that needed to be in the Lord's hands.

Todd shut his eyes. His heart pounded. During the time Shannon spent with Gary, he couldn't help but worry that she might like Gary better than she liked him. Regardless of what Todd knew or heard, he had to leave that in the Lord's hands, too. The battle of love wasn't always won by the person who was the most deserving. Not that he deserved Shannon. He was trying his best to make things right from the past, though. He could only hope and pray it was enough.

He opened his eyes and stared blankly at the wall. If Shannon did choose Gary over him and Todd came out the loser, then it would be inappropriate for him, as the Secret Admirer, to keep telling her how much he loved her, because her heart would belong to another.

But that didn't mean he wouldn't keep an eye on her, just to be sure she was safe and happy.

Chapter 12

Hey, Shan. Are you going out for lunch with Gary again today?"

Shannon cringed at Nanci's question. In the last couple of weeks, she'd gone out with Gary almost every other day. She hadn't realized it had become a topic of conversation among the other staff, although she hadn't been trying to keep it a secret. Before she could tell Nanci she wasn't going out today, Faye piped up.

"No, she went out with Gary for lunch yesterday. She'll be staying here today because it's Todd's turn."

Nanci drew in her breath sharply. "Wow. I wish I had your love life."

Shannon steeled her nerve and turned toward Nanci. "It's not like that at all. Todd and I are just friends. The same with Gary."

She could tell from Nanci's expression and the expressions of those around who were listening that no one believed her.

"It's true," she muttered, as she resumed her work.

Unfortunately, her words were truer than she wanted them to be. She didn't have a love life. Gary was a ministry. Nothing more, nothing less. She wanted to keep things as they were now, which was the occasional lunch on a weekday and church on Sunday.

Shannon's hands paused over the keyboard.

Church on Sunday.

Without Todd.

She couldn't believe how much she missed him. Not that she really saw him any less— she saw him every day at work, plus she saw him for various reasons several times a week after working hours and on weekends. But she missed not being with him during the Sunday worship services. She'd been with him two Sunday mornings, first at her old church, then at her new one; yet now she felt the loss when the seat on the other side of her was empty, which had been the last two Sundays.

Shannon sighed. She deeply regretted telling him not to come with her. After two weeks of being with him during the service, and now two weeks of not having him there, she had to admit she missed him. She wanted to take back her words but didn't know how.

Shannon glanced at the doorway leading to the dispatch office, where Todd was hard at work. He was still the same old Todd she'd always known, but at the same time, he was completely different. It didn't make sense, but it was true.

The day of their big argument about Gary, Todd had let it slip that he liked her. She could tell from his face he hadn't meant to say it out loud, which only emphasized he meant it.

She couldn't help herself. After all this time, she liked him, too. She didn't know when it happened, or why, but she found herself thinking about him often. If the man in question hadn't been Todd Sanders, she would have wondered if this was what it was like to fall in love.

Shannon closed her eyes. The pressures of her job were becoming too much for her. Surely, she was going insane.

She glanced to the side, at Faye, hard at work.

The meeting she'd set up between Faye and Craig had gone well. Craig, being Craig, had convinced Faye to attend a church service again. In fact, she'd heard about her first visit back to church in over three years from Todd, who sat with them that morning. He'd been relieved Faye was over the crush she had on him and encouraged she had responded well to the pastor's sermon.

She turned her head toward the doorway to the dispatch office.

She didn't want Todd to sit with Faye and Craig at her old church. She wanted Todd to sit with her and Gary at her new church.

She looked back at her computer screen, which had gone blank from inactivity.

It was true she had gone out to lunch a number of times in the last couple of weeks with Gary. She'd enjoyed the time she spent with him. But Gary mentioned repeatedly he felt rushed while they talked, and he didn't like it. Shannon felt the same way, as she had many things she wanted to say to him that couldn't be limited to five or ten minutes.

She wasn't sure when it started, but Gary began to ask, over and over, if they could go out in the evenings to talk. But the places he suggested weren't what Shannon considered conducive to talking about opening one's life to God. They were romantic getaways, places more expensive than she'd ever been. Even though Gary hadn't said so out loud, Shannon suspected that if she agreed, just by the atmosphere and what went with it, more would be expected of the relationship than ministry.

Lately, Gary had also been inquiring about a boyfriend. When she finally gave in and told him she had no boyfriend, his questions started becoming more personal, even suggestive.

She didn't want to cross that line or have that kind of relationship. At least, not with Gary.

Nanci's words about her "love life" replayed in her mind. Despite what Gary was hinting at, he was a ministry. For all the time she spent with Todd, he was an old friend, now that she could call him a friend. The only love she had in her life was her Secret Admirer, a man she didn't know. Or if she did know him, she didn't know who he was. So he didn't count.

Yet both Gary and Todd worked with her. In the months since she started receiving the notes, no other man in the office acted differently around her. Most of them barely noticed her at all; they only looked in her direction long enough to make sure their time cards landed in the right basket when they tossed them on her desk. Since she had no other candidates, either Gary or Todd could likely be the Secret Admirer.

Gary was a charmer. He knew what women liked, and women knew he knew. She could imagine Gary doing something romantic and fanciful to win the heart of a lady, especially because he was so aware that women soaked up his attentions. If pressed, Shannon had to admit she was not immune to Gary's charm, either. His polished manners and the way he presented himself suited the role of a handsome and dashing suitor.

The other possibility was Todd. Todd was—

Shannon shook her head. Todd was *not* the Secret Admirer.

She resumed her work until Faye told her it was time for lunch break. Faye ended up sitting with someone else, so she found herself once again sitting with Todd, as Faye had predicted.

As usual, Todd was in a happy mood, and soon, he had her laughing so hard she nearly choked on her salad.

Now was not the time to talk about Gary, about whom they had agreed to disagree. Before she could gather up her courage to ask Todd to join her and Gary the following Sunday morning, another employee appeared at their table to engage Todd in a conversation; one of the drivers had damaged a van.

While they talked, Shannon studied Todd. She would never have thought of him as responsible; yet he was a good fit in his position. He admitted the driver's degree of fault, but he also pronounced a fair judgment and recommended against disciplinary action for a number of good and valid reasons. Shannon knew Todd would stick up for her in the same way if something happened. Because Craig knew she had been seeing a lot of Todd, her brother continued to give her updates on his progress with the Lord. Yet, for all the changes, he was still the same old Todd.

When they were finally alone again, Todd turned to her and sighed. "I have to ask you something. I'm having my mom over for dinner tomorrow. Do you know what I can cook her that's good and healthy, too? Something with lots of vegetables. Remember it has to be easy, because I'm not very good in the kitchen."

Shannon smiled. Yes, he was still the same old Todd Sanders. She remembered one day when Todd and Craig had set something on fire in her mother's kitchen. Since it hadn't been an oil-based fire, Todd had used the sprayer from beside the kitchen sink to extinguish the fire. Her parents had arrived before the smoke residue cleared completely, but fortunately, the rest of the mess was cleaned up, except for one slightly blackened area on the hood above the stove, which remained to this day.

"I can't think of anything healthier than some nice stir-fried vegetables, maybe with cubed chicken and noodles. You can do that, can't you?"

Todd's eyebrows raised. "I don't know how to stir-fry noodles. I also don't know how to cook vegetables unless they come out of a can."

Shannon rolled her eyes. "Canned vegetables are already cooked."

"Really? Then I'm halfway there. Can I buy cooked noodles, too, and just mix them together?"

Shannon tipped her head to one side slightly. He looked on the verge of desperate. She didn't know why cooking vegetables for his mother was so important, instead of just cooking her a nice meal, but she didn't need to know. Something inside her wanted to help him. "I'm not doing anything tonight. If you want, we can go shopping together. I'll show you what to buy, and I can tell you how to cook it."

"I have a better idea. How about if I buy double of everything I need, you show me how to cook it, and then I'll cook the second batch tomorrow by myself?"

She wanted to protest and tell him he wouldn't enjoy the same thing two days in a row. But she often stir-fried a meal one day then enjoyed the leftovers more the next day when they were already cooked and all she had to do was reheat them.

More important, she needed a chance to be alone with Todd. It had been on her conscience for two weeks that she should apologize to him for the way she told him not to attend church with her when she took Gary. Also, she wanted to reinvite him and hope he accepted. She didn't know what was wrong between Todd and Gary, but ever since they'd attended church together Shannon detected a strain between them. Not only did Gary tend to be more critical of Todd, Todd stopped joking when Gary entered the room. She didn't want something she'd said or done to affect their working relationship, especially since Gary was Todd's supervisor. But first, she had to find out what was wrong so she could deal with it.

"That sounds like a great idea. It's time to get back to work. I'll see you at 4:30."

❦

An afternoon never passed so slowly.

Every minute felt like an hour.

At 4:30 sharp, Shannon walked into the dispatch office, her purse slung over her shoulder. "Ready to go?"

Todd looked up at the clock. "Actually, no. I have to wait for Dave to call in and let me know he doesn't need a helper. If he doesn't, then I can go."

"No problem. I'll be at my desk. I can always find something to keep me busy."

At 4:37, the radio beeped, signaling Dave's call. After Dave confirmed he didn't need a second man sent out, Todd packed up his paperwork and poked his head in Gary's office. Gary was busy typing on his computer, but he acknowledged Todd with a nod.

"I'm gone for the day," Todd said from the doorway, not stepping inside Gary's office.

"I hear you're doing something with Shannon."

Todd stiffened from head to foot. What he did on his own time was none of Gary's business. What he did with Shannon was especially none of Gary's business. But he wasn't going to hide the fact he spent time with her. Every day she didn't go out to lunch with Gary, Todd made sure he took his break at the same time as Shannon. Everyone saw them together, including Gary, and Todd didn't care. As far as everyone was concerned, they were old, childhood friends, and that was exactly what he wanted them to think. "That's right."

"She tells me she's not currently dating anyone. I trust that includes you, too."

Unfortunately, it did include him. In the time he'd spent with Shannon since he started leaving her the notes, the right moment had never come up to tell her how he felt. He rationalized the delay not by admitting his fear of rejection, but by telling himself she was still enjoying reading the notes every morning.

Todd crossed his arms and stretched himself to stand as tall as he could. "For now."

Gary continued to type on his computer. "Just making sure my options are open." Gary's hands stilled, and he raised his eyes to stare at Todd intently as he spoke. "And that they stay open."

"That's up to Shannon now, isn't it, Gary?" Before Gary could respond and before Todd said something he would regret later, he clamped his mouth shut. He spun around to leave and froze.

Shannon was standing in the doorway leading into the dispatch office.

Todd's heart pounded. She was standing where Gary couldn't see her. Since she hadn't spoken, he didn't know she was there. And Todd intended to keep it that way.

In two steps, he was at her side. Without speaking, he gently gripped her elbow, guided her so she turned around, and nudged her to start walking. She didn't say a word until they were outside in the parking lot.

"What was that all about? What's up to me?"

"Whether or not you decide to go out with him."

"Go out with him?" Shannon sputtered. "Why are you discussing with Gary who I'm going out with?"

Todd rammed one hand in his pocket for his keys. As he did so, his fingers brushed the note he'd intended to leave in Shannon's drawer but hadn't because they'd exited the building together. "I wasn't discussing anything. Gary brought it up, not me. I told him what you did is up to you. But I think you know by now how I feel about your seeing Gary."

Her face tightened. "And you know by now how I feel about him. This is my decision, as you said."

Todd's stomach clenched. He'd watched Gary pour his seductive routine over Shannon for the past couple of weeks. From what he'd seen, she was falling for it because she wasn't telling Gary to take a hike. She still went out with him for lunch about every other day. From the things Gary said to Bryan and Rick upon his return, he knew Shannon had omitted parts of the conversation when she recounted to him what was said. Not that she owed him an explanation. What she did and whom she chose to spend her time with was her decision. Regardless of how it hurt. "If you don't mind, I don't want to talk about it."

"Neither do I," she replied tersely.

Todd clenched his teeth then began to pat his pockets, making it look as if he couldn't find something. "I'll be right back. Or if you want, I'll meet you at my place. I have to go back inside for a minute."

Shannon sighed loudly. "Did you lose your keys again? We go through this same routine at least a couple of times a week. I think I'm going to buy you one of those key-chain things with a voice-activated signal."

He knew she thought he was a birdbrain, but if Shannon left at the same time he did, he wouldn't get a chance to slip a new note in her drawer. She had started coming to work earlier in the morning, so he was no longer certain he would arrive before her. He had to make sure he left each new note when he went home at the end of the day.

"Very funny," he grumbled, trying to make it sound as if he was annoyed. "I'll be right back."

No one was in the main office when he returned, making his mission fast and efficient. He was back in the parking lot at the same time Shannon's car pulled up to the exit. While she waited for an opening in the traffic, she turned around, so he held his keys in the air and waved. She waved back to acknowledge that he had them then turned back to the traffic and pulled out as soon as she had an opening.

Todd hurried home, arriving only a minute behind her. She left her car in the visitor parking and hopped into his car to go to the supermarket, where he pretended he knew what she bought, when he had no clue what some of the strange things were called. Soon they were in his kitchen, ready to start cooking. She showed him how to cut the chicken into small pieces and cook it. Then they added cut-up vegetables while the noodles cooked in another pot.

"This would go so much easier if you had a wok."

"I'm lucky to have this big frying pan. I just bought it a couple of weeks ago. I found it at a garage sale. I didn't know this was going to be such a complicated thing with so much to do."

"You said you wanted to make something that was mostly vegetables."

Todd lifted the lid to the pan and tested a noodle to see if it was cooked. "I know. My mother doesn't eat enough vegetables."

Shannon smiled. "Usually, it's the other way around. Mothers telling their sons they don't eat enough vegetables."

Todd didn't reply. Instead, he grunted so she would think he'd said something.

"How's your mother doing anyway? My mom was asking about her again. Lately, I've been seeing you more than Craig. In fact, I don't think you've done anything with Craig for a week, since he's been seeing so much of Faye. So Mom asked me instead of Craig to ask you about your mom."

"She's doing better," he mumbled.

"I'm sorry. I didn't know she was sick. You never talk about your mom."

"There isn't much to say," he muttered as he replaced the lid. "I don't think these are done yet."

He flinched as Shannon's fingers rested on his arm. Todd looked first at Shannon's hand on his arm, then up at her face to see the saddest expression he'd ever seen.

"I don't know what's wrong with your mom. My mom has been asking me about her ever since we've been working together, so I know it's not that she had the flu or something temporary. Todd, please tell me what's wrong."

"It's nothing."

Her grip tightened for a second as she gave his arm a gentle squeeze. "Maybe there's something I can do."

He stiffened. "There's nothing you can do. There's nothing anyone can do. Except Mom. When she decides herself."

Todd lifted the lid again and watched the noodles in the boiling water. Even though he doubted much had changed in the last thirty seconds, he poked at them with the fork, about to taste another noodle, which forced Shannon to release his arm.

He didn't want to talk to Shannon about his mother. Only a few people knew besides the social worker. Craig knew everything, but he'd said a few tidbits to Craig's mother in a moment of weakness. At the time, it felt good to get some of it off his chest; but later, he regretted saying anything because she kept asking how things were going, and he never had anything good to report. The only other person who knew what was going on was his pastor, and Todd planned to keep it that way.

In his peripheral vision, he saw Shannon shuffle around so she was behind him. He was about to scoop up another noodle when Shannon's arms slipped around his waist. He nearly dropped both the fork and the lid when she held him tight and pressed her cheek into his back between his shoulder blades.

"Come on, Todd. You can talk to me. I want to help you. Can't I do more than help you cook? Even if there's nothing else I can do, I can pray for her."

He clenched his teeth. But when she started rubbing little circles on his arm with her hand, he felt as if he would fall apart. He nearly threw the fork and lid onto the counter so he could peel her off him. As he covered her hand with his own, Shannon sighed. The heat of her breath through his shirt warmed a spot below his shoulder blade, and the movement of the sigh pressed her closer to him. Instead of pulling her hands off, he found himself holding them tighter, just to keep her there.

"You can tell me," she whispered against his back. "That's what friends are for."

Friends. Todd squeezed his eyes shut. He wanted so much more. Lately, he'd had dreams of spending his life with Shannon, not just at work, but living together as man and wife, with a dozen kids in a cozy, stable little house with a white picket fence and a big black dog in the backyard. Instead, Shannon was spending more time with Gary.

Todd had planned to talk to her today about Gary while they were cooking, although they were nearly finished and he still hadn't thought of a way to put his thoughts into words. He knew she liked Gary. But Todd couldn't tell her everything, especially how Gary threatened his job. Regardless of how she felt about Gary, if he told her what Gary had said, she was bound to say something to him that would get both of them fired. That would end the relationship, but Todd didn't want Shannon to lose her job because of something he'd started. He needed to think of a better way. He couldn't think properly with Shannon wrapped around him, though. But he didn't want her to be anywhere else.

Todd forced his thoughts away from Gary and back to what they were talking about earlier—his mother.

He tried to clear his throat, but his voice came out in a hoarse croak. "No one can help. She's been like this since my dad left when I was in my teens. I help her a little bit with the basics when she comes over for dinner on Tuesdays, and I go through her stuff."

"Go through her stuff? I don't understand." Todd's head swam. He chose his words carefully. "She's never been good with money or anything that required any planning or advance preparation. She doesn't take care of herself, and she's not good with commitments, but she will come here every Tuesday for dinner and for me to balance her checkbook. That's why I want to feed her something with lots of vegetables. It's the only good meal she gets all week."

Shannon's hands didn't move beneath his, but she gave him a short, gentle squeeze. "I can't imagine anyone cooking any worse than you do. Between you and Craig, I remember a few disasters in my mom's kitchen. But that's so sweet. Do you give her leftovers to take home?"

"Yes, but she eats everything when she gets home, and the next day it's back to the usual patterns."

He felt her arms stiffen. Part of him wanted her never to let him go, but the more sensible part of him told him to pick up her hands and push her away. Having Shannon's arms around him had altered his judgment, and he'd already said more than he should have.

"Usual patterns? What usual patterns?"

She gave him another gentle squeeze. All Todd's self-constraint melted away. He pressed his hands more firmly over hers, as if the closer contact could make everything better.

"On payday, if she's working, she blows all her money on stupid things—cigarettes, movies, clothes, things she doesn't need. I know a lot of the money goes toward illegal drugs, but I can never catch her with them. And then she has nothing. Often she can't pay the rent, and the landlord threatens to evict her. That's one reason why I go through her checkbook. I don't give her money because she'll spend it, then not tell me what she did with it. So I pay her landlord myself. I also give her groceries, but sometimes she sells them for much less than I paid for them, just to get a couple of dollars for more drugs. When she's completely out of food and money, I make her come here, and I feed her. When she's hungry enough, she comes, even if it isn't Tuesday."

Shannon squeezed him tighter. "I'm so sorry. I didn't know. Isn't there anything you can do? Can't social assistance help her? Or a counselor at church or something? There are agencies and all sorts of places she can go to for help."

Todd remained silent while he tried to maintain his composure, grateful Shannon was behind him and couldn't see his face. He did feel awkward talking to her this way, though it was easier. He'd talked to his mother's social worker and his pastor more times than he could count. As an adult, he understood more of her mental state than before, but in his teen years, he hadn't known what was wrong or what he could do about it. He only knew that none of his friends lived the way he did.

Craig had been the only one to see through the show he put on for the rest of the world. Todd had confided in him, especially when matters got bad and his mother started selling his belongings when he wasn't home. Whenever he confronted her about his things being missing, especially treasured or high-priced items, she either yelled at him or slapped him for accusing her of stealing.

Since she was his mother, he certainly couldn't hit her back, even when she went berserk and hit him repeatedly. Once, he remembered breaking down in front of Craig when he asked him how things were going. That was when Craig had involved his pastor, but his mother only got worse and kicked him out. It was the worst thing she could have done for herself, but perhaps it was best for Todd. By then, he couldn't do anything more, and it gave him the separation he needed. He'd been an adult then and already supporting her for the most part for years. Now he helped her from a distance, when she was desperate enough to accept it.

Todd stiffened as he repeated the words he'd heard so often and was helpless to do anything about. "She's not breaking into homes and stealing things, and she's not really hurting anyone but herself with everything else, so they say there's nothing anyone can do until she makes the decision to get help herself. My only choices are to have her arrested or committed. I can't do either one. She hasn't stolen from anyone else besides me, at least not that I know of. I'm certainly not going to press charges. Even if I did, they wouldn't lock up a first-time offender. And she's whacked out enough to be placed in a rehabilitation center without her consent. All I can do is be there to pick up the pieces and make sure she has a roof over her head."

Shannon pulled her hands away, releasing her backward hug, and stepped back. He didn't intend to move, but she latched onto his arm and turned him around until they stood face-to-face, leaving her hand on his arm. "I had no idea things were that bad. Why didn't you tell me?"

The pain in her eyes touched him deeply. The last thing he wanted was her sympathy. He was coping with everything—badly at times—but with help from the Lord, he was coping better than before.

Todd wanted to hold her tight, but he knew if she wrapped her arms around him again he would fall apart, and he couldn't let that happen. Instead, he smiled wryly and brushed a wayward lock of hair out of her eyes so he had something to do with his other hand. "We never had that kind of relationship."

"I guess. I'm beginning to see I didn't know you at all and am only starting to get to know you."

Todd didn't know if that was good or bad, so he chose not to comment. "I think the noodles are probably wrecked by now. I guess my cooking skills haven't improved over the years."

"Forget the noodles. I think you need a hug."

Without waiting for him to respond, she stepped forward and pressed herself into him. She slid her hands around his back and held him tight.

Todd couldn't have spoken if the roof had caved in. His heart pounded, his eyes burned, and he could barely breathe. He'd never thought of hugging as an answer, but she was right. Holding Shannon didn't solve anything, but he did feel better, and he had never loved her more.

Shannon spoke first. "Maybe we should check those noodles, before they burn in the bottom of the pan." She moved away from him.

He ached from the separation, but he didn't want to wreck his only good pan.

Shannon stepped in front of him, took a clean fork out of the drawer, and pulled a noodle out. Watching her pucker up and blow on the steaming noodle made Todd think of her puckering up for something much better than eating. When she blew on the noodle a second time, it almost hurt not to kiss her.

She slurped the noodle into her mouth and chewed it thoughtfully. "A little overdone, but not terminal." She turned off the heat and removed the pan from the stove top. "They're fine if we eat right now. You set the table, and I'll drain them and mix everything together."

Todd scrambled to set the table. They said a short prayer of thanks and began to eat.

Todd ate a mouthful then swirled some of the noodles with his fork. "I've been meaning to ask you something. About your Secret Admirer. Do you have any ideas?"

She laid her fork down. "Yes and no. Sometimes I think I know for sure it's Gary, then other times I don't think he's the one at all. Why do you ask?"

Todd tried to appear neutral. "I was just wondering how you feel about Gary."

"I'm not sure yet. Sometimes I have my doubts about his sincerity, but other times, I think he's struggling with something. I know what he's like with the ladies." She gave a little giggle, suddenly dampening Todd's optimism that she had seen through Gary's ploys. "But I can't help it. He's a lot of fun, and I think that when he decides to settle down, he'll make some woman a wonderful husband."

Todd's hopes sank. He knew he was lousy husband material. For all his hopes and dreams, his own home was as dysfunctional as they came. Before his father left, he had vivid memories of arguing and shouting. A few times his parents had resorted to throwing things at each other.

His only example on how to be a good husband, and even a good father, was Shannon and Craig's father. He loved and respected their parents immensely, but watching his own family had taught him the outside world rarely saw what went on behind closed doors. When it came down to the intimate workings of a relationship, he didn't know what to do.

Gary, on the other hand, knew exactly how to treat a woman, because all the women loved him, despite what he said to the other men when no ladies were present. Yet maybe what Gary said to him, Bryan, and Rick was only a macho front. Maybe he really did know how to treat a woman right.

"Yeah," Todd mumbled, as he stuffed a forkful of vegetables and noodles into his mouth. "Good luck."

Chapter 13

Shannon listened to Todd's laughter, echoing from the dispatch office all the way to her desk. The sound made her smile, without even knowing what was so funny. She peeked over her shoulder, confirming he had the same effect on Brenda and Nanci, who were both grinning for no apparent reason as they worked.

In so many ways, Todd was as big a mystery as her Secret Admirer. She'd known Todd came from a single-parent family, and she'd known something was wrong; but she had no idea his situation was so tragic. When she returned home after having dinner with him a few days ago, she'd buried herself in prayer, first for Todd's mother, then for Todd. The night they'd talked, she'd even shed a few tears for Todd. She'd prayed for him daily since then.

Knowing now what she didn't know before, she had to give Todd credit. Despite his hardships and heartaches, he had a marvelous sense of humor—maybe that's what had saved his sanity over the years. He sometimes overdid it, but he was honorable and sincere, two traits she valued. She'd always known his heart was in the right place, even before he accepted the sacrifice of Christ in his life.

For all he'd been through, he was remarkably well adjusted. He also handled his money well, if he covered his own living expenses, plus most of his mother's rent nearly every month. His actions also proved a kind and generous spirit. If the same thing had happened to others, most people would have simply left and not looked back. Not only was Todd taking care of his mother as much as she allowed him, he was also covering a large expense knowing he had no chance of repayment or even being appreciated.

This was the problem Craig wouldn't tell her about years before. She suspected Todd's pastor was aware of it, but she doubted anyone else was except her. And she knew only because she'd pried it out of him.

Others would have called him a sucker. Shannon thought he was a saint. She had underestimated him. Previously she thought Gary would have made some woman a wonderful husband, but she had revised that opinion. Gary was too self-centered and full of his own accomplishments and ego to be a good life's partner, at least for her. Todd, on the other hand, was everything she had ever dreamed of in a man. If she wasn't sure before, she was now. She didn't know exactly when it happened, but she'd fallen hopelessly in love with Todd Sanders.

But Todd only wanted to be friends. He'd told her so on more than one occasion. And she couldn't blame him. She was, after all, his best friend's kid sister. Regardless of her age, in his eyes, she would always be Craig's kid sister.

If being friends was the best she could be, then she had to accept that. Although it was only a teenage crush at the time, she had been in love with him before and lived through it. If all Todd wanted to be was friends, then being friends was better than not being friends.

Shannon glanced up at the clock. It was still hours before lunch break, but she could hardly wait. Not that she was hungry. Since Gary had a meeting with a client, she would be staying in the lunchroom and taking her break with Todd today.

At the thought of spending some time with Todd, whether or not anyone else joined them at the table, Shannon began to hum as she picked up her stapler and the statistical report for the graveyard shift's productivity. When she tried to staple the report together, she discovered her stapler was empty. She pulled the drawer open and groped for the box of staples, but instead, her fingers brushed the newest note from the Secret Admirer, which she'd left in her drawer instead of tucking it in the envelope in her filing cabinet.

Shannon glanced from side to side to make sure no one was watching. Ignoring her empty stapler, she picked up the note and read it for probably the fifth time that day.

Dearest Shannon,
Of all the things that make life worthwhile
Nothing makes me happier than your lovely smile.
You're bonded to my heart, as steadfast as with glue,
And that's why I write these words of love to you.
Your Secret Admirer

Usually, she didn't reread the notes until she got home, but this one she did. Not that it was better than the others; in fact this one seemed worse. The theme was still sweet and the message touching, but in this one, the pentameter seemed more off than usual, which made her think of all the notes and how they were constructed.

Gary had hinted he was the Secret Admirer, but he was a gifted speaker. His vocabulary was better than the words used in the notes, which she'd been studying at home. She had also discovered a pattern. The most elaborate words were those at the ends of the sentences, the words that rhymed, which didn't make sense. In today's note, however, she'd found an exception.

The word *steadfast* was a word she'd never heard anyone use in normal conversation. In fact, the only place she'd heard the word was at church.

Gary didn't go to church. Or rather he did, but that had only been for the past month. If Shannon were honest with herself, she wasn't sure how much he paid attention. She certainly didn't think he paid attention enough to make a word like "steadfast" part of his everyday vocabulary, especially in what was supposed to be a love sonnet.

After a month, she was starting to have some serious doubts about Gary's alleged interest in Christianity. She'd given him a Bible and pointed out some key verses for him to read, but every time she questioned him, he avoided answering or made an excuse about why he hadn't read that section. She now suspected he hadn't read a single passage she'd suggested.

At the sound of a chair scraping behind her, Shannon stuck the note in her pocket and picked up the box of staples from the drawer. She had almost finished tucking the row of staples into the slot when Rick walked through the doorway from the dispatch office and handed her an envelope.

"Kyle said to give this to you."

As she always did when she received something handwritten, she studied the writing, especially when the person wrote her name. She could easily compare the letter *S* from *Shannon* to the signature *Secret Admirer*.

Kyle on the north city route was not the Secret Admirer.

She quickly read the letter, which was Kyle's request to take a few days off and get his vacation pay. Even though he'd done it correctly by making his request in writing, he'd missed a step. Before she paid him, Kyle had to get permission from the department head to take the time off.

Letter in hand, she walked into Gary's office.

Gary read the letter quickly, called up the staffing schedule on the computer, then nodded. "Sure. He can have those days. I have a couple of guys on the casual list who aren't working and would be happy to get some hours."

Shannon started to turn around, but Gary spoke again.

"Shannon, do you have a minute? I'd like to talk to you about something."

She turned around and sank into one of the plush chairs in front of Gary's desk. "Yes?"

"I was wondering if you'd like to join me for dinner tonight." He quickly held up his hands to stop her from turning him down instantly. "I know what you're going to say, but this is different. I just received an e-mail from the customer I'm going to be joining for lunch, and he's given me a couple of tickets to the theater. They're for tonight, which doesn't give me a lot of time to ask someone properly. I know it's not much notice, but you'd be doing me a favor. I have to go because it's a business obligation rather than something I want to do, and you'd save me from going alone." Gary paused and flashed her a heart-stopping smile. "If you want to justify this, you can call it work related."

"I don't know. May I think about it before I give you my answer?"

"Of course. But I'd appreciate it if you let me know as soon as possible. And while we're out, I think it would be a good time to tell you about a little"—Gary dropped his voice to an alluring whisper—"secret."

Shannon's heart began to pound. She gulped, trying to make her voice sound normal. "What kind of secret?"

He leaned forward over the desk, not losing the smile Shannon knew melted women's hearts by the dozen. "If I told you now, then it wouldn't be a secret, would it?"

"I suppose not," she choked out.

"I've always *admired* a well-kept *secret*, haven't you?"

Shannon forced herself to breathe. She sprang to her feet. "I'll let you know about dinner after lunch." Before Gary could pressure her, Shannon left his office and returned to her desk.

A million thoughts zinged through her head. She didn't know what Gary was going to say, but she wasn't stupid. She could tell he was alluding to the Secret Admirer. Just because he knew, though, didn't mean he was the Secret Admirer. Faye knew, Todd knew, and she suspected Nanci did, too. She also had the impression Rick knew, because he worked closely with Todd and might have overheard them talking about it a couple of times.

Regardless of who knew, since the time she started receiving the notes, she was no closer to discovering the man's identity. The only thing that had happened was that she had gained three pounds. She attributed part of that to going out with Todd for coffee and dessert twice a week, but part of it also had to be a steady diet of a chocolate kiss every morning.

Shannon glanced at the clock. Little time had passed since she'd last checked, but now she wanted it to be the lunch hour more than ever. She hadn't talked much about the Secret Admirer with anyone, but this time, she had to. She had to know if it was Gary, and if it took going out with him in the evening to get an answer, then that was what she would have to do.

But first, she had to discuss it with Todd.

To make sure Todd didn't forget she was remaining in the building for lunch, Shannon returned to the dispatch area, staying clear of Gary's office door.

She found Todd alone in the room, not working, standing and staring out the window.

"Hey, Todd. Working hard, I see." She couldn't help but grin. "What's so interesting out there?"

He smiled. "I was just looking at the spring sunshine. See how it sparkles?"

Shannon grinned wider. Sunshine may be bright, but she'd never seen sunshine sparkle.

Only Todd would think of something so strange.

She stepped beside him, so she was looking out the same window. "It's bright and sunny out there, a nice spring day. But I don't see any sparkles."

He wrapped his hands around her shoulders and turned her in the direction of the trees in the corner of the parking lot. "I'm not talking about the glitter type of sparkles that kids use for their arts and crafts projects. Look." He pointed directly at the trees. "It stopped raining, and the sun came out right away. Everything is still wet. See how the sunshine catches the raindrops on the leaves? And see how the droplets of water shine on that big spider web? Do you see it? It's kind of like dew on the grass early in the morning, but the sun isn't bright enough at sunrise to make the dew sparkle. It's well past sunrise now, though, so the rain is drying fast. The sparkling spring sunshine happens only early in the day, when the weather is cool but not too cold, for that few minutes while everything is wet after a quick rain. Like today. It lasts a minute or two, if the angle of the sunlight is right, and then it's gone. Kind of like the commercial for those chocolate Easter eggs. They last only a short time, and then they're gone until next year. That's what makes it so special. It fascinates me every time, because it's unique and pretty. And now, I better get back to work."

Shannon looked outside at the tree, but she didn't see anything. Her mind was elsewhere.

Sparkling spring sunshine. She'd heard the phrase before.

One of the Secret Admirer's poems had used that phrase. She didn't memorize the poems, or even parts of them, but that one phrase had caught her attention at the time because it was so odd.

Todd had just said the same phrase.

It was Todd. Todd Sanders was the Secret Admirer. She pressed her hand over the top of her pocket with the Secret Admirer's latest note in it.

Todd's latest note.

Todd Sanders was the man who had been writing words of love to her, as today's poem had professed.

She turned to watch Todd busily typing at the computer, hard at work.

"Todd?"

He turned around, smiling. His eyes sparkled, just like his spring sunshine. "Yes?"

Behind her, footsteps approached, meaning either Bryan or Rick or both were returning. Gary's phone was ringing in his office. One of the dispatch phones started ringing, and a beeping and flashing light signaled that one of the drivers was calling in. It was payback time for the three minutes of silence.

This was not the time to tell him she knew.

Shannon cleared her throat, hoping she could make her voice sound normal. "I just wanted to see if we're on for lunch together, since I'm not going out."

He picked up the phone. "You betcha." He pushed the button to get the caller. "Dispatch. This is Todd."

Bryan appeared and reached for the radio. Rick started walking into Gary's office with a folder, but Gary met him halfway, and they both stepped into the dispatch area.

Without a word Shannon turned and returned to her desk, but she didn't sit down. Immediately, she removed the key to her filing cabinet from her pocket. Her hands shook so badly she didn't know how she got the key into the lock. She reached for Todd's personnel file. For all the years she'd known him, she'd never seen his handwriting. When the Secret Admirer notes started appearing, she'd checked the handwriting of a few of the men, but it never occurred to her to look at Todd's.

Shannon pulled out the tax form he'd filled out and studied Todd's signature at the bottom.

The *S* in Sanders was a perfect match.

The last note she'd read flashed through her mind. This time, instead of reading a message from a piece of paper, she imagined Todd's voice saying the words.

"You're bonded to my heart, as steadfast as with glue,
And that's why I write these words of love to you."

🌸

"Oh...Todd...," she whispered.

She replaced everything, locked the cabinet, and resumed her work. By the time her lunch break finally arrived, her stomach felt so fluttery she didn't know if she could eat.

Todd was his usual smiling self as he sat at the table in the lunchroom, waiting for her, the contents of his lunch tote already spread out.

Shannon quickly retrieved her lunch from the fridge and joined him.

So he couldn't see her hands shaking, Shannon didn't open her lunch but instead folded her hands in her lap. "Before we eat, I was wondering, is there anything you'd like to tell me? Something important?"

He opened one of his containers, removed a sandwich, and rested it on the lid.

"Not really. Give me a hint."

"Something that might be a secret?"

His eyes widened, and his smile dropped for a split second, but he recovered quickly. He rested his hands on the tabletop and leaned forward. "I hear everyone's going out for dinner next month, and one of the birthdays for the month is yours. Faye asked me to buy a card."

"That's not a secret."

He straightened, and his grin widened. "Sorry. That's the best I can do. If you want juicy gossip, you have to go elsewhere."

She realized he wouldn't tell her unless she forced it out of him so she tried to think of how she could reword her thoughts in a way that would pin Todd into a corner.

He sat there, staring at her, not eating, making her realize it was her turn to say grace. She led in a short prayer of thanks for their food, and they began to eat.

She thought she'd try again, perhaps coming at the issue another way. "I was wondering. Have you ever thought about—"

Todd's foot tapped hers under the table, halting her words. "Hey! Faye! What do you say?" Todd quipped while looking over Shannon's shoulder. Faye slid into the empty chair beside Shannon. After she was settled, Todd grinned at her. "Have a seat. Why don't you join us?"

Shannon couldn't help but smile, as did Faye.

Faye plunked a notepad on the table in front of her and focused her attention on Todd. "Someone suggested that you should be on the social committee. We're going to start making plans for the Christmas party next meeting, and Nanci and Brenda think you should be there."

Todd blinked. "Christmas? But it's only May."

"If we want to book the banquet room we like best, we have to do it soon. You wouldn't believe how fast the good places go."

"But I've never done anything like that before."

Shannon knew Todd would be good at administration.

"Oh, look," Faye said. "Here come Nanci and Brenda." She waved the duo over to the table. "Guess what? Todd said he's going to be on the social committee with us."

"I did?"

Both ladies winked at Todd as they slid into the last empty chairs at the table.

Shannon smiled. It appeared Todd's fate was sealed, with or without his approval.

Faye giggled. "I think this year the social committee stuff is going to be fun."

Rick also appeared. He pulled out a chair from another table, squeezed it in between Faye and Nanci, and joined them. "Did someone mention the social committee?" He turned to Todd. "Did they volunteer you? Faye said she was going to ask. And I know how Faye 'asks.'"

With the sudden appearance of the entire social committee at the table, Shannon had a feeling she wouldn't have the chance to talk to Todd without an audience.

Suddenly, Gary's voice sounded from behind her. "Rick, I've been looking for you. I need your report on John's accident. Sorry to bug you on your lunch break, but the insurance people need me to fax it to them by one o'clock, and I have to leave in five minutes to meet a client."

Shannon didn't look at Rick. While Gary was speaking, she watched Todd. She had told him about Gary's insinuations that he himself was the Secret Admirer. She could only guess now at how he felt. He had tried to get her to reconsider spending time with Gary for more than the fact he didn't like the man. It was because Todd knew the truth.

She clenched her fists under the table. Before she started receiving the Secret Admirer's notes, she had turned Gary down many times when he'd asked her for a date. She didn't know what he had planned for after attending the theater, but when she'd also been hesitant about that, even after he called it a business function, he'd insinuated he was going to tell her he was her Secret Admirer. By trying to make her believe he was the Secret Admirer when he wasn't, Gary was lying to her. Worse than lying, he was trying to take advantage of her, knowing she was in an emotionally vulnerable state.

She had no idea why he was trying so hard. But Gary didn't care about the hearts he broke. Jody was still nursing her wounded heart and had been for six months. He hadn't been interested in a relationship with Jody; he only wanted to have fun with her. Shannon wasn't interested in that type of relationship. She didn't want love or loyalty from Gary. She wanted his honesty, which she knew she wasn't getting. If he cared about her, he wouldn't lie to her. He wanted something else—probably the same thing he got from Jody—and Shannon wasn't giving that to him.

Apparently, Gary was using any means he could to break her down. After more than a month of leading her to believe he was interested in God, he hadn't read anything from the Bible she'd given him. Nor had Gary ever had any appropriate questions or comments on the pastor's sermons. Looking back, she doubted he was even paying attention to the pastor's words. Gary was using her desire to share her faith and attending church with her as another ploy to make her fall into his clutches.

Todd was right. She was completely out of her league with Gary. She didn't want to think of what would happen if she went out with him. If she had to imagine the worst that could happen, it would be her word against his, when she had voluntarily spent so much time with him over the past month, with many witnesses to bear testimony to the fact that she was a willing victim.

To allude to being the Secret Admirer was deceitful enough, but going to church under false pretenses intending to take advantage of her was reprehensible.

Slowly, Shannon turned around. After what she'd just thought of as a worst-case scenario if she did see Gary on her own time, what she was going to say was best stated in front of witnesses. "Gary, about our earlier conversation. I've decided not to go out with you this evening. You'll have to find someone else to schmooze the customers with you. In fact, I think it would be a good idea if we didn't see each other on weekends anymore, either. And that includes Sunday mornings."

Gary's smile faltered for a second, but he recovered quickly, putting on a great macho show in front of the other ladies. "You don't know what you're missing." He lowered his voice to a playful growl. "We'd have been good together."

After everything she'd been thinking, the concept of being coupled with Gary made her stomach churn. "I don't think so. I don't appreciate the way you've been trying to get me to believe something you know isn't true. I think it best if we only see each other at work, during working hours. And that includes lunch. Effective immediately."

Gary grinned and shrugged his shoulders. "It's all in the game." He glanced around the table at everyone sitting there, most noticeably Rick and Todd, as two single men who could supposedly relate. "Win some, lose some. Rick, I need that report. I have to get back because I have to leave."

Rick stood and walked back to the dispatch area with Gary.

Shannon felt as if she'd been stabbed. She wasn't playing games. She'd been serious about the time she'd spent with Gary, hoping for results and praying for his eternal salvation. She'd risked her friendship with Todd, knowing Todd disapproved; yet she'd gone ahead with her plans to minister to Gary anyway. All she wanted was for Gary to respect her faith and accept Jesus as his Savior. If not, she at least hoped to be friends so the door would be open for the future, when he was ready. She certainly hadn't expected to be brushed off like a toy he no longer had any hope of playing with.

She'd never felt so insulted in her life.

With Gary and Rick out of the room, Nanci turned to Shannon and giggled. "Good one, Shan. It serves him right for how he treated Jody. Score one for us girls!"

If Shannon had any remnants of her appetite left after talking to Gary, she had absolutely zero desire to eat now. She wasn't out to hurt people to avenge past wrongs, nor did she have any inclination to play gender battles. She also didn't want to talk to Todd about the Secret Admirer anymore. She couldn't look him in the face, not knowing if she'd see sympathy, anger, or pity in his eyes.

She just wanted to be alone.

Shannon snapped the lid back on her salad bowl. "I guess I wasn't as hungry as I thought. I'll catch you later." Since she didn't have anything else to do, Shannon returned to her desk ten minutes early and resumed her work. If she couldn't be alone, keeping busy was probably best, which was easy while she was at work.

At the end of the workday, she could go home and lick her wounds. She wasn't in a position to quit her job over a personal injury, and she knew Gary wouldn't, either. In fact, Gary probably didn't even consider her rejection of him an injury. He'd brushed off Jody, and Jody was madly in love with him. In Gary's mind, Shannon was nothing, which on top of everything else added insult to injury with her bruised ego.

Tomorrow, after spending some time alone with God and getting a good night's sleep, she knew she would feel somewhat better, and life could go on as normal.

But until then she had work to do.

Chapter 14

I can have the driver back there in twenty minutes. . . . You're welcome." Todd hung up the phone and paged the driver in question, but his mind was elsewhere. No matter how busy he was, he couldn't stop thinking about Shannon.

To the best of Todd's knowledge, only Faye knew about the Secret Admirer. Rick knew something was going on, but he didn't know what. He didn't think anyone else knew besides Gary, and that was because Gary had been snooping in Shannon's desk. From the way Shannon had worded her statement to Gary, no one except those who knew about the Secret Admirer would have been able to figure out the meaning of her words.

Somehow, since the last time he'd spoken to her about it, Shannon had determined the Secret Admirer wasn't Gary. Todd was more relieved than words could express that Shannon had decided not to see Gary outside of work. Last night, he'd hardly slept at all. He'd decided that, even if Shannon didn't want to save herself, Todd would. Whether or not it put him at risk of being fired, Todd had decided to confront Gary and put a stop to his pursuit of Shannon at the close of work Friday, which was that day. Now it appeared she had solved the problem herself, in the nick of time, without any input or help from him.

Of course he was relieved. And though the result was what he wanted, Todd didn't like the way Gary brushed off Shannon in front of everyone. Maybe he'd done it to cover up his own embarrassment, but he didn't need to wound her in the process. She tried to hide it, but he could see she was hurt because she couldn't even finish her lunch.

Todd wished he could do something about it, but there was nothing he could do or say except for giving her a few platitudes. For all the time he'd spent with her, and in all his efforts to treat her special, Shannon only thought of him as a friend and nothing more. He would have approached her on bended knee to propose love and marriage if he thought it would have helped. But he'd been on bended knee once before, singing "Happy Birthday" at the top of his lungs in the middle of a crowded restaurant to get her a free piece of cake. She didn't take him seriously then; she wouldn't take him seriously this time, even if he meant it from the bottom of his heart.

Last night he'd also thought about revealing himself as the Secret Admirer after the close of work today, whether or not he was still employed. That plan had also been squelched. After Gary treated her as little better than a piece of fluff in front of her work friends, she needed the Secret Admirer to hold her up and tell her how special she was more than ever. If she found out now that he was the Secret Admirer, the joy she'd received from the notes would only be a disappointment.

As the day continued, the phones eventually quieted down, and most of the drivers were told to start coming in as everything began to wind down for the close of business. Todd took advantage of a rare moment of silence to go to the supply closet for a computer disk to back up his work for the day.

When he walked into the closet, it suddenly dawned on him how quiet it was and how alone he was.

No one was in the closet except him and God.

Todd closed his eyes and prayed. He thanked God for Shannon's friendship, for the improvement in their relationship, and that she had put the past behind them. He praised God that Gary hadn't made a big scene or thrown his corporate weight around. After lunch, everything had gone on as usual, indicating no harm had been done, except the pain in Shannon's heart. He prayed for God to show him a way to help her deal with it, even if it meant continuing to be her Secret Admirer and hold her up. It wasn't what he wanted to do; but if that was what Shannon needed right now, then he would do it.

He wasn't quite finished when he heard someone coming. He opened his eyes, reached onto the shelf, and wrapped his fingers around a new disk just as Faye stepped into the closet.

She squeaked when she saw him. "Todd! You scared me!"

He scrambled to clear his thoughts, turned around, disk in hand, and grinned impishly. "Boo."

Faye giggled. "It's almost time to go home now. I guess I'll see you Sunday at church. Craig wants to go out for lunch afterward. Will you be coming?"

Todd shrugged his shoulders. He didn't feel like watching Craig and Faye cuddle up to each other when he couldn't be doing the same with Shannon, who would be at her own church. Gary wouldn't be with her, but she hadn't asked Todd to join her, as he had hoped she would. The lack of an invitation told him everything he needed to know. "Not sure. I might just go home after the service. Three can sometimes be a crowd."

Her smile widened. "As much as I enjoy your company, I won't argue with you there. We'll see what happens."

Todd nodded and left the room to get back to his job, feeling more alone than he had for years.

❧

Shannon glanced up at the clock. It was ten minutes past Todd's quitting time. Everyone in the main office had gone home, but Todd still hadn't appeared from the dispatch area.

If he wouldn't come to her, then she would go to him.

She found him bundling the last of the pickup sheets for the day. Bryan was on the phone, and Rick was leaning toward the opening to the drivers' area, talking to one of the casual drivers. Since Todd was the first person to start in the morning, he was first to go home while the others stayed to receive the paperwork from the drivers as they brought their shipments into the building for distribution.

Shannon stepped behind him as he bent over to toss the bundle into the box. "Are you ready to go, Todd?"

"Go? Go where?"

Shannon smiled. "Home, silly. Let's walk out to the parking lot together. Actually, I'm hungry because I didn't finish my lunch. How would you like to join me, and we'll go grab an early dinner someplace? I'll buy. There's something I need to talk to you about."

"I...uh..." Todd blinked, looked up at the clock, then back to her. "Sure."

Shannon waited until he tidied up his area, and they walked out of the building together.

Instead of laughing and telling jokes, Todd's mood was somber. They had reached his car before he finally spoke.

"I don't know if this is the right time or place to say this, but I'm going to say it anyway. I think you made the right decision about not seeing Gary anymore. If the day ever comes when he wants to search for God, he knows where to go and who to ask. I hope one day that will happen. I really do. In a way, I feel sorry for him. I don't know how he ever thought you wouldn't find out he was only leading you on. The big loser here is Gary, not you."

"Thanks. I appreciate your saying that." After thinking about Gary's rebuff, she'd come

277

to terms with it quickly. Her ego was still bruised, but the big loser truly was Gary. Worse than turning down Shannon's offers of friendship, Gary had rejected God.

Todd reached to pull on the handle to his car door, which of course was locked. "Oops," he muttered.

Shannon smiled at what she knew was going to happen. She could have counted the seconds each stage took as he performed his routine.

Todd straightened and stuck his right hand in his right pocket. He pulled his hand out, empty, then stuck his left hand in his left pocket. Again, when he removed his hand, it was empty. He began to pat all his pockets, but Shannon knew his attempts to find his keys would be futile.

"I have to go back inside. Wait here for me. I'll be right back."

Shannon reached out to touch his arm, barely able to hold back her grin.

When he turned around and looked at her, Shannon had to nibble on her bottom lip in an effort to keep a straight face. "Why don't you check the back pocket of your jeans? I think you'll find your keys there."

Todd reached behind him and patted both back pockets with both hands. "Well. How about that? You're a genius."

She couldn't hold back her grin anymore. "Not really. But you're the one who's going to have to be a genius to figure out another excuse to go back inside the building while you leave me here outside. I've got you figured out. I know what you're doing."

Todd's face paled instantly. He froze with his hands still covering his back pockets.

"Every time you've gone back inside for your keys, you've known where they were. Your keys weren't the issue. You've gone back to my desk when you knew I wouldn't see what you were doing."

"But. . ." Todd's voice trailed off.

Shannon reached forward and rested her hands on his arms and looked up into his eyes. Eyes that showed so many things—now his hesitation and uncertainty. Above all, his eyes showed depth of character—a man who was sweet and sensitive, despite the display of bravado he put on for the rest of the world. She mentally kicked herself for taking so long to see it.

Her voice dropped to a whisper. "It's you. It's been you all along."

Todd looked down at her hands. He stood, frozen, not moving a muscle. "I. . ." His voice trailed off again.

Shannon shuffled closer, not caring if anyone else they worked with saw them. "You might as well give me the note right here instead of making me wait until morning." Leaving her left hand still on his arm, she reached into her own pocket and withdrew a piece of paper. "But first, this is for you."

Todd accepted the paper from her hand. "What's this?"

"It's a note, silly. Read it."

Todd's hand was shaking as he read what she'd written.

Dearest Secret Admirer,
I have no chocolate kiss to share
All I have are my words and a prayer.
It's been hard to rhyme when my mind meanders
Because I'm in love with you, too, Todd Sanders.

Yours forever, Shannon

Todd stared at the note, read it a second time, and gulped. "I'm speechless." Still clutching the paper, he brushed his fingers against her cheek and looked deep into her eyes.

The parking lot, the vans, the traffic on the street behind her—the whole world around her faded into oblivion. Todd's beautiful brown eyes were warm and inviting and as sweet as the chocolate he had given her every day.

He cleared his throat, but his voice still came out so low and husky she could barely understand him. "Do you mean this?"

Shannon's heart pounded so hard she wondered if he could hear it. "As much as you've meant your notes to me."

He cupped both her cheeks with his palms. "I love you so much that words are inadequate."

Shannon started to open her mouth to respond, but before she could speak, Todd's mouth covered hers. He kissed her passionately but still cupped her cheeks gently, using no force to keep her there except for her own compelling need to kiss him back. His gentle touch emphasized that his kiss came entirely from his heart and that he truly loved her as much as his notes had said.

Shannon slipped her arms around him to embrace him fully. She kissed him the same way he was kissing her, because she loved him, too.

"Woo hoo! Go, Todd!" a male voice called out from somewhere in the parking lot. From the other side of the lot, a horn honked.

Todd drew back slightly, his face red. "I guess the drivers are starting to come in. We should go someplace else. You said something about supper?"

Shannon knew her own face had to be as red as Todd's. "Yes. Where do you want to go?"

He brushed a light but lingering kiss on her lips then released her completely. "I don't know. I'm so mixed up right now I can't think. I want to go someplace quiet and romantic so I can ask you to marry me, but it's probably too soon for that."

Shannon giggled. "I don't know about that, but if you wanted that tidbit to be a secret, you blew it. Now I won't answer until you ask me properly."

His cheeks flushed again. "Oops." They walked in silence to her car. Todd spoke as Shannon inserted the key into the lock.

"It's not very romantic, especially since we're taking separate cars, but there's a great place to eat not far from my apartment. It's called Joe's Diner. It's small, and it isn't fancy, but the food's great. The owners just got married, and the local paper said they've decorated the place like a wedding. The bride is wearing her veil all week, the groom is wearing a top hat, and the waiters and waitresses are wearing their wedding gear. They're also offering dinners for two at half price and giving away free cake, like wedding cake, to everyone for dessert."

"That sounds like your kind of place. I'll meet you there."

Shannon was so happy she felt lightheaded. As strange as it sounded, she couldn't think of a more romantic atmosphere for Todd to propose than in the midst of wedding decorations, even if the recent bride and groom were serving hamburgers. She could hardly wait to give him her answer.

Shannon pulled the car door open.

"Wait."

Before she could slide in, Todd's hands slipped around her waist. She turned around and rested her hands on his waist as well. They were hugging loosely, so that no one they worked with would tease or interrupt them.

Todd brushed a kiss on her temple, backed up a little, but didn't release her. "I have to tell you this now, or I'll forget. That was a good poem you wrote, especially in a short time."

Shannon felt her face grow warm at his compliment. "Thanks. I found out writing poetry isn't easy. Do you know how difficult it was to think of something that rhymed with Sanders?"

Todd grinned, stepped back, covered his heart with his hand, and cleared his throat.

"Finding rhymes is easy when you know where to look. All it takes is to love a special woman, and then go buy a book."

What's Cooking?

by Gail Sattler

Dedication

To Sandie, my friend and critique bud extraordinaire.

Chapter 1

W hat are you trying to do, poison me?"

Mitchell Farris watched as Jake covered his mouth with his hand, ran across the room, and leaned over the sink. Jake spat, turned the tap on full blast, filled a large glass with water, rinsed his mouth, then spat again.

"Come on, Jake, you're my best friend."

"With friends like you, who needs enemies?" Jake sputtered, standing over the sink with his head bowed, still gasping.

Mitchell tried not to look hurt. "I did my best."

Jake straightened and wiped his mouth with his sleeve. "What was that supposed to be?"

Mitchell skimmed his finger down the page of the cookbook on the counter. "Crab snaps."

All the color drained from Jake's face. "You fed me diseased seafood. I'm going to die of salmonella poisoning, and it will be all your fault!"

"I don't think you can get salmonella from seafood. And it wasn't that bad." At least he hoped it wasn't that bad.

"Did you try it?"

"Well, no. . ."

"Since you're soon going to be my brother-in-law, I'm going to save your life. Don't touch them. And don't give any to the dog, either, unless she has a horrible disease and you want to put her out of her misery."

Mitchell didn't find Jake's comments very amusing.

"Whatever possessed you to try this?" Jake waved his arm to encompass the array of dirty bowls and utensils scattered over every flat surface of the small kitchen.

"Ellen said I couldn't do it."

"Ellen was right."

Mitchell snorted. "Ellen and Mom and I were talking about the rehearsal party and what it's going to cost to have everything catered since Mom can't do very much with her arm in a cast. So I said I would do the cooking."

"We've been roommates for four years, Mitch, and I've seen the extent of your cooking talents. I'm not having hot dogs at my wedding rehearsal."

"I know. That's why I'm making these, uh. . ." Mitchell checked the cookbook one more time. "Crab snaps."

"I changed my mind. Take your life in your hands. Try one." Jake extended his arm toward the soggy blobs, still in neat rows on the cookie sheet. "Sorry, Mitch. I know how you cook. There is no way you can ever make these edible, much less in seven weeks."

"It's too late. I said I'd do it. My personal honor is at stake."

Jake disappeared into the living room and returned with the community newspaper. "If you're really going to insist on doing this, you should take a night class."

"Night school? Me?"

Jake nodded and opened the newspaper about two-thirds of the way through. "Look. Here's one. Creative Cooking for Entertaining. It's an eight-week course, and it starts in an hour. I'll bet you could still make it if you phone right away."

Mitchell glanced up at the clock, then the calendar. The session ended after Jake and Ellen's wedding, but he figured he could learn enough to do what he needed for the rehearsal. He'd made a promise, but he certainly didn't want to poison the wedding party. They were his friends, too.

"I'll do it. What's the number?"

❧

Mitchell arrived at the classroom door with one minute to spare. As he entered, the teacher raised her eyebrows at the sight of him, smiled a polite greeting, and shuffled a piece of paper on the table in front of her.

He scanned the room, looking for an empty chair.

A group of young girls who looked like they'd just graduated from high school filled the back area, about a dozen fortyish ladies filled the rest of the room, and center front, an elderly lady sat primly with her hands folded in her lap.

There was no one there his own age, and he was the only man present.

The last empty chair was in the very center of the classroom. Trying to act casual, he aimed himself for it and smiled at everyone as those in his path pulled up their knees to allow him access. He slid into the seat. Because he was a head taller than everyone around him, he slouched and leaned back, rested one ankle on the opposite knee, and tried to make himself as comfortable as possible.

The teacher frowned and ran her finger along a paper in front of her. "Excuse me, but I think you're in the wrong class."

Mitchell smiled. "I'm in the right class. I just signed up, and they said I wouldn't appear on your list. My name is Mitchell Farris. Stella at the office told me to tell you she'd fax a new list in the morning. I promise I'll be on it." He waited for a response, but she only stared back at him. "Stella gave me a registration number," he said.

The teacher blushed and scribbled something on the paper. The group of young ladies in the back row giggled.

"That's fine." The teacher checked her watch. "I think it's time we started. My name is Carolyn Rutherford, and I'm the home economics teacher here at Central High. This class is Creative Cooking for Entertaining." She paused for a few seconds and scanned the room, making brief eye contact with everyone except him. "Your original teacher, Edith Ramsey, had to go out of town for urgent family business, so I agreed to take her place. Today, we're going to prepare a few fancy finger foods, favorites at any gathering, casual or formal. We'll start with something basic so I can see the skill levels of everyone here. Let's get started."

Mitchell couldn't believe he was doing this. Jake had railroaded him into signing up so fast it hadn't occurred to him that only women would take such a class. And now that he was here, he didn't want to look like a coward and walk out.

The teacher donned her apron, opened her cookbook, and started explaining what she called "basics." She explained to everyone about putting the beaters in the freezer for a few minutes before whipping the cream, but he really didn't need to know why, only that he was supposed to do it. Instead of studying her food processor and all its wonderful features, he studied the teacher.

He guessed Carolyn Rutherford was a bit older than he was, probably in her late twenties. She was a little heavier than most of the women he went out with—not fat, but not skinny, which was probably a good testimony to her cooking skills. He pegged her height at just barely over the five-foot mark, nearly a foot shorter than he was.

She held up some other strange contraption, but instead of looking at the device, he looked at her hands. She had tiny hands, short little fingers, and no rings. Of course, she might have taken them off because she was teaching a cooking class, but he filed the information in the back of his mind.

She wasn't a classic beauty, but she had a cute little nose and pouty, cherub lips with a very attractive smile. Her glasses only seemed to make her face more delicate, and he smiled every time she pushed them up the bridge of her nose with her index finger and kept talking without missing a beat. She spoke slowly enough to be understood, but not so slowly that she seemed to be talking down to her students. Her cheery voice made him wonder what she sounded like when she laughed.

Her fluffy hair framed her face nicely, and even though he couldn't decide what color it was, he liked it. It was a very unique shade of brown—dark, not on the black side, but not red, either. Her eyes were brown, but he wasn't close enough to tell what exact shade.

Since she appeared to be almost finished with her demonstration, Mitchell thought it best to actually pay attention to what she was doing because soon she would be starting to cook. A glint of gold around her neck caught his attention. He squinted and was able to make out a delicate gold cross on a chain around her throat. He wondered if she was a Christian, if she attended church regularly, and how he could find out.

Before he could give it any more thought, she smiled and looked right at him. "And that about covers the basics. Now I'll show you today's creations, which are stuffed mushroom caps and hot tenderloin canapés on pumpernickel with blue cheese."

Before he knew it, she'd mashed a bunch of stuff together in a bowl, whipped it up, and stuffed it into a bag. Next, she squeezed it out in little patterns into the tops of the upside-down mushrooms. He didn't like mushrooms, but it looked so pretty, he thought he just might try one.

Then she mixed up another batch of ingredients, put a plop of the white stuff on a morsel of bread, then stuck a hunk of meat on top of each.

"Now it's your turn. I'll divide you into groups of four, assign each group to a kitchen unit, and you can all do this yourself, following the instruction sheets I've passed out."

Mitchell smiled and stood. This was going to be easy.

Carolyn fought to control a bad case of nerves. Men usually enrolled in the more basic class, Home Economics for Adults, because it was more suited to people with limited kitchen skills. The presence of a man in the more complicated course meant he was an accomplished cook, and rather than simply learning to make decent daily meals, specialty cooking was a personal interest.

She'd already noticed that Mitchell wasn't really paying attention when she ran through her basic spiel prior to her demonstration of their projects for the day.

Carolyn divided everyone into five groups of four, the last team being Sarah, one of the younger ladies; Lorraine, one of the over-forty crowd; the elderly Mrs. Finkleman, who didn't appear to have a first name; and Mitchell Farris.

She directed the last group to the kitchenette in the back and gave everyone a brief explanation of the setup. Before she returned to the first group, she turned to Mitchell. As they made eye contact, he smiled brightly.

Carolyn's breath caught in her throat. One dimple appeared with his lopsided smile, and his green eyes sparkled with humor. His light brown hair, shorter on the sides and gelled on top to hold it in place, set off his straight nose and highlighted his masculine features, making him more handsome than any man had a right to be. He towered above her, and she estimated his age to be about twenty-seven.

"I'll be back later to check on your progress," she mumbled and hustled away.

Spending time with each group, Carolyn answered questions and made sure everyone took a turn in the preparation of the mushroom filling. By the time she returned to the last group, she had to struggle to quell her nervousness. She expected this group would need little interaction and instruction from her, as Mitchell would be able to help them.

As she joined them, the group was preparing to squeeze the filling into the mushroom caps. Mrs. Finkleman had applied the star-shaped decorating tip and was busily stuffing the mixture into the bag.

Carolyn put on her best teacher smile to hide her jitters. "Why don't we give Mr. Farris the honor of filling the first mushroom cap?"

He flinched then made direct eye contact. "Please call me Mitchell. Mr. Farris is my father."

His gorgeous smile almost made her knees wobble. Carolyn forced herself to smile. "Mitchell, would you like to do the honors?"

He took the bag and positioned it in the strangest way she had ever seen, with the tip touching the mushroom. Anxious to see his method, she leaned closer.

When he gave it a small squeeze, nothing came out, so Carolyn had to assume he was testing the viscosity of the mixture, which probably wasn't a bad idea. She wished she could have made notes.

He stopped all motion and raised his head then stared straight into her face. "I'm not very good at this," he mumbled.

His modesty impressed Carolyn. "It's okay," she muttered, smiling in anticipation, waiting. "Take your time. I'm interested in your technique."

With a small shrug of his shoulders, he squeezed the bag of filling once more, but still nothing came out. Carolyn let her smile drop.

Again, he squeezed it a little harder, but still not using sufficient pressure to start the flow through the designing tip. Carolyn wondered if there was something wrong with the filling.

As discreetly as possible, she checked the bowl containing the mixture that had not fit inside the bag. It appeared to be the right consistency and texture, so she focused her attention back to Mitchell as he gave the bag a small shake then held it farther away from the mushroom.

He squeezed harder then gave an abrupt sigh when nothing came out. A quick glance told her the other groups were already half through pressing swirls of filling onto the neatly laid mushroom caps.

Mitchell mumbled something under his breath and squeezed again, much harder this time.

A stream of filling spewed out of the bag. Some of it hit the mushroom, propelling it to the end of the baking sheet and over the edge. The errant mushroom cap continued its trajectory and disappeared off the end of the counter. A long trail of filling zigzagged all over the baking sheet and countertop. With the sudden change in the thickness of the center of the bag, Mitchell lost control and fumbled as he tried to catch it, unsuccessfully. It landed on the counter with a plop, splattering the contents from the open end in a three-foot radius, most of which landed on Carolyn's sleeve.

Sarah and Lorraine stood with their eyes wide and mouths gaping while Mrs.

Finkleman lowered her head and stared at her feet. Mitchell stood motionless, staring at his hands, which were covered with the gray mixture. He rubbed his thumb and index finger together, feeling the texture of it, shuddered, and then stuck one finger in his mouth to suck it off.

"I told you I wasn't very good at this," he mumbled.

Carolyn hadn't seen even a high school student's attempts meet with such disastrous results. While she had to pay attention to each group, she had spent more time than she should have watching Mitchell's group's progress. He hadn't done anything in the preparation but had watched the women do all the chopping and mixing. At first she thought it was because he'd done it so often he was letting the novices learn. Now she wasn't so sure.

"You've never done this before, have you?" she asked.

A dead silence filled the room; all motion in the groups halted. Mitchell's face turned beet red. "Can you tell?"

She surveyed the mess on the table, as did everyone else in the room. Giggling drifted from the first group, along with a badly masked "shush" and a grunt from someone probably being poked in the ribs.

Carolyn squeezed her eyes shut and slowly opened them, releasing a sigh at the same time as she crossed her arms over her chest. "There's a basic home economics cooking class on Thursday nights. Perhaps you could practice some basic skills there before taking on a more advanced class such as this. I could have you transferred since their first class hasn't started yet."

He shook his head so fast, a lock of hair flopped onto his forehead. "I don't have time for that. I need to learn how to make all these fancy thingies in seven weeks. I'm staying."

She was about to tell him that the basic class included one lesson on entertaining but stopped short. Something in his eyes implored her to let him stay.

Carolyn sighed once again. "Okay, let's clean this up. Accidents happen."

He smiled and mouthed a thank-you, which she didn't want to acknowledge. Instead, she drew everyone's attention to the front, while Mitchell and Sarah dutifully wiped the counter and Lorraine salvaged what filling she could from the cookie sheet and put it back in the bag. Mrs. Finkleman wiped off her shoe then used a toothpick to dig what she could out of the tiny holes and crevices in the leather.

When Carolyn started the class on their second project, Mitchell stood back to watch instead of assisting with the preparation, and the remainder of the class time progressed without incident.

Everyone cleaned up their work areas and filed out. Mitchell's group was the last to leave, having had the most to clean up. Carolyn said her good-byes to Sarah and Lorraine and Mrs. Finkleman, but the cause of the flying filling lagged behind.

"I can see there's a trick to putting that stuff into the mushrooms. I was wondering if you could tell me what it is."

"All you have to do is increase the pressure gradually and. . ." She let her voice trail off as Mitchell stepped closer. Had he been anyone else, she would have been fine with his proximity. But for some reason, being in the same room with this man felt much too close for her liking. Not wanting to appear nervous, she didn't move away.

"It's really important that I learn how to do this properly."

"You just need a little practice. All you have to do is follow the instructions on the handout sheets."

"I'm really sorry about the mess." His voice lowered in pitch and volume, and he reached out to swipe something off the bridge of her glasses with his index finger. "By the way, I couldn't help noticing that little cross around your neck. It's very nice," he said as he lowered his hand to his side.

Carolyn caught her breath and stepped back. She wasn't sure what Mitchell meant by his comment, but good-looking men seldom looked at her a second time, if ever there was a first. And even for those who chose to ignore her plain features, once they got to know her better, men often ridiculed her for being "too religious."

If she let her imagination run wild, she could easily fantasize that Mitchell was attempting to make a pass at her. However, since he'd mentioned her gold cross, she figured he was simply doing his research so he could eliminate her from his list quickly, which was fine with her. She'd decided long ago only to date men from her church whom she already knew were Christians. It was less painful that way.

Carolyn gulped then swallowed hard to clear the lump in her throat. "It was a gift from my grandmother—when I was baptized a few years ago."

His mouth formed into a smile that made Carolyn's heart pound. "That's really sweet. Can I see you before next class?"

Carolyn nodded numbly. "Sure. I'll be here to set up half an hour before the class starts next week."

"I meant before that. Like during the week."

Carolyn could barely speak beyond the tightness in her throat. "Why?"

He shuffled closer then smiled, but his eyes held no humor. Instead, it was one of those slow, lazy smiles like she'd seen in movies—just before the tall, dark, handsome hero swept the heroine off her feet.

"So we can talk."

"Sorry. I don't think so," she muttered, deciding it was time to rein in her imagination.

"But I'd really like to get to know you better."

The custodian poked his head into the room, sparing Carolyn from needing to elaborate or discuss it further.

"It's time to go. The custodian needs to lock up the building for the night."

Mitchell blinked and stepped back, and his goofy grin disappeared.

Carolyn brushed her hair off her face, straightened her glasses, crossed her arms, and cleared her throat, grateful that he apparently understood her unspoken meaning. "I'll see you in class next Tuesday."

Slowly, he turned and left the room.

Instead of gathering her supplies, Carolyn stared at the open doorway and allowed herself to exhale, not realizing until that moment that she'd been holding her breath. Before she could fully relax, four fingers appeared in the doorway, grasping the door frame, followed by Mitchell's head. He smiled and winked. "Good night, Carolyn," he said and disappeared.

Carolyn closed her gaping mouth. "Good night, Mr.—Mitchell," she mumbled, but he was already gone.

Chapter 2

G ood evening, Carolyn."

Carolyn fumbled with the recipe sheets she'd been sorting. "Good evening, Mitchell. You're early."

All week long she'd been torn between wanting him to come to class early and dreading that he actually would. Every day, without fail, he'd invaded her thoughts. She couldn't decide if she should have been flattered by his attention or angry with him for teasing her.

He stepped forward and rested his palms on the demonstration table. "I wanted to get here early to ask if you would go out for coffee and dessert with me after class tonight."

The knife she'd so carefully selected fell from her fingers. "I don't think so."

"I guess you're right. It might be a little late for that, since we both have to get up for work in the morning. How about tomorrow, then? Maybe after dinner we can take in a show."

She stared blankly at him. Flirting she could handle, but she had no intention of being made for a fool. Other than his being hopeless in the kitchen, she didn't know anything about him. Most of all, she wasn't going to go out with a non-Christian. "No, but thank you for the invitation."

He stepped closer, so she pretended to be selecting matching forks.

"Why not? Are you already involved in a relationship?"

She'd been casually dating Hank off and on for a while. She couldn't quite call it a relationship, but Hank went to her church, and he was safe. "I'm seeing someone, if that's what you're asking."

He moved closer. Her hands froze. "Is it serious? Are you engaged?"

The perfectly matched forks dropped into the drawer with a clatter. "That's personal and none of your business."

He moved even closer. Carolyn's breath caught and her heart raced.

"I think it is since I want to get to know you better."

"I'm too old for you."

For a split second, he froze then blinked. "I don't care how old you are."

"Mitchell, I'm thirty-two years old. What are you, twenty-seven?"

"Twenty-four. But who's counting?"

She looked up at him. Mitchell was more assertive than she was used to, but he was well mannered and charming. He had a delightful sense of humor and was able to recover quickly when caught in a spot, something she always thought revealed a strong character. However, at nearly thirty-three years old, it was time for her to get serious and find someone to settle down with. Soon it would be her birthday, adding another year between them. She always preferred older men, but a nine-year age difference the other way was robbing the cradle.

Carolyn squeezed her eyes shut to clear her thoughts. "I'm sorry, Mitchell, I don't think it's a good idea."

He opened his mouth to speak but shut it quickly at the sound of approaching footsteps in the hall.

Carolyn quickly adjusted her glasses then greeted her incoming students.

After she welcomed them, she took her place at the front of the classroom and froze. Mitchell sat in the front row, center seat, right next to Mrs. Finkleman. He crossed his arms, smiled, and winked.

Briefly, Carolyn considered canceling the class.

She was barely conscious of what she was doing as she showed the class how to properly lay out decorative meat, cheese, fruit, and vegetable trays. Next, she demonstrated how to make rosette radishes, carrot spirals and curls, then her specialty edible decoration, an onion blossom. Throughout the entire process, Mitchell alternately groaned and joked with both her and the rest of the class, questioning his ability to do the fine detail required. His protests were promptly met with sympathetic comments and encouragement all around.

Carolyn smiled through gritted teeth. Very soon he would have every woman present eating out of his hand. She vowed to be different.

She continued with the second project, cream cheese veggie puffs, and sent everyone to try their hand at carving the raw vegetables and assembling the puffs. This time the pastries would be filled with a spoon, and she was almost positive Mitchell could handle that.

As everyone proceeded to their kitchenettes, she noticed that both Lorraine and Sarah had brought full-sized aprons and Mrs. Finkleman wore her canvas sneakers.

❁

Mitchell dragged his feet all the way back to the mini kitchen in the back of the classroom. Fortunately for him, today's projects looked easier, and he wouldn't make a fool of himself again.

After butchering the vegetables, he welcomed the chance to make the next project. He didn't attempt to cut the onion—after all, he doubted anyone at his sister's wedding would care if he set out onions that looked like flowers. After the mess he made with the carrot curls and radish rosettes, when he was asked if he'd rather chop the vegetables or do the mixing, he picked the mixing, even though he'd never operated an electric mixer before. This time he'd paid more attention to Carolyn's demonstration, so he knew he could do it.

Sarah smiled up at him with stars in her eyes, which bolstered his sagging confidence. He smiled back then quickly turned away. While she seemed like a nice kid, he didn't want to encourage her. What he really wanted was Carolyn's attention.

Mitchell caught himself grinning as he absently worked the beaters around the bowl. Carolyn's calm manner enchanted him. She hadn't made a big production out of his major disaster last week. Neither had she fawned all over him. She quite plainly expected him to clean up his own mess without embarrassing him about what he had done.

Also, the tiny gold cross Carolyn wore again this week intrigued him, especially after she told him she'd recently been baptized. She hadn't backed down and told him the cross was just a piece of nice jewelry or that it was simply a gift without an explanation. She'd had the guts to tell him in not so many words that she was a Christian.

After thinking about it all week, he realized he hadn't given her any indication of his own status in his relationship with the Lord, so, if he'd read her hint correctly, he couldn't blame her for not so subtly telling him to get lost. He wouldn't go out with a non-Christian, either.

With all that to consider, he'd had the whole week to think and pray about it, and this was one relationship he wanted to pursue.

"Can I add this now?" Sarah asked, holding a small bowl full of finely chopped green onions.

He nodded and made one final circle with the whirring beaters, taking care that he didn't bump the sides of the bowl. He raised the beaters and tilted the mixer to give Sarah room to dump in the onions when an onslaught of white projectiles flew out of the bowl, splattering everything in the near vicinity.

Still holding the bowl of onions, Sarah spread her arms and lowered her chin to look down at the front of her bright blue apron and the sleeves of her red shirt, which were now enhanced by odd-sized white polka dots.

"Oops," Mitchell mumbled as he turned off the mixer.

"What happened here?"

Mitchell cringed. Carolyn had abandoned whatever group she was with and was now standing beside Sarah, taking in not only the mess all over Sarah, but also the smattering of white blobs all over the counter and up the side of the cupboard.

Mitchell swished the electric mixer behind his back and grinned. "Nothing."

Carolyn bent her head forward, closed her eyes, and pinched the bridge of her nose. "You need to turn the mixer off before you lift the beaters out of the bowl. I really think you should switch to the more basic class on Thursday nights, Mitchell."

He shook his head. "No! I'll get the hang of this."

She sighed, which he thought rather endearing. She returned to the front, and Mitchell listened intently as she described how to properly dice the vegetables, which ones to chop finer, and recommended different types of knives and cleavers for the different jobs and techniques.

Mitchell now knew more than ever that he was in over his head. Besides the cutlery he ate with, he only owned one knife, and he didn't know the difference between it and any other. It had never mattered before.

When they were done, each group sampled the others' creations. Everyone else's radish roses and fruit carvings looked nicer than his, but he didn't care. He didn't want to decorate; he only wanted to serve good food and to say he made it himself.

He glanced up at the clock. Time never passed so quickly when he was at work. Yet they had finished their second lesson. Only five lessons remained before Jake and Ellen's wedding rehearsal, and he couldn't see himself being anywhere near ready to serve the kind of food he'd proudly told his family he would make.

Being the tallest in the group, Mitchell volunteered to do what he did best in the kitchen—putting everything away in the cupboards no one else on his team could reach.

Once more, he glanced to the front of the class at Carolyn, at the display table with all her perfect samples. They emphasized how pathetic his creations had turned out. He didn't know what he was going to do, but whatever it was, time was running out and he had to act fast.

❁

In all the time she'd been teaching, Carolyn had never been so relieved to see the end of a class. She dismissed everyone and busied herself with tidying up her work area. Everyone headed for the door except, to her dismay, Mitchell. He approached her, stood directly at the table in front of her, planted his palms firmly on the surface as she worked, and leaned forward, giving her no choice but to stop what she was doing.

"I can't do this," he said, waving his hand over her display of cut fruits and vegetables. "I need remedial help."

"Remedial help?"

"I peel carrots at home, but I certainly don't cut them into these fancy curly things. I really have to learn to do this stuff. Could you give me extra lessons during the week? I'm desperate." He grinned a cute little boyish grin that emphasized his charming dimple.

Carolyn nearly choked. She couldn't imagine why he was so adamant about learning to prepare fancy hors d'oeuvres or finger foods, and especially the delicate procedure of food decorating, when she doubted his ability to cook even a basic meal.

She continued to stare back at him across the table. If he needed help improving his basic cooking skills, it wasn't like she had anything better to do. Except for Wednesday night Bible study meetings, her evenings and social calendar were embarrassingly bare. She often assisted graduating students in acquiring basic cooking and home management skills, but Mitchell wasn't a student. He was a grown man.

She opened her mouth to decline, but before she could get a word out, he pressed his palms together, widened his grin, and opened his eyes even wider. "Puh-leeeeze?" he begged.

Carolyn folded her arms in front of her chest and openly glowered at him. In response, he pressed one palm to the center of his chest, fingers splayed, and batted his long eyelashes.

"Why is this so important to you?"

Mitchell's foolish grin dropped, and he straightened. "I promised my sister and my mother I would cook the food for her wedding rehearsal. Her fiancé is my roommate and best friend, and he doesn't think I can do it. But I can't let Ellen down. This is important to her."

"Oh." Whatever she had expected, this wasn't it.

"You can trust me. I'm a nice guy. I go to church every Sunday and everything. Promise."

Carolyn's breath caught. All week she'd been wondering why he'd really asked about the cross her grandmother gave her. Now she knew. That was, if she read his between-the-lines statement properly.

She cleared her throat, hoping her voice would come out even, and dropped her arms. "All right, I'll help you. I'm free Thursday night."

Mitchell moved his hands back to the tabletop and leaned closer. "And just to let you know, I was serious about taking you out for dinner sometime."

Carolyn gulped. What had she done?

❦

Carolyn stood in front of Mitchell's door but didn't knock. She wasn't sure she was doing the right thing in agreeing to tutor Mitchell outside of class hours. She'd prayed about it and received no clear direction, so she had to stand by her word. Besides, it wasn't like she was going to date the man. His age aside, so far she couldn't see anything wrong with him, but at the same time, she didn't see anything that made him right for her. If there were any man she would have considered right for herself, it was Hank, and Hank and Mitchell were as different as night and day.

However, she wasn't standing in front of Hank's front door. She was at Mitchell's, and she was not here as a social call. This was business. Or a favor. Or something.

Carolyn gathered her courage, raised her fist, and knocked. A dog barked, quieted, and Mitchell answered almost immediately. Some kind of midsize hairy brown dog stood at his side, indifferently sized her up, yawned, then turned and walked away, allowing her to follow Mitchell down the hall into the kitchen—where the counters were completely bare.

She waved one hand in the air above the empty countertop. "I thought you wanted me to show you how to cook something today. You don't have anything ready."

Mitchell raised his arms, palms up, then let them flop down to his sides. "I told you I needed help. If we went to the supermarket, could you show me what to get?"

Carolyn sighed. She hadn't counted on doing his grocery shopping. She opened her mouth to complain, but rather than watch his theatrics again, she gave in. "Okay," she muttered. "Let's go."

Minutes later, Mitchell pushed the cart as Carolyn selected the ingredients, in addition to some basics she doubted he had. Walking up and down the aisles, Carolyn tried to shake the cascade of mixed emotions as he teased and complained about the items she chose, acting as if they belonged together.

Once they returned to Mitchell's house, she spread everything on the table, ready to begin.

"Okay, where do you keep your bowls?"

"Bowls?"

Carolyn knotted her brows. "We need a bowl like the one we used in class last night."

"I don't have a bowl that big."

Carolyn sighed. "What do you mix things in?"

"Mix things? I put them in the pot."

She rested one hand on her hip and waved the other in the air in a circular motion as she spoke. "I don't mean when you're cooking something, I mean when you're mixing the ingredients. The bowl you use when you make cookies."

He grinned that impish grin she was seeing more and more often, giving Carolyn the feeling she wasn't going to like his answer.

"I buy the kind that comes in a tube. You just slice off pieces and put them in the oven."

"You don't own a mixing bowl. . . ." Her voice trailed off, and she let out a loud, exasperated sigh. "Okay, we'll use the pot. Where's your electric mixer?"

He raised one finger in the air in triumph. "I have one of those!"

Instead of opening a cupboard door, Mitchell left the room, the door to the garage opened and banged shut, boxes shuffled, and the door opened and closed again.

He returned with a large box, which he placed on the table then used a knife from the cutlery drawer to slice through the manufacturer's clear tape. He pulled out the protective foam packing, a warranty card and other literature, and finally, a brand-new electric mixer wrapped in a plastic bag.

Carolyn sighed again.

"You sure do sigh a lot."

She ignored his comment. "Why was your mixer in the garage?"

"I bought it after class last week and put it with my tools so I would know where it was when I needed it."

"You've got to be kidding."

This time, it was Mitchell who sighed loudly. "Carolyn, I'm starting from scratch here. I told you that."

She opened her mouth to suck in a deep breath, but after his comment about her sighing, she quickly closed it again and let her breath out slowly through her nose. "Do I dare ask if you own a wooden spoon?"

"Go ahead and ask, but I don't think you're going to like the answer."

Carolyn buried her face in her hands. "Mitchell!" she mumbled through her fingers. "How do you expect to prepare anything if you don't have the proper utensils?"

"I told you, I need—"

"I know, I know. You need—"

"Remedial help," they said in unison.

293

They stared at each other in silence until Carolyn gave up and reached for the pot. "Okay, we'll do our best with what you've got. But in the meantime, let's make a list of what you should have."

He nodded, and they set to work using whatever she could find to do the best job under the circumstances.

Carolyn guided him through the preparation process, and despite the extra time he took to write notes, things progressed well. His canapés didn't look quite as nice as hers did, and his cheese balls were a little crooked, but Carolyn assured him they would taste just fine.

Carolyn washed the dishes and Mitchell dried, pausing every once in a while to snitch a sample of their creations.

"You know," he mumbled as he licked his fingers, "I should probably have some of those fancy thingies for dessert."

"Fancy thingies?"

"You know. Those chocolate thingies. They have different fillings and that white swirly stuff on top. You know, when you to the coffee shop and you have coffee and one of those little chocolate thingies with the stuff in the middle."

Thinking he probably meant dessert squares, she nodded.

"Great! Can you show me how to do those, too? I'm going to make Jake eat his words. And I'll have you to thank for it." His charming grin made Carolyn's foolish heart flutter.

"I suppose I can. I have many recipes for chocolate dessert squares."

"No, I want a special one. I can't describe it, but I can show you."

"All right."

She barely had time to dry her hands when Mitchell gently grabbed her arm and pulled her toward the door. "Let's go."

"Wait! Where are we going?"

"We have to go to the coffee shop and buy some. They're only open for another hour. I hope they still have some left."

Carolyn let her mouth gape open. She hadn't expected to go out. She thought he would show her a picture in a cookbook. Then she remembered he said he'd borrowed a cookbook from someone he wouldn't name and he'd given it back.

In silence, she slipped on her jacket and followed him out the door to his car. Before she knew it, they had arrived at the local coffee shop.

As he opened the door, his other hand touched the small of her back and nudged her closer to him so he could lean down and whisper in her ear. "I see some people I know. Don't let them know why you're with me."

Carolyn's heart caught in her throat. She'd used the difference in their ages to discourage him from thinking she would go out with him, but even though this was merely the extension of their cooking lesson, it hurt to know she was now an embarrassment to him. She stiffened her back and accompanied him inside.

"Hey! Mitch!"

Two young men about Mitchell's age waved at them from one of the tables near the door as they entered.

"Gordie! Roland! How are you guys?"

To Carolyn's horror, the two young men rose and approached them.

"Carolyn, I'd like you to meet my friends Gordie and Roland."

Gordie and Roland nodded accordingly then quickly glanced back and forth between her and Mitchell. In response, Mitchell's arm slid around her back, then slipped to her waist. Numbly, she glanced down at his fingers. He grinned at his friends.

She probably should have felt very flattered that he was trying to make it look like they were on a date, but she knew he was trying to hide the real reason they were together.

His friends grinned back, nodded, and returned to their table.

"They're good guys, but I didn't want their company tonight."

Carolyn refused to look at him, wanting to cherish the moment, even if it was only in her imagination.

Mitchell ordered them each a cup of coffee and two chocolate dessert squares, one wrapped for takeout, claiming he wanted Carolyn to take it home and analyze it. She tried to convince him there was no need, but he insisted.

As she sipped her coffee, she could feel the stares of Mitchell's friends on her back. A tightening of his jaw signified their return. The chairs scraped on the floor as they sat, one on each side of her. Mitchell's jaw tightened even more. He opened his mouth to speak, but Gordie beat him to it.

"You know, Carolyn, this may sound like a line, but I know I've seen you somewhere before."

Not wanting to further embarrass Mitchell, she shrugged her shoulders. "It isn't exactly a large city. I'm sure it's possible."

"I suppose. It'll come to me."

Roland butted in. "Jake and Ellen's wedding is coming up fast."

"Just over a month from now."

"I can hardly wait to see you in a monkey suit, Mitch."

Carolyn wished she could see him in that monkey suit, too. He looked great in his jeans and loose shirt, but nothing made a man more striking than formal wear. Mitchell Farris in a tux would be a sight to behold. Not that she was interested. If she were interested in anyone, it would be Hank, whom she already knew.

The cutest dimple appeared in Mitchell's left cheek when he smiled mischievously at his friend. "You'll be wearing one, too. Now if you'll excuse us?"

At Mitchell's blatant hint, his friends left not only the table but the building, as well.

"Wasn't that a little rude?"

Mitchell shook his head. "Naw, they only came over here to check you out. You'd better get used to it."

Used to it? She didn't intend to be out with Mitchell in public again.

He changed the subject, and before long, he held her spellbound and laughing at his outlandish tales. She enjoyed herself more than she had in years.

"Oops," he mumbled as he checked his watch. "I think they're about to close."

They made pleasant conversation in the car while Carolyn sat holding the box containing the dessert square in her lap.

The garage door opened as they pulled into the driveway, then the garage. Carolyn wondered why he didn't simply drop her off beside her car, which was parked on the street in front of his house.

"Would you like to come in? We can put our feet up and watch some TV."

She shook her head. "I'd better go. I have classes in the morning, and I'm sure you have a job to go to." Carolyn supposed it would have been polite to ask what he did for a living, but she didn't want to encourage him in thinking she wanted to get personally involved.

He nodded then escorted her through the house and to the front door.

"I feel weird about this, Carolyn. After a date, a woman is supposed to see the man to the door as he goes home. It's so strange to escort you out."

He followed her all the way to her car.

"This wasn't a date, Mitchell. I'm just helping you with your cooking." She unlocked the car door, but before she had a chance to open it, his hands touched her shoulders and turned her around.

"The cooking lesson ended when we left the kitchen. Thanks for coming, Carolyn."

His gentle smile eased any nervousness she may have felt. Even though she didn't know him well, she thought him quite endearing. He made her laugh, and she'd never been so relaxed in a man's presence, either despite his youth or perhaps because of it.

Mitchell's hands remained lightly touching her shoulders, and he continued to watch her in silence. The dim shadow from the boulevard trees kept them out of the direct light of the nearby lamppost, but the light reflected in Mitchell's eyes.

Before she realized his intent, he bent and brushed a gentle kiss to her lips then backed up, his hands still resting on her shoulders.

A car drove by, drawing to Carolyn's attention that they were standing where his entire neighborhood could see them.

Carolyn felt the heat of her blush in her cheeks, making her very grateful for the darkness. Mitchell, however, showed no signs of chagrin.

His fingers lightly brushed her cheeks. "So," he drawled, "will I see you again tomorrow?"

It took Carolyn a few seconds to realize what he was asking. "Tomorrow is Friday. Surely you have other things to do on a Friday night than cooking lessons." She certainly didn't, but it was by her own choosing.

"Nope. But even if I did, I'd cancel, just to be with you."

With a line like that, she couldn't refuse without appearing churlish. "I guess we can do something tomorrow," she said then mentally kicked herself for agreeing.

Carolyn hustled into her car, gritted her teeth, and drove away.

Chapter 3

Mitchell shuffled the bags in his hands and knocked on Carolyn's door. While he waited, he wondered what the inside of her house looked like. He also wondered exactly how welcome he would be. He knew he'd pushed his luck by inviting himself. Yesterday, the cooking lesson was fun, but the time they'd shared at the cafe was better.

The night had gone by so fast, he missed the chance to question her about her faith, now that he'd established she was a Christian. Today, he planned to find out more. He took some comfort in that she'd finally agreed to see him outside of class after he managed to slip into the conversation that he attended church every Sunday, even though no opportunity presented itself to share any more. But she'd responded, and that was a step in the right direction.

For a brief second, Mitchell closed his eyes and prayed about it. He liked Carolyn. She had an easy sense of humor, yet at the same time, she was mature and responsible. Her smile warmed his heart like nothing else. He was even becoming fond of her endearing little sighs when she was exasperated with him. Once he determined they were compatible spiritually, he could see the beginning of a great relationship.

He knocked again, but instead of the door opening to her smiling face, he heard her voice calling him to come in.

He opened the door and entered, ready to reprimand her for leaving the front door unlocked at night, but before he said a word, he skidded to a halt. Across the room, Carolyn stood on a step stool, her back turned to him. She stood on her tiptoes holding a picture up against the wall, balancing it precariously by the bottom of the frame, a hammer poised in the other hand.

"What do you think?" she called over her shoulder. "Is this the right height?"

Immediately, he lowered the bags to the floor and jogged to her, removing the picture from her hands before she dropped it. "What are you doing?"

She sighed loudly as she sank to her flat feet and rested her fists on her hips, still gripping the hammer with one hand. "I'm trying to hang a picture. What does it look like I'm doing?" Even standing on the step stool, she just barely reached eye level with him.

Mitchell stepped forward, standing almost nose-to-nose with her. It would have been the perfect height for a kiss, but not only did they not know each other well enough for such familiarity, she looked too irritated. He sighed back, but she didn't get the hint.

"You're too short for that. I'll hold it up. You stand back and tell me when it's where you want it." When she hopped off the stool, he pushed it aside with his foot, stuck the nail in his mouth, and held the picture on the wall with both hands, awkwardly balancing the hammer at the same time. "Here?" he mumbled around the nail.

When she didn't answer, he peeked over his shoulder. His breath caught at the sight of her. Carolyn stood with her head tilted to one side, one arm over her stomach, and the index finger of her other hand tapping her pouty bottom lip. She looked so cute, he wanted to put everything down and give her a hug.

"A little to the right. There. Higher. Okay."

As she approached, Mitchell handed her the picture while he tapped the wall with his middle finger and listened. "You can't hang it here. There's no stud."

"But that's where it looks the best."

He tapped the wall again. "This isn't a good spot."

She exhaled another of her cute little sighs, crossed her arms, tapped her foot, and said nothing.

"All right, all right," he mumbled. "Do you have an anchor?"

"I'm not parking a ship. I'm only hanging a small picture. Give it to me and I'll do it."

Mitchell sighed back, but she still didn't get the hint, so he pulled the nail out of his mouth and dug the point into the wall to mark the place. Carolyn stood a couple of feet away holding the picture while he readied himself to hammer in the nail. He tapped the nail a few times gently with the hammer then took a good swing at it.

And hit his finger.

He clenched his teeth together and groaned, tucked the hammer into his armpit, and grasped his aching finger with his other hand. He hunched over and squeezed both hands between his knees.

Behind him, he heard a loud thunk on the hardwood floor and the crack of breaking glass followed by tinkling as the pieces bounced then settled in jagged shards around their feet.

Mitchell restrained himself from jumping up and down on one foot, while in his mind's eye, he pictured the frame falling on Carolyn's foot or her feet being cut by glass projectiles.

Both spoke in unison.

"Mitchell! Are you—"

"Carolyn! Are you—"

She stood in one spot, staring at him with her mouth open, the frame on the floor, her feet surrounded by broken glass. He supposed if she'd hurt herself, he should be able to tell by now. So far, he was the only one who'd been injured, and it was self-inflicted. He unclenched his knees and lowered the hammer to the floor. "I'll be okay. How about you?"

"Me? I'm fine. You're the one with the injury. Let me see that." She started to take a step toward him.

"No!" he shouted before she could move, and she froze on the spot. Mitchell lowered his voice. "I've got shoes on. You'll cut your feet if you walk in this. Don't move."

Mitchell crunched through the glass, scooped her off her feet, cradling her in his arms, then walked toward what he hoped was the kitchen.

She threw her arms around his neck to hold herself up. "Mitchell! What are you doing?"

"I'm escorting you to safety, milady."

"Really," she grumbled, squirming within his grasp. "I don't think—"

"Hush. I'm being gallant. Indulge me."

Her lips clamped shut. Mitchell didn't think she'd respond well if he laughed at her outrage, so he bit his tongue and continued.

On his way through the living room, he passed a photograph of a colorful sunset over a lake. Inscribed on a plaque embedded in the frame was a verse out of the book of Psalms, about the beauty of the Lord. On the coffee table he saw a Bible, opened and facedown to save the place where she was reading.

Mitchell smiled. The pain he'd suffered was well worth the result of his discovery.

His next goal would be to check out the guy she was dating and find out how serious the relationship was. She had very carefully avoided saying she was going to marry him when Mitchell asked, which gave him the answer he wanted.

He stood in the kitchen, looking around the walls for other hints of her faith. He saw plenty of cows all over the place, but he doubted she was into idol worship.

"You can put me down any time, Mitchell."

"Oops."

Gently, he lowered her feet to the kitchen floor.

She walked away as if he were on fire. "If you'll excuse me for a minute, I'll sweep up the glass, and then we can get started with your cooking lesson."

He followed her and removed the broom and dustpan from her hand. "I'm wearing shoes. I'll do it."

※

Carolyn watched Mitchell disappear down the hall with the broom in his hand. He didn't fool her. She doubted he was the least bit domestically inclined, so the only reason she could see why he was insisting on sweeping up was that he was trying to impress her. Knowing that, she tried not to be impressed.

She couldn't believe she'd dropped her picture, especially after all the money she paid to have it custom framed. She'd been so scared that Mitchell had seriously hurt himself she hadn't realized she'd dropped it until she heard the bang as it hit the floor.

He soon returned with the dustpan full of broken glass, which he dumped in the garbage.

"Thanks, Mitchell. Now let's start on your cooking lesson."

Mitchell retrieved his shopping bags, dumped the contents on her table, and proudly showed Carolyn his first batch of utensils and kitchen paraphernalia, claiming he wanted to be sure he'd bought the correct things before he removed the packaging. At her approval, he returned the bags to the door, and they were ready to start his next lesson.

Carolyn could barely concentrate. Today Mitchell insisted on doing everything with a minimum of assistance, only asking her when he wasn't sure of what it was he was supposed to do, which wasn't as often as their previous lesson. Normally this wouldn't have bothered her, but every time she showed him something new, he stood too close for her comfort.

When the lesson was completed, Carolyn packaged the food that wasn't eaten, insisting Mitchell take it all home with him. He set the bag on the counter and held the top open as she lowered the full containers inside, but before she was finished, he reached inside and grasped her hands. Slowly, he lifted them out of the bag and rubbed his thumbs on the undersides of her wrists, causing a shiver that made her heart skip a beat then start up in double time. All she could do was stare up at him, while he continued his gentle massage and smiled down at her.

After a few minutes of silence, he cleared his throat. "Is that blue container the one that has that stuff with that splatty glop on top in it?"

Carolyn tried not to stammer as she spoke. "That stuff is called toast points."

"Yeah. That. So that means the white container has those round things in it, right?"

"Those round things are called pastry cheese balls."

"Yeah, those, too. And where's that list of more stuff you said I should buy? Did you add one of those pastry-mixing contraptions? And don't you do that sighing thing again."

Carolyn clamped her lips shut and yanked her hands back. Her breathing didn't feel normal, and she didn't like it. "The list is in the bag, and yes, I did. Now I think it's time for you to leave."

"First there's something I wanted to talk to you about."

She checked her watch. "It's late. We can talk about it at class on Tuesday."

"But—"

"I think that's best. Let me see you to the door."

She scooped up a bag, prompting him to do the same. She led him to the door, where she handed him the bag she had carried. "Good night, Mitchell."

He shuffled everything into one hand, and instead of leaving, he slowly and gently brushed his fingers across her cheek. Carolyn closed her eyes. The moment was perfect for a good-night kiss that part of her wanted and part of her didn't.

"Good night, Carolyn." He dropped his hand, picked up the bags of supplies he'd left next to the door, and walked out.

A small sigh escaped as Carolyn watched him go. It was nothing she could put her finger on, but something deep inside of her found Mitchell interesting. However, from their conversation during the food preparation today, she knew more about his family than she knew about him. Other than that his sister was getting married soon, the only thing she knew about him was his age and that he attended church services. In some ways, she would have liked the age spread to be the other way around, but no amount of wishing he were older could make it so. She wished she knew why he wanted to see her so badly—but then decided the answer was obvious.

She was the cooking teacher, and he needed to learn how to cook in a hurry. He was simply being nice to her because she was doing him a favor. In a convoluted sort of way, she found it disappointing but, considering all else, for the best.

She didn't want to like him. Earlier, she thought he'd taken an interest in her favorite Bible verse, which she had on display on her living room wall. If she hadn't been in his arms at the time, she would have liked to talk about it, just to see where he was spiritually. Even though it was a good start, just because he said he attended church on Sundays didn't mean he was a committed Christian.

Not that it mattered. Except for class, she had no intention of seeing him again.

Carolyn shut the door, but instead of walking away, she pressed both palms into it, then leaned her forehead against the cool wood.

She prayed daily for God to send her a Mr. Right, a man who would be about five or six years older than her, educated, well into a successful career, and understand that her career as a teacher was important to her, too. Not that she was getting desperate, but soon she was going to be thirty-three years old, and she was more than ready to settle down. She wanted to fall in love with a man who would love and cherish her as much as she would him.

She needed a mature man who was a strong leader but was flexible and open to God's direction. Carolyn knew she had a tendency to be a bit headstrong, so she needed a mate who wouldn't stand back and let her make all the decisions or carry all the responsibility just because it was easier for him. But at the same time, she didn't want a man with whom every decision would be a battle. She needed a man who was regal and reserved and with the strength of character to stand by her side and be her equal partner in all things.

She didn't know much about Mitchell, but Mitchell was not that man. Even though she enjoyed her time with him, she doubted Mitchell could be serious about anything. There were more important things in life than simply having fun.

It didn't matter, anyway. She wouldn't see Mitchell until next class, on Tuesday, four days away, which was as it should be.

❈

Carolyn flicked off the vacuum cleaner switch and cocked her head to listen.

Sure enough, it was the doorbell she'd heard. Since she wasn't expecting anyone, she had no idea who it could possibly be.

When she checked through the peephole, a gorgeous green eye stared back.

She ran her hands through her hair to straighten it then opened the door.

"Hello, Mitchell. What are you doing here?"

He held a large, flat package. "I brought you something. Mind if I come in?" He grinned and stepped past her into the house without waiting for her reply.

Carolyn followed him to the couch and waited while he sat and tore away the white tissue paper surrounding whatever was in his hand. As soon as he made a large enough opening, he pulled out the newly framed needlepoint they'd tried to hang last night.

When she couldn't find it, she had assumed Mitchell had put it someplace safe and it would turn up later. It hadn't occurred to her that he'd taken it home last night, along with everything else.

He held it up for her to see. A shiny new piece of glass protected her work.

Her hands flew to her cheeks. "Oh, Mitchell! You shouldn't have!"

He grinned and, without comment, walked to the wall where the nail poked out, barely staying in place. "Where's the hammer?"

Still trying to let what he'd done sink in, Carolyn ran to the kitchen and grabbed her hammer off the pantry shelf. She nearly dropped it when she turned around to see Mitchell standing in the doorway.

"You keep your hammer in the kitchen?"

"So? You keep your electric mixer in the garage."

He laughed. "Touché." He removed the hammer from her hands and returned to the living room, proceeded to bang in some kind of plastic doodad, then tapped the nail into the center of it without mishap. This time he'd left the frame on the floor, leaning against the wall. When the nail was securely in place, he balanced and leveled the picture then stood beside her to admire it. "That sure is a pretty scene. I think I've been there. It's around Tofino, right? Did you do it yourself?"

"Yes, I did."

The project had taken her nearly a year to complete. She'd had a favorite photograph from her last vacation made into a needlepoint pattern, which she'd worked on diligently. That day had been the first and only time she'd seen a whale in the wild, and she'd managed to get a picture of it at just the right moment. The whale had jumped out of the water and made a big splash upon reentry against the scenic backdrop of a gorgeous bay lined with rocks and trees and seagulls in the misty blue sky overhead. The photograph was beautiful, but adding the texture of needlepoint made it a treasure. Someday, when she married and had children, she would eventually pass her cherished masterpiece on as a family heirloom.

"I don't know what to say."

Mitchell shrugged his shoulders. "It wasn't a big deal. Jake works for a place that makes windows, so I got him to make a piece that fit. He ended up using a piece out of the scrap bin, so all it cost me was a donut." He paused and grinned. "Of course I made him buy the coffee."

"You made him. . ." Her voice trailed off. "You've got to be kidding."

"It was his break."

She opened her mouth, but Mitchell quickly spoke up. "None of that sighing stuff. Just smile pretty and say, 'Thanks, Mitchell.'"

Carolyn pushed her glasses up the bridge of her nose with her finger. He would never know the restraint it took not to make that deep sigh.

Actually, she rather admired him for being so resourceful, but she wasn't going to admit it.

"Thank you, Mitchell."

He smirked. "Good. That's what I wanted to hear."

"I wasn't expecting you today, as you can tell." Carolyn jerked her head over her shoulder to indicate her vacuum cleaner in the middle of the living room, in addition to the dust rag still on the mantel. "I suppose I could think of something we could do as a cooking lesson."

"I'm not here for a cooking lesson."

Carolyn was touched that he would have made the special trip just to deliver her repaired needlepoint frame. In order to be polite, as well as to show her gratitude, she was about to ask him if she could make him a cup of coffee when he reached toward her, picked up one of her hands, then started massaging her wrist with his thumb in the same way he had last night before he left.

Her knees turned to jelly.

"I'm here to take you out for dinner."

"But—"

"And if you say one word about paying, you'll hurt my feelings, and you wouldn't want to do that, would you?"

"Well, I—"

"So lock up and let's get going so we can get a cozy table for two in a nice, dark corner."

"But I—"

"There are a few things I'd like to talk to you about, and none of it will have anything to do with cooking because, Carolyn, this is a date."

Before she could open her mouth to protest, he raised her hand, lowered his head, and kissed her palm. No man had ever done that before, and she froze at the soft touch of his lips on her skin. Carolyn stood with her mouth hanging open and her heart pounding as he smiled at her. She still couldn't imagine why Mitchell was doing this, but this opened up an opportunity to learn more about him—if she could get her brain to function properly.

Carolyn yanked her hand away and backed up a step. She ran her trembling fingers through her hair and straightened her glasses. "Excuse me. I have to change my T-shirt. I'll be right back."

Carolyn hustled to her bedroom and selected a baggy sweater to go with her jeans, quickly ran a brush through her hair, and returned to the living room, where Mitchell stood gazing at her needlepoint.

When the time came to eat, she would insist on pausing to say grace over their meal. That would tell her how willing he was to show he was a Christian in public.

Still, no matter where he stood in his Christianity, the bottom line was that he wasn't the type of man she saw as a suitable mate. Even though she and Hank didn't have what she could even remotely call a steady relationship, he appeared to be all the things she was looking for in a man. All the things Mitchell was not.

But if she had to have a reason for being with him, she knew Mitchell would make her laugh.

Carolyn sucked in a deep breath for strength. "I'm ready. Let's go."

Chapter 4

arolyn found herself sitting much too close to Mitchell, which was exactly what she wanted to avoid. She had nixed his suggestion of a quiet, cozy table for two at a small, intimate restaurant. Instead, they'd left his car at the Park and Ride and took the monorail to the crowded and busy public market.

Because of the Saturday crowd, the last available seats in their car were the sideways benches. As more people crammed themselves in, the seating became tighter and tighter until they were pressed together from knee to shoulder.

Carolyn refused to look at Mitchell. Instead, she watched two small children, heads plastered to the window, enjoying the ride. Mitchell barely had to move his head, and she could feel his breath on her cheek as he spoke directly into her ear.

"Those kids appear to be fascinated with the view."

She didn't know about the kids, but Carolyn didn't often take the monorail, and she found it fascinating.

The children's giggles set off a chord of longing deep inside her. With no marriage prospects in sight, Carolyn was starting to worry she might never have children of her own. She'd spoken with Hank casually a few times about marriage, and even though most men Hank's age were married, Hank had made it clear he wasn't quite ready to settle down. Up until recently she'd been satisfied to wait, but with her birthday coming soon, even though she wasn't going to get married just for the sake of being married, it was another warning that time was not standing still. She was the last of her friends still single, and her biological clock was starting to tick.

When more people exited than entered on the downtown stops, it allowed Carolyn to shuffle a few inches away from Mitchell until they reached their destination.

Throngs of people packed the aisles of the marketplace, which was a three-story building lined with booths and tables with sellers hawking goods from handmade jewelry to farm-fresh produce and everything else in between. The place looked fascinating, and she knew she could spend hours here.

Carolyn tugged on Mitchell's sleeve to get him to bend down so she could speak to him without raising her voice too much. "I can't believe you suggested this."

He straightened and shrugged his shoulders. "I come here every time I have company from out of town. We make it a day trip and take the monorail because it's so different and there's always neat stuff to see. Since it's Saturday, they'll have some kind of entertainment outside, too. If we'd left earlier, we could have gone to see a movie at the IMAX theater, but we'll only have time to look around here and have something to eat before we have to go home. It would be different if we'd brought my car instead of using the public transport."

Time flew by as they browsed through the tables and booths and stores.

The aroma of strawberries and fragrant fruit teased Carolyn's nose until they walked past the fish market with its pungent odor of fish and clams. As they continued, the strong smell of the raw fish changed to a delectable mixture of fresh-baked bread and cooking meat and spices, then to the heady bouquet of brewing coffee.

Carolyn didn't need to check her watch. Her stomach told her it was suppertime.

They stepped into the crowded food court. Very few tables were empty, but the area was large and people constantly flowed in and out.

"Pick what you want. My treat."

Carolyn glanced from one end of the court to the other. "There. The Greek place."

Mitchell smiled, nodded, and lowered his head to speak softly and still be heard. "A woman after my own heart," he said in her ear then straightened and guided her through the crowd.

The only table available was in the center of the crowded area. Mitchell lowered the tray to the table, and they removed their plates and plastic cutlery. "Not exactly a quiet table for two, but it will have to do."

With her food in front of her, she hesitated. This was it—the moment of truth. They were out in public, and it was time for her to broach the subject of praying in a crowd.

She opened her mouth, but before she had a chance to speak, Mitchell smiled and folded his hands on the table in front of him. "I hope you don't mind, but I always make sure to give thanks to the Lord before I eat, regardless of where I am or who I'm with, which sometimes can be awkward. Since you're a Christian, that does make things easier. Are you okay with that?"

He smiled again, waiting for her reply, but all Carolyn could do was nod. His words and actions pleased her more than they should have.

She lowered her head and folded her hands in her lap as Mitchell said a short prayer of thanks for their meal and their outing, as well as for a safe trip home.

He spoke without looking up as he pushed a tidbit of meat off the skewer with the plastic fork. "The verse you have on the plaque beneath the photograph on your living room wall made me think, so I'm going to add it to my list of favorites." He popped a french fry into his mouth and smiled.

"Thanks," she mumbled around the food in her mouth. She didn't want to know his favorite verses. The trouble was, she didn't know what she wanted.

Mitchell popped another piece of meat into his mouth. "I love this stuff," he said after swallowing. "I especially love that I didn't have to make it. Even though you seem to enjoy cooking, it still must be nice to have someone else do it sometimes."

She nodded as she pulled a piece from her own skewer. "Yes, it is nice, and you're right. This is too much preparation at the end of a long day to make for one person. I doubt I eat much different than most people, even though I make my living in the kitchen."

Mitchell froze then laid his fork down. "Hold on a minute. Before we left, I said we weren't going to talk about cooking."

She tried to bite back her grin. "You started it, not me."

"I suppose I did. Sorry."

At his grin, Carolyn stopped chewing. He really was charming in a boyish sort of way, and it was time again to remind herself not to get too involved with him. She still hadn't figured out why they were together. She was too old for him if he wanted a relationship. It wasn't like men usually sought her, because they didn't. She wasn't pretty, and though she wasn't fat, she was by no means slim. She wasn't glamorous or the life of the party type. She was just. . .ordinary.

Mitchell checked his wristwatch as he popped his last bite of food into his mouth. He took a sip of his drink and put his napkin on the table. "We should probably get going. We have a long ride ahead of us, and we shouldn't be home too late. We both have to get up for church in the morning."

Carolyn stood. "I just want to pick up a few things back at the farmers' market, then we can go."

❁

As usual, Mitchell joined Gordie and Roland in the foyer. They swapped stories of the interesting things they'd done all week then took their seats in the sanctuary.

Instead of continuing to talk until the service started, Mitchell only half paid attention to the conversation. Jake and Ellen had just entered the sanctuary. They held hands as they walked up the center aisle and separated only long enough to slide into the pew.

In just over a month, his best friend was going to marry his kid sister.

It made Mitchell wonder what it would be like to meet someone with whom he would want to spend the rest of his life.

He wasn't foolish enough to believe in love at first sight, but he sure did like Carolyn. It was sudden, but he wasn't going to let that scare him away. Instead, it intrigued him. In only a few weeks, he already knew she was different from any other woman he'd met—there was something special and right about her, and he wanted to get to know her better. Much better.

The lights dimmed, and the murmur of voices silenced as the worship leader greeted the congregation and invited everyone to stand.

Mitchell turned his attention to the words on the screen, but not before glancing quickly at Jake and Ellen, who were once more holding hands.

Right then, Mitchell knew that was what he wanted. It wasn't to sit with his goofy friends, but to sit quietly and participate in the Sunday worship service with that one special woman with whom he would spend the rest of his life.

He wondered what Carolyn was doing, who she was with, and if she was thinking of him.

❁

At the exact second Carolyn slipped her key into the lock, the phone rang.

She hadn't wanted to invite Hank inside, but with the insistent ringing, she didn't have the time to tell him good-bye without being rude, especially after he'd surprised her and treated her to lunch.

When she ran to catch the phone, Hank followed her inside, closing the door behind him.

"Hello?" she panted into the phone.

"Hi, Carolyn. Did I catch you at a bad time?"

"Mitchell?" Without thinking why, she covered the mouthpiece with her hand and stared at Hank, who was studying her needlepoint on the wall. The one Mitchell had hung yesterday.

The last thing she wanted right now was to talk to Mitchell. All throughout the church service, she couldn't stop thinking of him.

The pastor had read Psalm 50:1 and 2 as the theme of his sermon. The same verse engraved on the plaque. She glanced over and read it silently. "The Mighty One, God, the LORD, speaks and summons the earth from the rising of the sun to the place where it sets. From Zion, perfect in beauty, God shines forth."

Instead of reflecting on God's glory when the pastor read it, she thought of Mitchell's comment about adding the verse to his list of favorites.

Mitchell Farris was dangerous.

"Carolyn? Are you there?"

She fumbled with the phone. "Oops. Sorry. Yes, I'm here. I just got in the door and had to run to answer the phone. I'm a little out of breath."

As if Hank could tell she was looking at him, he turned toward her. "Carolyn? Who is it?"

Mitchell's voice immediately replied. "Who was that? Do you have company?"

"Yes, Hank is over. We went out for lunch after church."

"Oh. Does that mean you have plans for the rest of the afternoon?"

She turned to Hank. He hadn't asked her specifically to do anything, but he hadn't left her at the door when she ran in to catch the phone. But she had the feeling that if she told Mitchell she didn't have plans, he would suddenly show up on her doorstep. The only way to prevent that from happening was to do something with Hank.

"Yes. I think we'll be going out."

"Oh. I was going to ask if you wanted to join me for dinner tonight."

She wanted to tell him she'd just been out for dinner with him the day before, except that she wasn't sure if their trip to the marketplace and fast meal in the food court could be counted as dinner. "Sorry, not tonight."

"Oh."

The disappointment in his voice was almost her undoing. She didn't know if Hank was ever disappointed when she had other plans.

Good manners and guilt at his disappointment made her reply, "Maybe another time. Good-bye, Mitchell."

"I'll be sure to take you up on that. Good-bye, Carolyn."

The way he said her name made her quiver inside, like he was there, standing beside her, talking in her ear, just as he had on the monorail.

Hank's voice behind her nearly made her drop the handset.

"I see you have another picture hanging on your wall."

She struggled to control her trembling hands as she hung up the phone properly. "It's from my last vacation. Have you ever been to Tofino? I love it there."

"No, I'm not into wilderness. That's not a place I would ever go."

Mitchell had been there before. In fact, he'd recognized the bay in the picture. He liked it there, too.

Carolyn squeezed her eyes shut for a second to wipe the thought from her mind then turned to Hank. "Would you like to do something this afternoon?"

"I was going to invite you to the opening of the new wing at the art gallery."

She stifled her groan, but barely. "The art gallery?"

"Yes. Since you like scenery so much, I'm sure you'll find a few paintings there to your liking."

Carolyn glanced back at the silent phone. It was the art gallery or Mitchell Farris.

She turned and smiled at Hank. "Just let me put on shoes more suited for walking, and I'll be right with you."

"But those shoes look so nice with your dress. And they make you taller."

She almost snapped that she would change into her jeans and painting T-shirt to match her comfortable shoes but kept her control. "All right. Let's go."

Chapter 5

Carolyn watched Hank as he stood back from what could be loosely described as a sculpture and studied it in silence.

She couldn't tell if Hank liked it or not. Carolyn couldn't tell if she liked it, either, because she couldn't tell what it was supposed to be.

Mitchell would have said it looked like someone had an accident with a welder after a long day at the factory.

Carolyn squeezed her eyes shut. She didn't want to think of what Mitchell would have thought, but she couldn't help it. She was bored out of her mind.

At the market, she'd looked at everything imaginable with Mitchell—handicrafts, fruits and vegetables, jewelry, and items of every possible description. Mitchell had an amusing comment about nearly everything. She'd almost bought a little bunny ornament that had fascinated Mitchell because of its lifelike nose. In the end, she didn't want to buy anything that reminded her of Mitchell.

But now, even the bunny was preferable over the twisted metal that substituted for art.

When she thought she would fall asleep on her feet, Hank surprised her and took her out for dinner at an exquisite restaurant she'd never been to, which she supposed was an elaborate way of making up for the miserable time she'd had at the art gallery. Of course, that wasn't Hank's fault. He meant well, and she appreciated the thought.

She enjoyed Hank's company, as she always did, but when he took her home, she was glad the day was over and she could relax.

She didn't invite Hank in, so he left her with a chaste kiss on the cheek at the door.

The first thing she did was kick her shoes off her aching feet. Carolyn stretched and wiggled her toes then headed to the kitchen to make a pot of tea. On the way, the flashing light on the answering machine caught her attention.

When she hit the button, Mitchell's low voice greeted her.

"Hi, Carolyn. I see you're still not home yet. I wanted to say that I just got back from the evening service at my church, and I was thinking that it sure would have been nice if you could have been there with me. Bye."

Carolyn stared at the machine long after the beep, not knowing quite what to make of Mitchell's message.

She didn't want to wonder about Mitchell and his life outside of her classroom or how many times a week he participated in church activities. After his sister's wedding, which would be before the last class, she would never see him again.

She refused to let the knowledge cause her any regret. Instead, Carolyn sat in the kitchen with her tea, opened a cookbook, and started looking for chocolate dessert squares.

❁

Carolyn jumped at every little noise in the hallway. As usual, she'd come in early to set up for her class.

"Hi, Carolyn."

The box of rice nearly fell from her hands. "Hello, Mitchell."

He walked straight to her and removed the box from her shaking fingers then stood much too close. "I missed you on Sunday."

Although she hadn't exactly missed him, she did feel his absence after spending Friday evening and all day Saturday with him. With his odd message on Sunday, she'd expected him to call on Monday, but he hadn't.

She took the box of rice back from him. "You didn't call me yesterday," she mumbled.

"I had to work late yesterday."

"I don't know what it is you do for a living," she stammered.

"I'm a dispatcher for a commercial carrier. Monday is always a busy day, and the other guy phoned in sick on top of it, so it was nuts in there." As he spoke, he reached into his pocket and pulled something out. "I bought this for you. It's not a big deal, but I hope you like it."

Carolyn heard a little tinkle.

"Hold still," he muttered. "Let me do this before anyone walks in. I saw the cow stuff in your kitchen, and when I was in the mall today, I saw this. You can't decorate the high school kitchen with cows, but this little moo-moo can travel with you-you." She craned her neck and watched as Mitchell pinned a brooch of a small cow, complete with a mini cowbell, onto the bib of her apron.

"Thank you, Mitchell. It's so cute. I don't know what to say."

"You said thank you, and that's enough."

She kept her head lowered and studied the little cow. It was something small and rather silly but very much "Mitchell." She ran her fingers over the little black and white cow, tinkled the bell, then looked up at him. "Why are you doing this?"

He smiled and reached to touch her fingers, still resting on the cow in the corner of the bib of her apron. "Why do you think a man buys a gift for a woman?"

She didn't want to think about that. She didn't want his gifts, and she didn't want his attention. It was all wrong. It was flattering when one of her high school students had a crush on her, but those always faded quickly before she had to take steps to deal with it. This, on the other hand, was different. Mitchell was too old to be thought of as merely one of her students, but too young to be taken seriously as a suitor. Not that she could consider Mitchell a suitor, but she didn't know why he was going to so much trouble to get her attention.

Footsteps echoed on the tile floor in the hall, and Mitchell backed up, letting his hand drop to his side. He grinned then winked. "I can't wait to see what we're going to make today."

Instead of answering, she stood with her mouth open and watched Mitchell walk to the back row and sit without further comment. Last week he had been center front, where she couldn't help being keenly aware of his presence. She had thought he would do the same this time, but as usual, he never did what she expected. Now that she knew the true scope of his cooking skills, he should have been sitting center front to get the most out of the class.

When everyone had arrived, she started the lesson. Every time she moved, the tiny cowbell tinkled, reminding her where it came from. Now she didn't even have to be looking at Mitchell to be reminded of him.

When it came time to go to the kitchenettes, all the ladies smiled and giggled at his efforts. Carolyn didn't think Mitchell meant to be amusing, but she had to give him credit for accepting everyone's teasing about his ineptness in the kitchen with a smile.

By the time the class ended, even though he'd made progress, he still struggled with most of the basic skills.

There was only one solution.

Mitchell Farris needed more remedial help.

❁

Mitchell glanced at the different cow decorations all over Carolyn's kitchen as she paged through one of her many cookbooks. He'd found a message from Carolyn on his answering machine, telling him he still needed more help with his cooking skills. He didn't know what he'd done so wrong this time, but he was glad for the opportunity it gave him to see her again so soon.

"I know I said I wanted the same squares for dessert as the coffee shop's, but if it's going to be hard, I can always pick something else. I think I'm already in over my head."

"They're really not hard to make. I saw a recipe the other day for something similar. I just can't remember which book it's in."

Mitchell plunked his elbows on the table and rested his chin in his palms then crossed his ankles under the table. "I can take you out for coffee, and we can bring another piece home and use that for a sample."

She flipped another page. "Nice try, but you came here for help with your cooking. We're not going out. The only time I go out on Wednesday night is to Bible study, which I'm obviously missing tonight. I couldn't live with myself if I skipped Bible study to go out for coffee."

"Yeah. Tonight is my home-group meeting, too. Tell you what. Why don't we do the cooking tomorrow, and we can go to the study meeting together? You've already met Gordie and Roland. Jake will be there, as well as my sister, Ellen."

"I'd rather go to my own," she mumbled under her breath, barely loud enough for him to hear, as she flipped another page.

"You would? Well, okay. That would be nice. I'd love to meet your friends."

She froze with the page in midturn, still sticking up in the air. "Meet my friends?"

Mitchell stood. "Yes, that sounds good. Maybe next week you can come to my study meeting, but for this week, I accept your invitation. That was a great idea."

"But—"

"I parked behind you in the driveway, so we can take my car. You'll just have to give me directions."

"But—"

"And then how about if after it's over, we go out for coffee on the way home, and I'll buy an extra chocolate dessert thingy so you can compare pictures."

"I..." Her voice trailed off, a loud sigh escaped, and her whole body sagged.

Mitchell tried to contain his smile.

"All right," she mumbled. "Did you bring your Bible?"

"Nope—left it at home. I hadn't expected this, but it's a nice surprise. I'll just sit beside you so I can peek over your shoulder."

"You can borrow one of mine," she said then checked her watch. "We should leave now. Let me get the Bibles and my purse."

When they arrived, a hush fell over the room. Mitchell felt all eyes on him as they walked into their host's home.

Carolyn smiled graciously when she introduced him around, and they sat together on the couch until the leader began.

Mitchell enjoyed what the leader had to say, and it gave him a new perspective on the section they read. He wished he had his own Bible with him so he could have made notes.

When the study ended and it was time to mingle, he could tell everyone was trying to figure out his connection to Carolyn and why they were together.

Mitchell wanted to know the answer, too. He knew how he felt about Carolyn and what he wanted their connection to be. His biggest problem was to get her to take him seriously, but he didn't know how to do that—short of getting down on one knee and proposing, and they were nowhere near that stage in their relationship. He wasn't even sure what they had could be called a relationship.

After consuming too much coffee, Mitchell slipped away to use the restroom. He was just around the corner on his way back when he heard Carolyn's voice.

His feet skidded to a halt. He didn't want to eavesdrop, but he also didn't want to embarrass Carolyn by dropping into the middle of the conversation, especially if it was about him. He stayed where he was, out of their sight.

"It sure was a surprise to see you walk in with another man," a female voice said in hushed tones. "What's going on?"

"Going on? Nothing is going on. Mitchell and I are just friends."

Mitchell held his breath for a second. He wanted to be much more than just friends, but he supposed that being "just friends" was better than being "just a student."

The other voice hushed even more. "What about Hank?"

Mitchell heard a shuffle on the carpet, indicating someone else was coming. Not wanting to be caught listening, he stiffened, gathered his courage, and continued walking. The lady with whom Carolyn was talking blushed profusely at the sight of him, causing Carolyn to turn around and acknowledge his return.

Carolyn turned to him. "Are you ready to go?"

His ego made him want to slip his arm around Carolyn's waist to show what kind of friend he wanted to be, but Mitchell didn't think she would take kindly to that. And contrary to Carolyn's words that nothing had changed, everything had changed. Whoever Hank was, he now had competition.

Not long after they'd first met, he'd asked her point-blank if she was going to marry Hank, and all she said was that it wasn't any of his business. Her reaction gave him the impression first that the answer was negative and, most important, that she wasn't in love with Hank.

Now it was his business.

He smiled politely at the woman whose name he couldn't remember. "Thank you for opening your home. You and your husband have been gracious hosts. Please tell him I enjoyed his teaching and I hope to be back again soon."

Before either she or Carolyn could say anything, he hustled Carolyn out the door and to his car.

After they were seated at the coffee shop, Mitchell did his best to make cheerful, meaningless conversation, but he really wanted to bring up the subject of her relationship with Hank. Just when he was despairing of ever getting more information, Gordie and Roland walked in, straight to their table, and sat down.

"Would you care to join us?" he said as sarcastically as he could, not caring that he was being rude.

Gordie ignored him and turned to Carolyn. "You know, I finally figured out where I've seen you before. You're the home economics teacher at Central High. My brother is in your class this year. Steven Reid. Do you know him?"

Carolyn's eyes widened and her face paled. "Yes," she mumbled, "I know him. He's a nice kid."

Mitchell's favorite dessert turned to a lump of cardboard in his mouth. The last thing he needed right now was for Carolyn to be reminded that he and his friends were young enough to have a brother in her high school class.

He kicked Gordie under the table, but Gordie kept talking. "Steven has quite a crush on you, but I guess you know that."

The color in her face changed from a sickly gray to a deep blush. She picked up her coffee cup and stared down into it. "Yes. It's very flattering, but soon Steven will forget about me and focus on one of the girls his own age."

The word *boys* echoed in his head. Mitchell thunked his cup to the table and ran one hand through his hair. "Steven's a lot younger than we are."

"Yeah," Roland said. "I think you started teaching the year we graduated, right?"

Gordie closed one eye and started counting on his fingers. "Yeah. Too bad I didn't take cooking that year."

Mitchell gulped down the last of his coffee. He wanted to leave and get away from his friends, but Carolyn still had coffee and half her dessert to finish. He turned and made glaring eye contact with each of his friends. "Don't you two have someplace else to go?"

Gordie and Roland blinked and stared at Mitchell.

"No. Why?" Gordie asked.

Roland grabbed Gordie's arm and encouraged him to stand. He nodded and smiled again at Carolyn. "We were just on our way out." He gave Gordie a pull to get him moving then escorted him toward the door.

Mitchell couldn't help hearing them whisper as they walked away.

"What's he doing with the home ec teacher?"

"Gordie, you doofus. No wonder you're still single."

"What do you mean?"

The door closed, ending any further insight into Gordie's love life.

Mitchell quickly turned to Carolyn. He'd thought his worst problem was Hank, but he was wrong. Carolyn wouldn't look at him. She kept playing with a crumb on her plate, not touching the other half of her dessert. He didn't know what to say, so he pushed his mug and plate to the center of the table and stood. "Are you finished?"

She nodded, and they left in silence.

The ride home was short, but he didn't want a cloud hanging over their heads, and he certainly couldn't leave her for the night without saying something.

He walked Carolyn to her door. When she unlocked it, he didn't wait to be invited but quickly stepped inside. She blinked when he closed the door behind him but otherwise didn't speak.

"Carolyn, ignore them. It doesn't matter."

"It does matter. You could have been my student. This is so wrong."

He stepped closer. "That has nothing to do with anything. We're both adults now. I know you feel awkward about it, but it really doesn't matter, and it doesn't affect how I feel about you."

She looked up at him. As she raised her head, her glasses slipped down the bridge of her nose. He shuffled closer still, until he was directly in front of her, and gently pushed her glasses back into place. Instead of letting his hand drop, he cradled her face in his palm. She'd never looked so pretty or so fragile as she did right now. All her doubts showed in her eyes.

He wanted to find a way to tell her that age didn't matter to him; it was Carolyn the person who mattered to him.

She made one of her cute little sighs, but this time, for the first time, he was touching her when she did it. The movement and the feeling of her breath on his hand touched something deep inside him.

He couldn't stop himself. Mitchell rested his other hand on the side of her waist, pulled her closer, lowered his head, and kissed her. She felt small and delicate in his arms, and her lips were soft and gentle. He was lost. What little was left of his heart left him, and he kissed Carolyn the way a man should kiss a woman he was falling in love with.

When they separated, he couldn't take his hand off her cheek, nor could he make his voice work properly. His words came out too low and gravelly, but he was past caring. "Since we didn't have one today, can we have a cooking lesson tomorrow? At my house this time?"

His heart seemed to stop beating in the wait for her reply.

"Yes," she finally whispered.

Mitchell smiled then slid his index finger down her cheek and off the side of her chin. He backed up a step, making the separation complete. "Great. Tomorrow then. Good night."

He walked away before she could change her mind.

During the drive home, a million thoughts cascaded through his brain, but nothing came together.

Jake and Ellen were in the living room watching television when he walked in. For the first time, he didn't stop to chat. He grunted a greeting and continued into his bedroom without breaking stride, shut the door behind him, threw his clothes on the floor, and climbed into bed.

All he could do was stare up at the ceiling in the dark.

A knock sounded on his door, but it didn't open. Jake's voice drifted through the wood. "Mitch? Are you okay?"

"Yeah. I just need to think," he called back then rolled over onto his stomach.

The problem was, he didn't know what to think.

Mitchell closed his eyes and buried his face in his pillow. "Lord, what should I do?" he said aloud.

He couldn't deny that Carolyn had many hesitations about going out with him, most of which concerned his age, but there was also her mysterious relationship with Hank.

He could have been angry with Gordie and Roland for making the difference in their ages so obvious, but something else would have happened to bring it up. They'd only sped up the timing of when he had to deal with it. Unfortunately, when he tried to talk to her, he was the only one with anything to say. Mitchell didn't consider that a good sign.

He rolled onto his back and stared at the ceiling again.

Regardless, Carolyn had still kissed him. The experience was everything he thought it would be and more. He closed his eyes, remembering, then stared back at the ceiling.

Whatever happened with that kiss, there was still the major hurdle of Hank between them. He took solace in the fact that Carolyn would never have kissed him if she were truly serious about Hank.

Mitchell rolled over and punched his pillow. Even if she wasn't serious about Hank, the way things were now, she wasn't serious about Mitchell, either.

He couldn't change his age, but in order to compete with an older man, he could work on maturity. He hadn't considered settling down before now because he hadn't met the right woman. But now that he'd met Carolyn, he wanted what Jake and Ellen had. Commitment. Stability. A shared faith.

Love.

He didn't know if it was possible to really fall in love so soon, but the only way to know for sure would be to spend more time with her. Serious, quality time. In order to do that, Carolyn would have to be more receptive to seeing him instead of him forcing invitations where they really weren't wanted.

There was nothing he could do to make her want to see him, but he knew Someone who could give him guidance.

Mitchell closed his eyes and began to pray.

Chapter 6

Carolyn knocked on Mitchell's door and waited. His dog barked once then became silent as the door opened.

Another man stood in the doorway, holding Mitchell's dog by the collar. He was about Mitchell's age, but he, too, was a good-looking man. She thought of Gordie and Roland and wondered if Mitchell had any short, ugly friends. Or any that were older.

He smiled. "You must be Carolyn. I'm Jake. Mitchell had to work late. He called a little while ago to say he was on his way home, and he wanted me to ask if you'd mind waiting if you got here first."

"I don't mind at all." She stepped inside and closed the door behind her.

"Great." Jake released the dog, who sniffed up at her then left.

Now that his hands were free, Carolyn reached forward to shake Jake's hand. "I'm pleased to meet you, Jake. So you're the one getting married. Congratulations. I also want to thank you for replacing the glass in my needlepoint frame."

Jake smiled. "You're welcome. Nice picture, by the way. That means you're the brave soul who's trying to teach Mitch to cook something besides hot dogs. Good luck."

After experiencing firsthand the extent of Mitchell's cooking skills, she perfectly understood Jake's not-so-subtle wisecrack. She grinned to herself, knowing how much Mitchell had improved, but at the same time knowing Mitchell still had a lot to learn in the remaining four short weeks until the big day.

"Does he often have to work late?"

"Actually, yes, he does. His overtime hours are unpredictable because they always involve some crisis that can't be left until the next day. He never gets any advance warning or notice. It just happens." Jake checked his watch. "And speaking of late, I hate to be rude, but I have to take care of something for the wedding, and I'm already late. Would you like to watch television or something? Mitch shouldn't be much longer."

"That's fine; I don't mind."

Jake escorted her to the couch, turned on the television, handed her the remote, then left.

Carolyn started flipping through the channels when Mitchell's dog, who she knew was inaptly named Killer, entered the room. Killer looked at Carolyn, sniffed once in the air, then jumped up on the other end of the couch, curled up, and fell asleep, apparently quite comfortable with her presence.

Carolyn's finger froze on the remote's button while she stared at his sleeping dog, wondering how much longer she would have to wait for Mitchell to come home. She couldn't help being impressed that he was apparently dependable on the job. Still, she didn't know if the reason he had to often work late was because he was so good at what he did that the company depended on him in time of trouble or if he was the junior man and got stuck with all the dirty work no one else wanted.

Before she could think about it any further, the screech of tires sounded in the driveway. She stood just as Mitchell burst through the door.

At the sight of him, her hands flew to her mouth to cover her gasp.

"Don't worry, the blood's not mine. I'm fine." Mitchell was covered in dirt, his hair was streaked with a mixture of blue and orange, and a smear of blood marred the front of his shirt.

"You don't look fine."

He shrugged his shoulders. "One of the guys in the warehouse had an accident, and I had to take him to the ER, then drive him home. He's fine. It's just some heavy bruising and a few stitches. Do you have any idea how to get blood out of upholstery?"

"What about you?"

"I need a shower, but I think I should take care of my car first."

"Are you sure you're okay?"

He ran his fingers through his hair, studied his hand, then rubbed his fingers together. "Except for my hair, I'm fine. It'll probably wash out, but if not, I'll have the most trendy hair color at the wedding, don't you think?"

She blinked and stared at him. Now that the panic was over and she knew he was unhurt, she could look at him more objectively. "What is that? Or should I not ask?"

"It's some kind of dye or pigment used in paints. I don't know if it will come out."

"I think you should wash it right away, just in case. If you'll get me a sponge and a bucket, I'll see what I can do about your car."

While Mitchell was in the shower, Carolyn did the best she could to sop the blood out of the passenger seat. It wasn't a particularly expensive car, but it was sporty and fairly new, and she hated to see the interior spoiled, especially as a result of his helping someone else.

Only a small discoloration remained by the time Mitchell appeared.

He ran his fingers through his wet hair. "I didn't get much of the color out, but I'll need a haircut before the wedding, anyway. How's my car?"

She tossed the sponge into the bucket. "Pretty good. I think if we rent a steam cleaner and buy a good upholstery shampoo, the blood should all come out. It helps to get at something like this right away."

Since she didn't want to sit in the wet seat, they took her car to the supermarket to rent the unit.

"Now that we have a few minutes, can you tell me what happened?"

"The forklift driver tipped over a piece of machinery onto a skid of paint. Ted tried to run out of the way when everything toppled, but he didn't quite make it. I've got a first aid certificate, so I did my best to contain the bleeding and took him to the hospital myself rather than calling for an ambulance, since it wasn't life threatening. The next shift is going to clean up the mess, but tomorrow I have to fill out the accident and worker's compensation forms." He turned to her. "I also have to do an internal investigation on this. I used to drive the forklift before I got promoted to dispatcher. I know from experience that either the forklift driver was being irresponsible or the machinery wasn't packaged properly. It shouldn't have tipped over so easily."

"Does this kind of thing happen often? You had to work late one day last week, too."

"No. It's something different every time. I have to consider it an adventure or else it would drive me crazy. Did I ever tell you about the time one of the trucks got wedged in the underpass in rush hour?"

As they worked to wash the seat, he told her amusing stories of the various disasters that happened in his workplace over the years that sounded funny now, although she doubted they were even the least bit amusing at the time.

Before long, the seat was as good as new. After they returned the steam cleaner,

Carolyn pulled into the driveway behind his car and checked her wristwatch.

"I think it's a little late to be starting a cooking lesson."

Mitchell turned his wrist and also checked the time. "I guess. What about tomorrow?"

"Tomorrow is Friday."

"Oops. You're right. But if you don't have other plans, I'd appreciate it if you could come over tomorrow and we'll try again."

Carolyn closed one eye and tilted one corner of her mouth to think. She didn't know if spending so much time with Mitchell was wise, but she'd committed herself to helping him. As his teacher, if he couldn't do as he'd promised, his failure would also be her failure. She also wanted to bring him up to the skill level of the rest of the class—for the sake of her other students.

She grasped the steering wheel with both hands, sighed, and turned to him. "Your house or mine?"

❧

Carolyn knocked on Mitchell's door. As usual, the dog barked once and the door opened.

Carolyn tried not to let her mouth hang open. "Don't you think you're a little over-dressed for a cooking lesson?"

One dimple appeared in Mitchell's left cheek along with his lopsided smile. Instead of jeans and a T-shirt, he wore gray dress pants and a neatly pressed white shirt. Leather shoes replaced his worn sneakers, and his hair was meticulously gelled into a very attractive style. Carolyn narrowed her eyes and looked closer. She could still see some of the blue and orange from the day before, but somehow he'd managed to hide most of the damage. Also, unlike any other evening, night school classes included, he had recently shaved.

"I'm really hungry, and I'm tired of eating snacks. I want real food, so I thought maybe we could go out."

Carolyn crossed her arms and tapped her foot. "You don't intend to do any cooking tonight, do you?"

"I do so, but I gotta eat. Don't you believe me?" He splayed his fingers, placed his palm over his heart, and pretended to look wounded.

She wasn't falling for it. "No."

"Well, you're wrong. I just wanted to go somewhere nice, not too fancy, but not the local hamburger joint, and then we'll come home and get down to business. Please?"

Carolyn let out a long, exasperated sigh.

"You're doing that sighing thing again. I thought we could go to the new steakhouse. I've heard good things about it, although I haven't been there yet."

"All right, but you had better be prepared to do some cooking when we get back."

Mitchell reached into the closet and yanked out his jacket then stepped outside.

He opened the car door and waited for her to get in. "You look nice, by the way."

She wore her comfortable flat shoes and her denim skirt and a fuzzy pink sweater, which would be fine for where they were going; but for once, Mitchell was dressed better than she was. It felt strange. "Thank you. You look nice, too."

Not only did he look good, he smelled good. In the confines of the car, she could smell a spicy aftershave or cologne—something she'd never noticed about him before, which made her suspect that in his mind this was a date. And, contrary to her claims, she had indeed fallen for it.

When they arrived at the restaurant, he was the perfect gentleman.

Combining his new cultivated appearance with his polished manners, he looked and acted older, which was a perverse reminder of how young he really was.

As they talked, in the back of her mind, Carolyn thought of her own life and what she was doing when she was twenty-four years old. That was nine years ago, and she was just beginning her teaching career. So much time had passed, and she'd grown up a lot in those years.

When the waiter returned with their meals, Mitchell closed his eyes and bowed his head to pause for a word of prayer before they ate.

Something in Carolyn's heart went haywire. The young man before her, now dressed in his good clothes, ready to pray in public completely unashamed, was the same man who had given her a silly piece of tinkly cow costume jewelry only days ago.

Cow jewelry.

Hank would have given her diamonds. Diamonds and real gold were in Hank's nature. Mature. Dignified. Conservative.

Carolyn forced herself to stop staring at Mitchell and closed her eyes. Mitchell would never be conservative. It wasn't in him. He wasn't even wearing a tie to go out, which made her suspect that the only ties he owned had cartoon characters on them.

She recalled the three-piece suit with a matching monochrome tie Hank had worn to the last Christmas banquet. Hank was thirty-nine, six years older than she would be on her upcoming birthday. About six months ago, Carolyn had noticed a few gray hairs around Hank's temples and mentioned it to him. The next time she saw him, they were gone.

Carolyn didn't know how Mitchell had hidden most of the blue and orange, but it made her wonder if he would bother trying to hide any gray hairs when the time came. Instead, she suspected Mitchell would flaunt them as a sign of alleged maturity.

When Mitchell started to pray softly, Carolyn closed off her thoughts of Hank, prayed with Mitchell, and concentrated on having a lovely meal with him.

After the plates were cleared, the waiter returned to ask if they wanted dessert.

Mitchell shook his head. "No, thank you. We'll have the bill, please."

When the waiter left, Carolyn turned to Mitchell. "You could have ordered something if you wanted."

"We have to get back. You still have to show me enough so I don't make a fool of myself on Tuesday."

"Pardon me?"

"The cooking lesson? Isn't that why you came over in the first place?"

"You mean you really want to cook tonight?"

"Didn't I say that earlier?"

Carolyn struggled not to raise her hands to cover the heat in her cheeks. "I'm so sorry, Mitchell. I didn't believe you. I don't know what to say."

"This has been a real treat, not to have to grab something at a fast-food place. This isn't the kind of place a guy can go to eat alone. I got to eat a real supper today, and I enjoyed it."

She hadn't thought about what a single man usually ate. "You must eat fast food a lot, don't you?"

His cheeks turned red. Carolyn thought it quite endearing to see a man blush. "Most single guys do, you know."

As soon as they got back to Mitchell's house, he excused himself to change. Within minutes, except for the perfect hair and clean-shaven chin, he was back to the Mitchell she was used to.

Carolyn rolled up her sleeves and showed him how to properly separate eggs and beat the whites until they were just the right consistency. She then made him fold them into the mixture properly, being careful not to stir, resulting in the perfect texture.

"Is all this really necessary?" he grumbled as he spooned the filling into the pastry shells she had shown him how to make because he didn't know how to use a pastry cutter.

"As I recall, you're the one who said he would prepare all the food for the party rather than getting a caterer."

He mumbled something she couldn't make out, and she chose not to ask him to repeat himself.

The baked cuplets were as good as any she could have done herself, and she told him so. She struggled not to laugh as he tried to downplay the pride in his accomplishment.

"And on that note, it's time for me to go home."

"I'll walk you out."

He followed her outside to the driveway.

"It's a gentleman's duty to escort a lady to safety. If I can't escort you home, the best I can do is see you safely to your car."

Carolyn unlocked the car door and stood back before opening it. "This really isn't necessary."

"But it is. I won't be able to see you tomorrow because we have the fittings for the tuxes."

She hadn't intended on seeing him tomorrow, regardless. "But—"

Before she had the chance to move, Mitchell stepped closer and cupped her face in his hands. He leaned down until their noses were almost touching, and his voice dropped to a low whisper. "I'll miss you, Carolyn."

And then he kissed her, softly and gently and so fast that she didn't have a chance to respond. When he backed up, he let his hands drop and opened the car door for her.

His eyes shone in the light of the streetlamp at the end of the driveway as he smiled down at her. In a flash, she slid into the driver's seat and pulled the door shut.

He rested his hands on top of the car and bent over until his face was level with hers. "Good night, Carolyn. Sleep well." Then he stood and walked into the house.

Chapter 7

Mitchell wiped his palms on his pants and knocked on Carolyn's door. Her car was in her driveway, but there was a car behind it he didn't recognize. Part of him hoped this was his chance to meet the elusive Hank, and part of him dreaded it.

When Carolyn opened the door to see him, her face turned a ghastly shade of gray. Mitchell looked past her into the living room.

A man wearing an expensive three-piece suit and matching silk tie sat on Carolyn's couch, making Mitchell glad that in his mad rush to get out the door this morning, he had at least grabbed his good pants instead of the usual jeans.

"Mitchell," Carolyn stammered. "What a surprise to see you here. Please come in."

The other man stood.

"Hank, this is Mitchell."

Mitchell noticed the lines around Hank's eyes and the receding hairline.

Warning bells went off in Mitchell's head. Not only was Hank much older than he was, Hank appeared much older than Carolyn. Mitchell's stomach knotted, and he wondered if he might be sick.

Mitchell ran his fingers through his hair, giving the top a slight fluff to emphasize that it was still all his own and it was still all there, then forced himself to smile as he extended one hand. "Very pleased to meet you, Hank," he said, praying for God's forgiveness for the lie.

Hank offered his hand as if he hadn't a care in the world, while Mitchell was ready to break out into a cold sweat.

"Pleased to meet you, too, Mitchell. I hear Carolyn has been helping with your culinary skills."

He wasn't sure how he felt knowing Carolyn had mentioned him to Hank, but he had a bad feeling that because she had, she didn't see him as Hank's competition.

"That's right." Mitchell gave Hank's hand a little squeeze then released it, not breaking eye contact.

Carolyn rested her tiny hand on his arm, distracting him from sizing up Hank. Taking advantage of her attentions, Mitchell covered her hand with his and patted it as she spoke. "Not that it isn't nice to see you, Mitchell, but what are you doing here?"

"I was just in the neighborhood and thought I'd drop in to see if you were busy this afternoon."

"Actually, we're not—"

Hank stepped forward, close enough to Carolyn that she pulled her hand out and stepped back, and when she did, Hank reached behind her and rested his fingertips on the small of her back. "Actually, we were just on our way out. We're going to my nephew's junior golf tournament and then out for dinner afterward."

Carolyn stepped away from Hank's touch. "A golf tournament?" Carolyn turned to Mitchell. "Perhaps you would like to join us?"

Mitchell couldn't think of anything less fun to do. He'd only tried golf once in his life, and he didn't like it, even if he could afford the greens fees.

Hank's voice dropped in pitch and came out rather tight. "I'm sure your student has other things to do, Carolyn. With his friends."

Mitchell glanced quickly at Hank. He was able to ignore Hank's little dig, but he wasn't able to tamp down his triumphant smirk at Hank's indignation to Carolyn's invitation. However, after taking one look at Carolyn, he snapped his mouth shut and held back from commenting. Carolyn was holding her breath, her lips were clamped tight, and she stood as stiff as a board. She hadn't been this tense when she'd caught him using the largest meat cleaver to chop the lettuce in cooking class.

He could only imagine what it would be like for her with the three of them together for the afternoon. From Hank's demeanor, Mitchell anticipated more snide comments, which would make Hank look less than gracious but would put Carolyn in an uncomfortable position.

Mitchell pasted on a phony smile. "I think I'll pass. Have a nice time. If you'll excuse me, I think I should be going."

It was the hardest thing he ever did, but Mitchell said a polite good-bye and went home.

⚘

Carolyn adjusted the display mirror above her head. "Can everyone see now?"

When the class members nodded, she continued with her demonstration. Carefully, she pinched the edges of the bite-sized pastry and twirled it to seal it and make the correct shape. She raised her head and smiled at everyone. "There. Now it's your turn. Does anyone have any questions before we break into groups?" She surveyed the room then pointed to one of the ladies near the front whose arm was raised. "Evelyn?"

The young woman stood to be heard. "Yes, I was wondering if I could do the seal with a fork because I. . ." Evelyn's face paled, her eyes widened, and her gaze lowered, staring at Carolyn's feet. Her hands clenched into fists, and she pressed them to her mouth.

Carolyn lowered her head to see what Evelyn was looking at.

A blur of white streaked across her feet, and Evelyn screeched.

"A raaaaaaaat!"

The entire class erupted into a state of panic. Women screamed. Two ladies ran out the door. Most jumped onto chairs. Those that remained sitting lifted their feet up and scanned the area nervously, clutching their knees with their arms. Mitchell stiffly sat in his chair, his feet on the floor, his arms crossed tightly on his chest. She wondered what was going through his mind but didn't have time to think about it.

"Class! Wait!" Carolyn waved her hands in the air. "Please! Everyone, calm down! They're not rats! They're white mice! They escaped from the biology lab this afternoon. They're quite harmless. Most of them have been captured, but a few are still unaccounted for. Please, everyone sit down!"

Evelyn hunkered down on her chair, keeping her feet above the floor. "It was a rat," she whimpered. "I saw it."

Carolyn feared the poor woman was going to break into tears, but she had to think of the welfare of the class as a whole, not one single member. After a few minutes, order was restored, although no one had their feet on the floor except Mitchell, who was wearing cowboy boots that safely covered his feet and ankles.

Very slowly, he stood. "Is there something I can do?"

Carolyn nodded. "Yes. Would you please go find the custodian? And also we'll need a cage from the biology lab."

He glanced quickly at unit four, where the mouse had gone. "Sure."

"Thank you, Mitchell."

Everyone remained frozen to their seats while Mitchell walked out the door. All was quiet in the room, the only sound being the tap of Mitchell's cowboy boots echoing in the empty hallway and fading in the distance. Knowing that Mitchell had attended high school at Central, she wondered if he felt strange walking down the halls now, years later, at night when the school was relatively empty; but she had never been so glad he was there. He was possibly the only class member who knew where to find both the custodian and the biology lab.

The thought nearly caused her to drop the pastry roller in her hand. Even though she hadn't known him then, he'd been a high school student when she'd become a teacher.

Time stretched as no one moved or spoke. When Carolyn couldn't stand it anymore, she tried to distract the class with a few suggestions on menu planning.

Finally, Mitchell returned, cage in hand. "I couldn't find the custodian anywhere so I left him a note, but I thought I shouldn't wait to bring the cage."

Everyone in the class remained cowering in their chairs; although a few brave souls lowered their feet, they were still jumpy and kept anxiously searching the floor. Carolyn guessed that until the mouse was caught, no one would pay attention to anything else she had to say, much less actually walk across the room to the kitchen units.

She could no longer wait for the custodian to appear.

"Well, Mitchell, it looks like it's up to us to catch the errant rodent."

His face paled. "Us? Like, you and me?"

"We can't let it escape, and I can't continue class until it's caught. I saw it go under the sink in unit four."

His voice dropped to a whisper. "Are you sure it's just a mouse? Evelyn said it was a rat."

She walked toward the last known location of the missing mouse with Mitchell following close behind with the cage. "It's a mouse."

"Did you see it? Or are you just assuming it's one of the missing mice."

Both of them dropped to their hands and knees. She heard scurrying inside the closed cupboard under the sink. Mitchell laid the cage on the floor and jerked his hands away.

Carolyn narrowed her eyes. As much as he was trying to hide it, Mitchell's hands were trembling, and he wouldn't go close to the small hole through which the mouse had passed.

She couldn't understand why everyone was afraid of a little mouse. She'd often been in the biology lab to feed them kitchen scraps.

Being careful to be quiet since they were the center of attention, Carolyn lowered her voice to the faintest of whispers so Mitchell would be the only one to hear her. "It really is a mouse. I saw it. What's wrong?"

He spoke so softly she could barely hear. "I was bitten by a rat when I was a kid and had to undergo a series of very painful rabies shots. On top of that, my class had just studied the black plague. Even though the doctors insisted I wouldn't, I really thought I was going to die. I'm still skittish about rats—and mice, apparently. I feel like an idiot."

Her heart went out to him for admitting such a thing while they were in the middle of trying to deal with the fugitive mouse. "I don't know what to say. If you'd like to sit down. . ."

"No, if you say it's a mouse, I believe you. Besides, God has not given us a spirit of fear. Let's just catch the little escapist and get on with the class."

Slowly, they opened the cupboard door just wide enough to fit the opening to the cage, using the dustpan underneath to make sure it didn't squeeze through the space. Mitchell held the cage and dustpan in place while Carolyn shooed the little mouse into the cage with the broom. She worried Mitchell was going to faint, but he gritted his teeth and held himself together.

She heard him click the cage door shut, confining their prey. "Got him!" he called out in triumph. "I'll go take him back to the biology lab."

He held the handle of the cage containing the star attraction very carefully, cautious not to let his fingers get too close to the bars. As he stood, the class broke out into boisterous cheers and applause. At the clamor, Mitchell stood still, his eyes wide, and smiled so hesitantly his dimple didn't appear.

Since he wasn't moving, Carolyn sidestepped him and blocked his path. She clasped her hands together and tucked them beside her chin. "Our hero!" she singsonged.

She didn't know what made her do it. Maybe it was because she was so impressed at how he'd handled his obvious fear or maybe it was because Mitchell was already so flustered, but she couldn't help herself. She stood on her tiptoes, gently rested her hands on his shoulders, and gave him a quick and gentle peck on the cheek in front of everyone.

The applause and cheers increased in tempo and volume. Mitchell's face turned beet red, and he left without a word.

Carolyn adjusted her glasses then turned back to the class, which had finally quieted. "Okay, class, if we hurry, we can still make both projects. Divide into your groups while Mitchell goes to the biology lab, and let's get started."

The whole time Mitchell was gone, she couldn't help thinking of what she'd done. Judging from Mitchell's red face and the speed at which he left the room, she'd embarrassed him more than she had embarrassed herself.

Above all, she couldn't figure out why she'd done such a thing, as impulsiveness was not in her nature. It had only been meant as a joke, but Mitchell might have taken it the wrong way.

🌷

No matter how hard he tried, Mitchell couldn't concentrate on the lesson. He finally managed to push the memory of the rodent's beady little eyes out of his mind; but as if his humiliating admission about his childhood trauma hadn't been bad enough, every time he looked at Carolyn, he remembered her kiss.

Though it was only a quick peck on the cheek, Carolyn had kissed him in front of the class.

For the first time, he allowed himself to be encouraged that she might overcome her anxieties about their developing relationship. She'd responded the one time he'd kissed her properly; but this time she'd initiated it, and most important, she'd done it in front of the entire cooking class.

Unfortunately, the novelty of a man in a cooking class had lost its charm, so the ladies actually expected him to do his share of the work. He did his best to do what was required, but Sarah kept poking him every time Carolyn came near them. He would have done better if he hadn't known Carolyn was watching.

By the time the class was over, it had been the longest night of his life. He deliberately took longer than necessary to clean up so he would be the last person remaining except for Carolyn. He watched as she began to scoop up her bag of supplies, a huge cookbook, and her purse.

He joined her at the demonstration table. "I can carry some of that for you."

"Thanks, but we're going in opposite directions. I'm parked in the staff lot in back."

"I know that. I want to escort you safely to your car. It's dark out there."

She hesitated for a second and then sighed. Otherwise, she didn't protest, so Mitchell picked up the heavier items and walked with her toward the staff exit.

Unfortunately, the missing custodian was now standing in the doorway, awaiting their approach.

"Now he shows up," Mitchell grumbled.

"It's his job to make sure we get to our cars safely and wait until we exit the parking lot."

"Tell him his services are no longer required. It's now my job to be the hero."

She sighed again. Mitchell bit his lower lip to keep from smiling.

"District regulations, Mitchell."

The custodian didn't say anything, but Mitchell thought Mr. O'Sullivan looked at him strangely as he walked past carrying Carolyn's bags.

When they arrived at her car, Carolyn piled everything into his arms while she dug into her purse for her keys.

"See. You needed me after all."

"Yes. Thanks for helping catch the mouse. The whole class appreciated it."

He didn't care about the class. He only cared about Carolyn. He helped her load everything into the backseat then waited for her to be seated behind the wheel.

"About tomorrow night. I'll pick you up at seven for Bible study." He smiled and closed the door behind her then turned and walked away before she could respond or turn him down.

All the way home, he continued to think about what he could do to change the direction of their relationship. He didn't come up with an answer, but one thing he did know. It was time to quit fooling around and be more direct.

Once he climbed into bed, Mitchell closed his eyes, folded his hands over his chest, and lay still. What he wanted wasn't as important as what God wanted.

He opened his heart to God and prayed for a solution.

His eyes shot open. He had to prove his intentions in a concrete way, and nothing stated a man's intentions better than jewelry. Except for earrings and the cross necklace from her grandmother, Carolyn didn't wear jewelry of any kind. He didn't know if that was because she didn't like jewelry or simply that nobody else had given her anything to call special—besides the cow pin, which she had worn to every class since.

There was only one way to find out.

Mitchell smiled and rolled onto his side, pulled the blankets up to his chin, and closed his eyes. This time he would get her something more serious, something to better represent his intentions. Tonight his dreams would involve shopping.

Chapter 8

Mitchell managed to get off work on time Friday night. He didn't allow himself to be distracted by stopping for supper first. He headed straight for the mall and the jewelry store.

When he first made his decision to buy something for Carolyn, he hadn't considered how much he would spend; but now that he was in the store, he realized that different items would carry with them a different message. After browsing through everything the store had to offer, he narrowed his choices to either earrings or a ring.

"May I help you?"

He turned toward a middle-aged lady with a bad dye job, wearing a conservative two-piece dress. She smiled at him with a practiced smile as phony as her hair.

"I'm here to buy a gift for someone special."

The woman clasped her hands together. "You've certainly come to the right place. Did you want to look at engagement rings?"

Her question made him aware of where he was standing. He definitely wasn't in a position to buy an engagement ring. Such a commitment was for a courtship that had already withstood the test of time. "Not an engagement ring, no, but something special."

She led him to the next display case filled with rings of every size and color and description. The more he thought about it, the more he thought that a ring would be a good choice. A ring was a classic and tangible way to show how serious he was about courting her properly. If things went well, it might even be a precursor to that engagement ring.

However, most of the rings in the case were too flamboyant, the stones too prominent, or the settings too ornate. Not only did he not like a single one of them, he doubted Carolyn would accept something so large and obviously expensive. Her home was filled with simple things. He suspected every item she displayed held some degree of personal value to her.

"Those are too big. She's got really small hands. I want something delicate and understated. Nothing showy."

He was about to tell the woman that nothing in the case interested him and move on to the case containing the earrings when a selection of smaller rings in the corner caught his eye. In the middle of the grouping was a thin gold ring with a tiny diamond set in a dainty heart shape. Carolyn wasn't the flowers and lace type, but the simple understated message of the small heart was exactly right.

He pointed to it. "May I see that one?"

The woman pulled out the section, plucked the tiny ring from its velvet perch, and gently dropped it into Mitchell's hand. As he held it up, the small diamond twinkled brilliantly in the bright fluorescent light, and the gold reflected both the light above and the gleaming sparkle of the diamond.

"If you're looking for a promise ring, we have a better selection in the other case that I can show you."

"A promise ring?"

"A ring like that is called a promise ring, although often women choose to wear them as pinkie rings."

Mitchell smiled. Then the ring was all the more perfect. "This is exactly what I want."

"And what size will you need?"

He slipped the ring onto his pinkie, trying to picture the size of Carolyn's fingers. The ring barely went past the first joint. "I have no idea. This one is probably close, I guess. Can you size it after I give it to her?"

"Certainly."

Mitchell listened politely to the woman prattle away about promise rings in general as she processed his credit card and rang up the sale. When everything was completed, she tucked the ring into a small blue velvet pouch, dropped it into a store bag, and handed it to him.

Mitchell tucked it into his pocket, patted it, smiled a thank-you, quickly checked the time, and left the store.

Tonight he was going to present his gift to a very special woman.

❋

Carolyn turned off the electric mixer and listened. The doorbell rang again, confirming that she had not lost her mind. She hadn't arranged for Mitchell to have another cooking lesson this evening, and Hank never came without calling first, therefore she suspected that, perhaps because it was a Friday night, Wendy was paying her a surprise visit.

She peeked through the peephole. Instead of Wendy or a striking green eye staring back, she saw the entire owner of that eye.

She opened the door. "Mitchell? I wasn't expecting you."

"I was just in the neighborhood and thought I'd stop by."

She'd heard that one before. "What are you really doing here?"

His smile dropped, and she immediately felt churlish for being so abrupt with him. "I'm sorry. Please come in."

The smile immediately returned, making her wonder if she had just committed herself to something she might regret. "I just have to finish up what I was doing. I hope you don't mind."

"Not at all."

He followed her into the kitchen and sat in one of the chairs while she picked up the electric mixer and finished off the whipping cream.

"What are you making?"

"I might have found an alternative for you instead of those chocolate dessert squares." She tried to keep the blush out of her cheeks but felt them heat up anyway. "I first wanted to do it myself to be sure it was something you could handle."

Carolyn held her breath, waiting for his reaction to her lack of confidence in his ability.

"That's very nice of you. I appreciate it." He folded his hands on the table and smiled.

Carolyn opened her mouth, but nothing came out.

When she got home from school earlier, the first thing she had done was to continue searching through more cookbooks for the elusive chocolate dessert square recipe she had tried to find a few days ago. Instead, she'd come across something similar that looked really good, and before she thought about what she was doing, she had started making the recipe.

He watched her in silence as she added the whipped cream to the cooled creme mixture. The uncharacteristic silence and his constant goofy smile unnerved her so much that she threw herself into teacher mode.

"You've already learned how to fold ingredients together versus stirring. You do the same thing here to mix the whipping cream in with the filling. It's kind of tricky because you have to make the filling by adding everything individually, at the right time, in a double boiler. Here." She dipped a spoon into the filling to give him a taste.

He closed his eyes as he savored the rich chocolate cream filling. "Mmmm. This is great."

Carolyn waited for him to say more, but he only sat there and smiled at her. "Mitchell, are you feeling okay?"

He continued with his insipid grin. "Just fine. Why do you ask?"

"No reason," she mumbled then busied herself in spreading the filling on the first layer.

Mitchell continued to watch. It didn't take long before she couldn't stand the silence. "You said you were in the neighborhood. Where exactly were you?"

He smiled again as he spoke. "At the mall."

Any other day, Mitchell would not only have expounded on what he purchased, he would have also shown her and explained in full detail.

She placed the second layer on top of the filling then began spreading again. "I read in the paper they're going to be renovating the mall, expanding and modernizing it and maybe even adding a second level."

"That's nice. What's a double boiler?"

"And I hear they're putting in a new. . ." Carolyn blinked at the abrupt change of subject and tried to figure how long it had been since she'd mentioned the double boiler. "A double boiler is for cooking or melting heat-sensitive items that are prone to scorching. It's kind of an inaccurate name, because the water shouldn't actually be boiling, as that's too hot." Rather than explain, she rested the spreader on the side of the bowl and picked up the double boiler from the stove, where she had left it, separating the top, which still held a few dribbles of the filling mixture, and held the set up for him to see. "This is a double boiler."

"That's just two pots."

"They stack. First you put water in the bottom one and then. . ." Carolyn let her voice trail off. He hadn't come for a cooking lesson tonight. However, she didn't know what he really had come for.

She put the pieces back together, returned them to the stovetop, picked up the spreader tool again, and started mindlessly spreading the remaining filling. "How's your mom doing? Is she getting ready for the big day?"

He shrugged his shoulders. "Ellen says Mom's getting crabby. She says the cast is awkward and itchy, but I know she's enjoying the attention."

Carolyn waited for him to expound on the wedding plans, but nothing came out. She placed the last layer on top and began to spread the last of the filling.

"Mitchell, are you sure nothing is wrong?"

"No, everything is right. Just right."

"Then why are you looking at me like that?"

"I'm trying to figure out where to take you for dinner tonight."

"Dinner?"

"Yes, dinner. I hope you haven't eaten yet. I haven't, and I was thinking about asking you to go somewhere soft and romantic. Somewhere we can talk. Unless you already have other plans."

Her eyes opened wide. She didn't want to go somewhere to talk to him—not when he was acting so strangely. And she certainly didn't want to go anywhere romantic, but she couldn't lie to him. She didn't have plans. "How about Pedro's? I haven't had Mexican food for a long time."

"Pedro's? But that's so loud and crowded."

"I know, but the food is great. I'm really craving enchiladas. And I hear they have a new mariachi band that's really good."

He blinked twice in rapid succession then crossed his arms over his chest. "Are you serious?"

Carolyn nodded quickly. "I heard it's really good. And you don't need a reservation if you go early enough."

"That's not exactly what I had in mind."

Carolyn nodded so fast her glasses slid down the bridge of her nose. She pushed them up and kept talking without giving him time to protest. "We'll have to go now to get a good table. I think we're both dressed appropriately for Pedro's."

"Now wait a minute. I don't think—"

She rose and quickly set the bowl into the fridge, spoon and all. Without breaking her movement, she grabbed Mitchell's hand and started leading him to the door. "I can show you how to make that dessert another time. Suddenly I'm really hungry and really want to hear that new mariachi band. I just love the way they play those brass horns, don't you?"

"But—"

"Oops. Wait here. I have to get something."

Before he could reply, Carolyn ran into the bathroom and tossed the package of antacids into her purse, something she'd learned the hard way from her last visit to Pedro's.

Desperate times called for desperate measures.

🌼

Mitchell stared glumly at himself in his bathroom mirror, covered his stomach with one hand, and burped, making no effort to hold it back. The release of pressure didn't give him the relief he needed, and the taste of jalapeño peppers still tainted his mouth. He dumped another couple of antacids into his palm and popped them into his mouth just as Jake appeared behind him in the bathroom doorway.

"Did I hear you correctly? What did you do last night?"

Mitchell shook his head to try to clear the ringing in his ears. "I said we went to Pedro's and got a table right next to the band."

"The Mitchell Farris I know hates brass bands and can't stand real spicy food. Are you my roommate's evil twin?"

He burped again. "Shut up, Jake."

Jake shrugged his shoulders, unaffected. "Just checking."

Mitchell grumbled something rather impolite, but Jake ignored him.

"You were with Carolyn, the cooking teacher, right? I have a feeling there's more cooking there than food."

Mitchell pulled out his shaver. "Don't you have somewhere to go?"

Jake let out a boisterous laugh and left, leaving Mitchell alone in the house.

Last night had been a night to remember, although not in the way he would have preferred. Besides the fact that everything was far too spicy and it wasn't the private, romantic evening he'd planned, they had thoroughly enjoyed themselves over dinner. The band wasn't what he normally enjoyed, but Carolyn had, and for now, that was what mattered.

Even though he hadn't had the opportunity to talk to Carolyn about where he wanted their relationship to go or give her the ring, some good did come out of the evening. Since she had chosen the table right next to the band, he had moved his chair to sit beside Carolyn so they could watch the band while they played. He'd snuggled in beside her and held her soft little hand while she listened to the music. For his part, he had been thinking of someplace more romantic he could take her another time.

His bubble had burst when he took her home and she disappeared inside without letting him kiss her good night. Still, the fact that she had held his hand encouraged him. And no matter how slowly things were progressing, they were progressing.

He dumped dog chow into Killer's bowl and sat at the table to eat his own breakfast while Killer happily crunched hers beside him. He poured himself a large glass of cold milk to settle his stomach.

After he brushed his teeth, only one thing remained to do before he left.

Mitchell sat on the couch and prayed. Once again, he asked for guidance and maturity in his relationship with Carolyn, and he prayed for assurance that it was God's will, not just his own, that they would be together. He didn't know exactly what Carolyn was seeking in the man whom she would one day fall in love with and marry, but he prayed that he could be everything she needed and wanted.

She was certainly everything he needed and wanted. She was kind and gentle, yet held her own in trying times. She had certainly been braver than he had been in the skirmish with the killer mouse. Carolyn also possessed charm and a quick wit, which he enjoyed immensely. He didn't know what kind of activities she pursued on a routine basis, but so far what they had done together had been mutually enjoyable.

Again, he prayed for God to show him the right path.

When he was done, he grabbed his jacket and left. Today, whatever he did with Carolyn, it would be somewhere quiet, without a crowd.

An hour later, he found himself at the gopher enclosure at the zoo, Carolyn at his side, unable to figure out what convoluted process had gotten him there. Absently, his hand rose to pat the little ring still in the pouch, safely nestled in his pocket.

"Oh, look! They want my popcorn!"

"Carolyn, the sign says not to feed them."

She sighed and Mitchell smiled. Not only was he getting used to her cute little sighs, he was becoming adept at predicting them.

She pointed to one of the big gophers, which was sitting up on its haunches, looking at them. "Look at his face. He's so cute. I wonder if they practice so people will feed them."

"I don't think gophers practice being cute. They're too stupid to practice anything."

He received a smack on the arm for his knowledgeable deduction.

After an unreasonable length of time watching the gophers balance on their fat, pampered bottoms, they continued on their way.

When Carolyn tossed her empty popcorn bag into the garbage can, she inhaled deeply and raised her hands. "Spring is in the air!" she exclaimed as she twirled around.

Mitchell pulled his jacket collar tighter. Wind was in the air, and it was nippy. "That's not spring. It's manure. We're next to the pony rides."

He received another smack on the arm for his comment.

They kept walking, pausing for a few minutes to look at each animal as they wandered through the zoo.

When they stopped in front of the bighorn sheep enclosure, a large number of the magnificent animals grazed and a few bleated their opinions of whatever it was sheep thought about.

As Carolyn stood to watch, Mitchell rested his hands on her shoulders then shuffled right behind her so they were pressed together.

Carolyn tilted her neck to look up and back at him. "What are you doing?"

"I'm sheltering you from the wind so you'll stay warm."

She sighed again but didn't pull away, which he took as a positive sign.

A blast of wind came up from behind. Carolyn wrapped her arms around herself but otherwise didn't move. In an effort to warm himself, Mitchell dipped his head forward and nuzzled his face into the top of her head.

A pleasant herbal scent filled his nostrils. Mitchell closed his eyes and inhaled deeply in an effort to commit this moment to his memory forever.

Everything around them drifted into oblivion as he nuzzled Carolyn's forehead through her hair. The zoo in itself may not have been the most romantic place in the world, but where he was standing now, so close to her, touching her, it suddenly held a lot of promise he hadn't acknowledged before. The setting was casual, but he'd never been so close to her when she was relaxed, and all around them was quiet. She smiled up at him, and he was lost.

Very slowly, his fingers lifted from her shoulder to tip her chin up a wee bit higher. He leaned slightly forward, lowered his head, and kissed her lips. The position was a little awkward, but it was worth it to kiss her. The air around them was cool, but he ignored it for the heat of kissing Carolyn.

"Mommy, what are they doing?"

At the child's words, Carolyn pulled herself away and stepped forward to rest her hands on the railing, putting an inordinate amount of concentration on watching the sheep.

The mother's voice immediately followed the child's. "The boy sheep are butting heads. It's what sheep do to see who is the biggest and strongest of the herd."

"Why do they have to fight to do that?"

"Because the winner wants to be the husband of the prettiest lady sheep."

The little boy continued to ask countless questions about the sheep. Slowly, Mitchell approached Carolyn.

She glanced over her shoulder at the sound of his footsteps. "That shouldn't have happened, Mitchell."

"He wasn't looking at us. He was looking at the sheep." He reached out to touch her shoulder, but she shuffled away.

"It's not okay. This is a public place."

The only public around them was one small boy and his mother, who were now discussing what sheep ate for breakfast on school days; but if it bothered Carolyn, he wanted to respect her feelings. "You're right. I'm sorry. Would you like to keep going and see the rest of the animals?"

She nodded, so they continued their journey through the zoo; but for the rest of the day, he didn't make any attempt to hold her hand or touch her in any way. Eventually the tension left her, and they were able to enjoy the zoo as they had before the sheep enclosure. One thing he knew. After they left, he would never be able to think of sheep without remembering their kiss.

On their way out, since they had to exit through the gift shop, Mitchell decided to buy her something so she would remember the entire day as fondly as he knew he would. While Carolyn browsed at the souvenir T-shirts, Mitchell made his selection.

He suspected he might have made the wrong choice when, while sitting in the car before they left the parking lot, he presented her with a stuffed plush sheep.

He bit his bottom lip as she held it in her hand, staring at the poor thing like it was made of something toxic.

"Come on, you've got to admit it's cute."

"It's cute," she mumbled.

"And it's nice and soft."

Cautiously, she petted it then smiled just enough to give Mitchell some faint glimmer of hope. "Yes, it's soft."

"It's cuddly, too. Just like me."

She whacked him over the head with it before he had a chance to raise his arms.

On the way home, they chatted about the animals they had seen—every animal except the sheep.

His plan to give her the ring today didn't quite work out, but he'd managed to give her something else as a reminder of their time together. With any luck, tomorrow would present a better opportunity.

Again, she didn't give him a chance to kiss her at the door, but before the door closed, he did have the chance to say that he would pick her up for church, and she didn't turn him down.

Mitchell smiled the entire way home. As always, God had provided a way.

Chapter 9

"Good evening, everyone. We've got a lot of things to do today, so let's get started quickly." Carolyn prepared the pastry dough, warning everyone to work slowly to prevent it from tearing during the rolling process. She specifically cautioned Mitchell that too much handling would make it tough, but he took being singled out with a smile and a wink.

Next, she demonstrated making the strudel, rolling and shaping it, and showing how it was different than the previous project, then sent everyone to their kitchenettes to do it themselves.

As she walked from group to group, several times conversations stopped. Carolyn had already noticed many of the ladies glancing back and forth between her and Mitchell all evening, and the combination gave her cause for concern. It appeared many of her class members thought she and Mitchell were an item.

Even though she hadn't meant it that way, Carolyn now realized that she had fueled their thoughts when she kissed him on the cheek in front of the class. She'd only meant it in jest, but it had backfired on her. And, if the class took it the wrong way, she was afraid to think of how Mitchell felt.

She certainly didn't want to encourage him in whatever it was he thought he was doing by hanging around her so much. It was neither fair nor realistic for her to be spending so much time with him. She hoped and prayed that her actions had not given him the wrong impression, but she feared they had.

The truth was, she really didn't know exactly how she felt about Mitchell. She would have been lying if she tried to tell herself she didn't like him; but she was more than ready for a permanent relationship. Such a relationship had to be based on more than simply liking someone and being easily amused by them.

She forced herself to ignore the whisperings and pushed the class forward. Soon, everything was done, and the only person left to clean up his mess was Mitchell. He tucked the last baking sheet away as Carolyn gathered up her purse, bag of utensils, and cookbook and headed for the door.

The cupboard door closed with a bang, and his footsteps echoed behind her. "Can I walk you out?"

"The custodian will be watching to make sure I get to my car safely," she called over her shoulder, not slowing her pace.

"But I need to talk to you."

She didn't want to talk to him. She was too afraid she would weaken if he started talking about anything besides cooking, which he probably would, since cooking class was over.

"I'm sorry, but I have to go," she mumbled, not slowing her pace.

Carolyn didn't slow down until she reached the friendly custodian, who was standing dutifully beside the door. She nodded and mumbled a good night to Mr. O'Sullivan as he held the door open and she stepped outside into the brisk night air. Out of the corner of her eye, she saw Mitchell starting to exit, as well.

"Hold on, young man, wait a minute."

Mr. O'Sullivan blocked the path to the exit. Mitchell's sneakers squeaked on the tile floor as he stopped abruptly. Carolyn kept walking.

"I think I recognize you. Didn't you used to attend here?"

"Uh, yeah, I did, but—"

"Wait. Farris, right? I ran into those friends of yours at the coffee shop, Gordie Reid and Roland Carruthers. I remember the time the three of you—"

"Carolyn! Wait!"

She ignored his plea and quickened her step, managing to reach her car before Mitchell disengaged himself. She threw everything in without regard to neatness and drove off.

As soon as she arrived home, she dropped her bag on the kitchen counter, but instead of putting everything in its rightful place, she began to pace.

Things were getting out of hand, and she didn't know what to do about it.

She didn't know how it happened, but she'd been seeing Mitchell almost every day, starting not long after they met. It wasn't supposed to be this way, yet when she hadn't seen him Monday, she'd missed him.

It didn't make sense.

She was at a point in her life where she had to move forward with her future. She was settled into her career as a teacher. She was well involved in her church and the various activities there, and she was satisfied in her walk with the Lord. All else considered, only one very important thing was lacking in her life. From the bottom of her heart, she desired a special man who would love her the same way she loved him. And following that, she wanted to start a family.

She wanted to trust that God knew what was best for her and that whoever He sent would be the man she could be happy with for the rest of her time on earth. She'd even started praying for God to send such a man not long ago, and it was about that time God had sent Hank into her life. Yet as much as Hank matched all the things she was looking for in a husband, Hank had made it known he wasn't ready for marriage.

She thought the answer was simply to get to know Hank better, and the relationship God planned for them to have would work itself out over time. Yet, instead of spending her time with Hank and developing things there, she found herself spending nearly all her free time with Mitchell, a man who was wrong for her in every way that she could see.

Carolyn closed her eyes to pray for direction when the sudden jangle of the phone startled her. With a trembling hand, she picked up the receiver.

"I think we should talk. You ran off on me."

"Mitchell," she stammered. "We both have work in the morning. It's late."

"It's not that late. I think you were avoiding me."

Carolyn squeezed her eyes shut, not wanting to tell him the truth but knowing she had to. "I think the class is starting to make assumptions about us. . . ." She let her voice trail off.

She waited for him to say something, but he was strangely silent for the longest time. When he finally spoke, his voice was strangely soft. "Tomorrow is Bible study night. You promised me that this week we could go together again."

Her heart pounded in her chest. If it hadn't been for that promise, she would have told him she'd changed her mind. Hank had promised her that he would be a regular attendee at the meetings, but in the last few months, he'd only been to one. She knew what it felt like to have a promise broken, and she couldn't do that to Mitchell.

"All right. Pick me up at seven."

"Great. Since we won't be cooking, let's go out for dinner, too. Oops. Killer's outside barking. You're right; it is getting late. I can't let her disturb the neighborhood. Gotta run. Bye."

The dial tone sounded in her ear before she completely mumbled her good-bye.

She lowered the phone to its cradle and buried her face in her hands. What had she done?

Chapter 10

Mitchell rang Carolyn's doorbell and raised his hand to wiggle his tie then patted the pocket containing the little ring.

God's timing was perfect. After Tuesday's class, he had started to get a little nervous; but even though they rushed to be on time for the Bible study on Wednesday, they'd had a lovely dinner.

Mitchell smiled to himself. Tonight, neither of them had anything else to do, and neither had to get up early in the morning. Later, over candlelight and a juicy steak dinner, he would give her the little ring and tell her that he was falling in love.

The door opened. "Hi, Mitchell. Come in."

He wiggled the unaccustomed knot at his neck. "Sorry I'm so late. I often get stuck working overtime on Fridays."

"I'm finding that out, aren't I?" She smiled, and his heart rate kicked up a notch. Instead of her favorite fuzzy pink sweater and denim skirt, tonight she wore a pretty light purple dress and matching colored shoes that made her a little taller than usual.

His smile widened. "You look nice."

Her cheeks darkened, which he thought was kind of cute. It also told him she didn't hear enough compliments, something that was about to change. "Thank you. I was wondering, after dinner, would you like to see a movie? I saw a commercial for a new comedy that looked really good."

Taking a woman to a movie after dinner sounded more like a real date than ever, but he wasn't going to point that out quite yet.

He checked his watch. "I'd like that, but I think it's a little late to do both. What time is the late showing?"

"I don't know. Maybe we should check the paper."

Instead of taking Carolyn out to the car, he sauntered into the living room and planted himself on her couch while she spread the newspaper on the coffee table.

"Here it is. It starts at. . ." Her voice trailed off, and she pressed her finger to the newspaper. "Mitchell! Look!"

The sudden voice inflection made him jump. He leaned forward and looked at where her finger was planted.

"It's the Annual Cooking and Kitchen Showcase! It's this weekend, and the doors open at nine tomorrow morning!" As they made eye contact, the sparkle in her eyes disappeared. Her voice dropped. "Never mind." She turned back to the paper.

"What do you mean, never mind?"

"It's too late to ask anyone to go with me. I guess there's always next year."

Mitchell grinned. After all he'd learned about cooking in the past month, Mitchell thought that perhaps there might be something to interest him, too. "I'll go with you. It's probably just like the marketplace, and that was fun."

Her lips tightened. "It's not really like that at all, Mitchell."

"Even better. Something different will be fun."

Her head tipped to one side, and one eye narrowed. "Are you sure?"

"Sure. Why not?"

"Tickets are cheaper if you buy them in advance."

"Okay."

Before he could think about it, she rested her finger on the phone number listed in the ad, mumbled it a few times to memorize it, and ran into the kitchen. By the time he realized that she was paying for the tickets over the phone with her credit card, it was too late to do anything about it.

He stood when he heard her hang up. "I must be more tired than I thought. I didn't realize what you were going to do. I wanted to pay for those."

"Nonsense. It was my idea, so I'm paying. But if you want to appease your bruised ego, you can pay for my dinner tonight."

"I was going to pay for your dinner anyway. Where do you want to go?"

"Pedro's."

"No." He shook his head so fast that a lock of hair fell onto his forehead. "Anywhere but there." He rested his hand on his stomach. He'd felt the effects of that one dinner for two days afterward. He'd taken every last one of Jake's antacids before he felt normal.

"Please? It's the last night before the mariachi band moves on to another city."

He opened his mouth to protest, but her pleading eyes stopped him. "I give up. But before we go, I have to stop at the drugstore for something."

❧

"Look at all the cars," Mitchell grumbled as he turned into a parking spot that had to be at least two miles from the main entrance. He estimated about a thousand cars in the parking lot, and the line of people waiting for the doors to open was already around the corner of the building.

By the time they waited in line and picked up their reserved tickets at the entrance, another five hundred people had lined up behind them. They were each given programs listing all the display booths, a list of seminars, and a map. The enticing aroma of fresh coffee wafted through the air, teasing him. He'd been careful with his selections at Pedro's last night, and he'd had an extra dose of antacids before he left, so now he was more than ready for a large cup of hot coffee.

They stood to the side to look at the map and figure out the layout of the building. He'd almost figured out where the coffee concession was when Carolyn's hand blocked his view, pointing to a list at the side of the printed form. "We get one free class with the purchase of an advance ticket, so I signed up for this one." Her finger rested on some French person's name he couldn't attempt to pronounce. She looked up at him, blushed, then pointed to another seminar, a demonstration on some food item he couldn't pronounce either, even if he did know what it was, which he didn't. "I didn't know what you'd be interested in, but I signed you up for this one. If you don't want to go, I'll go instead."

He smiled. "It's all yours. Enjoy yourself."

She turned and pointed to an area in the far corner of the building. "There's a big screen television there for the guys. You can go there while I'm in the sessions, if you want. They last forty-five minutes each."

Mitchell grinned. A guy area. Perfect. He hoped they had a large coffeepot. "Let's start walking and see how much we can take in before your first class. How long until it starts?"

"We only have an hour, so we'd better get going."

"Only?" Mitchell scanned the area, trying to figure out what was here that would take more than an hour to see. In a room full of mainly women, he stood a head taller than most of the people there, so he could easily see almost everything. According to the map, there were hundreds of booths and displays, in addition to demonstration areas and rooms for the class sessions. He'd never seen anything like it. The annual auto show was nothing like this. However, since he couldn't imagine there could be that many ways to cook a meal, he figured that, unlike the auto show, they would be out of the cooking convention within a couple of hours, including her lectures.

Before they moved, he reached for her hand.

When she looked up at him, he gave it a gentle squeeze to stop her from protesting. "We don't want to get separated."

"Okay. Let's go this way first."

The first section was called Microwave Cooking. They managed to walk past the first booth with a cursory glance, but Carolyn stopped at the second one. They watched two women showing some kind of gadget that cooked rice in a microwave then had to wait while everyone tasted a small white paper cup full of the fresh cooked rice, followed by sufficient oohing and aahing about how tender it was. Then everyone, including Carolyn, walked away without buying one. Carolyn led him by the hand to the next booth, which was also preparing some kind of food and handing out samples. He was going to suggest that if she was hungry, they could go to the food court to buy something that was more than one nibble at a time, but Carolyn's attention was glued to the demonstration.

By the end of the hour, Mitchell had learned more about how to cook things in the microwave with strange utensils than he wanted to know in a lifetime. Worst of all, he was still hungry even though he'd eaten so many samples he'd lost count.

As he stood waiting while Carolyn inspected the latest and greatest version of some gadget he couldn't identify, Mitchell glanced around him. There weren't many men present, but those he had seen with their wives or girlfriends looked as bored as he felt.

"It's almost time for my first course. Shall we meet back here at ten forty-five?"

Mitchell looked up as a man pushing a stroller with an infant in it walked in the direction of the guy area.

He synchronized his watch with Carolyn's. "Gotcha. Ten forty-five."

❁

Carolyn hurried off toward the meeting room area. She could tell Mitchell was as bored as she predicted he would be, but he was being a good sport about it. However, just because she had warned him in advance didn't make her feel any better. Because of the guilt, she'd separated from him at the last possible second, which meant the only seats left were in the back.

She pulled her notepad out of her purse and adjusted her glasses as the class began. The chef displayed culinary techniques she could only dream of, making her wish she had more flair in the kitchen or, failing that, a specialty she could be proud of. The demonstration ended before she realized the time had gone by, and she enthusiastically joined the rest of the audience in a healthy round of applause. On her way out, she picked up a bag containing the recipe the chef had prepared—as if she could ever prepare it with such skill—a small booklet promoting the chef's newly released cookbook, and a small taste sample of today's demonstration.

Mitchell was already waiting for her by the time she reached the appointed meeting place. He held a steaming cup of coffee in one hand and a large bag in the other.

"Was there something interesting on television?"

He grinned then shook his head. "I didn't make it that far. Look what I bought."

Carolyn took one look at the bag and read the logo. "Oh, no," she groaned under her breath. "You didn't."

335

"It's a Handy Dandy Veggie-O-Matic Chopper. You should see what it does."

Carolyn forced herself to smile. She should never have left him alone. She should have personally escorted him to the men's area in the back and told him to stay put.

"It slices and dices and chops and everything. It even makes french fries, and you should have tasted them. Were they ever good."

She highly doubted Mitchell would ever attempt to make french fries from scratch, and it would be a pretty good guess that he didn't own a deep fryer. "Mitchell, when are you ever going to use such an item?"

He shrugged his shoulders. "I don't know. But when I do, I'll do the job in record time."

"I think that in a few years the Salvation Army will have a wonderful donation, still in the original packaging."

He ignored her as he dropped the chopper back into the bag and picked up a long, narrow box. "And look at this. I saw the guy cut a PVC pipe with this knife, and you should have seen how cleanly it cut through a big fat tomato after that. You said I needed a good knife."

Carolyn shook her head in disbelief. "Have you ever been to anything like this before?"

He dug through the bag as he spoke. "I go to the auto show every year, if that's what you mean."

"No, I mean something like this, where there are things to actively participate in, demos, door prizes, and booths with a million things for sale."

He stuck his head down closer to the bag opening, continuing to riffle through the contents until he found the specific item he was searching for. "No, never," he mumbled.

Carolyn didn't know whether to laugh or cry as she watched Mitchell pull out an assortment of gadgets, some of which might be handy to her but would be totally useless to Mitchell once he had finished the cooking class.

When he finished, she sighed and shook her head. "Come on. We still have a lot to see."

She grabbed his hand and led him to a section where his wallet would be safe. Together they nibbled samples and wandered around until they ended up at the food court. Carolyn couldn't stuff in another bite after everything she'd eaten, but Mitchell bought himself a corn dog on a stick, and they kept walking.

A scratchy voice she could barely understand boomed over the loudspeaker announcing the other session she'd signed up for was starting in five minutes. She tried to calculate how long it would take to escort Mitchell safely to the men's area and still be on time but knew she would never make it.

Guiding him to the side so people could walk around them, she held tightly to both his hands, forcing him to make eye contact. "Please, Mitchell, promise me you won't buy anything while I'm gone, okay?"

He held up one hand. "Promise. Scout's honor," he said while making the appropriate hand signal.

She didn't know if he had ever been a Boy Scout but didn't have the time to challenge him on it. "I'll meet you back here when it's over, okay?"

"Sure."

She dropped his hands and dashed off. Again, she had to sit in the back, but it had been worth it to extract a promise out of Mitchell.

The demonstration on Pâté Feuilletee was fascinating, but while she picked up some wonderful tips, Mitchell was always in the back of her mind. She left the room as soon as she could, missing the opportunity to ask the chef a few questions, and hurried to the appointed meeting place where, once again, Mitchell was waiting.

"What did you do this time while I was gone?" She was almost afraid to ask, but she had to know.

"Nothing bad. I didn't buy anything. I just entered my name in a bunch of free draws."

"Oh, no. Mitchell, they're going to phone and tell you that you won something, except you have to buy something or watch a demonstration for two hours to claim your prize, which is never worth the cost of getting there. And then they sell the names they've collected to mailing lists."

He shrugged his shoulders. "I don't care. I'd never buy anything I didn't really need."

Carolyn almost choked but held back her comment. "Come on. Over there, they're featuring a selection of new products for people with food allergies."

He checked his watch. "We've been here over seven hours. You mean there's still something we haven't seen?"

"Just two sections. If you want to go sit down and watch television, I don't mind."

"If I wanted to watch television, I would have stayed home. I came here to be with you."

Carolyn's throat tightened. By now, most of the men who had accompanied their wives and girlfriends were in the men's area, many of them having consumed far too much beer. Yet except for the time she'd spent in class, Mitchell hadn't left her side. Many times, when he didn't think she was looking, she'd glanced up to see him staring blankly at nothing, obviously bored to death, but he never complained.

"Forget the other two sections. I think we've seen enough, and I'm tired anyway. Let's go home."

His relief was almost tangible, and Carolyn knew she'd done the right thing.

On the way out, they passed a booth selling the same vegetable chopper he had purchased earlier in the day. He grinned and pointed but didn't slow down. "I got mine cheaper."

"It's only a bargain if you actually use it."

He laughed and held the door open as they left the building and began the long walk back to the car.

"I'm hungry. Can we go somewhere for supper?"

Carolyn rested one hand on her stomach. She'd consumed so many samples, she didn't think she'd be able to eat for a week. "I couldn't eat another bite, but if you're hungry, let's go through the drive-through."

"The drive-through? But. . ." Mitchell's hand drifted to the breast pocket of his leather jacket, he patted something tucked inside, then rammed his hands in his pockets as they walked. "I guess so," he mumbled.

They trudged in silence the rest of the way to the car, but once they were on the road going home, Carolyn could no longer contain herself. "Did you see that lady who was making the crepes? And how thin she could make them with that fancy pan?"

Mitchell checked for traffic over his shoulder. "Uh, yeah."

"And those tiny sausage rolls made on that specialty rack that fit into a toaster oven? I couldn't care less about the rack, but I wonder where those sausages came from. They were absolutely delicious and not dripping with fat."

"They were okay."

"And those brownies made in that special pan in the microwave. I've never been able to make cake with a decent texture in the microwave. But you know what was the most ridiculous thing I saw? That potato peeler tub thing, where you run water into it and between the water itself and the water pressure turning the grating unit inside, it peels the potatoes by itself. I timed it. Could you imagine taking fifteen minutes to peel potatoes?"

"I guess not."

When Carolyn didn't speak, silence hung in the air. Other than the soft music droning from the CD player and the hum of the traffic, the car was quiet.

"Mitchell, are you okay?"

"Huh? What? Oh, I'm fine. I'm just tremendously underwhelmed with the wonders of the modern kitchen. I didn't know what I was missing."

Not sure if his sarcasm was meant as a joke or not, Carolyn said nothing. After a few minutes of silence, she made a few more comments about things she'd seen, but he continued to respond with few words. When silence hung in the air periodically, he kept reaching to his breast pocket, feeling something, and then dropping his hand back to the steering wheel, making Carolyn wonder if he'd recently quit smoking.

Closer to home, he pulled into the drive-through of the local hamburger joint and ordered. Carolyn held the warm bag in her lap until they pulled into her driveway.

Carolyn made a pot of herbal tea while Mitchell ate the burger and fries, and then they moved into the living room.

Mitchell sat in the middle of the couch, which meant Carolyn had to sit beside him.

Carolyn stretched and wiggled her toes before sagging fully into the soft cushions. "I didn't realize my feet were so sore or that I was so tired until now."

Mitchell shifted his weight so she sank in his direction. "Same."

She flipped the television on for lack of something better to do. "I can't believe the time. We spent the whole day there."

"I can believe it."

She turned toward him. "Thank you for taking me, especially on short notice. I really had a wonderful time."

He smiled and slipped his arm around her back, drawing her against him. "It's also nice to be able to sit and relax with a good friend after it's all over, too."

Carolyn smiled back. She didn't think it appropriate for "a good friend" to have his arm around her, but she was so tired, she couldn't help snuggling into his warmth.

She thought of his words. If she had to put a label to what was happening between them, then calling Mitchell a friend was safe and probably quite accurate. She'd never before come to know someone so quickly or so easily. She already knew most of Mitchell's likes and dislikes, the movies he liked to watch, and the books he liked to read. She'd learned a lot about his job and told him a lot about hers. She enjoyed his quirky sense of humor, and she'd even started to miss him when they weren't together.

"Yes, this is nice," she muttered and sighed as she let herself continue to relax. "I'm so tired. I think it's tripled in size since last year."

He mumbled a reply she couldn't understand, and Carolyn didn't ask him to repeat it. Instead, she let herself relax even more with the steady and soothing rhythm of his breathing. Her eyes drifted shut of their own accord. She would open them in a minute.

She shifted with the movement as he reached up and patted his shirt pocket. Mitchell's voice sounded deeper when she was pressed up against him. "I was wondering. I've really enjoyed going with you to your Bible studies and church on Sunday morning. I'd like it if we went together all the time. What do you think?"

"Mmm."

"Was that a yes or a no? Carolyn?"

She wanted to answer, but she couldn't. All she felt was peace as everything faded into softness and warmth.

Chapter 11

Beeping sounded, jolting Carolyn from a sound sleep. She opened her eyes and started to roll over, squinting to focus on the time.

The clock was missing. And she wasn't in bed. She was on the living room couch.

As soon as she gained her bearings, she located the source of the beeping, which was a man's watch, lying on the coffee table. She picked up her glasses, which were beside the watch, and put them on.

Eight thirty.

Carolyn blinked, trying to figure everything out, starting with what day it was. The last thing she remembered was watching television with Mitchell after attending the Kitchen Showcase.

Her stomach churned. She'd fallen asleep on the couch. She clutched her blanket, which was the one from her bed, and glanced to her side. He'd also brought her pillow.

The warmth in her cheeks escalated to a burn when she found a note, next to where the watch had been.

Good morning, Sleepyhead!
I hope you had a good night's sleep. I had to use your keys to lock up when I left, so I'll be back for church in the morning. Expect me at 9:15. I'll bring breakfast.
Love, Mitchell

Carolyn buried her face in her hands. The thought of Mitchell tucking her in at night, even if it was just on the couch, made her cringe with embarrassment.

Without wasting any more time, Carolyn bolted off the couch, heading straight for the bathroom. She didn't know how she was going to get ready before Mitchell arrived.

She'd barely finished applying her mascara when the doorbell rang.

Mitchell stood in the doorway holding a brown paper bag in one hand and a cardboard holder containing two steaming cups in the other. He smiled brightly. "Good morning. Sleep well? You look nice. That color really suits you."

Carolyn opened her mouth, but no words came out.

"Aren't you going to let me in? I have food. And coffee."

She shuffled to the side to give him room to pass. "Of course."

Mitchell walked straight past her into the kitchen, but her feet remained glued to the floor. She didn't want to share breakfast in the kitchen with Mitchell. She didn't know how she was going to sit across the table from him and carry on an intelligent conversation.

When he was halfway through the living room, he stopped and turned around to smile so sweetly that she nearly cried. "Don't worry, you didn't snore or do anything embarrassing. Come on, before everything gets cold. These fast-food hotcakes are bad enough when they're warm."

Cold food was the least of her worries. Somehow she managed to talk to him while they ate their breakfast, although by the time she got to the last mouthful, it tasted like cardboard.

Sharing breakfast with him was one more reminder of how much Mitchell had become ingrained in her life.

Her friends now expected him regularly at the Wednesday night Bible study, and they asked about him when he wasn't with her on Sunday, whether Hank was there or not—which was rare. Her night school class definitely thought of them as a couple. Even his dog liked her.

Now they would be attending Sunday service together, again.

Mitchell rose and went into the living room to pick up his watch. "I guess it's time to go," he said as he walked back into the kitchen. "Are we going to your church or mine? I don't think I've been to my own church for over a month."

Carolyn sighed. She was too tired to meet new people, even though it meant that the entire congregation would be seeing her with Mitchell on yet another Sunday. "It's getting late. We can go to your church next weekend."

Carolyn bit her lip, but it was too late. The words had already been said.

"That's a good idea. You can also see it before the wedding. You are coming with me to Jake and Ellen's wedding, aren't you?"

"Uh..."

She opened her mouth to decline, but his eyes stopped her. She'd seen that look before, the day he begged her to give him remedial help with his cooking skills. She didn't want to go through that again.

Carolyn sighed again. "Sure."

"Before I forget, I can't see you for dinner tonight. I've got a family thing I have to do. Can we do dinner tomorrow night after work?"

Carolyn stood. There was no point in trying to decline. He would only bamboozle her into going out with him another time and another time after that.

When she sighed again, the corners of his mouth quivered.

"Yes, I'd like that."

Strangely, she meant it.

☙

Mitchell drummed his fingers on the steering wheel as he waited for the red light. If all the lights from here on out were green, then he had a chance of running into the cooking class on time—barely.

In the past, he had never minded the overtime. It wasn't like he ever had anything better to do, and the extra money on payday was always a treat. Now, he had changed his mind.

His supposed date last night with Carolyn hadn't happened. Just as he was about to leave, the dock foreman had come running in to say that someone had driven through the fence between their compound and the adjoining business. Not only did he have to call the police, but he also had to arrange to have someone come in at an unbelievable fee to fix the security fence at night. Then he had to deal with the police report and file charges, since there would be an insurance claim and criminal charges against the man who did the damages. Worst of all, he had to stay until the repair crew actually arrived and started working.

Instead of sharing an intimate dinner, he'd ordered a pizza, Carolyn heated up some leftovers, and they'd sat and talked on the phone while they ate, him at work and her at home. Again, he'd been unable to give her the ring, which seemed to have become a permanent fixture in his pocket.

He ran into the classroom to see Carolyn holding up some kind of gadget he'd seen at the cooking show, but he couldn't remember what it was called or what it was for.

The room suddenly went deathly quiet as he made his way to the only empty seat, which was in the exact center of the classroom—the same chair he'd sat in during the first class.

Without making a major production out of his late arrival, Carolyn held up a tray of food for all to see. "There was a question on the registration form asking if anyone here was allergic to seafood. Before we continue, does anyone here have allergies who may not have noticed the question on the form?"

When no one spoke up, Carolyn continued. "That's good. We're going to make battered shrimp, which will be dipped in various sauces. This works with many types of seafood, but shrimp is the most popular. It's much better to use fresh shrimp, so that's what we're going to do."

She then went through a gruesome process of pulling a shrimp apart, coating it with some stuff she mixed up, then frying it until it was cooked.

It smelled much better than it looked, and the mouth-watering aroma made Mitchell's stomach grumble—a nasty reminder that he hadn't had time to eat supper in his rush to get out of work and to class on time.

Carolyn then put together something else with a fancy name he couldn't pronounce and sent everyone to their kitchen units. As they got organized, she made the rounds to each kitchen, gave each person four shrimp, then returned to the demonstration table.

"Okay, everyone. As a change of pace, we're going to all do this together. Watch me, and we'll do it step by step."

Mitchell picked up one shrimp by the tail and examined it. He'd never seen a whole shrimp before. It wasn't what he'd expected. He thought shrimp were brown, but it was a grayish color.

"Is everyone ready?"

Several of the ladies around him nodded unenthusiastically.

"First you break off the legs, like this."

He did like she said, repeating in his mind that the poor creature was already dead and didn't feel a thing.

"Good. Now put your thumb and pointer finger at the point where the head meets the body and pull off the head."

If he was hungry before, he certainly wasn't now. His stomach contracted as he placed his fingers in the position Carolyn demonstrated.

"That's the worst part." Carolyn grinned, and he hoped she couldn't tell he felt sick. "The shell will peel right off quite easily now; just pull here and voilà!"

Mitchell pulled, but it didn't come out quite as easily as Carolyn's did. He pulled again and nearly dropped it at the unpleasant slimy feel of the thing inside. Canned shrimp didn't feel like this. He let it fall to the plate.

Carolyn held up her shrimp. "This next step is called deveining. Does everyone see that line down the back? Take your knife, make a quick slice down the back, and sort of scrape it out, like this."

Mitchell's stomach rolled. He sucked in a deep breath to stop it, but the smell of the raw seafood permeating the room only made it worse.

"You might think this is the shrimp's spinal cord, but it's not. It's just an intestine."

"Just" an intestine. Mitchell worked to control his breathing.

"You don't have to remove it, but it makes a more pleasant-looking appetizer."

With shaking hands, Mitchell inserted the tip of the knife and slowly ran it along the line, but the slice didn't go as neatly as Carolyn's. Instead, it made a jagged tear, and the shrimp started to come apart in his hands. For a moment he considered running to his car, first to get a breath of fresh air and then to bring back his needle-nose pliers to hold the shrimp steady so he could get the job done faster.

Finally, he managed to lift the dark, threadlike vein out, but in pieces, not like Carolyn had done. As soon as he did, he laid the shrimp down and looked away. Carolyn was trying to get an overview of everyone's progress from the central location of the demonstration table, so he concentrated on her until his stomach settled.

"You all look like you're doing fine. Now do the other three. And when you're done, we'll heat up the frying pans, dip the shrimp in the batter, cook them for four minutes, and then you can all do the next project without me."

He struggled through disemboweling the other three shrimp, but with each one, the process became slightly less revolting. By the time he began to cook them, the aroma made his appetite return, and he could hardly wait to eat them.

As they reached the point halfway through the second project, his stomach was grumbling so loudly that Lorraine and Sarah were giggling, and Mrs. Finkleman felt so sorry for him that she snuck him one of her shrimp to eat before Carolyn gave them permission.

When that permission came, not only was he the first one finished eating, but he'd managed to mooch an extra shrimp from Lorraine and Sarah, as well.

As usual, he loitered when class was over until he was the last person out.

"I'm sorry I was late, Carolyn."

She hesitated for only a second then continued packing up her area. "It's okay, Mitchell. I understand if you had to work late."

"Yeah, I did. I also haven't had supper, and I was wondering if you'd like to go grab a burger or something. The things we made today were good but not enough to constitute a real meal."

"I really can't, Mitchell. Believe it or not, I have a bunch of reports and tests to mark. Even the home ec department has to do them. I wish I could, but not today. How about tomorrow?"

His heart soared to think that she had suggested an alternate day, but just as quickly, his heart sank. "I can't. Our major competitor served strike notice today. That's why I had to work so late. Businesses can't afford to have their stuff tied up in a labor dispute, so a lot of people shifted over to us, and we weren't prepared. It will take a few more days before we've adjusted, and by then I'm sure the dispute will be settled and it will be back to normal. The way it looks, it's going to be like this all week."

"Then I guess I won't see you until the weekend."

"Yeah. It looks that way."

Mitchell raised his hand to his pocket. It was going to be a long week.

❁

Carolyn shut off the vacuum cleaner and ran to the door. She didn't have to wait a second time to confirm that she was hearing correctly. In a way, she was almost expecting Mitchell. She didn't want to admit it, even to herself, but she hadn't seen him since the last cooking class, and she'd missed him.

She turned the lock and flung the door open. "Mi—Hank? What are you doing here?"

Hank stood before her with his raincoat open. Beneath it he wore his usual dark suit and matching tie, which she thought odd for a Saturday afternoon. In his hand was a bouquet of red roses.

"May I come in?"

She stood aside and ran her fingers through her hair to straighten it and smoothed the folds out of her sweatshirt. "Certainly."

Hank walked past her with the flowers then waited for her to close the door behind him, which she thought rather strange. If it were Mitchell, he would have given her the flowers, tried to kiss her, and he would have closed the door behind himself. She envisioned Mitchell's impish smile, but as she blinked, Hank's solemn face came into focus.

He cleared his throat. "I brought these for you." He held out the roses.

Hesitantly, she accepted the bouquet. The only time Hank had given her flowers had been a corsage at last year's Christmas banquet because she had sung a solo. Other than that, the only time he had given her anything was at Christmas and on her birthday. Her feet didn't move as she stared down at the flowers, wondering what the occasion was to warrant them.

He straightened his tie. "I've been giving this a lot of thought lately, and I'm asking if you'll marry me. I didn't buy you a ring because I thought you might want to pick one out for yourself."

The roses trembled as her hands started shaking. Perhaps she had strange expectations, but she had always thought a proposal was accompanied by words of love and affection, followed by a hug or a tender touch, even a kiss. It should have been a moment to be remembered fondly for the rest of a person's life. The suit and the flowers seemed so prepared, even calculated, and not very romantic, despite the proposal.

"I can see I've caught you off guard, and I can't blame you. Would you like to think about it for a few days?"

She nearly choked. Obviously, another grand misconception of hers was that the day a man asked her to marry him, she would have been overjoyed, filled with excitement and visions of a happy future together. She should want to scream a big yes and throw herself into his arms.

She didn't know what to say, but one thing she did know. She couldn't marry Hank. Not when she was in love with Mitchell.

As the thought hit home, Carolyn felt the color drain from her face.

"Carolyn, are you okay? You don't look well."

He was right. She didn't feel very well at all. She was in love but with the wrong man.

But even if she wasn't in love with Mitchell, she couldn't marry Hank. She'd always thought marriage was a fulfillment of love and commitment. If Hank truly loved her, she should have been able to tell by now. She suspected that if men had a biological clock, Hank's was ticking. His proposal had nothing to do with love. She wanted to get married, too, but she wasn't desperate enough to be trapped in a loveless marriage. She would rather live alone.

Carolyn cleared her throat to get her voice to work properly. "I'm sorry, Hank, but I can't marry you. I don't need time to think about it. I like you very much as a friend, but I don't think it would work."

He shoved his hands into his pockets. "Well. I see. To tell the truth, even though we haven't exactly had a hearts and flowers relationship, I thought we were compatible enough to get married and raise a family. After all, neither of us is getting any younger."

Carolyn felt sick. Compatible. She wondered if she was supposed to be flattered. The roses, which she had always thought were the flowers of love, felt like a sham in her hands. She didn't love him, nor did he love her. But yet, Hank possessed everything she'd ever wanted in a man. He was mature, carried himself with class and dignity, was a marvelous host, and had a wonderful career as an accountant for a large corporation. He chose his leisure activities with great care—golf for fitness and the theater or gallery for something educational. Often his choices had involved business contacts, which allowed her to meet his peers in a social environment.

Hank's biggest shortcoming was his attendance at church and Bible study meetings. And come to think of it, in all they discussed, they never seemed to talk about God's Word, not even the Sunday sermon topics. She didn't even know his favorite Bible verse. She didn't know if he had a favorite verse. The more she thought about it, while she knew he was a believer, she didn't know exactly how important God was in Hank's life.

She couldn't love a man who didn't love God first.

She was in love with Mitchell Farris. How could her Mr. Right be so very Mr. Wrong?

"I think you'd better leave. And take these with you." She stood and held out the flowers, but he didn't accept them.

Hank's face hardened, and his lips tightened into a scowl. "Go ahead and turn me down now, but before long you'll be begging my forgiveness. If you're lucky, I'll consider you again. Just wait. When you're closer to forty, you'll see that life is passing you by. By then it will be too late. I'll be married to someone else."

Her mouth dropped open then snapped shut. "Get out," she ground out between her teeth. She thrust the flowers back into his hand, but he dropped them to the floor and stomped out, slamming the door behind him. As she stood transfixed in one spot, his car started then roared off into the distance.

Carolyn continued to stare at the closed door long after the sound of Hank's car had disappeared, stunned that he had asked for her hand in marriage not on the basis of love, but because he considered them—at least her—almost past their prime marriage years. She wasn't twenty-four years old anymore, but neither was she too old to desire a marriage based on mutual love and children conceived and raised in that love.

Rather than being sorry that she would never see Hank again, she was glad he was gone.

Her gaze drifted to the roses lying in a jumbled pile in the middle of the hardwood floor. Many of the velvety petals had fallen off and a broken leaf lay to the side, the heady rose scent made stronger by their disarray. Slowly, she counted a dozen roses, the flowers of love, lying at her feet as a wretched testimonial of the state of her love life. A man she didn't love had just proposed marriage, and the man she did love was completely wrong for her. Her throat tightened, and her chin started to quiver uncontrollably.

Tears welled up, and she couldn't hold them back.

She sank to her knees in the middle of the living room floor and, surrounded by the broken flowers, covered her face with her hands and gave in to sobs that racked her entire body.

The doorbell rang, but she didn't answer it. She couldn't allow anyone to see her like this.

Mitchell's voice drifted through the door. "Carolyn? I know you're in there. Your car is in the driveway."

She didn't answer. She couldn't have spoken a word if she wanted to.

He knocked again. "Carolyn? Are you all right?"

When she still didn't answer, the doorknob rattled then turned. The door slowly creaked open.

"Carolyn? The door was. . ." His voice drifted into silence.

Before she knew what was happening, she was pulled to her feet and locked solidly in a tight embrace, pressed against Mitchell from head to foot.

"What's wrong?" he murmured into her hair.

"It was Hank. He. . ." She couldn't finish.

His hands grasped her shoulders, and he pushed her away so he could look into her eyes. She turned her head so she didn't have to face him.

Mitchell's voice dropped to a low murmur, yet at the same time, it was very stern. "Did he hurt you?"

She shook her head, unable to stop the increased flow of tears or control the tremor in her voice. "N–no, n–nothing like that. H–he asked me to m–marry him."

In the blink of an eye, she was pressed into his chest again, but this time, instead of holding her by the shoulders, one of his large hands cupped the back of her head, gently pressing her cheek into his chest, the other hand pressed into the small of her back, and his chin rested on the top of her head.

With her ear pressed into the center of his chest, his voice sounded gruff and rumbly, and she could hear the rapid hammering of his heart. "And you said?"

She could barely choke the words out. "I said no. He didn't take it well."

His grip tightened, and he furthered the embrace by pushing his entire face into her hair. "Praise God. He's not right for you."

She shook her head, with her face still pressed into his chest, without answering.

He held her without speaking while she gained control then released her when her sobs quieted. Carolyn excused herself to splash some cold water on her face and blow her nose.

She didn't want him to see her like this, but she also didn't want him to leave. Since no amount of makeup would erase the evidence of what happened, Carolyn stiffened her posture and entered the living room, where Mitchell was waiting for her. Instead of sitting on the couch, she found him standing with his back to her, studying her needlepoint. She didn't know if he really was that interested in it, but she appreciated him knowing she felt awkward about what she looked like. She also appreciated that the flowers were gone.

She sniffled one last time and sat on the couch. "What are you doing here? I wasn't expecting you." She purposely neglected mentioning that even though she wasn't expecting him, she had spent the earlier part of the day hoping he would show up.

"I had a few errands to do, and now that I'm done, I thought maybe we could spend the rest of the day together."

"I think I'll just stay home. Thanks for the thought, though."

He turned around but kept his distance. "I think it would be a good idea for you to get away for a while. It's Saturday afternoon. Why don't we go to a matinee? We can pick some weepy chick flick, and everyone will think you've been crying over the movie."

"A chick flick?"

"You know what I mean. One of those gushy movies where all the women sit there and cry through the movie, giving the guys a chance to put their arms around them and be macho."

Except for the putting his arms around her implication, it sounded perfect. For a while, she could get lost in the sad story of someone else's life and forget about the mess of her own life. She forced herself to smile. "I think that's a great idea."

"Good. While you were. . .uh, busy, I looked through the paper and found one. We have just enough time to get there if we hurry."

Mitchell yakked nonstop all the way to the theater, for which she was grateful. True to his plan, when the plot of the movie started getting weepy, he slipped his arm around her shoulders, which again started the flow of tears, allowing her the release she needed to get everything out of her system.

The whole time she cried, Mitchell merely sat there with his arm around her, every once in a while handing her another napkin to wipe her eyes and blow her nose. At the end of the movie, they remained seated until almost everyone left, then they slowly shuffled out.

"See. I knew you wouldn't be the only one crying. Just why do women cry at stuff like that?"

Carolyn blew her nose on the last napkin and shoved it into her purse. "I can't explain it."

He smiled and ran his thumb beneath her glasses, under her puffy eyes. "It was a rhetorical question. I think it's time to take you home. Wanna order pizza for supper?"

Chapter 12

Mitchell sat at the kitchen table with the blue velvet pouch in his hand. With Jake gone and the dog asleep, the house was totally quiet, which gave him time to think before Carolyn arrived.

He couldn't count the times he'd tried to take her out for a quiet, romantic dinner, and each time something had happened or she'd managed to pick someplace not at all suitable to tell her what was in his heart and present her with the ring. Though often the activity was something fun—which in itself wasn't a bad thing—every time meant yet another delay and one more missed opportunity.

Again today, ideally they could have gone out for dinner. The competitor's strike had been averted, and not only did he not have to work overtime, he'd managed to get off early, which was a rare occurrence in itself. However, the rehearsal party was now only a few days away, and this was his last chance to practice what he needed to know before he had to do it for real, by himself.

Today was his last remedial cooking lesson, and Carolyn was due to arrive any minute.

It was less than the ideal situation, but if he didn't give Carolyn the ring today, he knew there wouldn't be a quiet day or time until all the cooking was done, the rehearsal party over with, and then after the big day on the weekend, the actual wedding. Following that, he would have to see Jake and Ellen off on their honeymoon, and then there would be the fallout with returning rented items and cleaning up. He didn't want to wait any longer.

He would give her the ring today. He tucked it into his pocket and patted it again.

Since the kitchen would be a mess when they were done, he'd prepared the living room as best he could. He'd vacuumed and dusted and done his best to pick as much dog hair off the couch as possible. For a romantic touch, he'd managed to find the one candle they owned and set it and a book of matches to the side, ready for the right moment.

Again, Mitchell pulled the pouch out of his pocket. He'd never thought much about jewelry before, but the little heart really was a perfect indication of his feelings for Carolyn. As delicately as he could, he plucked the tiny ring out of the bag and tipped it, making the small diamond sparkle in the light. He could see why such a ring would be called a promise ring. In a way, between the gold and the diamond, the ring resembled a miniature engagement ring. Hopefully, giving it to her could signify a promise of giving her a bigger diamond in the near future, along with the commitment of forever.

Both the kitchen and the living room were ready for Carolyn's arrival, but first, Mitchell needed to do one more thing. He tucked the ring back into the pouch, pulled the drawstring closed, dropped it back into his pocket, then folded his hands on the table and closed his eyes.

"Dear heavenly Father, thank You for bringing Carolyn into my life. She's exactly who I needed, and I pray that I am exactly who she needs as a perfect mate, designed and chosen by You. Again, I pray that tonight will present the perfect opportunity to give her this ring as a symbol of what our relationship could be and that You'll bless our time together. Amen."

At his closing amen, Killer started barking and ran for the door. Mitchell smiled and stood. God's timing was always perfect.

On his way through the living room, he could feel the pouch bouncing in his pocket.

He craned his neck to look down at it and realized he could see its outline through the pocket of this particular shirt. Rather than run to his bedroom to put it in the drawer, he detoured a few steps and tucked it beside the lamp on the end table, where she wouldn't see it until the time was right.

She hadn't knocked yet, but that didn't stop him from opening the door to watch Carolyn as she walked up the sidewalk. The streetlights had come on, but the sky was still aglow with pink and purple, vivid with the beauty of God's creation and very fitting for Carolyn's arrival.

"Hi," he said, making no attempt to stop the wide smile he knew was on his face.

Carolyn tilted her head and narrowed one eye as she walked past him. "We are cooking today, aren't we?"

He couldn't stop smiling. "Of course."

She marched straight into his kitchen, and he trailed behind.

"I guess this is the last time I'll be helping you at home. Have you decided what you need help with today? I see you have a cookbook out. You told me you didn't own one."

He could feel his blush warming his cheeks, and he chided himself for it. "It's my mother's. The thing I really wanted to make was her specialty—crab snaps. Actually, that's why I took the course, to learn how to cook well enough to make them. No one believes that I can do this except Ellen. She knows I'm taking your classes."

Carolyn ran her finger down the recipe, mouthing the ingredients but not saying anything out loud. Her finger stopped moving when she got to the instructions. "This doesn't look too difficult. I don't see that you'll have a problem."

He didn't have to close his eyes to envision his first attempt at making his mother's famous crab snaps. It still made him shudder to think about it. "You have no idea."

They both checked the clock on the stove at the same time. "I guess we better get started." She ran her finger down the list again. "I'm going to assume you're using canned crab and not fresh?"

Mitchell groaned aloud. "I wasn't going to take the chance it was like shelling shrimp. Yes, it's canned."

"Okay, then go get the—"

The light flickered once then went out.

Automatically, Mitchell walked to the wall switch and flicked it while Carolyn stared up at the dark fixture. "I don't believe this," he muttered under his breath.

Carolyn turned her head. "The living room looks awful dark. I don't think it's the bulb; I think the power just went out."

He strode to the window. The whole street was dark, as was his entire neighborhood and farther than he could see. "Houston, we have a problem," Mitchell mumbled and crossed his arms over his chest. He turned to Carolyn. "I don't have time for this. I have to learn how to make these things today. The party is Friday, only four days away."

He pulled open a drawer and grabbed a flashlight then opened the phone directory. "I'm calling the electric company." A few moments later, he hung up and turned to Carolyn. "The recording said they're aware of an outage and a crew was being dispatched to determine the cause. There will be updates on the radio. I'll be right back."

Mitchell took the flashlight and retrieved his radio from the garage, where he used it when he was working on his car. He turned it on and tried to find a good station as he headed back to the kitchen.

"Do you keep everything you own in the garage?"

"Not everything I own fits in the pantry."

She sighed then turned to study the stack of bowls and utensils he'd spread over the counters. "I don't know what to do. We could do this at my house, but by the time we get there, the power could be back on. Besides, all the ingredients are in your fridge, and I have a real aversion to opening the fridge when the power is out, just in case it doesn't come back for a long time."

Out of habit, Mitchell shone the flashlight on the battery-operated wall clock. "It's been out for twenty minutes already. I guess this serves me right for leaving the crab snaps until the last minute."

"Not really. Most of these things have to be prepared within a few days of the event. They get freezer burn quickly because of the individual-size portions. Besides, I doubt you have suitable storage containers."

He still had a couple of plastic containers he'd forgotten to give back to his mother the last time she sent him food, but other than that, whenever he had leftovers worth storing, he kept them in one of the two empty margarine containers he hadn't thrown out. Somehow he doubted Carolyn would consider those proper. He simply shrugged his shoulders, and her cute little sigh told him he was right in not replying.

"You shouldn't keep a seafood filling longer than overnight before serving. It would be best to make the pastries on Thursday, and then you could mix the filling and keep it in the fridge overnight and stuff them Friday before you have to go." She looked around the dark kitchen. "You really shouldn't prepare any of what you're going to serve until Wednesday or even Thursday. What else were you planning on making? Maybe we should go over your menu."

"I was going to make a few of the recipes we made in class and one of the things we did together. I really liked those rolled-up cheesy things that were dipped in the smashed-up nuts."

Carolyn sighed and crossed her arms over her chest. "Did I ever tell you that you have a unique way of describing these gourmet treats we've been making?"

"Many times. If we're not cooking, I guess we really don't need a lot of light." As if on cue, the beam of the flashlight faded, becoming slightly yellow. "It doesn't look like this battery is going to last much longer. I'd better get a candle."

He started toward the doorway when Carolyn's voice stopped him.

"Unlike your electric mixer, I can understand storing candles in the garage."

"Actually, I was going to the living room."

"I give up."

Mitchell soon returned to the kitchen. The smell of sulfur filled the air as he lit the candle and set it in the center of the table while Carolyn turned off the flashlight, which was almost dead anyway.

Carolyn pulled his mother's recipe book across the table. "What else were you going to make?"

He pulled up a chair and sat beside her. "Just the crab snaps. I wouldn't dare try to make anything else in there. I thought I'd stick to stuff I did in your class." He reached to the drawer behind him, grabbed the stack of handout sheets, and spread them over the table. "I know how to do these things, within reason. I was thinking I'd make the ones I liked best."

"You're just doing this now? You haven't decided on your menu or done your shopping yet?"

"I just bought what I needed to make the crab snaps because that's what I thought we were going to do today."

349

She grumbled something under her breath while she paged through the pile and pulled out the recipe he'd referred to earlier.

"Am I in trouble?"

"When did you expect to do this? Do you have a pen and paper?"

Mitchell found a pen, but he couldn't find an unused piece of paper in the dark, so he reached on top of the fridge and gave her the envelope from the phone bill. Her eyes narrowed as she accepted it from him, but she didn't say a word. He settled into the chair beside Carolyn and sat in silence as she skimmed the ingredients on the recipe he had selected and wrote out the shopping list in the flickering candlelight.

She slid the pile of paper back to him. "Which other ones do you want to make? And what did you do with the recipe for the dessert squares that I gave you?"

"It's in the pile somewhere."

Mitchell gave her his best smile, but it didn't ward off the annoyed sigh he knew was coming.

Together, they began the process of selecting the best choices for the party, and Carolyn dutifully added everything to the grocery list.

Instead of the romantic setting the candlelight was supposed to provide for the big moment he had planned, they now struggled to read by its questionable light; and instead of being receptive to him as he prepared to bare his soul, she was mad at him because he hadn't done his grocery shopping yet.

He couldn't believe how long the whole process took, nor could he believe that by the time she was finally adding the last of what they would need to the list, the power still hadn't come back on. The battery in his radio had expired during the wait.

Carolyn continued to write while he tried to think of a way to change the subject from cooking to how he felt about her when Killer ran to the door.

"I think your dog wants out."

"Killer would go to the back if she wanted out. She's at the front, and she's not barking, so that means Jake is home."

He heard Jake's voice before he saw him. "Wow. You should see the extent of this power failure. Did you know that it's dark all the way to. . ." His voice trailed off as he entered the kitchen. "Hello, Carolyn. It's nice to see you again."

She laid the pen down on the table. "Nice to see you, too, Jake."

Mitchell couldn't begrudge his friend's arrival. After all, Jake lived there, too. However, Jake's arrival had just disintegrated Mitchell's last hope of trying to have that private talk with Carolyn—unless the power failure was going to last a lot longer and they went to her house. "Did you have the radio on in the car? Any idea how much longer before the power comes back on?"

"They said about half an hour."

Carolyn stood. "That's too late to start, and it would take at least that long to pack up and move everything to my house."

Mitchell stood, as well. "What about grocery shopping? We can do that, now that we have a list."

"Sorry," Jake said. "Everything is out. They said on the radio that twenty-five thousand homes are without power."

Carolyn stepped toward the door. "Then I guess I'll be going."

Mitchell clenched his teeth and followed her to the door. Today, power failure or not, right moment or not, he could no longer wait. If he didn't give her the ring now, it would be another week before he could, and he didn't want to wait that long.

Since Jake's arrival meant no privacy inside, Mitchell followed her outside to her car parked on the dark street.

She reached for the handle, but before she opened the car door, Mitchell laid his hand on top of hers and gently pulled it to him.

"What are you doing?"

He massaged her wrist with his thumb. "I wanted to talk to you. I have to ask you something, and I don't know how to start."

Her smile made his heart flutter—something he thought only happened to women.

"It's okay. I know what you're going to say."

"You do?" He smiled back. That she had been thinking the same things was a positive and very encouraging sign about the growth of their relationship.

"Yes." She reached up with her other hand and gave his hand a tender squeeze. "I'm okay now. I'm not going to be seeing Hank anymore. It was a shock at the time, but I think I've known for a while that we weren't suited for each other. I'm sure that one day God will put the right man in my path. You're a good friend, Mitchell. I appreciate your concern."

"But—"

He let his hand go limp, and she moved away. "It's really late. I have to go home. The lack of electricity isn't going to prevent me from sleeping. Good night."

"Wait!" Out of habit, he reached up to his shirt pocket, but it was empty. He squeezed his eyes shut, remembering that he'd left the ring in the living room, ready for the right moment.

"I'll see you at class tomorrow."

Mitchell dropped his hand from his shirt pocket. "Yeah. Class tomorrow. Bye."

✿

Mitchell thunked his lunch pail on the counter and glanced at the clock, then at the calendar.

Today was Tuesday. Class night. It was also three days before the rehearsal party.

The power hadn't come on until after midnight Monday, when the only stores open were the convenience stores. He needed to start cooking as soon as he got home from work on Wednesday. That left tonight to do his shopping.

But tonight was cooking class. The last one he'd planned to take.

The clock on the wall ticked audibly.

He should have been shopping, not watching the clock.

Last night Carolyn called him a friend. She'd also said that one day God would put the right man in her path.

As far as he was concerned, God had put the right man in her path. She just didn't know it yet.

Mitchell grabbed his jacket and ran to his car. He didn't care if he was still at the grocery store at midnight when it closed, but he was going to class.

Chapter 13

O kay, class, today we're going to make some classic hors d'oeuvres, starting with stuffed celery, and then some meat and vegetable combinations. First you need to—"

"Sorry I'm late. Excuse me."

Carolyn waited until Mitchell shuffled into the last empty chair, crossed his legs, and leaned back. All eyes settled on him, then slowly everyone returned their attention to the front.

She sighed and carried on with the lesson, but her mind was no longer fully on the food preparation. Today Mitchell should have been doing his shopping, since the power hadn't come back on in time to do it last night. She really hadn't expected to see him, and his presence in the class rattled her.

It had been difficult, but she'd come to a decision on what she was going to do about Mitchell. The times he had kissed her were seared into her memory for a lifetime. They didn't have a future together, but she couldn't stand the thought of never seeing him again. To keep whatever was happening between them as a platonic friendship was the best solution.

Yesterday she'd done her best to summon her courage and tell Mitchell indirectly that she considered him a friend. Mitchell was an intelligent person. She knew he would understand her meaning. It was only the shock of Hank's proposal that made her think she was in love with Mitchell, because the more she thought about it, the more she knew it wasn't possible. Mitchell was twenty-four years old. He'd started his first job right out of high school as a warehouseman and worked his way into the dispatch office, where he now held a junior supervisory position. And he was happy with that.

She had to either continue to see him as a friend or not see him at all. She couldn't do that.

When the food preparations were done and all the creations eaten, Carolyn continued to walk from group to group, chatting and answering questions while everyone cleaned up. As usual, she arrived at Mitchell's group last.

Part of the routine she had set up was that every week the cleanup duties rotated, and today it was Mitchell's turn to wash dishes. He had his arms halfway to his elbows in the soapy water and his back was to her. She didn't mean to eavesdrop as she approached, but neither did she want to be rude and interrupt him.

"That's right. My best friend is marrying my sister, and I'm going to be cooking up all the food for the rehearsal party, which is Friday. I kind of backed myself into a corner. I took this course so I wouldn't have to eat crow."

Mrs. Finkleman started to chuckle. "That was a good thing. Crow would taste terrible." No one else laughed at her joke, but she didn't seem to notice.

Lorraine nearly dropped the pot she was returning to its place in the cupboard. "You're doing the cooking? You? The man who exploded an egg in the microwave trying to cook it faster?" She pointed her finger at him and burst out laughing.

"That was an accident," he mumbled while he scrubbed the last pan with far more force than necessary.

Carolyn gritted her teeth at Lorraine's barb and stepped into their little circle. "Everyone makes mistakes, especially when they're still learning. Mitchell is going to do just fine."

All noise and action immediately ceased, not only in Mitchell's group, but also the two neighboring groups. When the other two groups noticed the silence, they also suddenly quieted. All eyes turned to her.

Carolyn stiffened and made eye contact with everyone except Mitchell as she spoke. "Next week is our last class, and we're going to make a few dessert items. I look forward to seeing you all then. Good night, everyone."

She didn't wait for a reply but turned and headed for her demonstration table to tidy her own mess as the ladies began to filter out.

As usual, Mitchell was the last person besides her remaining in the room. This time, she really didn't want to talk to him. She'd made a public display of defending him when he was perfectly capable of defending himself.

Also as usual, he appeared at her side before she was finished cleaning.

"I need to talk to you."

He continued before she could protest.

"I have something for you, and this isn't exactly the way I wanted to give it to you, but I'm going to do it anyway." He patted his pockets until he found what he was looking for, pulled out a little blue velvet jewelry pouch, then handed it to her without a word.

She took the pouch from him but didn't check inside. "How did you know it was my birthday tomorrow?"

He hesitated but recovered quickly. "I didn't know it was your birthday tomorrow. If that's the case, then I'm going to have to figure out something special to give you to mark the occasion. This," he said, pointing at the pouch, "has nothing to do with your birthday. Quite honestly, I've been meaning to give this to you for a while and never got the chance."

Her heart started pounding, and she broke into a sweat.

Her hands trembled as she opened it.

When she saw what was inside, she couldn't keep the tremor from her voice. "It's a ring."

It was small and delicate and beautiful. A small, sparkling diamond in the middle of a gold heart glittered in the fluorescent light.

He scooted around the table and was beside her before she realized he had moved. "Try it on."

Her hands shook so much, she was afraid she would drop it. Very slowly, she slipped it on. It was a little too big for her ring finger so she changed it to her middle finger, which seemed to minimize its statement. A promise ring.

"I don't know what to say. Why are you doing this?"

He smiled that lopsided smile she was getting to know so well. When his dimple appeared, her throat went dry. "I'm courting you, Carolyn. Can't you tell? If you can't, I must be doing something wrong."

He had done nothing wrong, but until now, she had done a fine job of convincing herself that his constant appearances and the warm fuzzies she felt in his presence meant only friendship.

"Don't you remember that, as of tomorrow, I'm nine years older than you? You can't court me. It's not right."

"Age doesn't matter, Carolyn. At least it doesn't matter to me. You're the special person you are regardless of your age or mine. We share lots of common interests, and we share a common faith. Nothing else matters."

"I think it's a little more complicated than that." She still wasn't sure they had common interests, although they did enjoy their time together. While she'd always heard that opposites attract, she had a feeling she and Mitchell were too opposite for consideration. He was nothing like the man she had prayed for as her perfect mate. She almost shuddered visibly as she imagined Mitchell with all Hank's sensible and mature character traits. She didn't want another Hank. But Mitchell wasn't right for her, either.

While finding a woman with a strong faith in Christ seemed very important to Mitchell, she couldn't see that she could ever be the fun-loving and active woman he needed. Ten years ago she had tried skiing, hiking, and other more strenuous activities. Not that she was anywhere near a couch potato, but about the time she turned thirty, her interests turned to quieter and less demanding leisure pursuits.

"I don't know if I can accept this. I don't think this is such a good idea."

He picked up her hands then rubbed his thumb over the small ring on her finger. "The saleslady said it was a promise ring, and I am making a promise to you, Carolyn. But if you want to, we can start off slowly and call it a friendship ring."

"But it's a heart. Hearts don't mean friendship."

His hand rose to her cheek. Her eyes drifted shut as he brushed her skin with the backs of his fingers. "Then think of it however you want. All I want is for you to keep an open heart because I l–l–l. . . I like you a lot."

Footsteps echoed in the hall, drawing their attention to Mr. O'Sullivan checking the classrooms to make sure everyone had left the building for the night. No doubt he'd noticed that hers was the only car left in the staff parking lot and was dutifully checking on her.

She cleared her throat and opened her eyes, resisting as hard as she could not to lean her head into his fingers. "I think it's time to go home."

"I can't go home yet. I have to go grocery shopping."

"Pardon me?"

"I have to start cooking as soon as I get home from work tomorrow, so I'm going shopping tonight. The megastore is open until midnight, so I'll have just enough time. Wanna come?"

❀

Carolyn sent her high school students to the kitchenettes to do their projects then walked from group to group to supervise and assist.

Every time she moved her hand, she became aware of the unaccustomed ring on her finger. She'd never worn a ring before; no one had ever given her one. She enjoyed and appreciated both the look and the feel of the fine gold and tiny diamond on her finger, but conversely, it was a constant reminder of Mitchell.

She still didn't know what to do about him. A man didn't give a woman a ring with a heart on it to signify friendship.

The man was courting her. Part of her wanted it, and part of her said it wouldn't work.

A loud bang accompanied by teenaged laughter drew Carolyn's attention back to her class. Group three again needed more help than the rest of the class, so she stopped thinking about Mitchell and began showing her students how to properly separate an egg when the sound of footsteps clicked on the tile floor so loudly, it almost sounded like someone was wearing taps on their shoes.

"That's Miss Rutherford," a teen's voice piped up.

Abruptly, Carolyn turned to see a man in a horridly bright red bellhop uniform overly embellished with glossy black stripes down the sides of the legs and arms. The outfit was topped off with the ugliest hat she'd ever seen, and the man was holding a brightly wrapped parcel in one hand. He blew a tuning harmonica then ceremoniously cleared his throat.

"Happy birthday to you," he sang, drawing out the familiar refrain.

Most of the students burst out laughing.

Carolyn thought she'd die. But she would kill Mitchell first. Except that would probably be a sin.

Red faced and stiff as a board, she listened to the badly dramatized rendition wishing her a happy birthday. When the last torturous line was sufficiently drawn out, with a tip of his fez, the man offered her the gift. The class gave him a rousing round of applause to which he bowed with a flourish and left amidst another chorus of catcalls and whistles.

Carolyn continued to stare at the vacant doorway, barely aware of the brightly wrapped box in her hands. She couldn't believe the school secretary had allowed him in.

Another round of applause and cheers from the students snapped her mind back to what she was supposed to have been doing.

Carolyn cleared her throat. "That's enough nonsense. Let's finish up before we run out of time."

"What did you get?"

"How old are you?"

"Who sent the singing telegram? Your boyfriend?"

Most of the teenaged girls giggled.

Carolyn sighed. She didn't exactly think of Mitchell as her boyfriend, but the trouble was, she didn't know what to call him. The only thing she did know was that of all her friends, only Mitchell would do such a thing as send a singing telegram.

Again, her fingers drifted to touch the tiny promise ring, outlining the shape of the heart without looking at it. Certainly they'd gone beyond mere friendship, but she still hadn't figured out to what. In order to get the focus off her personal life and back to the home economics class she was supposed to be leading, she had to provide a response. "Yes, my boyfriend."

"Ooh," the students chorused.

"That's enough, class. Now get back to your kitchenettes."

Slowly, everyone shuffled back to their lesson project of the day, although she both saw and heard little whisperings in every group.

By the time the lunch bell rang, she was more than ready to be left alone. Rather than go to the staff room, Carolyn sat at her desk and stared at the brightly colored box. It was not professionally wrapped. The paper was cut crooked and the bow lay off center. Only Mitchell could have wrapped this.

Slowly, Carolyn picked off the brightly colored bow and stuck it to the side of her penholder. She unhitched the tape and pulled off the paper.

The box was from a specialty chocolate store, and inside was an assortment of foil-wrapped chocolate kisses and a small card filled with scrawling handwriting.

Happy birthday, Carolyn.
One sweet kiss for each sweet year. Enjoy them, and think of me.

Love, Mitchell

Carolyn squeezed her eyes shut and sighed.

She didn't know how to respond. As strange as it was, the gesture was unique and far more personal than any gift she had ever received. The addition of the chocolates made the whole thing rather romantic, in a Mitchell Farris kind of way.

She picked up the note and studied it. His handwriting was atrocious, but as bad as it was, the signature "Love, Mitchell" jumped off the paper at her.

She didn't want to think about the ramifications of the chocolate kisses.

Rather than dwell on it any longer, Carolyn popped one into her mouth, reread the note, and counted the chocolate morsels while the one melted in her mouth. To her dismay, the store had made a mistake, because, counting the one already in her mouth, there were only thirty-two.

She carefully closed the box, mentally kicking herself for having a chocolate before she ate her lunch, and tucked the box into her desk drawer. She checked the clock, picked up her purse, retrieved her lunch bag from the large fridge, and made her way to the staff lunch room, where she could phone Mitchell to thank him for a very unusual but very special birthday gift.

The second she opened the door, a chorus of "happy birthdays" greeted her, along with a cake with one large lighted candle. Carolyn clutched her purse tightly so she wouldn't drop it or her lunch. All the other teachers either cheered or laughed at her surprise.

Carolyn's eyes burned, but she blinked a few times, lifted her glasses, and wiped tears away. "Th–thank you," she stammered. In the six years she'd worked at the school, no one had ever acknowledged her birthday. Though the date was on her job application, she'd never told anyone. Of course some of them would have known because of the singing telegram, but she hadn't expected this.

Karen, the secretary, stood. "Come on, Carolyn. Blow out the candle before it burns the cake down or sets off the smoke alarm."

She sucked in a deep breath, blew out the candle, and everyone applauded.

Karen stepped forward, pulled the candle out of the cake, then hurried to run the smoking wick under the cold water. "Your boyfriend phoned first thing this morning and asked for permission and the best time to send the singing telegram, otherwise, I wouldn't have known it was your birthday. You should have said something." Karen placed a stack of paper plates and a knife beside the cake. "Here—we got you a card. Happy birthday."

Carolyn lowered her head. "Thank you," she mumbled as she tore the flap open. Everyone had signed it and added a silly comment.

Conversations that had ended when she walked in restarted, and soon it was just like any other lunch break. As everyone finished eating, Carolyn cut a piece of cake for each teacher. She'd barely finished her own slice when the bell rang to return to the classrooms, not allowing her the time to phone Mitchell.

The students all wished her a happy birthday as they filed in. Carolyn forced herself to smile and thank them all, knowing that the singing telegram had now become hot news throughout the entire school population during the lunch break. It also gave her a horrible premonition that there would be a picture of the young man and a summary of the incident in the school's yearbook.

The afternoon seemed the longest in the time since she'd begun her teaching career. By the time the bell rang signaling the close of classes, she was eager to go home.

She hurried to tidy her demonstration area and was almost finished checking all the kitchenettes to make sure everything was in order for the first class the next day when footsteps echoed through the door opening.

"Hi," a familiar deep voice drawled. "Happy birthday."

Carolyn spun around, her hand pressed to her heart. "Mitchell! What are you doing here? Why aren't you at work?"

"I have lots of time coming to me, so I took off early for a change." He grinned that same grin she'd come to know and love, and her heart pounded even more. "I brought you something."

"But you already gave me a wonderful birthday present. Thank you very much. It was really different."

He dangled something shiny in the air. "I brought you the last kiss."

She couldn't hold back her smile. The store hadn't made a mistake. "That's very sweet, but you didn't have to take time off and come all this way just for that." As she spoke, she walked toward him to collect it.

No sooner had she taken her first step than Mitchell hastily unwrapped the kiss and popped it into his mouth.

"Hey! That was mine!"

She watched as he guiltlessly grinned, chewed it, and swallowed. "Nope. That one was for me." He stepped forward. "This one's for you."

Before she realized what he was doing, he wrapped his arms around her and kissed her. And without thinking about it, she kissed him back. The combination of his embrace and the scent of chocolate on his breath made her head spin and her already pounding heart jump into overdrive.

The bang of someone slamming a locker in the hallway caused them both to jump. Mitchell released her and backed up a step, his confusion evident in his expression.

"I didn't mean for this to happen like that," he stammered then shook his head. "No, that's wrong. Yes, I did mean for that to happen. But not here."

If he suggested they go elsewhere and pick up where they left off, she thought she might run screaming for the hills.

"I had to come here to see you because it's Bible study night, and I know we said we'd go to mine tonight, but I'm going to have to get a rain check until next week. I'm going to start making the food for Friday tonight. Knowing my luck, something will happen, and I'll need two full evenings to do this. I hope you're proud of me for planning ahead."

She smiled. "Yes. I'm proud of you. If you need help, I can skip this one week."

He pressed one palm to his heart. "You're asking if I need help? You mean you actually considered that I could do this all by myself, without help?"

"Do you want me to be honest or make you feel good?"

His little grin made her breath catch. "I won't back you into a corner and make you answer that. Instead, I have an idea. How about if we pick up a couple of burgers, and I'd be forever grateful if you could join me in the kitchen this evening, just in case I need you."

There was no "just in case" to consider. "Yes, I think I'll do that."

Chapter 14

Carolyn opened the bag and slid the hamburger and large order of fries across the kitchen table, keeping the other hamburger and smaller order of fries for herself while Mitchell started a pot of coffee.

Killer lay in her bed in the corner of the kitchen, ignoring them while they prayed over the food.

"I've been meaning to ask you why you call that sweet animal Killer. That has to be the gentlest, most unexcitable dog I've ever seen."

Mitchell's ears reddened. "It was one of my lesser inspired moments. I thought if the dog was such a marshmallow, a name like Killer might preserve her reputation, but everyone just laughs."

"Is she so calm because she's old, or is she going deaf?"

"I'm not sure. I guess she's about five or so. I know she's not deaf. She appears the split second I open the cupboard where her dog cookies are."

"You guess? You mean you don't know how old your dog is?"

"Not really. We got her from the pound. Jake and I were looking for a watchdog because we'd just been robbed. We were looking at a bigger dog, but when we learned Killer was going to be put down, those big, sad eyes got to me, and I took her. We haven't been robbed since, so I suppose she's at least partly responsible for that. She's friendly, anyway. And she doesn't annoy the neighbors with tons of barking."

"That was a sweet thing to do!"

"Don't go getting gushy on me. It's just a dog."

She wanted to hug him just for being nice but didn't dare after what happened at the school.

As soon as they finished eating, Mitchell bundled the paper wrappings and they set to work. As a matter of pride, he insisted on doing the pastry while Carolyn mixed the fillings and pâté. Together, they shaped cheese balls and rolled them in the chopped nuts.

Killer jumped to her feet and ran to the door. She barked once then sat quietly and wagged her tail.

Mitchell wiped his hands on his pants, leaving floury handprints on his thighs, and headed for the door. "Killer barked, so it's not Jake. I'm not expecting anyone."

Carolyn stood in the kitchen doorway, watching.

Before Mitchell got to the door, it opened and Jake walked in, followed by Gordie and Roland.

"Mitch? What are you doing here? It's your Bible study night." Jake glanced at the flour on Mitchell's nose and burst out laughing.

Gordie stepped forward. "Hi, Miss Rutherford."

Carolyn cringed. Miss Rutherford. Is that what she would be to his friends? Not his companion or his girlfriend, but the teacher, Miss Rutherford? She smiled shakily. "Hi, Gordie," she mumbled.

Mitchell's posture stiffened as he faced his friend. "We're not in school anymore. Her name is Carolyn."

"Oops. Sorry, Miss—er, Carolyn."

Mitchell turned his back on his friends and moved to Carolyn's side. "We're busy here. Couldn't you go to the coffee shop?"

Jake ignored Mitchell's question. He crossed his arms over his chest and craned his neck in an attempt to see over Mitchell's shoulder into the kitchen. "What are you making?"

Mitchell turned his back on his friends and grabbed her hand. "It's a surprise," he grumbled. "Come on, Carolyn, let's finish up."

Unfortunately, Mitchell's friends trailed behind. They stood beside the table and gaped at the rows of hors d'oeuvres neatly set into the storage containers Carolyn had brought. Jake picked up a finished cheese ball and popped it into his mouth.

Roland stepped forward. "If you can have one, so can I." He followed Jake's example and snitched a cheese ball. Gordie took only a second to follow suit.

"Wow," Gordie mumbled. "Forget the wedding. All the good food's going to be at the rehearsal party."

Jake swept his hand in the air over the tray of goodies. "Did you really do this by yourself? Carolyn did it, and you've been watching, right?"

Mitchell raised one finger in the air and opened his mouth, but Jake interrupted him. "No, forget I asked. I can tell by the look of you that you've been doing more than watching. I wouldn't have believed it if I hadn't seen it with my own eyes. And there isn't a wiener in any of this."

Carolyn bit her lip. She had done some of the more difficult steps for him, but Mitchell really had worked hard, both in class and now, and he really had put what he learned into practice.

Jake pointed at the pastry shapes Mitchell had been in the middle of shaping when his friends had arrived. "What are those things?"

"Those things," Mitchell said as he crossed his arms and tapped one foot, "are going to be the pastry shells for the crab snaps."

"Well, what do ya know."

Roland pointed to the counter. "What are you doing with that bag of mushrooms? Making little teeny-weeny pizzas? Where's the pepperoni?"

"I'm making stuffed mushroom caps."

The three of them stood in one spot, staring at the bag of mushrooms as if it were some object from outer space.

Gordie shook his head. "Stuffed mushrooms? You? You've gotta be kidding."

"That does it," Mitchell muttered. "Get lost." Following his words, Mitchell practically shoved them out of the kitchen. "I wish kitchens had doors you could lock," he mumbled.

Carolyn grinned. "I think you should take it as a compliment."

He uttered something unintelligible in return.

The sounds of Jake and Gordie and Roland making themselves comfortable drifted from the living room. Killer returned to her bed in the corner of the kitchen and fell back to sleep, and she and Mitchell continued with their cooking. Jake reappeared in the kitchen to help himself to the coffee they'd made earlier then returned for a second cup, and not long after that he came back to make another pot. Considering the time it took him with every return trip, it gave Carolyn a sneaking suspicion that he was doing more than tending to the coffee. Jake was doing some serious looting.

After Jake's fourth trip into the kitchen, it finally dawned on Mitchell that his friend was pilfering the food. Carolyn struggled to stifle her laughter as Mitchell almost physically threw his best friend out of the kitchen, threatening Jake's life if he dared to return.

When they were done, Mitchell washed his hands in the kitchen sink with the dish detergent, and they carefully snapped the covers onto the containers.

Carolyn counted everything. "We did really well today. We only have a few things left to do tomorrow."

"Don't speak too soon. Since Jake seems to like these so much, I think it would all be safer if you took it home. Do you have room in your fridge until Friday? I know it's a lot to ask, but even the Bible says to remove temptation. I really don't think Ellen would be very pleased with me if her future husband showed up with a black eye on their wedding day."

"No problem. I can take most of this home." She picked up the remaining recipe sheets. "You don't even need to get off early tomorrow since there's only a few things left to do."

His triumphant smile would have made a winning toothpaste commercial. "Yeah. We did great."

"Since your mom still has the cast on her arm, who is going to put everything out and stuff and bake the crab snaps on Friday?"

"I am."

"Do you have any idea how long that's going to take?"

He shook his head. "I hadn't really thought about it."

"You've proved my point. You've prepared the food, but you're the best man. You should be with the rest of the wedding party, not spending all your time in the kitchen. If you want, while everyone is at the church, I could get the food ready if your parents wouldn't mind me being in their house when they're not home."

"No. I want you to come to the party as my guest, not the hired help."

"I don't mind. I could be both."

"I probably don't have a lot of choice, do I?"

"Not really. Someone has to do it."

"I won't let you do all the work. I made this stuff. I want to serve it."

"I'm sure you'll have plenty of opportunity. Now I think it's time for me to go."

He checked his wristwatch then glanced at the clock on the stove. "I'll help you carry this to your car."

Once everything was stacked securely, Mitchell stood in such a spot that she couldn't open the car door without hitting him with it.

"I'm really sorry that I didn't take you out for dinner on your birthday. You shouldn't have been working on your special day, but I was desperate."

"It's okay. I enjoy making things in the kitchen. Besides, the singing telegram more than made up for it. It was a birthday I'll never forget." Even more memorable than the young man in the horrid costume was the last of the kisses, but she wasn't going to admit that to him.

"Have I told you how much I appreciate your help?"

"A few dozen times, yes."

He grinned. "Then have I told you how much I'm looking forward to tomorrow, when we'll be finishing this up?"

"I believe so."

"Did I tell you that I can hardly wait until the rehearsal party, where I can show you off not only as the person responsible for teaching me how to make all this stuff, but also as my date?"

She wasn't sure he'd emphasized the part about being his date, although his meaning when he talked about it had been clear enough, so she nodded.

"Well, then, have I told you how much I love you?"

She opened her mouth, but no words came out.

Quickly, Mitchell stepped forward, tipped her chin up with his index finger, and brushed a light kiss to her lips. "Good night, Carolyn. Drive safely. I'll see you tomorrow."

As quickly as he had moved forward, he stepped back and opened the door for her.

"Good night, Mitchell," she mumbled as she scrambled behind the wheel and took off.

She obviously drove home, but Carolyn found herself standing in her kitchen loading the food they'd made into her fridge, remembering nothing of the drive. She only remembered Mitchell's words.

He loved her. She loved him, too, but that didn't make the relationship right or good. She couldn't believe Mitchell didn't see how wrong they were for each other.

For now, they had the excitement of a new relationship, but when everything faded to everyday routine, he wouldn't find her so interesting, especially when age started to creep up on her faster than it would creep up on him. Projecting further, she tried to imagine what it would be like when she was sixty-five, ready to retire, and wanting to travel and Mitchell was still fifty-six, with many more years of active employment ahead of him. By the time he reached sixty-five, she would be nearly seventy-four. She wasn't likely to be able to keep up with him then.

But for now, she wanted to have children and to do so before she was thirty-five. Her prospective mate had to be ready for an almost-instant family. While twenty-four was certainly not too young to be a responsible father, she didn't know if Mitchell wanted children. And if he did, she didn't know if he wanted them right away. She didn't even know if to him love meant getting married versus simply having a steady relationship.

Love was more complicated than a case of the warm fuzzies. She needed security, compatibility, and strength. But most of all, she needed to seek God's will for the man she saw as His choice for her.

She didn't want to think about Hank and his proposal. One thing she was sure of was that God wanted her to be happy.

Despite the late time, she knew she would never sleep. Instead, Carolyn picked up her Bible and turned to 1 Corinthians 13 and read all the things God said about love. Patience. Kindness. Not envious or boastful. Humble. She read the section a dozen times, and to the best of her knowledge, Mitchell was all of those things.

She didn't know what to do, so she buried her face in her hands and prayed for a sign that a relationship with Mitchell Farris was God's will for her.

❧

Carolyn helped Mitchell stack the containers of food into the back of his car, and they began the journey to his parents' house.

Today was the day.

She'd never been so nervous in her life.

It hadn't occurred to her until this moment that she hadn't considered the other members of the wedding party who would be there today—the bride's friends, or worse, Mitchell's family.

Realistically, she could expect Mitchell's sister to be at least one year younger than Mitchell. She would be participating in a social function with people who could possibly be her former students. She wouldn't be Carolyn, an acquaintance or possible friend. She'd be Miss Rutherford, the teacher from their high school days. As their teacher and person in a position of authority, she was careful to define the line between the generations. Except for helping the odd student with extra lessons, she kept her private life exactly that, private.

The name Ellen Farris wasn't immediately familiar, although she could hardly be expected to remember every student who passed through her class year after year. But even if she hadn't had Mitchell's sister as one of her students, the possibility existed that she had taught a few of the bridesmaids, some of whom would be friends of Ellen's from high school. She didn't want to think of the other guests at the wedding. Not that she'd never bumped into a former student at a social function, but this time it would be different because she would be accompanying Mitchell as a peer rather than an instructor.

Trying to be as discreet as possible, she glanced at herself in the rearview mirror to see if she looked her age, and she did. The beginnings of crow's-feet and other telltale signs of being over thirty couldn't be hidden, and since she rarely used anything more than a touch of eye shadow and lipstick, if she suddenly put on makeup to hide her age, it would only look worse.

"We're almost there."

Carolyn blinked and started paying attention to where they were. They had traveled about ten minutes and neither of them had spoken, which she found odd because Mitchell tended to be chatty in the car.

Upon the arrival of the wedding party, Mitchell planned to introduce her to everyone she hadn't met, and then everyone would leave except Carolyn. Then, once she was alone, she would start setting out the food and make the punch and put everything that required heating in the oven. Since the rehearsal itself wouldn't be long, she would have barely enough time to get everything done before the wedding party returned, and then it would be time to eat.

"Are you as nervous as I am?" she asked as she smoothed a few imaginary wrinkles from her sleeve.

Mitchell slowed the car, and they pulled into the driveway of a large white house with blue painted trim and a cheery flower garden in front.

He killed the engine but made no move to exit the car. He remained seated, rested one arm across the back of his seat as he turned the upper half of his body to her, and gripped the top of the steering wheel tightly with his left hand. "Before we go in, there's something I neglected to tell you. I've been afraid to mention it, but I think you should know this before you meet my parents."

Her stomach sank. She swallowed hard and listened.

"My mom and dad were only sixteen when she got pregnant. They got married when I was three. They became Christians when I was in kindergarten."

She waited in silence, but he didn't say anything more. "Why are you telling me this?"

He stiffened and grasped her hands as he spoke, holding them firmly enough that it would be an effort to pull away from him. The tightness in her stomach worsened her fear of what he was going to say.

"Just so you'll be prepared when you see them. I should have told you sooner, but I didn't know how. I'm sorry."

She stared at Mitchell, trying to picture an older version of him, which wasn't difficult, because she'd often tried to fantasize him into being older.

"It's okay," she said, still not sure she understood why he thought the state of his parents' early relationship was her concern. They were Christians now and had been for years, which was all that mattered.

Mitchell straightened and tugged at his shirt collar then ran his hands down his sleeves, straightening out the wrinkled fabric. "We'd better get moving. We have to get all the food inside and some of the work done before everyone gets here."

Walking side by side, they approached the house. Instead of knocking and waiting, Mitchell rang the doorbell and opened the door. He poked his head inside, calling out that they had arrived, walked in, and shut the door behind them.

A couple approached from the stairs. The woman was blond, tall, thin, and absolutely beautiful. She wore fashionably snug jeans along with a loose, short-sleeved, cotton pullover sweater. Her right arm was bound in a cast, which was supported by a sling.

The man was about the same height as Mitchell and just as attractive in a different sort of way because of the maturity that enriched his handsome features. He smiled a greeting that would have melted any woman's heart. He carried himself with a combination of good looks and confident manners that gave him a timeless appeal, except he wasn't old enough to need to be timeless. He was drop-dead gorgeous. It took a few seconds for it to fully sink in that this chic couple was Mitchell's mother and father.

The resemblance between father and son was striking, and he sported a physique identical to his son's. They almost could have been brothers, except for the fact that since Mitchell's mother was standing beside him, Carolyn could see some of her features in Mitchell.

"Carolyn, these are my parents, Kim and Roger. Mom, Dad, this is Carolyn."

Carolyn blinked, speechless. In a single instant, she understood the meaning of Mitchell's attempt to caution her about meeting his parents. She had friends the same age as Mitchell's mother, but that wasn't what hit her the hardest. Doing some quick math, she calculated that Roger was forty years old, only one year older than Hank—and closer to her age than Mitchell was by two years.

Carolyn felt sick.

His mother smiled. "So you're Mitchell's friend, the cooking teacher. We've heard so much about you. I'm so pleased to finally meet you." With her arm in the cast, she awkwardly glanced down while Mitchell's father extended his hand. Carolyn responded with the limpest handshake of her life.

"Yes, pleased to meet you, Carolyn."

The second his father released her hand, Mitchell slipped his around her waist and gave her a little squeeze, drawing both his parents' gazes to the obvious show of affection. His mother's eyebrows rose, but no comment was made. Carolyn should have parroted the usual polite reply, but for a moment she couldn't have formed words if her life depended on it. She didn't know how to address them. She had called Hank's parents by Mr. and Mrs. and besides, they were. . .older. If they were at school, she would have addressed a student's parents as Mr. and Mrs., regardless of the age difference, but in any other social situation, she would have greeted them using their first names.

In this case, she settled for, "Thank you. It's good to meet you, too."

Mitchell's mother cleared her throat. "Ellen and Jake phoned to say they're going straight to the church. We should get moving, too, or we're going to be late. While Roger and Mitchell empty the car, I'll show you the kitchen and where everything is, and then we'll be off." Carolyn followed Kim into the kitchen, but every word of explanation and directions went in one ear and out the other. Not only was Mitchell's mother a talented cook, she was gorgeous and slim. Carolyn wondered if her hair would go gray before Kim's did.

Thankfully, his parents left the house quickly, but Mitchell lingered.

"Are you okay?"

She wasn't, but she didn't know what to say. She nodded dumbly.

"We'll talk about it later." Before she could think or move, his fingers tipped her chin up, and he gave her a light, lingering kiss. Very gently, he stroked her cheek with his fingertips, tilted his head, and brushed one more light kiss to her lips. The sweetness of his actions nearly made her cry.

He spoke so softly, she could barely hear. "Remember, I love you."

Before she could collect her thoughts enough to respond, he turned and sprinted down the sidewalk, hopped into his car, and drove off.

Carolyn busied herself setting out the food on plates and preparing what needed to go in the oven. She didn't want to think about Mitchell, and she especially didn't want to think about his father. Instead, she paid an inordinate amount of attention to the exact amount of filling needed for each individual crab snap, and then put all her concentration on rearranging everything to make the most attractive display of all the food Mitchell had made.

Chapter 15

Mitchell smiled politely at a joke that had the rest of the wedding party nearly rolling in the aisles with laughter. He stood where he was supposed to stand and waited while the pastor instructed everyone on exactly what to do and how to walk.

She never said she loved him back. The first time he'd said it casually, just dropping it into the conversation, but he'd never been so nervous in his life. He didn't know how she would respond, so he left her an opportunity to bolt, and she had. This time hadn't been much different except that he was the one who ran, using the excuse that everyone was waiting for him. But before he took off, he had hesitated. He'd seen the shock on her face.

Ever since the first time he met Hank, Mitchell had worried about how Carolyn would react to meeting his parents, especially his father. At the time it had hit him right in the gut to see how much older Hank was than Carolyn. It had been almost like looking at his father, and it shook him.

It had taken him a long time to deal with the fact that his parents had been unmarried teenagers when he was born. Both his parents had continued with their schooling, except that his mother had taken a year off and graduated one year later. His grandparents, whom he loved dearly, had helped and supported them until his parents graduated, got jobs, and married.

His family had struggled, but now, twenty-four years later, his parents were happily married and in a few years would be celebrating their silver anniversary. Ellen had been born a year after his parents were married, after they had become Christians. Their story had a happy ending, unlike the story of so many teenage pregnancies.

As much as his friends had always been impressed with his youthful mother and father, Carolyn was having exactly the opposite reaction, and he couldn't blame her. He should have found a way to mention it earlier so it didn't come as such a shock.

Mitchell turned his head and stared blankly at the wall, ignoring the noise and clamor around him. He could only imagine Carolyn's misgivings about getting involved in a relationship with a man whose parents were only seven years older than she was.

Mitchell buried his hands in his pockets and continued to stare at the wall. He desperately loved Carolyn with all his heart and soul, but now there was nothing he could do. He had to leave it in God's hands and trust that if this was the woman God wanted him to have, then it would be so. If not, he would have to let her go.

He pulled his hands out of his pockets, stood the way he'd been told, and turned around to watch Ellen's friends walking down the aisle one at a time. Today they were all wearing jeans, but on Saturday they'd be in long dresses.

He looked at Jake, who was now standing beside him. Jake's hands were shaking as he watched the proceedings. For now, Jake rammed his hands into his pockets and grinned like an idiot trying to appear unaffected, but Mitchell wasn't fooled.

Mitchell thought back to when Jake announced his and Ellen's engagement. After he'd gotten over the shock that his best friend really was going to marry his sister, Mitchell had teased Jake about getting tied down and having to answer to someone else for almost everything he did.

Mitchell now knew differently. Jake was happy. He had the commitment, companionship, and love of a woman for the rest of his life—if he didn't do anything foolish enough to break that trust. Mitchell wanted the same.

He wanted to be Carolyn's soul mate for the rest of their lives. When he gave her the promise ring and then kissed her at the school, he hoped that she could love him and see a future with him.

Now, he wasn't so sure.

From the change in Jake's expression, Mitchell could tell it was Ellen's turn to walk up the aisle. As she hung on to their father's arm, Ellen was grinning from ear to ear, staring at Jake.

Jake was smiling, but his eyes were getting glassy, and even though it wasn't very macho, Mitchell envied his friend. He also wondered what it would be like on Saturday when everyone was all dressed up, the wedding march was playing, and everything was for real.

Once Ellen arrived at the front, the pastor talked to Jake and Ellen about their vows, exchanging rings, and signing the marriage certificate. When the pastor announced Jake would then kiss the bride, Jake grabbed Ellen around the waist and bent her backward. Ellen squealed in surprise and grabbed Jake's shoulders, and Jake kissed her fully while everyone else hooted and cheered.

Mitchell wanted to kiss Carolyn like that—willingly, before friends and family and before God.

When Jake and Ellen finally separated, the pastor directed the wedding party to pair up and exit the sanctuary as they would when the ceremony was over. As best man, he stepped out before the other attendants and escorted Melissa down the aisle immediately following Jake and Ellen.

Once they all stood in the lobby, the official rehearsal was finally over.

He wanted to be the first one back at the house to see Carolyn, but he had to wait while his mother talked to the pastor. He stood impatiently by the door, and soon his dad joined him.

"My baby girl is getting married tomorrow."

"Yeah." Mitchell wished his father's son was getting married, too, although the more he thought about it, the less likely it seemed that it would happen.

"That sure was nice of your friend to offer to help you with the food instead of hiring a caterer. We'll have to think of some way to thank her."

His friend. He wanted Carolyn to be more than just his friend. "Yeah, we should do that."

"I could be mistaken, but you appear to think of Carolyn as more than a friend."

Mitchell stared at his father. He figured it was a little late in his upbringing to be talking about the women he dated.

"How old is she, Mitch?"

"She's only thirty-three." Mitchell turned to his father, daring him to say anything more about Carolyn's age. He wanted to defend her, to justify to his father that it was okay for him to be dating an older woman and that Carolyn was more suited to him than any woman he'd ever met in his life.

"Is she a Christian?"

"Yes."

"You're in love with her, aren't you?"

"Yes, I am."

"Then I guess that's all that matters. I wish you God's blessings, Mitch."

Mitchell rammed his hands into his pockets and stared blankly out the window. "I don't know how she feels about me. The difference in our ages bothers her."

His father nodded and rubbed his chin with his index finger and thumb. "I've seen a few couples where the woman is three or four years older, but it doesn't usually go more than that. Women usually go for older men."

Mitchell's heart sank another notch. Up until now, Carolyn's preference had been for older men—something he didn't need to be reminded of. He couldn't do anything about his age, so he'd been trying to win her heart in other ways, although all he could do was simply be himself, and he wasn't sure that was enough.

His mom finally appeared, and his dad left his side to help tuck his mom's jacket over her cast then give her a small peck on the cheek.

"We'd better hurry. By now everyone's already at the house."

Mitchell gulped and swallowed hard. It was time.

❀

Carolyn smiled cordially at Gordie and Roland, who were the first to arrive. Fortunately, Jake and Ellen pulled in immediately after them, allowing her the chance to hide in the kitchen to wait for Mitchell. After that, she planned to stay only for as long as she needed to in order to be polite, then leave. She already had most of the food out and only needed to finish a few of the hot hors d'oeuvres. Then she would be free, and Mitchell could drive her home.

Silently, she kept busy doing things that didn't need to be done rather than standing around doing nothing while more and more people arrived. Just as she slipped on the oven mitts and was pulling the first tray of crab snaps out of the oven, she heard a female voice behind her.

"Miss Rutherford? Is that you? What are you doing here?"

The hot tray nearly dropped from her hands. She fumbled with it, letting it drop with a clatter to the top of the stove, and whirled around to see Melissa Roberts, one of her students from a few years ago, standing in the doorway, gaping at her.

She pulled the oven mitts off her hands and held them tightly. "I'm helping with the snacks, Melissa."

"I knew you were teaching night school, but I didn't know you were doing catering, too."

"Carolyn isn't here as the caterer, Melissa. She's here as my date."

The sound of Mitchell's voice nearly made her drop the oven mitts. Mitchell appeared behind Melissa, his face strangely pale, and his lips tightly drawn.

"Oh. Sorry." Melissa shrugged her shoulders and disappeared back into the living room, where the sound of laughter and conversation droned on.

Carolyn tried to force a smile and knew the effort fell flat. "You're the last one to get here. I was beginning to worry about you."

In the blink of an eye, Mitchell strode across the room until they were standing toe to toe. She would have backed up, except it would have sent her into the hot oven door, which was still open. He grinned, making his dimple appear. At the same time, the color returned to his face, and he rested his hands on her shoulders. "Did you miss me?"

"I wouldn't go that far."

It would have been impossible to miss him because even though he no longer lived in his parents' home, there were signs of Mitchell everywhere. She hadn't meant to snoop, but on her way into the kitchen after Mitchell and his parents left, she couldn't help but notice three eight-by-ten framed portraits prominently placed on the living room wall. One was his parents' wedding picture, with Kim and Roger in their wedding attire and a small child standing between them holding a ring bearer's silk pillow. Mitchell had been a beautiful three-year-old, and he'd grown into an equally handsome man.

The other two portraits were Mitchell's and Ellen's high school graduation pictures. Over the past six years, he hadn't changed all that much, except that time had matured his features.

After worrying about it, Carolyn had been relieved that Ellen hadn't been one of her former students, but Melissa had, and, of course, Melissa recognized her. She wondered if all the bridesmaids were former students.

She lowered her voice to a whisper to make sure no one suddenly appearing would hear. "Melissa was one of my students. What am I doing here?"

"You're here because you're with me. Don't worry about Melissa or any of Ellen's friends."

His hands moved from her shoulders to her cheeks. He lowered his head and kissed her gently then dropped his hands and backed up.

The oven mitts she was holding landed on the floor. She quickly picked them up, brushed them off, and turned to close the oven door. "If I don't get those crab snaps out, they're going to be so cold, no one will be able to tell they're baked. You'll want to show them off when they're at their best."

Together, they began transferring the crab snaps to a platter.

"I don't think I'm going to tell anyone I've done all the food until most everything has been eaten. I want it to be a surprise. Besides, a few of the people here wouldn't touch anything if they knew I did the cooking."

"I think you're exaggerating."

"Unfortunately, I'm not. I'll go put these on the dining room table, and then I have to help Dad with something. I won't be gone long, but it might be a good idea to join Ellen's friends and just talk to them. You know, to bridge the gap. They're all in the working world now. I think it's just hard for them to think of you as anything besides their former teacher. You know, like teachers aren't people or allowed to have a social life outside the school. Unless you show them otherwise, they're going to keep thinking that way."

"I don't know. . . ."

He smiled and touched her shoulder then lightly brushed one finger against her chin. "I'm serious. Show them the person you are outside of school."

Nervously, she glanced toward the doorway leading into the living room, as if by simply passing through it, things could be changed.

Most of her friends were her own age, but she thought of the people at her church, where the age gap was wide. There were women there who were in their mid to early twenties who addressed her by her first name, and to them, the age gap meant nothing because they had not previously known her. Likewise, she addressed ladies older than herself by twenty years or more by their first names, and the age gap meant nothing except more life experience. They were all equal in God's eyes as Christian sisters.

Again, she glanced to the doorway. "All right. I'll make the first move."

"Great. I'll catch you later when I'm finished with Dad." Mitchell picked up the tray and disappeared through the doorway, leaving her alone in the kitchen.

She didn't immediately follow him. First, she needed a few minutes to compose herself and work up her courage.

After multiple deep breaths, Carolyn ran her fingers through her hair, straightened her glasses, stiffened her back, and began the long journey into the living room.

Mitchell's older relatives sat on the couch and love seat, and the armchair remained empty. Ellen and the three bridesmaids stood in a small circle near the doorway, holding plates and nibbling at the goodies, totally engrossed in conversation. They didn't see her approach, giving Carolyn a chance to try to place them before she broke into their little circle.

She had never seen Ellen before, but Melissa had been in her homeroom a few years ago, and she recognized the other two as having attended her regular home economics class, but she couldn't remember their names.

Carolyn didn't want to eavesdrop, but her ears perked up when one of the girls leaned her head into the center of their little circle. "You won't believe this, but I saw Mitchell kissing Miss Rutherford!"

Chapter 16

Carolyn's feet skidded to a halt. Her heart pounded. She wasn't aware that anyone had seen what happened in the kitchen. Obviously, she and Mitchell were not as discreet as she had thought.

Melissa nodded her head. "I know. He said she was his date."

"Mitch? And Miss Rutherford?"

Carolyn heard a chorus of gasps. No one had seen her yet, but Carolyn feared if she moved, it would draw attention to her, and they would know that she had overheard. Her feet remained rooted to the floor.

All the heads stayed bowed in the small circle.

"He told me to call her Carolyn!"

"Get a life, Melissa. She does, like, have a name, you know."

"Yeah, but it feels so strange. She was my homeroom teacher. And now she's dating Ellen's brother."

"How old do you think she is?"

Carolyn watched the girls counting on their fingers and nodding. She wanted to yell out that she was only thirty-three, not ninety-three, and she had every right to date whomever she pleased, but she didn't want to make things worse.

She backed up a step then froze when they lifted their heads, fearing they would notice her if she continued to move.

Melissa covered her mouth with her hands. "Ew. That would be like me dating Gordie's kid brother."

Carolyn's stomach clenched into a knot. Gordie's brother, Steven, was sixteen, in one of her classes, and at the moment he was hopefully getting over a crush on her.

All four of them gasped again, and Carolyn thought she might throw up. She backed up another step until she was flat against the wall, but she couldn't get away.

The unnamed girl's voice rose a bit in volume, but she still continued to whisper. "You should have seen him kissing her. It was like in the movies. He was so romantic."

Melissa sighed. "Mitch can kiss me anytime!"

The girls giggled.

Carolyn no longer cared if they saw her. She turned and bolted into the kitchen. As she rounded the corner, she heard another round of giggles, telling her that her escape had been successful.

She drew in a ragged breath and slipped the last tray of crab snaps into the oven. This time, she would keep herself busy in the kitchen until Mitchell came back, regardless of his urging to let them get to know her as a person rather than a teacher. After hearing what Ellen's friends really thought, she couldn't face them alone. She wondered if she would be able to face them at all.

Just as she closed the oven door, Gordie and Roland appeared behind her. She wondered if they were ever apart.

Roland snitched a cheese ball from the tray on the table and popped it into his mouth. "Hi, Carolyn. I just wanted to say how great the food is. If I hadn't seen it for myself the other day, I wouldn't have believed Mitch did it. You helped him, didn't you?"

She turned and smiled at them, grateful for the distraction. "Except for the dessert, he made everything. I helped him a little, but not much."

"Mitch is a great guy, you know."

Her smile dropped. She had a bad feeling that Roland had come into the kitchen to talk to her about more than the food. She nodded and turned to check the last tray of crab snaps in the oven. "Yes, he is."

Roland swallowed a bacon-wrapped scallop then cleared his throat. "Are you and Mitch, you know, going to continue seeing each other?"

She gritted her teeth at his question. She didn't know the answer. She had already committed herself to being Mitchell's date for the wedding, but tonight had shown her that it simply wasn't going to work. Mitchell had almost convinced her it was possible to keep seeing each other, but even his friends were questioning their relationship. She really didn't know what was right anymore.

At this point in her life, she was seeking marriage. Mitchell had completely shocked her when he told her that he loved her, not once, but twice. The first time she could have let it go, but after the second time, she couldn't help thinking that the natural progression would point toward marriage.

Mitchell was nothing like the man she had been praying for. Yet, despite everything, she wanted to keep seeing him, which was selfish and wrong.

The right thing to do would be to tell him she couldn't see him again, to tell him to find someone else to love, someone more suited to him—a woman he could be with, without being the subject of everyone's gossip.

She couldn't say anything like that to his friends. She had to say it to him in person.

"Yes," she answered, justifying her reply in her mind, knowing she hadn't been specific. "I'll be seeing him after tonight."

For a few minutes, they simply stood and stared at each other, making Carolyn feel like a bug under a microscope.

Gordie stepped forward then fixed his gaze at some point on the wall behind her. "If you're wondering why we're asking, it's because Mitchell's been acting kind of funny. We haven't been seeing as much of him lately, and it's like when Jake started going out with Ellen, you know, seriously. We just wanted to know if you felt the same way."

Carolyn swallowed hard. Mitchell's quiet "I love you" echoed through her head, and her fingers immediately went to touch the little ring on the middle finger of her left hand—the little heart that said so much. It wasn't right, but she loved him, too.

"Yes," she whispered hoarsely. "I do feel the same way."

Gordie and Roland both nodded, then just as quickly as they arrived, they disappeared.

Carolyn's hands shook as she took the last tray of crab snaps out of the oven and set them on the counter to cool. She'd almost convinced herself to say good-bye to Mitchell, but the ache it brought to her heart was too painful. Using more concentration than needed for such a mundane task, she refilled the tray with goodies, leaving room for the last crab snaps, and told herself that now she had to stay put until they were cool enough to add to the tray.

While she waited, she tidied the kitchen until it was so perfect she had nothing else to do.

The time dragged. Laughter again drifted from the living room.

She stared out the window into the dark yard, where everything was quiet and still. Rather than joining the crowd or watching the crab snaps cool, she stepped out onto the

371

large wooden patio deck, where the cool night air was pleasant after being close to the hot oven most of the evening. She leaned with her hands against the cedar railing beneath a large tree, which stood regally alongside the structure, and looked over the property.

Suddenly, footsteps tapped on the path that led through the yard.

Jake's voice split the silence of the evening. "So, what are you going to do?"

"I'm not sure," Mitchell mumbled. She could barely make out his words as they walked farther away. "I can't help feeling sorry for her. I'll have to think of something extra special. I know she likes cows."

Their voices faded as Jake and Mitchell disappeared around the side of the house. The gate squeaked open then snapped shut.

Even though she still hadn't been able to figure out what it was Mitchell saw in her, she hadn't expected that he felt pity.

Immediately she thought of Killer, whom Mitchell had taken home rather than allow the dog to be put to sleep. One of the reasons she'd been so quick to fall in love with him was his kind and compassionate nature.

She could understand why he felt sorry for her. She was more than aware of the pathetic creature she'd been when Mitchell had walked in to find her sunk to her knees in the middle of her living room floor, crying like a baby over the fiasco with Hank.

She suddenly realized that in the same way Mitchell felt so sorry for a poor, pathetic dog, that he gave it a good and loving home, he had declared his love to her—out of pity. She felt a sudden, almost physical, pain in her heart.

Before Mitchell came to find her outside and realized she'd overheard, she hustled back into the kitchen and started transferring the cooled crab snaps onto the tray.

Footsteps tapped on the linoleum floor behind her.

"What are you still doing in here?"

"Getting ready to put this out," she stammered then cleared her throat. "Gordie and Roland were just here commenting on what a good job you've done with the food."

He glanced over his shoulder to the clamor coming from the living room. "They probably just came to snitch something while no one was watching." He faced forward and took one step toward her. "Never mind them. I came to pull you out of the kitchen. You've been spending too much time in here. You should join the party." He smiled wide and picked up one of the trays she'd finished preparing.

Her stomach tied into a knot, and she stepped closer to Mitchell so he couldn't see her trembling knees.

Their eyes met, steeling Carolyn's strength and nerve. She stood as tall as possible for someone barely over five feet tall and picked up a second tray of food. "Let's go."

She followed Mitchell into the living room, where everyone was engrossed in conversation.

Mitchell placed the tray on a table. In a flash, Gordie and Roland rose and headed for the food, causing everyone to groan.

Mitchell introduced Carolyn to everyone then reached for her hand and held it, as if it were a normal occurrence. She did her best to hide her shock, but when Mitchell ran his thumb over the small ring, she completely lost track of everything that had been said and pretended to cough so she didn't have to respond.

When only a few tidbits remained on the tray, Ellen called for everyone's attention. "I want everyone to know that all this food you've just eaten and thought was made by Carolyn was actually made by Mitch. Except the dessert, right, Mitch?"

Carolyn thought she could have heard a pin drop.

Mitchell gave a carefree smile, but the tightness of his grip on her hand gave him away. Besides, the dimple wasn't showing. He didn't speak. All he did was nod.

Ellen waved her hands in the air. "Don't worry. No one is going to die. Carolyn taught him everything he needed to know, and I have it from a reliable source that even though she didn't actually prepare the food, she was there to supervise. Let's give them a big round of applause!"

Her cheeks grew hot at the response, but it gave her some relief to see that Mitchell blushed, as well.

Fortunately, since the wedding was tomorrow, the party wound down and guests began to leave. Mitchell saw them out, while Carolyn helped Kim pack up the leftovers.

"I don't know how to thank you, Carolyn, not only for your help, but for teaching Mitchell what to do in the kitchen. I've tried to get him interested for years and failed."

Carolyn smiled. "Believe me, it's nothing I said or did. He'd made up his mind before he signed up for the class. Like anything else, when you have to do something, you do what you can to get the job done."

"Yes, I can tell he's quite proud of himself." Silence hung in the air for a minute, then Kim spoke quietly. "How long have you and Mitchell been, uh, dating? He hasn't been to church or Bible study in quite a while. I was starting to worry, and then I was told he's been going with you."

Carolyn snapped on the lids, and Kim tucked everything into the fridge. "We've been seeing each other quite frequently since he signed up for my cooking class."

"I guess what I'm trying to ask is if you're serious about him. He's my son, and I don't want to see him hurt. I also know that he'd be angry with me if he found out I've discussed this with you, but I had to ask. He hasn't seen much of us lately."

Carolyn forced herself to smile. "It's okay. You're not the first person to express concern."

Kim's face turned a dark shade of red, and she raised the uncasted hand to one cheek. "I'm so sorry! I don't know what to say!"

"It's okay, Kim. Or should I call you Mrs. Farris? It only shows how concerned everyone is about him. It's good to have such loving friends and family."

The red in Kim's face didn't change. "Please call me Kim."

All Carolyn could do was nod in agreement.

"I also hear you're coming to the wedding tomorrow as Mitchell's guest. I look forward to seeing you again."

Carolyn opened her mouth to speak, but Mitchell walked in before she could get a word out.

"You ladies finished? Or are you hiding in here because you're eating everything that's left?"

Kim smiled. "You did well, Mitchell. There's really very little left. Now if you two will excuse me, I'm off to bed. Tomorrow is a big day."

Carolyn picked up her purse and slung it over her shoulder.

Mitchell scooped up the bag of her empty containers. "Come on. I'll take you home."

She followed Mitchell to the car, and they made small talk all the way back to her house, where he left her at the door with a very sweet but chaste kiss.

She crawled off to bed, knowing she wouldn't be doing much sleeping.

Mitchell had told her that today, the day of the rehearsal, was the big day, but he was wrong.

Tomorrow was the big day. For the better part of the evening, she fully intended to enjoy every second she could with him because tomorrow she had to tell him of her decision—and stick with it.

Because after the wedding, she wasn't going to see him again.

❀

Carolyn studied herself in the mirror and tugged at the neckline of her snug dress. When she'd picked this dress specifically for Mitchell's sister's wedding, she only wanted to look good with Mitchell, who would be wearing a tuxedo, as would the rest of the men in the wedding party. She didn't know what had been running through her mind at the time, but her imagination and reality had suddenly collided, and it wasn't a pretty picture.

She sucked in her breath and turned sideways for one last view, then gave up and relaxed. The only person she was kidding was herself. She liked to eat and hated to exercise, which wasn't a great combination. She didn't know if it was realistic to hope for low lighting, but it was the only hope she had.

By the time the doorbell rang, she had nearly convinced herself to change. She ran her hands down her stomach one last time, sucked in her breath again, and walked to the door.

At the sight of Mitchell in a tux, her heart skipped a beat then started racing. His neatly styled hair sported a fresh haircut and was gelled into perfect order, showing no trace of the orange and blue she'd spotted only yesterday when she sat beside him on the couch at his parents' house.

The cut of the suit emphasized the width of his shoulders and tapered down to his narrow waist, trim hips, and long legs. The cummerbund wrapped around his midriff for that finishing touch of potent appeal.

The pristine formal wear made Mitchell look older than his years, which was another perverse reminder of how young he was. Still, the suit also emphasized his handsome face and physique, and when he smiled, that adorable dimple appeared in his left cheek. The combination of the total package of Mitchell Farris sent Carolyn's brain into a tailspin.

For lack of anything to say that wouldn't sound like a besotted teenager, she stood on her tiptoes and reached to straighten his slightly crooked bow tie.

He stiffened at her touch, which only confirmed her fears that she hadn't been seeing herself honestly in the mirror when she purchased the dress. To her surprise, when she wiggled his bow tie, his large hands settled on her hips. In a way, the contact helped to steady her but at the same time made her shaky inside.

She was in over her head. Way over her head.

Mitchell cleared his throat, then he reached up to touch the bow tie she'd just worked so hard to straighten. "You look great, Carolyn."

At his words, heat stained her cheeks. She sank to allow her heels to touch the floor, gave the bow tie a quick pat, and backed up a step. "You look great, yourself. I'm almost ready to go. I just have to get my shoes and a sweater in case it gets cool this evening."

She backed up another step to the closet, but instead of waiting outside, Mitchell also stepped inside and closed the door behind him.

"What are you doing? I thought we had to go."

His voice came out in a low growl. "This is going to be my last chance to kiss you today."

Before she knew what was happening, he'd backed her into the wall. He rested his hands on her shoulders then used one index finger to tip up her chin, and their eyes locked. She knew what he was going to do, and she knew why he stopped. He was asking her permission.

All her hesitations crumbled. She was in love with him, right or wrong, and today was all they were going to have. All night long, she'd tossed and turned, trying to decide what to do. She had decided to enjoy the day with him, and then she was going to tell him it was over. This wasn't just her last chance to kiss him today. It was the last chance she would have to kiss him ever.

Carolyn closed her eyes and let her lips part just a little, and his mouth descended on hers.

This was not a sweet, chaste kiss. This time he kissed her like he meant it.

Carolyn melted against him. She slid her hands under the suit jacket and around his back and held him tight, then kissed him back in equal measure because she meant it, too. No one had ever kissed her like this before, and she knew no one ever would again.

When they separated, she could feel his reluctance as if it were a tangible thing. Slowly, he backed up, and his eyes fluttered open. "You're right," he ground out. "We had better go."

Carolyn continued to lean against the wall, needing the support.

Silently, they stared at each other. Mitchell's cheeks were flushed, his eyes were glazed, and his breathing was labored. She didn't want to think of what she looked like.

As they continued to stare at each other, they both started to smile.

Carolyn couldn't help herself. She actually giggled. "You're wearing lipstick." Another giggle escaped. "There's a man in a tuxedo in my house, wearing lipstick."

Mitchell smiled wider, but he didn't giggle. "That's really strange, because I'm looking at a beautiful woman all dressed up, who isn't wearing any."

She couldn't stop herself. Carolyn continued to giggle as she straightened herself, took one step toward Mitchell, grabbed him by the wrist, and pulled him into the bathroom.

Instead of being embarrassed, Mitchell pursed his lips at his reflection in the mirror, made a loud smooch in the air, then smiled at himself. "Mm-mmm, I do look good."

Carolyn handed him a tissue. "Quit fooling around. Wipe off the evidence. You have to be there early."

While he wiped the lipstick off, Carolyn reapplied hers, and they were soon ready to go.

She slid on her shoes and glanced at him one more time, and in so doing, she once again felt the heat in her cheeks. "Wait. You didn't get it all off. You're going to be in a lot of pictures today. I'd better do it."

They returned to the bathroom, where he sat on the edge of the bathtub while she diligently dabbed off the last smear.

The situation they were in could have been quite intimate, if they weren't in the bathroom and she didn't have a wad of lipstick-smudged tissue in her hand.

"There. You're manly once more. Let's get going, or you'll be late."

"Carolyn, wait. Before we go, there's something I almost forgot to tell you."

"Oh?" She smiled on the outside but cringed on the inside.

"I have to warn you; you'll really like Uncle Vince, but don't let him get started talking about fishing or you'll be sorry."

Chapter 17

Once at the church, Carolyn sat and watched the preamble to the wedding from a different perspective than at any other time she had attended a wedding. She watched Mitchell, Gordie, Roland, and even Jake run around checking on last-minute things.

"Mind if I sit with you for a while?"

Carolyn looked up to find Mitchell's father standing beside the pew.

"Of course not." She slid over to the side to make room for Roger, surprised that such an important figure in the coming proceedings would take time to say hello to her.

"The father of the bride isn't allowed with his daughter until she's ready to walk down the aisle. I guess I'm at loose ends. A little nervous, too, I don't mind saying."

Carolyn smiled. "It's an important day."

"Yes, it is. I think not only for my daughter."

Carolyn's stomach tied itself into knots. His expression told her he had something specific in mind.

Roger sat and turned sideways to face her. "I think I'm just going to be blunt, because I don't know how much time we'll have before I have to go. Mitchell seems to be very serious about you."

All Carolyn could do was nod.

"I know you have some concerns about Mitchell being younger than you are, and it doesn't help that Kim and I are not all that much older than you."

She nodded again. She couldn't believe she was having this conversation, today of all days, and with Mitchell's father—not that she'd done much talking.

Roger continued. "I don't know how much Mitchell has told you about the start of Kim's and my relationship."

She cleared her throat, but her voice still came out far too unsteady. "I know you were both very young and were married when Mitchell was three."

He reached up and wiggled the knot of his tie. "That's right. We were young and stupid, and it was because of our age that we faced a lot of opposition, for a number of reasons. I know it's not quite the same for you and Mitchell, because Kim and I are the same age and we had each other." Suddenly, his ears turned red, making it apparent whom Mitchell got the trait from. "Kim is actually a few months older than I am. How about that, huh?"

She acknowledged that bit of information with a shaky smile, and he went on.

"All our friends were out having fun and letting their relationships mature the right way, before marriage, and especially before having children. Obviously we did it in the wrong order. Our parents helped, yet they didn't make it easy for us. We struggled and worked hard for a lot of years, even after we were married and managing on our own.

"When your kids are small, you tend to spend your time with people whose kids are the same age as your own. Because of that, we were ten years younger than the parents of Mitchell's friends, the people with whom we had the most in common and ended up spending most of our time with. We felt it then and we still do to a degree, but now that we're older, it doesn't make as much difference. I guess what I'm trying to say is that I know what it's like to face opposition and to struggle because something in your relationship is very different than the rest of your peers.

"Because we were so different than everyone in our circle, and because we made a lot of mistakes, Mitchell had to mature very fast for his years. Being so much older than all of his cousins and our friends' kids, he was the one to do all the babysitting and provide a good example. I wanted to ask you to give him a fair chance, based on Mitchell the person, not Mitchell the younger man."

Roger's presence and heartfelt words only confirmed what she already knew. Mitchell was serious—too serious to think she could fool herself into being just friends. They could never be just friends. With Mitchell, it was all or nothing.

Roger was called away, and soon it was time for Jake and his groomsmen to stand at their places at the front of the church. Of course, Mitchell looked the best of all of them. As the bridal procession began, Carolyn watched Ellen's friends making their way to the front, but she couldn't help sneaking a peek at Mitchell when Ellen and their father began their march up the aisle. She could see the play of emotions running through him from pride to confusion, then something else she couldn't even begin to guess as he discreetly glanced from his sister to his best friend.

Even though she didn't know anyone well except for Mitchell, Carolyn found herself getting misty eyed.

At the end of the touching ceremony, Carolyn stayed as much in the background as she could, standing silently by Mitchell's side as he chatted with other guests in the attached banquet hall.

She heard Mitchell's name being called in the background.

"Oops. I have to go to the park for the pictures now. Do you want to come?"

She shook her head. "It's okay. I see a few people I know from the school. It will be nice to talk to them."

He smiled, and Carolyn's foolish heart fluttered. "I'm glad you feel comfortable doing that. See you soon."

She walked with him to the church parking lot, where Mitchell slipped behind the wheel of Jake's vividly decorated car. As he drove the newlyweds to the park, he looked so happy that it made her regret what she would have to tell him at the end of the evening. Today was a wedding, a day to celebrate love. Despite what Roger had told her, it was not to celebrate hers and Mitchell's.

The guests mingled in every conceivable spot of the building, waiting for the wedding party to return. Carolyn recognized a few couples as former students or parents of present students. She strengthened her resolve and determined to see them as friends of the bride and groom. She was so successful that time passed quickly, and she was surprised when someone called out that Jake and Ellen had arrived.

Those who had not already found a table were quickly seated.

The speeches began, drawing everyone's attention to the front. Carolyn nearly cried at Mitchell's tender speech about his sister then laughed at the way he expounded on Jake's not quite finest traits, and the entire group roared at his comments concerning his best friend marrying his sister.

After the toasts to the bride, Mitchell's pastor prayed, then the room buzzed with conversation and laughter as the meal was served. After the meal, there was a short video presentation of Jake and Ellen's childhood and courtship.

When the official program ended, the wedding party left the head table to socialize, starting with Jake and Ellen cutting the wedding cake and visiting with their guests.

Mitchell slid into the chair across from Carolyn.

As quickly as he had sat, he stood. "I don't want to sit here and call to you from across the table. Come on, let's go someplace else where we can talk without having to raise our voices."

Carolyn glanced from side to side. Small groups congregated everywhere, standing and sitting, and many people had already filtered into the lobby to talk where it wasn't so noisy. She stood. "Sure."

❀

Mitchell led Carolyn out of the banquet room, through the nearly empty lobby, all the way outside. The sky was alive with the pink and purple hues of the sunset. The evening air was cool with the setting sun, and it was the perfect opportunity to wrap his arms around her, just to keep her warm because she'd left her sweater inside the banquet room.

"Mitchell?"

"I wanted to look at the sunset. It's kinda romantic, isn't it?"

"Romantic? It's the wedding getting to you."

"Maybe." He smiled and ran one finger over Carolyn's cheek. While he felt romantic, it had nothing to do with the beautiful sky or being at the uniting of two people before God. It was because he was with the woman he loved.

Despite the romantic atmosphere of the wedding and now the pretty sunset, all day long he'd had the nagging impression that something was wrong, but he couldn't put his finger on it. It had started long before the actual ceremony, when he arrived at Carolyn's house to pick her up. She'd been almost too responsive when they'd kissed earlier, like she knew something he didn't.

His stomach churned, despite his quickening heartbeat at the memory of a kiss that had rocked him to his soul. It was like the last kiss before the hero of the movie rode off into the sunset, never to be seen again.

Mitchell reached for her hand and twined their fingers together. This hero wasn't riding off into this sunset. He was staying, hopefully forever. Today, tonight, he was going to ask Carolyn if perhaps one day in the not too distant future, she would consider marrying him.

He wasn't going to rush her. After all, they hadn't known each other long, but all day he'd tried to squelch the panic he felt rising up, the fear that if he didn't do or say something right away, he was going to lose her.

"Listen! Do you hear the crickets chirping?"

He blinked, bringing his attention back to Carolyn beside him, which was what he had intended, not to go outside with her and be lost in his own little world. "There's a big piece of undeveloped land next door."

"Did you know that you can tell the temperature by a cricket's chirp? You count the number of chirps a cricket makes in fifteen seconds, and then add forty."

"That's very interesting. I never knew that." He almost started counting, but he stopped himself and squeezed his eyes shut. He wasn't there to learn about insect trivia. For weeks, he had waited for just that right moment to give her the promise ring, and it never happened. Then when he'd made his own moment after class, the wrong moment had turned exactly right.

Right moments didn't just happen, they were made, and he was going to make one right now.

He forced himself to relax, gave her hand a small squeeze, then turned and smiled at her. "Carolyn, I've been thinking. I know this is going to sound sudden to you, but will you—"

"Mitchell, wait."

Mitchell frowned. "Wait? But—"

"I know why you're doing this, and it's not necessary. You don't have to feel sorry for me."

"Sorry for you?"

"Because of Hank."

"But I—"

Suddenly, a voice called out. "Mitchell! Come on! Jake and Ellen are leaving."

"You have to go."

"No, we have to finish this."

"We can talk when everything is over. I have something to say to you, too."

❀

Once the last guest had left, Carolyn pitched in, and the cleanup progressed quickly. The mundane chores provided her the opportunity to be alone and allowed her time to think.

She could tell Mitchell knew what she was going to say to him. He wasn't his usual smiling self, and he was unusually quiet, while Gordie and Roland were unusually loud.

Also, his acquiescence meant that he had accepted what she was going to tell him.

To tell him she couldn't see him again was the most painful decision of her life. Over the last few days, she'd done a lot of thinking and even more praying, and she had concluded that Mitchell was not the man she'd been asking God for. She thought about all the qualities and criteria she asked for in the man who would be her husband, and of them all, Mitchell only met one—he was a Christian. She'd asked for God to show her whether Mitchell was right for her or not. For all her prayers, she hadn't seen anything that showed her Mitchell was the man God had chosen for her to share the rest of her life with.

Therefore, she had to quit fooling herself. A bad case of the warm fuzzies wasn't enough of a foundation on which to base a marriage. Something firm had to come first, something to help the relationship withstand the test of time. She'd had more reminders of everything wrong than the only thing right in their relationship, so she had to accept that as her answer.

There was no middle ground, because for this question, the answer was for keeps.

When the decorations were packed away, the room restored to its original order and properly cleaned, the wedding party left the building and walked to the parking lot.

Carolyn followed Mitchell to his car.

"Let's talk when you take me home. This isn't something I want to do in a moving vehicle," she said as he located his key ring and opened the door for her.

"Okay," Mitchell said quietly. He walked around to the driver's side and slid into the seat in silence.

She could tell that he had prepared himself for the worst, accepted it, and taken it like a man. A mature man.

She thought of what Hank had done when she turned him down. The older man, the one who seemed to be everything she'd ever wanted in the man who would be her mate. Mitchell rested one hand on the steering wheel and inserted the key in the ignition, but he didn't turn it. He sighed deeply then dropped his hands and turned his body toward her. "We don't have to have that little talk, Carolyn. It's okay. I know what you're going to say, and I won't insult you and keep hammering at you. Your decision is your decision, whether it's the one I want or not."

A burn started in the back of her eyes, but she blinked it back.

"I don't know if I'll have the strength to do this later, so I had better do it now." He reached behind the seat, pulled out a plastic bag, and handed it to her. "I got this for you. I forgot to give it to you before the wedding. You can ignore the note."

She opened the bag, reached inside, and pulled out a little plush ram that matched the sheep Mitchell had bought for her at the zoo. Stuck to it was a small note with Mitchell's scrawling handwriting.

To Carolyn.
  Husband attached.
    Love, Mitchell

She stared at the little ram, then at Mitchell.

He smiled weakly, like he was trying to lighten the heavy moment. "I hope this time you're not going to hit me over the head with it."

She petted the little ram, which was obviously the husband for the sheep now sitting on her bed, reread the note, and contemplated its message.

She swallowed hard. "Were you going to ask me if I wanted a husband, too?"

He smiled, but his face held no humor.

"Yes, I guess I was."

She stared blankly at the plush ram in her hands then raised her head to look across the space between them and studied Mitchell.

He was no longer the neat and tidy package he had been in the afternoon. The jacket of the tuxedo was crinkled. His carnation was squashed and missing half its petals. He'd spilled something on his shirt, the bow tie was crooked, and his hair gel had given up its hold long ago. And contrary to the claims of Mitchell's hairstylist, she could still see some orange and blue at the roots.

Mitchell never put on airs, nor did he pretend to be something he was not. Mitchell was, just as his father said, simply the person he was. Regardless of his age, his job, his visions for the future, or anything else—or maybe it was the combination of them all—Mitchell was the man she was madly in love with and always would be.

When it came down to the bottom line, Mitchell was a man of faith and character.

Suddenly, Carolyn had to force herself to breathe. Of all the Bible reading she'd done since she'd met Mitchell, one verse, Isaiah 32:8, sprang to mind. "But the noble man makes noble plans, and by noble deeds he stands."

For all his plans and reasoning behind them, whether it had been his strategy to prepare the food for the wedding, to his ideas for fun places to take her—in spite of her best efforts to avoid him—to his intentions to court her or the times they had simply prayed together, he'd always done the right and noble thing.

She'd never met a man nobler than the fine Christian man in the disorderly tuxedo in front of her.

She had been praying for the wrong things, but God had sent her the right man anyway.

Knowing that he had planned tonight to ask her to marry him, her eyes clouded, but she blinked back the tears. Before she spoke, she plucked the little yellow note off the ram, reached past the space between the seats, and pressed it onto the center of his chest. "Then the answer is yes."

Mitchell reached up to brush his fingers across the "husband attached" sticker in the middle of his chest, stared down at it, then raised his head, meeting her gaze. His voice came out gravelly and low, like he was having trouble comprehending what she'd just agreed to. "That's great. I feel all choked up. I don't know what to say."

Carolyn had no intention of becoming tangled in a big kiss in the bucket seats of a car in the middle of his church's parking lot. Instead, she leaned over the stick shift and rested her palm on the note stuck to the center of his chest. Beneath her touch, his heart pounded.

"Just say, Baa–aa–aa."

Sweet Harmony

by Janice Thompson

Dedication

In loving memory of one of my dearest drama buddies of all time, Robin Tompkins, currently performing on the greatest stage of all.

Chapter 1

Life is better in Harmony. If you don't believe me, come on up here and see for yourself." Tangie laughed as she heard her grandmother's cheerful words. Leaning back against the pillows, she shifted the cell phone to her other ear and tried to imagine what her life would be like if she actually lived in her grandparents' tiny hometown of Harmony, New Jersey. "Thanks, Gran-Gran, but I'm no small-town girl," she said, finally. "I've spent the last four years in New York, remember?"

"How could I forget?" Her grandmother's girlish laugh rippled across the telephone line. "I've told every person I know that my granddaughter is a Broadway star...that she knows all of the big names in the Big Apple."

Tangie groaned. "I might know a few people, but I'm no star, trust me." In fact, these days she couldn't even seem to find a long-term acting gig, no matter how far off-Broadway she auditioned. So, on Christmas Eve she'd packed her bags and headed home to Atlantic City. Tangie had spent much of the drive praying, asking God what she should do. His silence had been deafening.

Now Christmas had passed and a new year approached. Still, Tangie felt no desire to return to the Big Apple. Safely tucked into the same bed she'd slept in every night as a little girl, she just wanted to stay put. Possibly forever. And maybe that was for the best. She'd felt for some time that things were winding down, career-wise. Besides, she'd seen more than enough drama over the past four years...and not just on the stage. So what if her days on the stage were behind her? Maybe—in spite of her best efforts—she wasn't destined to perform on Broadway.

"I'm telling you, Harmony is the perfect place for you." Gran-Gran's words interrupted her thoughts. "You need a break from big-city life. It's peaceful here, and the scenery is breathtaking, especially during the holidays. It'll do you good. And it'll do my heart good to have you. I'm sure Gramps would agree."

"Oh, you don't have to win me over on the beauty of upstate New Jersey," Tangie assured her. She'd visited her mom's parents enough to know that Harmony was one of the prettiest places on planet Earth, especially in the wintertime when the snows left everything a shimmering white. Pausing a moment, she thought about her options. "Might sound silly, but my first reaction is to just stay here."

"In Atlantic City?" her grandmother asked, the surprise in her voice evident. "Would you work at the candy shop? I thought you'd given up on that idea years ago when you headed to New York."

"Yeah." Tangie sighed as she shifted her position in the bed to get more comfortable. "But Mom and Dad are about to head out in their RV again, so Taffie's bound to need my help, especially with the new baby."

Tangie couldn't help but smile as she reflected on her older sister's mothering skills. Baby Callie had lovely brown tufts of hair and kissable apple dumpling cheeks. And her big brown eyes melted Tangie's heart every time.

Yes, it might be nice to stay home for a change. Settle in. Hang out at the candy shop with people who loved her. People who would offer encouragement and help her forget about the thousand ways she'd failed over the past few years, not just professionally, but personally, as well. All of the parts she'd auditioned for but hadn't received. All of the plays she'd been in that had closed unexpectedly. All of the would-be relationships that had ended badly.

Tangie sighed.

"Let me tell you the real reason for my call." The determination in her grandmother's voice grew by the minute. "No point in beating around the bush. Our church is looking for a drama director for the kids' ministry. I suggested you, and the pastor jumped on the idea."

"W–what?"

"There's nothing wrong with your hearing, honey. Harmony might be small, but the church certainly isn't. It's grown by leaps and bounds since you were here last, and the children's ministry is splitting at the seams. Our music pastor has been trying to involve the kids in his productions, but he doesn't know the first thing about putting on a show. Not the acting part, anyway. We need a real drama director. Someone skilled at her craft. . .who knows what she's doing."

"Why hire one?" Tangie asked. "Why not just find someone inside the church with those talents and abilities?"

"No one has your qualifications," Gran-Gran stated. "You know everything about set design, staging, costumes, and acting. You're a wealth of knowledge. And you've worked on Broadway, for heaven's sake. Gregg doesn't mind admitting he knows very little about putting on shows. He attempted one with the kids last week. A Christmas production. But it was, well—"

"Wait. Who's Gregg?" Tangie interrupted.

"Gregg. Our music pastor. The one I was just talking about. You remember him, right?"

"Hmm." Tangie paused to think about it. "Yeah, I think I remember him. Sort of a geeky-looking guy? Short hair. Looks like his mother dressed him?"

Gran-Gran clucked her tongue. "Tangie, shame on you. He's a wonderful, godly man. Very well groomed. And tidy."

Tangie looked at the mess in her bedroom and chuckled. "Sounds like my dream guy."

"Well, don't laugh. There are reams of young women trying to catch his eye. Good thing they don't all see things the way you do. Besides, half the women in our Prime Timers class are praying for a wife for Gregg, so it's just a matter of time before God parts the Red Sea and brings the perfect woman his way."

"Mm-hmm. But let's go back to talking about that show he put on. What happened?"

"It was terrible." Gran-Gran sighed. "And I don't just mean terrible. It was awful. Embarrassing, actually. The kids didn't memorize any of their lines, and their costumes—if you could call them that—looked more like bathrobes. And don't even get me started on the set. He built it out of cardboard boxes he found behind our local hardware store. You could still see the Home Depot logo through the paint."

"Ugh. Give me a break." Sounded pretty amateurish. Then again, she'd been in some productions over the years that weren't exactly stellar. . .in any sense of the word, so who was she to pass judgment?

"The music part was great," Gran-Gran said. "That's Gregg's real gift. He knows music. But the acting part was painful to watch. If my best friend's grandkids hadn't been in it, Gramps and I probably would've left during the intermission."

"I've seen a few shows like that," Tangie said. She chuckled and then added, "I've *been* in a few shows like that."

Her grandmother laughed. "Honey, with you *everything's* a show. And that's exactly why

I think you'd be perfect for this. Ever since you graduated from acting school last spring, you've been trying to find out where you belong. Right?"

"Right." Tangie sighed.

"And didn't you tell me you worked with a children's group at the theater school?"

"Yes. I directed a couple of shows with them. They were great." In fact, if she admitted the truth to herself, working with the kids had been one of the few things she'd really felt good about.

"Think of all the fun you'll have working with the children at church, then," Gran-Gran said. "You'll be able to share both your love of acting and the love of the Lord."

"True. I was really limited at the school." The idea of working in a Christian environment sounded good. Really good, in fact.

"They need someone with your experience and your zeal. I've never known anyone with as much God-given talent and ability, and so creative, too. Gregg is pretty much 'in the box.' And you, well. . ." Her grandmother's voice trailed off.

"Say no more." Tangie laughed. She'd busted out of the box years ago when she dyed her spiky hair bright orange and got that first tattoo. Glancing down at her Tweety Bird pajamas and fuzzy slippers, she had to wonder what the fine folks of Harmony, New Jersey, would think of such an "out of the box" kind of girl.

Only one way to know for sure. Maybe it would be best to start the new year in a new place, after all.

Tangie drew in a deep breath then spurted her impromptu answer. "Gran-Gran, tell them I accept. Look for me tomorrow afternoon. Tangie Carini is coming to Harmony!"

�${}$

Gregg Burke left the staff meeting at Harmony Community Church, his thoughts tumbling around in his head. He climbed into his car and pointed it toward home—the tiny wood-framed house on the outskirts of town. With the flip of a switch, the CD player kicked on. Gregg continued to press the FORWARD button until he located the perfect song—a worship tune he'd grown to love.

Ah. Perfect.

He leaned back against the seat and shifted his SUV into DRIVE. As he pulled out onto the winding country road, Gregg reflected on the meeting he'd just attended. The church was growing like wildfire; that was a fact. And while he understood the need to keep up with the times, he didn't want to jump on board every trend that came along. He'd seen other churches pull out the stops to become hip and trendy, and some of them had lost their original passion for the Word and for prayer. No way would he go along with that.

On the other hand, some folks had accused him of being set in his ways. Unwilling to bend. What was it the pastor had just said at the meeting? "Gregg, you're the oldest twenty-six-year-old I've ever known." Dave's words had pricked Gregg's heart. He didn't want others to see him as stiff or unbending.

Lord, am I? I don't want to get in the way of whatever You want to do, but I think we need to be careful here. I know we need to do everything we can to reach out to people. I'm all about that. I just pray we move carefully. Thoughtfully.

As Gregg maneuvered a sharp turn, a bank of snow on the side of the road caught his eye. Late December was always such a beautiful time of year in Harmony, but this year he looked forward to the change of seasons more than ever. The countless piles of snow would melt away into oblivion. Gregg could hardly wait for the warmth of spring. Gramps—his adopted grandfather—had already informed him there were at least ten or twenty trout in the lake with his name on them. He could hardly wait to reel them in.

On the other hand, the eventual change in seasons forced Gregg to think about something he'd rather *not* think about—the Easter production he'd just agreed to do with the children.

At once, his attitude shifted. While Gregg wanted to go along with Dave's idea of reaching out to the community, the suggestion of putting on three to four musical performances a year with the children concerned him. First, he didn't want to take that much time away from the adult choir. Those singers needed him. Second, he didn't work as well with kids as some people thought he did. In fact, he wasn't great with kids. . .at all.

"It's not that I don't like children," he said to himself. "They're just. . .different."

The ones he'd worked with in the Christmas play were rowdy, and they didn't always pay attention. And, unlike his adult choir members, the kids didn't harmonize very well, no matter how hard he worked with them. In fact, one or two of the boys couldn't carry a tune in a bucket. Why their parents had insisted they participate in the musical. . .

Stop it, Gregg.

He shook his head, frustrated with himself for thinking like that. Every child should have the opportunity to learn, to grow. How many chances had he been given as a kid? He'd struggled through softball, hockey, and a host of other sports before finally realizing singing was more his bag.

The more he thought about it, the worse he felt. How many of those boys, like himself, were without a father? He knew of at least one or two who needed a strong, positive male influence. Had the Lord orchestrated this whole plan to put him in that position, maybe? If so, did he have it in him?

"Father, help me. I don't want to blow this. But I guess it's obvious I'm going to need Your help more than ever. Remind me of what it was like to be a kid." He shivered, just thinking about it.

Gregg pulled the car onto the tiny side street then crawled along the uneven road until he reached his driveway. His house sat back nearly a quarter mile, tucked away in the trees. At the end of the driveway, he stopped at the mailbox and snagged today's offering from the local mail carrier. Then he pulled his car into the garage, reached for his belongings, and headed inside.

Entering his home, Gregg hung his keys on the hook he'd placed strategically near the door and put his jacket away in the closet, being careful to fasten every snap. He placed the pile of mail on the kitchen counter, glanced through it, then organized it into appropriate categories: To be paid. To be tossed. To be pondered.

Oh, if only he could organize the kids with such ease. Then, perhaps, he wouldn't dread the days ahead.

Chapter 2

Tangie made the drive from Atlantic City to Harmony in a little less than three hours. Though the back roads were slick—the winter in full swing—she managed to make it to her grandparents' house with little problem. In fact, the closer she got to Harmony, the prettier everything looked, especially with Christmas decorations still in place. Against the backdrop of white, the trees showcased their bare branches. Oh, but one day. . .one day the snows would melt and spring would burst through in all of its colorful radiance. Tangie lived for the springtime.

"Color, Lord," she whispered. "That's what gets me through the winter. The promise of color when the snows melt!"

As she pulled her car into the drive, a smile tugged at the edges of her lips. Little had changed at the Henderson homestead in the twenty-two years she'd been coming here. Oh, her grandfather had painted the exterior of the tiny wood-framed house a few years ago, shifting from a light tan to a darker tan. It had created quite a stir. But other than that, everything remained the same.

"Lord, I'm going to need Your strength. You know how I am. I'm used to the hustle and bustle of Times Square. Eating in crowded delis and listening to taxicabs honk as they go tearing by. Racing from department store to theater. I'm not used to a quiet, slow-paced, solitary life. I—"

She didn't have time to finish her prayer. Gran-Gran stood at the front door, waving a dish towel and hollering. Tangie climbed out of the car, and her grandmother sprinted her way across the snowy yard like a track star in the making. *Okay, so maybe not everything moves slowly here.*

"Oh, you beautiful thing!" Her grandmother giggled as she reached to touch Tangie's hair. "What have you done now?"

"Don't you like it? I thought red was a nice color with my skin tone."

"That's *red*?" Gran-Gran laughed. "If you say so. In the sunlight, I think I see a little purple in there."

"Probably. But that's okay, too. You know me, Gran-Gran. All things bright. . ."

"And beautiful," her grandmother finished. "I know, I know."

Tangie grabbed her laptop and overnight bag, leaving the other larger suitcases in the trunk.

Gran-Gran chattered all the way into the house. Once inside, she hollered, "Herbert, we've got a guest!"

"Oh, I'm no guest. Don't make a fuss over me." Tangie set her stuff on the nearest chair and looked around the familiar living room. The place still smelled the same—like a combination of cinnamon sticks and old books. But something else had changed. "Hey, you've moved the furniture."

"Yes." Gran-Gran practically beamed. "Do you like it?"

Tangie shrugged. "Sure. I guess so." To be honest, she felt a little odd with the room all turned around. It had always been the other way. *Whoa, girl. You've never cared about things staying the same before. Snap out of it! Let your grandmother live a little! Walk on the wild side!*

Seconds later, her grandfather entered the room. His gray hair had thinned even more since her last visit, and his stooped shoulders threw her a little. When had this happened?

"Get over here, Tangerine, and give your old Gramps a hug!" He opened his arms wide as he'd done so many times when she was a little girl.

Tangie groaned at the nickname but flew into his arms nonetheless. Sure enough, he still smelled like peppermint and Old Spice. Nothing new there.

"How are your sisters?" he asked with a twinkle in his eye.

"Taffie's great. Motherhood suits her. And Candy. . ." Tangie smiled, thinking of her middle sister. "Candy's still flying high."

"Loving her life as a pilot for Eastway, from what I hear." Gramps nodded. "That's my girl. A high-flying angel."

"And you!" Gran-Gran drew near and placed another kiss on her cheek. "You're straight off the stages of Broadway."

"More like off-off-Broadway." Tangie shrugged, determined to change the direction of the conversation. "I come bearing gifts!" She reached for the bag she and Taffie had carefully packed with candies from the family's shop on the boardwalk.

Gramps' eyes lit up as he saw the Carini's Confections logo on the bag. "Oh, I hope you've got some licorice in there."

"I do. Three different flavors."

"And some banana taffy?" Gran-Gran asked.

"Naturally. You didn't think I'd forget, did you? I know it's your favorite."

Gramps tore into the licorice and popped a piece in his mouth. As he did, a look of pure satisfaction seemed to settle over him. "Mmm. I'm sure glad that daughter of mine married into the candy business. It's made for a pretty sweet life for the rest of us."

Tangie nodded. "Yeah, Mom was born for the sweet stuff. Only now she seems happier touring the country in that new RV she and dad bought last month."

"I heard they had a new one," Gran-Gran said. "Top of the line model."

"Yes, and they're going to travel the southern states to stay warm during the winter." Tangie couldn't help but smile as she reflected on the pictures Mom had sent from Florida a while back. In one of them, her father was dressed in Bermuda shorts on bottom and a Santa costume on top. The caption read Confused in Miami.

"I've never understood the fascination with going from place to place in an RV," Gramps said, as he settled into his recliner and reached for another piece of licorice. "Who wants to live in a house on wheels when you've got a perfectly good house that sits still?" He gestured to his living room, and Tangie grinned.

"You've got a good point," she said as she reached for a piece of taffy. "But I think Mom was born with a case of wanderlust."

"Oh yes," Gran-Gran agreed. "That girl never could stay put when she was a little thing. Always flitting off here or there."

"I'm kind of the same way, I guess." Tangie shrugged. "An adventurer. And I do tend to flit from one thing to another." She sighed.

"Well, we hope you'll stay put in Harmony awhile," Gramps said, giving her a wink. "Settle in. Make some friends."

A mixture of emotions rushed over Tangie at her grandfather's words. While there was some appeal to long-lasting friendships, she wasn't the type to settle in. No, the past four years had proven that. Jumping from one thing to another—one show to another—seemed more her mode of operation. Was the Lord doing something different this time? Calling her to stay put for a while?

"Let's get you settled in your new room." Gran-Gran gestured toward the hallway. "Do you need Gramps to get your things?"

"Oh, I don't mind getting them myself."

"Not while I'm living and breathing!" Her grandfather, rising from the recliner, gave her a stern look. She tossed him her keys then watched with a smile as he headed outdoors to fetch her bags.

Tangie traipsed along on her grandmother's heels until they reached the spare bedroom—the second room on the right past the living room. She'd slept in the large four-poster bed dozens of times over the years, of course, but never for more than a couple of nights at a stretch. Was this really her new room?

She smiled as she saw the porcelain dolls on the dresser and the hand-embroidered wall hangings. Not exactly her taste in decor, but she wouldn't complain. Unless she decided to stay long term, of course. Then she would likely replace some of the wall hangings with the framed playbills from all of the shows she'd been in. Now that would really change the look of the room, wouldn't it!

Tangie spent the next several minutes putting away her clothes. The folded items went in the dresser. Gran-Gran had been good enough to empty the top three drawers. The rest of Tangie's things were hung in the already-crowded closet. Oh well. She'd make do. Likely this trek to the small town of Harmony wouldn't last long, anyway. Besides, she knew what it was like to live in small spaces. She and her roommate Marti had barely enough room to turn around in the five-hundred-square-foot apartment they'd shared in Manhattan. This place was huge in comparison.

As she wrapped up, Gran-Gran turned her way with a smile. "Let's get this show on the road, honey. Pastor Hampton is waiting for us at the church. He wants to meet you and give you your marching orders."

"A–already?" Tangie shook her head. "But I look awful. I'm still wearing my sweats, and my hair needs a good washing before I meet anyone." She pulled a compact out of her purse, groaning as she took a good look at herself. Her usually spiky hair looked more like a normal "do" today. And without a fresh washing, even the color of her hair looked less vibrant. . .more ordinary. Maybe freshening up her lipstick would help. She scrambled for the tube of Ever-Berry lip gloss.

"Oh, pooh." Gran-Gran waved her hand. "Don't worry about any of that. We've got to be at the church at three and it's a quarter till. If you're a good girl, I'll make some of that homemade hot chocolate you love so much when we get back."

"You've got it!" Tangie pressed the compact and lip gloss back into her purse—a beaded forties number she'd purchased at a resale shop on a whim.

Minutes later she found herself in the backseat of her grandparents' 1998 Crown Victoria, puttering and sputtering down the road.

"This thing's got over two hundred thousand miles on it," Gramps bragged, taking a sharp turn to the right. "Hope to put another hundred on it before one of us gives out."

"One of us?" Tangie's grandmother looked at him, stunned. "You mean you or me?"

"Well, technically, I meant me or the car." He grinned. "But I'm placing my bets on the car. She's gonna outlive us all."

"I wouldn't doubt it."

Gramps went off on a tangent about the car, but Gran-Gran seemed distracted. She turned to wave at an elderly neighbor shuffling through the snow, dressed in a heavy coat and hat. "Oh, look. There's Clarence, checking his mail. I need to ask him how Elizabeth's doing."

She rolled down her window and hollered out, "Clarence!" The older man paused, mail in hand, and turned their way.

As the others chatted about hernias, rheumatism, and the need for warmer weather, Tangie pondered her choice to move here. *Lord, what have I done? If I've made an impulsive decision, help me unmake it. But if I'm supposed to be here...*

She never got any further in her prayer. Though it didn't make a lick of sense, somehow she just knew...she was supposed to be here.

❦

Gregg worked against the clock in his office, transcribing music for the Sunday morning service. The musicians would be counting on him, as would the choir. As he wrapped up, he glanced at his watch and sighed. Three forty-five? Man. He still had to call Darla, the church's part-time pianist, full-time self-appointed matchmaker, to talk about that one tricky key change. She'd struggled with it at their last rehearsal.

Leaning back in his chair, Gregg reflected on a conversation he'd had with Dave earlier this morning. Looked like the church had decided to hire a drama director. Interesting. In some ways, he felt a little put off by the idea. Was he really so bad at directing shows that they needed to actually hire someone?

On the other hand, the notion of someone else helping out did offer some sense of relief. That way, he could focus on his own work. Work he actually enjoyed. Music was his respite. His sanctuary. He ran to it as others might run to sports or TV shows. Music energized him and gave him a sense of purpose. Daily, Gregg thanked the Lord for the sheer pleasure of earning a living doing the thing he loved most.

Now, if only he could figure out how to get around that whole "productions" thing, he'd be a happy, happy man.

At four thirty, he finished up his tasks and prepared to leave. His thoughts shifted to Ashley, the children's ministry leader. At Darla's prompting, Gregg had worked up the courage to ask Ashley out and she'd agreed. Wonder of wonders! Would tonight's dinner date at Gratzi's win her over? From what he'd been told, she loved Italian food. For that matter, he did, too. Still, a plate of fettuccine Alfredo didn't automatically guarantee true love. No, for that he'd have to think bigger. Maybe chicken parmesan.

Deep in thought, Gregg left his office. He walked down the narrow hallway, arms loaded with sheets of music. Just as he reached Dave's office, the door swung open and Gramps Henderson stepped out. The two men nearly collided. Gregg came to such an abrupt stop that his sheets of music went flying. He immediately dropped to his knees and began the task of organizing his papers.

"Let me help with that."

Gregg looked up into the eyes of a woman—maybe in her early twenties—with the oddest color hair he'd ever seen. He tried not to stare, but it was tough. He went back to the task at hand, snatching the papers. She worked alongside him, finally handing him the last page.

"Ooo, is that the contemporary version of the 'Hallelujah Chorus'?" she asked, gazing at him with soul-piercing intensity. For a second he found himself captivated by her dark brown eyes.

"Yes." He gave her an inquisitive look. How would she know that?

She flashed a warm smile, but he was distracted by all of the earrings. Well, that and the tiny sparkler in her nose. Was that a diamond? Very bizarre. He had to wonder if it ever bothered her...say, when she got a cold.

Gregg rose to his feet then reached a hand to help the young woman up. By the time they were both standing, Mrs. Henderson's happy-go-lucky voice rang out. "Gregg, we want you to meet our granddaughter, Tangie Carini. She's from Atlantic City."

"Nice to meet you." As he extended his hand, Gregg realized who this must be. Earlier this morning, Dave had said something about counseling a troubled young woman who'd recently joined the church's college and career class. How could Gregg have known she'd turn out to be the granddaughter of a good friend like Herb Henderson?

His heart broke immediately as he pondered these things. Poor Gramps. How long had he quietly agonized over this granddaughter gone astray? Surely they still had some work ahead of them, based on her bright red hair—were those purple streaks?—and piercings that dazzled.

Not that you could judge a person based on external appearance. He chided himself immediately. He wouldn't want people to make any decisions based on how he looked.

Tangie shook his hand and then nodded at the papers he'd shoved under his arm. "Great rendition of the 'Hallelujah Chorus.' We performed that my senior year in high school. I'll never forget it."

"Oh? You sing?" When she nodded, he realized at once how he might help the Hendersons get their granddaughter walking the straight and narrow. If she could carry a tune, he'd offer her a position in the choir. Yes, that's exactly what he would do. And if he had to guess, based on her speaking voice, he'd peg her for an alto. Maybe a second soprano.

"We'll see you Sunday, Gregg," Gramps said, patting him on the back. "In fact, it looks like we'll be seeing a lot more of you from now on."

A lot more of me? What's that all about?

Oh yes, Gregg reasoned, it must have something to do with the snows melting. Gramps was anxious to go fishing. Still, the older fellow sure had a strange way of phrasing things.

As Tangie and her grandparents disappeared from view, Gregg made his way to his car. Tonight's date with Ashley would start a whole new chapter of his life. Suddenly, he could hardly wait to turn the page.

Chapter 3

On Sunday morning, Tangie and her grandparents left for church plenty early. With the roads still covered in snow and ice and Gramps's plan to stop for donuts along the way, they could use the extra time. Besides, she wanted to get to the church in time to acclimate herself to her new surroundings.

Tangie had given herself a quick glance in the mirror just before they left. She'd deliberately chosen her most conservative outfit—a flowing black skirt with a seventies hippie feel to it, and a gray cashmere sweater. Wrapping a black scarf around her neck, she leaned forward to have a look at her makeup. Not too much, not too little. . .just right. She chuckled, realizing how much she sounded like Goldilocks. If only she had the blond hair to make the picture complete. Nah, on second thought, she definitely looked better as a redhead. Or purple, depending on the angle and the lighting.

As they drove to the church, Tangie thought about the events about to transpire. A sense of excitement took hold. The more she thought about it, the more her anticipation grew. This wasn't about shaking people up, as Gran-Gran had said. No, Tangie had come to Harmony to help the kids develop their God-given talents so they could further the kingdom. She wanted to reach people for the Lord, and could clearly see the role the arts played in that. Oh, if only everyone could catch hold of that!

They stopped at the local bakery on the way and Gramps went inside. Tangie and her grandmother chatted while they waited in the Ford.

"I still can't wait to see the looks on everyone's faces when they find out you've been hired as drama director," Gran-Gran said and then snickered. "Ella Mae Peterson is going to have a fit. She thinks the church spends too much money on their arts programs, as it is."

Tangie sighed. How many times had she heard this argument over the years? "Mrs. Peterson needs to realize the arts are an awesome way to reach people. When you present the gospel message through drama, music, or other artistic venues, people's lives are touched in a way unlike any other. Performing for the Lord isn't about the accolades or even about ability. It's about using the gifts God has given you to captivate the heart and emotions of the audience member. You can't put a price tag on that."

"Exactly." Gran-Gran nodded. "Which is exactly what some of these set-in-their-ways folks need to realize. You're going to shake them up, honey. Give 'em a run for their money."

"Not sure I want to!" she admitted. In fact, this was one time she'd rather just fit in.

"Well, trust me. . .some people could use a little shaking. You'd be surprised how stiff people can be. And I'm not talking arthritis here." Gran-Gran winked.

Stiff? Oh, great. And it's my job to unstiffen them? Just as quickly she chided herself. *No, it's the Lord's job to unstiffen them. . .if He so chooses.*

Gramps returned to the car with a large box of donuts. He reached inside and snagged one, taking a big bite. Gran-Gran scolded him, but he didn't let that stop him. Finishing it, he licked his fingers, then set the car in motion once again.

They arrived at the church in short order. Tangie could hardly believe the mob of cars in the parking lot. "When did this happen, Gran-Gran? It wasn't like this last time I was here."

"Told you! This church is in revival, honey. We're bursting at the seams. Before long, we'll have to build a new sanctuary. In the meantime, we're already holding two Sunday services and one on Saturday evenings, too. Even at that, parking is a mess."

"Wow." Tangie could hardly believe it. Her church in New York City wasn't this full on Sunday mornings, not even on Christmas or Easter.

Once they got inside the foyer, she found herself surrounded on every side by people. "Man, this place has grown."

Gran-Gran flew into action and, over a fifteen-minute period, introduced Tangie to dozens of church members, young and old alike. She met so many people, her head was swimming. Tangie fervently hoped they wouldn't quiz her on the names afterward. She'd fail miserably.

As the word *fail* flitted through her mind, Tangie sighed. *Lord, I don't want to fail at this like I've done so many times.* How many times had she fallen short of the mark in her acting career? How wonderful it would have been to land a lead role just once. She'd dreamed of it all her life but never quite succeeded. Oh, there had been callbacks. Wonderful, glorious callbacks that got her hopes up. But each time she'd been disappointed, relegated to a smaller role.

On the other hand, Tangie didn't really mind the secondary roles. . .if only they had lasted more than a week or two. So many of the shows she'd been in had closed early, due to poor reviews. Was she destined to remain the underdog forever? Almost good enough. . .but not quite?

And what about her personal life? Would any of her relationships stand the test of time, or would she always bounce from one relationship to the next, never knowing what true love felt like? *I'm asking You to help me succeed this time. Not for my glory, but for Yours. Help me see this thing through from start to finish. I don't want to be a quitter.*

Through the sanctuary doors, she heard the beginning strains of a familiar praise song. As they entered the auditorium, she looked around in amazement. The place was alive with excitement. People clapped their hands along with the music, many singing with abandon. She followed behind Gran-Gran and Gramps to the third row, where they scooted past a couple of people and settled into seats.

Glancing up to the stage, Tangie watched Gregg standing front and center with a guitar in hand. His fingers moved with skill across the strings, and his voice—pure and melodic—immediately ushered her into the presence of God. *See, Lord? That's what I was trying to tell Gran-Gran. It is possible to stand center stage, not for the applause of men, but to bring people closer to You.*

She closed her eyes, thankful for the opportunity to worship. The music continued, each song better than the one before. Tangie watched as the choir geared up for a special number—the contemporary version of the "Hallelujah Chorus." The soloist—a beautiful young woman in her midtwenties—floored Tangie with her vocal ability.

"That's our children's minister, Ashley Conway," Gran-Gran whispered. "Isn't she something?"

"To say the least," Tangie responded in a hoarse whisper. "I think she rivals anyone I've ever seen or heard on a Broadway stage."

"Yep. We've got some talent here in Harmony, that's for sure." Her grandmother winked before turning to face the stage once again.

Tangie reached for an offering envelope and scribbled the words, "Why doesn't Ashley just help Gregg with the kids' production?" on it. She gave the girl another glance then penciled in a few more words: "She's got the goods."

Gran-Gran frowned as Tangie handed her the envelope. After reading it, she scribbled down, "Too busy. Ashley works five days a week at the elementary school and Sunday mornings and Wednesday nights at church. No time."

"Ah." Tangie looked up, focusing on the choir. With Gregg at the helm, Ashley and the other choir members performed flawlessly. They were every bit as good as the choir at her home church. Maybe better. And Gregg's heart for God was evident, no doubt about that. Tangie felt shame wash over her as she thought about the way she'd described him to Gran-Gran over the phone.

Lord, forgive me for calling him geeky. This is a great guy. And he's doing a wonderful work here.

In fact, she could hardly wait to work alongside him.

After the choir wrapped up its number, the singers exited the stage. Tangie watched as Gregg trailed off behind them. He reached to pat Ashley on the back, giving a smile and a nod.

"See? He has the gift of encouragement, too," Gran-Gran whispered. "That's a plus."

Finally the moment arrived. Pastor Hampton took the stage. Though she didn't usually struggle with stage fright, Tangie's nerves got the better of her as she listened for his prompting to come to the front of the church for an official introduction to the congregation. As she waited, she narrowed her gaze and focused on Gregg Burke, who now sat in the front row of the next section. He turned back to look at her—or was he looking at Gramps?—with a confused expression on his face. What was up with that?

She found herself staring at him for a moment. Maybe he wasn't as geeky looking as she'd once thought. In fact, that blue shirt really showed off his eyes...his best feature.

She'd almost lost her train of thought when Pastor Hampton flashed a smile and said, "I'd like to introduce our new drama director, Tangie Carini." With her knees knocking, she rose from her seat and headed to the stage.

🌺

From his spot in the front row, Gregg turned then stared at the young woman rising from her seat. Wait. *This* was their new drama director? Surely there must be some mistake. The woman Dave had told him about was polished, professional. He would never have described this girl in such a way.

Slow down, Gregg. Don't judge a book by its cover. People did that with your mom, and look what happened.

He forced his thoughts away from that particular subject and watched as Tangie made her way from the pew to the stage. Oh, if only he could stay focused. Her bright red hair—if one could call it red—was far too distracting. Underneath the sanctuary lights, it had a strange purple glow to it. And then there was the row of earrings lining her right ear. Interesting. Different.

She looked his way and offered a shy smile, as if she somehow expected him to know exactly who she was and what she was doing here. He hoped the smile he offered in response was convincing enough.

As she brushed a loose hair from her face, he noticed the tattoo on the inside of her wrist. He strained to make it out but could not.

"Dave, what have you done?" he whispered. "You've slipped over the edge, man." Tangie Carini was the last person on planet Earth Gregg would've imagined the church hiring. She was the polar opposite of everything...well, of everything he was.

On the other hand...

As she opened her mouth, thanking the congregation for welcoming her to Harmony Community Church, nothing but pure goodness oozed out. He found himself spellbound by the soothing sound of her voice—very controlled and just the right tone. She'd done this before. . .spoken in front of a crowd.

Then again, if what Dave had said about her was true, she'd performed in front of thousands, and on Broadway, no less. Suddenly Gregg felt like crawling under his pew. Just wait till she got a look at the video of the Christmas play. She'd eat him for lunch.

※

Tangie shared her heart with the congregation, keenly aware of the fact that Gregg Burke watched her every move. What was he staring at? Surely the pastor had filled him in. . .right?

Oh well. Plenty of time to worry about that later. With a full heart, Tangie began explaining her vision for the drama program.

"I'm a firm believer in stirring up the gifts. And each of these children is gifted in his or her own way. I plan to spend time developing whatever abilities I see in each child so that he or she can walk in the fullness of God's call."

She paused a moment as members of the congregation responded with a couple of "Amens." Looked like they were cool with her ideas thus far.

After that, she went into a passionate speech about the role of the arts in ministry. "God has gifted us for a reason, not for the sake of entertainment—though we all love to entertain and be entertained. However, He has gifted us so that we can share the gospel message in a way that's fresh. Creative. Life changing."

As she spoke, Tangie noticed the smiles from most in the congregation. Sure, Ella Mae Peterson, Gran-Gran's friend, sat with her arms crossed at her chest. Well, no problem there. She and the Lord would win Mrs. Peterson over.

As she wrapped up her speech, Tangie turned to nod in Gregg's direction. The music pastor flashed a smile, but she noticed it looked a little rehearsed. She knew acting when she saw it. He wasn't happy she was there.

Hmm. Maybe Ella Mae wasn't her only adversary. Well, no problem. Tangie made up her mind to win over Gregg Burke, too. . .no matter what it took.

Chapter 4

O n New Year's Eve, Tangie went with her grandparents to a party at the church. It sure wouldn't be the same as celebrating the New Year in Times Square, but she'd make the best of it. She decided to let her hair down—figuratively speaking—so that the people of Harmony could see the real Tangie. The one with the eclectic wardrobe. She settled on black pants, a 1990s zebra-print top, and a lime green scarf, just for fun. For kicks, she added a hot pink necklace and earring ensemble. Standing back, she took a look at the mirror. "Hmm. Not bad. Nothing like a little color to liven things up."

They'd no sooner arrived at the church than the chaos began. Kids, food, games, activities... the whole place was a madhouse. In a happy sort of way.

"Told you we know how to have fun," Gran-Gran said with a twinkle in her eye. "Now, just let me drop off this food in the fellowship hall and I'll introduce you to a few people your own age."

Minutes later, Tangie found herself surrounded by elementary-age kids. They weren't exactly her age, but they'd gravitated to her nonetheless.

A pretty little thing with blond hair tugged at Tangie's sleeve. "I'm Margaret Sanderson and I'm an actress, just like you," the girl said, puffing up her shoulders and tossing her hair. "My mama says I was the best one in the Christmas play. They should've given me the lead part. Then the whole play would've been better."

"Oh? Is that so?" Tangie tried to hold her composure.

"Yes, and I can sing, too." The little girl's confidence increased more with each word. "Want to hear me?"

Before she could respond, the little girl began to belt "The Lullaby of Broadway." To her credit, Margaret could, indeed, sing. And what she lacked in decorum, she made up for in volume. Still, there was something a little over the top about the vivacious youngster.

I know what it is. She reminds me of myself at that age. Only, she's got a lot more nerve.

Tangie released a breath, wanting to say just the right thing. "We'll be holding auditions for an Easter production soon and I certainly look forward to seeing you there."

"Oh, I know. I've been practicing all week," Margaret explained with a knowing look in her eye. "I'm going to be the best one there. And Mama says that if they don't give me the main part, I can't do it at all."

We'll see about that.

Tangie turned as a little boy grabbed her other sleeve. "Hey, do I have to do that stupid Easter play?" he grumbled. "I don't want to."

"Well, I suppose that's up to your mom and dad," she said with a shrug. "It's not my decision."

"I don't have a dad." His gaze shifted downward. "And my mom always makes me try out for these dumb plays. But I stink at acting and singing."

Tangie quirked a brow, wondering where he got such an idea. "Who told you that?"

He stared at her like she'd grown two heads. "Nobody has to tell me. I just stink. Wait till you see the video. Then you'll know."

"Ah. Well, I suppose I'll just have to see for myself, then."

From across the room, Tangie caught a glimpse of Gregg standing next to the young woman who'd sung the solo on Sunday. What did Gran-Gran say her name was again?

Determined to connect with people, Tangie headed their way. As she approached the couple, she could see the look in Gregg's eyes as he talked to the beautiful brunette. Ah. A spark. He must really like her.

Gregg turned Tangie's way and nodded. "Tangie Carini."

"Gregg Burke." She offered a welcoming smile. "We meet officially. . .at last."

"Yes. Sorry about the other day in the hallway. I didn't know who you were, or I would have said something then. I'm glad you're here."

"Thanks." Maybe this wouldn't be as tough as she'd feared. Looked like he was a pretty easygoing guy.

Gregg nodded as he gestured to the brunette at his side. "Tangie, this is Ashley Conway, our children's director."

Ashley. That's it.

Ashley looked her way with curiosity etched on her face. "Tangie?" she said. "I don't think I've ever heard that one before. You'll have to tell me more about your name."

Tangie groaned. Oh, how she hated telling people that she was named after the flavor of the month when she was born. Having parents in the taffy business didn't always work to a girl's advantage.

Thankfully, Pastor Hampton made an announcement, giving her a reprieve.

"I know the kids are anxious to see the video of the Christmas performance," he said. "So why don't we go ahead and gather everyone in the sanctuary to watch it together."

Gregg groaned and Ashley slugged him in the arm. "Oh, c'mon. It's not so bad."

"Whatever." He shook his head and then looked at Tangie with pursed lips. "Just don't hold this against me, okay? I'm a musician, not a drama director."

"Of course." With anticipation mounting, Tangie tagged along behind Gran-Gran and Gramps to the sanctuary to watch the video. Finally! Something she could really relate to.

"Now, don't expect too much," Gran-Gran whispered as they took their seats. "Remember what I told you on the phone the other day."

"Right." Tangie nodded. Surely her grandmother had exaggerated, though. With Gregg being such an accomplished musician, the production couldn't have been too bad, right?

The lights in the auditorium went down, and she leaned back against her pew, ready for the show to begin. Up on the screen the recorded Christmas production began. Someone had taped the children backstage before the show, going from child to child, asking what he or she thought about the upcoming performance.

"How sweet."

Tangie was particularly struck with the boy who'd approached her in the fellowship hall, the one without a father. Watching him on the screen, she couldn't help but notice how rambunctious he was.

"That's Cody," Gran-Gran said, elbowing her. "One of the rowdy ones that comes with a warning label."

"He's as cute as he can be," Tangie said. She wanted to ruffle his already-messy hair. "I wonder if he can sing."

At that, Gramps snorted. "Wait and see."

"Yikes." Didn't sound promising.

Tangie continued watching the video as the opening music began. The children appeared on the stage and sang a Christmas song together. "Not bad, not bad." Tangie looked at her grandmother and shrugged then whispered, "What's wrong with that?"

"Keep watching."

At this point, the drama portion of the show began. Tangie almost fell out of her seat when the first child delivered his lines.

"Oh no." He stumbled all over himself. And what was up with that costume? Looked like someone had started it but not quite finished. At least his was better than the next child's. This precious little girl was definitely wearing something that looked like her mother's bathrobe. It was several inches too long in the arms. In fact, you couldn't see the girl's hands at all. As she tried to deliver her lines—albeit too dramatically—her sleeves flailed about, a constant distraction.

"Ugh." Tangie shook her head. Only five minutes into the show and she wanted to fix. . . pretty much everything.

At about that time, a little girl dressed as an angel appeared to the shepherds and delivered a line that was actually pretty good. "Oh wait. . .that's the girl I just met," she whispered to her grandmother. "Margaret Sanderson."

"A star in the making," Gran-Gran whispered. "And if you don't believe it, just ask her mother."

Tangie's laugh turned into a honking sound, which she tried to disguise with a cough. Unfortunately, the cough wasn't very convincing, so she resorted to a sneeze. Then hiccups. Before long, several people were looking her way, including Gregg.

Focus, Tangie. Focus.

Turned out, Margaret was the best one in the show. Many of the really good ones came with some degree of attitude. Pride. Oh well. They would work on that. Maybe that's one reason Tangie had come, to help Margaret through this.

Tangie watched once again as Cody took the stage, dressed as a shepherd. Poor kid. He stumbled all over himself, in every conceivable way.

Maybe that's another reason I'm here. He needs a confidence boost.

Funny. One kiddo needed a boost. . .the other needed to be taken down a notch or two.

Oh well, she had it in her. Nothing a little time and TLC couldn't take care of. Determined to make the best of things, Tangie settled in to watch the rest of the show.

✿

Gregg cringed as the video continued. On the night of the performance there had been excitement in the air. It had given him false hope that the show was really not so bad. But tonight, watching the video, he had to admit the truth.

It stunk.

No, it didn't just stink. It was an embarrassment.

He glanced across the aisle at Tangie and her grandparents, wanting to slink from the room. Oh, if only he could read her thoughts right now. Then again, maybe he didn't want to. Maybe it would be best just to pretend she thought it was great.

He watched as Tangie slumped down in her chair. Was she. . .sleeping? Surely not. He tried to focus on the screen, but found it difficult when a couple of people got up and slipped out of the sanctuary, whispering to each other. Great.

Lord, I don't mind admitting this isn't my bag. But I'm feeling pretty humiliated right now. Could we just fast-forward through this part and get right to the next?

Gregg was pretty sure he heard the Lord answer with a very firm, *"No."*

✿

Tangie continued to watch the video but found the whole thing painful. Gran-Gran had been right. It wasn't just poorly acted; the entire show was lacking in every conceivable way.

And talk about dull. How did people stay awake throughout the performance? Looked like half the folks in this place had fallen asleep tonight. Not a good sign.

She glanced across the aisle at Gregg Burke, saddened by the look of pain on his face. Poor guy. He had to know this wasn't good. Right?

Surely a man with his artistic abilities could see the difference between a good performance and a bad one. And, without a doubt, Gregg Burke was a guy with great artistic skill. By the end of Sunday's service, both his voice and his heart for God had won her over. The way he led the congregation in worship truly captivated her. And though she'd performed on many a stage over the years, Tangie couldn't help but think that leading others into the throne room of God would far surpass any experience she'd ever had in a theater setting.

She snapped back to attention, focusing on the video. For a moment. As a child on the screen struggled to remember his lines, Tangie's thoughts drifted once again. She pondered her first impression of Gregg—as a stodgy, geeky guy. Tonight, in his jeans and button-up shirt, he was actually quite handsome. Still, he looked a little stiff. Nervous. But why? Did he ever just relax? Enjoy himself?

At that moment, a loud snore to her right distracted her. She looked as Gran-Gran elbowed Gramps in the ribs. Tangie tried not to giggle but found it difficult. She didn't blame her grandfather for falling asleep. In fact—she yawned as she thought about it—her eyes were growing a little heavy, too.

Before long, she drifted off to sleep, dreaming of badly dressed wise men and Christmas angels who couldn't carry a tune in a bucket.

Chapter 5

It didn't take Tangie long to settle into a routine at Gran-Gran and Gramps's house. Her creative juices skittered into overtime as she contemplated the task of putting on a show with the children. Oh, what fun it would be. She could practically see it all now! The sets. The costumes. The smiles on the faces of everyone in attendance. With the Lord's help, she would pull off a toe-tapping, hand-clapping musical extravaganza that everyone—kids and church staff, alike—could be proud of.

Tangie received a call from the pastor on Monday morning, asking if they could meet later that afternoon. She stopped off at Sweet Harmony—Gramps's favorite bakery—to pick up some cookies to take to the meeting. Unable to make up her mind, Tangie purchased a dozen chocolate chip, a half dozen oatmeal raisin, and a half dozen peanut butter. Just for good measure, she added a half dozen of iced sugar cookies to her order.

"I can't live without my sweets," she explained to the woman behind the counter. "My family's in the sugar business and I've been in withdrawal since moving away from home."

The clerk—an older woman whose nametag read PENNY—gave her a funny look as she rang up the order. "Sugar business?"

"Yes, we run a candy shop on the boardwalk in Atlantic City, specializing in taffy." Tangie pulled a cookie from the plain white bag and took a big bite. "Mmm. Great peanut butter. They're my favorite."

"You really do have a sweet tooth." Penny laughed as she wiped her hands on her apron. "Well, just so you know, I'm hiring. Sarah, the girl who usually helps me in the afternoons, has gone back to college. So, if you're interested. . ."

"Hmm." Tangie shrugged. "I'll have to see how it works with my schedule. In the meantime, these cookies are great. If you're interested in adding any candies, I'd be happy to talk with you about that. I'd love to bring some of our family favorites to Harmony. I think you'd like them."

"Let me think about it," Penny said. "And you let me know when you've made up your mind about the job. Otherwise, I might put a 'help wanted' sign in the window."

"Give me a couple days to pray about it." Tangie took another bite of the cookie then headed to her car.

By four o'clock, she and Gregg Burke sat side by side in Dave's spacious office, all three of them nibbling on cookies.

"I'm so excited about what God is doing, I can hardly stand it," Dave said between bites. "We've already got the best music pastor in the world, and now we've just added a Broadway-trained actress to our staff to head up the drama department. Between the two of you, the Easter production is going to be the best thing this community has ever seen."

Tangie felt a little flustered at the pastor's glowing description of her. If he had any idea of the tiny bit parts she'd taken over the past four years, he'd probably rethink his decision. On the other hand. . .

God brought you here, Tangie, she reminded herself. *So don't get in the way of what He's doing.*

"What are you looking for, exactly?" Gregg asked Dave as he reached into the bag for another cookie. "What kind of production, I mean? More of a variety show or an all-out musical?"

"Doesn't really matter. I just want a production that will work hand in hand with the outreach we'll be doing for the community," Dave explained. "I'd like to see something that's different than anything we've done before."

"Different?" Gregg's eyebrows arched as he took another bite. "How different?"

"That's for you two to decide," the pastor said. "We're going to be hosting an Easter egg hunt for the neighborhood kids, as always. But this year we're looking at this as an outreach—the biggest of the year, in fact."

"Easter eggs? Outreach?" Gregg shook his head. "Not sure those two things really go together in one sentence."

"Oh, I think it's a wonderful idea," Tangie said, her excitement mounting. "The Easter egg hunt will be a great draw. And people are always more willing to hear about the Lord during the holidays, so we'll have a captive audience."

Dave nodded. "My thoughts, exactly. We'll advertise the Easter egg hunt in the paper and draw a large crowd. Then, just after the hunt is over, we'll open up the auditorium for everyone to come inside for the production. It will be free, of course."

"I think that's a wonderful idea," Tangie said. "That way all of the kids can watch the show, even the ones who wouldn't be able to afford it otherwise."

"You've got it!" Dave looked at her and beamed.

Clearly, they were on the same page.

She looked at Gregg, hoping for a similar response. He sat with a confused expression on his face. What was up with that?

"I don't really have anything specific in mind, as far as what kind of production it should be," the pastor continued, "just something that appeals to kids and shares the real meaning of Easter in a tangible way. But different, as I said. Something kid friendly and contemporary."

Gregg looked a little dubious. "How will we get the kids and their families to stay for the musical? I can see them coming for the Easter egg hunt, maybe, but how do we get them inside the building once it's over?"

"I've been thinking about that." Dave rolled a pen around in his fingers. "Haven't exactly come up with anything yet, though."

"Oh, I know," Tangie said. "Maybe we could do some sort of a drawing for a grand prize. A giant Easter egg, maybe? The winner to be announced after the production. That might entice them to stay."

"Giant Easter egg?" Gregg asked.

"Made of chocolate, of course." Tangie turned to him, more excited than ever. "At my family's candy shop, we have these amazing eggs. . .oh, you have to see one to believe it! They're as big as a football. No, bigger. And they're solid chocolate, hand decorated by my sister. I know Taffie will help. She loves things like this."

"Taffy will help?" Gregg looked at Tangie curiously. "What does that mean?"

"Oh, sorry." She giggled and her cheeks warmed. "Taffie is my older sister. There are three of us—Taffie, Candy, and me."

"Tangie." Dave said with a smile. "Your grandmother told me they sometimes call you Tangerine, just to be funny."

"Terrific." Tangie groaned. "As you might imagine, Tangie wouldn't have been my first choice for a name. How would you feel if you were named after the flavor of the month when you were born?"

Gregg chuckled, offering Tangie her first glimmer of hope from the beginning of the meeting till now. His eyes sparkled and a hint of color rose to his cheeks. "So, we're giving away an egg, then?" he asked.

"If that's okay with both of you." Tangie looked back and forth between them "They sell for a fortune, but I'm sure Taffie would send one for free, especially if I tell her what it's for. My sister and her husband love the Lord and would be thrilled to see one of their candy eggs used for ministry."

"Eggs for ministry." Gregg groaned and shook his head. "What's next?"

"Oh, that's easy." Tangie nodded. "Sheep, bunnies, and chicks, of course. And anything else that might appeal to little kids. Oh"—her heart swelled with joy as the words tumbled out—"this is going to be the best Easter ever!"

※

Gregg watched with some degree of curiosity as Tangie and Dave talked back and forth about the production. Talk about feeling like a third wheel. Why was he here, anyway? He did his best not to struggle with any offense. He'd been through enough of that as a kid. No, in fact, he looked forward to Tangie's help with the production, though he still had a hard time admitting it to anyone other than himself.

Still, that bunnies and chicks line had to be a joke. Right?

Listening to her talk, her voice as animated as her facial expression, he had the strangest feeling. . .she was dead serious.

He glanced at his watch and gasped. "Oh, sorry to cut this short, but I've got a date with my mom. I'm taking her to the movies this afternoon."

"A date with your mom?" Tangie flashed a smile. He couldn't tell if she was making fun of him or found the idea thoughtful. Not that it really mattered. No, where his mom was concerned, only one thing mattered. . .convincing her that the Lord loved her. And there was only one way to accomplish that really. . .by spending quality time with her and loving her, himself. Not an easy task sometimes, what with her brusque exterior. But Gregg was really working on not judging people by outward appearance, especially his own mom.

"When can we meet to talk about the production?" Tangie asked. "One day this week?"

"Mornings are better for me," he said as he rose from his chair. "What about Thursday?"

"Thursday it is. Where?"

"Hmm." He reached for his coat. "The diner on Main? They've got a great breakfast menu. Very inspirational. I'm going to need it if we're talking about putting on a show, trust me."

Tangie grinned. "Okay. I'll see you there. Will seven thirty work?"

"Yep." He nodded. "Sorry I have to bolt, but my mom is expecting me." After a quick good-bye, he headed toward the car, his thoughts whirling in a thousand different directions.

Chapter 6

Tangie pulled herself out of bed early on Thursday morning and dressed in one of her favorite outfits—a pair of faded bell-bottoms and a great vintage sweater she'd picked up at a resale shop—a throwback from the 1960s in varying shades of hot pink, orange, and brown. Why anyone would've parted with it was beyond her. Sure, the colors were a little faded, but that just gave it a more authentic look. And coupled with the shiny white vinyl go-go-style boots, which she'd purchased for a song, the whole ensemble just came together. Once you added in the hat. She especially loved the ivory pillbox-style hat with its mesh trim. Marti said it reminded her of something she'd once seen on *I Love Lucy*. What higher compliment was there, really?

Tangie made her way into the living room, laptop in hand.

Gramps took one look at her and let out a whistle. "I haven't seen a getup like that since Woodstock. Not that I went to Woodstock, mind you."

"I believe I wore a little hat just like that on our wedding day," her grandmother added. "Wherever did you find that?"

"Oh, I get the best bargains at resale shops," Tangie said with a nod. "Who wants to shop at the mall? The clothes are so. . ."

"Normal?" her grandfather threw in.

Tangie laughed. "Maybe to you, but I think I'll stick with what makes me feel good."

"And all of that color makes you feel good?"

"Yep." In fact, on days like today—dressed in the colorful ensemble—she felt like she had the world on a string.

After saying goodbye to her grandparents, she eased her car out of the slick driveway. As she drove through town, Tangie passed Sweet Harmony and smiled as she remembered meeting Penny. What a great lady.

"Lord, what do You think about that job offer? Should I take it?" Hmm. She'd have to pray about that a bit longer. In the meantime, she had one very handsome music pastor to meet with.

Handsome? Tangie, watch yourself.

She sighed, thinking of how many leading men she'd fallen in love with over the past four years. Taffie and Candy had always accused her of being fickle, but. . .was she? After less than a second's pause, she had to admit the truth. She *had* been pretty flighty where talented guys were concerned. And the more talented, the harder she seemed to fall. All the more reason *not* to fall for Gregg Burke.

Not that he was her type, anyway. No, he seemed a little too "in the box" for her liking.

She arrived at the diner a few minutes early but noticed Gregg's SUV in the parking lot. "He's very prompt," she said to herself. Pulling down the visor, she checked her appearance in the tiny mirror. Hmm. The eyeliner might be a bit much. She'd gone for a forties look. But she'd better touch up the lipstick to match in intensity. Tangie pulled it from her purse and gave her lips a quick swipe then rubbed them together as she gazed back in the mirror. "Better."

Then, slip-sliding her way along, Tangie made the walk across the icy parking lot, cradling her laptop and praying all the way. She arrived inside the diner, stunned to find it so full. Gregg waved at her from the third booth on the right and she headed his way. As she drew near, his eyes widened.

"What?" she asked, as she put her laptop down then shrugged off her jacket.

"N–nothing." He paused, his gaze shifting to her hat. "I, um, just don't think I've ever seen a hat like that in person. In the movies, maybe. . ."

"I'll take that as a compliment." She laughed then took her seat. Glancing around, she said, "You were right. This place is hopping."

"Oh, this is nothing. Most of the breakfast crowd has already passed through. You should see it around six thirty or seven." He continued to stare at her hat, and she grew uncomfortable. Should she take it off? Maybe it was distracting him.

"The food must be good," Tangie managed. She reached to unpin her hat just as a young waitress appeared at the table and smiled at her.

"Oh, please don't take off that hat! It's amazing!"

Tangie grinned and left it in place.

The girl's face lit up. "You're Tangie Carini."

Tangie nodded.

"I knew it had to be you. That's the coolest outfit I've ever seen, by the way. Seriously. . . where did you get it? Is that what they're wearing on the runway this season?"

"Thanks. And, no. This is just vintage stuff. I love to shop in out-of-the-way places."

"I have a feeling I'm really going to like you," the waitress said. "I've been wanting to meet you ever since I heard you speak in church on Sunday morning."

"Oh?" Tangie took the menu the girl offered and glanced up at her with a smile. "Why is that?"

"Brittany is one of the leaders of the youth group," Gregg explained. "She was a big help to me with the Christmas production."

"I've always been interested in theater," Brittany said. "Our high school did *The Sound of Music* my sophomore year."

"She played Maria," Gregg said. "And she was pretty amazing."

Brittany's cheeks turned red. "My favorite role was Milly in *Seven Brides for Seven Brothers*. We did that show my senior year, and I loved every minute of it."

"Oh, that's one of my favorites," Tangie said. "I played the role of Milly at our local community theater back in Atlantic City."

"Oh, I can't believe you just said that!" Brittany clasped her hands together and grinned. "This is a sign from above. A community theater is exactly what I wanted to talk to you about." Brittany's eyes lit up and her tone of voice changed. She grew more animated by the second. "Several of us have been wanting to start a community theater group here in Harmony. There's an old movie theater that would be perfect. It's not in use anymore, but would be great. Just needs a stage."

"Do you have funding?"

Brittany shrugged. "Never really thought about that part. I guess we could hold a fundraiser or something like that. But I'd love to talk to you more about it. Maybe. . ." The teenager flashed a crooked grin. "Maybe you could even direct some of our shows."

"Ah ha." *I see.* So, that's what this was about. First she was directing at the church, now a community theater? *Lord, what are You up to, here? Trying to keep me in Harmony forever?*

Just then, the manager passed by and Brittany snapped to attention. "Are you ready to order?" she asked, grabbing her notepad and pen.

"I'll have two eggs over easy, bacon, toast, and hot tea," Tangie said.

"I'll have the same." Gregg closed his menu. "But make mine coffee. I'm not into the tea thing."

Brittany took their menus and headed to the kitchen.

"She's a great kid," Gregg said. "Very passionate about the theater. Hoping to go to New York one day."

"She's really talented, then?"

"She's pretty good, but I don't think she realizes what she'd be up against in the Big Apple."

"I could fill her in, but it might be discouraging," Tangie said with a shrug.

"So, you didn't just jump into lead roles right away?" he asked, peering into her eyes.

Tangie couldn't help but laugh. "I didn't jump into lead roles, period. Trust me, I was fortunate to land paying gigs at all, large or small. And they didn't last very long, sometimes. A couple of the shows I was in folded after just a few performances. Life in the theater can be very discouraging."

He shrugged, and his gaze shifted down to the table. "I guess it's the same in the music industry. I tried recording a CD a few years ago, but couldn't get any radio stations to play my tunes. Pretty sobering, actually."

"Man, they don't know what they're missing." Tangie shook her head, trying to imagine why anyone would turn Gregg's music away. "You've got one of the most anointed voices I've ever heard."

"Really? Thanks." He seemed stupefied by her words, but she couldn't figure out why. Surely others had told him how powerful those Sunday morning services were, right?

Brittany returned with a coffeepot in hand. She filled Gregg's mug. Then she started to pour some in Tangie's cup but stopped just as a dribble of the hot stuff tumbled into the cup. "Oops, sorry. You said you wanted tea."

"Yes, please." When Brittany left, Tangie smiled at Gregg. "It's funny. I love the smell of coffee, but I don't really like the way it tastes. My roommate back in New York used to drink three or four cups a day."

"It's great early in the morning." He took a sip then leaned back in his seat, a contented look on his face. "I've been addicted since I was in my late teens. My mom. . ." He hesitated. "Well, my mom sometimes let me do a few of the grown-up things a little earlier than most."

"Speaking of your mom, how did your date go?"

He laughed. "Good. She's a hoot. You'll have to meet her someday."

"Does she go to the church? Maybe I've met her already."

"The church?" Gregg's brow wrinkled. "No. I wish. But I'm working on that."

"So, she let you have coffee as a kid?" Tangie asked, going back to the original conversation.

"Yes." He grinned. "First thing in the morning, we'd each have two cups. Then she'd leave for work and I'd get on the bus to go to school. Wide awake, I might add."

"Well, maybe that was the problem. I was never up early in the morning when I lived in New York. I rarely got to bed before three or four and usually slept till ten or eleven in the morning. By the time I got up and running, it was practically lunchtime."

"Are you a night owl?" Gregg asked.

"Always have been." She smiled, remembering the trouble she'd gotten in as a kid. "So, life in the theater just works for me. . .at least on some levels. Shows never end till really late, and there's always something going on after."

"Like what?"

"Oh, dinner at midnight with other cast members." Tangie allowed her thoughts to ramble for a moment. She missed her roomie, Marti, and their midnight meetings at Hanson's twenty-four-hour deli after each show.

"I've always been a morning person," Gregg said. "Sounds crazy, but evenings are tough on me. When nine o'clock rolls around, I'm ready to hit the hay."

"That's so funny." Tangie tried not to laugh, but the image of someone dozing off at nine was humorous, after the life she'd led in the big city. She paused and then opened her laptop. "I guess we should get busy, huh?"

Gregg's expression changed right away. Gone were the laugh lines around his eyes. In their place, a wrinkled brow and down-turned lips.

Tangie studied his expression, sensing his shift in attitude. "You're not looking forward to this?"

He shrugged and offered a loud sigh in response. "In case you didn't notice from that video you watched, I'm not exactly a pro at putting on shows with kids. If we could sing our way through the whole performance, fine, but anything with lines and costumes sends me right over the edge."

"Well, that's why I'm here." She grinned, feeling the excitement well up inside her. "I want you to know I'm so hyped up about all of this, I could just...throw a party or something."

"Really?" He looked at her as if he didn't quite believe it.

"Yes, I don't know how to explain it, but there's something about putting on a show that makes my heart sing. I love every minute of it—the auditions, reading the script for the first time, building the set, memorizing lines. . ." She paused, deep in thought, then said, "Of course, I'm usually the one on the stage, not the one directing, but I have worked with kids before and I just know this will be a ton of fun."

"Humph." He crossed his arms at his chest and leaned back against his seat. "If you say so. I'd rather eat a plateful of artichokes—my least favorite food on planet Earth, by the way—than put on another show. But we'll get through this." He reached for his cup of coffee and took a swig, then shrugged.

"Oh, we'll more than get through it," she promised him. Reaching to rest her hand on his, she gave him a knowing look. "By the end of this, you're going to be a theater buff, I promise."

Gregg laughed. "If you can pull *that* off, I'll eat a whole plate of artichokes. In front of every kid in the play."

"I'm not going to let you forget you said that." Tangie nodded, already planning for the event in her head. "I'm going to hold you to it." She glanced at her laptop screen and then looked back up at him. "In the meantime, we should probably talk about the production. I had the most wonderful idea for the Easter play. I hope you like it."

"Wait." He shook his head. "You mean, you actually wrote something? Already?"

"Well, of course. You didn't expect me to get one of those canned musicals from the Bible bookstore, did you?"

He shrugged. "I didn't know there was any other way."

Tangie laughed. "Oh, you really don't know me. I don't do anything by the book. And while there are some great productions out there, I really felt like Pastor Dave wanted us to cater specifically to the community, using the Easter egg hunt as our theme. Didn't you?"

Another shrug from Gregg convinced her he hadn't given the idea much thought.

"Well, I don't know about all that," he said. "And I definitely think a traditional Easter pageant is the safest bet. People expect to see certain things when they come for an Easter production, don't you think?" He began to list some of the elements he hoped to see in the show and Tangie leaned back, realizing her dilemma at once.

She eventually closed her laptop and focused on the animation in Gregg's voice as he spoke. He hadn't been completely honest with her earlier, had he? All of that stuff about how he didn't like doing performances wasn't true at all. Right now, listening to him talk about his version of an Easter pageant—which, to her way of thinking, sounded incredibly dull—she could see the sparkle in his eye. The tone of his voice changed.

In that moment, she realized the truth. It wasn't that he didn't like putting on shows. He just hadn't done one he could be proud of. That's all. But if they moved forward with the pageant he had in mind, things were liable to fall apart again. She didn't see—or hear—anything in his plan that sounded like what Pastor Dave asked for.

Tangie swallowed hard, working up the courage to speak. *Lord, show me what to say. I don't want to burst his bubble, but we're supposed to be doing something different. Something original.*

When he finally paused, Tangie exhaled and then looked into his eyes, noticing for the first time just how beautiful they were.

He gazed back, a boyish smile on his face. His cheeks flushed red and he whispered, "Sorry. Didn't mean to get carried away."

"Oh, don't be sorry." She hated to burst his bubble but decided to add her thoughts. "I, um, was thinking of something completely different than what you described, though."

"Oh? Like what?"

"Well, hear me out. What I've written is really unique, something people have never seen before."

He gave her a dubious look.

"Just don't laugh, okay?" She proceeded to tell him about her plan to use talking animals—sheep, bunnies, baby chicks, and so forth—to convey the message of Easter.

"I've been thinking about this whole egg theme," she explained. "And I think we need to start the show with a giant Easter egg—maybe four or five feet high—in the center of the stage. We'll get some really cute kid-themed music that fits the scene, and the egg can crack open and a baby chick will come out. Of course, it'll be one of the kids, dressed as a chick. He—or she—can be the narrator, telling the rest of the story. There's going to be a shepherd, of course. He'll represent God. We'll need an adult for that. And then the little sheep—and we'll need lots of them—will be us, His kids. Make sense?"

Gregg stared at her like she'd lost her mind. Still, Tangie forged ahead, emphasizing the takeaway at the end of the play.

"See? It's an allegory," she explained. "A story inside a story. The baby chick hatching from its egg represents us, when we're born again. We enter a whole new life. Our story begins, in essence. The same is true with rabbits. Did you realize that bunnies are symbols for fertility and rebirth?"

"Well, no, but I guess I can see the parallel," he said. "Rabbits rapidly reproduce."

"Say *that* three times in a row." Tangie laughed.

He tried it and by the end, they were both chuckling.

Once she caught her breath, Tangie summed up her thoughts about the play. "So, the chicks and the bunnies are symbols of the rebirth experience. And the bunnies—because they rapidly reproduce—will be our little evangelists. Get it? They'll hop from place to place, sharing the love of Jesus."

"Um, okay."

"And the little sheep represent us, too. One of them wanders away from the fold and Jesus—the Shepherd—goes after him. Or her. I haven't decided if it should be a boy or girl. But there's that hidden message of God's love for us. . .that He would leave the ninety-nine to go after the one. I think the audience will get it if they're paying attention."

"Maybe." He shook his head. "But I don't know about all that. I still think it's better to do something tried and true."

"Like your Christmas play?" Tangie could've slapped herself the minute the words came out. "I–I'm sorry."

He shook his head. "I've already admitted that I'm no director."

"I'm sure that's not true," she said. "You just haven't found the right show yet. But I think this Easter production has the capability of turning things around for both the kids who are in it and the ones who come to see it." She offered what she hoped would be taken as a winning smile. "And you'll see. By the end of this, you're going to fall in love with theater. It won't just be a means to an end anymore. It's going to get into your blood. You'll be hooked."

"Somehow I really doubt it." Gregg took a swig of his coffee and gave her a pensive look. "But, for lack of a better plan, I'll go along with this little chicks and bunnies play you're talking about. Just don't credit me with writing any of it, okay?"

He dove into a lengthy discussion about how he'd already been embarrassed enough with the last play and how he had no intention of being the subject of ridicule again. Tangie listened in stunned silence, realizing just how strongly he felt about her ideas, in spite of her persuasive argument, seconds earlier. But, why? Was it just her ideas he didn't like. . .or her?

Tangie's heart plummeted to her toes. Not only did he not like her ideas, he acted like he thought she was crazy. Well, she'd show him a thing or two about crazy over the next few weeks. And then, if she ended up failing at this gig in Harmony. . .she might just give some thought to heading back home. . .to the Big Apple.

❧

Gregg could've slapped himself for making fun of Tangie in such a pointed way. From the look in her eyes, he knew he'd injured her pride. He knew just what that felt like. Still, he wasn't sure how to redeem the situation now. *Lord, I'm going to need Your help with this one. It's beyond me.*

Yes, everything about this was beyond him—the production, the outreach. . .and the beautiful woman in the nutty outfit seated across from him with the look of pain in her eyes.

Chapter 7

"Gran-Gran, you know I love you, right?" Tangie paced her grandparents' living room as she spoke with great passion.

"Of course!" Her grandmother looked up from the TV and nodded. "But you're blocking the TV, honey. We're trying to watch *Jeopardy*."

Tangie sighed and took a giant step to the left. Nothing ever got between Gran-Gran and her TV when the game shows were on. Still, this was important. Tangie attempted to interject her thoughts. "Gran-Gran, you know I would never do anything to hurt you."

"Never."

"What is *the Sears Tower*!" Gramps hollered at the TV.

Tangie looked his way and he shrugged. "Sorry, honey. The question was, 'What is the tallest building in America?' and I happened to know the answer."

He and Gran-Gran turned back to the TV, and Tangie knew she'd lost them. She took a seat on the sofa and sighed. Gran-Gran looked her way.

"You're really upset, aren't you?"

Tangie nodded. "Sort of." She worked up the courage to say the rest. "Now, don't be mad, but I'm giving some thought to only staying in Harmony till after the production, then going back to New York."

"What?" Her grandmother turned and looked at her with a stunned expression on her face then reached for the remote and flipped off the TV. "But why?"

How could she begin to explain it in a way that a non-theater person could understand? "I. . .I need artistic freedom." There. That should do it.

"Artistic freedom?" Gramps rose from his well-worn recliner and snagged a cookie from the cookie jar. "What did someone do, kidnap your creativity or something?"

"Very nicely put," she said. "That's exactly what someone did. He stole it and put it behind bars. And as long as I stay in Harmony, I'm never getting it back. I'm destined to be dull and boring."

Her grandmother's brows elevated slightly. "You? Dull and boring? Impossible." Gran-Gran stood up and approached Tangie.

"I can see how it would happen here," Tangie said. "I feel like my voice has been squelched."

"Impossible. You've got too much chutzpah for that. Besides, folks can only take what you give, nothing more."

"Maybe I just don't know enough about how to compromise with someone like Gregg Burke. But one thing is for sure, this gig in Harmony doesn't feel like a long-term plan for me."

Gran-Gran's eyes misted over right away. "Are you serious?"

"Yes." Tangie sighed when she saw the hurt look on her grandmother's face. "I'll stay till the Easter production is over at the beginning of April. But then I'm pretty sure I'd like to go back to New York."

"Really? But I thought you were done with New York," Gramps said, a confused look on his face.

"Well, see, I got an e-mail from my friend Marti last night. She just found out about auditions for a new show. They're going to be held a few days after the production and the director, Vincent, is an old friend of mine. He directed a couple of plays I was in year before last. I'll stand a better shot with this one, since I know someone."

"Honey, I know you enjoy being in those shows. You're a great little actress."

Tangie cringed at the words *little actress*. How many times had her father said the same thing? And her directors? She didn't want to be a *little* actress. She wanted to have a career. A real career.

Gran-Gran continued, clearly oblivious to Tangie's inner turmoil. "But, as good as you are, that's not your ministry. You're a teacher. You said it yourself when you stood up in front of the church to talk to the congregation. You're a gift stirrer. Your real ability is in motivating and teaching those kids. And if you go away. . ." Gran-Gran's eyes filled with tears. "Well, if you go away, nothing will be the same around here. There's no one to take your place."

Tangie shrugged. "Gregg will do fine. And Ashley. . .she's great with the kids."

"Yes, but she's too busy. That's what I was saying before. She has a full-time job at the school, teaching second grade."

"Right." Tangie sighed.

"That's why she couldn't help with the Christmas production. She was doing a show of her own. I know her pretty well, honey. She would probably agree to help, just to appease Gregg, but she's just too overwhelmed to take on anything else right now."

"I'm sorry, Gran-Gran. I just don't think I'm up for the job long term. It's going to be hard enough to make it through one show." Tangie tried not to let the defeat show on her face but couldn't seem to help herself.

Gran-Gran plopped down in a chair, a somber look on her face. "Well, I'm sorry to hear that. Very sorry."

As she left the room, Tangie reached for an oatmeal raisin cookie—her third. She took a big bite, pondering everything her grandmother had said. Looked like Tangie was right all along. She wasn't meant for small-town life.

What did it matter, really? Apparently she was destined to fail at everything she put her hand to—whether it was in the big city or in a tiny place like Harmony, New Jersey.

❋

Gregg picked up the phone and called Gramps for a much-needed chat. The elderly man answered on the third ring, his opening words packing quite a punch. "What took you so long, son?"

"H–hello?"

"I know it's you, Gregg. Saw your number on the caller ID. I've been sitting by the phone for the past hour, ever since Tangie talked to us about that meeting you two had at the diner this morning. She was plenty worked up."

"Oh, I'm sorry," Gregg started. "I—"

"Ruined a perfectly good round of *Jeopardy*," Gramps interrupted. "I figured you would've called me before this."

Gregg groaned. "I guess I should have. Things didn't go very well."

"So I hear. There's actually talk of her leaving. Going back to New York City. I'd hate to see that happen. Why, the very idea of it is breaking my heart."

"No way." She was giving up. . .that quickly? Why? "Can you put her on the phone, please?" Gregg asked.

He heard Gramps's voice ring out, "Tangie, you've got a call."

Seconds later, she answered. "Taffie, what happened? Everything okay with the baby?"

"Taffy?" Gregg repeated. "What does taffy have to do with anything?"

"O–oh, I'm sorry. I thought for sure Gramps said my sister was on the phone. Who is this?"

"Gregg Burke."

"Oh." The tone of her voice changed right away. In fact, her initial excitement fizzled out like air from a flat tire.

"I'm calling to apologize," he said, his words coming a mile a minute. "I've really messed this one up. Please don't go anywhere. I need you too much for that."

"You do?"

"Yes." He sighed. Might as well just speak his mind. "To be honest, I think I'm just insecure. I don't know the first thing about drama, but it's still hard to admit that I'm a failure at anything. Does that make sense?"

"More than you know."

"I think my pride was a little hurt, is all. I'll be the first to admit it." He paused a moment. "Your ideas about the Easter play are. . .different. Very different from anything I would've come up with. But maybe that's why they hired you. They want different. And this is for kids. Kids need kid stuff, and I'll be honest, I don't know the first thing about kid stuff. I think I proved that with the Christmas play."

"Well, I'm different, all right," Tangie responded. "But I don't want you to think I'm so off the wall that I'm going to end up embarrassing you or the kids in any way. That's not my intention. I can see this production being really cute, but if you'd rather do something more traditional. . ." Her words faded away.

"No, it's fine. I just think we need to meet to get this settled, one way or the other. Can you send me a copy of what you've written by e-mail attachment? I'll take a look at it and see what I can do with it from a music standpoint. Then we can talk again before next week's auditions. How does that sound?"

She hesitated but finally came back with, "Good. Thanks for giving me a second chance."

"No." He sighed. "I shouldn't have been so quick to shut you down the first time. I'm just used to being the creative one, and you. . ."

She laughed. "I know, I know. When God handed out creativity, He gave me a double portion. I've never understood why."

"Oh, I think I do," Gregg said. "He knew He could trust you with it."

She paused for a moment and then a much quieter Tangie came back with, "Thank you. That's the nicest thing anyone's said to me in a long time. I needed to hear that."

By the time they ended the call, Gregg felt a hundred pounds lighter. Until he thought about the giant Easter egg she'd proposed for the opening scene. Then his stomach began to tighten once again. *Lord, this is going to be. . .different. Give me patience. Please.*

❦

Tangie sighed as she hung up the phone. Gregg's plea for help had surprised her, especially after his reaction this morning. Who put him up to this?

"Gramps?" She called out for her grandfather, but he didn't answer. Tangie looked around the living room, but couldn't find him anywhere, so she bundled up in her coat and headed out to his workshop behind the house. There she found him, carving a piece of wood.

"Oh, wow." She looked around the tiny room, amazed by all of the things she found there. "You're very crafty, Gramps."

"That's what they tell me." He held out a wood-carved replica of a bear and smiled. "What do you think of this guy?"

"I think he's great. I also think. . ." The idea hit her all at once. "I also think I'm going to use your services for the kids' production."

"So, you're sticking around? Gregg did the right thing?"

"I'm sticking around." She shrugged. "I would've stayed till after the play anyway, remember?"

"Now you'll stay longer?"

She sighed and rested against his workbench, thankful for the tiny space heater at her feet. "I can't make any promises. Who knows where things will be in a few months? There's this really great show. . ."

"I know, I know." He sighed then reached to give her a peck on the cheek. "In New York. A chance of a lifetime. Something you've been waiting for. . .forever." He stressed the word *forever*, making it seem like a mighty long time.

"I know you want me to stay here," Tangie said. "And I promise to pray about it."

"That's all I ask, honey." He nodded and smiled. "But let me say one more thing." Gramps peered into her eyes, his gaze penetrating to her very soul. "Your mother isn't the only one with a case of wanderlust."

"What?"

"I mean, you have a hard time staying put in one place for long. And with one job for long." He paused. "Now, I don't mean anything negative by that; it's just an observation. Maybe your trip to Harmony is a lesson in staying put awhile."

"Hmm." She shrugged. "I don't know, Gramps. I just know that I always get this jittery feeling. And bolting is. . ."

"Easier?"

"Sometimes." She sighed. "I'm sure you're right. It's a learned behavior. I wasn't always this way. But when one show after another shut down, I just got in the habit of shifting gears. Now I've turned so many corners, I can hardly remember where I've been and where I'm going. And bolting just comes naturally. I'm not proud of it. I'm just saying it's become second nature, that's all."

"Well, pray before you bolt. That's all I ask this time." He wrapped her in his arms and placed a whiskery kiss in her hair. " 'Cause when you leave this time, it's gonna break some poor fella's heart." He dabbed his eyes then whispered, "And I'm not just talking about Gregg Burke's."

Chapter 8

On Friday morning, Tangie stopped off at Sweet Harmony, the bakery where she'd purchased the cookies. Penny greeted her with a welcoming smile.

"Great coat. Love the shoulder pads. Very 1980s."

"Thanks." Tangie chuckled. "That's the idea. I love wearing clothes from every era."

"Kind of reminds me of something Joan Collins would've worn in *Dynasty*." Penny paused then gave Tangie a pensive look. "Been thinking about that proposition I made?"

"I have." Tangie smiled. "I think I'd like to work here, but I might only be staying in town till the first week in April. Would that be a problem?"

"Hmm." Penny shrugged and wiped her hands on her apron. "Well, I can really use the help, even if it's temporary. I'll take what I can get."

"We'll need to come to some agreement about my schedule. I'm working part-time at a local church."

"Church?" Penny rolled her eyes. "I used to go to a church. . .back in the day."

"Whatever happened with that?" Tangie asked.

Penny shrugged. "Gave it up for Lent." She slapped herself on the knee and let out a raucous laugh. "Oh, that's a good one. Gave up church for Lent." After a few more chuckles, she finally calmed down. "Let's just say God and I aren't exactly on speaking terms and leave it at that."

"Ah."

"And I guess I could also add that the church hasn't exactly laid out the welcome mat for me. But, mind you, I haven't been to one since I was in my thirties, so I'm not talking about any church in particular here. I just know that churches, in general, don't take too kindly to unmarried women with kids."

"Whoa. Really?" Tangie thought about that for a moment. Most of the churches she'd attended—both at home in Atlantic City and in New York—had always reached out to single moms. But it looked like Penny had a different story. Then again, Penny was—what?—in her late fifties, maybe? So, anything that happened to her had to have happened twenty or thirty years ago, right?

"Back to the bakery. . ." Penny gave her a scrutinizing glance. "How are your cake decorating skills?"

Tangie shrugged. "We didn't do much pastry work at the candy shop, but I've decorated cookies and other sweets, and I've got a steady hand."

"You're hired."

"Just like that?" Tangie laughed. "You don't need references or anything?"

"Your grandfather is Herbert Henderson?" Penny stared at her thoughtfully.

"Yes. How did you know that?"

"He's my best customer, and he's been telling me all about this granddaughter of his from the candy shop in Atlantic City. He described you to a tee, right down to the tattoo on your wrist. What is that, anyway? A star?"

"Yeah." Tangie shrugged. "A theater friend of mine talked me into it years ago. She said I was going to be a big star someday, and that looking at my wrist would be a good reminder not to give up."

"Have you?"

"W–what?"

"Given up?" Penny gave her a pensive look.

"Oh, no. Not really. I, um, well, I'm just on hiatus from acting right now."

"Okay." Penny pursed her lips then spoke in a motherly voice. "Just don't let me hear that you've given up on your dreams. You need to go after them. . .wholeheartedly. I let mine die for a while." She looked around the bakery then grinned. "But eventually got around to it. Just wasted a lot of time in between."

"I understand. And part of the reason I'm in Harmony is to figure all of that out."

"Well, if Herbert Henderson is really your grandfather, I'd say you'll have a lot of wise counsel. He's a crackerjack, that one."

"You know him well?" Tangie asked, taking a seat at one of the bar stools in front of the counter.

"He buys kolaches and donuts for his Sunday school class every Sunday morning. He's got quite a sweet tooth. My boys were always partial to sweets, too."

"Tell me about your boys." Tangie leaned against the countertop, ready to learn more about her new friend.

"What's to tell? They're boys. And besides, if you go to your grandpa's church, you probably know at least one of them."

"Wait. Who?"

"My oldest, Gregg. He plays the guitar and sings."

Tangie stared at Penny, stunned. "Gregg Burke. . .is your son?"

"Well, sure. I thought you knew that. Figured your grandfather told you."

"Grandpa didn't say anything." Tangie would have to remember to throttle him later. How interesting, that she would end up working with Gregg at the church and with his mother at the bakery.

She startled back to attention. Turning to her new boss, she asked, "When would you like me to start?"

Penny reached behind the counter and came up with an apron with the words Sweet Harmony emblazoned on the front. "How about right now? I've got to make a run to the doctor in Trenton."

"Trenton?"

"Yep. Planned to close the place down for the rest of the day, but I'd rather leave it open, if you're up to it. Can you handle the register until I get back?"

"Mmm, sure." Tangie slipped the apron over her head. "I operated the cash register at our candy store for years as a teen. Anything else?"

"Yes, let me run over a few things with you." Penny quickly went over the price list, focusing on the special of the day—two cream-filled donuts and hot cocoa for three dollars. Then she gave Tangie a quick tour of the building. When they finished, the older woman turned to her with a smile. "Do you think you'll be okay?"

"Should be."

"Great. Oh, one more thing. When the timer goes off, pull those cookies out of the oven and set them on the rack to cool." Penny pointed to the tall chrome double oven and then reached for her purse. "Wish I didn't have to go at all, but I won't be long." She took a few steps toward the door but then turned back. "Oh, and if you see an older fellow—about my age—with white hair and a thick mustache, don't sell him a thing."

"W–what? Why?" Tangie asked.

"That's Bob Jennings. He's a diabetic. Comes in nearly every afternoon around this time, begging for sweets. His wife would kill me if I actually sold him anything."

"Why don't you offer sugar-free options?" Tangie asked. "We sell a whole line of sugar-free candies at our store."

Penny put her hands on her hips. "See! That's why I need you. Now that you're here. . ." Her voice faded as the door slammed closed behind her. Tangie watched through the plate-glass window as Penny scurried down the sidewalk toward the parking lot, talking to herself.

"Lord, how am I going to give her all of the help she needs in only three months?" Three years might be more workable. Still, all of that stuff about not giving up on your dreams. . .was the Lord speaking through Penny, perhaps? Stranger things had happened. Maybe God's plan for Tangie included at least one more shot at Broadway.

"April." She whispered the word. Auditions for *A Woman in Love* were going to be held just after the Easter production, according to Marti. And Vincent Cason, the director, had specifically asked about Tangie for the lead. Though flattered, the idea of going back home to the Big Apple scared her senseless. On the other hand, she didn't want to miss God. Was He wooing her back to finish what He'd started four years ago, perhaps?

Minutes later, a customer arrived—a woman ordering a wedding cake. Thankfully, Tangie had some experience with cakes. Her mom made ice cream cakes for brides all the time. How different could a baked cake be? She located Penny's sample book and walked the young woman—who introduced herself as Brenna—through the process.

"I've already talked to Penny about the size and style," Brenna explained. "We settled on a four-tier with cream cheese frosting. But I wasn't sure about my wedding colors until this week."

"Sounds like I'll need some specifics about the wedding, then," Tangie said, reaching for a tablet.

"The wedding is on April 14," Brenna responded with a smile. "I've waited for years for Mr. Right, and now that I've found him, I can't stand waiting three months. Is that silly?"

"Doesn't sound silly at all. What's the point in a long engagement when you've done nothing but wait up till then?" She scribbled the date on the notepad and then looked up at Brenna. "Where is the wedding taking place?"

"Harmony Community Church."

"Oh, that's my church," Tangie said.

"Really? I don't recognize you. But then again, that church is growing like wildfire, so it's getting harder to recognize everyone."

"I'm new. They just hired me to direct the children's plays."

"Oh, wait. . ." Brenna looked at her with renewed interest. "Is your name Tangie or something like that?"

"Yes."

Brenna nodded. "I was working in the nursery the week you were introduced, but my son Cody told me all about you. He's scared to death I'm going to make him be in the next play. He, um. . .well, he didn't have the best time in the last one."

"Ah." So this was Cody's mom. "Well, I think I can safely say this one will be more fun." She hoped.

"It's hard, being a single mom and trying to keep your son interested in things going on at church." Brenna's words were followed by a dramatic sigh. "I have to practically wrestle with him just to get him through the kids' church door on Sunday mornings. I'll be so glad when Phil and I get married. He's going to be a great dad for Cody."

Tangie paused to think about the little boy. Gran-Gran had mentioned he came from a single-parent home, but didn't say anything about an upcoming wedding. Then again, maybe she didn't know.

Nah. Scratch that. In Harmony, pretty much everyone knew everyone else's business. And then some.

"Let's talk more about the cake," Tangie said, offering Brenna a seat. "What are your wedding colors and what type of flowers will you carry?"

"The bridesmaids' dresses are blue and the flowers are coral and white. Lilies. I know Penny can make the lilies because I've seen her sugar-work in the past."

"Wonderful. I'll just write this down and give it to her when she gets back," Tangie explained. "If she has any questions, I'm sure she'll call. And I'll let her take care of getting your deposit."

"Oh, no bother." Brenna reached into her purse for her checkbook. "We've already talked through this part. I'm leaving a hundred-dollar deposit today and will pay the rest the week before the wedding."

They wrapped up their meeting and Brenna rose to leave. Afterward, Tangie went to work in the back room, tidying things up. Looked like Penny hadn't stayed on top of that. Likely her workload was too great.

About three hours later Penny returned, looking a bit winded. "Sorry, hon. But it's gonna be like this till my treatments end."

"Your treatments?"

"Forgot to mention that part, didn't I? I drive over to Trenton for chemo two days a week. Breast cancer. I was just diagnosed about two months ago."

"Oh, Penny. I'm so sorry." Tangie shook her head. "You should have told me."

With the wave of a hand, Penny went back to work. "I'm trying not to let it consume me. But I must warn you"—she began to look a little pale—"that sometimes my stomach doesn't handle the chemo very well."

At that, she sprinted to the back room. Tangie followed along behind her, stopping at the restroom door. "You okay in there?" she called out.

"Mm-hmm." Penny groaned. "Nothing I haven't been through before." After a pause, she hollered, "Would you mind putting another batch of sugar cookies in the oven? The after-school crowd will be here in less than an hour, and I'm not ready for them. The cookie dough is already rolled into balls in the walk-in refrigerator. Just put a dozen on each tray. Bake them for ten minutes."

"Of course." Tangie carried on with her work, silently ushering up a prayer for Penny. Looked like she needed all the prayers she could get.

❧

Gregg sat at his desk, reading over the script Tangie had e-mailed. Though different from anything he would have ever chosen, he had to admit the story line was clever, and probably something the kids would really get into. He would play along, for the sake of time—and in the spirit of cooperation. But as for whether or not he would enjoy it? That was another thing altogether.

He exhaled, releasing some of the tension of the day. In some ways, it felt like things were spinning out of control. Not that he ever had any control, really. But the illusion of having any was quickly fading. Gregg couldn't control the things his mother was going through. He couldn't control things with Ashley, who'd just informed him she might give her relationship with her old boyfriend another try. And he certainly couldn't control the madness surrounding Tangie Carini and the kids' musical.

"Lord, what are You trying to show me here?"

As if in response, Gregg's gaze shifted up to the plaque on the wall, one the choir members had given him for his last birthday. He smiled as he read the familiar scripture: FINALLY, ALL OF YOU, LIVE IN HARMONY WITH ONE ANOTHER. 1 PET. 3:8. He smiled as he thought about the irony. *Live in harmony.*

Sometimes it was easier living in the *town* than living in the sort of harmonious state the scripture referred to. Still, he'd give it his best shot. God was calling him to no less.

With a renewed sense of purpose, Gregg turned back to his work.

Chapter 9

On the following Sunday afternoon, Tangie stood in the fellowship hall, preparing herself for the auditions. She placed tidy stacks of audition forms on the table, alongside freshly sharpened pencils and bottles of water for the directors. Brittany had agreed to help, thank goodness. And Gregg would take care of the vocal auditions. Yes, everything was coming together quite nicely. Now, if only they could find the right kids for each role, then all would be well.

"Ready for the big day?"

She turned as she heard Gregg's voice. "Hey. Glad you're here. I want to run this form by you before the kids arrive."

"What form?" Gregg drew close and glanced at the papers in her hand. "What have you got there?"

"Oh, it's an audition form, designed especially for today. Look." She held one up for his inspection. "See this section at the top? Brittany and I will use this section for the drama auditions. There's a column for characterization—does the child really look and act the part? Then there's another for inflection, another for expression, and another for volume. It's pretty straightforward. You'll see a spot at the top where the child fills out his or her name, age, and prior experience on the stage."

"Ah ha." He seemed to be scrutinizing the page.

"I've created a separate section at the bottom for the vocal auditions," Tangie added, pointing. "It gives you a place to comment on things like pitch, projection, harmonization skills, tone, and so forth."

He pursed his lips then said, "Good idea. We could've used something like that when we auditioned the kids at Christmastime."

His words of affirmation warmed Tangie's heart. "Did you use some sort of form for the Christmas play?"

"Nope. The whole thing was organized chaos. We were all in the room at the same time."

"That's your first problem." Tangie laughed. "It's always better to hold auditions in a private setting, one at a time. Helps the child relax and that way they can't copy from one another." Tangie spoke from experience. She'd been through too many open auditions where candidates tripped all over themselves to one-up the people who'd gone before them. But none of that here. No sir.

"I never thought of doing it this way." Gregg shook his head. "But I'm always open to ideas. When we did the last auditions, it literally took all day. Each child wanted to audition for half a dozen parts. And then there were the would-be soloists." He groaned. "You wouldn't believe how many times I had to listen to "Silent Night." Trust me, it wasn't a silent night. Chaotic, yes. Silent, no." He offered up a winsome smile and for the first time, she saw a glimmer of hope.

"Well, here's something I've learned from other shows I've been in," Tangie said. "It's best to get the music auditions over with first. That way, you can mark on the form if you think the child can handle a lead role before I ever let him or her read for a part. Then I'll know which roles they can and can't be considered for."

"Sounds like a good plan. I'll have your grandmother bring the child's form to you after the vocal audition. That way the kids can't see what we're doing."

Tangie nodded. "Oh, one more thing. . ." She handed him a stack of the papers. "Some of the kids probably won't be interested in auditioning for vocal solos, so they can come straight to the drama audition. I've got plenty of roles to go around, and many of them aren't singing roles."

"I'd still like all of the children to be in the choir, though," he added. "We need as many voices as we can get."

"Well, let's talk about that afterward, okay?" She gave him a pensive look. "Not every child is an actor, but not every child is a vocalist, either. Some aren't crazy about singing in a group. So, why don't we pray about that?"

For a moment, he looked as if he might refute her. Then, just as quickly, he nodded. "I'm sure the sanctuary is about to burst at the seams with kids by now. Let's get in there and give our instructions. Then we'll start."

"Before we do, would you mind if we prayed about this?"

"Of course not."

As a matter of habit, Tangie reached to take his hand. She bowed her head and ushered up a passionate prayer that the Lord's will would be done in these auditions—that exactly the right child would get each part.

"And, Lord," she continued, "if there's a child here who hasn't come to know You, may this be the production that leads him or her to You. And for those who do know You, Father, please use these next few weeks to stir up the gifts You've placed in each boy and girl. Help develop them into the person they will one day be."

"And, Lord," Gregg threw in, "we ask for Your will regarding the ones who don't fit in. Show us what to do with the ones who are, well, difficult."

They closed out the prayer with a quick "Amen," and Gregg's smile warmed Tangie's heart. "Thanks for suggesting that. I always pray with the kids before every practice, but I never thought about actually praying for the audition process before the fact."

"It always helps." She shrugged. "And besides, if we ask God to be at the center of it, then—when we're in the throes of rehearsing and things are getting rough—we can be sure that we've really chosen the right people for the job. We won't be tempted to toss the baby out with the bathwater."

He quirked a brow and she laughed.

"I just mean we won't be tempted to take the part away from him—or her—and give it to someone else. If we pray about this ahead of time, then we're confident that God has special plans for that particular child in that role. See what I mean?"

"Yes." He nodded. "But I never really thought about it like that before. I guess I never saw this whole process as being terribly spiritual. It's just a kids' play."

"Oh no." She shook her head. "It's not just a kids' play. It's so much more than that." Tangie was tempted to dive into a lengthy discussion, but one glance at her watch served as a reminder that dozens of kids waited in the sanctuary.

"After you," she said, pointing.

He turned her way one last time, a curious expression on his face. "Before we start, I just have one question."

"Sure. What's up?"

"I just need to know. . .what *are* you wearing?" He pointed to her beret, which she pulled off and gripped with a smile.

"Ah. My cap. I always wear it on audition day. It puts me in a theatrical frame of mind."

"Mm-hmm." He chuckled, and they headed off together to face the energetic mob.

❧

Gregg looked up as Margaret Sanderson entered the choir room, a confident smile lighting her cherublike face. She wore her hair in tight ringlets, and her dress—an over-the-top frills number—convinced him she was here to do business.

"Good to see you, Margaret. Are you ready to audition for us?" Gregg asked, trying to remain positive.

Margaret nodded. "Oh, I am. And my mother says I should tell you that I'm interested in trying out for the leading role."

"Yes, but would you be willing to take any role if you don't get a lead?" It was a fair question, one Gregg planned to ask every child who auditioned.

Margaret paused and bit her lip. After a second, she said, "I, well, I guess. But my mom says I have the best voice in the whole church."

"Ah." Gregg stifled a laugh and looked down at his papers. "You do have a nice singing voice," he said, "but, of course, we have to listen to everyone before making our decision."

He took a seat at his piano and began to play the introduction to "Amazing Grace," the song he'd instructed all of the children to prepare in advance.

Margaret interrupted him, setting a piece of music down in front of him. "I've brought my own audition music. I would prefer to sing it—if you don't mind. My mother says it showcases my voice." She belted out "The Lullaby of Broadway," which to her credit, did sound pretty good.

Gregg covered her form with high marks then handed it to Tangie's grandmother, who had agreed to run interference between the music department and the drama department.

Next Cody arrived. His mother practically pushed him in the door. "Go on in, son. You can do this."

"But I don't want to!" He groaned then eased his way toward the piano.

"Lord, give me strength," Gregg whispered. "This one tries my patience." He turned to the youngster with a smile. "Cody, let's hear a couple lines of 'Amazing Grace.'"

The boy groaned. "Remember we did this last time? I stink. Why do I have to do it again?"

Gregg began to play. "Well, you've had some musical experience since then. Maybe there's been some improvement."

Cody began to sing, just not exactly in the key Gregg happened to be playing at the moment. Looked like nothing had changed, after all. After just a few notes, Cody stopped and crossed his arms at his chest. "See what I mean? I stink."

"Well, I understand Miss Tangie has some drama roles that don't require singing this time around," Gregg said. "So why don't you head on over to the fellowship hall and audition for her?"

"Really? I don't have to sing?"

"That's right."

When Gregg nodded, the youngster looked at him as if he'd just been offered an eleventh-hour stay. He sprinted out of the door with more exaggerated energy.

The next child in the room was Annabelle Lawrence. She was a sweet thing—probably eight or so—but a little on the shy side. Understandable, since her family was new to the church. As Gregg listened to her sing, he was pleasantly surprised. Nice voice. Very nice. "Have you done any performing, Annabelle?"

She shook her head and spoke in a soft voice. "No, but I think I would like it."

He filled out her form, smiling. Over the two and a half hours, the kids came and went from the room. Gregg heard those who could sing, and those who couldn't. A couple of them insisted upon rapping their audition and one sang "Amazing Grace" in Spanish. In all, the variety was pretty interesting. His favorite was a little boy named Joey who proclaimed, "I want to sing. . .real bad!" Unfortunately his audition proved that he could. Sing bad, that was.

By the time the afternoon ended, Gregg had a much clearer picture of where they stood. Thankfully, there were some great singers in the bunch. Looked like the Easter production might just turn out okay, after all.

🌺

Tangie scribbled note after note as the children came and went from her room. Some were better than others, naturally, but a few were absolutely darling. And, as they read the lines from the play she'd written, the words absolutely sprang to life. There was something so satisfying about hearing her words acted out.

Not that all of the kids were actors. No, a few would be better served in smaller roles, to be sure. And a couple of the ones who could act—though good—struggled with a little too much confidence. There would be plenty of time to work on that.

By the time the last child left, things were looking a little clearer. Yes, Tangie could almost see which child would fit which part. Now all she had to do was convince Gregg. Then. . .let the show begin!

Chapter 10

After the auditions ended, Tangie sat with papers in hand, going over every note. Looked like this was going to be easier than she'd first thought. Some of the kids were obvious; others, not so much.

She laughed as she read some of the forms. Under Prior Experience, one little boy had written *I sing in the shower*. One of the girls had scribbled the words, *Broadway, Here I Come!*

Ah, yes. Margaret Sanderson. Tangie sighed as she looked at the youngster's resume, complete with headshot. "She really wants the lead role something awful."

Awful being the key word. The little darling had pretty much insisted she get the part. That didn't sit well with Tangie.

She flipped through the forms until she found one for a little girl named Annabelle. Though Annabelle had no prior experience, there was something about her that had captivated Tangie right away. Her sweet expression as she read the lines. Her genuine emotion as she took on the character of the littlest sheep. Sure, she needed a bit of work. Maybe more than a bit. But Tangie always rooted for the underdog. Nothing new there. And from Gregg's notes, she could tell the child had a wonderful singing voice.

Tangie yawned and looked at Brittany, who laughed.

"Had enough fun for one day?" the teen asked.

"Mm-hmm. Don't think I could do this for a living." Tangie paused a moment then added, "Oh, yeah. I already do." A grin followed.

"I'm still hoping you'll think about that community theater idea," Brittany said, her brow wrinkling as she spoke.

Tangie sighed, not wanting to burst the teen's bubble. How could she tell her she was thinking of leaving Harmony in April? Today wasn't the day.

Tangie turned her attention back to the audition forms, placing them in three stacks: To be considered for a lead. To be considered for a smaller role. To be dealt with. Thankfully, the "To be dealt with" pile was the smallest of the three. Still, it contained Cody's form. Poor guy couldn't sing or act, at least from what she could tell. "Lord," she whispered, "show us where to place him. I don't want to put him—or us—through any more agony than necessary."

As she pondered the possibilities, Gregg entered the room, a look of exhaustion on his face.

"How did the vocal auditions go?" she asked. "Or is that a silly question?"

He shrugged. "Not too bad, actually. Things were a lot smoother with the forms you created. Still, if I have to hear 'Amazing Grace' one more time. . ." He laughed. "I just don't know if I can take it."

"Any ideas about lead roles?" Tangie asked, preparing herself to show Gregg the completed audition forms. "Because I have so many thoughts rolling through my head right now." She picked up the first stack of papers, ready to dive in.

He looked at the papers and grinned. "I have a few ideas, but let me ask you a question first."

"Sure."

"Did you really stack those forms like that, or did someone else do it?"

"I did it." She shrugged. "I'm usually right-brained, but not when it comes to something like this. When it comes to the important stuff, I have all my ducks in a row." She paused a moment then added, "Why do you ask?"

He shrugged. "It's just that I'm like that. . .pretty much all the time. You should see the stacks of mail at my place." A boyish grin lit his face. He paused a moment then asked, "Are you hungry?"

"Starved." Tangie nodded, hoping her grumbling stomach wouldn't show him just how hungry she was.

"Want to go to the diner for some food? It's open late and we can eat while we talk. I'll drive, if it's okay with you."

"Sounds amazing."

"As in '*Amazing* Grace'?"

Tangie laughed.

Brittany spoke up, interrupting their conversation. "Tangie, I told my mom I'd be home right after auditions. I've got school tomorrow."

"Thank you so much for your help." Tangie smiled at the exuberant teen. "Don't think I could've done it without you."

"Sure you could've." Brittany grinned. "But I'm glad you didn't choose to."

Ten minutes later, amid steaming cups of coffee and tea, Tangie spread the audition forms across the table. "Let's start with the ones who can sing."

"Sure. We have quite a few in that category." Gregg took a drink of his coffee, thumbing through the forms. "Now, Margaret Sanderson will play the lead, right? She's by far our best singer."

Tangie bit her tongue, willing herself not to knee-jerk. This was bound to be a source of contention.

"She's our strongest vocalist *and* has a lot of experience." Gregg looked over her form, nodding as he read the comments. "And she's tiny enough to play the role of the little sheep, don't you think?"

"Yes, she's the right size, but. . .well, experience isn't always the only thing to consider."

"What do you mean?" He looked up from the form, a puzzled expression on his face.

Tangie leaned her elbows onto the table and stared at Gregg. "Don't you think she's a little. . .well. . .stuck-up?"

"Hmm." He shrugged. "*Stuck-up* might not be the words I would've come up with. When you're really good at something, sometimes you come across as overly confident."

"She's overly confident, all right. She pretty much told me I was giving her the lead in the show. And you should hear what her mother's been saying to people."

Gregg laughed. "She's used to getting her way. I've seen that side of her before."

Tangie opted to change gears. "What about Annabelle? How did she do in the vocal audition?"

"Annabelle Lawrence? The new girl?" He shuffled through his papers until he found the right one. "Oh, right. She had a nice voice for someone with no experience. Pitch was pretty good. Nice tone. But she's not a strong performer."

"What do you mean?" Tangie felt more than a little rankled at that comment. "She did a great job in the drama auditions."

"Really? Hmm." Gregg shrugged. "Well, maybe you can give her a small part or something. And she can always sing in the choir."

"I don't think you're hearing me," Tangie said, feeling her temper mount. "If Annabelle can sing, I'd like to consider her for the lead role."

Gregg paled then took another swig of his coffee. "Lead role? Are. . .are you serious?"

"Of course." Tangie stood her ground. "Why not?"

He shook his head and placed his cup back on the table. "Look, I already botched up the Christmas play. I have a lot to prove with this one. My best shot at pulling this off is using kids who are seasoned. Talented."

"So, this is about making you look good?" Tangie quirked a brow. Looked like he was trying to prove something here, but at whose expense? The kids?

He groaned and shook his head. "Maybe I put too much emphasis on that part. But I feel like I need to redeem myself after what happened before."

"But at whose expense?" She stared him down, curious how he would respond.

"Whose expense?" Gregg looked flustered. "What do you mean?"

"I mean, Margaret Sanderson is at a crossroads. She's a little diva and she needs to understand that she won't always be the one in the lead role. Sometimes the underdog needs a chance."

At once, Tangie's hands began to tremble. Something about the word *underdog* sent a shiver down her spine. How often had she been in that position over the years? Too many to count. Take that last play, for example. The one where she'd been promised the lead but had had to settle for a bit part in the chorus. She'd handled it as well as could be expected, but when would she get her turn? When would she take center stage?

Tangie sighed then turned her attention back to the forms. This time she could actually control who landed in which spot. And she would make sure she didn't botch it up.

❦

Gregg stared across the table at Tangie, confused by her words. "Tell me what you're really thinking here, Tangie. How many grown-up Margaret Sandersons have you had to work with?"

"W–what do you mean?"

"I mean, maybe you're sympathetic toward Annabelle because you can relate to her. That's my guess, anyway. How many times did you try for the lead role and someone like Margaret got it instead?"

Ouch. "A million?" Tangie responded, after absorbing the sting of his question. "But I got over it."

"I'm not so sure you did. I think maybe you're still holding a grudge against leading ladies and want to prove a point. So, you're going to use Margaret to do it. If you prevent her from getting the lead, it will be payback to all of those leading ladies who got the parts you felt you deserved over the years."

Tangie's face paled. "Nothing could be further from the truth," she argued. "It's just that the character of the baby ewe is a really sweet personality and Annabelle can pull that off. Margaret couldn't pull off sweet without a significant amount of work."

"But I want her in the lead because she's the strongest vocalist." Gregg stood his ground on this one. If they put anyone other than Margaret in the role, it would double his workload.

"I have to disagree." The creases between Tangie's brows deepened and she leaned back against her seat, arms tightly crossed.

Gregg stared at her, unsure of what to say next. Why was she going to such lengths to challenge him on this? Margaret was the better singer. Who cared if she had a little attitude problem? They could work with her and she would get over it. Right? Yes, this production would surely give them the platform they needed to further develop her talents while giving her some gentle life lessons along the way.

Tangie began to argue for Annabelle, but Gregg had a hard time staying focused. Thankfully, the waitress showed up to take their order. That gave him a two-minute reprieve. After she left, Tangie dove right back in. They were able to cast everyone in the show—except Margaret and Annabelle. This was an easy one, to his way of thinking. Give Annabelle a smaller part and let Margaret take the lead.

Unfortunately, Tangie refused to bend.

They finished the meal in strained silence. Afterward, Gregg led the way to his car. He'd never had someone get him quite as riled up as he felt right now. As he opened the car door for Tangie, he paused to tell her one more thing. "It's obvious we're two very different people with two very different ways of looking at things."

"What are you saying? That I'm too different for this church? For this town?"

He paused, not knowing how to respond. "I just think we need to pick our battles, Tangie. Some mountains aren't worth dying on."

She stared at him, her big brown eyes screaming out her frustration. "We both need to go home and sleep on this," she suggested. "I'm too tired to make much sense out of things tonight. And besides, we're meeting tomorrow afternoon at the church to finalize things, right? Let's just drop it for now."

"But I don't want to leave it hanging in midair till then." Gregg shook his head. "I want to understand why you're being so stubborn about this. What are you thinking, anyway?"

"I'm thinking this will be a good time to teach Margaret a couple of life lessons. The top dog doesn't always get the bone, Gregg."

"She's a kid, not a golden retriever," he responded.

Back and forth they went, arguing about who should—or shouldn't—play the various roles in the play. All the while, Gregg felt more and more foolish about the words coming out of his mouth. In fact, at one point, he found himself unable to focus on anything other than the pain on her beautiful face and guilt over the fact that he'd put it there.

Tangie's hands began to tremble—likely from the anger—and he reached to take them, suddenly very ashamed of himself for getting her so worked up.

With hands clasped, she stared at him, silence rising up between them. Except for the sound of Gregg's heartbeat, which he imagined she must be able to hear as clearly as he did, everything grew silent.

Then, like a man possessed, Gregg did the unthinkable.

He kissed her.

Chapter 11

On the morning after auditions, Tangie wandered the house in a daze. *He kissed me. He. Kissed. Me.*

"But, why?" She'd done nothing to encourage it, right?

Okay, there had been that one moment when she'd paused from her righteous tirade, captivated by his bright blue eyes. . .eyes that had held her attention a microsecond longer than they should have, perhaps. But had that been enough to cause such a reaction from him? Clearly not. And wasn't he interested in Ashley, anyway? Why would he be so fickle as to kiss the wrong woman?

Hmm. She couldn't exactly accuse others of being fickle when she had flitted from relationship to relationship, could she?

"Still. . ." Tangie paced the living room, her thoughts reeling. "What in the world is wrong with him?"

"Wrong with who?" Gramps asked. "Or would it be whom? I never could get that straight."

"Oh, I. . ."Tangie shook her head, unable to respond. She raked her fingers through her hair. "Never mind."

"What has Gregg done now?" Gramps asked, putting up his fists in mock preparation for a boxing match. "If he's hurt your feelings or gotten you worked up over something, I'll take him down. Just watch and see. I'm not too old to do it."

Tangie chuckled and then released an exaggerated sigh. "Gramps, there are some things about men I will never understand. Not if I live to be a hundred."

"I feel the same way about women, to be honest," he said and then laughed. "And I'm three-quarters of my way to a hundred, so I don't have a lot of time left to figure it all out. So I guess that makes us even. We're both equally confused."

Yes, confused. That was the word, all right. Everything about the past couple of weeks confused her. Driving in the dead of winter to a town she hardly knew. Taking a job at a church where she didn't fit in. Working with a man who. . .

Whose eyes were the color of a Monet sky. Whose voice sounded like a heavenly choir. When he wasn't chewing her out or accusing her of being too outlandish.

She turned to Gramps with a strained smile, determined not to let him see any more of her frustration or her sudden interest in the music pastor. He'd seen enough already. "Are you hungry? We could go to the bakery."Tangie reached for her keys and then grabbed her coat from the hook in the front hall. "My treat."

"Sweet Harmony? I'd love to!" His eyes lit up. "I'm always up for an éclair or one of those bear claw things. Or both. Just don't tell your grandmother when she gets back from her nibble and dribble group."

"Nibble and dribble?"Tangie turned to him, confused.

He shrugged. "You know. That ladies' tea she goes to every month. It's just an excuse for a bunch of women to sit around and sip tea and nibble on microscopic cookies and cakes and dribble chatter all over one another. Never could figure out the appeal. I'd rather have the real thing from Sweet Harmony. Now there's some sugar you can sink your teeth into."

Tangie laughed. "Ah, I see. Well, I'm in the mood for something over the top, too. But you'll have to hide all of the evidence if you don't want Gran-Gran to know."

"Good idea. I'll bring some chewing gum with me. That'll get rid of the sugar breath and throw your grandmother off track."

"You sound like you've done this before."

He gave her a wink. "Let's hit the road, girlie."

"I'm ready when you are."

All the way, she forced the conversation away from Gregg Burke and toward anything and everything that might cause distraction.

Her thoughts kept drifting back to the auditions. The kids expected the cast list to be posted on Wednesday evening before service. How could they post it if she and Gregg couldn't even come to an agreement? When they met together this afternoon, they would come up with a logical plan. Surely the man could be reasoned with. Right?

Every time she thought about spending time with him, Tangie's thoughts reeled back to that tempestuous kiss. Sure, she'd been kissed before, but never by a man so upset. Gregg had been downright mad at her just seconds before he planted that kiss on her unsuspecting lips. She hadn't seen either coming—the anger or the startling smooch. And both had left her reeling, though for completely different reasons. She didn't know if she wanted to punch his lights out or melt in his arms.

The former certainly held more appeal than the latter, at least at the moment.

Tangie did her best to focus on the road, happy to finally arrive at the bakery. With Gramps leading the way, she entered the shop.

"Hey, Penny," Gramps called out.

"Well, Herbert, it's not Sunday," Penny responded, her brows rising in surprise. "What brings you to the shop today?"

"This granddaughter of mine. She talked me into it. Tangie's got sugar in her veins. It's from all those years working at the candy shop in Atlantic City."

"She's working for me now, you know," Penny said. "And we're talking about adding candies to Sweet Harmony."

"Ya don't say." His eyes lit up.

"Yes. And by the way, Tangie can take home leftovers any afternoon when we close. So, between you and me, you don't have to pay for your sweets anymore. Except on Sundays."

"Are you serious?" From the look on Gramps's face, he might as well have won the lottery. He turned in Tangie's direction. "Well, why didn't you tell me?"

She shrugged. "I didn't know. But we'd better take it easy with the sweets. Don't want your blood sugars to peak."

"My blood sugars are perfect," he explained. Turning to Penny, he said, "So I'll have a bear claw, an éclair, and a half dozen donut holes for good measure."

"Sure you don't want a kolache to go along with that?" Penny asked.

"Why not?" He shrugged. "Tangie's paying."

"Penny might have to mortage the business to cover that order," she said with a laugh. When his eyes narrowed in concern, she added, "But that's okay. You're worth it, Gramps. You're worth it."

On Monday around noon, Gregg slipped away from the office to grab a bite to eat at home. After taking a few bites of his sandwich, he paced his living room, thinking back over the events of the past twenty-four hours.

427

He still couldn't get over the fact that Tangie didn't want to cast Margaret Sanderson in the lead role. Didn't make a lick of sense to him. Then again, women didn't make a lick of sense to him.

On the other hand, his *own* actions didn't make sense, either.

Had he really kissed Tangie? Right there, in the diner parking lot for the whole town of Harmony to see? Why? What had prompted such irrational behavior on his part? Something about her had reeled him in. *What is my problem lately? Why is everything upside down in my life all of a sudden?*

Something about that crazy, unpredictable girl had gotten to him. And it frustrated him to no end. Gregg took a seat at the piano. . .the place where he always worked out his troubles. Somehow, pounding the black and white keys brought a sense of release. And there was something about turning his troubles into beautiful melodies that lifted his spirits. No, he certainly couldn't stay upset for long with music pouring from his fingertips, could he?

Gregg was halfway into a worship medley when the doorbell rang. He answered the door, stunned to see his younger brother.

"Josh?" Gregg swung the door back and grinned. "You should tell a person when you're coming for a visit."

"Why?" Josh shook off the snow and shivered in an exaggerated sort of way. "It's always so much more fun when I just show up. Besides, you know I don't stay in one place very long. I always end up back here, in Harmony."

"Yes, but you're back sooner than usual this time. What happened in New York?"

Josh shrugged as he eased his way through the front door. "Oh, you know. A little of this, a little of that. More this than that."

"Mm-hmm. What's her name?"

After a moment's pause, Josh offered up a dramatic sigh. "Julia."

"She broke your heart?"

"No, but her boyfriend almost broke my nose." Josh grinned then rubbed his nose, making a funny face.

"You've got to get past this thing where you jump from girl to girl," Gregg said. "It's not healthy—for you or the girls."

"Might work for you to dedicate yourself to one at a time, but I'm not wired that way." Josh shrugged. "Got anything to eat in that refrigerator of yours?"

"Sure. Help yourself." Gregg sat back down at the piano and continued to play. A few minutes later, Josh showed up in the living room with a sandwich in hand. "That's a great piece you're playing. What do you call that?"

Gregg looked up from the piano and shook his head. "Not sure yet. I'm just making it up as I go along."

"No way." Josh smiled. "I thought it was a real song."

"It will be." Gregg allowed a few more notes to trip from his fingertips then turned around on the piano bench to face his younger brother. They hadn't seen each other in months. And knowing Josh, he wouldn't be here for long.

Gregg spent the next hour talking to his brother—catching up on the time they'd been apart.

"I've been talking to Mom at least once a week," Josh said. "So, I know everything that's going on. She's doing better than I thought she would."

"Yes. Does she know you're back?"

"Yeah. I stopped by the shop just now. She seems to be doing okay. I hear she's hired someone to help."

"Yes. Someone I know pretty well, actually. A girl from church."

Josh's brows elevated. "Oh?"

"She's not someone you would be interested in. She's a little on the wacky side."

"I like wacky. You're the one who picks the straight arrows. Not me."

Gregg changed the direction of the conversation right away, realizing he and Josh were now talking about two completely different things. "I'm glad you're back. Mom really needs us right now."

"I know." Josh nodded. "I might be a wanderer, but even I know when it's time to head home for a while."

"Good." Gregg released a sigh, feeling some of his anxieties lift. "Well, I'm glad you're home. He glanced at the clock on the wall, rising to his feet as he realized the time. "I hate to cut this short, but I've got a meeting at the church in twenty minutes."

"Oh? Should I tag along?"

Gregg shrugged. "A couple of us are meeting in the choir room to talk about the Easter production. Pretty boring stuff, unless you're involved."

"Any beautiful females in the mix?"

Gregg hesitated to answer, knowing his brother's penchant for pretty women. "Oh, you know. Just church ladies." That was only a slight exaggeration. Tangie did go to the church after all, and she was a lady.

"Church ladies." Josh laughed. "Sounds intriguing. Thanks for the invitation. I'd be happy to."

Chapter 12

Tangie looked up from her notes as Gregg and the handsome stranger entered the choir room.

Her heart began to flutter as she turned her attention to Gregg. *Lord, help me through this. I don't know if I'm ever going to be able to look him in the eye again after what happened last night.* If she closed her eyes, she could relive the moment over and over again. Why, oh why, hadn't she pulled away when he leaned in to kiss her? Why had she lingered in his arms, enjoying the unexpected surprise of the moment?

Because she was a fickle girl who fell in love more often than she changed her hair color. And that was pretty often.

As Gregg made introductions, her gaze lingered on Josh. So, this was Gregg's brother. They resembled each other in many ways, but there was something different about Josh. He was younger, sure. And trendier. He certainly wore the name-brand clothes with confidence. The look of assurance—or was that cockiness?—set him apart from Gregg in many ways.

"So, where do you hail from?" she asked Josh as he took the seat across from her.

"Manhattan."

That certainly got Tangie's attention. She turned to him, stunned. "You're kidding. Where do you live in Manhattan?"

"East end. I love the city life. Always seems strange, coming back to Harmony."

"Oh, I know. Tell me about it."

Within seconds the two of them were engaged in a full-on conversation. Tangie could hardly believe it. Finally! Someone who shared her enthusiasm for big city life.

"What do you do for a living?" she asked.

"I'm a reporter. Did some work for the *Times*, but that's a tough gig. A couple of the local papers bought my pieces, but the competition in the city is fierce. So, I'm back in Harmony."

"As always." Gregg walked over to the coffeemaker and switched it on.

"Yeah." Josh shrugged. "I usually come back home when things slow down. The editor at the *Gazette* always gives me my old job back."

"Oh? They let you come and go like that?"

"He's a great guy." Josh sighed and leaned back against the seat. "Not that there's ever much news in this town. But I can always write stories on Mr. Clark's rheumatism and Mrs. Miller's liver condition." He laughed. "Not quite the same buzz as New York City, but it pays the light bill."

"Oh, I understand. I love the city. And you're right. . .it's filled with stories." Tangie dove into a passionate speech about her favorite places to go in Manhattan and before long, she and Josh were in a heated debate over their favorite—and least favorite—restaurants.

"What did you do in New York, anyway?" he asked.

"Tangie's a Broadway star," Gregg interjected.

That certainly caught Tangie's attention. She'd never heard him describe her in such a way. Glancing at Gregg, she tried to figure out if his words were meant to be flattering or sarcastic. The expression on his face wasn't clear.

"Really?" Josh looked at her with an admiring smile. "You're an actress?"

"Well, technically, I only did a couple of bit parts on Broadway. Most of my work was in theaters a few blocks away. But I did have a few secondary roles that got written up in the paper."

"Which paper?"

"The *Times*. It was a review of *Happily Never After*. I played the role of Nadine, the embittered ex-girlfriend."

"Wait, I saw that show. It shut down after just a couple of weeks, right?"

Tangie felt her cheeks warm. She looked at Gregg, wondering what he would make of this news.

"Yes. But that's okay. It wasn't one of my favorites. We never found our audience."

"Lost 'em, eh?" He laughed. "Happens to shows all the time. I just hate it for the sake of those involved. And I especially hated writing some of those reviews. It's always tough to crush people."

"Wait. . ." She paused, looking at him intently. "You said you wrote for the paper, but you didn't mention you were a reviewer."

"I'm not. . .technically." He laughed. "But whenever the other reviewers were too busy, I'd fill in. I got stuck with a lot of off-off-Broadway shows and some of them were, well, pretty rank."

"Mm-hmm." A shiver ran down Tangie's spine. Before long, he might start naming some of those not-so-great shows.

"How does a reviewer receive his training, anyway?" she asked. "On the stage or off?"

"Both." Josh shrugged. "In my case, anyway."

"Oh, he's got a lot of experience." Gregg approached the table with a cup of coffee in his hands. "Josh here quite the actor. He's been in plays since we were kids."

"Really." Tangie scrutinized him. "We need someone to play the role of the shepherd in our Easter production. Would you be interested in auditioning?"

Josh turned her way with a smile. "Now that's a proposition I just might consider."

🌺

Gregg could have kicked himself the minute he heard Tangie's question. Putting on this Easter production was going to be tough enough. Factoring Josh into the equation would only complicate things further.

"Josh is too—" He was going to say *busy*, when his brother interrupted him.

"I'd love to."

"It's for the church," Gregg explained. "And I'm not sure you're the best person for the job."

"Why not?" Josh gave him a pensive look. "You said you needed an actor. I'm here. What else is there to know?"

Gregg bit his tongue. Literally. Josh's walk with the Lord wasn't as strong as it once was. In fact, Gregg couldn't be sure where his brother was in his spiritual journey. In order to play the lead—the character of the Good Shepherd—the actor should, at the very least, understand God's heart toward His children. Right?

Gregg sighed, unsure of where to take this conversation. He'd have to get Tangie alone and explain all of this to her. However, from the enthusiastic look on her face, persuading her might not be as easy as he hoped.

Lord, show me what to do here. If You're trying to nudge my brother back home—to You—I don't want to get in the way.

"Okay, everyone." Tangie's words interrupted his thoughts. "Aren't we here to cast a show? Let's get to it."

With a sigh, Gregg turned his attention to the matter at hand.

🌺

Tangie arrived home from the meeting, her thoughts going a hundred different directions. Gregg had finally agreed that Annabelle could play the lead, but he wasn't happy about it. Tangie couldn't help but think Gregg was put off by her ideas, across the board. Of course, he just seemed "off" today, anyway. That much was obvious when he knocked over her cup of tea, spilling it all over the table. She could also tell the stuff about his brother being in the play bothered him...but why? Sure, Josh was a schmoozer. She knew his type. But Gregg was acting almost...jealous. Surely he didn't think Tangie would be interested in Josh.

No, guys like Josh were too familiar. They came and went through your life. Besides, she and Josh had far too much in common. What would be the fun in that?

As she entered the house, Tangie made her way into the kitchen to grab a soda and a snack. With all of the goodies from the bakery on hand, she felt sure she'd end up packing on the pounds before long. Especially if she couldn't get her emotions under control. Still, she couldn't stop thinking about Gregg. About that kiss. Was it keeping him preoccupied today, as well? She hadn't been able to tell while they were together. Maybe he was a better actor than she thought. Or maybe... She sighed. Maybe he regretted what he'd done.

As Tangie left the kitchen, a soda in one hand and two peanut butter cookies in the other, she ran into Gran-Gran in the hallway.

"Well, there you are. That meeting went longer than you expected." Her grandmother gave her an odd look. "Everything okay?"

"Yeah." She shrugged. "It took us a while to figure out which child should play which part, and we didn't all agree, even in the end. I guess you could say not everything is as harmonious in Harmony, New Jersey, as it could be," she admitted with a shrug. "Let's just leave it at that."

"Well, don't get too carried away thinking about that," Gran-Gran said. "While you were out on your date with Gregg last night—"

"Date?" Tangie gasped. Did Gran-Gran really think that? "We were having dinner after auditions to discuss casting the play. That's all."

"Okay, well while you were having dinner with Gregg—for two and a half hours—Pastor Dave called, looking for you. He wants you to sing a solo at the Valentine's banquet next week. He said to pick out a love song and e-mail the title to him so Darla can find the piano music."

"W–what? But he's never even heard me sing. How does he know that I can..." Tangie pursed her lips and stared at her grandmother.

"What?" Gran-Gran played innocent. "So, I told him you could sing. So what? And I happened to mention that you'd done that great Gershwin review a few years ago off-Broadway. What can I say? The man likes his Gershwin."

"Mm-hmm." Tangie sighed. "So, what am I singing?"

"Oh, that's up to you. Just something sweet and romantic. It is Valentine's, you know." Gran-Gran disappeared into the kitchen, chattering all the way about her favorite tunes from the forties and fifties.

Oh, Gran-Gran, you're the queen of setting people up, aren't you? You planned this whole thing.

Tangie sighed as she thought about Valentine's Day. Last year Tony had taken her to La Mirata, one of her favorite Italian restaurants in the heart of the city. It had been a magical night. This year would be a far cry from that romantic evening.

Not that romance with Tony was ever genuine. No, ever the actor, he'd managed to convince her she was his leading lady. But, in reality...

Well, to say there were others waiting in the wings would be an understatement.

Tangie put the cookies and soda down and went to the piano. Once there, she pulled back the lid, exposing the keys. She let her fingers run across them, surprised to hear the piano was in tune.

"We had it tuned the day you said you were coming," Gran-Gran hollered from the kitchen. "That way you wouldn't have any excuses."

Tangie shook her head and continued to play. Before long, she picked out the chords for one of her favorite Gershwin songs, "Someone to Watch over Me." After a couple times of running through it, she felt a bit more confident.

The words held her in their grip, as always. A good song always did that—grabbed the listener and wouldn't let go. Just like a good book. Or a great play. Yes, anything artistic in nature had the capability of grabbing the onlooker by the throat and holding him or her captive for just a few moments.

Isn't that what the arts were all about? They lifted you from the everyday. . .the mundane. . . and took you to a place where you didn't have to think. Or worry. All you had to do was to let your imagination kick in, and the everyday woes simply faded away.

❧

Gregg fixed a peanut butter and jelly sandwich, carried it to the small breakfast table, and took a seat. He went back over every minute of today's meeting in his mind. Tangie had been awfully impressed with his brother, hadn't she? For some reason, a twinge of jealousy shot through Gregg as he thought about that.

Josh came across as a suave, debonair kind of guy, no doubt. But his motives weren't always pure, especially where women were concerned. And he seemed to have his eye on Tangie. Should Gregg say something to warn her?

No. Not yet, anyway. Right now, he just needed to finish up his sandwich and head over to Sweet Harmony. His mom needed him. And, unlike his brother, when Mom called. . . Gregg answered.

Chapter 13

As the evening of the Valentine's banquet approached, Tangie faced a mixture of emotions. She found herself torn between being drawn to Gregg and being frustrated with him. Clearly, they were as different as two people could possibly be. And while he seemed attracted to her—at least on the surface—Gregg had never actually voiced anything to confirm that. Other than that one impulsive kiss. The one he never mentioned, even in passing.

Maybe he had multiple personality disorder. Maybe the man who kissed her wasn't Gregg Burke. Maybe it was his romantic counterpart. Tangie laughed, thinking of what a funny stage play that would make. *Slow down, girl. Not everything is a story. Some things are very real.*

The fact that her heart was getting involved after only a few weeks scared Tangie a little. She didn't want to make the same mistake she'd made so many times before. . .falling for a guy just because they were working on a show together. She'd had enough of that, thank you very much. Still, Gregg was different in every conceivable way from the other men she'd known. And his heart for the Lord was evident in everything he did.

Tangie smiled, thinking about the night they'd posted the cast list. The children—well, most of them, anyway—had been ecstatic. Margaret had sulked, naturally, but even she seemed content by the time Tangie explained her role as narrator. Excited, even. Of course, they hadn't faced her mother yet. And then there was the issue of Josh. He'd shown more than a little interest in her, something which ruffled her feathers. She'd finally put him in his place, but would he behave himself during the rehearsals? Had she made a mistake by putting him in such a pivotal role?

With the casting of the show behind her, Tangie could focus on the Valentine's banquet. On the evening of the event, she looked through her clothing items for something appropriate to wear. Thanks to her many theater parties in New York City, she had plenty of eveningwear. She settled on a beautiful red and black dress with a bit of an Asian influence. Tony—her onetime Mr. Right—had said she looked like a million bucks in it. But then, he was prone to flattery, wasn't he?

At a quarter till seven, a knock sounded at the door.

"Come in." Tangie sat at the small vanity table, finishing up her makeup, but paused to look up as Gran-Gran whistled.

"Tangie." Her grandmother's eyes filled with tears. "I don't believe it."

"Believe what?" She slipped her earrings on and gave herself one last glance.

Gran-Gran drew close. "You look so much like your mother did at this age. And I just had the strangest flashback."

"Oh?" Tangie looked at her with a smile. "What was it?"

Her grandmother's eyes filled with tears. "This was her bedroom, you know. And I remember the day she got married, watching her put on her makeup and fix her hair in that very spot." She pointed to the vanity table then dabbed at her eyes. "Look at me. I'm a silly old woman."

Tangie rose from her seat and moved in her grandmother's direction. "There's nothing silly about what you just said. I think it's sweet. And it's fun to think that Mom used to get ready in this same room. I guess I never thought about it before." She pointed at her dress.

"What do you think? Do I look okay?"

"Oh, honey." Gran-Gran brushed a loose hair from Tangie's face, "I've never seen you look prettier. In fact, I want to get some pictures of you to send to your parents. They're never going to believe you're so dolled up."

"Sure they will. Remember the bridesmaid's dress I wore at Taffie's wedding on the beach? And don't you remember those dresses we wore at Candy's wedding last year?"

"Yes." Gran-Gran nodded. "But I think tonight surpasses them all."

Gramps stuck his head in the door and whistled. "I'm gonna have the prettiest two women at the banquet. How lucky can one guy be?" After a chuckle, he headed off to start the car, hollering, "Don't take too long, ladies. The roads are bad and we'll need a little extra time."

Tangie donned her heavy winter coat and reached for a scarf. After one last glance in the mirror, she grabbed her purse and followed along on her grandmother's heels to the garage, where Gramps was waiting in the now-heated Ford.

"Are you ready for the program tonight?" Gran-Gran asked as they settled into the car.

"I guess so. I found the perfect song."

"Oh?"

"Gershwin, of course. 'Someone to Watch over Me.'"

"I heard you playing it. Of course, I've heard you play a great many things over the past few days. It's good to have music in the house again. But I'm tickled you chose that particular song. It's one of my favorites from when I was a girl."

"Really?"

"Oh yes. I used to be quite the performer. I'd stand in front of that vanity—the same one you used to put on your makeup—and hold a hairbrush in my hand, pretending it was a microphone. Then I'd sing at the top of my lungs. And I was always putting on little shows and such in the neighborhood."

"Yes, she's always been quite the performer," Gramps added. "She even had a starring role in a community theater show about twenty years ago. Back when we had a community theater, I mean. It's long since been torn down."

"So, what happened?" Tangie asked. "Why did you stop?"

Gran-Gran sighed. "I don't know. Just fizzled out, I guess."

"I can understand that."

"Dreams are like flowers, honey," her grandmother said. "They need watering and tending to. If you neglect them, well, they just die off."

Sad. But true. And hadn't Penny pretty much said the same thing? Dreams needed to be chased after. Tangie wondered if the Lord might be nudging her back to New York to pursue some of those dreams she'd given up on. Perhaps the answer would be clearer in time.

In the meantime, Tangie focused on her grandmother's words as they made the short drive to the church. When they arrived, Tangie searched for Darla, the pianist. Hopefully she would have time to run over her song one last time.

As she rounded the corner near the choir room, Tangie paused. The most beautiful tenor voice rang out. The voice drew her, much like one of the Pied Piper's tunes that captivated children.

She peeked inside the room and caught a glimpse of Gregg, dressed in a dark suit. He stood with his back to her, singing another one of her favorite Gershwin songs, "But Not for Me." She listened intently as he sang the bittersweet words about a man who feared he would never find love. Tangie heard genuine sadness in Gregg's voice. Either that, or his acting skills really were better than he'd let on.

She slipped into the room and sat in a chair at the back. When he finished, she applauded and he turned her way, his cheeks flashing red. "Tangie. I didn't know you were here."

She slowly rose and walked to the piano. "Dave asked me to sing tonight, too. Hope that's okay."

"Of course. He told me. Your grandmother thinks very highly of your singing abilities."

"Hmm." Tangie shrugged. "Well, we'll see if anyone else agrees, or if her opinion of me is highly overrated."

She handed her music to Darla, and the introduction for "Someone to Watch over Me" began. With Gregg standing at her side, Tangie started to sing.

❀

Gregg could hardly believe what he was hearing. Tangie's singing voice blew him away. And as she sang the familiar words, he almost felt they were directed at him. *She's looking for someone to watch over her.*

Just as quickly, he chided himself. They were here to work together. Nothing more. Still, as the music flowed from page to page, Gregg found himself captivated by this chameleon who stood before him. She was both actress and singer. And amazing at both, from what he could tell. Not to mention beautiful. In this red and black number, she looked like something straight off the stages of Broadway.

When she ended the song, Gregg shook his head but didn't speak. He couldn't, really. Not yet, anyway.

Thankfully, he didn't have to. Darla clapped her hands together and turned to him. "I have the most amazing idea," she said, turning pages in the Gershwin book. She dog-eared a couple of pages then kept flipping, clearly not content as of yet with her choices. "You two need to sing a song together."

"W–what?" Tangie shook her head. "But the banquet starts in ten minutes and we haven't rehearsed anything."

"You won't need to." Darla began to play, her fingers practically dancing across the keys. "You two can pull off a last-minute performance, no problem. Trust me. You don't need rehearsal time. You each have the most beautiful voices. And I'm sure the blend will be amazing." She turned to face Tangie. "Now, you sing alto, Tangie. And, Gregg, you sing lead."

"B–but. . ." He gave up on the argument after just one word because the first verse kicked in. He began to warble out the first words to "Embraceable You," fully aware of the fact that he was singing directly to—and with—one of the most beautiful women he'd ever laid eyes on. Within seconds, Tangie added a perfect harmony to his now-solid melody line and they were off and running. *Lord, what are You doing here? First I kiss her, now I'm singing her a love song?*

After just one verse, Darla stopped playing and looked back and forth between them, shaking her head. Her gaze landed on Tangie. "You know, for an actress, you're not giving this much effort."

"E–excuse me?" Tangie's eyes widened.

"You're not very believable, I mean. This is a love song. You two act like you're terrified of each other. Can't you hold hands and look each other in the eye while you sing? Something like that? Isn't that what they teach you to do on Broadway? To play the part?"

"Well, yes, but. . ."

Drawing in a deep breath, Gregg took hold of her hands. "We don't want to get Darla mad, trust me. I did that once in a vocal team practice and she knuckled me in the upper arm."

"Did not," Darla muttered.

"Did, too," he countered. Gregg turned to look at Tangie, unable to hide the smile that wanted to betray his heart. "We might as well go along with this. Besides, tonight is all about romance, and half the people in the room are huge Gershwin fans. So, why not?"

"O–okay."

Darla began the piece again, and this time Gregg held tight to Tangie's hands, singing like a man in love from start to finish. Tangie responded with passion in her eyes—and her voice. If he didn't know her acting skills were so good, Gregg would have to think she really meant the words of the song.

He could barely breathe as the music continued. The voice flowing out of her tonight was pure velvet. And the way they harmonized. . .he could hardly believe it. While he'd sung with hundreds of people over the years, none had blended with his voice like this. Never.

As they wrapped up the last line, Dave stuck his head in the door. "Gregg, are you ready?" He took one look at the two of them holding hands and stared in silence. "Whoa."

Tangie pulled her hands loose and started fidgeting with her hair. She reached to grab her purse and scooted past him. "I'll see you in the fellowship hall. Just holler when you're ready for me."

Darla rose from the piano bench and gave him a knowing look. She, too, left the room. Dave took a couple of steps inside. "Someone having a change of heart?"

"I. . ." Gregg shook his head. "I don't have a clue what's happening."

"That's half the fun of falling in love," Dave said, slapping him on the back. "What fun would it be if you knew what was coming? Let it be a surprise. Besides, you could use a few surprises in your life. You're a little. . .predictable."

"Not always," Gregg countered.

"Oh yeah?" Dave laughed. "Do you realize you always order the same meal at the diner?"

"Well, yeah, but. . ."

"And what about your clothes? Did you realize you always wear a blue button-up shirt on Fridays?"

"Well, that's because Friday was our school color day when I was a kid."

"This isn't grade school, my friend." Dave chuckled. "And what's up with your hair? You've combed it exactly the same way ever since I met you."

"I have?"

"You have. And I'd be willing to bet you're still listening to that same CD I gave you for Christmas last year."

"Well, it's a great CD. I love those songs."

"Mm-hmm." Dave paused, his eyes narrowing. "You eat the same foods, you keep the same routine, you wear the same clothes. And your office is meticulous. Can't you mess it up, even just a little? Do something different for a change! Live on the edge, bro."

Gregg sighed. "Okay, okay. . .so I'm predictable. But I'm working on it. Wait till you see that new song we're doing in choir on Sunday. I'm trying to stretch myself."

Dave grinned. "That's great. But don't jump *too* far out of the box. Might scare people."

"There's little chance of that." Gregg chuckled as he thought about it. No, where music was concerned, he was liable to stick with what he knew. But in matters of the heart? Well, that was something altogether different.

❁

Tangie somehow made her way through the meal portion of the banquet, nervous about the music, which was scheduled to begin during dessert. Something rather magical had happened in that choir room, something undeniable. She and Gregg sang together as if they'd been born to do so, but there was more to it than that. Chemistry. That was really the only word to describe it. And not the kind in a science lab.

As she nibbled on her baked potato, Tangie caught a glimpse of Gregg, who was seated across the table and down a few feet. In his dark suit and tie, he looked really good. She watched as a couple of the young women from the church vied for his attention. Though polite, he didn't seem particularly interested in any of them.

"Where's Ashley tonight?" Tangie asked, turning to her grandmother.

"Ah. She's out with an old beau." Gran-Gran's eyebrows elevated. "A guy from college."

"Oh, I'm sorry she's not going to be here. I was looking forward to hanging out with her."

"Well, get to know some of the other people your age," her grandmother suggested. She nodded in Gregg's direction. "I see someone about your same age sitting right there."

"Gran-Gran. No matchmaking."

"Matchmaking? Me?" Her grandmother shook her head. "Heavens, no. I wouldn't think of it."

"Sure you wouldn't. And I'm pretty sure you didn't put Darla up to any tricks, either."

"Darla? Hmm? What did you say, honey? I'm having a little trouble hearing you tonight with all of the people talking."

"Sure you are."

The meal wrapped up in short order, and the lights in the room went down as the small stage area at the front was lit. Tangie smiled at the decorations. Cupids, hearts, and candles. . . as far as the eye could see.

As Gregg sang his song, Tangie closed her eyes and listened. With her eyes shut, she could almost picture him singing on a huge stage at one of the bigger theaters in New York. He had that kind of voice—the kind that landed lead roles. Why hadn't he gone that direction? He could've made a lot of money with a voice like that.

Just as quickly, she knew the answer. His love was the Lord. . .and the church. She saw it on Sunday mornings as he led worship. She'd witnessed it on Thursday nights as she walked past the choir room and heard him leading the choir.

Still, as he crooned the familiar love song, she couldn't help but think of all the possibilities he'd missed out on.

When his song came to an end, Gregg introduced her to the dinner guests. "Ladies and gentlemen, one of our newest members—straight from the stages of New York City—Tangie Carini."

Gran-Gran nudged her. "Your turn, sweetie. Show 'em what you've got."

"I–I'll do my best," she whispered. "But remember, I'm an actress, not really much of a vocalist."

"Humph. That's for us to decide."

As she made her way to the stage, Tangie whispered a prayer. She somehow made it through her song but found herself facing Gregg, who'd taken a seat at the table nearest the stage. The words poured forth, and she allowed them to emanate with real emotion. How wonderful would it be, to have someone to watch over her? To love her and care for her? Someone with sticking power.

As the song came to a conclusion, the audience erupted in applause. Tangie's cheeks felt warm as she gave a little bow. Then, with her nerves climbing the charts, she nodded in Gregg's direction and he joined her on stage.

"We've decided to try our hand at a duet," he said, after taking the microphone in hand. "Though we haven't had a lot of practice." He turned to Tangie and whispered, "You ready for this?"

She nodded, realizing she was, indeed, ready. . .for anything life might throw her way.

Chapter 14

The Valentine's banquet ended on a high note, pun intended. Everyone in the place gathered around Tangie and Gregg after they sang, gushing with glowing comments. She heard everything from, "You two are a match made in heaven," to "Best harmony in Harmony!"

Oh, but it *had* felt good to sing with him, hadn't it? And gazing into his eyes, their hands tightly clasped, she could almost picture the two of them doing that. . .forever.

Of course, she might be leaving in April. That would certainly put a damper on forever. Still, she could imagine it all, if even for a moment.

After the crowd dissipated, Tangie helped her grandmother and some of the other women clean the fellowship hall. She noticed that Gregg disappeared and wondered about it, but didn't ask.

Gran-Gran's voice rang out, interrupting her thoughts. "Honey, they need your help in the choir room."

"They? Who are *they*?"

"Oh, I'm pretty sure Darla and Dave are in there with Gregg. Seems like someone said something about putting music away. Or maybe they said something about music for the Easter production. I can't remember." Gran-Gran yawned. "I just know I'm tired."

"Oh, I'm sure this can wait till later. I'm ready to go."

"No." With the wave of a hand, her grandmother shooed her out of the room. "You go on, now. Do whatever you have to do."

Tangie headed off to the choir room, where she found Gregg alone, seated at the piano. With his back turned to her, he didn't see—or hear—her enter. She found herself intrigued by the piece of music pouring out of him. It was truly one of the most beautiful melodies she'd ever heard. Truly anointed.

He continued to play and she drew near, pulling up a chair next to him. Not that he noticed. No, as the music poured forth, his eyes remained closed. For a moment, Tangie wondered if she might be invading his privacy. *Lord, is this how he worships?*

There wasn't time for a response. The music stopped abruptly and Gregg turned her way, a startled look on his face.

"I–I'm sorry." She stood. "I didn't mean to interrupt."

"No, it's fine." His eyes flashed with embarrassment. "I just needed a little alone time after that banquet. Might sound weird, but I usually don't leave the church until I've spent a little time on the piano. It helps me wind down."

"Makes perfect sense to me." After pausing a moment, she asked the question on her heart. "Did you write that piece?"

He nodded. "I have quite a few worship melodies like that. If you listen on Sunday mornings, sometimes I play them during the quiet times in worship, when people are at the altar praying. There's something about worship music that's so. . ."

"Anointed." They spoke the word together.

"Yes." Gregg nodded. "And to be honest, I like to close out the day with worship because it helps me put things in perspective."

"Me, too," she said. "But I usually just listen to CDs or songs on my MP3 player. Can you play something else?"

He looked her way, their eyes meeting for one magical moment. Then, just as quickly, he turned his attention to the keys. The music that poured forth was truly angelic. She'd never heard anything quite like it. Tangie closed her eyes, lifting her thoughts to the Lord.

As the song ended, she sighed. "Thank you for that. It's good to just slow down and spend some time focusing on the Lord, especially after such a hectic day."

"It was hectic, wasn't it?"

"Yes." She smiled. "But it was wonderful, too. I had such a great time."

He gazed into her eyes, a hint of a smile gracing his lips. "I don't mind saying, you've got one of the best voices I've ever heard."

"I was just going to say the same thing to you." A nervous laugh erupted. Then Tangie glanced up at the clock on the wall and gasped. "Oh no. Gran-Gran and Gramps are waiting for me. I have to go."

"Kind of like Cinderella at the ball?"

She looked at Gregg, curious. "What do you mean?"

He shrugged. "Just when things were getting exciting, Cinderella took off. . .left the prince standing there, holding a shoe in his hand."

"Well, my feet are aching in these shoes, but I promise not to leave them with you." Tangie rose and grinned. *Though you definitely look like prince material in that suit.* "But I do have to go. Thanks again for the great evening."

"Hang on and I'll walk with you. I just need to turn out the lights in here." He led the way to the light switch by the door. As he flipped it, the room went dark. Standing there, so close she could almost feel his breath against her cheek, Tangie's heart began to race. Seconds later, she felt Gregg's fingertip tracing her cheekbone.

"Life is full of surprises, isn't it?" he whispered.

"Mm-hmm." She reached up with her hand to take his then gave it a gentle squeeze.

He responded by drawing her into his arms and holding her. Just holding her. No kiss. No drama. Just a warm, embraceable moment, like they'd sung about.

Gregg finally released his hold and stepped back. "They're going to come looking for us if we don't get out there."

"R–right." Tangie smiled at him, wishing the moment could have lasted longer. Still, she didn't want to keep her grandparents waiting.

She walked back into the fellowship hall, stunned to see Gran-Gran missing. "That's so weird. Well, I know Gramps was tired. They're probably waiting in the car." Gregg helped her with her coat, and she wrapped her scarf around her neck.

"I'll walk you out." Gregg turned out the lights and locked the door and they headed to the parking lot, chatting all the way.

She wanted to reach for his hand. In fact, she felt so comfortable around him that she almost did it without thinking. But Tangie stopped herself, realizing that others might see. She didn't want to get the rumor mill started.

When they reached the parking lot, she gasped. "What in the world?"

"Did they leave?" Gregg looked around.

"Surely not. Maybe they just took a spin around the block to warm up the engine or something like that."

She picked up her cell phone and punched in Gran-Gran's number. When her grandmother's sleepy voice came on the line, Tangie realized she must be in bed.

"Gran-Gran?"

"What, honey?"

"Did you forget something?"

"I don't think so." She gave an exaggerated yawn. "What do you mean?"

Tangie shivered against the cold, and Gregg pulled off his coat and draped it over her shoulders. She turned to him with a comforting nod as she responded to her grandmother. "I mean, you left me here."

"Oh, that." A slight giggle from the other end clued her in immediately.

"Gran-Gran, what are you up to?"

"Up to? We were just tired, honey. We're not spring chickens, you know. Gramps has to be home to take his blood pressure medication at a certain time every night."

"He took it before we left. I saw him with my own eyes. And besides, I was only in the choir room fifteen minutes," Tangie argued. "I thought you were waiting on me."

"We started to, but then I noticed Gregg's car was still there, and he lives so close and all. . ."

"Gran-Gran." Tangie shook her head. "You're up to tricks again."

"Me? Tricks?" Another yawn. "What do you mean?"

"Nothing. Just leave your granddaughter stranded in the cold on a winter's night. No problem."

Gran-Gran laughed aloud. "I daresay that handsome choir director will bring you home. And I'm sure there's a heater in his car. So, don't you worry, honey. Just enjoy your time together."

Enjoy our time together? Yep, we've been set up, all right.

As Tangie ended the call, she turned to Gregg, trying to decide how to tell him. Thankfully, she didn't have to.

"They left you?" he asked, his brow wrinkled in concern.

"Yep." She turned to face him with a sigh. "I don't believe it, but. . .they ditched me."

❧

Gregg couldn't help but laugh at the look on Tangie's face. "So, we've been set up."

"Looks that way."

"Someone's doing a little matchmaking."

"Gran-Gran, of course. But I didn't think she'd go this far."

Gregg reached to take Tangie's hand. "Oh, I'm not complaining, trust me. This is probably the first time in my life I'm actually thrilled to be set up."

"R—really?" Tangie's teeth chattered and he laughed.

"Let's get you out of the cold." He walked over to his car and opened the passenger side door. She scooted into the seat and smiled at him as he closed the door in the most gentlemanly fashion he could muster. Then, he came around to the driver's side and settled into his own seat. Turning the key in the ignition, a blast of cold air shot from the vents. "Sorry about that. Takes a while for the air to warm up."

"Good things are worth waiting for," Tangie said, giving another shiver.

He looked her way and smiled. "Yes, they are."

Their eyes met for another one of those magical moments, one that set a hundred butterflies loose in his stomach.

Gregg finally managed to get a few words out. "I. . .I guess I'd better get you home."

They made the drive to Tangie's grandparents' house and Gregg pulled the car into the driveway, his nerves a jumbled mess.

441

Tangie smiled at him as he put the car into Park. "Thanks for the ride. Sorry about all of this."

"Oh, I'm not, trust me." Gregg watched as she opened her door but then stopped her before she stepped out. "Hey, can you wait just a minute?"

"Oh, sure." She looked at him with that piercing gaze, the one that made him a bumbling schoolboy once again. She pulled the door shut then turned back to him. "What's up?"

"I, um. . .I just wanted to say something about the other night when I, um. . ."

"Ah." She smiled, suddenly looking like a shy kid. *"That."*

"Yeah, that." He looked down to hide the smile that threatened to betray his heart. "First, I was out of line."

"Oh?" She sounded a little disappointed.

"Yes. I feel like I took advantage of the situation. But"—he looked at her—"I'm not sorry I did it."

In that moment, the tension in the car lifted. Tangie's voice had a childlike quality to it as she whispered, "I'm not sorry, either."

At once, Gregg felt as if his heart might burst into song. Maybe even another Gershwin tune. She wasn't sorry he'd kissed her. That answered every question.

"I'm usually the most predictable guy on planet Earth," he said. "But that kiss. . ."

She grinned. "Was unpredictable?"

"To say the least." He paused a moment. "It was downright impulsive. And it totally threw me." He couldn't stop the smile from creeping up. "In a good way, I mean."

"It feels good to be unpredictable every now and again, doesn't it?" She giggled, and he thought he might very well go sailing off into space.

Yes, if felt good. Mighty good. In fact, he could go on feeling this good for the rest of his life. "I want to say one more thing. I had a great time singing with you tonight. I felt like our harmony was. . ."

"Amazing?"

"Yes." He smiled. "Sometimes life does surprise you, doesn't it? And how interesting that two very different people could sound so totally perfect together."

"Mm-hmm." Tangie sighed. "Just goes to show you. . . We have to give things a chance."

"Yes, we do." He smiled, thankful she'd given him the prompt for what he wanted to say. "And that's really what I wanted to ask you. . .if you'd be willing. . .to give a boring, predictable guy like me a chance."

"You mean *un*boring and *un*predictable, right?" Tangie grinned, her eyebrows elevating mischievously. "I think you've crossed the line into a new life, my friend."

"You—you do?" Gregg never really had time to add anything more than that. Tangie's lips got in the way.

Chapter 15

Rehearsals for the children's production began the last Saturday in February. The children gathered in the sanctuary and, after a quick prayer, were immediately divided into two groups—singing and nonsinging. Gregg took the vocalists into the choir room to practice, and Tangie worked with the actors and actresses. For weeks, she'd planned how the rehearsals would go, had even mapped them out on paper, accounting for every minute of time. But now that the moment had arrived, things didn't go exactly as planned.

For one thing, several kids were missing.

"Where's Margaret Sanderson?" she asked, looking around.

"Margaret's not going to be in the play," a little girl named Abigail said. "She's really mad."

"Oh?" Tangie forced herself not to knee-jerk in front of the kids, though everything inside her threatened to do so.

"She wanted to get the main part." Abigail shrugged. "But she didn't."

"All parts are equal in this play," Tangie explained to the group. "There's a saying in theater: 'There are no small parts, only small actors.' In other words, whether your part is little or big isn't the point. It's how much effort you put into it that counts."

"Well, she's not going to put any effort into it, 'cause she's not coming," Abigail said.

Tangie's mind reeled. She'd specifically asked Margaret if she would be willing to accept any role she received and the little girl had agreed. And now this? *We're not off to a very good start, Lord.*

Out of the corner of her eye, she caught a glimpse of Gregg's brother, Josh, as he swaggered up the center aisle of the church. Tangie glanced at the clock. Yep, just as she thought. He was ten minutes late. Looked like he wasn't taking his role very seriously, at least not yet.

He drew near and whispered, "Sorry I'm late," in her ear then muttered something about his mom not feeling well. Tangie softened immediately. "Ah. Okay."

After a few seconds of glancing over her notes, she began to call the children to the stage. "Missy, you stand over here. Kevin, stand over there. Cody, take your place upstage right."

"Upstage right?" He gave her a funny look, and she pointed to the spot where he needed to go.

Once all of the players were in place, Tangie clapped her hands. "Now, let's do a quick read-through of the first scene. Starting with the narrator."

She looked center stage, remembering Margaret—the narrator—was missing. "Hmm. I guess I'll read the narrator's lines." She began to read, but off in the corner one of the boys distracted her. Tangie stopped and looked at Cody, who'd just punched Kevin in the arm. "Cody! What are you doing?"

"He called me a chicken."

"Well, you *are* a chicken," Kevin said with a shrug. "Aren't you playing the part of a chicken in the play?"

"Yeah, but that doesn't mean I want to." Cody groaned, his hands still knotted into tight fists. "My mom is making me do this dumb play just like she made me do the last one. I'm going to be a lousy chicken."

Kevin began to squawk like a chicken and before long, everyone was laughing.

"Hey, at least you're not one of the singing rabbits like me," one of the other boys said. "Can you imagine telling your friends at school you have to wear rabbit ears in a play?"

"Yeah? Well what about me? I'm a sheep," one of the little girls said with a sour look on her face. Everyone began to *baa* and before long, the stage was filled with squawking, bleating, squealing noises representing the entire animal kingdom.

Finally, Tangie had had enough. She felt like throwing her hands up in the air and walking away. If she felt this way on the first day, what was the week of performance going to be like?

A shiver ran down her spine as she thought about it. *One mountain at a time, Tangie. One mountain at a time.*

❧

Gregg sat at the piano, playing a warm-up for the children in the choir. As they "la-la-la'd," he listened closely. They sounded pretty good, for a first rehearsal. One or two of the kiddos were a little off-pitch, but this was certainly better than the Christmas production. Tangie was right—it worked out best for the nonsingers to take acting roles. That way, everyone was happy. Well, mostly. Some of the boys still balked at the various roles they'd been given, but they'd get over it. In time. With therapy. Perhaps before they went off to college.

Out of the corner of his eye, Gregg saw someone come in the back of the room. Margaret Sanderson. According to his schedule, Margaret wasn't supposed to come to the vocal room for another half hour. Perhaps she'd missed the memo. He paused as she approached the piano.

"My mom said I should talk to you." She pushed a loose blond hair behind her ear.

"Oh?"

Margaret crossed her arms at her chest and glared at him. "She's mad."

"Ah ha."

"Really mad." Margaret began to tap her foot on the floor.

"Margaret, I'm sorry she feels that way." Gregg lowered his voice. "But this isn't the time to talk about it. Perhaps you could tell your mom that I'll be happy to meet with her after we're done with the rehearsal."

Margaret sighed. "I don't think she'll come." She shuffled off to the side of the room and took a seat, a scowl on her face.

Wow. Tangie was right about that one. The child did have some major attitude problems. Even more so when she didn't get her way.

The rehearsal continued with few mishaps. Afterward, Margaret's mother met with Gregg in the hallway, voicing her complaints, one after the other.

Gregg did his best to stay cool. "Mrs. Sanderson, I'm sure you can see that we have a lot of talented children in this congregation."

"Humph."

"And we did our best to put the children in the roles where they could grow and develop."

"How is playing the narrator going to help Margaret develop? There's no vocal solo. We're talking about a child with an extraordinary gift here, one who's going to go far. . .if she's given the right opportunities."

"Actually, she does have a solo in the midst of the group numbers. And the narrator threads the show together, after all. Margaret is onstage more than any other character, in fact. So, in that sense, I guess you could say that she's got the lead role."

Mrs. Sanderson's face tightened even further—if that were possible. "Mr. Burke, you and

I both know that Margaret should have been given the role of the littlest lamb, the one with the beautiful solo. Instead, you gave it to an unknown."

An unknown? Was she serious? These were children.

For a moment, Gregg had the funniest feeling he'd slipped off into another galaxy, one where determined stage mothers ruled the day and lowly music directors became their subjects. Only, he didn't want to subject himself to this madness—not now, not ever. He immediately prayed that the Lord would guard his tongue.

"Mrs. Sanderson, I'm sorry you and Margaret are disappointed, and I will understand if you withdraw her from the play. However, I want you to know that we've prayed over these decisions. At length. And we feel sure we've placed the children into the roles they have for a reason."

The woman's countenance changed immediately. "So, this is God's doing? Highly unlikely. The God I serve doesn't like to see church folks embarrassed. And this play is going to be an embarrassment to our congregation, just like the last one."

Hang on a minute while I pull the knife from my heart, and then I'll respond. Gregg exhaled slowly. *One. Two. Three. Four. Five.* Then he turned to her, determined to maintain his cool.

"I'm not saying we're perfect, and I certainly can't guarantee this show will be any better than the last one. I can only assure you that we prayed and placed the children accordingly. Again, if you want to pull Margaret from the play, we will miss her. But we will certainly understand."

At this point, he caught a glimpse of Tangie coming up the hallway. She looked as exhausted as he felt. Mrs. Sanderson turned to her, an accusing look in her eye. "We all know who's to blame for this, anyway."

"W–what?" Tangie looked back and forth between them, a shocked look on her face. "What am I being blamed for?"

"You know very well. You waltz in here in those crazy clothes and with that ridiculous spiked-up hair and stir up all kinds of trouble. Obviously, you need glasses."

"G–glasses?"

"Yes. Otherwise you would have already seen that Margaret is the most talented child in this church." Mrs. Sanderson grabbed a teary Margaret by the hand and pulled her down the hallway, muttering all the way.

Tangie looked at Gregg, her eyes wide. "Do I even want to know what that was about?"

"No." He gestured for her to follow him into the choir room, where they both dropped into chairs. "Let's just say she was out of line and leave it at that. And I also need to say that you were right all along about Margaret. Though, to be fair, I can't really blame the child when it's a learned behavior."

"Right." Tangie nodded. "I've met so many drama divas through the years. . .they're getting easier to recognize. Still, I can't help but think Margaret is supposed to be in this play. The Lord wants to soften her heart."

"Sounds like He needs to start with her mom."

Tangie gave Gregg a look of pure sweetness and reached out to touch his arm. "Let's pray about that part, too, okay? I honestly think God has several plans we're unaware of here. Putting on a show is always about so much more than just putting on a show. You know? God is always at work behind the scenes, doing things we can't see or understand. We see the outside. He sees the inside."

Gregg took her hands in his and sighed. "Tangie, you've managed to sum up so many things in that one statement."

"What do you mean?" She looked puzzled.

"I mean, man looks at the outward appearance. God looks at the heart. He's not interested in the clothes we wear—colorful, outlandish, or otherwise."

"Hey, now."

Gregg chuckled. "You get what I'm saying. He's too busy looking at our hearts. And you're right. He's working behind the scenes. I know He has been in my life. . .ever since you arrived. And now you've made me look for the deeper meaning, not just in a kids' play, but in my own life. That's one of the things I love most about you. You *always* look for deeper meaning in everything."

Almost immediately, he realized what he'd said: *One of the things I love most about you.* Wow. A slip of the tongue, perhaps, or was Gregg really starting to fall in love? Gazing into Tangie's eyes, he couldn't help but think it was the latter.

Chapter 16

On the Monday after the first rehearsal, Tangie went to work at the bakery. The place was buzzing with customers from early morning till around eleven. Then things began to slow down.

"People like their sweets early in the morning," Tangie observed, pulling an empty bear claw tray from the glass case.

"And late in the afternoon. The after-school crowd can be quite a handful." Penny wiped her hands on her apron then leaned against the counter and took a drink from a bottle of water.

"How are you feeling, Penny?"

Penny shrugged as she went to work putting icing on some éclairs. "Chemo's making me pretty squeamish. I've lost ten pounds in the last three weeks alone. And I want to pull this wig off and toss it across the room. Makes my head hot. And it itches."

Tangie offered up a woeful smile. Penny's last statement confirmed a suspicion she'd had all along. So, she did wear a wig. The hair seemed a little too perfect. But if anyone deserved to look extraspecial, Penny did. Especially now.

Tangie paused to whisper a little prayer for her new friend. Penny had made it clear how she felt about the Lord, but that didn't stop Tangie. She'd started praying daily about how to reach out to her. What to say. What not to say. She didn't want to get in the way of what God might be doing in Penny's life. *Use me in whatever way You choose, but help me not to overstep my bounds.*

Though she'd worked several days at the bakery now, Tangie still felt a sense of disconnect between herself and Penny. Seemed like the older woman kept her at arm's length. Not that Tangie blamed her. Penny had plenty of other things on her mind right now.

In the meantime, Tangie had a couple of questions, from one female to another. "Penny, can I ask you something?"

"Sure, kid." She continued icing the éclairs, never looking up. Still, Tangie knew she was paying attention.

"Have you ever been in love?"

Penny snorted, nearly dropping her icing bag. "Only ten or twenty times."

"Really?" Tangie looked at her, stunned. "Are you serious?"

"Yes." Penny nodded then went right back to work. "Remember, I told you those church folks didn't know what to make of me. I was a single mom with two boys and no husband in sight. I guess I was so desperate to find a father for them that I checked under every bush."

"Including the church."

Penny shrugged. "Maybe my motives for attending weren't exactly pure. But, hey, I thought a good Christian man would be just the ticket for my kids, ya know? Most of the ones I knew were pretty nice."

"But, you never found one?"

"Oh, I found a few." She winked. "Problem was, a couple were already involved with other women. And I, um. . .well, I broke up a couple of relationships."

"Ah." Tangie pondered those words. "But you never married any of the men you fell for?"

"No." Penny's expression changed. "Never found one that really suited me or my boys."

"How did Gregg end up working in a church, then?" Tangie began to stack fresh bear claws on the empty tray, more than a little curious about the answer to this question.

Penny closed the glass case and shrugged. "There was one man, a youth pastor, who took an interest in the boys when they were in their teens. Offered to drive them to church. Even paid for Gregg to have voice lessons. He was a great guy. And I seem to recall a female choir teacher at school who spent a little extra time with him. She was a churchgoer. So, I guess he got sucked in that way."

"Ah." So not everyone had rejected them, then. After a moment's pause, Tangie couldn't hold back one particular question. "Has, um. . .has Gregg mentioned anything to you about the play we're doing with the kids?"

"Heavens, yes." Penny laughed as she began to roll out dough for cinnamon rolls. "I've heard all about it. He says you wrote it, too. Is that right?"

"Yeah."

"He told me about the singing rabbits and the little sheep. That part sounded cute. And then there was something about a chicken hatching out of an egg. Did he get that part right?"

"He did." Tangie realized just how silly the whole thing sounded, when described in only a sentence or two. Still, the idea worked for the kids, even if the grown-ups couldn't quite figure it out.

"Well, all I know is, it's a kids' play and I'm no kid." Penny went off on a tangent, going on and on about singing rabbits and dancing chickens. Tangie couldn't tell if she was being made fun of, or if Penny really found the whole thing entertaining.

"I want you to make me a promise." Tangie stopped her work for a moment. She took Penny's hand and squeezed it. "Don't let anyone else's opinions sway you. Promise me you'll come see the play for yourself. The performance is in a couple of weeks. You decide if it's too much fluff or if it's something the kids can relate to."

"You're asking me to take sides?"

"No. I really want to know what you think. Besides, Gregg is working hard at this and I know he'd love it if you came."

Penny shook her head. "He knows me better than that. I haven't graced the doors of a church in years."

"Well, this Easter might just be a good time to give it a try. What have you got to lose, anyway?"

Penny snorted then turned back to her work, muttering under her breath. Still, Tangie would not be swayed. Somehow, knowing that this woman—this wonderful, witty woman—was Gregg's mom, made her want to pray all the harder. . .not just for her healing, but for her very soul.

❀

On Monday afternoon, just as Gregg closed the door to his office, his cell phone rang. He looked down at the caller ID and smiled. "Hey, Mom," he answered. "What's up?"

"Pull out your rabbit ears, son. Mama's coming to church."

"W–what?" Maybe he was hearing things. "What did you say?"

"Said I'm coming to church. Oh, don't get all worked up. I'm not coming this Sunday or even next. But you give me the date for that rabbit and chicken show you and Tangie are directing and I'll be there for that."

"Mom, I really wish you'd come on a regular Sunday first. I think your opinion of me will be much higher."

"Are you saying the play's going to be awful?" she asked.

"Well, I can't imagine it will be awful," he said. "Not with Tangie behind the wheel. But let's just say we're off to an interesting start."

"Interesting is good." She let out a yelp, followed by, "Oops! Gotta go. Burned the oatmeal raisin cookies."

As she disappeared from the line, Gregg pondered his mother's words: *"Pull out your rabbit ears, son. Mama's coming to church."*

He couldn't help but laugh. After all these years, the Lord had finally figured out a way to get his mom back in church. And to think. . .she was coming because of a goofy play about singing rabbits. Gregg shook his head and then laughed. In fact, he laughed so loud—and so long—that the door to Dave's office opened.

"Everything okay out here?" Dave gave him a curious look.

"Yes, sorry." Gregg chuckled. "It's just. . .the strangest thing has happened. I think God has cracked open my mom's shell." Images of the four-foot Easter egg floated through his mind, and Gregg laughed again.

"Oh?" Dave gave him a curious look.

"Let's just say God is using Tangie in more ways than we thought. She's somehow managed to convince my mom to come to church to see the play."

"Oh, really?" Dave's face lit into a smile and he whacked Gregg on the back. "Well, why didn't you say so? That's awesome news, man."

"Yes, awesome." Just as quickly, the laughter stopped.

"You okay?"

"Yeah." He nodded toward Dave's office. "Is it okay if I come in?"

"Of course. I'm done with my work for the day."

Gregg's emotions took a bit of a turn.

"Why don't you tell me what's going on?" Dave took a seat behind his desk.

"Ever since my mom was diagnosed, I've been so worried that she might. . ." He didn't say the word for fear it might somehow make it true.

"You're afraid she might not make it." Dave leaned his elbows on the desk and gazed at Gregg. "Is that it?"

"Yes. And I think Josh must be worried about that, too. That's why he came back to Harmony, I think. But neither of us has said it out loud. Till now."

"It's good to get it off your chest," Dave said. "Helps you see what you're really dealing with."

"I've been trying to figure out a way to witness to her for weeks now," Gregg admitted. "And every attempt has failed. I couldn't get that woman through the doors of a church if my life depended on it. And now Tangie's done it with a goofy kids' musical."

"First of all, you've been living your life in front of your mom. That's the best witness of all. Second, we can never predict what might—or might not—be a good avenue to get someone in church. That's why we try so many different things. Different things appeal to different people."

"Right." Gregg sighed.

Dave paused a moment, rolling a pen around the desk with his index finger. Finally he looked up. "Can I ask you a question?"

"Sure."

"You somehow feel responsible for what's happened to your mom?"

"Responsible? For her cancer?" Gregg tugged at his collar, unhappy with the turn this conversation had taken.

"Well, not just the cancer. I mean the way her life has turned out. The fact that she's in her early sixties and living alone."

"Ah." Gregg didn't answer for a minute. He needed time to think about what Dave had said. "I guess I do in some ways. I was always the man of the house, you know?"

"Right."

"Had to practically raise Josh. There was no dad around to do it. And I always took care of everything for my mom. I thought I could save the day. You know?"

"I know. I'm an oldest son, too."

"As a kid, I prayed every day for a dad. And when Mom married Steve—my brother's father—I thought I'd finally found one. But then. . .well, anyway, that didn't pan out. But I guess there's some truth to the idea that I somehow feel responsible for my mom. That's why this cancer thing has been so hard."

"You can't fix it."

"R–right." Gregg sucked in a breath, willing the lump in his throat to dissolve. "I, um, I want to see her healed. Whole. And in church, going to those crazy teas and socials and stuff with the other ladies. She's all alone over there at that shop and I feel so. . ."

"Responsible."

"Yeah. That's why I spend so much time with her and make sure I call her every day."

"Gregg, it's natural for the oldest son to feel responsible, especially one who had to be both father and son at the same time. But I want to free you up by telling you something. Only God can be God."

"W–what?"

"Only God can be God. You can't fill His shoes. They're too big. You've taken on the responsibility of looking after your mom, and that's a good thing. Especially during the chemo. But she's a feisty one. Independent."

"Always has been."

"Yes. And you can't change her now any more than you could when you were little, no matter how hard you try."

"I know." Gregg slumped down in his chair, thinking about Dave's words. "But that's never stopped me from trying."

"God has a plan, and it's bigger than anything you could concoct. He sees the whole stage of our lives. Knows whether we're going to move upstage or down. Knows if the next song is going to be a heart-wrenching melody or a song and dance number. So, go ahead and pray for her. Spend time with her. Make sure her needs are met. But don't overstep your bounds, and don't take on guilt that isn't yours. You were never intended to save your mother's soul."

"W–what?"

"You heard me. You can plant the seeds. You've already done it, in fact. You've lived your life in front of her, expressed your faith and not held anything back. She's been watching those things, I guarantee you. But, Gregg, it's not your fault she hasn't come to know the Lord yet."

At this point, the dam broke. In one sentence, Dave had freed him from the guilt he'd carried for years. He'd never admitted it to anyone but himself, of course, but that's exactly what he'd believed. . .that he had somehow been responsible, even for his mother's very soul.

Dave rose from his chair and came to Gregg's side of the desk. He laid his hand on his shoulder and spoke in a gentler voice than before. "Witnessing to someone isn't like writing one of your songs."

"What do you mean?"

"I mean, when you write a song, you control where the notes go. Whether the melody moves up or down. When you witness to someone, it's like throwing a few notes out into space and then handing the melody off to that person and to God. It's up to them how the song turns out. Not you."

Gregg thought about Dave's words as he left the office. In fact, he couldn't get them off of his mind for the rest of the evening. By the time he rolled into bed that night, he'd made up his mind to let the Lord write the song that was his mother's life.

Chapter 17

The following Saturday, rehearsals for the play moved forward. This time, things were even more chaotic than before. For one thing, Josh didn't show up. Tangie asked Gregg about him about five minutes after two, the projected start time.

"Have you heard from your brother?"

Gregg shook his head. "I know he's been staying at Mom's place, but I don't have a clue why he's not here."

"Ah. I'll try your mom's phone, then." Tangie punched in the number, but there was no answer. She turned back to Gregg with a sigh. "Do you think we made a mistake casting him in such a large part? What if he doesn't show?"

"Hmm. I don't have a clue. But I'll try him on his cell." Gregg did just that, but Josh didn't answer. Looked like Tangie would have to read the lines of the Good Shepherd from offstage. Not that it really mattered. Nothing today seemed to be going according to plan. A couple of the kids were missing, due to the stomach flu. And the ones who attended were rowdier than usual. Take Cody, for instance. Tangie hardly knew what to do with him. As the rehearsal blazed forward, he ran from one side of the stage to the other, making airplane noises, disrupting the work at hand.

Finally, Tangie snapped. "Cody, I'm trying to block this scene, but it's difficult with you moving all over the stage."

That stopped him in his tracks. He froze like a statue then turned to her in slow motion, an inquisitive look on his face. "What does *block* mean?"

"To block a scene means I tell the players where to stand and where to move. When I say move downstage left, you go here." She pointed. "And when I say, "Move to center stage, you go here." She pointed to the center of the stage and the kids responded with a few "Ah's" and "Oh's."

Oh, if only she could block the kids in real life. Tell them where and when to move. Then they would surely be more obedient. Unfortunately, the characters in her play were better behaved than the kids performing the parts. Over that, she had no control.

Control. Hmm. Seemed she'd lost it completely over the past couple of weeks. And with the Easter production just a month away, Tangie felt like throwing in the towel. But every time she reached that point, the Lord whispered a few words of encouragement in her ear, usually through someone like Gran-Gran or Gregg. Then determination would settle in once again. Tangie would stick with this, no matter what.

Thankfully, there was one piece of good news. A humbled Margaret had come to her during the second rehearsal, asking if she could still play the role of the narrator. Tangie wasn't sure what was behind Margaret's change of heart but had smiled and responded with, "Of course, honey."

Looked like the Lord was up to something in the child's life. Could it be the result of Tangie's and Gregg's prayers, perhaps? Surely faith really did move mountains.

She watched from the edge of the stage as Margaret delivered each line with rehearsed perfection. Then Tangie turned to Annabelle, listening carefully as the youngster sang her first solo. The precious little girl, though shy, proved to be a great lead character, in spite of her inexperience.

About halfway into the final scene, Gregg's phone rang. "Sorry," he called out. He sprinted to the far side of the stage. From where she stood, Tangie could see him talking to someone, with a look of concern in his eyes. Glancing at her watch, she took note of the time. Three fifteen. The parents would be arriving soon, and she needed to update them on costume requirements. Still, she couldn't focus on that right now. No, she couldn't see past Gregg's wrinkled brow to think of anything else. Something had happened, but what?

When he ended the call, he took a few steps her way and whispered in her ear. "That was Josh. He's taken Mom to the hospital in Trenton. She's had a really bad reaction to her latest round of chemo."

"Oh, no."

Up on the stage, the kids began to recite lines on top of each other, most of them standing in the wrong places or facing the wrong way. Tangie would have to correct them later. Right now she needed to hear the rest of the story about Penny.

Gregg sighed. "She's been having trouble keeping anything down since her last treatment. She's a little dehydrated, is all. They've got her hooked up to IVs."

"Do you need to go? I can handle the kids."

"No, Josh said they're just keeping her on fluids another hour or so and then releasing her. He, um. . .he asked if I would read his lines for him." Gregg smiled. "Actually, he told me how much he missed being with the kids and how much he's looking forward to being in the show."

"Aw, I'm so glad. Maybe God is working on him."

"No doubt. He's also using this situation with Mom—and the play—to accomplish something pretty amazing."

"Sounds like it." Tangie turned her attention back to the kids, who were now scattered every which way across the stage. "Boys and girls, we need to run though that scene again," she called out. "I noticed that some of you weren't standing in the right places and a few of you need to work on your projection skills. Give it your best. Okay?"

They hollered out a resounding, "Okay!" and she began again. Still, as the rehearsal plowed forward, Tangie's thoughts were a hundred miles away.

With a heavy heart, she did her best to focus on the kids.

❁

After the children departed, Gregg and Tangie spent some time cleaning up the mess the kids had left behind in the sanctuary. Then she headed to the office to use the copier. Gregg retreated to the choir room, taking a seat at the piano. Before touching his fingers to the keys, he made another quick call to Josh, and was grateful to hear his mom was now on her way home from the hospital.

Gregg's fingers pressed down on the ivory keys, and he felt instant relief. As the melody to one of his most recent compositions poured out of his fingertips, he reflected on the conversation he'd had with Dave about his mother less than a week ago. "Lord, I don't understand." He pounded out a few more notes. "Why don't you just reach down and touch her? Heal her? Why does she have to go through all of this?"

A few more notes rose and fell from the keys and then he stopped. Gregg stared at his trembling hands, realizing just how worked up he was. He shook his head, feeling anger rise to the surface like the foam on top of his coffee.

"What is it, Gregg?"

He turned as he heard Tangie's voice. She stood behind him, holding a stack of papers in her hand. When he shook his head again, she placed the papers on the top of the piano

453

then reached out and put her hands on his shoulders. He relaxed at her touch. Tangie offered a gentle massage as he returned to the keys once more. When he finally stopped playing, she whispered, "What has you so upset? The news about your mom, or something to do with the play?"

"Both." He played a few more notes, finally pausing again.

"I'm ready to listen whenever you want to talk."

This time, Gregg pulled his hands away from the keys. His thoughts shifted to the kids, then back to his mom.

"Might sound crazy," he said at last, "but when I see Cody, I see myself at that age." He turned to face Tangie, emotion welling inside of him.

"You were rowdy and unmanageable and sang in twelve keys at once?" The laugh lines around her eyes told him she didn't quite believe his story. "I'm sorry, but after getting to know you, I'd have to say that's a pretty tough sell. Not buying it."

"No. Just the opposite. But I was the kid from the single-family home with the mother who never seemed to fit in." He paused a moment then whispered, "Did you hear about his mom?"

"Brenna?" Tangie took a seat on the piano bench next to Gregg. "What about her?"

"You know about her wedding and all that."

"Right." Tangie smiled. "Your mom is doing the wedding cake."

Gregg sighed. "Not anymore. Cody took me aside after the rehearsal and told me the wedding is off. Phillip took off to Minnesota without so much as a word of warning to either of them. He sent Brenna an e-mail after he arrived."

"Oh, that poor woman." Tangie rested her head against Gregg's. "And Cody. I can't even imagine how he must feel."

"I can." He drew in a deep, calculated breath as the memories flooded over him. "I grew up in the same situation basically, but back then, people in churches weren't always as kind to single moms. I'm not sure you would believe me if I told you some of the stuff we went through."

"Surely that didn't happen here. . .in Harmony?"

"No, I grew up in a small town called Wallisville, not far from here. Just small enough for everyone to know everyone's business, if you know what I mean."

Tangie laughed. "Harmony feels like that to me, after living in Atlantic City, then the Big Apple."

"Well, I'm talking about a group of people who weren't as kind as the people from Harmony. Instead of befriending my mother, they judged her. They were pretty harsh, actually."

"Whoa." After pausing for a moment, she added, "I know what it feels like to be judged, trust me. Been through my share of that."

A pang of guilt shot through him, and for good reason. Hadn't he once made assumptions about her, based on her appearance?

"Here's the thing. . ." He rested his palms against the edge of the piano bench and peered into her eyes. "My mom wasn't married when she had me."

"Right, I know. She told me all about that." Tangie nodded. "But that's not so uncommon these days, and it's certainly not the fault of the child."

"Oh, that's not what I was getting at. It's just that I was always looking for a father figure. Kind of like Cody." Gregg leaned back in his seat to finish the story. "My mom married Josh's dad when I was three. My dad never even stuck around to see me born. To my knowledge, he has no idea who I am or where I am."

"I–I'm sorry, Gregg."

He shrugged it off. "Anyway, when Mom married Steve, she was already pregnant with Josh. They had him a few months later, but the marriage ended before his first birthday, so it was a double slam dunk. I *finally* had someone to play a fatherly role and he didn't stick around. That's why. . ." He groaned. "That's why I empathize so much with Cody. It has nothing to do with his ability to sing, or the lack thereof. It's just his situation."

"Well, let me ask you a question," Tangie said, the tenderness in her voice expressing her concern. "Your mom told me a little of this, but she mentioned a couple of specific people who took an interest in you."

"What do you mean?"

"I mean, you eventually got your life on the right track. And you figured out you could sing. Who were those people who took the time to pour into your life? Who led you to the Lord? Who stirred up your gifts?"

"Oh, that's easy. One of the men in our church always treated me kindly. Mr. Jackson. It was through his witness that I came to know Jesus as my Savior. And as for the music, I have my sixth grade choir teacher, Mrs. Anderson, to credit with that. She went to our church, too." As he spoke her name, a rush of feelings swept over him. He hadn't thought about her in years. "To this day, I still remember the joy in her eyes as she talked to me about music and the tenderness in her voice as she responded to my never-ending questions."

Tangie looked at him with interest. "Okay. So, she saw a spark of something in you and fanned it into a flame."

"Right. I remember the day she asked my mother to come to one of those parent-teacher meetings. She told my mom that I was born to sing, that I'd been given a gift."

"Sounds like she and Mr. Jackson played a pretty big role in your life."

"Actually. . ."—Gregg felt tears well up in his eyes as he thought about it—"I used to credit them with saving my life. I was at a crossroads that year. I was going to go one way or the other. And they caught me just in time to point me down the right road. The right road for me, I mean."

"Wow. That's pretty amazing. God's timing is perfect."

"It is." *Thank You, Lord. How often I forget.*

"Okay, well let's go back to talking about Cody, then," Tangie said, her eyes now glowing. "We just need to figure out what his real gift is, so we can begin to stir it."

"Well, he's not a singer, that's for sure." Gregg groaned. "Not even close."

"He does have some minor acting ability."

"Acting up, you mean." Gregg grinned.

"Well, that, too. I could probably turn him into an actor if I could just keep him focused, but I haven't been able to do that," Tangie admitted. "Have you ever heard him talk about anything else?"

"I know he wanted to play baseball last year, but his mom couldn't afford to sign him up. I heard all about it."

"Really?" Tangie's eyes widened in surprise. "Well, I'm not a huge sports fan—haven't really had time to focus on any of them—but it might be fun to test the waters with Cody. When does the season start?"

"Oh. This coming week, I think. I saw a poster at the grocery store just last night."

"Well, here's an idea. If his mom can't afford to sign him up, why don't we raise the funds through the church's benevolence ministry and do it ourselves?"

"Baseball?" Gregg groaned. "I'm terrible at baseball. Don't even like to watch it. It's so. . .slow."

"I know. I feel the same way, but we're probably biased. Besides, I'm not asking you to *play* baseball, just to watch Cody do it. Help him discover his dream. If it is his dream, I mean." Tangie laughed. "It's so hard for me, as an artist, to understand the love of sports. But I suppose some people are as passionate about baseball and basketball as I am about acting and singing."

Gregg shook his head. "Crazy, right?"

"Very. But I definitely think this is something we can do. His mom is probably plenty distracted right now, and I know her finances are probably tapped out, like so many other single moms. We can do this for her. Don't you think?"

Gregg didn't have to think about it very long. "It's the perfect idea. We should do it. And when we do. . ." He looked at her with a smile. "He's going to need someone in the crowd, cheering him on. Want to come to a few practices with me?"

Tangie paused. "If. . .if I'm still here."

Gregg's heart hit the floor. "Are you still thinking of leaving?"

She released a sigh as she gazed at him with pain in her eyes. "I don't know, Gregg. If you'd asked me a couple weeks ago, I would've said yes in a heartbeat. I have so many opportunities waiting for me in New York. But now. . ." She shrugged. "Now I'm not sure which way to turn. But I promise to pray about it."

"Me, too." In his heart, Gregg wanted to add, "I'll pray that God keeps you here, in Harmony." However, he knew better. Tangie needed to chase after her dreams, too.

Even if they didn't include him.

Chapter 18

The week before the Easter performance, the kids met with Tangie and Gregg for their first dress rehearsal. Although Gramps had worked long and hard on building the set pieces, he hadn't quite finished several of them. And though the kids had been told to have all of their costumes ready, many did not. Tangie ran around like a chicken with her head cut off—ironic, in light of the many chicken costumes—looking for feathers, rabbit ears, and so forth. She tried to keep her cool but found it difficult.

In fact, she couldn't think of one thing that had gone as planned, and now that the performance date was approaching, Tangie had to wonder if she'd made a mistake in promising she could pull this off.

As she paused to pin a tiny microphone on a little girl, her thoughts gravitated to a call she'd received just this morning from Marti in New York, urging her to come back for auditions for *A Woman in Love*. Tangie's heart twisted within her as she contemplated the possibilities.

"Vincent says he's had his eye on you for two years," Marti had said. "He thought you did a great job in *Brigadoon* and wants to see you audition for the role of Gina in his new play. You're coming, right? This is the opportunity of a lifetime, Tangie. It's what you've waited for—the lead in a Broadway show."

"I don't know." Tangie's response had been hesitant, at best.

It sounded wonderful, of course, especially in light of the chaos she was facing with the kids. But every time she thought about leaving Gregg. . .well, the lump that rose in her throat grew harder and harder to swallow. She'd fallen for him, from his schoolboy haircut to his geeky tennis shoes. She loved him, and there was no denying it.

Of course, they hadn't really had time to develop their relationship. Who had time to date with a show under way? But if she stayed in Harmony after the production, there would be plenty of time to see where life—and love—might take them. Right?

Oh, Lord, show me what to do. I don't want to miss You this time. If this opportunity on Broadway is what You have for me, then speak clearly, Lord. But if I'm supposed to stay here. . .

The road back to New York might not be a long one, but from where she stood, it seemed like a million miles.

"Miss Tangie!" Cody's scream startled Tangie back to reality.

"W–what, honey?"

"I can't go out there wearing this costume." He pointed to his chicken suit, and a sour expression crossed his face.

Tangie tried to hide her smile as she responded. "Why not?"

"My friends will make fun of me." He plopped down on his bottom on the stage. "Besides, I think I'm getting sick. I have the flu." He sneezed, but she could tell it was forced.

"Well, I'll tell you what," she said, "if you will do this one show dressed as a chicken, I promise never to cast you in a part like this again."

"I don't want to be in any show again," he muttered, pulling at his feathers. "When will people get that?"

Oh, she got it all right. And she had a wonderful surprise for him as soon as the rehearsal ended—a full scholarship to play baseball. She could hardly wait to tell him. And if he chose not to do another show, that would be fine by her, as long as he got to do the things he longed to do, develop the gifts he wanted to develop. But, for now, the boy was going to play a chicken, whether the idea settled well with him or not.

Minutes later, Tangie and Gregg prayed with the kids. Then it was time for the rehearsal to begin. Darla, who'd been looking a little pale today, sat at the piano, ready to play the intro music. The song sounded great. At the end of it, Tangie turned to Gregg and gave him a thumbs-up. He responded with a smile.

At this point, Margaret Sanderson moved to center stage, dressed as a baby chick, ready to deliver her opening lines. Her expression was clean, and her lines were flawless. However, a couple of the kids who followed bumbled theirs pretty badly. Tangie stopped the rehearsal to say something to the cast.

"Kids, I told you we would be *lines off* today."

Cody raised his hand. "What does lines off mean?"

Tangie groaned. "It means you can't use your scripts anymore. The lines are supposed to be memorized."

A round of "Oooh's" went up from the cast, and Tangie slapped herself in the head. She should've explained the term.

"How many of you know your lines?" she asked.

Annabelle and Margaret raised their hands.

"Anyone else?"

A couple of others half raised theirs. Tangie sighed then went back to directing the rehearsal. When it came time for Annabelle to sing her solo, Tangie breathed a sigh of relief. Surely this would redeem the day. Or not. Ironically, Annabelle sounded a little. . .strange.

"Everything okay, honey?" Tangie asked, trying not to overreact.

The child pointed to her throat. "I feel a little scratchy, and it hurts when I swallow."

"Oh no." Tangie shook her head. "Well, have your mom talk with me after the rehearsal." She would tell her to have Annabelle gargle with warm salt water and drink hot tea with lemon. Tricks of the trade for actors who'd overused their voices. In the meantime, they'd better get back to work. The show must go on, after all!

☙

Gregg watched Tangie at work, his heart heavy. With just one week till the production, he had to face the inevitable. She would be leaving him soon, going back to New York. Every fiber of his being cried out for her to stay, but he would never suggest it. No, he of all people understood what it meant to respond to the call of God. If the Lord was calling Tangie to New York, she had to go.

On the other hand, the whole New York thing might just be a distraction, right? Should he mention that? Maybe if he told her that he loved her. . .

No. He wouldn't do that. If she stayed, he wanted it to be because the Lord had spoken, not because Gregg had spoken.

But I do love her.

As he watched her work with the children, he realized his feelings—once small—had grown into a wildfire. Listening to the sound in her voice as she soothed Cody's ruffled feathers. Watching her as she diligently poured into Margaret's life, in spite of the youngster's attitude. Observing the way she continued to nurture the gifts in little Annabelle's life.

Yes, Tangie was truly one of the most amazing women he'd ever met, and easy to love.

But he couldn't tell her. Not yet, anyway.

Chapter 19

Two days before the show, Tangie received a phone call from Annabelle's mother. She could tell by the sound of her voice that something was amiss.

"I'm afraid our little lamb is really sick," Annabelle's mom explained.

"No! What's happened?"

"I don't know. It started out as some sort of virus, I guess. I did everything you said. She gargled with warm salt water and drank hot tea. We've been loading her up on vitamin C and even making her drink orange juice, which she doesn't like. But every day is worse than the day before. What started out as a scratchy throat is now full-blown laryngitis. She can't speak a word."

"Yikes." Tangie wanted to dive into one of those, "Oh, man! What are we going to do now?" speeches but stopped herself short of doing so. *It's not about the show*, she reminded herself. *It's about the kids.*

Instead of saying too much, she simply offered up a few kind words. "Please tell Annabelle how sorry I am. I hope she feels better."

"I will. And please don't give her part away just yet. We're going to keep her home from school for the next two days, so I'm hoping that will help," Mrs. Lawrence said. "But I wanted to let you know so that you can begin to look for an understudy. . .just in case."

"Right. Good idea."

As she ended the phone conversation, Tangie's mind reeled. An understudy? At this late date? Which of the children was savvy enough to pick up the role this late in the game?

Really, only one person made sense. But Tangie would have to eat a little crow to make this work. She picked up the phone and punched in Margaret Sanderson's number. The child's mother answered on the third ring.

"Mrs. Sanderson, this is Tangie Carini from the church."

"Yes?"

"I, um, have a little problem and I'm hoping you and Margaret can help me with it."

"Oh?" She could read the curiosity in the woman's voice. "What's happened?"

Tangie went on to explain the predicament, finally asking to speak to Margaret. When the child came on the phone, she listened quietly and then responded with words that stunned Tangie. "But Annabelle needs to do her part! She's the best at it. Her song is bee-*you*-tee-ful!"

Tangie laughed. "You're right. It is."

"How can I be the narrator and the littlest sheep, too?" Margaret asked.

"Oh, that's easy. The narrator costume covers you from head to toe. It's also very tall, so you look bigger in it. The little sheep costume is completely different. I don't think the audience will even realize it's the same person."

"So, you're saying I get to do both parts?" Margaret's voice began to tremble. "Both? Not just one?"

"If Annabelle can't be there, yes."

"Mom! Guess what!" Margaret hollered. "They want me to do two different parts." She returned to the phone, sounding a little breathless. "But I don't know Annabelle's song. Not very well, I mean."

"Can you meet me at the church in an hour? We'll go over it then."

"Okay. I'll ask my mom." The youngster hollered once again, finally returning to the phone with, "She says it's fine. We'll see you in an hour." After a pause, Margaret said, "Oh, and Miss Tangie..."

"Yes, honey?"

"I hope Annabelle gets to do her part. I'm fine with the narrator. Really I am."

Tangie smiled all the way to her toes. "Oh, honey, I'm so proud of you. And I have to tell you, you're doing an awesome job with your part. I couldn't be prouder."

As she ended the call, Tangie realized just how true those words were. Margaret had come such a long way. Then again, they'd all come a long way.

Oh, but what a great distance they had left to go!

❀

Gregg sat on a bar stool at the bakery, chatting with his mom as she made some of her famous homemade cinnamon rolls.

"Mom, can I ask you a question?"

"Sure, son." She continued her work but glanced up at him with a smile. "What's up?"

"I love you so much, but I'm worried about you."

"I know you are, but I'm going to be just fine."

"Still, with all you're going through, why don't you just sell off this place? Kick back and relax a little? You deserve it."

"W–what?" She looked at him, a horrified expression on her face. "Close down Sweet Harmony? But why?"

"The shop has brought in all of the money you could need to retire in style." He shrugged. "You could live stress-free for the rest of your life. I think it would be good for you. All of this work is...well, it's work. And Josh and I want you to be able to take it easy."

"But honey, I'm only sixty-one. I'm not ready to retire yet. Besides..." Her eyes filled with tears. "Coming here every morning gives me a reason to get out of bed. People need me. And I need this shop. It's..." She shook her head. "It's keeping me going. I'm surprised you can't see that."

Immediately, shame washed over Gregg. He'd never considered the fact that his mom would respond with such passion. "Ah. I'm sorry I brought it up. We just want the best for you, I promise."

"I know you do, honey, but this *is* the best for me. If I keep my body busy, then my mind stays busy, too. If my mind stays busy, then there's no time left over to..."

"To worry?"

"Yes." She nodded then stretched out the dough for the cinnamon rolls, adding cinnamon, sugar, and butter before rolling them. "It's all part of this great plan I've got for getting through this. Keep working. That's the answer."

"Working helps keep your mind occupied," he said. "But Mom, there's really only one answer to getting through this, and it has nothing to do with work. It's—"

"No lectures, Greggy." She turned to him with a warning look in her eye. "We've been through this. I don't mind hearing you talk about all of the things this God of yours has done for you, but I've managed pretty well without Him for the first sixty years of my life and I'll do just fine for the next sixty."

She gave him a wink, but it didn't ease the pain in his heart. What could he do to get through to her?

Just love her, Gregg. Just keep on loving her.

Chapter 20

The afternoon of the final dress rehearsal, Tangie's nerves were a jumbled mess. The kids somehow made it through the show, but there were problems all over the place. Margaret seemed really unsure of herself in Annabelle's part, so she dropped quite a few lines. Darla wasn't feeling well, so Gregg had to play the piano in her place. The set was still incomplete, and some of the costumes still needed work. Tangie didn't know when she'd ever been more stressed or *less* ready to pull off a show.

As the rehearsal continued, Tangie offered up a plea to the Lord for both His mercies and His favor. She also spent a lot of time muttering "The show must go on" under her breath.

The rehearsal ended soon enough and Tangie prayed with the children then handed out flyers with instructions for tomorrow's curtain call. She went over her notes one last time before releasing them. "Be here an hour before curtain. Have your hair and makeup done ahead of time. Get into costume immediately upon arrival. Meet in the choir room for vocal warm-up and prayer. Do everything you're told to do when you're told to do it."

"I'm never gonna remember all of that stuff," Cody muttered.

"That's why I've given you the flyer," Tangie explained. "Just make sure your parents read it. Oh, and kids. . .spend some time praying for our performance and for the people who will come to see it. That's the most important thing we can do."

That last part hit her especially hard. There would be people in the audience who didn't normally attend church. Some who had never heard the gospel message before. Would they really see the heart of the Good Shepherd shining through in her little play? Could a silly production about bunnies and baby chicks touch people's lives?

Suddenly, she wasn't so sure. All of her confidence faded away, leaving behind only doubt.

As they rose from their places on the stage, Tangie used her most animated stage voice to holler, "Break a leg!"

Cody, who'd taken off running the other direction, turned back to look at her with a questioning look on his face. "Huh?"

Tangie hollered out, "Cody, be careful! The set pieces still aren't finished and I don't want you to—" She never got to say the words "hurt yourself." Cody tripped over a piece of wood behind one of the flats and down it came on top of him, the canvas ripping straight in half.

He stood silent and still in the middle of the torn piece, his eyes as wide as saucers. All around the other children froze in place.

"I'm sorry, Miss Tangie." He groaned and slapped himself in the head. "But I told you I'm no good at this. I don't belong on the stage." He rubbed his ankle. "Besides, you *told* me to break my leg."

Tangie groaned then rushed to his side to make sure he was okay. Convinced he was, she finally dismissed him. Ready to turn her attention to the ripped backdrop, she switched gears. With Gramps's help, they would get the rest of the set pieces ready before the show.

Less than a minute into the process, she heard her grandmother's voice ring out.

"Tangerine! Yoo-hoo!"

She looked up as Gran-Gran approached the stage, carrying a small box. "I, um, need to talk with you about these programs, honey." She handed one to Tangie, who looked at the cover and smiled.

"Oh, they turned out great."

"Yes and no."

"Yes and no?" Tangie looked at the cover again.

"Well, open one and see what I mean."

Tangie opened the program, realizing right away the text on the inside was upside down. "Oh, yikes."

"The printer sends his apologies," Gran-Gran said with a shrug.

"Can't he redo them?"

"Unfortunately, he has a big order for another church in town and doesn't have time. But there's some good news."

Tangie handed the program back to her grandmother. "I could use some good news, trust me."

"He gave them to us for half price."

"Well, yippee." Tangie sighed. "I guess we don't have much choice, do we?"

"Look at the bright side. . ." Gran-Gran paused for a few seconds, her brow wrinkled.

"What's that?" Tangie asked.

"I'm trying to think of one." Her grandmother laughed. "But nothing's coming to me."

Tangie knelt to fix the torn backdrop, seaming the backside with heavy tape. However, just a few minutes into it, she heard Gregg's voice ring out from the auditorium. "Tangie, I hate to tell you this. You have no idea how much I hate to tell you this." He climbed the steps to the stage.

With exhaustion eking from every pore, Tangie looked up at him. "What's happened now?"

"It's Darla."

Tangie's heart quickened. "Darla?" She put down the roll of tape and looked into Gregg's eyes. "What's happened to her? She hasn't been in an accident or anything, has she?"

"No, nothing like that." Gregg shook his head. "It's her appendix. They've taken her to surgery to remove it. Doctor says if they'd waited another day it could've been deadly."

"No! Oh, Gregg." Tangie crumpled onto the floor, and the tears started. "What are we going to do? How in the world can we pull this off without Darla? We can't have live music without a musician." On and on she went, bemoaning the fact that the show couldn't possibly go on without the pianist.

Finally, when she regained control of her senses, Tangie sighed. "I'm so sorry. That was completely heartless. I should be saying how bad I feel for Darla, and instead I'm thinking only of myself."

"Well, not only of yourself." Gregg gave her a sympathetic look. "You're thinking of the kids. And the parents. And the other musicians. And the audience. And then, maybe, at the bottom of the list, yourself."

"Right." Tangie shook her head then whispered, "I give up."

"W–what?"

"You heard me." She looked at him, determination setting in. "I give up. I can't do this. I'm not cut out to handle this much pressure."

"B–but. . .whatever happened to 'The show must go on'? Doesn't that stand for anything?"

"There's a time to admit defeat, Gregg, and this is it. Our leading lady has laryngitis, our set is in pieces, Cody very nearly broke his leg when he tripped earlier, the programs are upside down, and now Darla can't be here to play the piano for the show."

"Anything else?"

"Yes." She stared at him with tears now flowing. "The drama director is having a nervous breakdown!"

He joined her on the floor and opened his arms to comfort her, but she wasn't having any of it. No, sir. Not today. Today she just wanted everyone to go away and leave her alone.

※

Gregg watched all of this, completely mesmerized. First of all, he'd never seen a grown woman throw a tantrum like this before. He found it almost comical. Entertaining, at the very least. Still, he did his best to hide any hint of a smile. Might just send Tangie over the edge. Looked like she was pretty close already.

Chapter 21

On the Saturday of the big show, Tangie was a nervous wreck. Before she left for the church, she spent some time praying. Only the Lord could pull this off.

She rode to the church with her grandparents, script in hand. Nestled beside her on the back car seat, the box holding the football-sized chocolate egg. Taffie had sent it, along with a note reading, BREAK A LEG. Tangie was half tempted to pick up the phone and tell her about Cody's mishap. Maybe she'd have time for that later. Right now, they had a show to put on.

After the Easter egg hunt, anyway.

She arrived at the church to find Ashley and other children's workers hard at work, putting out Easter eggs in designated areas, according to the ages of the children. Tangie looked at her with a smile. "How's it going?"

Ashley smiled. "Great!" She drew near and whispered, "Have you heard my news?"

"News?" Tangie shifted her script to the other arm and shook her head. "What is it?"

Ashley displayed her left hand, wiggling her ring finger so that there would be no doubt. A sparkling diamond adorned that finger, nestled into a beautiful white-gold setting.

"Oh, Ashley! You're engaged?"

When she nodded, Tangie's joy turned to sorrow. "Does. . .does that mean you're leaving?"

"Nah. Paul and I have talked about it. He has his own web-design business. He can do that here, in Harmony. So, it looks like we'll settle in here, raise a family. You know." She gave Tangie a wink.

Tangie's stomach tumbled to her toes. *She's assuming that's what Gregg and I will do, too. But I'll be in New York, not Harmony.*

Tangie forced her thoughts back to the present. "I'm thrilled for you!" After a few more words of congratulations, she heard Gregg's voice sound from behind her. Tangie turned around, smiling as she caught a glimpse of him.

"Ready for the big day?" he asked, drawing near.

"As ready as I'll ever be." She sighed, and he gave her an inquisitive look.

"What?"

"Well, I guess I should just admit that you were right all along. Doing a play with kids is a lot tougher than it looks. And all of the Broadway experience in the world didn't prepare me for this."

Ashley laughed. "Nothing can prepare you for the chaos of kids, but they're worth it."

"They are."

"And I heard there's some good news where Annabelle's concerned," Gregg said.

"Yes." Tangie grinned. "Her mom called this morning and said she's got her voice back. Said it was a miracle. When Annabelle went to bed last night things weren't any better. But this morning. . ."

"Was a brand-new day." Ashley laughed. "Oh, God is good, isn't He?"

"He is." Tangie smiled—and all the more as guests started arriving. Within the hour, the whole church property was alive with activity. She had never seen so many children. And the Easter baskets! Nearly every child held one.

Except the kids in the production, of course. They hadn't come to hunt for Easter eggs. They were here to do a show.

Tangie glanced at her watch. One o'clock. Time to meet with the cast and crew in the choir room for final instructions. She and Gregg made their way inside, finding a lively crowd waiting for them. She managed to get the kids quieted down, and Gregg opened in prayer. Then he nodded for Tangie to begin.

"Kids, I know you've missed out on some of the activities outside," she told them with a playful smile, "but it will be worth it when that auditorium fills up with neighborhood kids."

Cody raised his hand. "My best friend is here. I already told him I'm wearing a chicken suit and he didn't laugh, so I don't think I'll have to give him a black eye or anything."

"Well, that's nice." Tangie stifled a laugh.

Annabelle's hand went up, too. "My aunt came and she brought my cousins. They've never been in a church before. My mom says it's kind of like a miracle."

Tangie's heart swelled with joy. "It is like a miracle." *Lord, You're proving what I've said all along. . .the arts are a great way to reach out to people who don't know You. Use this production, Father. Reach those who haven't heard the gospel message before.*

"Kids, let's pray before we do the show." Tangie instructed them to stand and get into a circle. Some of the boys were a little hesitant to join hands, but eventually they formed a large, unified ring. At this point, she encouraged the children to pray, not just for the show, but also for those in attendance. By the end of the prayer time, Tangie had tears in her eyes. For that matter, Gregg did, too. From across the room, she gave him a wink then mouthed the words, "Break a leg." He nodded then ushered the children toward the stage.

❀

Gregg took his seat at the piano, stretched his arms, and then whispered a prayer that all would go well. He could take Darla's place as chief musician, ensuring the show would go on, but that was where his role ended. Everything from this point forth was up to the Lord. Would He take the little bit they'd given Him and use it to His glory? Only time would tell.

The lights went down in the auditorium, but not before Gregg saw his mother slip in the back door. He whispered a quiet, "Thank You, Lord," then began to play the opening number.

The stage lights came up, and the colorful set came alive. The colors had seemed bright before, but not like this. Maybe it was the energy of the crowd. There were, after all, over three hundred elementary-aged children in the room. Everything seemed brighter and happier.

In the center of the stage, the spotlight hit the giant Easter egg. Then, as the music progressed, the egg began to crack from the inside out. "Good girl, Margaret," he whispered. "Come on out of that protective shell of pride you've been wearing. Show 'em what you've got."

She did just that. As she emerged dressed as a baby chick, the audience came alive with laughter and joy. "It's a chicken!" one little girl hollered.

Not swayed, Margaret delivered her line with perfection. Then Annabelle entered the stage. Oh, how cute she looked in that little lamb costume. Tangie had been right. The kids loved this sort of thing. Annabelle opened her mouth to sing, and a holy hush fell over the audience. In fact, by the end of the song, Gregg could hardly see the keys. His eyes were, after all, filled with tears.

❀

When the show ended, Tangie rushed around backstage, congratulating the children and thanking them for doing such a terrific job. When the last of the kids had finally gone, she plopped down into a chair, completely dumbfounded. "You did it, Lord. You pulled it off." And, with the exception of a couple of minor glitches, the show had been as close to perfect

465

as any show could be. "Lord, I believe in miracles. I've just witnessed one." She paused for a moment to think of all He had done. More than anything else, the Lord had convinced Tangie that she did, indeed, have a call on her life to work with kids. Maybe it hadn't always been easy. . .but it had been worth it. No doubt about that.

"A penny for your thoughts." Tangie looked up as she heard a familiar voice. Gregg's mom stood in front of her, a broad smile on her face. "I liked your bunny show."

Tangie laughed. "Seriously?"

"Seriously. Lots to chew on. I'll have to get back with you on all of that. But I wanted you to know I think you and Gregg did an awesome job." Penny leaned down and whispered, "And didn't he sound great on the piano?"

"He sure did. You should hear him on Sundays. He's the best." Tangie stopped herself from saying more. Didn't want to push the envelope. Still, Penny was right. Gregg had saved the day by stepping into the role of pianist.

Penny glanced at her watch. "Well, I've got to scoot. Thank goodness Sarah was home from school and could babysit the store for me this afternoon."

"I'm so glad." Tangie smiled.

"You coming in on Monday?" Penny asked. "There's going to be a lot of cleanup."

Tangie gave a hesitant nod. "M—maybe. I'll get back to you on that."

Penny nodded but took off in a hurry.

Tangie rose and started cleaning up the stage area. As she reached the farthest corner, a couple of familiar voices rang out.

"Tangerine!"

She turned, stunned to see her sisters and their husbands standing there. "Taffie? Candy!" Tangie sprinted their way, her heart now beating double time as she saw her little niece cradled in Taffie's arms. "What are you doing here?"

"You didn't think Gran-Gran would let us get away with not seeing the show, did you?" Candy said, her words framed in laughter.

"And besides, I wanted Callie to see her Aunt Tangie in her first church performance," Taffie added, passing the darling baby girl off to Tangie.

She held the beautiful infant, her heart suddenly quite full. "Did you come alone, or. . ."

"Oh, you mean Mom and Dad?" Candy shrugged. "They're in Texas this week. But Mom sends her love. And Dad says—"

"Break a leg!" they all shouted in unison.

"So, you saw the show?" Tangie gave her sisters a hesitant look. When they nodded, she asked, "W—what did you think?"

"You're kidding, right?" Candy shook her head. "It was amazing, Tangie. I got it. Every bit of symbolism. Every nuance. It was all there. And the kids were amazing."

"So was their director," Taffie added with a wink.

"Yes, you're a natural," Candy agreed as she reached to give her a hug. "You were born for the theater." She said the word *theater* in an exaggerated British accent, making everyone laugh.

Tangie wanted to ask her sisters' opinion, whether she should—or shouldn't—go to New York to audition for *A Woman in Love*. But this wasn't the time. No, this was the time to cuddle her niece, chat with her sisters. . .and introduce everyone to one very special music director.

Chapter 22

The Monday after the big show, Tangie received a call from a very hyper Marti.

"You're coming home, right? Vincent called again, and he said to tell you to be at the Marlowe Theater at two o'clock on Wednesday afternoon. That's the final day of the auditions. In my opinion, it's better to go last than first. You'll leave a lasting impression on him that way."

"I guess." Tangie sighed. "I've been praying about it, Marti, but I'm just not sure." Every time she prayed, images of Gregg's face popped up in front of her. And the children. . .she would miss them something fierce. She would miss Penny, too. And her grandparents. Would it really be worth it—to trade in the people she now loved. . .for a production?

"We're not talking forever," Marti reminded her. "It's just one show. And what can it hurt to audition? You don't have to bring all of your stuff when you come. Just bring a bag or two. Come tomorrow and stay at my place for a few days. You can make your decision after you get here. If you get the part, maybe that will be a sign you're supposed to be back here. If you don't. . ." Marti paused. "Well, I don't want to think about that because I really want you back in New York. But you can decide for yourself, okay?"

"Okay." Tangie realized this was really the only thing that made sense. If she didn't go back to New York and audition for this role, she'd never know for sure whether she belonged in the Big Apple or in Harmony. And, if she didn't at least give this a shot, she'd never know if she had what it took to be a leading lady.

Tangie settled down onto the bed, reaching for one of the programs from the children's musical. The kids had signed it—using their childish scribbles to offer up their thanks for the role she'd played. She grinned as she saw Cody's signature, followed by, *Break a Leg!* And then there was Annabelle's childish script, followed by, *Thank you for believing in me.* Her favorite, however, was Margaret's. After the beautiful, well-placed signature, the tempestuous little girl had written, *This was the best play ever! Thanks for letting me be the narrator!*

"Lord, I'm going to miss these kids. And my grandparents. And. . ."

She sighed. Most of all, she would miss Gregg. She'd miss the look of disbelief in his eyes when she said something outlandish. She'd miss the way they harmonized together. Most of all, she'd miss the way he looked deep into her soul, challenging her to be a better person.

Determined to get through this, Tangie made her way to the living room. She found her grandparents watching TV.

"I, um, I need to talk to you."

"Not now, honey." Her grandmother shooed her away with the wave of a hand. "We're watching *The Price Is Right.*"

"Yes, but. . .I need to tell you something."

Gran-Gran looked up, and for the first time Tangie noticed the tears in her eyes. "We know you do, honey. But not right now." The way her grandmother emphasized the last four words stopped Tangie cold.

Ah ha. She just doesn't want to face the fact that I'm leaving. Well, fine. I'll talk to them later. Right now, she needed to head over to Sweet Harmony to let Penny know about her decision. Then, of course, she had to talk to Gregg.

Every time she thought about telling him, Tangie felt a lump in her throat. The sting of tears burned her eyes. She'd fallen for him. No doubt about that. But then again, she always fell for the leading man. Right? What made this one different from the others?

She drove to town, noticing, for the first time, the green leaves bursting through on the trees. "Oh, Lord! I've been so busy with the show I almost missed it! Spring!"

Yes, everywhere she looked, the radiant colors of spring greeted her. They were in the blue waters of the little creek on the outskirts of town. They were in the tender white blossoms in the now-budding pear trees. Even the cars seemed more colorful than before, now that they weren't covered in dirty snow.

Yes, color had come to Harmony at the very time she had to leave.

"Stop it, Tangie. It's springtime in New York, too." She forced her thoughts to Manhattan as she pulled her car into the parking lot at Sweet Harmony. By the time she climbed out of the car, Tangie had a new resolve. "I can do this. What's the big deal, anyway?"

She pushed open the front door of the bakery, the bell jangling its usual welcome. Tangie drew in a deep breath and approached Penny, who was working behind the counter.

"Well, hey, kiddo. I wondered if you might come in today. Made up your mind yet? Are you staying or going?"

Talk about cutting to the chase. Penny was never one to mince words. Well, fine. She wouldn't either. "Penny, I hate to tell you this, but. . ."

"You're leaving for New York."

"Yes."

Penny set down the mound of dough she'd been kneading and gave Tangie a pensive look. "Well, look, kid, I've been preparing myself for it for weeks. I'll just put a sign in the window, and—"

"No, please don't do that. Not yet anyway." Tangie's nerves kicked in. "I'm going to New York, but I don't know if I'm going to stay. Auditions are on Wednesday, so I need to leave tomorrow. I should know something a few days later. Can you give me a week, Penny? I'll call if I'm not coming back."

"Sure." With the wave of a hand, Penny dismissed the idea. "I'll get Josh to help me till then. It won't hurt the boy to work with his mama. Go on and go to that audition. Might do you some good." She went to work washing out one of the mixing bowls. "'Course, if you stay in New York it'll break our hearts, but don't fret over that." She turned back and gave Tangie a wink. "Kidding, kiddo. You chase after your dreams."

"Thank you for understanding, Penny. I'm praying about what to do, but God hasn't really given me a clear answer." She glanced down at the tattoo on her wrist, pondering the little star. *Is this really where I'm supposed to go, God? To follow that star? To see where it leads me?*

Everything in Penny's demeanor changed at the mention of the word *God*. Her happy-go-lucky smile faded, and she exhaled. Loudly.

"What?" Tangie approached with a bit of hesitation.

"Well, since you brought up God and all. . ." Penny began to fidget.

"What about Him?"

"I just wanted to tell you something. I've been thinking a lot about this. That play you and Gregg put on with the kids. . .it was, well, it was great."

"Really?" Tangie's heart wanted to burst into song with this news.

Penny's eyes filled with tears. "This is going to sound nuts, but that scene where the little sheep has the conversation with the shepherd about wandering away from the fold. . ." Penny's eyes misted over. "I got it, Tangie. I understood what you were trying to say. I'm that little sheep."

"Yes." A lump rose in Tangie's throat, and she could hardly contain her emotions. "T–that's right."

"Let me ask you a question. Did you write that play with me in mind?"

Tangie smiled. "To be completely honest, no. I just wrote it with *people* in mind. God loves people, Penny. All people. And He desires that we love Him back. It's really pretty simple. That's why I used such a childlike platform to get that message across."

"So childlike an old fool like me could get it." Penny smiled as she gazed into Tangie's eyes. "Oh, by the way, thanks for letting Josh play the role of the shepherd. I haven't seen him this excited since I gave him that *Star Wars* lunch box in the second grade."

Tangie laughed. "He did a great job. And I think memorizing those lines about how much God loves His kids really did something to him."

"I think you're right." After a moment, Penny's brow wrinkled. "Seeing God as a shepherd really messed up my thinking, I'll have you know."

"It did?"

"Yes." Penny exhaled, pursed her lips, then said, "I never saw Him as kindhearted or loving before. I guess I always figured God was as mean spirited as some of the people who say they represent Him."

"He's not." Tangie shook her head. "And I'm sorry your experience with the church was painful. I can only tell you that the people I know who love the Lord are just the opposite of what you've described. They're loving and giving, and they accept people, no matter what." She gestured to her bright red hair, her tattoos, and then the tiny diamond stud in her nose. "I speak from experience. No one there has ever judged me."

"Except me."

The male voice sounded behind her, and Tangie turned to find Gregg standing there. He must've slipped in the back door, but when?

"W–what?" Tangie turned to face him.

"I judged you." He sighed. "I don't think I did it on purpose, but I'm pretty sure I didn't give you a fair shake in the beginning. I'm not sure why."

"My appearance?" she asked.

"I don't know. I think it's just that we're so opposite. It took me a while to adjust to the fact that I'd be working with someone who's my polar opposite."

"You two are about as different as singing rabbits and dancing chickens," his mother threw in. "But that's what makes relationships so interesting."

"Yes, opposites do attract." He took Tangie's hands in his and stared into her eyes. "But the real question is, can this relationship stand the test of time?"

※

Gregg's heart thump-thumped so loudly, he could hear it in his ears. He'd walked in at just the right moment—or maybe just the wrong moment, depending on how you looked at it. Tangie was leaving. She'd confirmed it. And he wouldn't stop her, though everything within him rebelled at the idea of losing her.

And all of that stuff his mom had said to Tangie about the play. Had she really come face-to-face with the Good Shepherd, thanks to a kids' Easter production? If so, then God had truly worked a miracle.

His mom gave him a wink then disappeared into the back room. Gregg took this as his cue. He wrapped Tangie in his arms, thankful there were no customers in the store.

"So, you're leaving tomorrow?" he whispered, leaning in to press a kiss onto her cheek.

"I am." She lingered in his arms, giving him hope.

He reached to brush a loose hair from her face.

"I'll never know what might've happened if I don't go."

"I understand. And I support you. It's killing me, but I support you."

Tangie gave him a playful pout. "You'll wait for me?"

"Wait for you? Hmm." He paused a moment, just to make her wonder, then grinned. "Till the end of time."

"Very dramatic. Spoken like a true theater person." Tangie winked then kissed the tip of his nose.

He wanted to grab her and give her a kiss convincing enough to stay put, but the bell above the bakery door jangled. A customer walked in. At that same moment, Gregg's mother reappeared from the back room.

"You two lovebirds need to go build your nest elsewhere." His mom snapped a dish towel at him. "I'm trying to run a business here."

"Mm-hmm." He nodded, gingerly letting go of Tangie's hands.

"I need to get to work, anyway," Tangie said, reaching for an apron. "This is going to be my last day. . .for a while, anyway."

"Last day." Gregg swallowed hard and settled onto a bar stool. If this was her last day, he wanted to spend every minute of it with her.

"Oh, but, Gregg, before I go." She turned to him with a winning smile. "There is one little thing you need to do."

"Oh?"

"Yes." She nodded, a hint of laughter in her eyes. "I seem to remember someone once promising he would eat a whole plateful of artichokes in front of the kids if the performance went well."

Gregg groaned, remembering. "You're going to hold me to that?"

"I am." Tangie nodded. "And, in fact, it might just be the thing that woos me back to Harmony. I'd pay money to see you eat artichokes."

"What? Artichokes?" Penny laughed. "This boy of mine can't stand artichokes."

"I know, I know." Gregg sighed. Still, he had promised. And Tangie had given him hope with her last statement, anyway. Maybe she would come back to Harmony. When the time was right. For that, he would eat all the artichokes in the state of New Jersey.

Chapter 23

Tangie made the drive to New York, her mind going a hundred different directions. She arrived in short order, marveling at the noise and fast-paced chaos she found. Had it always been this crazy?

Seeing Marti was such a thrill. They spent Tuesday afternoon visiting all of their favorite places—Hanson's Deli, the art museum, FAO Schwarz, and Macy's, of course.

On Wednesday morning, Tangie shifted gears. Before she even climbed out of bed, she ushered up a lengthy prayer, asking for God's will. She wouldn't dare make a move outside of it, not with so much at stake.

At one thirty, she caught a cab to the Marlowe Theater. At a quarter of two, she walked through the back doors into the familiar auditorium. At once, her heart came alive. Oh, how she'd missed this place! It captivated her, set something aflame inside of her.

She filled out an audition form, reached into her bag for her music and resume, and passed everything off to Vincent's assistant, a girl named Catherine. Then, when her name was called, Tangie walked to the center of the stage, ready to audition. She drew in a deep breath and sent one last silent prayer heavenward. Then the music began.

With as much confidence as she could muster, she sang the first few lines from "On My Own," one of her personal favorites. Closing her eyes, she allowed the melody to consume her. It felt so good to be back on the stage. And that Vincent hadn't cut the song short yet. That was a good sign.

Not only did he *not* cut her short, she actually sang the entire piece. When the music drew to a close, Tangie smiled in his direction. Even with the stage lights in her eyes, she could see the contented look in his eye. So far, so good.

"We'd like to hear you read, please," he said.

Catherine crossed the stage with a script in hand, which she passed off to Tangie.

"Start at the top of page 4 and read for Gina," Vincent said. "We're going to bring in one of the guys to read against you."

He looked around the empty auditorium and then shrugged. "What happened to our guys?"

Catherine gasped. "I'm sorry, Vincent. I really thought you said you were done with the guys until callbacks."

"Did I? I can't remember."

Tangie shrugged. "I can just read both parts if you like. Or maybe you could call out Harrison's lines."

Just then, a noise at the back of the auditorium startled her. With the stage lights in her eyes, she could barely make out the figure of a man walking down the aisle toward the stage.

Vincent rose and greeted him. "Perfect timing. You'll need to stand center stage next to this beautiful young woman to read for Harrison."

The man stopped, and Tangie squinted to see him better. Was. . .was that. . . ? No, it couldn't possibly be.

Just then, a familiar voice rang out. "You. . .you want me to read for a part?"

Gregg!

"Isn't that what you're here for?" The director sounded a little perturbed.

His voice rang out loud and clear. "Oh, well, actually I. . ." He climbed the steps leading to the stage and for the first time, came into full view.

Tangie gasped as she saw him. "Gregg, w–what are you doing here?"

"I. . ." He squinted against the bright lights then put his hand over his eyes.

"He's here to audition for Harrison," the director said, the impatience evident in his voice. The older man climbed the steps to the stage and pressed a script into Gregg's hand. "Top of page 4. Read Harrison's lines. We'll listen to you sing afterward."

"E–excuse me?" Gregg's face paled, and the script now bobbed up and down in his trembling hand.

"Just do what he says," Tangie whispered. "Please."

Gregg looked down at the script then began to read the lines, sounding a little stilted " 'Gina, I don't know any other way to say it. I've told you a hundred times in a hundred different ways. I love you.' " He looked up from the script, his eyes wide.

Tears filled Tangie's eyes as she took his hand in hers and read her line. " 'Sometimes we only see what we want to see. It's so hard to crack through that protective shell we all wear. So, maybe you've been saying it, but I didn't hear it. Does that make sense?' "

" 'Perfect sense.' " Gregg looked up from the script as he continued. " 'Sometimes we resist the very thing that's meant to be because it's different from what we're used to, or because we're afraid.' "

Tangie almost laughed aloud at the words. *Lord, what are You doing here?* Her hand trembled in Gregg's, but it had nothing to do with the audition.

He tossed the script on the stage and stared at her. "Tangie, I've been the world's biggest fool."

"Wait, that's not in the script!" the director hollered out.

"I should have told you that I loved you before you left. I drove all the way here just to say it." Gregg spoke with deeper passion than Tangie had ever heard before. Tears covered his lashes as the words poured out. "I don't know what took me so long. Guess I let fear get in the way."

"That makes two of us," she whispered, her voice filled with emotion. "I've been afraid to say it, too." The script slipped out of her hands and clattered to the floor.

"We're as different as night and day, just like my mom said. But, you are who you were born to be," he responded, taking both of her hands in his. "And so am I. But being without you these past two days has almost killed me. I can't eat. I can't sleep. I can't even play the piano anymore. Everything in me stopped functioning when you left, and I don't know what I can do to make things normal again."

Tangie smiled and squeezed his hand. "Oh, we're halfway to normal already, trust me."

He took her in his arms and cupped her chin in his palm. Such tenderness poured out of his eyes. She'd never known such powerful emotions.

"I love you, Tangie. I love every quirky, wonderful, unique thing about you. I love that you're different."

"Hey, now—"

"In a wonderful, glorious sort of way. And I love that you love me, even though I'm just a boring, predictable guy." He leaned into her, a passionate kiss following his words.

For a moment, time seemed to hang suspended. All that mattered was this man. *He loves me!* Tangie whispered the words, "*That* wasn't boring," in his ear then giggled.

They lingered in each other's arms, whispering words of sweetness. Until a voice rang out.

"Best version of that scene I've seen all day. Where have you two been all my life?"

Tangie opened her eyes, suddenly blinded by the stage lights. Squinting, she made out the face of the director. "Oh my goodness." How could she possibly make Vincent understand. . . they weren't acting!

"I love the way you took the lines and made them your own." The older man spoke in a gravelly voice. "Brilliant. No one else has taken the time to do it. And there's a chemistry between the two of you that's. . .well, wowza! We don't see a lot of that. People can act like they're in love, of course, but to actually pull off a convincing love scene? Almost impossible."

Tangie laughed until she couldn't see straight. Gregg joined her, of course. The only one who wasn't laughing was Vincent.

"I'm glad you think this is so funny," he said. "You're going to have to clue me in on whatever I've missed. But in the meantime, you've got the part." He looked at Tangie then shifted his gaze to Gregg. "And if this guy can sing half as well as he can act, he's got the part, too!"

Tangie's head began to swim, and the laughter continued. Then, quite suddenly, she stopped and looked Gregg in the eye. "Let me ask you a question."

"Shoot."

"You once said that I had issues with leading ladies, that I was secretly jealous of them."

Gregg groaned. "I wish I could take that back. I'm so sorry."

"No, you're missing my point." She grinned at him. "I just need to know one thing, Gregg Burke. Do you think I'm leading lady material?"

"Always have been and always will be."

"Okay, then." She turned back to the director with a smile. "In that case, forget the play." Tangie looked at Gregg with her heart overflowing as she spoke the only words that made sense.

"This girl's going back to Harmony."

Chapter 24

Tangie finished painting the set piece and stepped back to have a look at the stage. She smiled as she looked at the road sign she'd just put in place. One arrow pointed to Broadway, the other to Harmony, New Jersey. Perfect.

Gramps entered, covered in paint. "Do you think we'll get it done in time for the show? We're on at two, right?"

"Yes. Still not sure about the backdrop, though. Do you think it will be dry?"

"Won't make any difference if it's dry or not. The show must go on, honey." He walked out backstage, muttering all the while. "You're a theater person. I would think you'd know that. Doesn't matter if the set isn't built, if the costumes aren't ready, if the lines aren't memorized. The show goes on, regardless."

Tangie laughed until she couldn't see straight. *Thank You, Lord, for the reminder.*

"Honey, what are you doing in here?" Her mother's voice rang out.

"Yeah, don't you have a wedding to go to or something?" her older sister Taffie said with a laugh.

"Yes, I do." Tangie looked down at her hands and sighed as she realized they were still covered in paint. "I don't exactly look like a bride, though, do I?"

"You will soon enough," Candy said, drawing near. "But first we've got to get you into costume."

"Oh, it's no costume, trust me." Tangie sighed as she thought about the blissfully beautiful wedding dress her sisters had helped her choose. "This is one time I'm going with something traditional."

"Well, it's going to be the only thing traditional at this wedding," Candy said, coming up the aisle. "I've never known anyone who got married at a community theater before."

"You're a fine one to talk!" Tangie laughed. "You got married on an airstrip." She turned to Taffie. "And you got married on the beach."

"I guess all of the Carini girls went a different direction on their wedding day," Candy said with a giggle. "But I still think getting married in a theater—especially one this beautiful—tops them all."

"It's the perfect way to christen the building!" Tangie looked around the theater, marveling at the changes that had occurred over the last six months. The whole thing had been Penny's doing. She'd hung posters around town, asking for the community's support. And, once the funds started rolling in, the old Bijou movie house had morphed into the most beautiful community theater ever.

The artichoke thing had been a big hit, too. Tangie didn't mind taking the credit for that one. Folks had contributed up to a hundred dollars per artichoke. Gregg had downed nearly two dozen of them, all funds going to the new theater, of course. Then again, the artichokes didn't stay down long, but that part didn't matter. The money had come in, and the old movie house was now a fabulous place for folks in the town of Harmony to put on productions.

Tangie still marveled at the transformation.

Of course, she marveled at a good many transformations, of late. Take Penny, for instance. Now that her chemo treatments were behind her, she was feeling better. So much better, in fact, that she'd joined the church. She now thrived on providing sweets for the monthly women's tea. And Tangie had it on good authority that Penny also slipped Gramps free donuts for the Prime Timers. He wasn't complaining.

No, these days Gramps had little to complain about. He was too busy working on the theater and celebrating the fact that Tangie had come back. Well, that and driving Gran-Gran back and forth to auditions. She'd reluctantly agreed to be in the community theater's first performance of *The Sound of Music*. Tangie hadn't shared the news yet, but she'd be casting her grandmother in the role of the Mother Superior. What havoc that would wreak at home!

But no time to think about productions now! Only the one at two o'clock mattered today.

Tangie stepped back, looking at the fabulous décor on the stage. "All things bright. . ."

"And beautiful," her grandmother whispered, stepping alongside her. "It's fabulous, Tangerine. You've done a great job, and this is going to be the best wedding ever."

"I do believe you're right." Tangie turned with tears in her eyes. "I do believe you're right."

🌸

Gregg left the ball field at one fifteen, racing toward the theater. He hadn't wanted to miss Cody's game, of course, but there were more important things on his schedule today. His wedding, for instance.

Gregg pulled up to the theater, amazed to find so many cars out front. "Oh no. I hope I'm not later than I think." He leaped from the car, pausing to open the back door and grab his tuxedo and shoes.

When had his life become so chaotic? Where had all of the organization and structure gone? And then there was the wardrobe! These days, he was more likely to wind up wearing a chicken suit than a suit and tie.

Not that he was complaining. Oh no. Falling in love with Tangie meant falling in love with theater—lock, stock, and barrel. And there was no turning back, especially today, when he faced the performance of a lifetime.

Still, there would be no funny costumes on today's stage. They'd agreed to that. She would wear a white wedding gown—one he looked forward to seeing—and he would look top notch in coat and tails. Bridesmaids and groomsmen would wear traditional garb, as well. No, nothing to take away from the beauty of their marriage vows or the amazing work God had done in their lives. Besides, there were sure to be costumes in abundance over the years to come.

Gregg sprinted into the theater, pausing only for a moment to look at the stage. "Whoa." Talk about a transformation. Tangie and her grandfather had done it again. Then again, she always managed to pull rabbits out of hats. Sometimes symbolically, other times for real.

Gregg reached the men's dressing area backstage, finding Josh inside, already dressed.

"You had me worried, man." Josh grinned as he ushered Gregg inside then closed the door behind him.

"Sorry. Didn't want to miss Cody's game. You should see him, Josh. He's incredible. I think we've really discovered his true gifting."

Scrambling into his tux was the easy part. Getting the tie on was another matter. Thankfully, his mother rapped on the door just as he gave up. After he hollered, "Come in," she entered the room, her eyes filling with tears at once.

"Oh, Greggy." She shook her head. "You're quite dashing."

"Very theatrical response." He gave her a wink and she drew near to fix his tie. "I need you, Mom."

"It feels good to be needed." She worked her magic then stepped back and sighed. "That Tangie is a lucky girl."

"No, I'm the lucky one." Gregg paused, thinking of just how blessed he felt right now. In such a short time, the Lord had brought him his perfect match—someone who also turned out to be his polar opposite. What was it Tangie had said again? That God was always at work behind the scenes, doing things they couldn't see or understand?

Lord, it's true. You saw beyond my stiff, outward appearance to my heart, and You knew I needed someone like Tangie. She's perfect for me.

He allowed his thoughts to shift to the day they'd met. . .how she looked. What she was wearing. Then his thoughts shifted once again to that day in the diner when she'd shown up in that crazy hat. Funny, how he'd grown to love that hat over the months.

"Look at the time!"

Gregg snapped to attention at his mother's words. This was not the time for daydreams. Right now, he had a wedding to attend!

Tangie stood at the back of the theater, mesmerized by the crowd, the beauty of the stage, and the look of pure joy in her future husband's eyes. She thought back to her first impression of Gregg. What was it she'd told Gran-Gran, again? How had she described him over the phone that day? *"Sort of a geeky-looking guy? Short hair. Looks like his mother dressed him?"*

Oh, how her impressions had changed. Then again, the Lord had changed a great many things, hadn't He? He'd washed away any preconceived ideas of how a person should look or dress and dug much deeper—to the heart of the matter. And just as she'd predicted, He'd been working in the backstage areas of her life, fine-tuning both her career and her personal life.

And what a personal life! The familiar music cued up—the theme song from *A Woman in Love*, of course—and she took her father's arm, taking steps up the long aisle toward her husband-to-be. *Just stay focused. Just stay focused.*

Somehow they made it through the ceremony, though the whole thing flew by at warp speed. She spent the time in a beautiful whirlwind of emotions.

Finally, the moment came, one she and Gregg had kept secret from their friends and family for weeks. Darla took her seat at the piano and the familiar music for *Embraceable You* began. Tangie looked at her amazing husband with a grin. She mouthed the words, "You ready?" and he nodded.

Then, the two of them joined heart, mind, and voice. . .for a harmony sweeter than the town itself.

Epilogue

Ten Years Later

Tangie tucked her daughter, Guinevere, into bed and gave her a kiss on the forehead.

"So, is that the whole story, Mommy?" Gwen asked with an exaggerated sigh. "You met Daddy doing a play at the church?"

"That's right. We met doing a play, and we've done dozens of them since...at the church and the community theater."

"I love it when you and Daddy sing together. You sound bee-*you*-tee-ful! And your plays are so much fun. But"—the youngster's angelic face contorted into a pout—"when can *I* be in one of them?"

"Hmm, let's see." Tangie thought for a moment. "You're nearly seven now. I guess that's old enough to start acting. But only if you want to. Mommy and Daddy want you to be whatever you feel God is calling you to be."

The youngster's face lit up, and her brown eyes sparkled as she made her announcement. "I'm going to be an actress and a singer, just like Margaret Sanderson!"

Tangie had to laugh at that one. Her daughter had fallen head over heels for the community theater's newest drama director. Then again, Margaret had come a long way from that stubborn little girl who'd insisted upon getting the lead in the shows. These days, she was happier to see others promoted while she worked behind the scenes. Funny how life turned out.

"Honey, just promise me this." Tangie looked her daughter in the eye. "Promise you'll use whatever gifts God gives you to tell others about Him."

"Oh, I promise, Mommy. I'll sing about Him...and I'll act for Him, too." Gwen giggled.

"And if you decide you want to be a softball player or something like that...well, that's okay, too."

"Softball?" Gwen wrinkled her nose. "But I don't know anything about sports."

"You are your mother's daughter, for sure." Tangie laughed.

"And her father's daughter," Gregg called out as he entered the room.

Tangie looked up as her husband drew near. Her heart still did that crazy flip-flop thing, even after all these years. Oh, how she loved this man! He sat on the edge of the bed and kissed their daughter on the forehead.

"So, your mom's been telling you a bedtime story?" he asked.

"Mm-hmm." Gwen yawned. "It was the best ever, about a singing rabbit and a dancing chicken."

"I know that story well." Gregg laughed. "Did she tell you that they lived happily ever after?"

Gwen shook her head and yawned once more. "No, I think she left that part out."

Tangie smiled as she watched her daughter doze off.

Gregg rose from the bed and swept his wife into his arms. Brushing a loose hair from her face, he whispered, "You left out the happily ever after part?"

Tangie chuckled. "Well, the show's not over yet, silly. How can I give away the ending?"

"This one's a given." He kissed the end of her nose then held her close.

As she melted into his embrace, Tangie reflected back on that day when Gregg had come to the theater in New York to tell her he loved her. On that magnificent Broadway stage—with the lights shining in their eyes—they'd tossed all scripts aside and created lines of their own, lines better than any playwright could manufacture. They were straight from the heart, words that set the rest of her life in motion. They'd sent her reeling. . .all the way back to Harmony.

And now, as she gazed into her husband's loving eyes, Tangie had to admit the truth. She knew exactly how this story would end. The singing rabbit and the dancing chicken. . .well, they would live happily ever after. Of course.

Wanda E. Brunstetter

New York Times and *USA Today* bestselling author, Wanda E. Brunstetter, known for her novels about the Amish, also enjoys writing historical and contemporary stories. Wanda and her husband, Richard, live in Washington State but take every opportunity to travel throughout the States in order to research her books. When she's not writing, Wanda enjoys photography, gardening, beach-combing, spending time with her family, and using her ventriloquist skills during some of her speaking engagements.

Gail Sattler

Gail Sattler was born and raised in Winnipeg, Manitoba and now lives in Vancouver, BC (where you don't have to shovel rain) with her husband, three sons, two dogs, three lizards, and countless fish, many of whom have names. Gail and her husband were baptized together in 1983. Between acting as a referee for her three active boys and half the neighborhood, her day job as office manager for a web design company, her evening job as Mom's Taxi Service, and being the bass guitarist for her church's adult worship team, Gail loves to glorify God in her writing. Gail also writes for Barbour's Heartsong Presents line, where she was voted as the Favorite Heartsong Author three times. Gail has also written a number of novellas for Barbour's fiction anthologies.

Janice Thompson

Janice Thompson, who lives in the Houston area, writes novels, non-fiction, magazine articles, and musical comedies for the stage. The mother of four married daughters, she is quickly adding grandchildren to the family mix.